*From the Depths of Despair—
to the Heights of Glory*

Frank Clair was an artist who loved and hated beyond
his understanding . . . whose only passion was power
. . . who abandoned the women able to save him . . .
and who recovered, at last, the golden vision that
could fulfill him . . .

THERE WAS A TIME

Novels by Taylor Caldwell
from Jove Books

TAYLOR CALDWELL

THERE WAS A TIME

A JOVE BOOK

AUTHOR'S NOTE

All the characters in this novel and all the incidents and situations mentioned are fictitious and do not relate to any person living or dead; and any possible coincidences are accidental and unintentional.

Thirteen previous printings
First Jove edition published October 1977

10   9   8   7   6   5   4   3

Jove books are published by Jove Publications, Inc.,
200 Madison Avenue, New York, NY 10016

PART I

There was a time when meadow, grove, and stream,
   The earth, and every common sight,
      To me did seem
    Apparell'd in celestial light,
The glory and the freshness of a dream.
                  —*Wordsworth*

CHAPTER 1

HE ASKED his mother: "How old was I when we lived in Higher Broughton?"

"You were only two and a half years old," his mother answered. "Then we went to High Town, and then to Reddish. You couldn't remember Higher Broughton."

But he remembered. There were two things which he remembered with much more poignancy, and power, and clarity, than he could remember yesterday in his manhood. He said to his mother: "We lived in a house that was part of a row of gloomy, red-brick, semi-detached houses, with a stone yard, and a stone wall that enclosed the yard. I used to sit on the water-closet in that yard, and eat bread with currant jam, while you hung out the washing. In a house across the street there was a family by the name of Burns. They had a little girl named Nellie."

His mother was incredulous. "You weren't but a little over two. You couldn't have remembered that. You heard your father and me talking."

But he remembered.

He was only two years old at that time, but he remembered the yard clearly. The wall had seemed enormously high to him. It could not have been more than six feet in height, but to him it appeared to touch the clouds. The green, wooden door was an impassable bastion, with the latch so high on its side that he could not dream, as yet, of lifting it. On the lower reaches, the dim paint was a mass of fascinating blisters. He spent hours pulling these blisters from the dark wood underneath. Hours spent in blister-pulling, and filled with vague ecstasy and the movement in himself which was so deep and profound, like the movement of slow and sleeping tides. The warm and gauzy sun would lie on his back and filter over his busy, abstracted fingers. He could feel it now, if he wished, and could see his grubby little fingernails, with their black tips, and experience the flowing ecstasy again. He hardly saw the blisters. They were merely something to

9

divert his conscious mind from the quiet exaltation which submerged him.

He knew himself to be waiting for something, but waiting without impatience and restlessness, and only with a kind of bottomless peace and still rapture. He did not feel young. He did not feel time at all. He was existing in a boundless timelessness, wherein there was nothing but that strange beatitude in himself, and everything outside himself was a diffused and swimming glory, gentle, harmonious, trembling with a shining and halcyon tranquillity. It was not joy, he now knew. Joy was something men know, after pain, after success, after attainment. This was only awareness, and bliss, beside which the joys of men were nothing and only petty and mean and shameful, entirely of the flesh. I was not young, then, he would say when he was a man. In losing what I had at that time, I lost maturity and became emptily young.

His mother had been frightened by gypsies, who were lurking somewhere in the lanes, and so had compelled his father to add a bolt to the latch. Gypsies were inveterate child-stealers, though why they should bother with the only man child of lower middle-class people was something she never halted in her emotionalism to discover. The boy never saw the bolt consciously, but he knew it must have been there. That is why what happened remained forever inexplicable.

By this particular day he had torn away all the blisters he could reach. He stood on the toes of his small boots and groped. There was a delicious blister just beyond his reach. It held a promise of retaining, and enhancing, his powerful serenity. He must have that blister, which was the grandfather of all blisters. He looked about him with hunger.

The yard was full of soft English light. Insofar as he knew, nothing existed beyond those towering walls and that green door—no other human soul, no bird, no tree, no voice, no laughter, no being. Behind him stood the soot-stained brick outline of the house in which he lived. That, too, had no being, though he knew his mother was busy inside. His mother lived on the outer fringe of his consciousness, and did not impinge on his reality. He saw a plume of smoke wandering over the hard gray slates of the roof, which cut into a pale blue sky. Everything was silence. Everything swam in a flood of warm, floating light. He saw the crevices between the flags of the stone flooring. They were wet and green with moss. Restlessly, still hungering, he squatted, and rubbed his dirty little finger on the lichens; his frock pulled back over his thighs, he felt a cool wind on his round buttocks. He plucked at the moss, and looked about him petulantly. His eye fastened on the door and the wonderful blisters so far out of his reach.

The green door was opening softly, without sound, almost without perceptible movement. He watched it incuriously, his mouth open, his large blue eyes staring vacantly. The door was opening, despite latch and bolt. This did not seem odd to him, for in his universe there were no latches and no bolts, and queer things happened for which he had no question and no answer.

The door stood wide ajar. A lady entered the yard and closed the door soundlessly behind her. Frank stared emptily, his small finger still rubbing the moss, the wind circling about his bare bottom, the frock and the pinafore slipping back completely. The lady was extremely tall, or so she seemed from his squatting position. She was very beautiful. Even his infant intelligence recognized that. She was slender and young. She could not have been more than twenty, and her hair, falling heavily over her shoulders and far down her back, was as yellow as daffodils. She wore a long and glistening robe of pure whiteness, massive, delicate or stiff by turn, as the sunlight struck it. It was impossible to guess its substance, so changeable was it in its texture. Her white arms were bare and very soft. Her red lips smiled; there was a pulsing and ebbing rose in her cheeks.

She came close to him, and he pushed himself awkwardly to his feet, rubbing his dirty hands together to rid them of soil and the moss. He stared up at her, still incuriously, his mouth still gaping. He felt nothing of fear or embarrassment, and nothing of his usual shyness when in the presence of strangers. He sniffed loudly. He wiped his hands on his filthy pinafore, which was already stained with jam and soup, and which he had busily used as a handkerchief.

"Do you know me?" asked the lady kindly, in a soft and vibrating tone.

He did not answer. He was not a baby who had learned to talk early in his existence. He knew only a few words. None of them seemed appropriate at this time. He continued to stare at her vacantly. The sun was warm and bright in the silent yard. But there was another light about the lady, a concentration, a beautifulness, which was akin to the rapture he felt when tearing blisters from the door. He smiled at her tentatively. She smiled in return; her smile became audible in gentle, murmurous laughter. He began to laugh too—timidly, eagerly.

She put her hand on his rumpled mass of thick chestnut curls. She pulled the ringlets through her fingers. He felt the caress; it ran all through him like a tongue of flame. He came closer to her; he pressed his head against the white gown. He felt its texture: it was like the touch of sweet and silken wind, like the surface of a lily petal. He smoothed it timidly, enchanted by it. The lady was murmuring; she stroked his cheek. She bent down and kissed his forehead, and sighed, and the thin tongue of fire widened all through him to a sheet of hot joy, extended beyond him, became part of the beauty and the light. He looked up at her lovely face; it was still smiling, but now it was sad also. She had the most vivid blue eyes in all the world, and they swam, now, in what could only have been radiant tears. She pressed him against her body almost convulsively. The whole world throbbed with brightness, with tenderness, with rapture, with fulfilment, but the throbbing was all in shining silence, too intense for movement or even for breathing.

Somewhere, there was the sudden thunderclap of a door opening and shutting, and a peevish voice cried: "Baby! Baby! What are you doing? Don't you want your tea? Didn't you hear me calling you?"

He heard his mother's footsteps on the flags, quick, impatient, rapping footsteps. He saw his mother with the outer circle of his eye, beyond which she never entered. He clung to the lady. She was very pale now, and tenuous, and the robe he held in his fingers had no substance at all. He cried in himself: "Don't go! Don't go!" He glanced at his mother with rage. He screamed: "Go 'way!" He tried to grapple the lady closer to him. But she had gone, gone completely, like sunlight, and the green door was closed again and firmly latched.

His mother grasped him by the arm and shook him. "Oh, you dirty baby!" she exclaimed. "Look at your frock and your hands! It doesn't do any good to wash you. Soap is useless. Look at you! Into the closet with you, and then I'll have to wash you all over again before you can have your tea!"

The door of the water-closet creaked loudly, and a flood of sunlight entered into its narrow dank interior, which smelled heavily of paraffin and chloride-of-lime. He was plumped on the wooden seat, and his mother stood over him, bewailing the lot of a woman with a tiresome child. He sat there, and the tears ran down his cheeks, and made wide white paths in the grime. He wept as he had never wept before, with a sense of overpowering loss and endless sorrow, while his mother scolded and wiped his face with her apron.

He could remember nothing more of that day, or of any other day in that yard, save one, and he could not remember whether he had ever reached the blister, or whether blisters had ever played an important part in his life again.

Had it been a dream? But he had been too young, he recalled later, to have created such a lady in his own mind, and to have clothed her in garments so dissimilar to those worn by his mother and her neighbors. How could he have dreamed such a visitation? Years later, he was convinced that it must have been a dream, strange and lovely though it had been, and beyond all reason.

He waited for the lady every day after that, for he recalled that there was in his mind always the emotion of waiting, deprived, restless and unsatisfied.

He never saw the lady again in Higher Broughton, but she haunted him once or twice later in life, and always, afterwards, he asked himself whether it could have been a dream.

Only one more memory of Higher Broughton, and it was less than a memory and really more of a sensation, an awareness.

The day had been dim and cloudy, and now the sky was heliotrope mist, and a heavy still silence hung over everything, and filled the yard, with its stone walls. Frank had been playing with a chair and a doll, but now he had become listless and bored. He wandered about the yard. He touched the green door, wandered away again.

Then he heard a sound, only the ghost and breath of a sound, immeasurably sweet and piercing. He stood still, head lifted, eyes staring at the sky, from which the sound seemed to drop like rain. It was not the call of a bird, or the singing of a human voice, or like the sound of any instrument he was ever to hear. Neither flutelike nor tinkling like a harp, resembling neither a trumpet nor a violin, it yet seemed to encompass all these instruments in one sustained and ineffably lovely note.

Entranced, Frank listened. The music did not ebb and flow in any tempo or cadence. But it became louder, clearer, more imminent, until the sky, the yard, the walls, the flags under his feet, were permeated with it, echoed it back, were drenched with it as with light. Indeed, there was a quality of light and airiness about it, in spite of its surging and impelling quality, its triumph and power. Frank stood, and now all the world was filled with that almost intolerable majesty and sweetness, that profound and depthless music, at once impersonal and full of meaning.

How long he stood there he had no way of telling. But slowly, imperceptibly, the music withdrew rather than faded or grew less. It was like the passing of a host beyond the sky. He held to it as he had held to the lady, until the last whisper of it was gone.

He never forgot the joy and the solemn rapture that filled him that day. But, he asked himself, years later, had that, too, been a dream? He could never tell.

CHAPTER 2

HE REMEMBERED nothing of High Town, though the family must have remained there two years. But he remembered Leeds, where his grandmother lived and conducted her "genteel lodging house for select guests." Or, rather, he remembered his grandmother, and her house, the water-cress sandwiches on thin brown bread, sparingly buttered, the Shrewsbury tarts, stuffed with raisins and citron.

His memory of Leeds was of stark, cold streets, endlessly gray in the day, flickeringly lamplit at night, of tall brick houses stained with soot, of ever-present coal gas floating in the speckled wet air, of small dim fires lurking under ponderous mantelpieces, of skies like wet gray blankets, eternally dripping, of colds in the head and scratchy clothing. And of hatred.

He accepted hatred as he accepted his colds, his aching belly, and the omnipresent rain. He accepted it, with the placid knowledge that he had always known it; it was part of his life, and there was nothing else of particular vehemence. It was the one positive in an atmosphere of saturated negation. It did not seem to him possible that there was anything else, and he never wondered.

Mrs. Jamie Clair had her house on a street that was like a score of others in Leeds, no more dank, no more chilling, no more dreary. But it was larger than the house in Higher Broughton. It had nine bedrooms, two water-closets, and a single bath, which no one used. It was thin, and it was three stories tall, crushed between replicas of itself, and its windows were narrow slits eight feet in height, and not more than thirty inches wide, and clothed in Nottingham curtains of coarse, intricate lace over which were looped draperies of dusty crimson velveteen. Mrs. Clair was an excellent and un-remitting housekeeper, and her only assistant was an im-becile slattern of a girl of fourteen with a running nose (ank, wispy hair, and a perpetual grin. But in spite of torrents of soapy water, sedulous brushings, yards of unending cloths and bricks of whiting, the soot and the coal dust were every-where, like a plague. The girl scrubbed the steps, and the walk before them, every morning. By night they were blotched with wet blackness. The brass knocker was polished daily; by night it was spotted and grimed. The sound of brushes went on far into the day, sometimes until teatime, but the dust gathered in crevices and in the folds of draperies. The Nottingham curtains were washed every fortnight. At the end of fourteen days they were gray webs, filled with black filaments. Each week the walls were dusted vigorously, with cloths on brooms, but by the next Friday there were nests of black threads in every corner, trailing downwards over the violent wallpaper. The carpets were brushed every day, after first being sprinkled with bits of paper soaked in water, but by the next morning their patterns were dimmed, and their nap felt gritty to a bare foot. Each Saturday morn-ing the windows were made sparkling clean, almost invisible in their brightness. By the following Saturday they were opaque smears of flat light through which the street outside was seen dimly.

If the sun ever shone in Leeds, Frank Clair did not re-member this phenomenon. He remembered only the melan-choly dripping of eaves, livid water in small pools on the brick streets, and the sound of low, wailing wind. He remem-bered umbrellas that showered grimy drops over one's shoul-ders, and galoshes, and for some reason these things in Leeds always reminded him of fish frying, spluttering away in grim, damp kitchens.

He must have been four years old when he first became conscious of Leeds as fixed in time and place. But he did not remember the trains that took him there and took him away. He could not have visited his grandmother more than five or six times. He soon became aware that his grandmother disliked his father, despised his mother, and hated himself. All this was inextricably involved with the lodging house.

There was a long thin parlor, its incredibly high ceiling always lost in gloom, its corners dark as if the crimson roses of the wallpaper had been washed over with a gray paint brush. No sun ever penetrated in broad shafts into that room;

it was always filled with a crepuscular light, as if filtered through a fog, as it often was. There was an imitation black marble mantelpiece against one wall, bulky, flaked and chipping, showing its bleached plaster flesh under the painted skin. The hearth was made of black flags, unavailingly polished. The mantelpiece itself, draped in dark crimson velvet, balled and looped, frowned at the room with beetling brows, and the tiny red fire far back in its recesses was a cold and cheerless snarl. But the brass fender and the andirons glowed as brilliantly as whiting, salt and vinegar could effect it. Above the mantelpiece glowered a somber portrait of the late Mr. William Clair, but soot had obliterated everything about it except a pair of fierce and beetling eyes. They followed little Frank everywhere, full of censure, indignation and umbrage. He hated the portrait, and was afraid of it.

Brussels carpeting, red, ribbed and worn, covered the floor to the walls. The walls flanking the fireplace boasted two huge "Chinese" jars filled with drooping ostrich plumes, tinted a sickly violet. They were Mrs. Clair's pride and joy. She dipped the plumes several times a year in a concoction of water and violet ink. The fronds were filled with frail dark webs strung with tiny beads of soot. (Frank would often surreptitiously rub the dry fronds between his fingers, and look at the black streaks with fascinated wonder. Again, when his grandmother was absent from the room, he would climb up on the steel stool beside the fireplace and minutely examine the red-and-purple vases on the mantelpiece, and insert his little finger tips in the intricate convolutions along the necks and around the twisted handles. It was his greatest ambition to have enough time, some day, to examine every other article on that cluttered, draped shelf.)

Mrs. Clair's parlor furniture was very "elegant." It was all ponderous swelling mahogany, covered with black horsehair or red velveteen, sofas like big-headed recumbent monsters, rockers that creaked and rumbled, stiff chairs devilishly contrived so as not to conform to the human contour. A huge round table stood in the center of the room, covered with a dusty spread of crimson velveteen, balled and draped. It held a brass-and-china lamp, which smelled of paraffin, and its round shade was painted with viciously scarlet roses and poisonous green leaves. The lamp was never lit. The parlor basked in the pride of the hanging gas chandelier, which, when the Welsbach mantles were lighted, flickered and glared with stark ferocity. Sometimes, when a mantel was changed, Frank was allowed to take the discarded article to the kitchen, there to stand over the sink and crumble it finely into a china dish. The ashes were used to polish silver. He loved the feel of the delicate tracery dissolving into nothingness between his fingers.

But he did not love the parlor. It was a horror to him. It had a dry smell of lavender, which he associated with his grandmother, and an overpowering stench of coal gas and damp cold. The carpet, he observed, gave off a peculiar woolly and dusty odor when he sat upon it. Sometimes the parlor was pervaded with the effluvium of boiling cabbage and mutton, of barley and onions, and, on the one Christmas he was there, with sage and the fat heavy smell of roasting goose. The parlor was airless; it held the ghosts of many meals within its sweating walls.

He remembered nothing of the rest of the house, and of the kitchen he could recall nothing but the black iron sink, where he crumpled Welsbach mantles. But from his mother he learned that Mrs. Clair housed nine impeccable "ladies and gentlemen" of great respectability: anaemic milliners, dressmakers, clerks, bookkeepers and an artist or two, apprentices to lithographers. He never saw any of them; they lurked in their dark and cheerless cubbyholes. Mrs. Clair did not dine with them. "Familiarity breeds contempt," she would say, with great unction and majesty. Frank could often hear them muttering and coughing in subdued voices in the dining room beyond the folded doors. Most of them suffered from "Lancashire catarrh," and he would hear their choked sneezes, apologetic and meek. Later, slow dragging footsteps would creep up the back stairway; a door or two would open and shut with a long echoing boom. Then there would be only silence, settling heavily over the house to the accompaniment of the dripping rain. What these poor creatures did in the dim and voiceless misery of their rooms he never knew. It did not concern him in childhood. But in manhood he was often seized with a wild sense of desperation and sadness, as he remembered this, and a kind of hating fury.

Memories of Leeds were all confused in his mind, flowing together like gray oily water, sluggishly moving and melting into one another. But he distinctly recalled one day, for on that day he experienced once more the ecstasy and exaltation of his babyhood.

Remembering, he could feel again the scratch of the horsehair on his bare legs beneath the tight little serge trousers into which he had lately graduated. He was sitting in a monster rocker in the parlor, but he dared not rock. He must sit "like a mouse, and behave himself." His hands were spread on the curved mahogany arms of the chair; the surface beneath them sweated and dimmed from the moisture and heat of his little palms. He vaguely rubbed those palms back and forth, feeling the polished chill of the wood, and constantly seeking for another cool spot when he had heated the current one.

He could see his black ribbed stockings, which did not quite meet his trousers when he sat down, and his black buttoned boots, which had been vigorously polished that morning. The buttons winked at him in the bleak firelight. He moved his feet, so he could catch its light on the buttons, then extinguish it when he dropped his feet. His mind was all suffused, empty, vegetative, as it usually was. It was like something waiting, filled with nothingness, not even emotion or longing, but often huge formless shadows would drift through it, foglike, without outline or feature.

He seemed immune to stimuli, he remembered years later. He could not remember any peevishness on his part, any sharp desire, any response to outside goads or stresses. Nothing provoked him, angered him, delighted him. He was, in his memory, a very obedient little boy, dull and silent, docile and hardly existing, though doubtless, considering his grandmother's aversion to him, he must at times have been very annoying, if for nothing else but his complete blankness and lack of response to the impact of unfolding life. Once his grandmother had called him "a dolt." He had gazed at her, his mouth open, his eyes fogged with heavy, sleeping dreams. "The lad's not right in his head," she would say, sharply, to which his mother would reply, in her whining but respectful voice: "The lad is good. He never mithers me." "You'll be putting him away if he doesn't improve," said his grandmother, grimly. He thought nothing.

This pungent exchange, quite familiar to him, occurred on this day also. He rocked slightly; the buttons winked at him, dropped into darkness. One coal in the grate cracked; a little tongue of flame licked upwards. Frank watched it, enchanted. It was like an eager red flower, opening, leaping, falling. The chandelier had not yet been lit. The parlor was filled with ponderous cold gloom, enlivened only by the twinkle of the fender and the andirons. He liked to watch them; they were alive, and curious thin images flashed over them.

Up to this time, he had never been really conscious of his parents, or of his grandmother, or of anyone else, as having pertinence or existence in his private universe, which was so immense and shadowy and voiceless. But all at once he was conscious of the others in the room, and he looked up alertly. Now his blue eyes became poignant, brilliant.

For the first time in his life, the world rushed in on him, loudly, unbearably, filled with clamor and awareness, too vivid, too intense, and he felt a wild swirling in himself, a terror, a fright, a sudden impulse to cover his ears with his hands. His small pale face, triangular and wizened, whitened. His slack mouth dropped open. It was as if his damp nostrils had been pinched together, for his breath stopped. He could feel the scratching of his starched, frilled blouse about his neck and wrists; he could feel the harsh wool of his shirt, his serge trousers, his stockings, lacerating his sensitive flesh. He could feel his body, and never before had he been conscious of it. He could feel the movement of his heart, leaping affrightedly in his meagre chest, and the length of his long thin legs, and the hair on his head. The horsehair that rasped his flesh made his skin cringe. The chill of the room, its bleakness, its smells, the sight of the fog at the windows, the drip of the rain, the presence of the three adults, penetrated like agony to his very bones. The protoplasm of his body, sleeping sluggishly for four years, was suddenly drenched with soul, and became conscious, and could not endure the consciousness.

He really saw his parents for the first time. There was his father, a little withered man of some thirty-five years, sitting opposite the grandmother. He had a completely bald head, polished, gnome-like, too large for the small frame that supported it. The flat and angular face was decorated with an immense pair of waxed black mustaches, like symmetrical stiff wings on the facade of a skull. There was such a meek, wary, blinking and apologetic aura about poor Francis Clair, that one knew he possessed no will-power, no impulse to revolt, no passionate emotion in his soul, despite the fierce mustaches. One saw at once that this little thin man was afraid, nebulously but enormously afraid of everything, that never would he assert himself, that never had he known more than the most furtive gleam of grandeur or exaltation. He had little bright blue eyes, shifty, timorous, placating, though often they were sly and cautious and frightened, as well.

He wore black broadcloth, which was so "genteel" and "respectable." His waistcoat, his best, was of black sateen, with a vague pattern of leaves which shivered over the tiniest of paunches. The sharp flaring corners of his stiff white collar appeared to choke him, as did the bulky black silk of his cravat, which was stuck through with an immense artificial pearl pin, gleaming in the firelight like a glaucous eye. He had a scrawny neck, and the keen edge of his collar had left a chronic red line upon it, angrily suggestive of the scars of a hangman's rope. His hands trembled continually; his right hand had a habit of clenching his right knee, all the fingers spread and tense, like a convulsive claw. Then he would move that hand to his jutting little knob of a chin, there to finger an astonishingly deep cleft or to rub his very insignificant and pointed nose. It was evident that he feared his mother, that her every gesture and word were, to him, fraught with apprehensive anxiety, that he wriggled before her like a worm on a pin, helplessly cajoling her to be kind to him with every fearful skulking of his eyes.

At his right hand, away from the fire, sat his wife, Maybelle. (Such a vulgar name! Mrs. Clair was wont to say, with a snort.) She was five years Francis' senior, and was never allowed by her mother-in-law to forget it. She had been a seamstress before her marriage, and even now, five years later, her fingers were rough, like a grater, and their plumpness had a calloused feel. She was a small, very buxom woman, with untidy auburn hair, huge masses of it forever tumbling around her small round cheeks, which were as hard, as red, and as firm as apples. Her breast impinged on her short neck, for it was full and swelling. Her skin was the easily flushing skin of the red-haired woman, and the least excitement sent warm moist waves of color over her throat and face. Her features, small, plump, pursy, seemed stuck on her broad countenance haphazardly, like lumps of pink dough, and the peevish pouting of her lips, by turns chronically frightened and anxiously belligerent, betrayed a most commonplace and servile mind. Her brown eyes were wide, blank, staring, full of suspicious wariness, and like her husband, she blinked rapidly when the least confused, her reddish lashes standing out in a hard fringe from her eyelids. Despite her plumpness and shortness, all her movements were uncoördinated and rapid and blundering. Sometimes, when on the most insignificant mission about the house, she would wave her short fat arms distractedly, and her fingers bumbled at button-holes if she were pressed for time.

She had made her light-fawn shirtwaist herself, but had made a dolorous error in the huge frou-frou of lace puffing from the high neck to her belt, for she lacked any semblance of taste. "Really, May," Mrs. Clair would say, disdaining the "Maybelle," "I cannot understand, really, how you ever made a living at sewing, with your complete ignorance of style!" The light dull color of the fabric was liberally spotted with remnants of the last meal, evidences which Maybelle repeatedly tried to obliterate by rubbing futilely at them with a messy handkerchief. Her skirt, of heavy navy-blue serge, was awkwardly cut and badly fitted, and kept slipping away from the belt. Her buttoned boots, wide, squat and swelling with bunions, were toed-in nervously, as she looked fearfully at her mother-in-law and tried to smile appeasingly.

Frank stared at his parents, stunned, not by any real critical apprehension, but by his conscious awareness of their existence, and his awareness of his own. He stared for a long time, for in the room there had fallen a prolonged and uneasy silence. Then he heard his grandmother's harsh voice, and he started violently and looked at her.

No one knew why Mrs. Clair was known as "Jamie," a distinctly masculine name, but "Jamie" it was, and the devil with those who cavilled. She sat bolt upright in her stiff chair, for there was no nonsense about her. She was the reasonably prosperous landlady of a most respectable lodging house, had a "nice bit of money tucked away in the bank," and was proud of it. She was also proud of the fact that she had supported herself and her son since he had been six years old, "and never a penny from a soul, and never beholden to anybody." This was no mean accomplishment to boast about on this tenth day of November in the year of Our Lord 1904. Everything in her house, she would say, was paid for, from the carpets on the floor to the curtains at the windows, and every pot and dish and spoon in the kitchen. "A creditor is a bad friend, and I want no kind," she was fondly, and loudly, accustomed to say. These were no empty words. She considered it a kind of special virtue that she had no close acquaintances. "I walk like a queen among the neighbors," she would declare, "and there's none can say a word against me, and precious few to me. Never a friend, never an enemy, is my motto. Pay your debts and hold your head high, and put your shilling in the collection box of a Sunday, and you can face God and man with a clear conscience." She was not one to speak loosely; her lodgers never spoke much of anything to her except a meek "good morning, Mrs. Clair," and as meek a "good evening." Only one or two dared venture an opinion of the weather in her presence. She kept their rooms expertly cleaned, and demanded her rent of a Saturday, nor did she expect them to regard *her* as a human being. It was a matter of business. If one of them sickened, a tray might be dispatched to his room by the slattern, but not many of them. Two days' sickness and they were "out of the house," God knows where. That was no concern of hers.

There she sat, conscious of her character and her courage, with her indomitable faith in industry and money in the bank, and no debts. She was very tall and lean, and until this day Frank had never been aware of her face. Now he saw it, rigorous, full of rectitude and firmness, all gray bone and drawn hard flesh, all piercing hazel eyes, jutting nose, grim wide mouth in a nest of wrinkles, and a chin like a spade. She wore black, both because she was a widow and it was "wearing." Her shirtwaist was of some stiff black silk, which gleamed, rattled with her movements, and seemed spun of cast iron, the collar highly boned, and innocent of even the smallest edging of lace. About her neck was hung a thin golden chain, from which a locket, containing a lock of her husband's hair, was suspended. Her skirt, black also, was so rigid as to give the illusion of wood, and it covered her feet. Not for her the disgraceful display of ankle or buttoned boot. In fact, one could not imagine that she had ever been young, or that the unpliant gray pompadour, fortified with "rats," had ever been any other color. It was not possible to believe that she uncoiled it at night and let it down upon her unbending neck, or that she wore a nightdress. Her frightened lodgers sometimes were positive that she never slept, but sat always in that chair in that precise position, waiting for Saturday night. A bunch of keys jingled at her belt.

A desiccated scent flowed from her when she moved, compounded of soap, old lavender, chloride of lime, and righteousness. This scent struck on young Frank's nostrils, and he winced. But he did not look away from his grandmother. He was fascinated by his consciousness of her. He was not afraid.

"Put a few coals on the fire, Francis," she said peremptorily to her son. "But not too many. A pennyworth's only. It costs money."

She became aware of Frank's concentrated regard. She turned her head quickly, rigidly, in his direction. The boy was "touched." There was no doubt of it. Such vacant big eyes, such a slack, hanging mouth, such a stare. She pointed a long hard finger at him, and said, with more concern than derision: "The lad's a ninny, May. Britched, and no more life than a sick cat. And next year you send him to school! Humph. He'll be back on your hands, I warn you."

"Don't gape," said his father, with quick irritation, and a glance at his mother. "Close your mouth, lad. You're drooling out of the corners." Forgive me, he seemed to be pleading with the formidable Mrs. Clair. But she brushed aside his plea with an arch of her long neck.

"Frank's a good lad," said Maybelle, with a faint rare spirit. "Wipe your nose, lovey, and don't glower at your Grandma; there's a dear."

" 'Frank!' " snorted Mrs. Clair, with a toss of her head, and a meaning look at her grovelling son. "His name is Francis. I never held with nicknames. Francis is an honorable name. Or are you ashamed of it, May? If I remember rightly, you were glad to be able to say it, after you had your marriage lines."

How unbearably close and near those voices were! Not louder than ordinarily, but to the awakened consciousness of the child they were filled with clangor, with ripping intensity. The figures opposite him did not move, but it appeared to him that they rushed upon him through space, like menacing presences. Their faces swelled, became enormous, full of eyes and mouths and roaring tongues and frightful tumult. He cowered away from their rush, from their voices. He thrust out his hands, to keep them away. He burst into wild sobs of sheer terror. He clapped his hands over his ears. There was no help, no refuge. He curled his legs under him, as if hiding, trying to make himself tiny like some threatened small animal in a forest full of wild beasts. He clasped his arms over his head, and screamed.

May, her instinctive motherhood surging over her fear and respect for her mother-in-law, cried shrilly: "There, look what you've done to my laddie, Mrs. Clair! Nagging and gnawing at him until he has fits!" She jumped up on her short fat legs and waddled rapidly to the shuddering child. She snatched him up in her arms and smothered his face against her breast, and his cries came in a muffled blur from that welter of lace, warm flesh and buttons. Amidst the multitudinous folds of that bosom a treacherous pin had been concealed, to close an empty button-hole, and the point pierced Frank's cheek like a touch of fire. He pushed his hands against that overpowering bosom, and screamed in mingled terror and pain, a drop of blood welling up through his skin.

"Oh, oh, the poor little creature!" Maybelle almost sobbed,

rubbing frantically at the red moisture with the rough lace of part of her jabot. "It might have been his eye!"

"For Heaven's sake, make him stop that skriking," demanded Mrs. Clair, unmoved, and only annoyed and disgusted. "And if you will wear pins, as no neat woman would, you'll have to bear the consequences. You'll find arnica upstairs. Where's your handkerchief?"

Francis Clair had sprung helplessly to his feet, torn between his natural affection for his wife and his awe of his mother. He was enraged with "that brat" for being the cause of all this disturbance. His mother was right; Ma was usually right. The lad was a ninny, a dolt, and Maybelle was "touched" on him, for all her cloutings and rages when the little fool irritated her.

"Shut him up, or I'll clout him!" he exclaimed, with thin ire. "You'll have the house down around our necks. What'll the lodgers think?"

"I don't care about the blinking lodgers," replied Maybelle, aroused. "I'll not have the little thing mithered, just because he ain't—isn't—too bright. There, there, lovey," she crooned to the child, who was writhing in her arms as if possessed. She pumped him up and down in her arms. Her auburn pompadour had come loose and was falling into her eyes. Her hot wet face was the color of a poppy, her eyes suffused with easy tears, her thick little lips trembling. Her breath came fast and noisily with her indignation. "There, there, it's Mama that's got you, safe and sound. Would you like a Shrewsbury tart, lovey? A nice sweet Shrewsbury tart?"

"There are no Shrewsbury tarts to be had. Just enough for the lodgers' tea," remarked Mrs. Clair with pointed indifference. "He can have some bread and gooseberry jam."

"He hates gooseberry jam," protested Maybelle. She waddled up and down the room, agitatedly tossing the boy about in her arms. His cries were becoming feebler, but his hands were pressed convulsively over his eyes.

Mrs. Clair shrugged her lean shoulders. The pleated black silk of her shirtwaist crackled. She gave her son a prolonged and deadly glance, which called upon him to accept his fate with fortitude, while she, his mother, knew he was foredoomed to defeat.

Maybelle's anger against her mother-in-law was subsiding. She knew that she would be "in for" a berating from her husband later for this show of rebellion and for her "language." Now she began to feel annoyance and impatience with the frenzied child. "Hush, hush," she said, with something of shrewishness in her voice. "Stop your skriking, or I'll thrash you, that I will. A big lad like you!"

In her fast perambulations up and down the dark parlor she paused momentarily before the mantel. There was a suspicious dampness against her forearms. Surreptitiously, turning her back to her mother-in-law, she felt of the small trousers. There, he'd done it again, and what would Mrs. Clair and Francis think? They would be confirméd in their opinion about the child. Now she was angered, and shook the cowering boy. "Do you want a clout?" she demanded fiercely.

The boy was abruptly silent, but his whole body shivered violently. He opened his eyes. They were not wet, but they were stark and wild. He glared about him. Then his mouth fell open. He was on a level with the mantelpiece, and he suddenly pointed a finger at it, mumbling thick sounds in his throat.

Maybelle followed the little finger, craning her tousled head over her fat shoulder. "No, no, mustn't touch. Grandma's things."

"What does the lad want?" asked Mrs. Clair, unexpectedly and with alertness. In truth, she was somewhat disturbed at the passion the child had displayed, for he had always been so silent, so docile, so lumpish. "He can't have my vases, or my bric-a-brac, not even to quiet him."

Maybelle moved backwards, still craning. Frank's hand shot out and clutched a large pink shell, all convolutions. He clasped it to his breast like a precious treasure. His white little face glowed.

"It's the shell," Maybelle surlily informed her mother-in-law. "No, no, lovey, mustn't touch. Give it back to Mama, and she'll put it back in the right place."

She tried to wrest the shell from the moist small fingers, but Frank screamed again, with so piercing a note that Maybelle recoiled involuntarily, and Francis again sprang to his feet as if touched with a hot iron, doubling his fists savagely. Mrs. Clair's ears deafened. Her voice rose over the tumult, firm and harsh: "Let him have it, for God's sake. He can't hurt it. It isn't worth anything; a lodger left it."

She added, "Put the brat down on the hearth, May. I've got a lot to talk over, and we can't waste time with him."

Maybelle set Frank down with a thump. She viciously hoped his wet trousers would soil the Brussels carpeting. Then, frightened, she snatched him up, looked about, met Mrs. Clair's eye, hastily dropped the boy on the hearth again.

He forgot everything, the voices, the faces, the smart in his cheek. He held the shell in his hand. He tipped it towards the fire.

CHAPTER 3

THE SHELL was about six inches long and four inches wide. The outer surface was rough and ridged. But the interior was shaded from the most delicate pink at the edge to the softest, brightest rose-mauve towards the center. Moreover, the inner surface had a smooth cool feel, and was streaked with living silver that flashed and changed in the firelight.

Frank cradled the wondrous treasure in his hands, breathlessly, worshipfully. There was a religious ecstasy in him, an awed bliss. He felt his little heart swell with a kind of nameless exaltation. His body was held rigid, lest he disturb the flow of frail silver that darted in little streaks and rivulets over the lovely pink-and-mauve sheen. His hands shook; the silver flowed, brightened, became moons and rivers in microcosm. A rosy island rose momentarily between silver streams, fell and was lost.

Something like a suppressed sob choked the boy's throat. His chestnut ringlets brightened to flame in the firelight as he bent his head over the shell. His cheeks flushed, his lips quickened with color. A dreaming and rapturous light drowned his features, which had suddenly become beautiful.

Even Mrs. Clair was not insensible to that sudden and incredible beauty of the crouched child on the hearth, the shell trembling gently in his hands. She said reluctantly: "He should have been a girl. I never knew he was so pretty. If he'd 'a' been a girl, it wouldn't matter that he wasn't bright." She added, in a softer voice than usual: "Francis, put the shell to your ear. You can hear the sea."

The boy started. He glanced up, dazed. But he had heard her. Obediently, he put the shell to his ear, though he knew nothing of the sea, and to him it was only a word.

He heard a long sonorous note, a miniature thunder, a soft majestic droning. Entranced, not daring to move, he listened.

There was a faint singing sound rising over the deeper notes, a sound of fairy music, sweet and compelling. It was a voice full of joy and tenderness and glory, and now other voices joined it. The universe was filled with the singing, with long bassoons in accompaniment, with tremendous drums from a distance, with the far blazing of celestial trumpets.

Frank forgot time and place. He forgot his newly discovered entity, the world, his parents, the room, his being. He was only a core of consciousness, acutely burning, concentrated passionately on the music which swelled ever louder, so that the utmost limits of space were drenched with the power and the force of the overwhelming harmony.

Clouds of light flowed over his vision. Dark abysses rolled towards him, were cleft asunder with swords of fire, filling up with swimming radiance. Mountains, chaotic and tumbling, rose in gray majesty before him, blazed blue, purple, scarlet, gold, until he could no longer look upon their brilliance. Oceans of flame whirled dizzily away from him, burning with apocryphal colors; incandescent rainbows, shedding lightning, flashed over the bottomless depths. And everywhere was the music, ever louder and louder, like a thundering and universal paean of triumph. It was more terrible in its splendor and grandeur than the music he had heard in the yard at Higher Broughton. Then it had been the faintest and noblest of echoes. Now it was an unbearable rapture, a wild glory, almost terrible.

Such a joy seized him that he could not endure it. He seemed to know everything, to understand everything. His unseeing eyes stared at the firelight, reflecting the flickering light. His expression was transfixed. There was a sound of bursting in his chest, as if something had been released, had been freed. He sat in a trance, his soul in the music, the visions.

The thunder became shattering; it was like great wings, beating, palpitating, frightfully imminent. Then, all at once, he saw a hand emerge from the fire and the crashing radiance. It was a most enormous hand, yet delicately fashioned, long and slender and strong. It held a ball of clay in its palm. The fingers closed about it, lifted, thrust forward, opened. The ball of clay sprang as if alive from the fingers, and went hurtling forward and downward into space, into the rainbows, into the dissolving mountains of light and conflagration. It was illuminated by them; tinted lightnings flashed about it. A brilliant halo encircled it. It disappeared into darkening space, spinning like a top, dizzily and help-lessly spinning. but pregnant with meaning.

The hand extended, the fingers spread, lifted a little, as if giving a blessing. It remained for a time like that, the light shining through it, falling like beams from its palm, falling in golden cataracts through the gathering darkness, so that their rolling and tumbling were momentarily illuminated.

The hand withdrew, slowly, reluctantly, yet with finality. The light flowed in after it, and everything dimmed and paled. The voices sank lower, became sonorous and diffused thunder again. It retreated like a melodious and meditative tide into the far reaches of the universe from which it had come. Now it was only a murmur.

And at last there was only silence and darkness and empti-ness, and the crushing wild grief and sense of dreadful loss in the heart of the child.

"The lad's fallen asleep, thank goodness," said Mrs. Clair. "No, don't disturb him, May. Let him sleep. He will only skrike again. No, let him keep the shell, if he wants it. He'll drop it and break it soon."

"He's anaemic," said Mrs. Clair, uncomfortably. "Why don't you give him iron? He looks as if he has the rickets."

"He gets good food," replied Maybelle, defensively. She was frightened by the boy's pallor, by his flaccidity.

Mrs. Clair shrugged eloquently. She turned her attention to her son. "So, it's settled, then. I leave for America in January. I've got a good price offered for the furnishings of the house, and the lodgers have had their long notice. Francis, you'd best go to America, too."

"What'd I do in America?" asked Francis Clair, with a weak attempt at facetiousness. "Work as a navvy on the streets, sweeping up the gold that's supposed to be there?"

"I dislike levity," said Mrs. Clair, with grand sternness, and rocking herself a little in her rockerless chair. "You'd do just as you do here: work in a chemist's shop. You're a good chemist, if I do so say, myself, from what Mr. Sawyer says. Then, you've got your fiddle. You might have op-portunities for it there."

Francis was silent. His hand squeezed his knee; he stared into the fire. His face was still, blank, frozen.

"I fancy they have public houses there, too," went on Mrs. Clair inexorably.

Francis Clair did not move, yet he appeared to jerk violently, as if twisted with despair. He said in a low voice:

"I wouldn't play in the public houses in America. Just as I won't play here."

Mrs. Clair tossed her head impatiently. "You don't play it at all. Does he, May? After all the money I spent, trying to lift him above himself, though a lodging house is no disgrace. I can tell you. It's given us bread and butter, and good clothes, and a roof over our heads, for years. It's honest and respectable. I have no regrets. I had no one to turn to—"

"I'm not saying anything, Ma," said her son. But his thin tones were abstracted.

"And it'd be a caution if you did! And ungrateful. Well. I had high hopes for you, Francis. Your father kept a shop. That's respectable, too, and I'm not one to think different. But I wanted something a little better for you. You wanted fiddle lessons. You got 'em—"

"Violin," murmured Francis, wincing.

"Fiddle. Fiddlesticks! What does it matter? It was called a fiddle in my day, before people got fancy. Fiddle. Well, you got your lessons, and what do you do with them? Nothing. You don't even practice, do you?"

"It's been years. I've been busy."

What could he tell his mother? What could he say to her? My teacher told me I had no real talent, and could only memorize, in spite of what I heard inside myself. I couldn't make it come out! It came out in wheezes and dribbles. My teacher told me I would do well in a public house, or perhaps in a cheap music hall, or perhaps I could teach. That wasn't enough. It wasn't enough for what I heard inside me! I couldn't. I really couldn't. With me it was all or nothing. It's nothing. The case is covered with dust. That's me. Covered with dust. I haven't any soul; that's what's the matter. No soul.

"Busy!" snorted Mrs. Clair. "A body's always got time to do the things he wants. It's just an excuse. Well. Do as you wish. I'm not one to impose my opinions on anyone else. Mind your own business, is my motto. Live and let live. Do right, and don't bother about your neighbors. Anyway, you'd do well in America."

"You're right, Ma. It's a fiddle."

Maybelle looked up quickly. She knew that tone of voice, which was almost malignant.

"Eh?" said Mrs. Clair. "Well, then. A fiddle's a fiddle. No use despising any way of making a living. Then, you're a chemist, too."

Rolling little white pills, green pills, red pills, for sluggish bellies, for dull aching heads, for all the chronic and nameless ills that afflict the human body. Capping, wrapping in striped paper. String. Looking at great glass jars, and sometimes seeing crystals like sparks of yellow and red and blue fire. A chemist! He thought of the great pioneer chemists of history. Once he had dreamed of being one of them, of discovering a cure for consumption, for cancer, for sick hearts, for tumorous intestines. He thought of kneeling before the Queen—it was the King, now. "Rise, Sir Francis Clair." Silk breeches and silk stockings, and a ribbon on his chest, and newspapers and the noble of the world paying him honor! My God, a chemist! A chemist on a side street in High Town, with lamplight blinking in his eyes, and the bell tinkling on the door, and the smell of dirt, dust, rain and sweat and dripping umbrellas! His hand clenched his knee so that it bit into the flesh.

America. The gripping fingers slowly relaxed. There was money in America. Money made up for a lot of things. What was that chap's name who came back to Manchester for his wife and children? Francis couldn't remember. But he had a pocket full of pounds—dollars. He showed them lavishly. He was making three pound a week in some shop in a place called Philadelphia. Bragging. His clothes were good. Money to burn in America, he had said. Pubs flowing with cheap beer, and "vaudeville" houses, and a chance for everybody. America was the land of money; jobs were to be had for the asking, for four or five pound a week! Francis calculated. He was lucky to bring home three pound ten every Saturday night. He couldn't remember when he had last seen a sovereign. There might even be hope in America. What had the chap said? Beastly hot in the summer in Philadelphia. But there was the sun. One never saw the sun in Lancashire. All at once his thin blood and his meagre body strained, turned urgently towards the sun he had never seen. And he heard the rain running down the spouts; he heard it in the eaves. It was washing the windows in yellow-gray streams. Fog pressed against the glass; a dray rattled on the bricks outside.

"America," he said, aloud. "I'll give it thought."

"Oh, Frank, you'd never leave dear old England!" cried Maybelle, incredulously. Her lips pouted; her eyes filled with tears. "Among strangers!"

"Don't be a ninny, May," said Mrs. Clair. She nodded approvingly at her son. "That's the ticket, Francis. Assert yourself. You know best. I've got it all planned. I'll open a lodging house in America. There's my friend—you remember her, Mrs. Blossom that was. She's a Mrs. Jones since she married in America. She lives in Bison, in a place called New York. You remember me telling you. She's got a lodging house, and charges the lodgers fifteen shillings a week. Think of it. My best front room brings in only eight. And she's not got a fine place, from what she says. Just working-class. I'd do it up much better. Clerks and bookkeepers and shopkeepers. I could charge more. I'd make a fortune. Haven't I got the best feather beds money can buy? And good linen sheets and feather pillows? I know quality. People'd appreciate it in America, where they're little better than savages. Give them a taste of good old English cooking, too. Dashes of sage and onions and thyme and sweet marjoram. I fancy they don't have such things there."

Maybelle rubbed her eyes with her moist knot of a handkerchief. Frank always listened to the old devil. She had him in a spell. Maybelle heard the rain, too, but it was a friendly and familiar voice. She shrank from the thought of America.

"It's settled, then," said Mrs. Clair, who always settled things at once, so that her audience was helplessly swept away with her. "You'll follow me. What have you in the bank, Francis?"

He cringed. "Well, Ma, you see there was Maybelle's bronchitis last winter, and the lad had something wrong with him, so there was cod liver oil in wine, and I had to buy a new coat, the old one was patched—"

Mrs. Clair gave Maybelle a baleful glance, as if these things were all her fault. "I see," she said ominously. "You've got nothing."

"Two pound three shillings."

"I see. Sometimes a man can't get ahead. I'm not blaming you, Francis. I know what you have to buck up against. If nothing keeps you back, what could you save in a year?"

Francis smiled wryly. His face was gnomelike. "Two pound three shillings, if I'm lucky."

"When you sell your furniture, that will bring you in something. You've got some good things there; I gave 'em to you, and I know their quality. Get a good price." She paused, struggled with herself. "I'll send you the difference. You can pay it back so much at a time. Without interest," she added, battling her instincts.

Without interest, he thought. But life is never like that. The interest piles up, and then it is more than the principal.

It becomes a mountain. A man can never climb it. He is buried under it.

"I'll think about it," he said again.

"Well, I'm glad it's settled," said Mrs. Clair firmly. "I'll get the tea. I've got a treat for you tonight. Cold sliced ham and fresh tongue, sliced thin. Brown bread and butter, and some plum preserves. A bit of raisin cake. Water-cress—the last. You always liked water-cress, Francis. Good hot tea. You can put a few more coals on the fire. But be careful. Waste not, want not, is my motto."

CHAPTER 4

MRS. JAMIE CLAIR, competent and sure as always, "sold up" her household goods, and armed with a few retained lares and penates, set sail for America in January. But Francis Clair secured a "post" in a larger chemist shop in Reddish, with an increase of fifteen shillings a week, and Maybelle, overjoyed that the threatened hegira was at least postponed, accompanied him happily to the little suburb of Manchester.

The house on Mosston Street was almost identical with the ones in Higher Broughton and High Town, except that it was somewhat sootier and a trifle more dreary, if possible. There was a cotton mill in Reddish, where young children, youths and maidens, men and women, toiled at the looms in wet and steaming heat, almost unclothed, and coughed themselves into bronchitis or "the consumption." The neighbors of the Clairs were composed of these poor people, but Maybelle was contented. There were shops nearby, and one could purchase fish and chips conveniently, and there were the eternal stone yards and walls and green wooden doors to take away the sting of homesickness. She was by nature a friendly soul. She was soon standing on the outside of the green door, her arms folded under her apron, exchanging symptoms, gossip and "receipts" with the wives of the cotton-mill workers. She hypocritically bewailed her sad lot in not producing more children, carefully refraining from announcing her age, but, in truth, she was really complacent at the benevolence of nature. One had only to look upon the anaemic, half-starved, rickety children that flocked, whining, about the bedraggled

skirts of the envious neighbors to understand that one was
blessed of God. Moreover, all this gave her an opportunity to
exercise that egotistic and really cruel "virtue" called magnanimity. She was enabled, by reason of Francis' better
wages and her one-child condition, to run into the neighbors'
sordid kitchens and there leave a pot of jam, a loaf of
bread, a "bit" of meat, or a head of cabbage, as a kind of
offering to the Moloch of nature, who had been so inexplicably kind to her. Sometimes, evading Francis' watchful eye,
she would present some worn shoes, some out-grown clothing
of little Frank's, as an additional offering to the malignant
gods of all the poor and the child-ridden and the hungry.

It gave her a happy glow when she saw some poor woman
"traipsing" down the street in one of her mended shirtwaists
or discarded serge skirts or old, moth-eaten shawls. It pleased
her to sit in some stricken kitchen, wailing and rocking, and
comforting a mother of many children on the occasion of the
calamity of her man being "sacked" from the mill. Sometimes
she could afford a shilling or two, or a bottle of cod-liver oil
for a racked man coughing his lungs away in a dirty bed, or
a new christening robe, made of coarse cotton and coarser
machine-made lace, for a newborn infant. Once, she had the
delicious opportunity of ministering to a collapsed mother,
whose little girl of ten had lost three fingers of her right hand
in the mill. Maybelle thought the occasion merited a whole
pound of tea, and she heroically put aside the sad thought
that now she could not buy those white kid gloves for church
on Sundays.

Frank could remember her singing happily as she ironed in
the kitchen at night:

> "Before I was married, I used to wear a shawl,
> Now I am married, I haven't one at all!
> Oh, what a life, a very hard life;
> It's better to be single than a poor man's wife!"

To the end of his life, that foolish song was to haunt him,
to make the rain, the soot, the agony of the poor, the cotton
mills, and all the misery of the helpless as poignant in his
memory as when he had first heard it. It seemed to him that
it was the real song of England, the real song of the people,
the song of those who labored, time out of mind, and whose
mute voices could not express their anguish.

How clearly, even at forty, he could remember that house
on Mosston Street!

There was a small "garden" outside, a strip of moldy moss

eight feet by twelve, carefully guarded by a low iron railing. The steps to the house, scrubbed every Saturday morning, glimmered like snow, for it was a matter of pride to the local housewives to be first on their knees on that day with pail and scrub-brush and a brick of whiting. A woman who neglected that public task was considered entirely worthless and contemptible, and received only curt nods from the neighbors. Only childbirth constituted an excuse.

The parlor, carefully shaded, was not a "living" room, in any sense of the word. Frank could not remember ever having sat in there for a single moment, until the day arrived when he was allowed to perch on the wooden crate containing the family belongings, a crate already stamped: "Baltic. White Star Line." But he did remember the rubber plant in the window, tall, lanky, repulsive, in its green majolica pot, the Nottingham curtains parted carefully, and slightly to inform the neighbors that within everything was orthodox and in order, and a rubber plant in residence. He remembered the red Turkey carpet on the floor, the red plush chairs and settee, the plated silver candlesticks on the stone mantelpiece, which was draped in red crimson velveteen, and the sprawling red roses on the wallpaper. Mrs. Clair had bestowed that large round table in the center of the room, with its crimson balled cover, and the china lamp with its odor of kerosene. Above it was the cheap gas chandelier, lately installed. Mrs. Maybelle, who had a penchant for red, was enraptured by her parlor. She would often stand reverently in the doorway, and murmur: "Rich." She would turn to Frank, lurking at her skirts, and say, proudly: "Rich, lovey, isn't it?" She never lit the fire on the stone hearth, but the fender and the andirons were polished religiously.

The family lived in the room behind, which was entered by a short narrow hallway. Here there was less "richness" but more comfort. It was an ugly room, but enlivened by a constant fire, and the mantelpiece was a clutter of bric-a-bric, glasses containing wax tapers, an imitation marble clock, and a few photographs. A cheap rug covered the floor; the dining table stood in the corner, between two windows set at right angles to each other. There were wooden rockers, with cushions, and the glaring gas chandelier, and a steep staircase leading to the bedrooms, always cold and bleak, and, best of all, a bathroom, without water closet. The latter ugly utility was, as in Higher Broughton, in the stone yard. Frank never remembered having a bath in the shining white monster upstairs. He, as well as his parents, bathed in a tin tub before the living-room fire, an ordeal accompanied by pungent harsh soap and stiff hard towels.

Beyond the yard was the Common, where the children played, and beyond the Common, the elevated street called Sandy Road. This road led to "town," on the left. To the right, it led to the cotton mills, the open country, and, over a mile away, the free school.

He remembered some of the neighbors vividly. To the left, the Wordens. The father, Jim, was a worker in the cotton mills, the mother, a hag-ridden and desperately silent woman who spent her life in a fever of "making ends meet." There was the older daughter, Bertha, a grown woman of sixteen, already a worker in the mills, a frail pretty girl with a white face and a crown of fair curling hair and protruding blue eyes. There was Will, fourteen, who came home at noon, to enter the mills without the preliminary of halting for a meal, then Jim, eleven, who was to die in France in 1916, then Jack, eight, then Helen, seven, who was fat, bold and noisy, then Lassie, a pretty child of five. There was a nebulous child in arms, who whined constantly and died of rickets before he had seen his first birthday. This, then, was the Worden family, who dined almost exclusively on fish and chips, boiled potatoes and cabbage, limp carrots and boiled onions, tea, flabby white bread and jam, and, on Sundays, a "bit" of boiled beef or mutton.

The neighbors opposite, across the red-brick road, remained nebulous to Frank, except for the Durhams. He, the father of one lone child, was a physician, and was denounced enviously as a "quack." But he wore a black broadcloth coat with a velvet collar, an elegant derby hat, carried gloves and cane, and went on his rounds in a rented carriage. His wife, petulant, well-dressed, snubbed the neighbors very effectively, and guarded her son, Eddie, an obnoxious snob of a boy who went to a private school far up on Sandy Lane, from the encroachment of the "common" children.

This school, attended by Eddie Durham and a few other children in Reddish, cost only four shillings a week, and Francis Clair, flushed with his larger wages, decided that young Frank also must attend it. He discouraged Frank's frightened overtures to the Worden children, and was acid in his comments on his wife's traffickings with them. "Have some pride, Maybelle," he would say. "You've got to hold your head up. I'm not a snob, but after all, there are limits." Young Frank was not allowed to wear clogs, like the other children, though he thought the clatter fascinating, and was envious. He must be washed and brushed meticulously when his father returned home for dinner and tea. He must not play on the muddy Common, which he did, naturally, on every occasion when his father was absent. Maybelle had no snobbery whatsoever, and she thought Mrs. Worden a "good, respectable woman, poor soul," and preferred the hot dirty kitchen next door to sitting in the elegant Durham parlor, sipping tea from bone china and eating caraway-seed cake. She allowed Frank to go with her, and often left him with the Wordens when she went on her "messages," her market basket over her arm.

It was with trepidation that she tearfully watched her husband march Frank to school on the first day. In spite of her maternal stoutness of mind, she remembered her mother-in-law's warnings. She was quite convinced that the afternoon would see Frank ignominiously rejected. How, then, would she be able to hold up her head? The law demanded that a child begin school at the age of five, but what if he was "touched"? But Frank was not rejected. He was brought home that evening frantic, bewildered, tearful, and completely disheveled, his new white blouse stained with ink, his new blue serge jacket and trousers crumpled, his black stockings hanging dolorously, and his sailor hat on his neck, strangling him with its elastic.

Francis Clair was infuriated. He came down the street, jerking the child viciously by the hand, so that sometimes the small feet were lifted clear of the pavement, and muttering fiercely to himself. "I'll clout you, I'll clout you!" he would say, gritting his teeth. "I'll show you! Wait till I get you home!"

Upon entering the house, and carefully closing the doors and all the windows against the "neighbors," Francis assaulted the frightened Maybelle with furious shouts.

"D'ye know what he did, this fine lad of yours? Sat like a lump all day, and then just before I came, he picks up an ink-pot and throws it at some kid, and knocks a lump up on her head! Gets it all over him, too! Look at him! And I lay it all at your door. You've spoiled him beyond repair."

Frank was soundly thrashed, of course, first by his father, then by his mother. The latter thrashing was administered less in anger than in an attempt to placate Francis. Frank uttered no cry during the rough ordeal, though his small face turned ashen. He was sent to bed without his tea, and there he lay, shuddering and shivering, a ball of terrified misery, a loud roaring in his ears. He did not sleep until morning.

He had no words. He had no speech at all to make articulate his boundless and frightful terror and wretchedness. He knew what hatred was. He had encountered it in his grandmother. But he had made his first, large-scale acquaintance with it that day, and its smell was in the very folds of his fragile flesh.

The school had been established by a decayed gentlewoman of a faded but malicious temperament, and consisted of two large rooms over her lower living quarters. The first room was the classroom, fitted out with a long narrow table surrounded with chairs. A lithograph of the late Queen adorned the plaster wall. There was no fireplace, and the chill damp of autumn filled the room with a fetid, chalk-like, dusty smell. The second room had another long table, also surrounded with chairs, on which the children were served lukewarm and weak tea, sweetened with condensed milk, and stale cake and biscuits. There the children would dine, their hands dusty from their slates, their faces intent and wary.

There were only eight children, the offspring of those who had pretensions to gentility, such as Francis Clair. Their fathers were small shopkeepers or public-house owners, bookkeepers, or starveling clerks. In comparison, the poverty-ridden Worden children were buxom, healthy and strenuous; each wizened face was completely pallid, every nose ran with Lancashire catarrh, or colds, every thin throat coughed incessantly. But no sturdy clogs protected any foot; buttoned boots, thin but well-polished, clothed the pedal extremities that hung over the sides of the chairs. The girls wore neat, ruffled pinafores. The boys were immaculate.

Suppressed, poorly fed, constantly shivering with cold, the children ranged in age from five to fourteen. All were ardent snobs, all envious and full of malice, all carefully elegant of speech. Their natural childish instincts, so well concealed and denied and corrupted, turned from a normal robustness to thin and poisonous cruelty. With the prescience of children, they had only to glance once at Frank Clair to know him as an eternal alien, as strange and threatening. They did not know what it was in themselves that he threatened, but they felt his difference from them, and hated him, and immediately began to plot torments for his separateness, for his daring not to be one of them.

Nor were they alone in their hostility. Miss Elizabeth Ballister recognized Frank immediately. Her meagre instincts bristled at the sight of him. Her hackles rose. She hated him at once. She could not say to herself: "Here is a stranger, and strangers are dangerous, particularly a stranger like this. He menaces something in me. He fills me with uneasiness and discomfort; why, I do not know." She merely looked at him and thought: Here is a very stupid and unpleasant child, and I simply do not like those staring, empty blue eyes and that open, drooping mouth. He does not look very intelligent, and I shall have trouble with him, I daresay.

But four shillings a week were four shillings a week, so she smiled with languishing affection at the terrified child, who was straining back against his father's grip, and simpered daintily at Francis. "What a dear love," she cooed. "And how delighted I and all these dear children are to have our little Francis with us. I know he'll be very happy, indeed."

She was a tall spinster of some forty years, emaciated but very elegant in her blue silk shirtwaist, with her gold locket, wide black belt, and blue serge skirt. Her faded pompadour was incredibly neat. Not a wisp of hair escaped pins and combs. She exuded an odor of intense gentility and of Pears' soap and eau-de-cologne. She had bony cold hands, damp and lean, and her waist was as thin as a stem. Her faded skin creased into a score of fine dry wrinkles when she smiled, and this smile displayed a row of suspiciously fine big teeth, too large for the long thin face, which was without a vestige of color. Her pale blue eyes were framed in red rims, and the prevailing catarrh had reddened the nostrils of her great bone of a nose. But Francis, overpowered by the gentility, by the saccharine condescension, by the thin swaying figure and high-born airs, thought of his ruddy, plump Maybelle with distaste.

Frank had previously been lectured on the importance of school, and warned that he must not cry, that he must be a little gentleman, and behave himself. Silently, with docility, he had listened. He had been neither attracted nor repelled by the discourses of his good luck in having been accepted at this school. He felt, and thought, nothing at all, sunken, as always, in his nebulous dreams. But when the school became a sudden and terrible reality, when he was actually there, when he saw Miss Ballister's eyes, and the watchful, piercing eyes of his dear new schoolmates, he burst into screams. He could not control himself. He screamed wildly and tearlessly, quivering with terror, straining away from his father, impelled only by a blind impulse to escape.

Francis lifted his hand in an impulsive gesture of threat, his face turning the dull purple color of his mother's ears, visions before his eyes of being hurried ignominiously into the street and being forever shamed before the neighbors. But before the blow could fall, Miss Ballister, fearing for the new four shillings a week, had deftly whisked the child away from his father, and was bending over him like an angel of mercy. The delighted children watched avidly.

"There, there, now," crooned Miss Ballister, stroking the disheveled chestnut curls. "We are just strange. We shall be calm in a few minutes. We shall send his papa away at once, and everything will be just splendid, won't it?"

Francis, sweating and quaking, took the hint, and went rapidly out of the room and down the stairs, the shrieks of his son in his ears until the closing door mercifully shut them from him.

Suddenly, Frank knew that he was alone, that his father was gone, and he subsided abruptly, trembling violently from head to foot. The handkerchief which mopped his tearless face sickened him with its sweet scent, but he stood and endured it. The gentle touch had become vicious now. It scrubbed and flayed. The languishing voice had lost its crooning quality. It was hard and hateful: "Now, you'll sit down and behave yourself, and no nonsense, sir. We know what to do with bad laddies, and I warn you you won't be pleased."

He found himself sailing through the air. He was set down with a thump on a chair; the table loomed, chin-level, before him, with its papers and its slates. He saw the faces of the children, gloating, greenish, disembodied faces, spaced in a row on the opposite edge of the table. He saw the blank, curtainless windows, and the eyes of Miss Ballister glaring down at him. He saw it all, in a clear, glittering crystal light which seemed inimical and appalling to him. He saw it all, and was still.

Miss Ballister, her lips compressed and spiteful, sat down. She lifted a lead-pencil, tapped it peremptorily on the table, and said, "Children, we will get at our lessons at once."

She had quelled more obstreperous children than this odious little wretch. She was mistress of the most distressing situations. She opened a book, began to give out sums. She watched Frank out of the corner of her gelid eye. She'd endure no nonsense from this horrid monster. She saw him staring at the children opposite, and thought: He is completely off. Whatever shall I do with him? All I ask is that he sit quiet. I have no fear of that, however. He hasn't the intelligence to do otherwise, with that silly face of his, and those awful gaping eyes.

CHAPTER 5

Miss Ballister was not without some knowledge of children, whom she hated. She had had to develop this knowledge in self-defense. So she pushed a book full of pictures before him, and opened it. Then she rapped on his head with her pencil, to the delighted giggles of the others, and said: "Look at that, and amuse yourself for a little while."

There is the Enemy, thought the children, not in actual words, but only with their instincts. He is the Outlaw. He is the Alien, formed of other flesh and filled with other spirit, whom we hate bottomlessly.

The profound and primordial tide flowed back and forth between Frank Clair and the children, the tide of recognition and denial, of understanding and hatred. It flowed all the morning, while Miss Ballister complained, reprimanded, questioned, and assigned. A boy or girl stood up to drone from a book; a late fly buzzed dizzily at the windowpane. The smell of chalk and slate pencil became acrid in a gathering dimness before the coming rain, and the air progressively chilly. Frank stared at his book, his cold fingers numbly turning pages. He saw strange scenes: storks nesting on roofs, a child in the arms of an ice goddess who fled through snow and storm, a child in a magic boat of gold with red silken sails, a girl with scarlet shoes racing through a dark forest, a beautiful lady asleep for one hundred years on a blue satin couch, a slattern on a hearth, among ashes, and a pumpkin coach beside her drawn by little white mice. He saw, in short, his first book of fairy tales, and immediately he was one with the creatures in the colorful pictures. He sat in a trance, dreaming, leagues deep in formless meditation, so that his own identity was lost, and he was not cold or terror-stricken or alone.

Miss Ballister was pleased at his stillness. At least, she thought, he is not incorrigible, as I had feared. I shall be able to control him. But what a stupid, stupid, empty face! No expression at all. He might be asleep with his eyes open. She was surprised when she saw the pages turned, softly, slowly, by a little bluish finger.

The children did not forget little Frank, though he had now forgotten them. He was completely unaware of their presence, and this, too, their instincts resented, almost more intensely than their knowledge of him. Sometimes he would lift his heavy blue eyes and stare at them, but it was as if they did not exist. Their warm and savage young hearts rebelled at this dismissal of them into nothingness, into insignificance. Had he, but for an instant, smiled at one or two of them, shyly, hopefully, had he really seen them, he might have made a friend.

At noon, the children smelled tea. A little maidservant entered the other room with a loud tramping of boots, carrying a tray on which were steaming hot water and tea, a slop-bowl, a cannister of hard biscuits encrusted with slate-like sugar or seeds, a plate of thin bread and butter, a jar of jam, and, for Miss Ballister, a small saucer of sliced cold beef. The children greeted her entrance with joy, put aside their slates, slammed shut their books.

Miss Ballister assembled them with some order, and marshalled them into their places at the tea table. Happily noisy and released, they frolicked, pushed each other, grinned, chatted. Miss Ballister sat down, smiling thinly, her avid eyes on the beef. It was then that she became aware that Frank was not among the children.

Angrily, she glanced back into the other room. There sat Frank, his head bent over his book, the faint glimmering light from the windows hovering over his bright hair. He sat like a young neophyte poring over mystic parchments, transfixed with holy awe. Even Miss Ballister became aware of some deep quality of stillness about him, some absorption that had drawn him away into a region of eternal dreams. The stillness of him seeped through the deserted room, so that it was like a well of motionless water, gray and soundless. He did not seem to breathe.

In spite of herself, Miss Ballister shivered, and thought vaguely of her shawl. Then a hot little spark of hatred and impatience glowed in her. The lad was impossible. Some impulse made her rise swiftly from her chair, rush to the boy, and seize him by a flaccid arm. She shook him with quite unusual violence. "You little ninny, what is wrong with you?" she exclaimed. "Come at once and have your tea!"

The child's head lolled on his shoulder. Then she felt his trembling, his startled return to reality. He looked up at her, and a glaring light flashed over his eyes. He allowed her to drag him into the other room. The children were again delighted and eager. Miss Ballister set him with a smarting thump on a chair, and stared at him balefully as she poured a cup of tea for him and clattered three biscuits into his saucer. She buttered a slice of bread for him, covered it with a thin skin of jam. Her mouth was tightly closed against any display of temper and disgust, and something nameless which she had never felt before. He watched all her movements, as if hypnotized. Then he sat and looked at his plate.

"Eat!" said Miss Ballister furiously, while the children watched, full of glee.

Obediently, for he had found that obedience brought him inattention, he put a biscuit into his mouth. He carried the teacup to his lips with both his cold little hands. The warmth penetrated into his flesh, and it was comforting. He even looked up.

The children, disappointed that they had been deprived of scenes and screamings, were talking and laughing with one another merrily, clattering their spoons in their cups, teasing one another with friendly malice, passing the plates, gossiping and disagreeing. One of the children was the son of Reddish's richest shopkeeper, and he was treated with respect and servility, and his slightest word greeted with quick nods though he was a fat young bully and a fool. Eddie Durham came next in respect. He was the only one who knew Frank, and he kept whispering viciously to his neighbors, who answered with malevolent giggles and stares at the silent little boy. The children were still too young to have acquired that hypocritical veneer of civilization which pretends to accept even the stranger. Savage, cruel, uninhibited and naturally bestial, they were themselves—truly human and as yet uncorrupted by courtesy and tolerance.

Frank sipped his tea. But now a mortal despondency had him, a sickness of heart which he was too young to understand. He had these periods quite often, though he had no words for them and became only more silent. He looked up, and met the row of grinning faces, saw the sly noddings of heads, heard the spiteful whispers.

Children had never impinged on his consciousness before, not even the Worden children, who endured him with healthy indifference because they were so busy and poverty and hunger were so exigent. But now he saw the children objectively, and knew that they had thrust him outside the pale, that he would never be one of them.

He was seized with an immense loneliness and isolation, a horrible and indescribable grief. His human flesh cried out for a human touch, a human hand, a human word of affection and closeness. All his heart, all his being, craved a glance of brotherhood and friendliness, a confiding laugh, a gesture of acceptance. His loneliness became a huge and crushing thing, an illness of the spirit, a desperate and bottomless hunger.

Stare, stare, thought Miss Ballister, disgusted. Has he never seen children before? He looks like an imbecile. Perhaps he is an imbecile. Well, four shillings extra a week is four shillings extra a week, and beggars cannot be choosers, unfortunately.

"Drink your tea, Francis," she said crossly. She snapped open the watch that was pinned on her shirtwaist. "We have exactly five minutes left."

But Frank could not drink his tea. His hands were reaching toward each and every one across from him, hands extended as if for alms. But the children, with the cruelty and the viciousness and malice of their childhood, looked at those hands and remained gloatingly silent.

Then Frank knew that he was finally, irrevocably, rejected, and that it would always be so, unless he disguised himself behind another face that was not his, unless he learned an alien and hateful language, unless he became what they desired all others to be. The asking hands withdrew. He sat in cloudy silence, not in rebellion, but in resignation, not in anger, but in perplexed sorrow.

The children went back to their schoolroom, and Frank followed, stumbling awkwardly over his feet. He pulled himself silently up on his chair. The book lay before him, but now it had lost its enchantment. All his flesh was wounded, aching, bleeding, his sickness a knot in his vitals. He sat in his chair, bowed, his head on his chest, his eyes closed.

He's really asleep, thought Miss Ballister, relieved. I do hope he will sleep until school is over.

But Frank was not asleep. He sat, completely inert, as the noisy lessons went on. He was too young to think in images or words, but his emotions were immense. They were storms and lightnings and seas and wearinesses and despairs. All sound retreated from him, and he was alone as he had always been alone and as he always would be alone.

The hours crept by. It was two, three, four o'clock. The children, having completely forgotten Frank, prepared to go home. But Francis had promised to come early for his son. Tomorrow, one of the older children, or perhaps Dr. Durham, who sometimes called for Eddie, would accompany him home until he knew the way.

During the past hour or so Frank had stirred feebly from his lethargy, but he was still not present among the other children. He watched them, his eyes moving listlessly in their direction when they recited. He watched Miss Ballister as she moved behind the chairs. The vagueness and heaviness were like a mist over his face.

Now the children, exuberant at release, hung up their pinafores, gathered together their books, giggled and pushed each other cautiously. The girls tied on their hats; the boys pulled caps from their pockets. Frank still sat.

He suddenly attracted the attention of the sister of the boy whose father was the rich shopkeeper. She was a green-faced little girl with bright orange hair and mean darting eyes. She had taken a vast dislike to Frank. She paused suddenly opposite the table, leaned across it, stuck out her tongue, and made a rude sound. Her saliva splattered him.

Frank had never known rage before, never so awful and appalling a rage. But all at once his eyes cleared, saw everything brilliantly, saw the hateful child across from him. She was all that was hideous. His gorge rose that she had dared even to be aware of him, and the anger that made all things so clear was a knowledge of all loathesomeness and outrage. She embodied, for him, a repulsive world that insisted on breaking in on his privacy, on invading that in him which was inviolate.

He had only one desire: to destroy that face, to eliminate it, drive it from his consciousness, force it into nothingness, out of his memory. His hand shot out instinctively, grasped an ink-pot, and hurled it at the child. It struck her forehead with a loud crack. Its contents ran in thin black streams over her face, down her neck, over her crimson wool frock.

She stood there, stunned. Others, hearing the noise, whirled and stared. When they saw what had happened, their delight was violent. They shouted; they jumped up and down. They clapped their hands in the excess of their excitement. But the brother of the girl rushed upon Frank and knocked him out of his chair, and kicked him. He continued to kick him, and then something voluptuous, murderous, rose in his narrow chest until it seemed unbearable. He writhed; he moaned; he was beside himself. Now, as he felt his foot sinking into the soft thin body of the prostrate child on the floor, thrills of sharp ecstasy shot all through his nerves, quivered over his back in tendrils of delicious fire.

Miss Ballister, horrified, watched for a moment in complete paralysis. Then she leapt upon the boy, dragged him away, shaking him vigorously, boxing his ears. He turned upon her furiously. He sank his teeth in her hand, grunting loudly.

She pulled away her hand with a yell, and sent the boy flying with a well-aimed and vigorous blow. She, too, felt delight. She knew children, and hated them. It gave her an enormous pleasure to strike the boy, and she followed him up with a clenched fist.

He stood at bay, sobered, blubbering. "I'll tell my father, that I will!" he sobbed, rubbing his eyes. "He'll take me and Mary away from your rotter of a school! And then, won't you be sorry!"

Mary jumped up and down, delirious with excitement, and the other children joined her, caught up in the prevailing intoxication. They chanted with her: "Won't you be sorry! Won't you be sorry!"

Cold sobriety fell upon Miss Ballister. She rubbed her bitten hand. She panted. She was a lonely and deprived spinster; she had nothing but her fees. She would starve. She knew that. Suddenly she was overcome with terror, and her mouth turned dry. What had she lost by defending a miserable little wretch who had deserved his punishment!

Her heart became a pulse beating feebly and rapidly. Her face grayed with fear, her body lost its rigidity, became old and limp. She took out her handkerchief and wiped the eyes of the shopkeeper's son. "There, there," she said. "You were very wicked. Frank Clair is only five years old, Bobbie, and you are nearly twelve. He's only a baby. Look, you've hurt him. He doesn't move; he doesn't even cry."

This was such an interesting piece of news that Bobbie Tompkins pushed aside her trembling, ministering hand, and craned to see the prostrate Frank. It was true. The little boy lay as he had fallen, lay as he had lain while being kicked, his arms instinctively clasped about his head to protect it. He might have been dead.

Miss Ballister had an inspiration. She straightened up, fixed all the children with a stern eye.

"You know what the law does when someone is hurt and kicked like that?" she demanded, with new courage and slyness. "They put the kicker in prison. Think, Bobbie. If Frank is very hurt, they will take you away, away from your mama and your papa, and your little sisters. You may never see them again. They might even send your papa to prison, or fine him a lot of money."

Bobbie Tompkins had a sudden and horrid vision of his father. He was not Mr. Tom Tompkins' favorite child, but

Mrs. Tompkins had "spoiled" him, a matter which the father had found it hard to forgive. Mr. Tompkins was also a very irascible man, with a bad temper and a very heavy hand. Bobbie saw his father dragged away by the "bobbies." He heard the wails of his mother. He saw the family funds confiscated, and the whole family sent into exile far from the pleasant suburbs of Sandy Lane, and forced to live on one of those horrible streets in "town." His father would kill him, as he had often threatened to do. "I tell you, Sally, I'll kill that boy some day, if I have to hang for it!" he had screamed on occasions of great provocation.

Bobbie shook so violently that he almost fell. He blubbered louder than ever. He clung to Miss Ballister. "You'll not tell my dada, please, Miss Ballister?" he pleaded, almost in a shriek. "You'll not tell my dada?"

Miss Ballister, who was fervently thanking God for her inspiration, would not immediately relent. She tried to calm the frantic Bobbie. "How can I help it?" she said sternly. "All the other children know. How will you explain Mary's inky frock and the bruise on her head?"

In a rage of fear, Bobbie tore himself away from his teacher, and, with clenched fists and bared teeth, swung on his companions. "I'll murder the first one as speaks!" he shouted, forgetting the elegant language taught him by Miss Ballister. "I'll smash his bloody head! Just one word, and there'll be an end to him! Hear?"

He turned from one to the other, panting, glaring, wild with fright and hate. The children recoiled from that savage eye, from that very real threat. They burst into a chorus of trembling denials. "We won't tell, Bobbie. You can rely on us, Bobbie. You can trust us, Bobbie!"

Satisfied, his breath loud and rasping, Bobbie turned on his whimpering sister. "If you say a word to dada, I—I'll smash every blasted doll you have, and break your nose!" he exclaimed.

The girl scrubbed her frock with a black handkerchief. "What'll I say to Ma about this?" she demanded feebly. "She's got to be told something."

Bobbie considered, his fists still clenched. He knew his mother's adoration of him. His face began to clear. "Tell you wot," he said thoughtfully. "Ma won't mind. We were having a jolly time, and I knocked it over your head, accidental. But we'd best get home before dada comes."

The matter was adjusted, decided. He resolutely pulled his

cap on his head, caught his sister's hand. He rushed out of the room with her.

Miss Ballister, breathing easier, now admonished the other children: "It will be best if nothing is said of this. I am sure you understand that, my dears. Bobbie has a very nasty temper."

She dismissed them, and they went out in a silent and subdued file. The danger was over. She was safe. None would dare defy Bobbie Tompkins' blackmail.

Then she started, newly terrified. During all this, Frank had not moved. He lay as if dead. And, almost any moment now, Mr. Clair would arrive for his son. She dragged the boy to his feet. He swayed against her, his eyes half shut. But he was conscious. She brushed off his clothing with her hand. She ran for water, and bathed his bruised face. She did all this automatically, rapidly forming a story in her mind. The child was too young for self-control. His father must be told a portion of the truth. She knew her Francis Clair. She knew that he was flattered that his son had been "accepted" by her; she had noticed how he had fawned on her during the negotiations. He could be relied upon not to broadcast the story.

Now her fear became rage against the suffering child. "You nasty, nasty little thing!" she exclaimed. "Whatever am I to do with you? Oh, if your father had just not brought you here! I don't know what to do! Here, drink this water. Watch that you don't choke. There. Oh, dear, why am I tried so? Come with me at once, you naughty lad. You may wait for your papa downstairs, in my sitting room. To hit poor little Mary with an ink-pot! I am sure I don't know what your father will do to you for this! And how angry he will be to know how you provoked poor Bobbie, who had to defend his little sister!"

She paused, hoping the latter artful statement had penetrated to that dull and sluggish brain behind the boy's blank face. But he said nothing. She thought: I doubt if he knows how to speak. I haven't heard him say a word all day.

She knew fresh relief. But still, his stained and dusty clothing, his bruises, had to be explained.

She carried him downstairs to her musty little sitting room, sat him down in the semi-darkness, shut the door behind her, and waited for Francis Clair.

Frank was alone, as he had not been alone all day. He lay back in the horsehair chair, and closed his eyes. A frightful exhaustion overpowered him. He sank into semi-sleep, retreating away from the aching of his body.

Years later he remembered that dark and silent half hour. Had he later dreamed that he was a child again, in that little dank parlor, and had another dream flowed into that one? He could not know.

But somewhere, after a time, there was mauve twilight and mauve rain, and a woman standing with white lilacs in her arms, her eyes shining in the dusk. Somewhere, peace and all sweetness, and the smell of the lilacs all about him, and silver drops falling in the silence. Somewhere a thrush singing far in the dimness of unseen woods, and those shining eyes gazing at him with so deep a love and tenderness. He could feel the fulfilment in his heart. Yes, yes, it must have been a dream, for he was a man, not a child, as he had dreamt it!

Miss Ballister met Francis at the door and gave him a slightly changed and expurgated version of the affair. Frank had been naughty. He had thrown an ink-pot at a child. But perhaps it had been only childish high spirits, after all. She, Miss Ballister, understood high spirits. Of course, it was unfortunate, and she was very vexed with little Frank. But the least said the soonest mended. Shall we not forget it, Mr. Clair? I am sure that little Frank is very sorry, and these things do happen among children.

Francis was aghast. He could only stammer his abject apologies. He could not know that Miss Ballister was worried about her extra four shillings a week, worried lest some natural paternal concern might cause him to doubt her story, especially when he saw the child. She need not have alarmed herself. Francis Clair was too abject, too frightened, too craven a man, to feel anger for a palpable injury done to a child, especially where his precarious social position was concerned. In truth, had Miss Ballister told him the real story, including the assault on Frank by the depraved Bobbie Tompkins, Francis would have exclaimed: "Good job! Serves him right!" Tompkins was a rich man; his children were sacrosanct. Francis, the chronically fearful, and possessed of quite an imagination, would have had visions of lawsuits directed against himself.

He was overwhelmed by Miss Ballister's graciousness. The woman, the lady, was so damned civil and well-bred! There she stood, making such kind excuses for the little beggar, and pleading with him with her eyes not to be angry at him! He was touched to the heart, and infuriated that his boy had dared to cause her a moment's inconvenience. So much above him, too, she was. One could see her breeding, her gentility. And there she stood, talking to him. Francis Clair, as if he were her equal! A phrase rang through his tumultuous mind: " 'Kind hearts are more than coronets— and Norman blood.' " It was plain to see she had "Norman blood." It would serve the little devil right if she expelled him, that it would!

"He is really such a nice little boy," Miss Ballister was saying, enthusiastically, her mental eye sternly fixed on the four shillings. "We've had such a jolly time together. He read his little book, and asked me to tell him what the pictures meant. Perhaps he was just a wee bit excited over it all. In looking back, I can almost believe he did not know what he was doing! I had been telling him the tale of Jack the Giant-Killer, and it might possibly be—yes, it might possibly be— that he was reaching for a stone to throw at the wicked giant! The fantasies that children have!"

"I'll give him fantasies!" muttered Francis, between his teeth.

Frank lay in his chair in the mauve and silver twilight of his dream. He heard the door open. He sat upright. Then all at once one clear quiet thought came to him with powerful surety: "What am I doing here?"

What am I doing here! The dark room rocked about him. He shuddered. He gazed about him, stupefied. Why was he here? What had happened to him? He knew nothing of this room, of the man and woman standing like wan shadows in the doorway, staring at him. They were strangers. He had never seen them before.

The room dissolved about him like mist, the walls sloping grotesquely, the door with its shadows slanting away from him into space. He was sitting upon an enormous top, which revolved, at first slowly, then faster, faster, and the walls, sloping, retreated, and the shadows in the doorway fled away.

He felt himself dragged by some force from the top. He felt a sharp impact on his cheek. It was not until he was on Sandy Lane that he became aware of anything at all, and then he burst into dreadful tears.

"I'll give you something to blubber about when we get home," Francis promised, jerking his son by the arm. "You damned little pig, you."

CHAPTER 6

FRANK learned slowly and painfully anything that did not pertain to letters and words.

Within a week, he could trace very sure, delicately strong letters, but it was months before he could recognize figures easily. For a long time, for instance, he would write the figure "nine," under Miss Ballister's impatient tutelage, but reversed; then, with silent triumph, he would add another circle and murmur: "B!" Letters had significance for him; figures were cabalistic characters that one only guessed at, dreamily, and, with luck, arrived at the correct conclusion.

He seemed to love the sound of words, formed surely from the letters he traced. He was face to face with a miracle, and when the word "cat" had been spelled out by him, and he understood that it referred to the creature pictured in his book, his eyes would glow and he would seem on the verge of tears. He had a low, uncertain voice, a rusty young voice, which was rarely used except to cry out the magic groupings he had achieved, or which he had learned to recognize in his books. Now he began to listen to all words, as if they were music, sometimes repeating them silently with strong motions of his lips, as the speaker enunciated them. It was as if he were intoxicated by words, any words. They were flashes of light; they were windows suddenly thrown open upon a land drenched with moon and enchantment. They were the blaze of trumpets raised visibly in darkness, haloed with radiance. They were drums that thundered, and filled the silence with wings.

How could he ever explain the intoxication of words, mere disjointed words, words in themselves, the butterflies of color, the rainbow bridges over voiceless abysses, the sudden flight of birds like the rising and wheeling of gulls with sunset on their wings?

Instinctively, he knew the richness, the succulence, the suety opulence of words. Sometimes a new word would remind him of a little fat man, waddling, full of chuckles. It was the sound of them, the mere sound of words (for he could not as yet know the meaning of one-tenth he heard) which entranced him. It was the rhythm and the spacing of them, the flow, the pianissimo or the fortissimo of accent, the sudden curve of a syllable like the swell of a glass vase, the sudden and abrupt rise, as if a hand had been lifted peremptorily. Sometimes they were ugly words, unpleasant raucous words, hideous little spoons of words that contained a lump of poisoned jam. He listened for words on the street; he listened for them in houses, in the shops, in corridors, halls, rooms. He listened when his father read from the Manchester *Guardian*, and the measured pace of these words was like a procession, a somber parade, a conclave of kings, an old man talking gravely in the night. Best of all, when his father read some incomprehensible comic comment, the words were like tumbling clowns at the pantomime, rollicking little dwarfs with large red noses, tiny tinselled fairies pulled by strings, Punch and Judies with cackling voices, or a silly little bang of happy drums. And some words were cold and stiff, like twigs in winter, or hard, like stone, or pungent, like the striped peppermint canes given to children at Christmas. But still they carried no actual projection of their intrinsic meaning to his brain. It was the mere sound of them which held him transfixed.

There were letters from Mrs. Jamie Clair, in America, which Francis read aloud to Maybelle. Mrs. Clair lived in Bison, New York, but she wrote grandiloquently (to show her new, cosmopolitan character) of heroic words like Oregon and Philadelphia and California. Oregon! Frank felt a profound silence like marble. The "Ore" was a man's stern voice, the "gon" was loneliness and adventure. Philadelphia! It was a word with velvet around the edges, the "del" in the center was a sweetness, the "phia," a soft excitement. California! There was the sweetness, also, in the first syllable, but a sweetness as of a cheaper grade, sugary, like jam which had begun to crystallize, and the "for" was hard as a wooden almond in toffy, and he did not like the "nia" at all. No, it was not nearly the delightful word that Philadelphia was, nor did it have the heroism of Oregon. He repeated these words over and over to himself, for the sheer ecstasy of the sound of them.

When, in his manhood, he remembered this, he was amazed, and bitterly envious. What a pristine and lovely frenzy had been his! What would he not now give to feel again that keen and terrible rapture, that fresh glory, at the mere sound of words! A voice on the street, just an ordinary, flat voice of a child or a housewife, but a voice enunciating a cadence of syllables that caught the ear with their poignant dissonance, or their thin little runnings like a brown rivulet in spring. Images flashed through his awakened mind at a mere exclamation. He heard a child demand something petulantly of its harried mother, and he heard a young rook complaining in the bare trees of winter. A young shopgirl spoke in the sweetest trill of a voice to his mother, and he heard a sleepy thrush awakening in the morning. He heard a woman laugh, and it was the tinkle of a four-sided cow-bell in the evening. Lovely, lovely words, entrancing sounds, excitements in a harsh grunt, enormous fears in the growl of the shoemaker!

He had a deep aversion for the word "platter." It had a flat, dead sound. He disliked "ham," for it was smug and thick. But serviette! What tender frolic, what grace, what sparkling fingers, what arching of pretty neck! "Tablecloth" suggested wool that scratched, and he itched at the sound of it. "Jam" set his teeth on edge, and made him annoyed with his mother when she spoke it. His father spoke of "Torquay," and he did not know whether it was a city, a place, a proper name, or something to eat, but the articulation of it made him feel wild and strange and full of hot bright wind. He heard the word "somber," and he saw a face turning in darkness, full of meaning. There was no relationship between the words and what he saw and experienced in his trembling heart. It was enough that he heard them.

Long before he knew their meaning, there were words that he could not endure. "Snob" was one. It made him think of thick catarrh. He could not stand hearing his mother say "messages." Such a fussy, blurred, silly word, like unravelled yarn. His father called an acquaintance a "gambler," and Frank held a stone in his hands, a stone of rough angles and jutting edges. Once his mother complained of "diarrhea" and Frank saw a little pile of stones with sharp corners glimmering in a brook. He heard Miss Ballister say "glittering," and he remembered the gritty, sickening feel that had cut his flesh when he had furtively played with his father's razor. And then there were words that raised gooseflesh on his skin, and one of them, foolishly, was the name "Myrtle." He thought of his father sharpening the carving knife on Sunday. No, there was no sense to it, none at all.

Miss Ballister could not understand why he listened to her with such intensity, why his eyes fixed themselves upon her as if hypnotized, whenever she spoke. But she was surprised and pleased. Perhaps the boy was not an imbecile, after all. Sometimes he glowed, palpitated, when she made the most ordinary remark. Also, he was learning. In three months he could read as well as little Herbert Kemp, who was eight years old. In another month, he had surpassed Master Kemp, and was reading with the brightest nine-year-old. But he could not understand that the cipher "2" and the cipher "3," had any meaning whatsoever, and when she showed him, over and over, that they equalled five, he would only stare at his slate, dumfounded. She would give him another sum: 4 and 2, and hopefully, hopelessly, he would put down the answer as five, as three, whatever the answer to the preceding sum had been. It was useless: it was cabalism; he could not fathom it.

Finally, in desperation, she had an inspired thought. She took out five large copper pennies from her purse and laid them on the table before him, and demonstrated addition and subtraction. Now he was fascinated. Something had been projected objectively; it was reality. He stared at the pennies; he looked at the slate. He was suddenly filled with joy. He looked at Miss Ballister and laughed excitedly. He learned to add, to subtract, to divide. But, to the end of his life, that was all, and whenever he was to add a column of figures, abstract figures, he was compelled to think of them as apples, as copper pennies, as oranges. He never mastered algebra, and geometry was always cabalism, the answer to which forever remained in the realm of luck or crystal-gazing.

He learned to write with amazing speed, and even at six, his script was small and swift, angular and running, and full of fever. He could write his name the first week; in five months, he was writing exercises with nine-year-olds.

But let another subject arise, apart from writing, hearing, reading, and he retired into apathy and inertia, like an emerald-winged butterfly metamorphized again into a sightless, blind pupa. Then blankness would slide over his features like lava, so that all the quickness and clearness of them were only vague sockets and formless lumps.

Once his mother gave him a broken prism from one of her lamps. At her suggestion, he carried it into the wan spring sun. Instantly, as he held the prism before his eyes, the world was split up into a thousand shattered colors. The stones of the garden wall were edged with crimson, with purple, with an intense golden yellow. He looked at his hand, and each finger became incandescent, streaked with colored fire. He could not get enough of this wonder, of this awesome excitement. Emotion welled up in him; he stood mute, understanding that there were thresholds which words could not cross. But something could cross, and the knowledge of that something hovered just beyond his memory. Then he remembered the strange music he had heard in an old garden and in the shell his grandmother had given him. Only music could render this exquisite play and fantasy of hue and shining light, and he felt a devouring hunger for exultant and passionate sound that lived beyond the enunciation of words.

Later, as now, he realized that the thoughts and the emotions which surged through the human mind were like multi-colored, radiant and gleaming fish, darting, leaping, veering, gliding, which could not be captured in the coarse net of words. Words were like thick and clumsy fingers which tried to catch drops of quicksilver rain. A vast unrest, a sadness, a muteness, filled him.

His mother, who was hanging clothes in the yard, said to him: "Frankie, don't keep that glass at your eye all this time. You'll hurt your eyes."

Years later, when he remembered her words, he thought: Yes, it will always hurt the eye, to know that what it sees can never be fully expressed, that what the heart knows can only be made audible in uncouth grunts.

More and more, as the months passed, he felt the thickness and heaviness of his tongue, the inadequacy of the words he knew and heard. They were like the dumb gestures which the deafened and speechless make, to communicate with others so afflicted.

He did not know what happiness was, the happiness of the thing expressed. He only knew that peace and joy came to him when his eyes were full with seeing, his ears filled with hearing. He cared for nothing else.

He accepted the ostracism imposed upon him by his schoolmates as he accepted the air he breathed. Sometimes, but only sometimes, he was wistful when he saw them romping and laughing and giggling together, and he experienced a kind of bitter young pain when he noticed that on his approach they became silent, their eyes glittering with detestation and hostility, and that, after a moment, they would turn their backs upon him and walk away. He did not know why they did this. He was beginning to talk well, exceptionally well, to quote the surprised Miss Ballister, and he had eager young things to say. But his schoolmates would have none of his company and none of his speech. Then he accepted this, with only a few first pangs of rebellion and perplexity.

But sometimes, only rarely sometimes, he would wonder if it were because he was dirty, or ugly, or repellent in some mysterious manner. Slowly the conviction began to grow up in him that he was repulsive to other eyes, and he would stand on the stool in the kitchen and peer at his reflection in the mirror over the sink. The mirror showed a young, slender, very pale face with brilliant blue eyes, a wide sad mouth almost colorless, a rather large and prominent nose, and a tangled mass of chestnut curls. It was the face of a budding ascetic, an intense thinker, a creature afflicted with too much perception and an agonizing sensibility. It was a strange face, and a compelling one, reminiscent of the faces of old Grecian statues, for the line from the hair to the tip of the nose was almost unbroken, and there was a classic roundness of chin and fullness of lower lip. An artist would have recognized that face. But the children were neither ancient Greeks nor artists, and they knew only that he was different from themselves. They called him "mud-face," "worm-face," "clown-face." They called him "Punch-and-Judy." They told him he was ugly. They had no other words to express their unease in his presence.

In consequence, he avoided other children as much as possible. The Worden children were more friendly, or, rather, indifferent to him, the result of Maybelle's warm generosity to the family. He found comfort in the big dark kitchen of the Wordens, which smelled of wet wool, drains, soap, grease and cabbage. Here he was tolerated. Maybelle was too rigorously clean in her own house, so that there was always a chill and ugly stiffness about every article of furniture. But in the Worden house everything was happy, dirty, disordered, and cluttered, and full of shouting young voices. The younger children could squat or lie on the gritty hearth and inhale a mixture of coal gas and blazing heat in utter content. Mrs. Worden was too exhausted, too enfeebled, to have control over her children and over her disheveled household. One found the most entrancing things everywhere, under heaps of damp shawls on scarred chairs, under the beds, under the edges of discolored rugs and linoleum.

Maybelle was careful of Frank's "food." But no such concern was exhibited in the Worden household. The children, including the rachitic baby, ate everything wherever found: on the table, on the chairs, on the mantelpiece, on the stove, in the skullery. One even found remnants of cake on the beds, where they could be munched in happy immediacy. The Wordens ran heavily to fish and chips, generously sprinkled with salt and deliciously pungent with vinegar. Frank was not allowed much of this delicacy in his own home, as Maybelle condemned it as unfit for young stomachs. But the Wordens had no such repressions. Mrs. Worden, right in the midst of weary washing at the wooden tubs, would shake her macerated hands free of soap and water, and "put on a pan" for chips. (There was fish only occasionally.) Then, delicious sound! the fat would pop and crackle, and a cloud of steam would arise as the raw potato chips were dropped in the boiling grease, and the children would crowd around, dancing in anticipation. The older girls would eagerly roll newspaper into cornucopias, and lay them ready on the splintered wooden table. The rain would drench the dirty window in cataracts; the fire would play shafts of ochre light over the chaotic kitchen and over the children's excited faces. The chips would turn yellow, faintly brown. The pan would be removed from the grid with a grating sound. Mrs. Worden would take a ladle and smile with fond wanness at the avid eyes. Now each hand held a waiting cone of newspaper, on which shocked headlines reported the San Francisco earthquake. The ladle hovered over each cone, the smoking chips fell therein, imparting a heart-lifting warmth to chilled little fingers. Up to the brims of paper relating tales of devastation, death, fire and horror poured the chips. Then there was a rush for the crusted salt-shaker on the table, the bottle of vinegar through whose cork a small hole had been bored. Then the piquant fragrance would fill the kitchen, a fragrance combined of mouth-watering tartness, hot fat and crisp potato. The children would run about the kitchen, looking for places to sit and enjoy and savor. Heads and bodies would tumble to the hearth; others perched on the table, pushing aside dishes caked with egg and crumbs; others stood near the stove, devouring. Frank always had his twist of newspaper filled with chips, and never again in his life would he taste anything half so delicious.

But Shrove Tuesday was the delight of all delights. It was a holy day, and sixteen-year-old Bertha came home from the mills at noon, and the children were not at school. Bertha, who was the acknowledged expert at pancakes, would deliberately set about her preparations to bring the food of the gods down into the Worden kitchen. Long before she made her appearance, wrapped voluminously in a faded apron, the children were gathered, waiting for her. She had the air of a priestess. Not for her the loud voices, the clattering, dancing clogs, the shrieks and clapping of hands, which her mother countenanced. The children had to find places to sit, and be quiet, and there they would crouch, hands clenched together, every face turned toward the stove as toward an altar, every exalted and dedicated young profile outlined with leaping firelight.

First, a big yellow bowl, then wooden spoons, then flour and salt and sugar and carefully skimmed milk standing in its white, cracked pitcher. Flour poured in a snowy cataract; the sugar was measured with the care of an alchemist, the salt was sparsely used, the milk was poured, drop by white drop, into the batter. Now came the tattoo of the spoons, beating against the hollow sides of the bowl. Now seven-year-old Helen, newly initiated, was allowed to put the great black frying-pan on the heated stove, and to drop a lump of precious golden butter into it, where it melted with a subdued and reverential splutter.

Frank forgot the faces of all the other Wordens, but he never forgot Bertha, with her pale bright tendrils of hair curling about her pale, pretty face, her snub nose, her coral mouth set in concentration and solemnity, her slender figure with the very full breasts, and her plump, work-scarred young hands. She was priestess of all the rites; she was Hebe and Athena, Diana and Juno. He never forgot the eternal rain that poured against the windows, the fire, the smell of melting butter, the intensity of emotion that simmered all through the clammy, odoriferous old kitchen.

Now the excruciating moment arrived. Bertha moved solemnly to the stove, so absorbed in her religious rites that she was unaware, ostensibly, of her neophytes, her altar boys, her as yet mute chorus of voices soon to be raised in orisons. A big spoon, dripping with cold white nectar, lifted, dropped its burden slowly and religiously into the pan. Splutter! Pop! Seethe and crackle! Now one or two children stole, trembling, to the stove, to watch the whiteness spread, expand, become thin and bubbling. Bertha permitted this to only one or two at a time, then their places would be taken by others, in subdued order. One might see the nectar seeping to the outermost rim of the black and fuming pan, another might see the bubbles begin to appear, another would see the edges turn up, crisp and yellow, another would see the last rite, as the huge thin pancake was turned, and its crusty brown back appeared, hissing, succulent and unbearably luscious.

Plates were waiting at the table. The children were lined up in order. Jim, eleven years old, presided over the sugar bowl. The children, too excited to speak, brought their plates to him, fragrant plates that almost fell from shaking fingers.

Jim, his mouth pursed judiciously, would sprinkle a thin layer of sugar on the steaming pancake, then the grimy fingers of the owner would roll it up. Then back to the allotted corner, with a fork, and bliss unimaginable.

Some of the older children, slightly blasé with memory, would taste critically, and give vent to such comments as: "Rich." "Lovely." "Better than last year's." "Well, I don't know. A bit soggy, mine is." "A bit more salt, perhaps, Bert." But the younger children, unspoiled by worldliness and recollection, enjoyed, speechless with rapture, taking slow sips of hot weak tea on the side.

Oh, happy, happy days of shelter and fire and smells and soapsuds, gray water in everlasting wooden wash-tubs, and chips and hot grease and sugary pancakes! Oh, days of supreme delight for all the palate! Oh, days of acceptance and peace and rich sensation, and warmth and squabbling children's voices! Much of England was forgotten by little Frank Clair, but never Shrove Tuesday, never Bertha and her yellow bowl and her ladle and her smoking pans, and her big brown teapot.

Forgotten was the livid rain, the hatred at school, the fear, the bewilderment, the pain, the silence, the loneliness. It was the Lenten season, and Shrove Tuesday was its summit of glory. The English pancake remained, for Frank, the holy bread of the crucifixion. It was God's manna on the poor, the true sacrament of His body and His blood.

All guilt was washed away with the tea. All fear and self-conviction were dissolved with the pancakes. Now he was at peace. His was the grace of the temporarily redeemed. His soul expanded with knowledge, with prayerful tranquillity.

CHAPTER 7

HE COULD not understand why the Worden children seemed so happy, self-confident, serene and sturdy. They had a robust objectivity of temperament, though they were so miserably poor and lived so precariously. They were loud of voice and blustering, and had human faults. Their clothing, patched, neatly mended, reflected the catholic tastes of more prosperous neighbors. But, with the exception of the rachitic baby, most of them had rosy cheeks, bright eyes, and a ready laugh. Their little father, a twisted, black little gnome of a man, often smelling of beer, and possessing a profane tongue, had a droll way with him, and he could whistle and imitate with fidelity many birds. His meekness was not craven, as was Francis Clair's; rather, it was a "respect for his betters" which did not reduce his own natural dignity in the slightest. He had no ambitions, except the simple one of keeping his job, of marrying off his daughters to "sound" young men, and helping his sons to jobs beside him in the mill. On Saturdays, he had his "pint of beer," and his cricket or football games, and his fish and chips at night. On Sundays, he had his "good sleep" of a morning, a "jolly good breakfast," his place by the fire with his newspapers, his walk after a dinner of boiled meat, hot potatoes, cabbage, suet pudding and tea, and his long arguments with his fellow-workers on the streets, during which politics were discussed and much dark head-shaking indulged in. "That Kaiser feller, now, I don't trust him; though, mind you, he's the old Queen's grandson. Ah, it's not been the same since she died, God bless her. There's goin's on in London, these days, as couldn't be investigated, and I daresay we'll never know. There's a barmy feelin' in the air; not like in the old days. The papers tell you nothin'."

Jim Worden possessed the ancient pride of the English workingman, the inviolate faith, the knowledge that his house was his castle. He could "look the bobby in the eye" and know himself for an honest man. He had none of the pretensions of the wretched "middle class" to which Francis Clair belonged. He had none of their fears, their anxieties, their pallid concern for caste, their necessity to "hold their heads up." And he was richer in his dignity than they were in their cautious and pitiable snobbery. He did not quail before a haughty glance; he was never afraid that he had "said something" which might not be genteel.

He had no fears, except the ones of being "sacked" and of his daughters "going wrong." So long as these fears did not materialize, he was happy and secure. He loved his wife, in the half-bullying, half-affectionate way of his class, regretted that she was so fecund, and honored King and God, in that order. He brooded tenderly over the photographs of the royal family which appeared in his newspapers. He discussed their affairs intimately, sometimes with scorn, sometimes with perplexity, but always with affection. He knew that they lived in their palaces because he acquiesced. He knew that it was by his will that they were guarded well, and he was proud and delighted when he saw magic-lantern pictures of the noble grenadiers' red coats. The carriages in which they drove, the jewels they wore, the garments which clothed their backs, were theirs by his consent. Without arrogance, but with honest beaming pride, he knew his power. He knew the power of the millions like him, who had only to rise in their might for all this granted panoply to disappear, for those gilded coaches to disintegrate into firewood, for those palaces to be made empty. And it was because of the knowledge of his potency that he loved them, brooded over them as if they were his dependent children, and cherished them. He was prepared to fight for them to the very death, for they represented his enormous power of consent, his unshakable stability, his invulnerable dignity, his strength as an Englishman. He pitied the Americans, who changed their Presidents regularly. He scorned the Germans, who were ruled, rather than rulers. He despised the Russians, who were oppressed by bloody czars and murderous clergy. There was no peace in change, no dignity in being ruled, and no manhood in slavery. He, an Englishman, accepted the laws he had made, for he had made them; he loved his rulers, for he had vouchsafed to them the honor of ruling him. Who could prevail against him, except death?

He looked at such as Francis Clair, and laughed: "Bloody little snobs! Can't call their souls their own!" He went to his local chapel of a Sunday, and grinned to see the shabby but haughty middle-class going into the "High Church." He did not mind the "High Church." It existed because he allowed it to exist, because he was a tolerant, just Englishman. But just let anyone try to "come over him" with their "fathers" and their "nuns" and their "popery." He'd "show 'em, he would!" Live and let live, was his credo. But God help the man who tried to change that by a jot or a tittle.

He thought Maybelle Clair a "nice little woman." But he had nothing but disdain for Francis, whom he would greet with a curt nod of the head. Like most Englishmen, he was not overly fond of children, and sometimes scowled at little Frank, when he found him hovering wistfully in the noisy, crowded kitchen. Then he would shrug and mutter: "Poor little beggar," and go about his business.

Frank found comfort in the Wordens, though they robustly ignored him, or teased him on occasion. They had no malice. They visited no bestialities on him, as did the children at his school. They openly pitied him because he did not attend their own huge, roaring school, and because his mother would not let him wear clogs. They did not think buttoned shoes superior. Did they not each possess a pair to wear on Sundays? They were stronger than he, and they often had chips to eat, and they could have a sip of beer when their father was generously inclined. They knew, instinctively, that the penny they each received on Saturdays was far more valuable than the many pennies which Frank possessed. They were much richer in the bag of toffy they could buy only at weekends than he was, because he could buy toffy almost any time he wished. He had many toys; the one or two poor cheap things they received at Christmas were infinitely more precious. So, they pitied him, suffered him, out of their riches, and their magnanimity, and were kind to him in their indifferent way.

He never remembered attending any church or church-school, and only the fact that his mother possessed a certificate which testified that he had been "christened" guaranteed that he was not a heathen. Maybelle, who was a Baptist, dared not suggest that the boy attend the local Baptist "chapel," so Frank must have accompanied his father to the "High Church." If he did, he retained no memory of that event, or events.

Once he asked his mother why the Wordens did not attend his father's church. "Well, it's this way," said Maybelle, reflectively, not knowing in her simplicity that nothing she would ever say again in her lifetime would have so profound an effect upon her son, "some people believe one thing, and some another. There's the McNultys, across the road. They're Romans. They go to that little church on Sandy Lane, near the fish shop. And there's the Horowitzes on the corner, him that's a tailor. They go to their own church. Your pa goes to his, and sometimes I go to mine. Some likes music with their sermons, and some don't. Some likes candles, and some wouldn't have candles for love nor money. Some goes to a certain church because they're snobs and put on airs. Shabby genteel. And some goes to other churches because they're handy. Mrs. McNulty likes her church because she can drop in any day or time, and say a prayer. That's nice. My church is open only on Sundays. And there's the Seventh Day Adventists, who think Saturday is the Sabbath.

"It's all the way they look at it, Bunting. No one really knows. But they do their best, and that's what matters in the long run. It's the same God. But some people think they're the only ones as have God's ear. Like kids, who think they're their pa's pet. When all the time God is thinking of all His children, and no favorites."

She paused, and looked with astonishment at her son, her reddish eyelashes stuck out sharply from her wide brown eyes. "You know, Bunting, people used to kill one another because they thought God liked them best and hated the others! That's what your pa tells me. I couldn't say. Sometimes I don't believe it. Rum, isn't it?"

They laughed together, deliciously, completely incredulous of this rumored absurdity. Later, many years later, Frank remembered his mother's rich laughter, which seemed the wisest comment on hatred he had ever heard, or would ever hear. His mother's words were, to him, all that was England, and for that reason alone he was to cherish for England the reverent respect and love which one gives freely to a great and honorable man.

Once, when he was out with his mother on her "messages," he saw his first dark-skinned man, who, his mother explained, must have "come from some place called India." The man wore conventional English clothes, but his head was wrapped in a turban. His features were beautiful, his skin the color of Maybelle's cherished mahogany settee. A crowd of curious little boys, silent but unafraid, staring but without hostility, followed him. He appeared not to care. In fact, a small half-smile tugged at the corner of his handsome mouth.

Frank was immensely interested, but his mother would not allow him to follow. "Embarrassin' to the man," she said, severely. "Though God knows why those kids follow him, like kittens after a cat. He's got a darker skin than ours, but is that any reason people should stare? God made red and white and blue flowers, and everything's different in the world, yet some people are ninnies enough to think it's eccentric to be different. What do they expect? Everybody to have the same gawps as they do?"

Even when he was still a child he gathered that politics were the life-blood of the Englishman, no matter how poor he was, or how preoccupied with his terrible necessity to keep from starving. Even the uneducated Englishman's comments on politics were pungent, wise and apt, and the doings of Parliament were of the most immediate concern to him. It was in America that he was to discover that politics were the degraded circus of the fools, the pantomime of idiots, the "hobby-horses" of rascals. The superior American, either out of inertia or dismay, avoided them.

He often listened to Jim Worden, in Reddish, and to his

father, and he acquired for all government a deep respect and reverence. For it was evident to the Englishman that his government was himself, and he must preserve that self from indignity, defilement and mendacity. The "nobs" might "swank abaht" in their carriages, but the Englishman knew that before the law he and the "nobs" were equal, that one suffered the same punishment for the same crime as did the other. The government did not declare that "all men were equal," but unhampered by this hypocritical fallacy, it could administer the law with full justice. British law declared that the privileged man and the underprivileged both owed a duty to the laws they had made and sanctioned, and that duty was neither increased nor decreased by social position or wealth. It was inexorable.

Sometimes the Englishman was disturbed by the uneasy suspicion that all was not entirely well "at 'ome" and throughout the Empire, that there were grave injustices and undeserved afflictions and many bunglings by too-cautious or too-expedient men.

But he had the unshakable belief, also, that in good and proper time he could, and would, rectify these things, that it lay in his power to do so, that salutary changes did not occur overnight, except in disastrous convulsions which he earnestly repudiated and rejected, but came like the slow and implacable and resistless swell of the ocean, the flooding-in of the main. After all, had he not given the Magna Charta to the world? Had he not been the first to declare himself free of clergy and tyrants? Had he not been the first in history to establish a "Parliament by argument" and to enfranchise himself? These things had not come between dawn and sunset. They had come over the centuries, and were rooted in his own strength and in his own indomitable heart. Evil came like devouring locusts, but was gone on the morrow. The forest grew slowly, and no casual wind could uproot or disperse it.

What the Englishman finally decreed was done, and it remained.

CHAPTER 8

EVEN in Frank's memory it did not always rain in England.

He remembered that last summer. He remembered his mother taking him by the hand and walking with him down Sandy Lane, past the last shops and the last houses, and down over a small wooden bridge, and down into Reddish Vale. Here he saw the quiet blue water lying between high green banks, and misty English skies flooded with soft, gauzy sunlight and afloat with silent clouds. Here, too, he saw lavender twilights and mauve mists and great oaks set ruggedly on great emerald knolls, lonely against empty heavens.

Sometimes he and Maybelle sat on still hillsides, the gentle sun warm on their shoulders, their eyes encompassing rolling meadows filled with tranquil cows, their senses aware of the sweet smell of dreaming earth, and of hawthorn, and of scented breezes as bland as milk.

He never knew where it was, nor could his mother tell him, but he remembered a blue twilight after rain, the fragrance of drenched roses, which shook crystal drops from their bowed heads, and the slow moving of snails on a flagged garden path. He remembered lilacs around the ancient door of a thatched cottage, white and purple lilacs with a scent that pierced the heart, and the poignant singing of a thrush.

He remembered spring woods, filled with frail white light, and carpets of tiny, yellow-eyed violets, and green mist in the awakening trees. He remembered millions of miniature white daisies clinging to brown spring earth, like drifts of snow, and, overhead, a dreaming purple sky.

He remembered the market place, full of grapes and yellow apples, plucked fowl, baskets of clean potatoes, the smell of fish and chips and beer, the laughter of women and the cries of playing children, and, over all, a sun like a benison. He remembered Stockport, where he rode in the upper deck of the omnibus, and his parents ate blood-puddings contentedly, as they sat, and gave him a bag of toffy. He remembered Belleview, the shrieks of the monkeys, the roar of the lions, the riding on the backs of the elephants, and monkey-nuts to be peeled and crunched eagerly between his teeth, and young women, with enormous hats and parasols, and feather boas about their necks, sitting on benches and laughing with dapper escorts.

He remembered the pantomime at Christmas, his stocking hanging by the crackling fireplace, packages marked with the sooty fingers of Father Christmas, peppermint sticks and roasted chestnuts and browning goose, and the frozen pond where he skated amid the sharply cast shadows of crystal sun and gaunt trees. He remembered the carols that came sweetly through snow that fell like small white butterflies, and the sweetness and content of a blazing hearth in the black night.

He remembered water-cress sandwiches and hot sweet tea, and daffodils in a yellow bowl on the white-spread tea table, and his mother placing a pot of honey and a plate of thinly sliced bread beside his plate, and his father by the window, reading the Manchester *Guardian* and commenting on various items in a sardonic voice.

He knew, by now, that they were going to America, and he heard his mother's loud grief and protests, and his father's impatient replies that it would be only for a few years. "Good God, you're not going into the wilderness!" Francis would say, throwing aside his newspaper. "Never mind what you heard about Indians, blast it! There're no Indians in Bison, in spite of the name. It's a big country, and it's got cities, and the blinking place is full of money. What do you expect me to do? Stay and rot here the rest of my life?"

But, most intensely of all, he remembered his first sight of death.

He did not remember going to that farmhouse, but there, in his memory, he was, accompanied by two or three of the Worden children. He was in the big bare kitchen, standing beside a tiny coffin in which a baby lay, while the mother of the child, seemingly quite casual and undisturbed, combed her long, yellowish hair before the mirror that hung over the sink. Frank remembered disliking her, for, though he had never encountered death before, he knew that it was accompanied by grief, and he knew this instinctively. But there the stout young woman stood, swirling the straight tan lengths of her hair, carefully inserting her "rats," meticulously and competently plunging hairpins, which she held ready in her firm mouth, into the masses of her coiffure. She had on a white shirtwaist, a locket about her neck, and a coarse brown skirt beneath which her hips bulged solidly. From time to time, abstractedly, she glanced in the mirror at the children who surrounded the small coffin, and Frank never forgot the cold hard glint of her green eyes, and her busy hands, and her air of brutal unconcern.

The coffin stood on a table. It was white, and lined with cheap white silk, all ruffles. The baby lay under its white shroud, like a sleeping doll, its tiny hands curled limply at its sides. It could not have been more than five months old. Death had not removed all color from the round still face; golden lashes curved on its miniature cheeks. Its sweet little mouth smiled faintly. The child was like a flower dropped from its stem, and finality lay over it, with gentleness and silence.

Frank gazed at the dead infant. He saw the golden curls lying so pathetically on the white cushion. He saw the smile, and the vulnerable, fallen hands. Suddenly, though he knew nothing of death, he was plunged into a terrible sorrow. His heart ached; his eyes burned, and there was a creeping heaviness in his limbs. He was a child who cried easily. He could not cry now. In some way he knew that he was in the presence of something inexorable, something profound and without explanation, before which tears were impotent.

He stretched out his hand and touched the small marble fingers of the baby. He felt the coldness, the chill. It ran up his arm and engulfed his warm heart, and he experienced terror and grief and bitterness and a knowledge of mystery. The child was to be buried, he knew that. But he did not see the child in the earth, closed over forever in darkness and mould. He saw the child journeying through long and shifting mists, alone, clothed in awe, lost and mute.

He did cry that night, at home, and Maybelle was very vexed. "Why did you go there?" she demanded, wiping away his tears. "You didn't tell me. It's not for a kiddie your age to see—death."

In an effort to console him, she told him of "heaven," and she said that the baby was doubtless, at that very minute, playing in a garden and surrounded by angel infants like himself. Frank listened obediently, but his tears still flowed. He did not believe his mother. He did not know why he did not believe her. He could see only the baby floating away into the mists and the mystery, forever lost, forever silent, the ghost of a petal on dark seas.

CHAPTER 9

AND now they were going to America!

The February sun was warm. The fields were adrift with the exquisite little white daisies to be found nowhere but in England. The branches of the trees had softened, become gentle, and seemed pregnant with life. Here and there, the hawthorn bushes had tangled green gauze in their twigs. All the earth smelt of sweetness and freshness, and the water in Reddish Vale was slowly turning as blue as windy spring skies.

The Clairs were to sail from Liverpool on February 22, 1907. Now all the neighbors were friendly, crowding into the house to give their best wishes. Dr. Durham, dignified, sand-colored and cold, unbent so far as to pat Frank on the head and to shake hands with Francis. Mrs. Durham spoke sweetly as she sat near the fire and graciously sipped tea. The Wordens surged in and out of the rapidly emptying house, and the children were fascinated at the sound of hammers on the huge crates in the parlor. Maybelle wept; but she, too, was caught up in the general excitement. She was not an adventurous soul. However, she plainly saw the envy and wistfulness on her friends' faces, and she acquired a new dignity and importance among them.

Surprisingly, Miss Ballister expressed sincere regret to Francis, and she held Frank by the hand as she spoke: "This little boy is really clever, Mr. Clair. Really clever! He was a little hard to understand at first. He has very strange ways, which need understanding. He has a very bad temper, I am afraid, but don't you like a child with spirit, Mr. Clair? He is shy, but takes what he wants. If he thinks he might not get it, he takes it and lets the fur fly afterwards. A little—a little—ruthless, you might say? He is very determined, for all his quietness, and he obeys just so he won't vex. You say that is sly? Dear me, I don't know. I really wouldn't want to say. But it is my opinion that he is a very peaceable little boy, quiet and docile when he isn't attacked or annoyed, but full of quite—quite—furious fire when someone gets in his way or is unjust. You can trust him, if you understand him. But if he is your enemy, you couldn't trust him, not one inch, and he has a most prodigious memory for slights and unjust offenses against him."

Francis, scoffingly polite and protesting at this extravagance, shook his head. However, he was pleased. He looked down at Frank with objective appraisal. Well, yes, the little beggar did have a "different" look. He had lost that doltish expression, too. Almost intelligent. Perhaps more than intelligent. He was a pretty kid, too. Something like Maybelle in his coloring, but with sharp clear features. Perhaps he, Francis, would "make something" of him yet. After all, there was good blood in the family.

So elated was Francis at Miss Ballister's appreciation of his child that he gave her eight shillings as a "remembrance."

He was very kind to Frank for some time after that episode.

The Clairs were to sail second-class, and this, too, was a source of envy among the neighbors on Mosston Street. No steerage, for the Clairs! Cabins and stewardesses and dining rooms full of silver and fine china and dignity. Mrs. Jamie Clair had sent fifty pounds towards the passage. She was "rolling in money" in America, the neighbors said impressively. She had her own carriage, and lived like a queen. She had sent her son photographs of herself, sitting in her carriage, clad in black silk with a good sable over her shoulders and a black frilled parasol over her head. Her expression had been full of majesty and stately forbearance. Behind her, the facade of an imposing house was faintly seen, with the lower reaches of white skirts, men's trousers, and polished boots shown standing on the steps. Her lodgers, doubtless. But now she referred to them as her "guests."

Francis and Maybelle and little Frank were finely outfitted for the journey. For some reason which was never quite fathomed, Francis had equipped himself with a pair of black leather leggings, with straps and buckles. These were for America. Little Frank, who knew nothing of America, nevertheless had a sudden vision of black, impenetrable forests, of wild landscapes full of boulders, of mountains which had to be climbed on foot. He, too, wanted leggings, which were refused, of course. He came to the conclusion that his father would carry him constantly in America, for his own polished boots were not fit for such arduous exploration. In addition to the leggings, Francis had purchased a strange, black cloth hat, or cap, with a large visor, and very exciting in appearance. No one in Reddish had ever seen such a hat, and it inspired wonder. But Francis importantly informed his friends that such things were widely worn in America.

Francis had acquired a handful of "cents." These he gave to Frank and the Worden children. They never tired of these strange copper coins, so small, half the size of English pennies. "Cents." Why, that was very odd. Everyone knew that a "scent" was a smell, a fragrance. But these strange Americans called their coinage by the name of perfume. Very strange people, indeed. Once Francis told his son, facetiously, that all American men ate with their feet on the table, and Frank had a dizzy vision of rows of tables, endless rows of men in shirtsleeves, eating ravenously, their boots crossed on white tablecloths.

Mrs. Clair, from her advantageous position of two years' residence in America, had written to warn them of the local climate. "It's not like England, Francis. You'll find it winter, when you land in March. Snow, and ice, and blizzards. That's their name for the snowstorms. It goes on like that far into the end of April, and often into May. So, dress warm."

But Francis and Maybelle laughed richly at the absurdity of a winter extending into summer, even in that fantastic America. Why, one could plainly see, by the map, that Bison, New York, was farther south than Manchester, much farther south! Mrs. Jamie was "exaggerating." However, as a concession to her weird notions, Francis bought himself a thick tweed suit (for which he was to thank God, later) and Maybelle outfitted herself in a pale-blue wool jacket and skirt, with blue silk facings. After some consideration, she decided to carry a warm coat also, but only over her arm. Why, it would be March, warm March, when they reached America!

Little Frank had his two new blue serge suits, new polished boots, new round sailor hats, and new jackets with rows of white sailor braid on the collars. He never tired of looking at this magnificence, lovingly and carefully hung in his wardrobe. One was to be worn on shipboard, along with his old clothes. But the other was for "landing." The rich Americans would have little cause to look down their noses at the Clairs when they arrived.

For the first, and the last, time in his life, Francis Clair was not afraid, not cautious, not apprehensive. Some excitement had taken hold of him, some adventurousness. His very features changed, briefly. He was alive, his eyes sparkled, his uncertain voice became firm and strong. During the last week in England he walked with quiet arrogance down Mosston Street. He nodded with stately courtesy to greeters. He was important; he was envied; he was "looked up to."

Now an exhilaration flowed through his narrow veins. Anticipation threw back his shoulders; a new dignity caused him to move his head slowly on his neck and favor acquaintances with a remote look. His tones had authority and pride. Even Dr. Durham treated him with respect. This small, meagre little man, bald, equipped with newly fierce mustaches, was suddenly clothed in excitement and consequence. His speech was trenchant, listened to reverently. Like all meek men of his sort, insignificant and timorous, he took advantage of this transient prestige, and the mill folk hardly dared speak to him. He was bathed in glory.

"Of course," he said loftily to his new dear friend, Dr. Durham, "we'll only have to stand it a few years. Then back we'll be, with our pockets full of money. I expect to set up my own shop, perhaps in Manchester, or go into another line of business entirely. There are one or two formulas I've been going over in my mind. My own concoctions. There's a fortune in them. But it needs money to launch them in the patent medicine market."

He thought of Beecham's Pills. Why, the chap was a baronet now! And all out of a few pills. Pears' Soap. Why, he knew the damn formula. Too simple for words. He, Francis Clair, had a formula for a much better soap, at much less cost. Some rare exquisite scent, now, to start the people sniffing, and a novel way of wrapping. It all needed money, of course, and money was to be had with absurd ease in America. He toyed with the idea of making his formulas in America, then shook his head. No, it was England, for him. Perhaps a baronetcy even. Let the nobs look down their noses. Titles built on pills, laxatives, hair tonics and soap were not to be jeered at, after all, especially when they had money behind them. His heart beat wildly. His own carriages; his own little place in the country; winters at Torquay, or on the Riviera. Servants for Maybelle, a good public school for the boy. Hadn't Miss Ballister said there was something in him? Arise, Sir Francis Clair. And then home to a banquet at Russell Square, and the carriages of the nobs seething in the streets of London around his great house. He might even get one of those steaming new motor cars for himself, and go swanking about with the best of them. Perhaps even a shooting-box in Scotland. Arise, Sir Francis Clair.

He seemed to vibrate as he walked through the streets. He was no longer in Reddish, on Mosston Street. He was strolling through the streets of Paris, with gray gloves and a gold-headed cane in his hand, and gaiters on his feet.

These, now, were the last days. Maybelle had given to the Wordens much of what could not be sold. The parlor, the living room, the bedrooms, were denuded. Crates stood before the cold parlor fireplace, huge crates filled with Maybelle's precious feather beds, blankets and best linen sheets. Crates of her best china and silver, and ornaments and bric-a-brac. She packed them, hiding her silent tears. When she heard Francis hammering the tops on the crates, it was like the sound of nails being driven into a coffin.

The last day came, a day of warm sun, of brilliant blue skies, of freshness and fragrance and teeming soft wind. It was February 22, 1907, and the air was like a holiday, even in Frank's memory. A few last neighbors came to say goodbye. He had never heard the word before, and it, too, had, for him, a deathly sound of finality. The crates were gone. The rooms were empty, filled with sun for the first time in Frank's memory. Now the house echoed, and all the rooms were strange, remote, closed against him in their emptiness.

He ran upstairs, just to hear his footsteps echo through the barren corridors, just to hear the booming of a slammed door. Oh, he had never slept here, in this room with the sloping high roof! He had never seen a fire in this ash-filled grate. He had never seen the sun through this dusty window! He was a stranger here, in a strange house, and ghosts in every corner. He ran down the stairs, faster, faster, trembling with fear.

Now the carriage which was to take the family to the station was at the door. There it stood, twinkling in the warm spring sun, the horses with gleaming black silky hides. A man was putting small bags on the floor. There was his father's new London luggage, and a mysterious bundle of his mother's, wrapped in an old Paisley shawl. Francis was disgusted. He pulled his luggage over the shameful thing. Maybelle would never learn. There was something common about Maybelle.

The family, after much last bustling on Maybelle's part, were finally ensconced in the carriage. The neighbors were on the street, waving, blowing kisses. Mrs. Worden had her apron to her eyes. The warm wind blew the women's shawls, the little children gaped. The sun lay on the slate roofs, over which coiled the acrid smoke from the chimney-pots. Maybelle wore a dark-brown suit, new and handsome, and a big brown straw hat, heavy with pink roses. The jacket was too tight. It strained at the seams and in the middle. She smelt of rose perfume, lavishly sprayed upon her person. Her brown buttoned boots glittered in the clear lucid light. Frank's woolen shirt scratched his sensitive flesh. His face was moist. Francis, lifting his new derby hat with dignity, nodded a last farewell to the chattering women. The carriage began to roll. Francis sat, staring straight ahead, his gloved hands folded on his cane. Maybelle sobbed, her arm about her little boy. But Frank gazed about him eagerly, delighting in the motion of the carriage. He had never been in such a vehicle before.

The carriage rattled briskly over the bricks of Mosston Street. It rose at a sharp tilt, and reached Sandy Lane. Now the shopwindows gleamed in the morning light. Now the street tilted downward, and Frank saw the ineffably blue sky, adrift with snow-white clouds like huge mushrooms.

Maybelle wept. Francis moved his head majestically. The harness jingled. The horses trotted. There was a pungent smell of manure.

CHAPTER 10

FRANK'S next memory was of a street in Liverpool, a street filled with the pale wan light of evening. And, at the end of the street, a vast gray wooden wall, which his mother told him was "the ship."

He was disappointed. He had seen pictures of great sailing ships in his picture books, and he had had visions of standing on a polished deck and seeing the mighty sails spread far above him. This was no ship of his dreams. It was only a wall, and nothing else, a drab wall pressed hard against the end of the street. How could a wall carry the family over seas, to America? He was very tired, and his feet hurt in his new boots. He began to whimper a little.

The next thing he remembered was the cabin of the ship, where he was to spend twelve whole days. He knew that the name of the ship was the "Baltic," and that the Captain's name was Smith. Years later, when the "Titanic" died in the waves of the terrible Atlantic, his parents told him that the Captain of this ship had been their own Captain. He remembered one or two glimpses he had had of Captain

Smith: a tall, quiet and rugged man with a gray Vandyke beard, and kind and distant eyes.

The cabin was quite commodious, with a most fascinating washbowl that folded into the wall, and three fixed bunks, soft, covered with good blankets, and very comfortable. There was a closet for clothes and luggage. But this is all that Frank ever remembered of the cabin, though his mother lay there, moaning in sickness, during most of the passage.

He had only one poignant memory of that day of sailing. The portholes were open to the warm sea breezes. His mother had opened her bags and bundle on one of the beds. Now she lifted her head, and looked through a porthole. Frank stood beside her. He, too, looked. He was not conscious of movement, of motion. But he saw a silvery and shimmering expanse, softly heaving, and beyond that, the purple shores of England, dropping slowly behind the curve of water. "There, that's England, good old England, dear old England," said Maybelle, and Frank looked until the purple cloud that was his native country sank behind the swelling sea. And then he heard his mother's weeping. But Francis was up on the second-class deck, his arms on the railing.

It was on shipboard that Frank discovered that not only himself, but all others, were distinct personalities, and that each had his secret life which did not impinge on the rim of the consciousness of his fellowmen.

His mind had always been involved in dreams, in huge cloudlike emotions and reactions, in tidelike responses to stimuli. But now, as he moved about the ship, his eye became more objective, and the amorphous clay of his mind took on patterns of thought, conscious conjecture, deduction and silent comment. If he looked at the sea in the morning, it was not only with responsive rapture and awe, but with the thought: How beautiful it is! When his father pointed out a whale to him, far off on the vast level of the ocean, a thin fountain of water betraying his great, indifferent presence, Frank was no longer merely excited. He projected himself into the whale, became part of the enormous monster, felt his dim consciousness and content, and imagined the green universe that flowed in the subaqueous depths. When he saw the leaping dolphins in the wake of the ship, he wondered at their life, and was filled with marvelling at the unknowable mysteries of existence. He no longer, with thoughtless joy, accepted the limitless red sunsets that turned the amethystine waters to fire, but he wondered about the sun and its journeyings, and tried to solve the puzzle in his thoughts.

Now, wandering about the deck, and observing the passengers in their chairs, or at the rails, or conversing with one another, or strolling briskly, he no longer accepted their presence with vague indifference, as one accepts shadows. He began to stare at them eagerly; he listened to them; he followed them about; he watched the play of expression on their faces. His sensitivity, like delicate antennae, extended to them, feeling the substance of their being, their thoughts, their passions, their despairs and their responses to all about them.

In so projecting himself into these others, into the feel of the air, the movement of the stars, the meaning of a voice, he discovered himself, and this was the most exciting discovery of all.

On the morning of the third day out, Frank came up on the second-class deck and found his father leaning on the railings, and talking to some shipboard acquaintances. He wore the astonishing cap he had so proudly purchased in Manchester, and his leggings. His cane hung over his arm. The cap shadowed his small meagre face and enhanced the black belligerence of his mustaches. The leggings betrayed the spindling thinness of his calves. The cane was a pretentiousness.

There he stood, with the air of a blasé voyageur, his voice dogmatic and affected, his gestures languid and continental. He was the traveller bored with Paris, with London, with Copenhagen and Berlin and Stockholm. He was the independent seeker after novelty in America. Casually, he gave the impression that he was on some mission of experimental research in certain American cities, and that he was to compare notes with mysterious colleagues on the subject of scientific chemistry. As he had read much on the subject, possessed more than the low average of intelligence, and had a quick mind which raced neatly over gaps in his knowledge, he was not too unconvincing to his audience. It was fortunate, however, that all of them were of his own class, pathetic poseurs in their own right, seekers after an importance they instinctively knew was not and never would be theirs, and each eager to impress the other. You believe this tale of mine, about my significance and value, and I will believe yours, they seemed to say. Grant me my miserable false glory, my little hour in the sun of your admiration, and I will grant the same glory to you and let you bask in my sun. Pretend to believe that I am a person of consequence and dignity, and I will pretend to believe the same of you.

Young Frank stood at a distance, watched and listened. Only a short time ago he would have noticed his father listlessly, and would then have made himself scarce. Adults were boresome creatures who had no perceptible reason for existence. But now, his supersensitive antennae reached out restlessly towards his father and the other elaborately nonchalant men, and, though as yet untouched by experience, the child knew and understood.

He did not as yet know exactly why they were so pathetic, why there was a quality of terror in their being, why they should so wring his heart. But all at once he was flooded with a bitter and tearless compassion, a burning sadness. He saw his father as he had never seen him before. He saw his pitiable pretenses, his elaborate and touching gestures. The cap, the leggings, the cane, were points of pain to the boy, individual blows on an excruciatingly sensitive spot of perception. He wanted to cry, but no tears came to him out of his adult sorrow. He wanted to run to Francis, to grasp his hand, to cry out to him in anguish: "I know! I know!" He wanted to look up into Francis' frightened blue eyes, and say to him out of the depths of his suffering spirit: "I understand, Papa. And I am so sorry. I want to help you, but I know there is no help anywhere."

But the paralyzing impotence of childhood was heavy upon him, and he had no real words to express his new knowledge, and no means of communicating his pity. He turned away, and went back to the salon, and there he sat for over an hour, enduring his first agonizing compassion for his father, his first understanding. And he knew his first abstract anger against all the world, his first comprehension that it was a shameful and terrible thing that anything in the world should be able to arouse pity, that the necessity for pity was evil and outrageous.

Frank did not recall ever having made any shipboard acquaintances among the children. Not one young face ever rose up in his memory. He remembered the handsome dining room, the stewards and stewardesses, the afternoon tea on deck, the little cups of chicken bouillon, the sound of the dinner-gong, and the vast breathing floor of the ocean. He remembered fog, and the uneasy foghorns at night, and the sound of music.

On the fifth day, the "Baltic" moved out of its course because of storms and the threat of icebergs. Now the warmth of the Gulf Stream was gone. The dolphins no longer playfully chased the ship. The blue glory of the water gave place to a mist-covered grayness, and the ship heaved and tossed and rolled incessantly. The dining room grew emptier with every meal. Captain Smith's face was anxious and absorbed. For three days no one was allowed on deck.

Steam hissed in the pipes along the companionways and in the cabins. But a pervading chill penetrated every cabin and stateroom and down into the crowded steerage. When the passengers were again allowed on deck, they shivered, turned blue. It was early March, and they were approaching America. Francis wore his tweed suit and thanked God for it. Frank's woolly shirts no longer itched him. Maybelle put on her coat, even in the cabin, even when she lay on her bed. Stewardesses brought rubber bags full of comforting hot water. English blood congealed in English veins.

On the sixth of March the ocean rose in smooth, gray and oily swells, but the fury of the gale had subsided to a constant low thrumming. The sky boiled with thick whitish clouds, streaked with coiling black mist. The bitter cold "froze a man's marrow," to quote Francis Clair, whose short sharp nose was constantly blue. Never had he felt such piercing wind, such grim temperatures. His mother had been right. He thought of the warm English breeze, the daisies, the low purple hills, the green meadows, and for the first time he was sick with longing.

On the morning of the seventh of March, Francis rushed down into the cabin and excitedly demanded that his wife and son come up on deck with him. But Maybelle, whose fresh pinkness had faded into a permanent sallowness, was listlessly packing the scattered luggage, and denied that she felt any desire to see the New York coastline. To her, the ship had become her tie with England. She clung to this umbilical cord to the last moment. Frank, however, raced upstairs with his father. Francis had provided himself with a pair of binoculars. He pushed his son ahead of him through the crowds to the rail, focused the glasses for the child.

Frank, trembling with excitement, stared through the binoculars. There, right on the floor of the thick heaving ocean he saw a low sharp wall, broken and chaotic, blue and lavender and pale yellow. The wall appeared to sink, to rise, to grow steadily brighter and firmer. Now the ship, jubilant, brayed out its greeting to America, and the deck was inundated with smoke. Voices rose on a happy storm of exclamations and laughter. The perilous journey was over. Frank became conscious of a strong sickish smell, sweet and overpowering. Gulls swooped over the deck, their shrill cries mingling with the gray wind. Frank saw small busy tugs, black and important, moving over the water towards them, belching smoke and making a prodigious noise.

His next memory was of American Customs and Immigration officials filling the cabin. As the Clairs were second-class passengers, they were not compelled to undergo the indignity of examination at Ellis Island. There was a little doctor among them, who applied stethoscopes to the chests of the three Clairs in their cabin.

Then Frank heard his father's angry, protesting voice: "What're you talking about, man? I've never had consumption in my life! Nonsense. I'm as sound as a nut!"

The doctor shook his head, listened again. Francis had removed his "weskit" and shirt. He stood in his woolen underwear, his meagre little face sparkling with ire and fear, his eyes darting about restlessly, his mustaches bristling, his tongue moistening his lips. Maybelle stared blankly, her face paling.

The doctor put away his stethoscope, and said: "There are rales there. Ever had bronchitis?"

"Who hasn't?" scoffed Francis. "It's the bloody national disease of England."

The doctor examined some papers in his hand. "Chemist, eh? Not a laborer. Well. We've had enough laborers coming from Europe. Don't be alarmed, Mr. Clair. I haven't said you have consumption, or, rather, tuberculosis. I merely remarked that you show some tendency to it. Probably chronic bronchitis. We find a lot of that coming from England." He smiled, clapped his hand on Francis' quivering shoulder, which was so thin, so bony. "We have a lot of sun here, and maybe that'll fix you up. But if you develop a cough, or show blood, better go to a first-class doctor as soon as possible."

When the doctor and the officials had gone, Francis collapsed on the bed. His breath came labored and heavy. He was white with desperate fear. He coughed tentatively. Maybelle said: "I told you you should wear your woollen scarf, but you would traipse around showing your neck!"

"Shut up!" replied Francis savagely. He coughed again and again, and listened with utter and passionate absorption to the sound. The cough was dry, forced. Francis began to tremble as he listened. "Honey and lemon," suggested Maybelle anxiously.

"Shut up!" screamed Francis. He coughed and coughed. He put his handkerchief to his mouth. It remained dry and clean.

The little man's face cleared. "Did you ever hear me cough at night?" he demanded of his wife, excited.

"No, lovey."

"Do I get flushes, or sweats, in the night?"

"Certainly not."

Francis sprang to his feet, triumphant. "These American doctors! Don't know anything. I've heard about them. They go to school for two years. That's what Durham told me. Consumption! Never had a day's illness in my life. Did you hear that cough? I had to force it."

CHAPTER 11

FRANK CLAIR'S next memory did not include New York, except for a vague impression of gray cold and patches of snow, and a chaotic confusion of buildings. Nor did he recall the four-hundred-and-fifty-mile journey from New York to Bison by train.

But he did remember leaving the train at the Lackawanna Station. Before him and his parents rose a long snowy incline, bleak, dirty and bitterly cold, which ended on lower Main Street. On either side extended deserted warehouses, saloons, suspect rooming houses for derelicts and those who sailed the Lake boats in the summer. A fetid odor of sewage, filth, alcohol and bad cooking filled the ashen air. Overhead, Frank could see the northern sky, heaped, overflowing, tumultuous, with heavy and swollen clouds the color of ash. He felt the paralyzing gale from the river and the Lakes, the sting of sand-like particles of snow and ice in his face. He was exhausted as he climbed the incline with the shivering Maybelle. Francis, capped, caned and resplendent in leggings, climbed ahead, carrying his precious London luggage. Frank never forgot the twinkling legs, the wiry little figure in its tweed suit, climbing with spry alacrity up the slippery slope.

They reached the upper level of lower Main Street, and Frank saw the street before him, lined with tumbled heaps of shops, restaurants, saloons and rooming houses. Everything appeared to cower before the huge and overwhelming winter sky. The streets, the curbs, the roofs, were heaped with dirty snow. There was a frontier air about this city of some three hundred thousand souls. Perhaps it was the endless winter, the cold, the proximity of those great bodies of fresh-water lakes and the fierce Niagara River which imparted this air, but though Bison was to grow to a population of some seven hundred thousand people, it never lost its frontier quality, its winter desolation, its atmosphere of isolated rigor. It was the second largest city in New York State, but between it and New York City were hundreds of towns, villages and smaller cities which seemed as remote from either as if separated by thousands of miles. Crouched on Lake Erie and the Niagara River, Bison faced the long snowy desolation of Canada, and drew into itself the freezing impact of polar air and the quality of lonely plains and forgotten mountains.

Mrs. Jamie Clair, who never mixed "family" with business, had made no provision for the immigrants in her own grim lodging-house on Porter Avenue, not far from the river. She had engaged two "housekeeping" rooms for Francis and his family on Vermont Street, near Normal Avenue. Nor had she met them upon their arrival in this forlorn amd melancholy city. They had their directions. Somewhere, Francis found a cold cab, and the family, shivering uncontrollably, climbed in and were driven off.

Frank was too young to feel much physical discomfort, though his feet were numbed and his ungloved hands blue with cold. He stared through the dirty windows of the cab, absorbed in seeing. He saw endless streets of drab, dark, wooden houses, the curbs high with snow, the roofs leprous with mingled white and black, the air aswirl with white sand and furious wind. No one seemed about, at ten o'clock in the morning of this March 8th. The veils of snow blew through deserted streets, coiled and twisted on deserted street corners. The houses were only dim, dark blotches behind these dancing and shivering scarves of thin whiteness.

"We've come to the end of the world," whimpered Maybelle, wretchedly, cowering in her coat.

Francis did not answer. He, too, stared through the windows of the cab, which were frosted with ferns of ice. His small face was tight and pent; he kept blinking his little blue eyes. Frank felt more sorry for his father than he did for his mother, though he could not have told why. The cane lay forgotten beside Francis; the valorous little leggings seemed vulnerable and pathetic, the cap too large for the face beneath it. Even the magnificent mustaches had begun to droop.

After endless heavings and rockings through streets rutted with frozen ice, the cab came to a halt on Vermont Street.

Frank saw a grocery shop, a tailor shop, and a row of shabby wooden houses, gaunt-looking and abandoned to the assault of winter. He climbed a long flight of steep wooden stairs, dark and gritty. A door at the top opened, and a vicious fat harridan looked down at them, staring in silence from behind a pair of steel-rimmed glasses.

Maybelle tried to smile. "Good morning," she said, and her voice was hoarse. "We're the Clairs. Just arrived."

The obese old witch stepped aside, not speaking. She sniffed loudly, though whether with a cold or with disdain, no one could tell. A blast of chill dusty air struck the travellers. Maybelle looked about her, and her warm heart sank, never fully to arise again in America.

There were two rooms awaiting them. One was a large bedroom and sitting room, containing a big iron bed, all filigree, covered with sunken dank blankets and a patched white bedspread, a couch with a heap of soiled blankets at its foot, obviously for young Frank, a leaning oaken dresser with a blurred mirror, two wooden rocking chairs, a round, uncovered oak table, and, on the floor, worn and patched linoleum of an indefinite brown pattern. A tiny gas heater had been grudgingly lit; its yellowish red flames gave off a stinking odor of unconsumed gas. A gas chandelier, without mantles, hung from the calcimined ceiling.

The other room was a kitchen, containing a "hot plate" on a wooden box, an iron sink, with a faucet that dripped only cold water, a bare table, and three or four wooden chairs with imitation leather seats. All the coarse cotton curtains hung limply, filmed with soot. An empty wooden cupboard yawned against a wall.

Every window, narrow and dirty, framed a scene of desolation: wooden roofs, smoking chimney pots grim and black, the sides of wooden house walls, and the dreadful street below.

For this magnificence, the Clairs were to pay three dollars a week, which Mrs. Clair had assured them was very cheap, as everything was "found," the heat, the illumination, the furniture.

"Well," said the witch, her arms folded under her apron, "you got here all right. Expected you two days ago."

Francis removed his cap. He dropped it on the large damp bed. "We had a storm," he said, trying to make his dwindled voice strong and confident. "Delayed three days." He paused. "You're Mrs. Watson, I presume."

The old woman grunted. She had an enormous belly under

her dirty dress of some black cotton material. Her whitish hair had been screwed into a small knot on the top of her huge head. There were white hairs growing profusely on her chins. Her whole appearance was brutish, callous, suspicious.

Francis indicated his wife and son with a wave of his hand. "Mrs. Clair, and my little lad, Frank," he said.

Maybelle nodded. She dared not speak for fear of bursting into sobs. Frank stared. The old woman deliberately scrutinized Maybelle and the boy. She said: "I hope the kid ain't a nuisance. First time I let the place to a family with a kid."

Francis said: "The lad's well behaved." He glanced at Frank fiercely.

"There's a school, number 38, up the street," said Mrs. Watson. "He's old enough, ain't he?"

"Frank's been to school for a year." Maybelle spoke for the first time, and with wan spirit. "He's very good."

"Hope he don't wet the bed," responded Mrs. Watson, sourly. She stuck out her hand. "Three dollars. That's to Sunday. It ain't but four more days, but I've kept the rooms for you nearly a week, so you owe it."

Francis brought out his money. His fingers shook a little as he counted out three bills. He gave them to the witch, who snatched them from him, stared at them suspiciously, folded them, and popped them into her bosom. She hated "foreigners." She particularly hated English folk.

"You've gotta use the bathroom that goes with the flat," went on Mrs. Watson. "It's my bathroom, too. You'll find it, going through my rooms, in the rear. There's a rule about it. You gotta ask me first about a bath, and no more than one bath a week." She sniffed. "Got any china and things?"

"Our crates are at the station. I've arranged for them to come this afternoon," said Francis. He seemed smaller in the bleak half-light of the rooms than in England.

"I have my own bedding," said Maybelle, with a horrified glance at the bed and sofa. "Good feather beds, and sheets, and pillows."

Mrs. Watson looked scornful. "Well, you can use your own. I don't care. Just hand 'em back when you're ready."

She trundled to the door, shaking the worn floor-boards as she walked. She went out and slammed the door.

Now there was silence in the ugly, poverty-stricken rooms. Maybelle sat down on a wooden kitchen chair. She began to take off her fine kid gloves. Her fingers trembled violently. Francis moved from window to window, gazing through them. The rooms darkened steadily. The luggage stood abandoned, its good brown leathers seemingly withdrawing into themselves.

Then Maybelle began to cry wildly. She bowed her face into her hands. Her hat tilted like a huge, flower-trimmed plateau. She crouched on her chair, and gave herself up to her misery. Frank pressed against her, too wretched and frightened for tears. Francis turned from the window and glared at his wife. He said, but his voice was tremulous: "For God's sake, give over, Maybelle. It can't be helped. It's only temporary."

But Maybelle cried incoherently: "To think I gave up my nice cosy home for this, with the polished fenders and the fireplaces, and my good beds, and my lovely furniture! To think we left England for this!"

Francis spoke harshly, out of his own despair and depression and fear:

"It's only temporary, I told you. It's cheap. We'll save all our money, and go home. Perhaps in two or three years. Ma's got me a good job in a chemist shop, a drugstore they call it. Twenty-five dollars a week! That's more than five pound! I'll get more a little later. We can save fifteen dollars a week; that's three pound. Three pound a week is seven hundred eighty dollars a year, one hundred fifty-six pound. I'll be getting more, too. Why, it'll soon be two hundred pound a year, a thousand dollars! Three, four, five years, and we'll have a fortune, and back we'll go. A thousand dollars a year, at least. We can put up with anything for that money."

He waited for Maybelle's comment, but none came. He twirled his mustaches hopelessly. "Think of it as exile," he said, with less confidence. "Just exile. We're still young. We can put up with anything for a few years. Then back we'll go, with our pockets full of money."

"Years out of our life in this God-forsaken place," sobbed Maybelle.

Francis began to bluster. "You talk like a fool. Where'd we ever get in England? There's money here. Keep a stiff upper lip, for God's sake. D'ye think it's easy for me?"

He glanced down at his tremulous hands. "I've got to wash up," he said. "There's the bathroom. In the meantime, you'd better change, and find something warm to put on. The rest of the luggage'll be here this afternoon. Buck up, Maybelle. Wash the kid's face. Ma expects us. She'll have a good dinner ready. Buck up. Things're never as dark as they seem."

He walked out briskly. Maybelle continued to cry with complete desolation. Frank timidly put his arm about her. He could feel her plump shoulders heaving: he could feel the utter abandonment of her grief. "Ma," he said feebly.

She caught him to her so vehemently that the breath was knocked out of him. "Oh, my lovey, how can I stand it?" she cried. "This terrible country! I knew we shouldn've left home. We'll never go back, Frankie, we'll never go back. I feel it, I feel it in my heart! We'll never see England again —never, never, never!"

CHAPTER 12

MRS. JAMIE CLAIR'S rooming house, "genteel furnished rooms with excellent board and home cooking," was situated on Porter Avenue near Niagara Street, where it had the full advantage of petrifying gales in winter and cooling breezes in summer. It had once been a mansion, built according to the tastes of somber-souled people of the seventies and eighties, and was painted a dark chocolate brown. It had twin "tower" rooms, excrescences which were like a pair of bulging bellies extending on each side of the second floor. Directly below each truncated tower was a "bow" window, crowded by four narrow panes of rounded glass. One was the window of the parlor, the other the window of the dining room. There was a third story, also, consisting of four tiny dormer windows set in a slate roof. A deep gloomy verandah surrounded the house on three sides, artfully contrived to shut out every vestige of sunlight that might incontinently pierce its way through crowding chestnut trees on the narrow strip of lawn. The trees effectually prevented grass from growing on this lawn, and so a dank area of moss, unhealthily green and spotted, served the same purpose. Almost identical houses stood on either side of Mrs. Clair's, so close that the side windows of the houses adjoining could be reached by an outstretched hand. The alleyways between them were narrow, dank, gritty with soot. But each house could boast a "back yard," where attempts were made to raise flowers, mostly sunflowers and nasturtiums and peonies, during the short summers.

Frank Clair could discover very little difference between

this house on Porter Avenue, Bison, New York, and the house in Leeds. Mrs. Clair had succeeded, miraculously, in transferring her atmosphere almost intact to this alien land. There was the same dank air, chill, clammy and shuttered, the same plush and horsehair furniture, the same long gloomy windows shrouded in coarse net and crimson draperies, the same dark carpets and long crepuscular stairways and narrow corridors. Instinctively, she had chosen this house the moment she had seen it. The air was pervaded by the same smell of boiling cabbage, barley, mutton, potatoes and suet puddings, and there was an odor of mingled chloride of lime, wax, coal gas and linoleum which made Francis and Maybelle sniff and stare nostalgically at each other each time they smelled it.

With the same instinct that had made her choose this house, and furnish it, she had picked her "guests" carefully. Frank heard the same hollow meek coughs in the dining room and hallways and bedrooms. He heard the same apologetic rustlings, the same hushed and apprehensive voices. As in Leeds, these guests were clerks, milliners, dressmakers and bookkeepers. The house was respectable, run like a military barracks, and the food was good. Mrs. Clair invariably had a full house. The hot and tiny rooms under the roof rented for seven dollars a week, apiece, with board, "two meals on Sunday." The second-floor rooms brought in nine dollars a week, and there were two large front rooms, "parlors," which paid the incredible sum of twelve dollars each. One was occupied by a Mr. Farley, who owned the drugstore where Francis was to work, and the other had been rented by a "refined" middle-aged widow, a Mrs. Prescott, who boasted an annuity of twelve hundred dollars a year, a fortune. To these, and to these only, did Mrs. Clair unbend. Mr. Farley and Mrs. Prescott were welcomed into the downstairs parlor at any time, and they dined in state with their landlady.

Mrs. Clair had been forced to increase her household staff to two, a mother and daughter. "These Yankees are so independent, you wouldn't believe it," she told her son. These two occupied a lightless little room at the rear of the third floor, and received ten dollars a week between them. "Two pound! said Mrs. Clair with tragic pride. "Think of it! A week's wages for a family!" She confessed that she had to handle Mrs. Clark and her daughter, Sally, "with kid gloves." "No sense of responsibility and duty," she complained to Maybelle. "And impudent. They demand every second Sunday off after four o'clock, and no work after ten at night! It's unheard of."

The Clairs were invited to dinner every Sunday, where Frank sat and shivered in silence, even in the summer. His perceptiveness had increased. He hated this gloomy house on Porter Avenue. He was beginning to hate his grandmother. He rarely, if ever, spoke to her, and this confirmed her in her opinion that the boy was "barmy." She was sorry for her son, she told Francis, with a deadly expression on her iron countenance. But then, one must always consider the blood of the mother.

Mrs. Clair was increasingly annoyed with Maybelle, for she had lost the warm pinkness of her English complexion. She had become permanently sallow, with freckle-like blotches on her cheeks. The bright coral of Maybelle's lips had faded for all time. Now their small pudginess was livid and dry. Even Maybelle's hair was beginning to lose its flamboyant auburn tint; it had faded, too, become drab and streaked, and its curl had turned into lank strings. But her plumpness remained, not round and firm as before, but flabby, unhealthily limp and shapeless. Her brown eyes, which had never been too vital and sparkling, became heavy and dull. A change was taking place in her, and the change was not comely or pleasant.

In England, Maybelle, despite her secret dislike of the older woman, had lived in awe of her mother-in-law, and she had rarely betrayed her natural spirit in any clash or encounter. Now Maybelle was becoming sullen. "She never has a civil word for me," Mrs. Clair would complain privately to her son. "She snaps and snarls at everything. I thought the lad was the apple of her eye, but now she clouts him at every opportunity, and sometimes even I rebel. What's come over her?"

Francis did not know. He did not even care. He was a man of shallow instincts and timorous expediency. He was a "pharmacist" in Mr. Farley's prosperous drugstore on Niagara Street, near West Ferry, and he was receiving twenty-five dollars a week. He had his own problems. It was hard for him to acquaint himself with the new methods of dispensation. He could not reconcile himself to the necessity of learning to mix "sodas," which he thought vile concoctions. He could not understand why a "chemist's shop" should sell candy and ice cream and tobacco, in addition to drugs. Moreover, he could not understand Mr. Farley.

Mr. Timothy Farley was Irish. Francis was at first outraged that he was to work for an Irishman. He'd soon "put the beggar in his place." But Mr. Farley seemed sincerely and warmheartedly unaware that he had "a place." He was a kind, fat, jovial little man, with remnants of red hair on a big bald pate, sparkling greenish eyes, a wide and engaging smile, a heavy gold watch chain, and a fine taste in good tailors. He was a widower, with no children. He had the deepest affection for young creatures, either human or animal, and his pockets were always full of candies and gumdrops and chewing gum, which he dispensed with tenderness. He had a rich and booming laugh, hard to resist, though Francis resisted it successfully. In England, of course, Mrs. Clair would never have dreamed of having an Irishman for a "guest." But things were different in America, and, as she frequently said to Francis, "when in Rome, do as the Romans do."

But Francis could not reconcile himself to working for an Irishman. It was "demeaning." He was as impertinent to his employer as he dared to be, for he was not a man of courage, and his impertinences were almost imperceptible. Mr. Farley did not recognize condescension. He thought Francis "a funny little feller, with no blood in his veins." He pitied Francis with all the power of his warm and generous heart, and so he was almost excessively kind to his new pharmacist, and invariably included a box of chocolates for Maybelle, a bag of candy for little Frank, and a quart of ice cream, in the salary he paid Francis every Saturday night. Francis accepted these gifts, given out of instinctive compassion and understanding, with stately graciousness. The gifts soothed him.

Francis was a conscientious if uninspired pharmacist. Mr. Farley was grateful. He had almost become reconciled to incompetence, slackness and irresponsibility in his employees. And even to cheating at the till. But Francis could be relied upon to be at the shop at exactly eight o'clock in the morning, superintending the cleaning of the floor and the windows, and even doing these tasks himself if the lazy schoolboy on certain mornings decided against the effort of appearing. Francis could be trusted at the till, as was evidenced by a marked increase in receipts. Francis was courteous, if cold, to customers, and his filling of prescriptions was exact, so careful and exact, in fact, that he acquired a reputation among local doctors, even among those who ordinarily did not recommend Mr. Farley's drugstore.

Francis' white coat was invariably immaculate, his hands

scrubbed and clean, his person impeccable. He was an automaton, apparently tireless and always precise After six months, Mr. Farley increased his salary to thirty dollars a week, and gave him a check of twenty-five dollars at Christmas.

Mr. Farley secretly wished that Francis would invite him to his home. He had become very fond of young Frank, who he thought had the face of some fiery but silent saint. He was very sorry for Maybelle, and plied her with patent medicines, to which she was becoming addicted. He listened with endless patience to her complaints of vague and ominous pains, and thought nothing of running back to his shop on Sunday and mixing up a special concoction for her. He would stare compassionately at her fat, flabby face with its petulant lips and shadowed eyes, and say a silent prayer for her in his heart.

But the Clairs never invited Mr. Farley to their miserable home on Vermont Street. It simply never occurred to Francis. Mr. Farley was his employer; it was the duty of employers to "keep their distance." Employees never presumed on an employer's humanity. Employers were a distinct and elevated race. Francis found no inconsistency in his profound conviction that Mr. Farley, being Irish, was his inferior, and, simultaneously, that Mr. Farley, being his employer, was his superior.

Maybelle, not having had the advantage of middle-class breeding, thought Mr. Farley a very nice man indeed. She was respectfully humble before him, as the source of her bread and butter, but sometimes he could make her laugh. He always listened to her when she bewailed her exile and spoke with tears of England, and though he privately thought England "a hell of a country," he always sympathized with the poor woman.

If Maybelle was changing, Francis was changing, also, and just as inexorably. These changes were not apparent to Frank for at least two or three years. Francis, always apprehensive and anxious, with a tendency to cringe before any manifestation of the innate malevolence of fate, was beginning to know fear in its most crippling aspects. He never knew why. Years later, Frank sometimes wondered, with a determined access of compassion, if this change had not begun to take place on the day of the immigration doctor's examination on shipboard.

But this imperceptible and implacable change in his parents

was not as yet the most pressing problem in young Frank Clair's life.

To Miss Jones, the children of the first grade were not a mass of anonymous afflictions who represented her livelihood. They were individuals, intensely set apart from each other, dissimilar souls endlessly exciting and new. Most of the children were the offspring of poor working-class parents, dull, insensitive and hopelessly inferior in intellect. For these, Miss Jones had a despairing compassion, not because they were poor and patched, but because their minds condemned them to a half-life, hardly superior to that of a beast of the field. They were eternal embryos, half-formed, expelled from the womb of life before final development.

CHAPTER 13

THERE were three teachers in Frank's life who had a profound effect upon him, and whom he never forgot. Two were women, the other a man. They were entirely dissimilar in character, in appearance, and in age. Yet they had one thing in common: a certain heroic sensibility and perception.

Frank's first teacher in America was a spinster of some fifty years, a thin little woman with a face like a raisin, and a huge, untidy black pompadour. In contrast with her diminutive size, everything about her was enormous, from her pompadour to her great boots, from her great hands to her watch, which was pinned on her shirtwaist. This gave her a rakish and picaresque air, which was increased by her sudden grin, wide, full of large white teeth, and delightfully humorous. This little cricket of a woman would rise with alacrity from her chair and race to the blackboard, her vast boots stomping the wooden floor like the boots of a grenadier, her pompadour a mighty swelling tumor over her miniature face, her immense watch flopping on her shrivelled bosom, her silver bangles clattering on her bony wrists. And, as she raced, she would give voice to a series of high, chirping notes, notes without words, which seemed the natural expression of her personality, and were as much a part of her, and to be expected, as the shrilling of the cricket she so much resembled. Her name was Emily Jones.

Frank was enchanted by her. He loved her from the moment she pulled his ears playfully, and called him her "honey." She had a rough and sprightly manner, and would cuff the boys with heavy-handed affection, tug the girls' ribbons into place and dismiss them with a smack on their gingham bottoms, and then look about her with an exhilarated and expectant air. She was all flash, all awkward running movements, all tenderness and understanding, and all discipline. The children laughed at her and adored her. Three boys and two girls attained varying measures of fame later in their lives, and they always spoke of Miss Jones with laughing love. Only one, and that one was Frank Clair, ever suspected that she was half starved on the four hundred and fifty dollars a year she received, out of which she supported herself, her mother, and a crippled sister. Only Frank sought her out later, to discover that she had died of malnutrition.

She would look at each new class of six-and-seven-year-olds, studying each babyish face, searching. Four or five times in the long years in which she taught she had perceived a certain flash of an eye, a certain turn of a head, a certain gesture, and heard a certain intonation, which filled her with a sudden energy and a great exultation. Here was one, not of this heavy clay mass, who was potentially a full human being, something to be sought out, cherished, guided, one to be prayed over and treated with respect and honor.

No one brought Frank to school that first day. Maybelle had merely pointed out the school to him, which was the distance of two blocks, on Vermont Street, and was numbered thirty-eight. She dressed him in his second best serge sailor suit, warned him to behave himself, tightened one of his garters, wiped his nose and tucked the handkerchief in his pocket, and told him not to linger on the way home. Then she dismissed him, and returned to her new occupation of brooding over her wretchedness and trying to remove at least part of the accumulated grime and dirt in her miserable rooms.

Frank entered the school at a quarter to nine in the morning. He was dismayed by the children playing on the sidewalks, awaiting the ringing of the bell. They were rough and riotous children, and they jostled him without thinking. He went into the dark hall of the old-fashioned brick school, timidly accosted a teacher, who took him in charge and brought him to Miss Emily Jones.

Miss Jones was busily writing the alphabet on the blackboard when Frank was pushed into her room by the other teacher. The splintered desks were empty, the gray windows admitted the cold March sunlight, and the room smelt of chalk dust, sweat and wood. Miss Jones turned rapidly from the blackboard, surveyed Frank with her tiny, restless black eyes, smiled at him hugely, and exclaimed: "Oh, a new boy! What's your name, dear?"

She clumped over to him, playfully pulled his ears, and stared down at him searchingly. She saw his pale, slender face, his clouded blue eyes, his chestnut ringlets, and his tall, thin body. He smiled at her miserably, his wide mouth moving without real mirth. She saw his long pale hands with the smooth fingers and the strong knuckles. And then she felt once more that rare quickening and excitement in herself, that strange breathlessness, that acute recognition.

She took him by the hand and led him to her desk. She sat down, clasped her great hands tightly together, and stared at him for a long time. Oddly, Frank felt no embarrassment or shyness under that intense regard, but only a kind of urgent response. He told her his name, his address, the names of his parents, his place of birth. She listened, her head cocked, the mighty pompadour glistening in the spring sunlight. She seemed to be listening to something else besides his voice.

Miss Jones knew, from her few questions, that Frank belonged in a higher grade. The boy could read and write; he could figure indifferently. But she could not send him away. She knew she must keep him, that she must help him, that he was one of the rare ones. She assigned him a seat at the rear of the class, just as the children poured into the room.

They recognized a stranger immediately, and peeped at him all through the long morning. A few of his neighbors smiled at him tentatively, and he smiled back. But all at once their smiles unaccountably ceased, and Frank saw again that hard mask of hostility sliding over their features. He was familiar with that mask, and he experienced, for another heart-sickening moment or two, that conviction of guilt, that awareness that he was outside the pale. He felt, again, that certainty that he was repulsive, ugly beyond redemption, a monstrosity that must always be repudiated, oppressed and cast out. He braced himself for his inevitable ostracism, his exile from his fellows.

Always hypersensitive to environment, always possessed of an uncanny ability to "feel" atmosphere, and the very exhalations of human temperament, Frank spent the morning sensing the schoolroom, the teacher, and his companions. The antennae of his mind searched the dusty blackboards, the narrow, grimy windows, the faces of the little boys and girls around him. It was as if he had no integument. The nerves of his body were acutely exposed, and they felt upon them the brief little winds of emotion that stirred all about him. Nothing was without personality for him. The walls were not only drab; they had a dull unfriendliness for him and possessed an inanimate soul which regarded him blankly yet with awareness. There was a long and jagged crack in the ceiling, blackened and peeling. He looked at it, and was overwhelmed with depression. There was a lithograph of a gentleman on one bleary wall. The gentleman had curious white hair, cut and shaped to resemble a pyramid, and he wore the most extraordinary garments. Frank did not know that this was a lithograph of George Washington, but he found himself absorbed in the steadfast quiet eyes, in the faint, enigmatic smile, in the lofty aloofness of the painted expression. He wondered if this were a portrait of the head schoolmaster. He was certain that this man would like him, and that he himself would respond to the strong kindness so evident in the calm face. He felt something like an urgent blood kinship between himself and the painted gentleman, an understanding.

The bleak March sunlight poured into the classroom, and Frank was again overcome with melancholy. He saw, outside the window, a projecting brick wall of the school, and the rough faces of the dark red bricks were alien to him, remote from him. His melancholy intensified. The nerves of his body ached with the impact of new awarenesses.

Miss Jones did not call upon him, nor give him pencil and paper, or a book. She let him soak in his environment, wishing him to become accustomed to all this strangeness. But she watched him, even while she read to the children, or scrawled large letters on the blackboard, and she saw his bewildered eyes, the way he studied the others about him, and his absorption in the crack on the ceiling, and in the lithograph. She also saw the glances the other children gave him, and she sighed.

Her cheerful and chirping voice rang all through the morning. She had a genius for holding the most childish attention. After an exercise with the alphabet, she added eyes, a nose and mouth to the fat A and B on the blackboard, made a squirrel's face on the C, a witch's leer on the E. The children laughed happily. Then Miss Jones, with a glance at the door, hastily wiped away the gay little caricatures.

She knew that Frank was condemned to unhappiness by his own peculiar character and strangeness. She knew also that children will admire and respect even the ostracized, if the latter demonstrates an unusual ability. She knew that Frank could read well. So, at eleven o'clock, she said, in her high crisp tone: "My dears, I usually read you one or two of Grimm's Fairy Tales at this hour. But we have someone new in the class, who can read as well as I, and so I am going to ask him to read to us."

The children stared in astonishment. Miss Jones smiled brightly and gayly, and, carrying the book, walked to Frank. When she paused by his desk, he gazed at her in fright, guessing her intention. She looked steadily into his eyes, and now her expression was grave and quiet. She laid the book on his little desk. "Francis Clair," she said, clearly, "will you oblige me and read to the children? We have reached page 157."

Frank was numbed with terror and confusion. But he could not look away from Miss Jones. She was telling him something with her birdlike eyes, and what she said to him gave him courage. He bruised one of his trembling knees as he stood up. He took the book in his shaking hands. Miss Jones retired to her desk. Her smile, her faith in him, struck him like a beam of light over the heads of the staring children.

Frank began to read, at first almost inaudibly, then with gathering certainty. The story was familiar to him, and one of his favorites. His young voice, clear and well-bred, filled the room. The children listened. One or two snickered at his broad English "a's," his careful enunciation, so different from their own gobbling and careless speech. Now Frank forgot his audience. He saw dark forests, drenched in golden sunlight; he saw the red roof of a witch's house crouching under twisted trees; he saw the white faces of terrified children, the blue and white of their garments in the shifting gloom. He heard the songs of strange birds in the leafy roof, the whisper of small animals under flowering shrubs, the stir of wind in the high cold sky. He imparted to the story his own emotional response to these things, so that the children, despite themselves, listened breathlessly, straining towards Frank so as not to miss a word of the adventure of the lost babes. The clock ticked on the calcimined wall; the March sunlight paled yet brightened, and illuminated the brick wall outside the window. A wagon rumbled heavily on the cobbled street below. A dog, in the distance, emitted a hollow bark. The children listened and did not stir a muscle.

The story was finished. Frank sat down, dazed. He had transported himself to the forest, and the song of the birds was still in his ears. It took him several moments to orient himself.

Miss Jones was speaking, brightly and firmly: "Children, I hope you listened carefully to Francis' reading. I hope you will remember how English should really be spoken. Try to remember how Francis pronounced his words, clearly and distinctly, and not as if his mouth were filled with bread and butter. English is a beautiful rich language, and it deserves to be spoken well, as Francis has spoken it."

The children stared with round eyes at Frank. Their unfriendliness was open. But he could feel their admiration in spite of this. He was a stranger, but he had learned that even the stranger can be tolerated and respected, if he be superior in some manner, though he may never be able to win affection. He must use his superiority to compel admiration, and now Frank understood that, from one's inferiors, admiration and respect are more desirable than acceptance.

Maybelle, instructed by Mrs. Watson, her landlady, had put up a small package of sandwiches and an apple for Frank. The other children had also brought their lunches. They went into the dark basement to eat them, sitting on gritty benches in full view of the furnaces. Frank found a quiet spot, and began to eat. His isolation closed about him like the walls of a small fortress. The other children ate, screamed, ran and played about the furnaces. Frank was content. He had come to hope that he would always be ignored. He listened to the voices of the children, and he thought that they sounded like the squealing of pigs, the baaing of young lambs, the mewing of kittens.

Then he became aware that a large and lumpish boy about eight years old was standing stolidly before him. He recognized the boy, who sat near him in the classroom. Frank glanced up, first with his usual preliminary shrinking, then with distaste. The boy had a big stupid face, vicious and dull, a cropped yellow poll, a fat body and big brutish hands. He was the largest child in the class, this Herman Kolzmann, for he had been obliged to remain in the first grade for two years. He malignantly resented this, so had appointed himself the class dictator and bully. The children hated, feared, admired and followed him, aware of his strength and his cruelty and the potential menace of his fists. He was one of the incorrigibles.

He glared down at Frank, his hands on his hips. "Bloody, bloomin' Englishman," he said, with derision. "Vat you doin' in our country? Ve beat you in sefenteen-sefenty-six. Remember?"

Frank looked at him, fascinated. He felt the presence of something blindly malevolent before him, something that could crush with inhuman brutality. His acute ear detected the unfamiliar accent. He said: "You speak in a funny way." What had his father told him only yesterday? "This is an English country, Frank. We've got more right here than all these blasted foreigners living around us. Remember, you're English, and this is your country, too." Frank said: "You don't speak English very well. This isn't your country, then."

The boy's large and bloated face turned crimson. He doubled up his fist and thrust it under Frank's nose. But Frank, for the first time when in contact with strangers, did not wince. His great blue eyes widened, dilated, with scorn. He felt something surge up in him, something rise and fill him like a power. He pushed aside the meaty fist, and stood up. He was tall and thin, and his eyes were almost on a level with Herman's. Now he was trembling, not with fear, but with a desire to strike that dull and savage face, to beat it down and away from him.

"Get out," he said, quietly.

Herman stepped back a pace or two, his little empty eyes, hazel and lightless, blinking. Several of the other children, smelling danger, gathered about them. Herman was enraged, but his naturally cowardly temper was taken aback at Frank's bitter scorn and fearlessness. He chewed his lip and stared at the strange little boy, and one could see his uncertain and fragmentary mind trying to orient itself.

"I could beat you all to hell," he growled, but his voice was thoughtful, almost whining.

"Try it," suggested Frank. For the first time in his life he doubled up his fists and felt a hot red rage in himself, and a certainty that in combat he would be the victor.

Herman felt this certainty also. He tried to grin. "Tryin' to pick a fight?" he said. "Vat's de matter wid you, anyway? Bloody, bloomin' Englishman."

The children, surprised and delighted, began to chant: "Bloody, bloomin' Englishman!" Several of the little girls clapped their hands and jumped up and down. More children gathered.

"Beat him up, Hermy," suggested one bloodthirsty little boy.

Herman would have liked nothing better, but animal caution kept him still. "Aw, I vouldn't dirty my hands wid him," he said, scornfully. He had another thought. "Vat're you, anyway? A Mick?"

Frank's hands unclenched. He was sorry that he was not to knock this hateful boy down. Then he was baffled. "A Mick?" he repeated.

"Yeh. A dirty Mick." Herman waited. Frank still stared at him, perplexed. Herman added, impatiently: "You know: a Cat."

Frank was silent with bewilderment. Herman was elated. "Aw, you don't know nothin', you bloody, bloomin' Englishman! He don't know what a Mick or a Cat is," he informed his faithful followers with scorn, glancing over his heavy-set shoulder at them. The children laughed loudly, triumphantly. Frank looked at them, more and more perplexed. Then he saw one little girl and one little boy, their faces pink with embarrassment, drifting away from the group about him. They disappeared behind one of the furnaces.

"I don't know what you're talking about," said Frank, with new anger. "What's a Mick or a Cat?"

Herman bellowed with brute laughter. "A dirty Pope-lover. That's what a Mick and a Cat is. They'll kill you soon's look at you. You're dumb, you bloody, bloomin' Englishman. Don't they have Micks and Cats in your country?"

Frank considered. He had never heard of people who made it a point of going about killing their neighbors. He said: "The bobbies wouldn't let Micks and Cats kill us." He was curious. "What do they look like?"

Herman and his friends bellowed with fresh laughter. Herman looked about him. "Hey, vere's Tom Murphy and Mary Flynn? They vas here. Vell, they ain't now." He returned to Frank. "They got black hearts, and they're Pope-lovers, and they'll kill soon's look at you. We gotta kill 'em first."

Frank was alarmed. What a frightful place this must be, when one had to defend himself to the death! It was strange that his parents had never warned him of this dangerous contingency.

Herman asked: "Are you a Protusunt?"

Again, Frank was bewildered. "A Protusunt?" he asked. "What's that?"

Herman banged his breast mightily, while the children howled with mirth. "I'm a Protusunt, you dumb ox. Like all these other kids. Well, are you?"

"I don't know," confessed Frank. "I never heard of Protusunts. Perhaps we don't have them in England."

Herman glowered at him. A red, kindling spark appeared in his eyes. "Veren't you efer baptized, you dumb ox?"

Here was another word unfamiliar to young Frank Clair. He rubbed his forehead. "I don't know," he said. "I never heard of it."

Herman could not believe his delighted ears. The red spark brightened between his short yellow eyelashes. He shouted.

He pointed his finger at Frank, while the children, entranced, stared.

"Then, you ain't only a bloody, bloomin' Englishman, you're a dirty kike, too!" he shrieked.

The children clapped their hands, jumped up and down. "A dirty kike! A dirty kike!" they chanted, overcome with ecstasy.

Herman grinned. "Vat's you real name, kikey?" he asked. "Levy?"

Frank was silent. Again, rage was rushing up through him like a torrent. He could feel it beating, burning, in his arms, through all his flesh, and rising to his head in a resistless wave of hate. He took a step towards Herman. Herman became suddenly quiet; he licked his lips. He tugged at his trousers. The children, sensing drama, became still and watchful.

"Aw, you can't be a kike," said Herman, in a conciliatory tone, watching Frank with some nervousness. "Kikes don't fight. Listen, dumb ox, I don't want no fight wid you. Look, what church you go to?"

The rage still palpitated in Frank. All his muscles were tense with lust for combat. He took another step towards Herman, who backed away. "Look," said the German boy, "I don't want no fight wid you. Don't you know what church you go to?"

Frank stopped. Now his curiosity temporarily overcame his fury. "It's none of your affair," he answered scornfully. "But I don't mind telling you, you dirty thing. I went to High Church with my papa, in England, but my mother went to the Baptist chapel. What does it matter? What has it got to do with you?"

Herman was relieved. He did not like Frank's expression, nor the sight of those doubled fists. He said, in a whining and more conciliatory tone: "Aw, well. Then you're a Protusunt, too, like me, and the other kids. You ain't a Cat or a kike. I'm a Luthern." He paused hopefully. "Know what a Luthern is?"

"No, and I don't want to know," said Frank angrily. "If

you're a Protusunt, I don't want to be one. I won't be one."

He waited for a few moments. But Herman did not answer. Only cowardly and furtive hatred blinked in his eyes. Then Frank, with scorn, turned away and went upstairs to his classroom.

This was his first encounter with prejudice and ugly hatred in the free and noble Republic which had been founded by Englishmen on the premise that all men are equal in the sight of God, that all men are privileged to live within its borders in tolerant safety and justice.

And it was his first, and most exhilarating, awareness of the power that lived in himself, a power that could arouse respect in others. He had felt his first pure rage and disgust, his first recognition that brutal cowardice can be halted by the scorn and indignation of clean men. He knew the answer lay in his own indomitable heart.

Even when the children followed him home every day, screaming: "Bloody, bloomin' Englishman!" even when they threw stones at him, and leered at him, and swore at him, in their childish, unthinking hate, he was not afraid. He had learned what oppression and persecution are, and he never forgot. He had learned the answer to them: Scorn and courage.

He never agreed with friends, later in his life, that the answer to oppression, ignorance, hatred and persecution was "education." For he knew that education cannot enter brute and subhuman minds, that these minds are impervious to gentleness and knowledge. No, the answer must always be scorn and courage, armed strength if necessary, and an unrelenting pride.

CHAPTER 14

MAYBELLE looked at the bank book in her hands. Francis stood over her, smiling with satisfaction. "Another fifteen dollars—three pound," he said. "At this rate, we'll soon have a fortune."

Maybelle smoothed the small pages with a reverent hand. The book had become the book of life to her. She looked at the many blank pages following. She could see them, filled up, rich with promise and hope. She turned to the last page.

Oh, surely to God, when that was filled and totalled at the bottom, they could go home! But how long would it take? The first four entries filled such a little space. She concentrated again on the last page. When that was filled up! Her eyes burned with tears.

"I want to go home just as much as you do," said Francis, defensively, knowing her thoughts. "I'll promise you: when the book is full, we can go."

"It'll take years," said Maybelle, mournfully.

"Not at this rate. We don't spend a penny unnecessarily. We can sacrifice. That's why I was so vexed when you wanted to buy the lad an extra pair of boots. Kids grow fast. One pair at a time is enough. No use wasting money buying extra things and luxuries. I still regret spending that one dollar and fifty cents last Saturday at Crescent Park. We could've put it in the bank."

"We've got to have a little change sometimes," said Maybelle, with sad spirit and regret.

"Well, you don't always look ahead," Francis reproached her. "Many a mickle makes a muckle, as the Scotch say. Little leaks sink big ships. A penny in the bank is worth two in the pocket. Look ahead. Sacrifice. Save."

Maybelle turned the book over and over in fingers that were suddenly clammy and trembling. She was helpless. She could do nothing. They must save money. But what if something happened, and they couldn't continue to save? Maybelle well knew the unforeseeable vicissitudes of life. If they could not save as much as they hoped, then they would be exiled forever.

Young Frank was in the kitchen, reading one of the books which Miss Jones had lent him. He felt something strident, something terrifying, in the atmosphere. He looked up. But nothing seemed wrong. His mother and father had been writing out the weekly budget on the kitchen table, and now they had a little gray book in their hands. Everything was quiet and peaceful. No one was speaking. Yet, something most terribly wrong was in the air, something cowering and fearful and frightening.

He always remembered that cool dim April evening. Was it then that his parents began to change perceptibly? Or had the change been coming on for weeks before? When had he begun to smell fear in those dreadful rooms over a grocery store on Vermont Street? When had it begun to permeate the lives of his parents and to make their days hideous? When had it started to corrode their average English characters and to deteriorate them, so that they became vicious and cruel, hysterical and intolerant, hateful, not only to each other, but to him who was still so young and helpless?

He never knew. He knew only that his mother had once been fond of him, in England, and during the first weeks in America, that she had defended him against his often irritable and peevish father, that she had delighted in his progress at school, and had listened to his evening prayers with tenderness. He remembered that in England she had been given to singing in a rather pleasant voice, that she had laughed frequently, and that often she had had little surprises for him in the way of toffy or a picnic or a gay visit to the shops. He remembered that his father had sometimes laughed and had been playful, teaching the boy checkers in the firelight, and taking him for walks in the country and helping him gather the first wild flowers in English fields. In England, there had been comfort and some solid, middle-class pleasures.

Frank recalled that in England he had frequently been thrashed, but it was a brief, healthy thrashing, and he admitted, honestly, that he must have been a hard child to understand. But now the thrashings he received seemed less in punishment for a childish crime than a sadistic catharsis for the fear that dogged his parents. Francis was beginning to pinch, to pull the ears of the boy, sometimes to punch him, his tongue stuck, animal-like, out of his mouth, his teeth clenched on it. Sometimes, for the mere misdemeanor of lingering over his dinner, he hammered Frank about the head with his fists, with obscene grunts of pleasure. Sometimes, for the slight sin of spilling tea on his blouse, Maybelle literally tore his hair from his head, scratched him, gashed him with her nails, her eyes sparkling with cruelty.

"They must have been mad," he would say in later years. "Mad with fear. Nothing but fear could have made them so murderously brutal to a child, whatever his crimes."

Was it in those early days that their fear began to cover all things in their lives with a gray and stinking fog? Frank knew only that they soon began to fear everything, a knock at the door, a certain note in Mrs. Watson's voice, a strange letter which later turned out to be an advertising leaflet, the neighbors, the people on the streets. And inevitably the fear became hatred, hatred of everything, hatred of the "Yankees," Mr. Farley, the weather, the house, the money which they had to spend for bare subsistence, Mrs. Clair, the sun in the streets, the snow in the winter. And, even more inevitably, each other.

It must have been Frank's strangeness, of which they were increasingly aware, which so infuriated them. Had he echoed their own fears, had he trembled at an unaccustomed footstep, had he evinced an interest in saving the rare pennies that came to him, they would have recognized him as their own, and, seeing themselves mirrored in him, would have loved him.

Had he screamed when they attacked him with such monstrous and demented fury, had he yelled and cried, it would have made his life easier, for they feared "the neighbors" with an unreasoning terror. But he made no outcry, and so they could torture him with impunity, leaving him bruised, breathless and panting.

It seemed incredible to him, in later years, that such madness could have come upon two formerly average and undistinguished people. When he spoke of this madness, not in anger but in perplexity, to others, they looked at him incredulously. But then, not many people are so beset by insane fear as were Francis and Maybelle.

Frank would not have been human had he not sought to protect himself from his parents. He knew that the slightest infringement of any small rule, the slightest complaint of a neighbor against him, the slightest annoyance which some adult might display towards him, would result in a dreadful beating. If Maybelle sent him to the gorcery store, and he returned with a penny short, she would assault him madly. So Frank, in self-defense, became a liar.

He never forgave his parents for that. Out of his understanding, he could forgive them their craven fears. But he could not forgive them for forcing him to soil his young life with lies. He could not forgive them for darkening his existence by the necessity for falsehood.

Miss Emily Jones was increasingly worried about Frank Clair. He had passed from her schoolroom in June, 1908, and had gone to the indifferent mercies of Miss Leona Burkholz. The latter teacher did not like children, and had tolerance only for those who caused her the least trouble. Frank was not one of these happy ones. He was inattentive, inert and extremely dull when a subject did not interest him, and was given to scrawling odd faces, triangles and other irrelevancies in the midst of an arithmetic or grammar or spelling lesson. So far as the arithmetic was concerned, it was still cabalism to him, though occasionally, purely by luck, he believed, he hit upon the right answer. He could read and write brilliantly; correct grammar came to him instinctively, and it was not necessary for him to study spelling. In consequence, his mind wandered off into fog and dreams during these lessons which Miss Leona persistently forced into the heads of the other children.

He thought Miss Leona of no importance, for her voice was without accent or richness, her ways lackadaisical, her interest in her subjects completely absent. He never remembered her face or her figure. She was a vast boredom to him. He was still young enough to betray his opinion frankly. Moreover, the other children no longer frightened him, nor was he docile among them. Their initial antagonism had increased. He returned it with contempt, and not infrequently was the party of the first part in a brawl.

His clothing became shabby, too small for his quickly growing body, and was patched. This was because of Maybelle's growing penuriousness and his father's emotional refusal to spend "an unnecessary penny." Also, Maybelle was beginning to show a veritable genius for ferreting out cheap shops where discarded and unfashionable clothing was for sale. The few garments bought for Frank were peculiar, badly cut, poorly made, and ill-fitting. These things aroused the other children's risibilities, and nothing could have delighted them more than the occasion when Frank appeared at school in a pair of extraordinary shoes which possessed toes and heels of brilliant "patent" leather and tops of gray cloth with black buttons. The shoes had been made for a youth several years older than Frank, and were of a style of some ten years previous, having "toothpick" toes of a triangular shape. Maybelle had thriftily stuffed the vacant two inches above Frank's big toe with wads of cotton-batting. Even Miss Burkholz smiled broadly at the sight of them. No one but Miss Jones suspected that these shoes tormented Frank with intense mental and physical anguish, for not only did everyone stare and grin at them but their very shape distorted and twisted the boy's feet in a veritable agony.

Worst of all, to Miss Jones, was another change that was becoming evident in Frank. Added to his growing dreaminess and absorption in some subjective universe of his own was a disquieting and extreme tenseness and nervous instability. He had always been pale. Now his color was almost ghastly, and there were mauve circles under his eyes. His hands trembled at the least excitement. His lips were dry and parched, and had a bitten look. His eyes, always large, were now too brilliant, too alert.

She was too astute, too sensitive, to believe that all this was caused solely by the hostility of the other children. Some other chronic misery had come upon the boy. She made discreet inquiries, and learned that Frank was the only child of his parents, and that his father was a chemist of no small salary. Why then these atrocious clothes? Why then this expression of acute anxiety and nervousness? She had never met Frank's parents, and knew no way to call upon them without a reasonable explanation.

She managed to arrange with Frank that he come into her room after school hours. She would talk with him affectionately, sometimes holding his hand. She borrowed books for him, and was touched and amazed at his eagerness and understanding, for his appetite for reading seemed insatiable, and he was no longer satisfied with fairy tales and stories of childish adventure. When in her presence, when talking to her, the taut stiffness of his young face would relax, the abnormal brightness of his eyes would lessen, and sometimes he would laugh. He spoke to her eagerly and listened to her words almost with hunger.

The boy haunted her. She would manage a few words with him in the corridors. She would bring him candy, which he devoured with such avidity that she was sickened. When he suddenly developed a tendency to stammer, she would gently turn her head aside and refrain from looking at him. To the end of her life she could hear that pathetic stammering and see the look of helpless and suffering suffocation on his face as he struggled to speak.

In November, 1908, she missed him. She made inquiries of Miss Burkholz, who said, indifferently, that the boy had been absent for several days. "He can stay away forever, as far as I am concerned," said the teacher spitefully. "Of all the mean, stupid, contrary, bad-tempered young ones, he is the worst! He ought to be in a home for the feeble-minded."

Miss Jones bought five suckers, three oranges, two bananas, and armed herself with several books from the library. She went to call upon Frank and his mother.

The neighborhood was poor, she saw. But not so poor as many homes in which healthy and happy children lived and thrived. The dark stairs leading up to the Clair rooms were, she noted with approval, clean and scrubbed. She knocked on the upper door. She waited. She heard stealthy footsteps within, then silence. She knocked again, more vigorously. There was no sound, but, mysteriously, she felt alarm and wariness behind that shut door. and she was positive that she heard sharp breathing, as of someone in stress and fear. Anxious now, she knocked once more, and called out: "Is anyone home?"

Again, the sensation of fear, of some presence near the door. Then she heard a woman's voice, sullen, suspicious: "Who is it? What do you want? We don't want agents."

Miss Jones was perplexed. Agents? Agents of what? Not familiar with English terminology, she could not know that "agents" means salesmen or peddlers. She said, loudly and clearly: "I am Miss Jones. Frank's teacher. I'd like to see him, please."

To her surprise there came, after another prolonged silence, the scraping of a chain-lock, the drawing of a bolt. The door opened an inch or two, and she caught a glimpse of auburn hair, of dilated brown eyes, and an apron. "Mrs. Clair?" she asked, smiling brightly, and inserting a toe in the opening. "I'm Miss Jones. Frank has been absent from school, and I've been worried."

The door opened wider, and Miss Jones stepped into a dismal kitchen, which, clean as it was, smelled unpleasantly of disinfectant and harsh soap and kerosene. She looked at Maybelle, whose surly under lip was thrust out, and whose eyes were blinking watchfully. She thought: What a peculiar little woman! This must be Frank's mother. She looks—she looks—just a little queer.

"I'm very glad to see you, I'm sure," said Maybelle, in a mincing voice, removing her apron from a very patched cotton dress. She smiled an artificial and unfriendly and still suspicious smile. "It was very kind of you, indeed. Frankie has the measles. He is always getting something wrong with him," she added, and now her face became almost vicious. "Sickly," she amended, with an intonation as if she had said: "Criminal."

She resents him. He costs money, no matter how little. Miss Jones' thoughts came to her with such perception that she was momentarily dazed, for there was something of clairvoyance in them. Now, in only an instant or two, she understood.

Maybelle did not ask her guest to sit down. It was evident that she wished her gone, that she actually feared her. Does she think I will steal something? thought Miss Jones, incredulously. And then, with anxiety: Will she punish the poor child because I came?

She looked at the bundles and the books in her arms. "I brought these for Frank," she said, trying, with a hopeless smile, to win some responsive friendliness, some human interest. Maybelle did indeed smile, but it was still artificial and false. "It's very kind of you, I'm sure," she answered, and now with some nervousness.

"I do hope Frank isn't very ill," said Miss Jones, after a pause during which the presents had been turned over to Maybelle. "What does the doctor say?"

"Oh, we didn't have a doctor," said Maybelle, with actual, defensive alarm and definite umbrage. "I'm sure I'm capable of doing what's best. And I do hope you won't say anything. We don't want a placard on the door. Measles are nothing."

It's a reportable disease, thought Miss Jones, with indignation unusual to her. And the poor child hasn't even a physician! I see. It would cost money.

"Oh, naturally, I'll not say anything! But could I see Frank for a moment or two, if he isn't very sick."

"Sick?" repeated Maybelle, frowning and suspicious again. "Oh, I understand. You mean 'ill.' I'm not used to Yankee language yet," she added, with a smile that was clearly malevolent and intentionally derisive. "No, little Frankie isn't very ill." She hesitated. "If you won't mind an upset room, he is in the bedroom."

Reluctantly, and with every line of her plump little figure expressing resentment, she led the way into the next room. There, on his hard and lumpy divan, lay Frank, flushed, blotched, half asleep, and manifestly sick. He opened his eyes languidly at the entrance of the two women, and his eyes, reddened, swollen and painfully rheumy, stared at them. Then, recognizing his former teacher, he smiled weakly, and his face lit up with incredulous pleasure.

Miss Jones bent over him tenderly. She laid her large cool hand on his forehead. Its heat frightened her. She said softly: "My poor child. I didn't know. I missed you so much."

Frank glanced at his mother, anxiously, and that glance filled Miss Jones with sudden anger and pity. He stammered: "I—I'm not very ill, Miss Jones. I—I'll be better soon."

"Of course," said Miss Jones brightly. "Measles are nothing. Nothing at all. Everyone has them. Several of my children are out right now. Nothing at all, Frank." I'm babbling, she thought. She was surprised that she was trembling. She saw the broad November light in the room, unshaded, beating down on the child's sore and aching eyes. He coughed, deeply and hoarsely. The lumpy feather bed that covered him was obviously distressing.

Miss Jones turned to Maybelle, who was watching sourly and closely. She coughed. "We have a new notion, now," she said, with appeasing apology and a little false laugh. "We think children's eyes should be guarded when they have the measles. What do you think? Perhaps if the blinds—" her voice died away into silence when she saw Maybelle's resistive and sullen expression.

Busybody, thought Maybelle. She gave a parody of a smile. "Air and light's good for him," she said. "It's nonsense about the blinds. Can't have it dark."

Miss Jones sighed. She had a fleeting and rebellious impulse to notify the Board of Health. No, that was impossible. Frank would suffer.

She bent over the boy again, and bit her trembling lips. She smiled at him with tenderness and yearning. "I've brought you some fruit and candy, dear. And some books. But Frank, you must promise me something, and I know you will keep the promise. You must not read a line, not a single line, until you are completely better. You will remember? You won't use your eyes? You will give me your promise?" she added with deep urgency.

He nodded. Maybelle tumbled the gifts on the bed. He began to open them eagerly, his hot hands fumbling. Miss Jones removed the books and laid them on the dresser. Should she take them away? But the boy had promised, and she knew he would remember. She could trust him.

She helped him peel an orange, and he sucked it with passionate delight, moistening his parched mouth with the fresh juice. A look of pure bliss came into his eyes. Something tightened and twisted in Miss Jones' meagre breast. When he gave her a wildly grateful glance, full of love, tears blinded her.

Maybelle was speaking in a whining and resentful voice that cracked and wavered with self-pity: "He's never been well since we came here. He was never sickly before. Now he ails all the time. It's a burden. And me with my bad health, too. It's enough to make you wonder. I never thought I'd be mithered by a sickly child. It's a burden, with everything else."

Miss Jones' hands clenched. But she kept her voice soothing: "Oh, he isn't sickly, I'm sure. He's really a healthy little boy. All children have the measles. It's nothing at all. One expects these things."

Maybelle moaned faintly. "I don't know why I've been so cursed. Never a well day since we came here. Bottles and bottles of physic. Pills galore. I never had to take them in England. But this climate is killing."

"It is a little—difficult," said Miss Jones. She bent over Frank and kissed him, not once, but several times. I can gargle when I go home, she told herself. One must protect other children. She looked at the glaring window. If only she dared pull down those ragged shades!

"Get well soon, darling," she murmured, her eyelids hot with salt tears.

She stood up. Maybelle, with melancholy pride, was pointing to the rows of bottles ranged on the dresser. "That's me," she said, in hollow tones.

"How unfortunate," said Miss Jones, trying to be sympathetic. She wanted to smash the bottles. What is she doing for Frank? she asked herself. But she knew nothing was being done for him.

Maybelle, whose old, natural friendliness had withered into poisonous hostility in America, scrutinized Miss Jones with wary suspicion. She had taken a dislike to the little teacher and thought her excessively ugly. There Miss Jones stood, with that painful, appeasing smile on her raisin of a little face, her cricket eyes lively and intelligent, her old black velvet hat perched high on her monstrous black pompadour, her gray wool skirt and jacket obviously old in spite of the sedulous brushings and pressings, her gloves neatly darned, and her huge boots polished like twin mirrors. No, Miss Jones was not prepossessing, and her attempts to be charming for Frank's sake only gave her a mendacious air which Maybelle had detected at once, and which she distrusted.

They went out of the bedroom together. Maybelle, melancholy again, began to complain: "I don't know what's got into the lad. He was always so well in England. It isn't for lack of good food. We don't begrudge anything." She pointed to the kitchen table, and Miss Jones, with surprise and pleasure, noted the groceries laid out upon it. There was a fresh chicken, plump and appetizing, a package of lamb chops, a joint of really excellent beef, eggs in profusion, butter, fresh vegetables, loaves of bread, and milk. Miss Jones, with gratitude, decided that Maybelle was a good cook. A large kettle of soup stood cooling on the miserable hot plate, and now Miss Jones caught a whiff of something very flavorsome.

"He's getting gruel, made with sugar and milk," offered Maybelle, "and I've just made him a drop of Scotch broth. But he doesn't eat anything. Miserable appetite. We have to force him."

Miss Jones anxiously recalled Frank's growing tenseness and nervous instability. It was not for lack of excellent food, then. It was something emotional. She suspected she knew the cause.

"We live for the day we can go home," said Maybelle, her voice breaking. "We're wretched here. We don't like Yankee-land."

A hot little prickle touched Miss Jones' heart. But she quelled her natural and stinging retort to this remark.

"We lived comfortable in England," Maybelle went on. "Our own place, and lovely furniture. Rich. We lived like kings, compared to this. Now we live like beggars."

Miss Jones had to make some mental readjustment. Immigrants frequently made such disparaging remarks, in order to add superiority to themselves. But all at once she knew that Maybelle spoke truly. She was amazed, and now genuinely sorry. But was it necessary to live like this? It was apparent that the Clairs were saving every penny in order to return to England. Again the hot little prickle of indignation touched Miss Jones. She felt an anger against these people who regarded her beloved country as the Cave of the Forty Thieves, to be ravished, to be robbed of its jewels, to be sacked, in order that the sackers might carry off the treasure to an alien land. How dared they come like this, landing on the golden shores at midnight, seeing nothing of the beauty, hearing nothing of the great strange music, carrying their bags, which they hoped to fill with gems, and then depart! Was it for these that Americans had dreamed, had died, had prayed, and had hoped? God had blessed this huge and lofty land, had touched it with supernal loveliness, had dyed cliff and mountain with flaming cataracts, had sunken tremendous rivers in the midst of teeming plains, had set the very light of the sun on endless yellow meadows.

How dared Maybelle speak like this, with such mean contempt, such imperviousness, such lack of understanding! Miss Jones felt a constriction in her throat, and a new surge of anger. And then she knew what she must do. She had only to be patient.

She said, murmurously: "Well. Things change. I'm sorry you are unhappy here, dear Mrs. Clair." She paused. "But I know you have some happiness, really. Frank is a wonderful little boy. Really wonderful. But, of course you know that."

Maybelle listened restively, Then, to Miss Jones' gratification, the dark and melancholy look lifted from Maybelle's face, and it was reluctantly pleased. Natural maternal love still lingered, then, in this wretched little woman so beset by self-pity and resentment and homesickenss.

"Well, I don't know," said Maybelle, trying to be harsh. "His new teacher doesn't think much of him, according to the report." But a light of eagerness, pathetic and cautious, touched her eyes.

Miss Jones went on with real and earnest enthusiasm. "It takes a great deal of discernment to understand Frank. I think I understand him. He has a great mind. Some day he will, I know, do great things."

Maybelle smiled and simpered. "Funny, but that's what his teacher in England said. It was a private school," she added with pride. "Miss Ballister said he had great dreams." She paused, eagerly waiting for more.

"Oh, I am sure he has great dreams! He reads so much. He is fascinated by words. He is so sensitive and subtle. Why, he reads far beyond his age, with the most marvelous understanding. He plays with words as artists play with paints. He loves poetry, and I have taught him a lot of it. Even Shakespeare."

Maybelle bridled, simpered again, tossed her head. "Well, he doesn't hear trash in this house. His father and I are great readers. We go to the library every week. His father likes history, and he tells it to Frank. And reading's my greatest pleasure."

Miss Jones was doubtful for only an instant, and then again, with incredulity, she knew that Maybelle spoke with truth. These were not the average run of immigrants. In some way she had always known it. She thought: They are of my own blood, English. And it was Englishmen who had made America, and it is English blood which will always save it. She had had her own anxious fears at the sight of the increasing number of young aliens in the schools, who spoke in broken accents, and whose faces were strange in the brilliant light of America. The Celts and the English: these were truly the blood of her country, and so long as they remained in the majority, America was safe.

Moved, she impulsively laid her hand on Maybelle's plump soft arm. "Frank is fortunate in his parents," she said; and now without hypocrisy "But he is such a nervous little boy. That is what makes me think he has genius. Do you know, Mrs. Clair, I have a feeling he will be an artist of some sort. A writer, perhaps."

They parted on a surge of great amity. and with a lighter heart, now, Miss Jones went down the dark clean stairs.

Maybelle put the pot of soup on the fire. She poured a huge bowl full of the steaming and appetizing liquid. She brought it to Frank, who had fallen into a half doze again. She awakened him. When he saw and smelled the food, he turned away, sick.

"You've got to eat," said Maybelle, with determination. Her sallow face softened. "Look, Frankie. Good, rich soup. You'll enjoy it. Now, eat, or I'll bash you."

Later, Frank lay on his hot pillows, and sank again into a half doze. Maybelle stood, looking down at his red and crusted eyes. Then, impatiently, she pulled down the shades. She stood looking at the brilliant cracks and pinpricks of light which imprinted themselves on the dark cloth. Her eyes filled with tears.

Frank was only partly asleep. Words were forming in his mind as stars appear in a darkening sky. Lovely words, marching together with hushed majesty, his own words rising out of the abyss of his being:

"Now God walked in the Garden all alone.
A mist was lingering where the sun had shone,
A mist of light in which the forest bowed
And murmured in a gentle monotone."

He saw the dark and murmurous forest, deep as velvet in the shadows, the tree-tops afloat in pale golden mist. He saw the trunks of the trees, purple in the fading light; he saw the aisles, adrift with shadow. He saw a Presence moving there, radiant as with moonlight, the branches gathering in canopies above the lofty head. He saw the Presence come upon a fallen tree, and seat himself upon it. All was silence, all was strengthening darkness, somber stillness, and peace. And then, far off in some distant and unfathomable reach, a thrush began to sing, and God lifted His head and listened.

CHAPTER 15

MISS EMILY JONES, who had so little time in her harried life, now devoted fragments of hours to her protégé. Sometimes, on Saturdays, she prevailed upon Maybelle to allow her to take Frank to The Front, her favorite spot. Only rain prevented these excursions.

They would stand, this little wizened woman and this young boy, and gaze at the Niagara River, gray as ashes under an ashen sky, its current boiling swiftly and powerfully as it sped towards the Falls. They would watch sunsets splash the river with running scarlet streaks. Sometimes the sky would be flat and cold and the color of tarnished silver, and the waters would turn white and deathly under it. And once they were rewarded with such beauty and such majesty that they could not speak of it again to each other.

It was at sunset, in July, 1909, that they saw this ineffable and solemn thing. There had been a storm during the day, but now the air was full of strong freshness. The Canadian shore, usually a blurred green wall across the river, had disappeared in a mist, so that the river was without boundaries. The sky, vast and motionless, had become a wrack of color, almost violent in intensity. From the cobalt zenith, westward, it merged from profound purple to amethyst, from amethyst to brilliant lavender, from lavender to an enormous arch of vivid and pulsating green that imperceptibly quickened to tender rose, from rose to scarlet, from scarlet, as it neared the horizon, to a bloody crimson. The sun was gone. But the colors overhead brightened, widened, deepened, moment by moment, as if the palpitating sun would not depart, but must throw his vaults of color, his rainbows of burning green flame, eternally over the dark earth, engulfing the universe in unbearable effulgence.

But wonderful though the sky, the rushing Niagara surpassed it. Dark purple at the watery horizon, it faded to deep but delicate violet towards the observers, the crests of the impetuous waves touched with pinkish mauve, their hollows shining with evanescent fire. The small waves lay in scallops on the glistening beach, and these were of the purest turquoise, like liquid enamel, reflecting the green of the sky, and as they retreated and advanced, slowly and gently, they left glowing shreds behind them on the wet shingle.

Between earth and heaven hovered a mist, heliotrope and mysterious. A lighthouse to the left, set far out on the water on a heap of dark rocks, threw its fragile beam into that mist so that it brightened momentarily to a cloudy lilac.

Alone together, Miss Jones and Frank stood hand in hand. They were only a consciousness, awestruck, worshipping, in the midst of that unbelievable glory. They breathed softly. They felt near to a Presence moving with majesty about them. They stood like this for a long time, for heaven and earth seemed reluctant to give up this tremendous splendor to the night.

Then Miss Jones whispered, her face flooded with a peaceful but exalted light: "When I was a little girl, my grandmother told me a very strange story. She said that when God recalled His artists from the earth He permitted each one to paint a sunset for Him, for the joy of the men he had left behind. So, each sunset, the selected artist would take up his great palette of paints, and turn his brushes to the sky. There he would paint the most wonderful sunsets, lovingly, carefully, and then wait, with hope, for what men would say.

"But men are very careless. They seldom look at the sky, and sometimes the artist must have only the admiration of the angels. Even to the last moment, before night came, the artist would wait. If only one man saw, and praised in his heart, and thanked God and the artist for the beauty, then the artist was happy."

Frank, his heart swelling, looked at the tremendous glory of sky and water, and his eyes were drowned in tears. He said, in himself: "Thank you. Thank you."

In his later years there was seldom a sunset for which he did not spare a moment or two, no matter how hurried, and though he smiled at himself, he would invariably whisper: "Thank you. Thank you." Even when, for him, "the glory had passed away from the earth," he could still feel a gratitude for it, could still see it though he could not feel it. "I see, but do not feel, how wonderful it is," he would say to himself, in the words of Coleridge. But, though emotion was gone, the gratitude was always there, and this gratitude was like a soundless mirror which could only reflect, which could know nothing in itself.

Sometimes they would lie in the grassy park of The Front, watching full white clouds that mushroomed in the intense blue sky. Sometimes they would sit on the old Spanish-

American War cannons, swinging their feet, and singing together. They would go down to look at the soldiers, who marched before their barracks, and the sight of the Stars and Stripes, blowing free and brilliant in the windy sunlight, would strike strongly on Frank's heart. Then Miss Jones would say, in a trembling voice: "It is such a noble flag, such a dear, dear flag! Only bars, red and white, and white stars on a blue sky. But what it means! Freedom, safety, opportunity, instinctive kindness, largeness, hope and integrity. Men are weak, Frankie, but the blood of great men colors those stripes, their faith is white and clear between them, the stars of their souls shine always in that sweet blue sky. If America does not live, then the whole world must die. What does it matter that there are so many evil men in the world, even here, faithless men, wicked men, treacherous and ugly and greedy men? The flag remains, and the things which it represents remain, and so long as that flag flies under heaven, so free and noble and bright, the faith of good men can never pass from the earth."

Frank would feel the benediction of the sun on his shoulders, a stronger, warmer sun than England's. He would feel in himself a burgeoning, a passion, as he looked about him. He would hear the music of wild and tender and majestic words rising in him, like chords of disconnected harmony heard at a distance.

How ecstatic were the days of his childhood, how tranquil were the evenings of his youth! Beset though he was by the hysterias and dementias of his parents, he could forget these when he was alone, or with Miss Jones. His soul was drenched in light and sound, in glory and music, in the guessed movement of vast forces beyond the reach of eye or ear. Then, indeed, there was a glory and a mystery upon the earth, a rapture and a splendor, a leaping of the universal heart, a oneness with God. The great trees were his friends; he touched their bark lovingly. The grass was his sister. The sky was the roof of his temple. The winds at midnight were the high shouts of strange adventure, of mighty spirits flowing over the world. When snow fell on his arm, he would hold it to the light of the gas lamps, and marvel over the intricacies of each perfect and minute shape, and worship in his soul. There was no aspect of the golden spring, the green summer, the crimson autumn, and the white and blazing winter, which did not stir him with passion.

Often he would see the ball of the burning sun through the narrow aisles of dark mean houses, and it was like the call of

God in the desert. Often he would look at the pale blue of a
winter sky and feel himself caught up into the crystalline
radiance of the company of the angels. When he saw the
first tender shoots of the iris in his grandmother's garden, he
was so overcome with emotion that he wept. The first buds on
the trees were an ecstasy. A crimson leaf, drifting to his feet,
was an exalted message, for him alone.

Sometimes, on a summer dusk, he would sit on the stone
step of the grocery store, and listen to the distant voices on
nearby verandahs and the strident shrieking of neighborhood
gramophones. He would hear laughter, softened by evening,
and sometimes a song, simple, pure and happy. The hideous
words and music of "Meet Me in St. Louis, Louis!" would
seem gay and joyous to him, and he would laugh softly in
answer. Fleets of young men and women on bicycles would
fly by, streaming merriment, and he would watch them disappear into the dusk with love in his heart and a strange
sadness. He would sit there until the windows opposite were
only disjointed rectangles of broken light, and the stone grew
cold under him, and his mother called him to bed. There
were children in the neighborhood, but he never spoke to
them, nor they to him. He was not lonely any longer. He was
lonely only in the enforced company of others. His thoughts
and his emotions were enough for him, and his brightening
dreams.

He loved the chuckle of the rain in the eaves. He loved
the sparkles of mica in the cement sidewalks. He loved the
sight of dust turning gold in the sun. When March winds
tossed and tore at him, with giant buffetings, he would
laugh aloud. He would plunge his feet into white drifts, and
stand, for long moments, watching the blue light on the snow.

He was eleven years old when he wrote down his first
poem, and gave it to Miss Jones.

> "Light of the lilac dawn,
>   Scent of the lilac tree,
>   Bud on the dripping thorn,
>   Silver mist on the sea!
>   I have passed this way before."

Yes, thought Miss Jones, you have passed this way before.
She said: "Frankie, you will be a poet, or a writer of great
books. Never, never, must you forget this. Let no one stop
you, hinder you, or turn you aside, my dear. There is an
increasing purpose in you, a promise. If you fail that, you

will have failed more than your life. You will have failed God."

She looked at this tall boy humbly, strongly. "Remember, Frank. Always remember."

She bought him a book of heroic poems for Christmas. "Perhaps you won't understand all of them now. But later you will."

He was in the fourth grade now, and was well disliked by his teachers, who invariably had an aversion to him. He was indolent, they said, and disobedient, and sly. He would not study. He evinced no interest. Moreover, he was belligerent. He sought out quarrels with the other children. "He is defending himself from their hostility," Miss Jones would protest. The children called him "Jonesy's pet." He looked at them with contempt, turned away from them in silence.

Then one day he informed Miss Jones that his parents were leaving Vermont Street and were moving to Albany Street, and that he would have to attend another school. His face was full of grief and despair. But though the news was a shock to her, she pressed his hand and smiled. "Never mind, Frank. You must come often to see me, and I will go to see you, too."

But she never saw him again. He came to see her two months later, but she had been transferred to a school miles away. He waited for her to come to him. She had intended to, with the firmest determination. But her mother died, and she herself became dangerously ill. Then her crippled sister sickened, and she was obliged to care for her for several weeks. She was finally forced to place this sister in a public charitable institution, for she had no means and no way to care for her. She visited this sister on week-ends. Then, less than a year later, she herself died. Insufficient food and clothing, exposure to severe weather, caused her to contract pneumonia. She was buried in a humble spot in the cemetery supported by her church, and the grass grew thick and rank and sheltering over her grave. It was marked only by a stick of wood and a number, and Frank Clair could never find it.

CHAPTER 16

THE exodus from Vermont to Albany Street was no casual affair, nor voluntary on the part of the Clairs. It occurred because Mrs. Watson's newly widowed daughter and her two children were coming to live with her.

With what lamentations, revilements, agonies and despairs was the news received! Had death come to those wretched rooms, had Francis been stricken down with a fatal illness, had young Frank committed a most awful crime, the demonstrations could not have been excelled by the ones that took place when Mrs. Watson made her announcement. Francis pleaded cravenly. Maybelle bewailed. Mrs. Watson was stirred out of her malevolent indifference by such antics. She told them they were "crazy." There were plenty of rooms and flats in Bison. They had only to look for them. "You're the dippiest folks I ever saw," she told them frankly. "You'd think I was taking a million dollars from you."

Even she, who pared her cheeses and utilized her crusts with the utmost thrift, could not understand with what horror Francis regarded the moving bills, small though they might be. Had she suggested a pint of his blood in lieu of the moving, he would gladly have agreed. She stared at him, despising him, and then waddled away with a shrug. Moving bills! Two dollars, at the most, and him making good pay in that drugstore! She knew. She had listened at the door when Francis, in jubilation, had announced that Mr. Farley had increased his salary to thirty-five dollars a week. That was nearly a year ago. Maybe he was making more now.

After the stunning initial shock, it was Maybelle who recovered first, and a look of speculation came into her eyes. She, more than Francis, had suffered in these rooms. Now there was a possibility of a "place of our own." A flat, perhaps. A little cottage. As in England.

She went out, searching. A few days later she found on Albany Street the most minute house imaginable, a house with so small a facade that it appeared to be of toy dimensions. But, surprisingly, it had a large "front" room and a big kitchen, one bedroom, and "our own toilet." It had no bathroom, but there was a huge back yard, grassy and full of trees and clumps of golden-glow. The rent was no more than what the Clairs had been paying to Mrs. Watson.

"That's all very well," groaned Francis, in anguish. "But we'll have to buy furniture."

"It won't cost much," replied Maybelle, sturdily. "Secondhand shops all over Connecticut Street. I've priced some things."

She bought two secondhand beds, one of brass, the other of iron, the latter for Frank. She bought linoleum, brown and shiny, for the front room, which was to serve as a bedroom for herself and Francis. Then she purchased a hideous oaken dresser for that room, a table, and a single wooden chair, and a gas heater full of clay rings, with windows of isinglass. This was the furniture for the marital chamber. Frank's room was much more spare, containing the iron bed, a table and a stool, with a strip of nondescript carpet for his feet. A kitchen range, thick with grease and stove polish, was set up in the kitchen and flanked by a secondhand wooden table and three chairs, and an ancient, imitation black-leather sofa was installed near one window. This was to be the combined kitchen and living room of the Clairs for a long time.

The cost of this munificence came to exactly thirty-five dollars.

"Thirty-five dollars!" lamented Francis. "Two weeks' savings! We're that much behind, now. You're out to ruin me; I can see that."

But Maybelle, secretly delighted that she was to have "a place of our own," was more optimistic. "You can cut down a dollar on the food bill, and I'll go without that new winter coat, and you can manage without a suit for another year," she said. "We won't miss the money. And we'll be alone! Private."

She was temporarily happy, as she scrubbed and polished and scoured the tiny house, and arranged the furniture. It was true that neither the house nor its furnishings could compare with the comfort of the home in England, but it was her own now. She was freed from the everlasting presence of "a stranger." To the Englishwoman, privacy and independence were sacred things, to be desired above all else. "A garret, if you are alone in it, is better than sharing a palace with others," she told young Frank happily.

She even felt a new fondness for her husband and child, which lasted all of two months.

The house was less than two blocks from Niagara Street,

where Frank discovered a fascinating blacksmith's shop, stables, granaries near the river, the Erie Canal, and the ferry dock. Also, trains swept by at the foot of the street, and he was never tired of watching their roaring passage. He got to know the hours when they could be expected, and would go down the long incline, beyond Niagara Street, past brothels, saloons and shacks where fishing bait and tackle were sold, and there await the trains. He loved the fishy smell of the river, the hot and splintery ferry dock, the brawls he could hear behind the swinging doors of the saloons, the sight of dubious ladies sunning themselves on rickety wooden galleries above the filthy and narrow street, the fishermen, with their bending rods, sitting on the piles, and even the stench of beer and dust that permeated the little stretch from Niagara Street to the river.

It was an odoriferous neighborhood, and an evil and violent one. But it was full of zest, noise and vitality, and he preferred it to the dirty dull quiet of Albany Street, on the other side of Niagara, where the cobbles were gray and decorous, and where West Avenue, solidly middle-class in 1912, bisected it.

He delighted in the strenuous little ferryboats which plied between Bison and Canada, and the sight of the huge ice floes grinding and tilting in the spring as they thundered towards the Falls was a most exciting thing to him. Sometimes he was rewarded by the sight of long and smoking lake boats moving sluggishly down Erie Canal, heavy with cargo from far, strange cities. What a sight it was, after the shrieking of the whistles, when the bridge lifted to accommodate the smoke stacks of the large boats. Sometimes he saw that women and children lived on these vessels, and he thought the lines of miscellaneous laundry fluttering in spring and autumn breezes the gayest of all things. Often there were dogs aboard, who barked importantly at the little boy standing on the stony edge of the Canal. To his nostrils would come the rank smell of stagnant water, of stinking aqueous vegetation, of water fungus, evilly green, which spread from the shore halfway across the Canal. But it did not revolt him. Adventure lived here among these rough and roaring men, among these boats, in these dilapidated squatters' shacks along the edge of the Canal, in the passing of trains, in the spluttering plowing of the ferry vessels.

There was bliss in the aspect of the Canadian shore opposite, all broken green, smiling little hills, tiny white houses, and, far down the river, the delicate black span of the International Bridge. As yet he had not set foot in Canada, though each summer Francis had faithfully promised to take his family to Erie Beach, "when things look up." They had still not "looked up."

Here he spent his days after school, vanishing discreetly from the miniature house on Albany Street and returning at dusk. He wished Miss Jones could see this new wonder, and he looked for her. But she never came.

He explored the squatters' colonies, was chased by their savage dogs, was enchanted by the slatternly women and the filthy children who romped about among piles of ashes and tin cans and discarded beds and springs. Once he had the joy of witnessing a ferocious fight between two male squatters, and he saw the flash of a knife, and blood, and heard the shrieks of drabs.

He was not lonely, but now he began to long for some companion with whom he could share these stimulating wonders. He wanted to hear someone comment excitedly on his discovery of the impressive water-works at Front Park, and the armory on Niagara Street. Often he ran after lumbering wagons, and climbed up on the backs of them, thus going for a long and blissful ride, or, in the winter, he "hitched" onto the sleighs of milkmen and explored new neighborhoods. Each Saturday, Maybelle gave him six cents for carfare, and he would visit the Public Library on Washington Street, downtown, and come home with armfuls of books. Sometimes, when Maybelle felt particularly benevolent, she gave him two or three extra pennies and, thriftily investing the return carfare in additional candy, he would walk the three miles home, sucking, chewing and dreaming. To him, every street was a mercurial adventure, where the strangest and oddest things might happen, and each new face a fairy tale.

No, he was not lonely, but he longed for a companion, for an ear.

Later, he discovered the homes of the rich, on Richmond and Delaware Avenues, and in Delaware Park, and the beautiful cemetery called Forest Lawn.

CHAPTER 17

IT WAS one of those summer days which seduce the senses into a languid unreality, when there is nothing but a long hazy warmth and utter, golden silence. Even the shadows of the heavy trees blurred on the dancing sidewalks, and the houses had an unsubstantial look like the painted houses on a stage backdrop, and the streets had this look, too, deserted, vista-less, hotly blank. If a sound came, the shutting of a distant door, the bark of a dog, the rumble of a wagon over shimmering cobbles, it was a sound like the echo in a dream, bodiless and meaningless.

It was the sort of a day that Frank Clair loved, for all disturbing human elements had melted out of his awareness, and he was alone. In his dreams, he often dreamt that he was the only living soul in a great abandoned city steeped in sheltering peace, and that he could wander through the long avenues with only trees for company, and with no face to stare at him with hostile derision. The silvery hushed light of a Never-never land would gleam in the far distances, and would lurk in the drooping branches under which he would pass. Then he would be happy, serene and full of content, looking at mighty mansions which held no enemies, pausing by lawns on which faint shadows played.

This was one of the days that brought his dreams back to him vividly. Of all those who slept, inert, in shaded bedrooms, or drowsed in hammocks under back-yard trees, or rocked silently on verandahs, he alone was alive, restless, seeking. The city was his. He walked for two or three miles, reveling in the desertion under the hazy, smothering sun, encountering nothing but an occasional panting dog or a beer wagon slowly heaving along, the teamster asleep on his high seat. A shop-window or two glinted back at him dustily, but nothing stirred behind them.

Now he was on a wide and stately avenue, clasped in trees, the lawns all level plush in the silvery, windless air. He saw low gray walls and terraced grounds, silk-shrouded windows and sun-bathed slate roofs, flower beds and distant gardens. Here, too, nothing moved.

He paused at the gate of a stone wall about four feet high,

and peered through it. He saw winding drives dark with warm trees, shrubbery, the gray wall of a far house, and the latter's immense and shining windows. Nothing lived or moved in that spreading vision of calm majesty and silence. He clutched the gate and gave it a tentative shake. It opened. Without thinking, he stepped into the fragrant enchantment of the grounds, heard the faint crunch of gravel under his feet. He moved dreamily towards the house. On one side he saw arbors covered with vines, on the other side a wall of evergreen shrubbery. And now all the adjoining houses vanished, and he was alone in a garden of mystery and soft, shadowless light.

He was only a young boy, and none too clean, his face was dirty, his hair uncombed, his shoes were scuffed. Yet he did not feel himself an intruder. It was right that he should be here; this was his home. He had found his way back; he belonged on this drive, walking towards the looming mansion at the end of it.

Absorbed in his dreams and his pleasure, he did not see a little girl approach him from the direction of the house. It was not until she stood directly in front of him, staring at him with enormous dark eyes, that he became aware of her. She was a very pretty little girl, with a mass of black ringlets on her shoulders, smooth slender legs in red socks, with patent-leather slippers on her feet. She wore a bright pink dress, all ruffles, ribbons and edges of lace, and there was a pink bow high on the top of her curls.

"Hello," she said, gravely, gazing at him with expectation.

He did not answer. He only stared at her. He had never seen anything half so beautiful, so sweet and entrancing. His hostility toward girls was much less than his hostility toward boys. Girls were gentler, not so brutal or vicious. But they had malice and slyness, and he was more afraid of these than he was afraid of brutality. One could cope with physical brutality with one's fists; but there was no coping against malice and slyness, no defense against soft treachery and malignance. The little girl delighted him with her beauty, but he remembered that girls were cunning and mean. So he only stood and stared at her, ready for flight when her eyes would light up with the nasty expression with which he was familiar.

But, to his surprise, she remained grave and expectant, and she seemed even pleased. "What's your name?" she asked.

"Frank," he answered, warily.

"Mine's Jessica," she confided. Her eyes opened a little wider, as she waited for him to make the next move. But he merely rubbed the gravel under his foot, and looked at her. Her face was like a doll's face, perfectly tinted, and she had a full coral mouth like a nasturtium. She regarded him eagerly.

Then he said rustily: "You live here?"

She shook her head while her ringlets bounced. "Oh, no, just my uncle. I live on Porter Avenue with my daddy. But it's my birthday, and my uncle's giving me a party. He bought me this dress. Isn't it pretty?" and she spread out the pink ruffles until they were a rosy gauze about her little figure. "Are you coming to my party?"

"I guess—not," he stammered. "I wasn't invited. Your uncle doesn't know me."

She dropped the ruffles and regarded him with disappointment. Then she brightened. "Well, you can stay, anyway, though it isn't until four o'clock." She had a high sweet voice. She gazed at him with fond and complete acceptance. "I like you," she announced. "I don't like boys, much. But I like you. Do you fight?"

"Only when I have to," he said. "Then I fight hard. That's because I'm English," he added proudly, and now without the defiance he always felt when he was obliged to admit his race.

She admired him with her eyes. She looked him up and down, and found all of him admirable. She gave a little skip. "I've got a kitten in the summerhouse," she said. "I'm not going to let the others see it, but I'll let you."

She turned and beckoned, ran on before him. He followed, watching her pretty little legs flashing behind her. She was a fairy, a rosy fairy, floating over the green grass, and he followed like one hypnotized. She led him along the side of the great gray house, and he saw the wall of it towering above him. And now he was in a garden, a garden of dreams, glowing with flowers, dotted here and there like a park, with vast willows and elms. There was a white summerhouse at the end of the garden, covered over with a green and scarlet blaze of climbing roses. Here was set white wicker furniture with red cushions. A kitten mewed in a little basket on a white table.

Frank was tentative about the kitten and more than a little wary of it. He had never been permitted close contact with animals. Dogs, according to his mother, were likely to go "mad," and cats were "dirty." He watched little Jessica take up the white kitten in her arms and nuzzle its fur with her small nose. He stood and watched, fascinated, then stretched out a grubby and hesitating hand and patted the animal's head.

Jessica sat down and held the kitten on her knee, and Frank sat on the edge of a chair. He could not look away from the little girl. Each moment her face became lovelier to him, more enchanting, a face out of his dreams. He felt the strangest sense of familiarity. He watched the girl; she did not babble or twitter as other girls did, or squirm or giggle. She just sat quietly, stroking the kitten, and gazing at the young boy with her grave dark eyes. Her mouth opened on the very slightest and most thoughtful smile, and her expression was expectant.

"You are somethin' like my daddy," she confided at last, as if puzzled.

Frank laughed his rusty, hesitating laugh. "Oh, gosh, I'm not so old," he said.

But she frowned a little, still gazing at him, and the gravity became deeper in her eyes.

"My daddy is a great—artist," she said. "He plays beautiful, on the piano."

"My father used to play the fiddle," boasted Frank.

Jessica brightened. "Maybe he knows my daddy." When Frank shook his head, she was disappointed. She looked down at the kitten, and even Frank could see that she had become saddened.

The hot and hazy silence of the summer lay over the little summerhouse. Insects buzzed on the flowers outside. A wasp bumped in, then bumped out. A cloud of yellow butterflies blew by the door. The two children sat and looked at each other solemnly.

"I wish you could stay for my party," said Jessica at last. But he knew from her tone that she well understood why he could not. She sighed. "I like you," she said, and now her voice was clear and strong. "I like you, Frank. I wish you'd never go away again. But I suppose you must."

He looked through the open door of the summerhouse at the wide, parklike grounds, and at the trees standing in their own gauzy shadows. "I'll come back some day," he said, softly. "Yes, I bet I will. And I won't go away again."

He did not know why he felt so at ease with this little girl, why her presence did not disturb him, why she gave him so much consolation when she looked at him, and so much quiet joy. She did not seem like a child to him, but part of a lovely dream. It was as if he had always known her, and always would, as if he understood that some day he would come back to her. She sat so quietly, stroking her kitten, and just gazing at him.

He said: "Do you like your party, and—everybody—that's coming?"

She shook her head. "No, but my Uncle Wentworth—he's Daddy's brother—says I don't know how to play, or anything, and that I ought to know other girls, too, and maybe some boys. But Daddy doesn't think so. Besides, I'd rather be with Daddy, and listen to him play. Sometimes he goes away on long trips, and plays, and then we have some money. And then we don't have," she went on, frankly, "and we have to let Mrs. Marks go—she takes care of me when we have money—and then Daddy just waits and plays until he goes away again, and then he sends for Mrs. Marks, and she comes back."

"You must have a nice uncle," said Frank, entranced.

Jessica shook her head emphatically. "Oh, no, he's terrible. He doesn't like me or Daddy. But he hasn't a wife, or anything, and Daddy says maybe Uncle Wentworth wants to leave me his money, and Daddy says he doesn't want me to have it. But he let Uncle Wentworth give me this party, because we're going away to New York next month, me and Daddy, and so it doesn't matter about the party."

"You are going away?" cried Frank, aghast.

Jessica nodded, and beamed. "Oh, yes, and we'll never come back, maybe."

Then her face changed, became oddly somber for one so young. And again she waited.

Frank clutched his knees with his hands and stared at her. Then he said: "You'll come back. I know you will! And I'll come around a lot, and wait for you, Jessica."

She regarded him in silence for a long time, then she nodded, very slowly. "Yes. I guess you will, too. I won't ever like any other boy but you, Frank." She lifted her small white chin, and her deep eyes smiled at him.

Frank did not know the meaning of charm, but he felt it. Everything about the little girl was grave and reflective, mature and understanding. She had strength and gentleness, and he felt them, and they were like a consoling sweetness to him.

He got up, as if something was temporarily over, and said: "Guess I ought to go now."

She nodded, rose and put the kitten back in its basket. Then she gave him her small hand and smiled at him.

She watched him go. She did not accompany him back to the driveway. Once he turned and waved to her. She stood in the door of the summerhouse, like a large rosy doll, and waved in return.

He came back the next day, but he did not see her. He hardly expected to, however. But still he came. He came when it was autumn, and the leaves were flying and crackling under torn dark skies. He never saw her. But it was enough to be near the place where he had seen her.

He never forgot Jessica. Even when he met Paul Hodge, who became so much a part of him all the rest of his life, he did not forget. Once or twice he thought of bringing Paul to this house, but something restrained him. He could not tell even Paul. And then as the years went on, he forgot the exact location of the house, and even the street. But he never forgot Jessica. Jessica, and the awful burden of his life, prevented him from developing any strong interest in other girls, except in the most casual and most exigent sense.

He never forgot, but finally he came to believe that he had dreamt another dream, part of the many beautiful and lost dreams of his childhood. Yet always, when he heard a girl laugh in a certain way, he would turn his head and look, and watch, and wait, until the girl had passed.

CHAPTER 18

SCHOOLS, parents, home, had become faint and disagreeable unrealities to him.

The school on West Avenue, near Hampshire Street, numbered eighteen, was larger than the school on Vermont Street, but just as old and grimy. He found that by lurking in the basement after classes were dismissed at three, he could avoid the jeering and obnoxious children. Then he had the suddenly quiet streets to himself, lined with noble trees and full of sunlight. There, walking home slowly and dreamily, he could evolve tales of stupendous magic and adventure, stories of the discovery of strange and spicy islands set in turquoise seas. He was beginning to write these down in his notebooks, during lessons in history and mathematics and grammar. No one saw them as yet. Sometimes he composed poems, filled with leaping and colorful words, which quieted his spirit as well as made it restless.

Then, on a dreary day in November, he found his friend, his ear, his alter ego, and his companion.

It was an ashen November day, with brief wild sunlight as colorless and dazzling as water, and with wilder and briefer gales of astringent wind. It was at recess that Frank found his friend, hovering uneasily in a corner of the playgrounds, hovering uneasily as he was doing, himself.

Beyond the iron palings that circumscribed the schoolyard could be seen the bare lashed boughs of trees, the dun roofs and sides of shabby houses, the dull vista of empty, littered streets. There was a parched silence in the air. From a side street came the monotonous bell of a scissors-grinder and umbrella mender, and the occasional echo of a horse's trot and the grind of heavy wheels. These only enhanced the silence beyond the schoolyard, and made it more melancholy and somber.

The schoolyard itself was unattractive, and contained no swings or other implements of play. Its ground was covered by small sharp white stones, which crunched under the feet of the children with loud, snapping noises. There was no ease between the sexes. When the sun went behind mounds of black clouds, the red tam o'shanters of the little girls sprang out like dull yet animated fires in the sudden gloom. But the fires bobbed decorously among themselves, and did not mingle with the black caps of the little boys. The teacher, exhausted and drained, went back into the school and then reappeared, shivering in the sheltering doorway in her thick cloak, and rubbing bony hands that appeared never to have been soft and warm and tender. It was her week to watch the children, and she stood in her doorway, regarding them with a hatred that shot from her red and swollen eyelids. She only hoped that the boys would not begin to fight again, or invade the ranks of the little girls for a session of hair-pulling and punching.

Frank Clair never played with the others. They would not have accepted him. Nor did he desire their company. He wandered about near the brick wall of the school, scuffing the gravel. Even the little girls, in spite of their apparent indifference, coyly conscious of the other sex, did not glance at him, though he had a strange handsomeness which was daily growing more evident.

He suddenly collided with another boy, who was leaning

against the wall and staring sullenly and impassively before him.

Frank did not know what made him pause so suddenly and stare so frankly at the stranger. He vaguely remembered having seen him in class that morning, but he had forgotten him until now. Was it the boy's expression, fixed and abstracted, which caught Frank's attention, or something deeper, some kindred chemistry of blood and spirit? He never knew. He could only look at the boy, and find him familiar in some mysterious and nameless way.

The other was as tall as himself, and of about the same age. Frank saw a small pale face, rather insignificant eyes of no definite color, pale hair well-brushed and sleek, a tilted nose with sensitive nostrils. Hair, skin and eyes seemed of one vague and colorless hue, verging on a greenish yellow, overcast with somberness. The face was utterly without expression, frozen and immobile rather than blank, but the eyes held in them the watchful and apprehensive quality of something almost feline; they were greenly luminous, unearthly, full of fear, suspicion and cautiousness.

The boy was very thin, and all his bones were delicate. His clothing was less soiled and patched than Frank's, and was excessively neat. His listless, relaxed hands hung at his sides. When he saw Frank gazing at him with such steadfast alertness, he moved uneasily, as if to go away, and a flash of fright and wary desperation showed in his eyes.

"Hello," said Frank, and he was surprised at the confident sound of his own voice.

"Hello," replied the new boy, faintly, and without inflection. His voice had a certain lack of timbre, a certain lack of strength. It was almost a girl's voice, fluting and piping.

All at once, Frank felt that he had known this boy always, that never, with him. would he experience the old shrinking and dread in himself, that he would be understood, not misconstrued, not ridiculed or despised. There was a wooden bench nearby, and he sat down. The other boy, as if compelled by some stronger will, sat down, too. His listless hands relaxed on his knees; they lay there, clean and empty. He looked at Frank, with a certain expectancy, indeterminate and vigilant, which was to become as familiar to Frank as his own face. Something warm and contained began to swell in Frank. He who had always avoided strangers, had turned aside from lingering groups on the street, had walked blocks out of his way to evade the necessity of recognizing acquaintances, felt master of a chaotic and miserable existence.

He had a rather grim if infrequent sense of humor, and tremendous depths of sympathy and prescience in his nature, which no one had ever suspected. He smiled reassuringly at the other boy, who was regarding him with that curiously apprehensive distrust. Perhaps it was that distrust which touched Frank, which made him feel strong and assured.

"You look scared," said Frank, with friendly candor. "What are you scared of? That old dummy teacher up there, or the damn kids? I'm not. All she can do is screech, and that's all they can do, too: screech. Even in their minds they screech. And their fathers and their mothers screech in their minds, just like them. The whole world screeches. I'm sick of it."

Into the strange boy's face there crept a strange expression. It was as though the tight and somewhat wizened greenishness of it was melting and softening. The living blood mounted through the film of that pallor, warming and timid. He still regarded Frank in silence, but it was a comprehending silence, full of gratitude and wonder. His catlike eyes became translucent, like emeralds struck with sunlight. His mouth parted eagerly, showing a row of big, perfect white teeth. His whole expression was that of someone who had suddenly heard a familiar voice, a familiar language, in an alien and lonely land.

"What made you think I was scared?" he asked in his thin and neutral voice, after a prolonged interval.

Frank shrugged. "I—I guess I can—can—recognize being scared when I see it. How old are you, and what's your name?" he asked abruptly, for meagre contact with others had not imparted to him a smooth and tactful approach.

The tense nervousness of the other boy's figure relaxed; his legs untwined from clutching the leg of the bench. "I'm thirteen, almost fourteen. And my name is Paul Hodge. We just moved into Bison a couple of days ago. From Erie, Pennsylvania. My father and me, and my brother, Gordon. Gordon's in first year high, and he's two years older. I haven't any mother." His voice became plaintive and wistful. "My father's a bookkeeper in some store on Main Street. I don't remember what it is." He paused. He seemed astonished at his own loquacity. "What's your name?"

"Frank Clair. I've got my mother yet, and my father." He went on: "I'm just as old as you are. And my father is a chemist—a druggist. That's all. Where do you live?"

"I live down on West Avenue, near Connecticut."

"I live on Albany Street. Near the river. Ever see the river?

I can show you a lot of places. There's boats, on the canal, and going across to Canada. And fishermen, and saloons, and trains."

They stared at each other, rapt. The cold and dismal yard disappeared from their consciousness. The screams and shouts and laughter of the other children were less than the wind in trees.

"What do you do?" asked Frank softly.

It was the completeness of the odd communication which had sprung up between them which made the other boy understand immediately. He murmured: "I play the violin. I take lessons." Now his face glowed. "My teacher says I'll be a great violinist, if I keep on taking lessons."

Frank felt the sweetness of bliss. "I write," he said. "I write stories, and soon I'm going to write a book."

"Books!" said Paul, with entire and wonderful acceptance. "May I read what you write?"

"Yes. If you'll play for me, sometime. I—I like music so much. My father played the violin once. We've got the violin in the cellar. He won't let me touch it, though."

The recess was over. Frank and Paul fled up the stairs to their classroom, running close together as though escaping from a common danger which threatened them if alone. There was a thunder and rumble of feet all about them, classes returning from recess, classes impatient and noisy, going to recess. The corridors seethed with children, and the dank air was full of dimness and dust. Paul and Frank hugged the walls, slipped past their natural enemies, pushed into their room ahead of the returning class.

The classroom was dingy and dark and scuffed, with old ink-stained desks and grayish blackboards. An odor of chalk, decaying wood, dampness and chill hung in the motionless atmosphere. The two boys sat down and smiled at each other like conspirators. Paul's eyes were no longer afraid. They were full of trust as, frequently during the afternoon, they rested on Frank.

He watched Frank almost with fascination. He was so silent, so impassive of face, that it was not possible to read his thoughts. He was a naturally obedient and well-behaved child, and Miss Hempstead, with thankfulness, decided that the new boy would give her little or no trouble, not like that horrible Frank Clair, who displayed towards her and her teaching an open mixture of carelessness and indifference which was infuriating. He never knew his lessons, except spelling and "English." He showed no interest, except when, during the last half hour, she read from *The Child's History of Napoleon*. Nor did he appear to care that he was at the foot of the class. Often he was insolent, but in so subtle a way that she could not find a clear-cut occasion for which to punish him. There he would sit, scowling emptily, twisting scraps of paper in his hands, or he would stare through the windows with an utterly vacuous look, while only his body remained behind like a discarded heap of clothing. She, however, respected his marvelous talent for writing "compositions," and would reluctantly read them to the class. A boy who could write like this, with such lucidity and mature wisdom and beauty, should certainly learn long division and fractions with ease. A boy who could read aloud with expression, understanding and clarity, ought to have no difficulty with history or geography. But he rarely, if ever, attained a passing mark in these subjects, though he would astonish her, during a written test in history, by his awareness of some sidelight which she had not mentioned at all.

Frank dozed with his eyes open all afternoon, though during the morning, when the class had been ordered to write a composition about the sea, he had been all alertness, all excitement. Then at half past two Miss Hempstead began to read from *The Child's History of Napoleon*, and Frank came to life again, visibly rising from some bottomless depth into which he had moved, semi-conscious.

It seemed, from the history, that Napoleon's youthful nose had been his most conspicuous feature, and all through the reading the eyes of the children turned, with grins and snickers, to Frank. Now Frank's nose, though classic and well-formed, was, in the opinion of the others, overlarge and too emphatic, and he felt self-conscious when the passages referring to Napoleon's nose were read by Miss Hempstead. In some fiendish and subtle way which only children command, his classmates had divined his sensitiveness. Also, a very popular comic strip was now being run in a local newspaper about an old horse ludicrously christened Napoleon. Never was there such a delightful grouping of circumstances.

So it was, as the reading proceeded, that nearby boys would whisper spitefully at Frank: "Giddap, Napoleon, it looks like rain!" Frank pretended to ignore these comments, fixing his attention upon Miss Hempstead. He was afraid to glance at Paul Hodge, for fear of seeing derision on his face. But when he finally could not refrain, he saw that Paul's expression was blank and inscrutable, and that he was giving the teacher proper and oblivious attention. Frank understood. Paul, too, was apart from the others.

Then Frank, with a peculiar thrill, noted something else. In addition to Paul Hodge, there was another stranger that day, a quiet little girl with pigtails and a freckled face. She sat near Paul, with decorous politeness. The other children, tired of baiting Frank under their breath, turned their attention to Paul and the little girl, with that monkey-like curiosity and speculation which distinguishes the anthropoid race. Not yet civilized, they had not learned that one gives the stranger at least a tentative and courteous acceptance, and hides antagonism as smoothly as possible. They studied the little girl. Mysteriously, almost as though by open vote and acclaim, they accepted her without reservations. She belonged to them, and this decision had been arrived at instinctively. They forgot her, until she could be more completely explored in a friendly manner at a later opportunity. They turned their satisfied attention to Paul. Immediately, there was a quickening about his vicinity.

Paul sat, listening to the teacher, his quiet, well-shaped hands on the desk before him. There was nothing in his face or his dress that was unusual or odd, as there was in Frank's, nothing odd about his attitude, nothing outlandish in his expression. He looked as colorless as the majority of the others; he appeared completely conventional and acceptable. Nevertheless, not a glance that touched him warmed or became interested. Each eye turned from him, bored, returned to him, sharpened vaguely into dislike, then into aversion.

"I'm afraid that's a very stupid child," sighed Miss Hempstead to herself, as she glanced up from her book and looked at Paul Hodge. "He hasn't a bit of expression. Just a dull blank face. He's worse, in his way, than that awful Frank Clair." She felt no alarm, however. She knew instinctively that Paul would never cause her anxiety. His report card from Erie had shown him to have attained average marks.

When three o'clock came, the children surged downstairs for their clothing. Frank, as usual, hung behind. He always waited until the others had gone, in order to escape their persecutions outdoors. He made a great play of looking for his books, putting away his pencils. He was hoping that Paul would wait for him, but it was more a depressed wish than an expectation. He was much surprised, therefore, to discover Paul sitting silently in his seat in the empty classroom, watching him.

"Hullo! Aren't you going home?"

"Um. I don't want to go out just now," replied Paul, in his fluting tones.

Frank stared at him, astounded. Paul returned the stare. He smiled a little, and again his greenish eyes glowed and welled. Frank slowly put down his ragged books.

"Say," he said slowly, "you don't—you don't hate the kids the way I do, do you?"

Paul shrugged. All at once he did not look fearful; there was a sort of livid contempt on his face. But he made no answer. Frank glanced through the window. The street was almost cleared of children.

"I guess we can go—now," he muttered, his voice dropping on the final word. In silence, they left the room together.

CHAPTER 19

THE malignancy of the children seemed to permeate the street for some distance about the school, and Frank and Paul hurried through it until they came to other streets where they would be less likely to encounter tormentors.

"Gosh, I have to twist like a corkscrew to get home," said Frank, with some humor. "First the kids, here. Then I have to pass a parochial school. You know, a Catholic school, where they have nuns for teachers. The kids chase Protestant kids and yell 'A.P.A.'! and 'dirty Black Protestant'! Sometimes they throw rocks. One of the kids in our class almost lost his eye." He added reflectively: "I'm a Protestant. I didn't know we were Protestants until we came here. Never heard of it in England."

"In Erie," said Paul Hodge, "we do the same thing to the Catholics. Serves them right."

Frank scuffed his toes with dissatisfaction on the concrete sidewalks. "Why do they do it, anyway? There's no sense to it."

Paul set his pale lips tightly and did not reply.

Frank's nervous tension relaxed. He slowed down, shifted his books, and said: "I've got five cents. Want some candy?"

Paul assented without much interest. He rarely showed interest in anything, but it was characteristic of him that he studied the candy counters in the little dark shop with sudden avidity. Frank took his time in choosing. He bought two little pink paraffin bottles, which, when bitten, poured out a rich red sweet syrup, nectar to the tongue. Then, after due consideration, he bought ten little chocolate "niggers" for another cent, two tiny tin skillets filled with pink soft candy (to be eaten with minute tin spoons), and a length of licorice string. They strolled down the street again, while Paul ate his full share with a sort of hidden greediness and pleasure which had more than a little of the feline in it. When he had finished, he licked his lips delicately with the clean tip of a very pale tongue. Walking beside Frank, his carriage and his posture were superior. He had a kind of cold and negative dignity. Frank almost slouched along, both aggressively and warily, and now there was an exaggerated fierceness on his face.

For the first time in his short life he felt both strangely expansive and at ease. He felt unknotted. Because of this, he became witty, and Paul laughed, listening as if in surprise to his own mirth. Inspired by this laugh, Frank's conversation became, in his own ears, quite brilliant. His humor flowed out, sly, subtle, pungent, unusually intelligent and discerning. He kept glancing at Paul, hopefully. Paul's greenish eyes sparkled with enjoyment and pleasure, and sometimes he looked at Frank with amazed and dawning affection. Frank's voice became louder, more excited and eager, voluble and colorful, full of stammering crudity but also full of power and authority. His gestures were violent and lavish. Adults, passing them on the street, were much amused. Frank was not conscious of this, but Paul was, and he colored duskily. His sympathy for Frank increased, became mysteriously strong and protective. Nevertheless, he said mildly: "Don't shout so, Frank. The fools are staring at us."

Frank scowled after two passing women. "Damn fools," he muttered, ferociously, but with uneasiness. Paul said nothing, but there was a smooth malevolence on his quiet face as he looked at the adults. Frank saw that look, and he experienced a shock of confusion, almost of repugnance.

"Oh, hell, who cares about old people?" he said carelessly. "What was I saying? Oh, yes. Well, I write poems and stories. I'm going to write a whole book, soon. About the French Revolution." He swelled with pride. "I had a teacher once. She said I would be a writer. Seems I always was, even when I couldn't write." He paused. "I've got a poem in my history book. I'll read it to you when we can sit down."

Paul turned and smiled at him, and all at once it was a

soft and radiant smile, full of tenderness, and a sharp little thrill of joy, almost of pain, twisted through Frank's heart. Neither of them had spoken of parting immediately. Frank was going some streets out of his way to be with his new friend as long as possible.

Frank began to speak about his parents. He said: "Well, my father is a pharmacist. He works in a drugstore. They have all kinds of candy there, but he won't let me go in when he's working, or any other time. Says it doesn't do to get too 'familiar.' He's funny. He never takes Ma anywhere, and she rows about it. He doesn't care what she says, though. Acts as though he's heard her rowing so long that it's just like a noise in his ears that he doesn't hear. Pa says we've got to save money so we can go back to England before he and Ma are too old." His face changed, darkened, grew more intense as he struggled with his thoughts. "He isn't so old, though. He's only forty-two, but Ma is forty-seven. When Pa talks about England, he looks alive. He walks about, some-times, and talks excited. He's not so old. But I guess he walks about so he can feel important. When grown-up people are scared, they just feel they have to do something im-portant. When they haven't anything important to do, they look dead, don't they? Funny?" He stared with intent eyes of sudden excitement at Paul's face, so impassive, so inscrut-able. "Maybe we all got to feel important or we just die, whether we lie down or not. When we get older. That's why I don't ever want to grow up and get old. That's what my poem is about."

They reached the corner of a quiet street, where grassy lawns spread about them, and the houses, in the waning November light, had an air of secretive withdrawal. There was an iron railing near the sidewalk, and Frank, with sudden shyness, drew out a sheet of scrawled paper from his history book.

"I wrote this while old Hempstead was howling about fractions," he said. "I never can learn fractions. I don't see any sense in it."

Paul raised one fair eyebrow. The two boys leaned com-fortably against the railing. "Please read your poem," he said politely.

Frank cleared his throat shyly, staring down at the paper. His colorless cheek turned pink. "Well," he said, and now he did not stammer, "I call it 'If I Must Die'—"

He glanced up to see if there was any ridicule on Paul's

face. But a strange look, almost too intense, had come into Paul's eyes. Frank began to read:

> "If I must die, then let me die
> While still my lute is strung,
> Before the birds have left the sky
> And all their song is sung.
> If I must go, then let me go
> While still I feel, and still I know,
> That earth is fair and all aglow,
> And God and I are young.

> "If I must sleep, then let me sleep
> Before my hours are run,
> Before the winter snows are steep
> And summer's day is done.
> If I must fade, then let me fade
> Before my faith is all betrayed,
> And hope and I too deep are laid
> For any morning sun."

His young voice had become vibrant, rich and compelling, during the reading of his crude but vital poem, and it seemed to hover in the drained light about the two boys. Paul did not move; he leaned against the railing. He watched Frank and listened. But a quickening tenseness had whitened the area about his impassive lips, and his eyes had widened enormously in their sockets. He did not speak while Frank awkwardly folded the poem and replaced it with feigned carelessness in the leaves of his book. "Well, I guess it isn't so much," he said. "Maybe I'll do better later on."

But he waited, his heart beating. Paul still did not move.

"A lute," said Frank, faintly, "is a kind of stringed instrument. The ancient Greeks used to play it. It has a pretty sound, hasn't it? Lute." He frowned. He repeated softly: "'Before my faith is all betrayed,' I don't know just exactly what that means—I think. I suppose I really meant before I got to feeling that nothing was beautiful any more. Yes, that was it. When you look at grown-ups, you know there isn't anything beautiful for them in the world. It—it's as if they had got color-blind, or something, and saw everything just in grays and blacks and dirty whites."

Paul drew a little breath. There was a tiny vivid light in the corners of his eyes.

The brief November day was dying. The dry, astringent

gales had fallen, and the static air hung, quiet and dead and very cold, about the children. The streets were almost empty except for an occasional hurrying housewife with a basket of groceries, a brave child on a velocipede, a beer wagon that rumbled by, its barrels thumping, or an automobile, clanging, roaring, smoking, leaving a stink of gasoline behind it. The windows of the shabby but large frame houses began to glow and flicker with yellow gaslight, and chimneys smoked languidly, throwing up twisting serpents of dark vapor against a darkening sky. Doors slammed eerily in the dusk; once or twice a hungry dog barked. Underfoot, the sidewalk was gritty, and on the brown lawns there swirled little eddies of dried chaff. The trees stood spectrally along the curbs, their bare branches merging indistinguishably. Now an arc light on the corner began to hiss and splutter, tearing the twilight apart with its shooting and glaring beams.

Everything had been drained of color, dusted over with a grayish powder that seemed to make everything of the same deathly hue. But the heavens had escaped this universal decay. Though the zenith was dark and somber, the low west was flaring with a dull red fire, intense and wild. Above this belt of flame, the skies were a softer rose, melting yet bitterly cold, and above this was a pale lake of translucent jade filled with a flock of golden birds.

Frank saw the sunset, but he never spoke of things that clutched and tormented him with their lonely beauty. He was too afraid of the old ridicule that had followed his earlier attempts to speak. Paul, too, was seeing the sunset. He regarded it, absorbed. But his face was rigid, almost frozen, full of inarticulate and motionless pain. He experienced none of the exaltation that so stirred and invigorated Frank, and none of his prayerful ecstasy. He felt only despair without words, hopelessness and longing beyond his power to understand.

Then Paul said, speaking in his soft and reluctant voice: "Your poem was wonderful, Frank. It—it is like that sunset. Isn't it?" he added, almost inaudibly.

"Oh, I don't know," said Frank, with fine loftiness. "I've done better." But now his heart was beating with rapture. He took Paul's arm, and they went down the next street together. And then the next, in a deep and absorbed silence, seeing nothing but each other.

They had reached West Avenue and Massachusetts Street. Paul stopped in front of a little house of gray wood, the windows tall and narrow and unlighted, the chimney without smoke. A little rickety stoop stood before the closed door. The house looked cold and gloomy and poverty-stricken. Its lawn had been neglected all summer, and dry faded grass stood upon it almost knee-high; it was beginning to move and rustle in a little bitter wind which was rising. Frank looked at it with vague discomfort. The house chilled him, seemed to send out its dusty aura to surround and choke him. He half waited for Paul to invite him in. But Paul did not invite him. Intimacy had not gone that far in that cool and reticent young heart. He merely looked at Frank without expression.

"Tomorrow's Saturday," said Frank suddenly. "I'll come down to your house."

"All right," responded Paul, indifferently. But he was inwardly excited and warmed. Now his face became humid, gentle, and he smiled.

Frank scuffed his toe. He glanced up at Paul fearfully.

"Do you like football?"

"No!" For the first time, real emotion sounded in Paul's tones. He made a faint gesture of involuntary repugnance. Frank grinned delightedly.

"Neither do I. Fool business. Do you like anything else of that kind?"

"No, I don't!"

"Neither do I."

They were caught up in intimate pleasure. They laughed. They were friends. Frank laughed loudly and joyously, but Paul's laughter, so rare and niggardly, was a shrill and musical piping. They stood together, facing each other, these tall and emaciated young boys with the strange faces. Frank, even in the dusk, exuded vitality and fire. But Paul, standing there, gave an impression of immovable integrity. Frank was swift and brilliant lightning leaping across the skies, but Paul was granite rock that the lightning might play upon with only a distant threat of sundering it.

Frank went down the street alone. He was very late, but he was not concerned about it. When he looked back, he saw Paul still standing on the sidewalk, watching him. He waved affectionately. It was now too dark for him to see whether Paul had responded or not. But Paul had not responded.

Now that Frank was leaving him, the warmth and comfort and assurance were seeping out of Paul at every psychic crack, and fear crept in again. He went into the house.

Frank walked on home, whistling softly, staring at the sky, which was now awakening with silvery stars. An active little man, a lamplighter, ran ahead of him, turning on the gas-lamps, lighting them, so that it was as if pale golden suns preceded Frank upon his way, and glowed into life as he approached.

He reached the corner of a street. A girl was approaching, in a red coat and a red hood. She had dark curls on her shoulders, and a round pink face. Frank waited, and the hands in his pockets clenched. She came under the lamplight. It was not Jessica. She stared at him impudently, then looked away. He went on, desolate.

CHAPTER 20

PAUL's brother, Gordon, was just lighting the flaring gaslight in the cold and miserable little parlor when the younger boy came into the house.

Gordon was taller and broader than Paul, and much healthier in appearance. His lean face was fair, very intelligent, and had a good color. Moreover, it was mobile, sly and expressive, which Paul's was not. He had lively gray eyes, even though they had something of Paul's cold suspicion in them, though none of Paul's integrity. His wide white forehead, below a well-cut mop of light brown hair, showed intellect, but its tendency to wrinkle constantly betrayed lack of self-control. His mouth was almost pretty in its color and shape, but satirical.

He cultivated small ills of the body, which relieved him of sundry responsibilities and duties. In this he displayed a good deal of genius, for he was naturally indolent and possessed of no strong emotion.

"Hello," he said in a voice of ironic amusement as he saw his brother. "Who was that funny-looking little boy you were talking to out there? The little boy who made his hands fly? He jumped around like a flea."

Paul's lips compressed angrily, but he shrugged with carelessness.

"Just a kid from school who walked home with me."

Gordon chuckled spitefully.

"Well, that kid was certainly queer-looking," he said.

Paul's light brows drew together harshly, though his face otherwise changed hardly at all. He was conscious, again, of a sudden possessiveness with regard to Frank. The memory of his new friend became precious, became part of himself. His mind closed on the memory of Frank like the shells of a clam, absorbed it, digested it, made it a portion of his own substance.

"He's not queer-looking. He's a fine boy. He's coming to see me tomorrow."

Gordon gave a display of mock stupefaction. "What! Since when did you start to make friends with school kids? And what a kid! While you were at the business of making friends, why didn't you pick out someone more presentable and civilized?"

"You don't know anything about him, Gordon. He's the only boy I ever could stand, and I don't want you to make fun of him tomorrow. His father's a pharmacist, in a big drugstore," he added, with a shrewd appeal to Gordon's intense snobbery.

Gordon was still unconvinced. "He doesn't look it. I mean, he looks queer and has funny clothes. As if his father was a day-laborer. I hope this doesn't mean that you are going to be like other people and fill the house with a pack of Toms, Dicks and Harrys. You know Dad would never stand for it, and I don't want the place cluttered up with kids, myself. By the way, did you forget to bring home the bread and milk?"

"Yes," Paul said angrily.

"Well, for the Lord's sake, go out and get it! And don't yell at me like that. You're no tenor. And Dad'll be sure to forget the paper, so you'd better get that, too. There's a couple of cents on the kitchen table. You might clear off the table while you're there, so I can start supper."

Paul stood in silence, glancing disconsolately about the room. A sick depression rolled over him. The Hodge family had moved in from Erie only three days before, and had not yet got settled in. The place had not been cleaned before the new tenants had arrived, and every object, from the scarred window-sills to the hideous oak "mission" furniture and frayed, discolored Brussels rug, was covered with a patina of oily dust. No mantles had as yet been put upon the gas jets, and the light was flickering, dim and yellow, and full of desolation. The wallpaper, discolored and dirty, and of an ugly brownish shade, would have darkened even the brightest light. On the bare oak table, square and ink-stained, stood a brass lamp with a brass-framed shade of milky colored glass, several bits of which were missing. Besides the mission furniture, there was an imitation black leather chair, cracked and peeling and showing the stuffing through an occasional small rip. The only piece of furniture belonging to the Hodges was a beautifully polished and simple mahogany chest of drawers in one corner, but its beauty was temporarily eclipsed by heaps of small newspaper parcels, match boxes, a bag of apples and one of grapes, a shabby violin case, and kindred trivia. A shivering small fire burned in the little iron stove; the room was both airless and acridly cold. Between the two small windows, curtainless and dismal, were several scuffed old suitcases. Gordon had lit the gas in the kitchen and the bedroom, and Paul could see the littered breakfast table, the dusty range, the disheveled and littered beds

Paul shivered. Resentment flashed up in him like gunpowder. Gordon had complained of a headache that morning, and had not gone to school, where, in three days, he had distinguished himself. Despite his claim to indisposition, he looked extraordinarily fresh and complacent.

"You've been home all day, Gordon," said Paul. "You might have cleaned up a little of this mess and unpacked our things."

Gordon glanced up swiftly from the little stove, whose stubborn contents he had just been poking. His sandy brows drew together irritably. "I've had a headache. Besides, Dad ought to have had a woman in to clean up before we unpacked. But it seems that he expects us to do the scrubbing."

"Of course. Who else? Gordon, you talk so silly. You know Dad hasn't any money at all. He can't spare a cent. And now he'll soon be home from the office and there's nothing to eat in the house, and you haven't even made the beds."

Gordon shrugged with contemptuous indifference. "All right, if you want things done, Cinderella, do them yourself." His fair face tightened and colored vindictively; he went into the bedroom, turned up the gas, snatched a book from a broken and littered chair, tucked a soiled pillow under his sandy head, and collapsing onto the creaking bed, calmly began to read. "I've got to make up for missing today," he said. "Run along, now, and get the bread and milk. You can put some potatoes on to boil, too, and you might get some boiled ham or some lamb chops while you're out. And a can of beans and a couple of cupcakes from the bakery. Oh, and some tea. And don't bother me."

Furious anger tore at Paul's throat and heart. His long pale hands clenched. He had a mad longing to lay those hands on Gordon, to rip and slash and destroy with them.

Nothing of what he felt showed on the small expressionless face, which seemed to lack the very muscles to reveal emotion. He merely looked tight and blank, though under his brows there was a strong and yellowish glare.

After a moment, he went into the kitchen. He was trembling all through his thin body, and he felt sick. He gingerly washed some potatoes and lit the gas under them. On a filthy shelf was the family treasury of small coins, and he picked up several. He glanced into the bedroom. Gordon was serenely reading. His chilly lips were compressed in a stony silence, and Paul went out.

The little corner store, dirty and smelly and cold, yielded up some boiled ham, a can of beans, and some bread and butter and tea. Paul looked at a basket of oranges, and hesitated. His father loved oranges, but the family purse was very thin, and it would be four days until pay day. Paul fumbled in another pocket where he was hoarding ten cents. He bought half a dozen oranges for his father, and asked that they be put into a separate bag. He would have to hide them from Gordon, who would eat them immediately, and would laugh in Paul's face while doing so. Gordon's dislike for his brother was even greater than his love for his father. The fact that he had deprived his father occupied less space in his mind than the fact that Paul would shudder with rage and "look ridiculous" in his helplessness.

Paul bought an evening paper at the store, and while his purchases were being wrapped, he glanced listlessly at the headlines. He was rarely really interested in anything. He read of two suffragettes who had died during a hunger strike in London prisons. There was a forum of indignant ministers who were vigorously denouncing the modern hobbleskirt and its display of feminine calves when the owner climbed into a public vehicle, and one clergyman became lyrical about the effect this display would have on a tender, rising generation. "Women have lost all modesty," he proclaimed. "Decorum is going the way of the horse and carriage and church attendance." Paul yawned. He was not of the company of young boys who hung about corners where streetcars stopped for passengers, in hope of seeing the female limb exposed. He saw the headline: "King George visits Kaiser Wilhelm," and was not interested. There were dire prophecies by Republican politicans that the recent election of Woodrow Wilson would result in "panic, depression, inflated money and disorganization, the usual concomitants of Democratic administration." Mr. Taft, who had been defeated, had only dignified and restrained comments to make, but Mr. Theodore Roosevelt was less ambiguous, in his usual vitriolic manner. An embargo on war munitions into Mexico was announced. Everyone was very excited.

A miserable woman, poorly dressed and with raw red hands, entered the store with a little girl of about five years. The woman's face was pinched and white and fierce with chronic despair, and the child looked hungry and cold. The grocer was gathering Paul's oranges up from the counter and was putting them into a bag, when the child snatched one greedily and thrust the thick yellow fruit against her chapped lips.

"Here, you mustn't do that," began the grocer with uncomfortable kindness. But before he could take back the orange, Paul had pounced on the child. He snatched the fruit violently from the thin and dirty little fingers. "Pig!" he exclaimed, his voice shrill and keening. The woman, the grocer, the baby, stared at him, paralyzed. For his face had turned to gray stone, and in his eyes glared the mortal and loathing hatred that was so inexorably a part of his character, and which not even his father suspected. Between his livid lips, his large white teeth had a wet and ferocious glitter. He was only thirteen years old, but he looked, at that moment, like an insane and vicious old man.

The baby began to cry suddenly, with fright. But the woman and the grocer were still petrified. In silence, they watched Paul leave the shop. Then the grocer breathed deeply, and grinned at his customer. "Well!" he exclaimed. "Did you ever see the like? Here, sweetheart, Mr. Murphy'll give you a nice big orange. There's the girl!"

CHAPTER 21

PAUL, back in the miserable little cottage on West Avenue, washed dishes and looked at the shabby violin case on the chest of drawers. His brows contracted in a slight frown; he was full of sudden pain. He secretly believed that regular lessons would reveal the fact that he was a genius; his dreams at night were golden and flaming with visions of a world's homage, a world's adulation, and of having expressed himself in the noblest of music.

The house was almost warm, the supper almost ready, when Edward Hodge crept wearily up the board sidewalk in the darkness. A few flakes of dry snow powdered his old overcoat with its threadbare sleeves and frayed collar. His hat was too large for him. Under it, his gentle wry face, with its one-sided, twisted smile, looked too small and angular. His trouser legs, though narrow in the prevailing style, still flapped emptily about his emaciated calves and thin ankles. He walked like a man who had reached the last boundary of exhaustion, and could go no farther. His shoulders were bent and huddled; he seemed to shrink from the bitter wind. He was of medium height rather than tall, and his lack of flesh made him seem even shorter.

Edward Hodge was in reality a very sick man, and to the discerning and interested eye this was self-evident. He would have appeared pathetic had it not been for his continual sweet and sadly satirical smile; that smile saved him from appearing defenseless, warned off sympathy. Though only forty years old, he appeared older. It was not that he was prematurely gray or wizened or slow of gait. It was more in the expression of his fine, mild and intelligent blue eyes. In the sweetness and steadiness and endurance of his delicate features was a whimsicality and a wisdom that at times gave him a puckish look. He despised everyone, himself included, with fragile humor. A strange and devoted little man was Edward Hodge, of immense tenacity and a certain fine-drawn grimness.

Edna Hodge, his wife, had died when Paul had been but six months old. She had never seemed real to her husband; she was even less real to her sons. Edward had a faded photograph of her; Gordon resembled her closely, but there was a certain catlike fixity about her eyes which recalled Paul. However, Paul resembled his father, though he lacked the delicate mobility of the latter's features. He possessed, however, their general contour and dignity, their reserve and secretiveness.

It seemed to Edward, tonight, that he did not have the strength to push open the splintered wooden door of his new home. He had been certain all day that he would not be able to go on, that he must lie down and give up. Perhaps die. But he had not really believed that. There was nothing for him to do but to go on, to educate his sons, to give them an opportunity to be more than he had been.

Until they no longer needed him, were no longer defenseless, he could not die, however his sick body ached and thirsted for death. His will kept him alive, his sons' need of him. He had come to Bison from Erie because Bison was much larger, had better schools, chances for scholarships, and a State College, where tuition could be had for almost nothing.

When he entered the little house, its close warmth seemed to enfold him and greet him with affection. Gordon, who was belatedly gathering up newspapers, immediately told his father of his headache, which had prevented him from going to school. Edward had no breath as yet to speak; he merely smiled. His pale and delicate face lit up. Paul ran in from the kitchen with a knife in his hand, and when he saw his father a radiance came into his eyes and he looked glorified as at the coming of a beloved. He said nothing, however, but helped his father to remove his coat.

"Well, boys," said Edward, faintly. He glanced about the living room, and his thin nostrils distended for an instant. The boys had done nothing today, in spite of his requests that morning; he could see that. But he never complained; that was both a virtue and a source of irreparable injury to his children.

"Supper's almost ready," said Paul. He saw that his father was completely prostrated. But he never had any words to express what he thought and he lacked the tenderness to show it.

Edward went into the bedroom to take off his shoes. He saw that the beds had been roughly made. The bare floor was splintered and stained; on the one rickety oak bureau was a pile of trash and odds and ends. The gaslight flared dimly from the wall. Suddenly, with a gesture of utter surrender, he threw himself face downwards across one of the beds, and lay as if dead, unmoving. An air of collapsed resignation enveloped his slight body in its worn and shabby serge suit. One arm hung limply over the edge of the bed in an attitude of dissolution. In his breast was a sick and intolerable pain, and he closed his eyes, swimming away on a dark and rolling tide.

He could hear the boys squabbling ill-naturedly in the kitchen as the last touches were given to the dinner, but he was too ill to arrange the words that entered through his ears. All at once nothing mattered, nothing was important, except death. He dared not give way to this treacherous betrayal of his children; groaning inwardly, he pulled himself into a sitting posture, and pressed his wet and trembling hands over his eyes. He became aware that Gordon was standing in the doorway and talking peevishly, as though he had been trying to attract his father's attention for some time. "Supper's ready, Dad. I called you a couple of times."

"Yes, son, I hear you," said Edward faintly.

He crawled, shivering, into the warmth of the dirty little kitchen. He looked at his sons, and smiled at them with a selfish and passionate devotion. There was something terrible in his love for them, for it was too personal, too grasping and tenacious a love, and it excluded the world, repudiated it, held it off with gestures of suspicion and fear. His compassionate love for his children had deprived him of compassion for others.

He tried to eat, but the food sickened him. He listened to all the slight and trivial things his sons had to say, and, as he listened, he smiled his sweet and quizzical half-smile, and his eyes roamed slowly from one to the other with a feasting expression.

When he spoke to them tonight, it was in his usual manner, soft-voiced, wry, tolerant, and thoughtful. He treated them as men his own age. He discussed things with them. His interest in their thoughts and their days was not the sedulously cultivated interest of adults who think it their duty to appear interested. He was genuinely, passionately, greedily, absorbed in everything they thought and did.

Paul spoke little. Between his father and himself was a great understanding, too complete for words. He ate steadily, his small pale face disinterested, self-bewitched, almost avaricious, and this infuriated Gordon, as it always did. His young nerves began to crawl with the old disagreeable sensation, as he watched Paul daintily extract every ounce of flavor from the poor dinner. He would roll a morsel delicately in his mouth, as if savoring it gloatingly; he would swallow it, and his yellow-green eyes would show a faint glaze, as if in ecstasy. "Like a cat," thought Gordon, with sudden hatred.

"Tell Dad about the funny little boy who came home with you today, Paul," he said, with a laugh.

Edward looked at Paul in smiling surprise, raising his eyebrows.

Paul colored unpleasantly. "He's not funny," he said, coldly. "He's not like other kids. He's different, and bright. He's coming to see me tomorrow."

"Tomorrow!" exclaimed Edward.

"He looked as if he needed a bath," said Gordon, with enjoyment. "And his clothes were three sizes too small. Looks like a shabby, overgrown puppy, all legs and knobs, and he jumps around like a puppy, too. You'll laugh when you see him, Dad. Paul wouldn't pick out a nice boy. You'd know he'd pick out a freak."

Paul glared. "He's not a freak. He's just not stupid, like everybody else." And then he was suddenly ashamed. He remembered all Frank's strangeness and awkwardness, his queer rapid speech and grandiloquent gestures. Then his shame passed, and was replaced by a warm and affectionate indulgence and superiority. "He's the only boy I ever liked."

Edward said nothing, but he was disturbed and puzzled.

"Bah, you never liked anyone but yourself! I never saw such a selfish little beast as you, Paul," said Gordon, with smiling carelessness. "You've always grabbed off things for yourself, even when you were just a baby. This new boy has probably got something you'd like, or he toadies to you."

Paul and his father exchanged a glance. Then Paul said: "You're stupid. I don't want anything from Frank, and he doesn't toady. Besides, he writes books, and poems and things."

Now Edward's lassitude lifted, and a tight jealousy squeezed his heart. He smiled indulgently. He said: "How children boast. They often try to gain importance that way." He dismissed Frank as something too pettily amusing for discussion. But, for once, Paul was not in accord with him. His mouth tightened, and he looked away, with obstinacy. Edward, seeing this, was vaguely perturbed.

They were eating their dry and sawdust-like bakery cupcakes when there came a smart though discreet knock at the door. The November wind has risen to a mournful howling, but the knocking sounded through it. Gordon rose and went into the living room where the gas, turned down, was dimly flaring. When Gordon opened the door, letting in a swirl of gritty wind, it was a woman's voice that Edward and Paul heard, rich, warm, apologetic.

"I'm sure you must excuse me, Sonny," it said, laughing a little. "My, it's cold tonight, ain't it? Well, I thought, the poor boys and their Daddy will be having a hard time getting settled and everything, and no woman to cook anything for them, so, seeing I'm your neighbor, I thought I'd bring over a nice hot apple pie for your supper. Here it is. Be careful, the bottom's hot. Your Dad home, honey?"

Gordon's affirmative answer, though reserved and diffident, was still pleasant and grateful. Edward, staring at the doorway, frowned. Paul laid down his knife and fork. Above their silence the gas flared, the rusty stove smelled of grease and dirt. In the doorway appeared a plump, buxom woman of about forty, with firm red cheeks, flashing teeth, and thick black hair in a rather disorderly knot on the back of her head. She was clad in stiff blue gingham and had a black shawl about her shoulders. Both Edward and Paul regarded her with the pale and affronted apprehension of those who suspect strangers. Edward did manage a stiff and frightened smile, but Paul glared at the woman. She beamed at them from the threshold. Gordon, behind her, was murmuring.

"No, I won't bother you folks," she said heartily, bestowing her smile on them all like the anonymous heat of a friendly fire. She had just come from the shining cleanliness of her own snug home and she thought the dirt and indifferent slackness of this house frightful. "Of course," she said later to her husband, "he's a man, and they're boys, but you'd think they would notice dirt, wouldn't you, and want to do something about it?" But now she continued to beam upon them without betraying what she was thinking.

"Awful night, ain't it?" she asked cheerfully, pulling the shawl closer about her as she prepared to leave. Edward murmured; Paul continued to stare at her with fixed affront. His small body was stiff with dignity and outrage. "Well, winter's coming, and everything—Say, I hope you folks are comfortable? You got everything you need? I know how it is when you're moving."

Edward murmured again. He had not risen; he half turned away from her now, and played with his fork. There was something deathlike in the waxen fragility of his fingers. He did not ask his generous guest to sit down. He moistened his lips and moved his head slightly, as though looking for an escape. The woman's vitality and the lush quality of her body and spirit made him shrink from her with pallid timidity and the unspoken epithet: "Vulgar."

The woman chattered on from her doorway. Gordon stood beside her, smiling uneasily. She folded her robust arms across her full bosom. "Your Missis been dead long, Mr. Hodge?" she asked sympathetically.

"Yes," replied Edward, faintly. The dusky and unhealthy tint of anger surged up into Paul's face.

"That's too bad," she commented. She heaved a big sigh. "Well, here today, gone tomorrow. You never can tell when it's going to be your turn. That's life. I hope you like the pie," she added.

She bustled out of the house, missing nothing, on the way, of the dirty and dreary confusion of the living room.

At the outside door, she stopped to chat a moment with Gordon, who was burning with mortification at the conduct of his father. "If you need anything, honey," she said, kindly, "just run in and ask. Don't be backward." She patted his shoulder and went out into the dark gale of the wintry night. Gordon, indignant, returned to the kitchen seething with reproaches. But they died in his throat when he saw that Paul was just in the act of throwing the hot and spicy pie into the garbage pail. There was something so vindictive, so savage, in his gestures, that Gordon stood there petrified, unable to say a word. Edward made no effort to restrain Paul, but sat in silence in his chair, smiling faintly, almost indulgently.

"Interfering old pig!" exclaimed Paul in his fluting voice, as he gave the pie a last vicious poke in the bottom of the pail. "What business was it of hers if our mother is dead? Or anything? Why doesn't she mind her own business?"

Gordon made a prodigious effort to speak. "Why—you!" he cried hoarsely. "Why—" Rage exploded in him, rage lighted and fed by a thousand faggots: his father's impotence and gentle obstinacy, his father's and brother's patronizing smiles, their blanknesses and silences, their unhealthy immobilities, the whole sordid and dank dreariness of his life and his home. There was a dimness before his eyes and a salt sickness in his mouth. And then he knew it was no use, no use at all.

CHAPTER 22

WHEN Edward came home at noon on Saturday, he found a very odd young boy about thirteen with his son Paul.

It had turned extremely cold during the night, and morning light had revealed the iron earth, corrugated and stiff, wrinkled and patched with the first snow. The trees had tangled themselves together in a bony confusion against an iron-colored sky. The shabby houses along the street hugged their clapboards about their thin walls as if for protection against the corroding air, and the smoke that came from their chimneys was thin and grudging.

Paul and Gordon had made only languid efforts to clean up the dirt and confusion of their new home. The last packing case had arrived that morning and stood squarely on the dusty carpet of the living room, still untouched. Just as Edward entered the house a pale and watery beam of sunlight filtered in through the dusty windows, which were streaked with old finger marks. It revealed all the dustiness and squalor and disorder of the room.

Gordon was sitting on top of the packing case, eating a cheese sandwich with great relish. His fair and intelligent face was full of amusement, and his eyes were laughing with indulgent malice. At a little distance Paul rocked lazily in the old leather chair. Between the brothers stood the tall strange boy.

Just before Edward had opened the door, the weary man had had a dim impression of a new excited voice, strong and vehement. Then Gordon had begun to laugh. But now the new boy was silent, staring at Edward with the shy and half-hostile eyes of a young and frightened animal.

Edward had no reaction towards other children than that of acute indifference and ennui. Therefore, he merely twitched his eyebrows absently, immediately and apparently becoming unconscious of the stranger. But under this obvious indifference, there was an uneasiness in himself.

However, he was too exhausted to think of the matter. Paul had come to him and was helping him off with his coat. But Edward's usual weariness had sharpened to pain today in the region of his heart, and for once the squalor of the house penetrated through his lassitude.

"Children, children," he said, faintly, "why haven't you straightened up a little?"

"O Dad, you should hear this boy!" cried Gordon, shrill with glee. He stuffed the last of the sandwich into his mouth, and chewed rapidly. "He says the most ridiculous things! You ought to hear him! I never heard anything so funny, all the ideas he has—"

"Dad," broke in Paul's fluting voice, "this is Frank Clair, the boy I told you about last night."

Edward glanced briefly and without interest at Frank, with the absentminded expression of one whose attention is forcibly attracted. He made his cold lips smile, and he again forgot the boy except for that slight feeling of irritation. "Paul, did you find the hammer? We must open that packing case at once. Almost everything is in there."

There was no midday meal in readiness for him. The monstrous selfishness and self-absorption of his children had prevented them from thinking of such a thing. And, in truth,

he would have liked a meal. His poor body would have rev-
elled in a hot cup of tea, a bowl of soup, and a sandwich.
He was too tired to get these for himself, and it did not
occur to him to ask his children. One of his firmest theories
was that parents should not "impose" upon their children,
nor ask of them anything that they would not ask of a
friendly acquaintance.

Almost without his direction, his aching feet found their
way into the bedroom. The beds, of course, had not been
made. He sank upon one of them; there came to his nostrils
the moldly smell of unaired bedding, of none too clean
blankets, and old body smells. He did not care. He shut his
eyes and sank into a confused nightmare of pain, into utter,
though temporary resignation. He was too tired to sleep.

Paul had found the hammer and was trying to persuade the
perched Gordon to abdicate. Gordon, in response, settled
himself more firmly, began to tease his brother.

"Come on, Gordon, get off," said Paul, half crying.

"Don't feel like it," replied Gordon. "I want another sandwich. Get me another cheese sandwich, and after I eat it I'll
get off. But here I stay until I get the sandwich."

"But we need the stuff. I need my sweater and my rubbers
and my mittens."

"Piffle. Why are you so energetic all of a sudden? This
thing's stood here since eight o'clock this morning, and you've
never stirred to open it. What have you done, anyway? You
slept until eleven. I never saw such a sleeper; you might as
well be dead, and even when you are awake the few hours
during the day, you are still half dead. Lazy little pup. Well,
I'm staying here until I get my sandwich."

Frank had been watching interestedly, and with disgust.
Young though he was, the disorder, the odors and dust, of
this house had already affronted him. His own home, though
cold and comfortless, was clean and well-ordered. Dirt was
alien to his experience. As he was of an ardent and positive
temperament, he could not understand Paul's impotence. He
said: "If I were you, Paul, I'd hit him with the hammer,
good and hard." He did not like Gordon, in spite of the
latter's surface pleasantness and amiability.

"Oh, you would, would you, Charles Dickens?" asked Gordon, smiling goodhumoredly. "Read me that poem again, the
one you just read, about 'If I die.' I like it."

Frank glowered, and dug his foot into the carpet.

"You're just a fake," added Gordon, prodding him delicately with his toe. "I don't believe you wrote it. You

copied it out of some book. You can get into trouble that way."

He found Frank enormously amusing. He had not been so diverted for a long time. He regarded the other boy steadily and smilingly. Was there ever such a raw wrist and long bony hand, such big feet, so big a nose, such tight trousers and touselled hair! Like a farm boy, he thought with pleased disdain. Yet, under his teasing, he was sorry for the child, almost liked him. He had come to the conclusion, though, that the boy was "deep" and would bear watching.

For the past hour or two, before the arrival of Edward, Frank had been full of spirits. He had a gift for pantomime and a keen sense of the ludicrous, and when he spoke to a sympathetic audience his hands, his feet, his whole body, became virtual extensions of his speech. He had been "taking off" some of his neighbors for the edification of Paul and his brother, and the little house had been full of shrieks of laughter. Once or twice, Gordon had paused in his mirth to stare curiously at Paul. He had rarely heard Paul laugh, yet today Paul's musical and piping laughter had been as frequent as Gordon's.

But the warmth and light had gone from Paul's face now as he resumed his urging that Gordon get off the packing case.

"I tell you what," said Gordon, smirking comfortably. "Play me something on your violin, Paul. I feel in the mood for music. Then I'll get off."

"Slam him," suggested Frank. "I'll take one arm, and you take the other, Paul. We'll pull him off together."

But Paul sighed exhaustedly. He was really somewhat relieved, for he had an excuse for not attacking the packing case just yet. There was plenty of time. "All right," he said. He went to the chest of drawers, tenderly opened the violin case and took out the instrument. Frank glanced at it, and was disappointed. He saw at once that it was a very poor violin, cheaply made, not at all like the quite excellent instrument of his father's, which he had examined secretly at home. He had an idea! Some way, somehow, he would obtain his father's violin for Paul! He had a sudden vision of himself presenting his father with a sheaf of green bills, and grandly buying the violin. He took the instrument from Paul and examined it scornfully. "That's awful," he said. "Why, it's nothing but an old five-seventy-five thing! Just an old soap box with strings on it. I thought you had a real violin."

Paul colored furiously, and snatched back his treasure. Then Frank knew that he had wounded his new friend, and was abjectly sorry. He said: "Well, I don't know anything about these things. Bet you'll have a fine one, one of these days. That's good enough to practice on."

Paul looked at his brother, ignoring Frank. "Shall I play the Spanish Fandango?" he asked disdainfully.

"You might as well," replied Gordon, pulling a small apple from his pocket and beginning to chew on it. "You do that best of all, Mouse."

Paul tucked the violin under his chin and lifted his bow. He began to play.

He played miserably, and with absolute correctness. Under his bow the sprightliness of the simple Spanish folk song became dead and cold and perfect as a wax flower, the bright and childish life of it beaten out under those small stiff hands, which were without passion or feeling. It was not that Paul made a single error or faltered once in his playing. He played with exactitude and precision. And because of these, he made a hideous thing of a little dancing song that was created for young feet, the feet of those who love life and are innocently happy and gay. It became a melancholy dirge, amazingly played in a quick tempo. There was no emotion or laughter in it, no fire, no ardor. It was a reproduction, in gray and dun-white, of a riotous scene of color and joy.

Smiling faintly and amusedly, Gordon chewed on his apple. He chewed contentedly, occasionally glancing at his brother, and idly hummed an accompaniment to the selection. He had no particular opinion as to Paul's ability, and merely supposed the boy played rather well.

He gave Frank a curious look, and was surprised. Frank's face was an exaggerated mask of utter incredulity and astonishment and pain. His eyes blinked as he listened, and once or twice, as Gordon watched him, he shook his head sharply, vigorously, as if to clear something away. He frowned, jerked his features, thrust his hand into the pockets of his tight trousers. Finally, as the selection labored towards its end, he moistened his lips. His expression became grave, his eyes full of adult pity. Why, he can't play at all! he thought, and there was sadness in his heart.

The last note shivered into silence, and Paul relaxed. He did not look at Frank; his face had become blank and impassive again. He lifted his bow and examined it critically. "I thought so," he muttered, angrily. Then for the first time he looked at Frank, with something like smugness. And Frank looked back at him, without speaking.

Paul was languidly rubbing his fingers over the strings.

It was as if Frank no longer interested him, or, as Frank guessed, his opinion of Paul's ability was too unimportant to affect his friend. But Frank was not offended. He had little real conceit, and he was only sad. He said, nervously: "That was awful pretty, Paul." But he winced inwardly. It seemed to him that the very air was still quivering from the insult of Paul's music, and that the hard notes, the acid vibrations, would remain forever suspended in space, and he could not bear it.

He suddenly took the violin from Paul's limp hands and grasped it feverishly. He drew the bow over the strings; he was trembling. But only a harsh and whining note rewarded him. He could not bear it. He had no power to evoke what he heard in himself. The instrument was only wood in his hands, and he was agonized with the terrible necessity to externalize his inner music. He had only words. He looked up, and his eyes were shining vividly. He would write a poem! He would force words into harmony to express, to some small degree, the unutterable.

"That kid looks crazy," commented Gordon, wiping his mouth. "Say, Frank, you look dippy. What's the matter with you?"

Edward was still lying in his stupor of exhaustion in the fetid bedroom. But he had heard his son's playing, and his dark smile was peaceful in the gloom. He was certain that Paul had great genius. Now the pain began to ebb from him, and the voices in the other room came to him clearly, and they gave him peace.

"Nothing. I—I'm going to w-write a poem about that song Paul played," Frank stammered. Then he seemed to sink into revery, and a brooding shadow covered his face.

Gordon laughed lightly. "I like your poems, you little plagiarist," he said. Frank looked at him, as did Paul. "Plagiarism," said Gordon, smugly. "Know what that is? You take what someone else wrote and call it your own. How could a kid like you write poems, or anything? You don't know enough."

Frank stared at him, and his eyes were heavy with dreams. "I don't know," he said softly. "Words come to me. Sometimes I—I don't know just what they mean. But they come. Like music. As they did to me last night, and I got a pencil and paper and went to the window and wrote one down, just by the light of the lamp outside."

"Well, let's hear it," suggested Gordon, winking at his

brother. "I still think you pinched it from somewhere. I'll have to look it up."

Edward, in the next room, smiled contentedly. In some odd way, the mysterious threat which he had felt in Frank Clair was gone. He listened. Now Frank was reciting his poem, and his young voice came clear and rich and exultant, yet tender and meditative, to the man on his bed:

"I stood alone where green-limbed Neptune plowed
Dark furrows in a lambent sea of gold.
The black rocks, drowned and wet, and yet uncowed,
To heaven turned foreheads rimmed with scarlet cold.
The sky was like a silence, filled with light,
A hope of joy before the march of night.

"And yet, thou wast not there. The fire of eve
In her great beauty had but power to grieve.

"I saw the pulsing beauty of the stars,
Like drops of dew upon the robes of night.
The moonlight lay on earth in shadowed bars
Of mingled darkness and of whisp'ring light.
The world was but a cup of shadow, tipped
To catch the silver wine that in it dripped.

"O lovely night, that stilled the cry of care!
It stilled me not, for lo! thou wast not there."

Edward raised himself on his elbow. There were painful little pulses all over his body, in his neck, his arms, his legs. He was a devotee of poetry, and understood it. He knew that this poem he had just heard was childish, crude and awkward. But he felt the grandeur of the images which it expressed, even in its crudity. He sensed the mind which could feel and evoke them, and a kind of jealous terror, overpowering and reasonless, seized him.

"You never wrote that poem," said Gordon, accusingly.

No, no, he never wrote it! said Edward fervently and wildly in himself. His gripping hands clutched the bedclothes, and he felt anguish all through his body. How dared that little wretch come here with his stolen lies and so affront Paul! My boy, my boy, he murmured prayerfully.

The early winter twilight was already thick in the room, and now it seemed to gather itself into mists of unbearable pain. Edward pushed himself to his feet. He stood on the threshold of the other room. Then, slowly, as he looked at the boys, unaware of his presence, something like a bitter and deathly cold crept over his flesh.

The strange boy was vehemently defending himself against the charge of plagiarism. He was shouting: "T'isn't so! I don't have to copy! I can write things myself! You're a liar, Gordon Hodge! I—I'll k-k-knock your damn head off!"

Gordon laughed delightedly. He imitated Frank's angry stammer.

Edward rubbed his hands over his eyes. He knew. He knew that Frank was no plagiarist, and that what he had tried to tell himself was a lie. He dropped his hands, and looked at Paul with a dreadful yearning, as if to throw a protecting arm about him. And then he paused in amazement.

For Paul had become alive, shakingly alive, like a glass flower miraculously blooming into color, and bending before a wind. His motionlessness had become motion, his pallor had become tinted. He was gazing at Frank, as if the other boy's poem were still ringing in his head, and the more he gazed the brighter the life glowed on his hushed face.

Then Edward started, as if licked by flame. Here was the Enemy, in the shape of a young boy he had never seen before this day. Not like the ordinary enemies, familiar and contemptible, but an enemy, alien and powerful.

Edward put his hand to his throat. He tried to speak, and his voice emerged as a croak.

"Isn't it late, boys?" he said. He leaned against the doorway, faint and sick. He heard an obscure scurrying, and a match flared as it was applied to the gas-jet. It came to Edward that the sudden scratch of the match, the low muttering of the wind against the windows and the doors, were obtrusively loud, significantly loud, fatefully loud. All sound, for a few moments, had in it something malefic.

Paul was not looking at his father. He was looking at Frank. And his face was full of shy laughter, moved and poignant and eager, and something more which suggested worship and love.

Frank was awkwardly tugging his cap from his pocket and smiling shamefacedly. "Guess it's time for me to go," he said, uneasily aware of the frail shadow of the man in the doorway, and aware, too, of a suggestion of enmity in him. Paul sighed. He put his violin in its case. Always acutely aware of anything his younger son did, Edward felt that in Paul's gestures was a renunciation, not without bitterness and pain and rebellion. Edward closed his eyes in a spasm of intolerable suffering."

Then he said: "It's almost five o'clock. What did you boys buy for supper?"

There was something in his voice that dismissed Frank contemptuously, and Frank was overcome with mortification. Again, he was inferior, cast out; and his cheeks turned hot. Edward's manner, that vague smile, the thin, unseeing light in his eyes, struck him down.

He went towards the door. Paul went with him. They stood, silently staring at each other a moment, then Paul smiled. It was a smile without fear, utterly natural and young. "I'll see you tomorrow," Frank muttered, defiantly, going out into the winter twilight.

"Funny little fellow," murmured Edward amusedly, as Paul came back to him. "Where on earth did you pick him up, son?" Always before, this attack had been attended with success on the few occasions when Paul had struck up a feeble friendship with another child, and Edward waited.

But Paul flung up his delicate and narrow head and looked squarely at his father. He said, with gentleness, almost as if he understood, and warned: "He's in my class at school. I told you, Dad."

CHAPTER 23

How ineffably lovely and palpitating with color and light were the days and the weeks and the months! Now the earth was an orb of gold afloat in rainbows, and it spun in rings of music. Everything was lost in harmony and radiance. Everything had become resolved and exalted, full of tender and majestic meaning. Everything widened and contracted in a kind of shouting incandescence. Angels stood in the morning, and God walked in the stars. Luminous figures moved in tinted dreams, and the glory that lay upon the world deepened and brightened with every hour.

"I don't know what's come over the lad since he began to traipse around with that Paul Hodge," complained Maybelle to her husband. "He never was normal, but now he's worse. It won't do any good to warn him to keep away. He's gone, right after school, and doesn't come back until tea."

"He needs a good belting," said Francis. "He needs to go to work. How old is he? Fourteen? Old enough for him to go to work. He doesn't do anything in school, anyway. And we need the money."

"I was earning my own wages when I was his age," agreed Maybelle. "I just got a note from his teacher. She says he never gets his homework, or anything, and that he's impossible. Never obeys. Sneaks away from school at lunchtime, and sometimes never comes back. Threatens me with the truant officer, or something. But she says he has a good mind," added Maybelle with wan pride. "He could do wonders. He's interested in ancient history, she says. But he'll have to stay in the seventh grade again, because he can't even do his sums right, and there's something called civics which she says he doesn't know a thing about. And doesn't try to learn." She hesitated. "The teacher seems a decent sort. Says Frank's sure to get the gold medal for an essay in June. It's a competition, she says. And she wonders why he doesn't do well in the other things."

"He needs to go to work," repeated Francis. "Gold medals!" He snickered. "Wonder if it is a five-dollar gold piece? That would be more like. What a lot of rot! A job—that's what he needs and is going to get. Take the damned nonsense out of him."

But Maybelle was uneasy. "The teacher says he could get a scholarship, if he only tried. Go to college."

Francis was frightened at this potential threat to the possibility of an additional wage in the family.

"College! It's work for him, curse it! When can he go to work? In England he'd be working in the mills at his age." He went on: "I don't know where we got him. He was wished on us. No sense, no intelligence. Just a big gawping fool, stumbling around over his big feet, and writing his damn poems. Didn't I tell you to stop him, take away his paper and pencils when he comes home from school?"

"I did," Maybelle defended herself angrily. "Then I found him writing on toilet paper. What can you do? There's no stopping him."

She was pricked by an obscure pain and misery.

Francis clenched his teeth on his tongue. "Just let me catch the ruddy beggar writing anywhere!" he shouted. "I'll hammer the nonsense out of him, and damned quick! It's work for him. These cursed Yankees! They won't let him leave school until he's sixteen, but he can work this summer, and perhaps we can keep him going if nothing's said."

"Well, that's Yankeeland for you," whined Maybelle peevishly. "Keeping the kids in school to all years. Better off if they worked. Keep them off the streets, and give them something to do."

There were six thousand dollars in the bank now. Enough to go home on, thought Maybelle, with the sick wrenching in her heart. But Francis said it was not enough. "Ten thousand dollars, and we'll go home, Maybelle. That's my solemn word."

Maybelle looked at her husband. She heard him cough dully, and then with a heavy and choking paroxysm. His cough was getting worse daily. Honey and lemon didn't help at all, nor did the cough mixtures he concocted for himself in the pharmacy. He needed a rest. But he would not take a single day off, though Mr. Farley had promised to pay him for a week's vacation a year. Then Francis slyly, but with revolting pathos, had suggested that Mr. Farley pay him overtime for the vacation to which he was entitled but never took. Mr. Farley had stared, then shrugged, and had scowled. He paid for the vacation, and the one for next year, and the next. Francis exultantly carried the money to the bank. It made him wonder, though, why Mr. Farley was less friendly now, why he rarely spoke to his employee with his old geniality. Sometimes this frightened Francis, made him work harder in an attempt to appease this mysterious hostility. "Don't know what's come over the beggar," he would say to Maybelle. "I do my best."

"You can't trust the Irish," Maybelle would reply, as if that settled everything.

Francis' fringe of dark hair had turned gray. There were thick gray threads in his mustache, which was not so jaunty now. As for Maybelle, only auburn streaks in her masses of hair revealed its once riotous color, for now it had faded and whitened, and her face was wrinkled, flabby and extremely sallow. But she had grown fatter and more shapeless, and an expression of chronic petulance made her mouth droop and twist.

She had forced Francis to take her and Frank to Erie Beach a few times in the summers. They would take the little chugging ferryboat across the river to Canada, where the sight of the Union Jack blowing in the warm lake breezes would fill her eyes with scalding tears. Then they would wait for the tiny train which would lurch them, over tracks surrounded by woods and sand, to the beach.

It was a pleasant beach, there on Lake Erie, with the blue

waters shimmering in sunshine, and the bathers on the sand, and the concessions blaring away merrily. Sometimes she could prevail on Francis to give young Frank twenty-five cents, so that the boy could ride the merry-go-round or the "figure-eight." She and Francis would sit on a grassy knoll near the beach, and comment acidly and vindictively on the strollers on the boardwalk below them. It was the day of huge, awning-striped skirts for women, and Maybelle would laugh endlessly at the wearers of this outlandish style. Once or twice they would even dine in the pavilion, where they discussed and disparaged the fifty-cent dinner, and compared it invidiously with the ones "at home."

Here, as in Bison, Frank would wander away from them, but would always appear just in time to go home. Where he went they never knew, and cared less.

Sometimes, but again not often, they would go to Crystal Beach. The boat that conveyed them there, larger and more impressive than the ferryboats, made Maybelle think of the journey across the Atlantic, and when the shores of the lake disappeared for a short time she would imagine that they were homeward bound and that soon she would see the purple line of England rising like a cloud out of the ocean.

Francis managed to force Maybelle to make up for these sinful and wicked excursions, which robbed the bank of extra quarters and dimes and dollars. On the journeys home, his face would become thick and dour with resentment and rancor, no matter how much he apparently enjoyed the day.

Edward Hodge, with incredulous distress, read the note from Miss Gorman about his son, Paul, while Paul stood over him impassively.

"Why, Paul!" said Edward. "I don't understand. You playing truant! It's impossible. There's some mistake."

Paul said in his colorless voice: "I guess there's no mistake. I did, Dad. I'm sorry." For a moment bewilderment flashed in his eyes. "I don't know why—"

"I know," said Edward, with pallid grimness. "It's that Clair boy. He makes you do the most astonishing things, Paul; you know he does. Why? Why, for Heaven's sake? What is the matter?"

"I don't know," muttered Paul. But again that sickening expression of imperviousness, of warning and shutting-out, appeared on his face, and seeing it, Edward was despairingly impotent.

"Paul, you must promise me not to do it again. This is

terrible! Paul, you know that the only hope we have of you boys' obtaining an education is to win scholarships. How are you going to do it with this attitude? You are in your last year. The record you make during the next four years will determine your future. You know that I have no money—"

"I know," whispered Paul, with real and helpless grief.

"Paul, you have always had such an excellent record at all your schools. You were always on the honor roll. Now, you are a truant! Paul, I just can't stand it. I don't know what it is all about. Promise me, Paul."

Paul was silent. Why did he follow Frank Clair everywhere, involving himself in dangerous and unpleasant situations? He did not know. He only knew that he would trail Frank, complaining: "We can't do that, Frank, we can't do that!" But they always did. There was something so exuberant, romantic about Frank, and Paul inevitably, and defenselessly, followed him. It was as if he were hypnotized!

"Promise me, Paul," Edward was pleading. He never disciplined his children; he never commanded them. It was his theory that one should "reason" with the young, and that there was something absurd in parental authority and pompousness.

Paul had gone from him. His mind and thoughts were on that day on the ferry docks, when the ice floes had churned like the crunching and gritting of giant and hungry teeth! The Niagara River had been black as shining ink between the blue and gray cakes, and the spring sky had been an arch of ultramarine filled with crystal light. The boys had felt the heavy wall of cold air in their faces, and Paul, all at once, as he stood beside Frank, had known the uplifting and nameless ecstasy of freedom and joy. Always, he knew this ecstasy with Frank Clair. It was life to him, who had never known life before. When he approached his friend, it was as if he came into the aura of violet rainbows, the sound of musical thunder, and laughter and excitement and immense anticipation.

"What's school compared with this—and foolish books?" Frank had asked him, was always asking him. "Sunshine and air and light and beauty—aren't they more important than dust and the thoughts of old dead men?"

Paul had assented, with a still rapture, and he knew that his assent contained the ultimate truth.

Now he was threatened with the cloister again, the old gray cloister of nothingness, of blankness, of the sound of

dusty voices and the foggy movement of lightless days. No!
He could not return to it. He could not relinquish the reflection of glory and splendor which touched him in the presence of his friend.

He said dully: "I'll try not to play truant again, Dad."
How could he say to his father: "You want me to die again,
to be lifeless grub in the cocoon of loneliness and coldness?"
He could not say it. He knew that Edward would never understand, and suddenly he was filled with pity for his father.

It was this pity which made him refuse the next two in-
vitations to truancy. He watched Frank slip away at noon,
and he felt no smug righteousness but only a sense of loss
and nostalgia. Where was Frank going? To what ebullient
excitement and to what new discovery of grandeur and loveliness and strangeness?

The next invitation came on an early day in March. The
winter had been endless. Drifts, many feet high, had filled
the streets, hidden the houses. Then, miraculously, there had
come two or three days of clear mild weather, smiling, passionate, and the songs of returned robins had greeted new
dawns in bursts of poignant music. Frank had said: "Let's go
away at noon. I've got ten cents. Have you any money?
Fifteen cents? Swell. We can go across by ferry to Canada.
I want to get out in the fields and the woods. I always go,
on the first nice days. Nothing to see yet, of course, but
there's something—"

Paul had slipped away. They could disappear like shadows,
for all the watchfulness of the teacher. They went down to
the ferry docks through silent hushed streets. They heard
a hurdy-gurdy in the distance, playing the Intermezzo from
Cavalleria Rusticana, and the song came through the aisles
of the abandoned and ashen streets like the voice of all
love and sweetness and hidden beauty, softened and melancholy. They heard hammering at a distance, too, and the
sound was a hollow echo. They might have been alone in a
dead city, in which only the song and the hammering were
alive.

The sky above them was pale, misty, through which the
spring sun came in long and slanting bars, light from a far
heaven. They invested five cents in a bag of peanuts, and
blissfully chewed the nuts as they went aboard the deserted
ferryboat. Now they were moving across the river. As far as
they could see, to Lake Erie itself, there lay a blue mist. The
ice floes about the boat were like restless sharks, bumping
into the sides and careening off, and between them the water

was the color of a cloudy turquoise. The Canadian shore awaited them, brown and sleeping in the sunlight.

They were almost the only passengers to disembark. Now the wind was clear and strong in their faces, and cold and pure as crystal water. The little village of Fort Erie slept; here and there a farmer's wagon rumbled through the cobbled streets. They climbed a hill, walked down a muddy road, heard the far barking of a dog, but saw nothing. Then, there lay the woods before them, and they plunged into them. They did not speak very much. It was not necessary now. They knew each other too well.

Now the woods closed about them, slim pallid birches, old maples, chestnuts, beeches, elms. Their branches were still bare, but their limbs were softly brown, and pregnant with life. The buds on the maples had turned red and fat. The elms had tiny yellow tufts on the twigs. The birches were like tall and slender youths, naked and solemn. A white dim light pervaded the aisles of the trees, a misty light like a gentle fog. They could see the sky through the branches, pale, shadowy blue, and very far and serene. There was only silence, yet they heard the swell of life, the ground swell of nature coming awake after a long death.

The ground all about them gleamed pallidly with pools of water. They saw ferns bending over marshy patches. Their boots sank into brown mud. Deeper and deeper they penetrated into the woods, hurrying, holding their breath as if escaping, as if fugitives. Now as far as they could see the woods had closed them in, and they were held against the heart of nature. Somewhere, there was a low and watery chuckle, but no other sound, not even the call of a bird.

They stood side by side, and looked, and felt, and smiled at each other, and moved their arms as if just released from chains.

How long they stood there they did not know. But then, all at once, as if some invisible choirmaster had lifted a baton, the woods, the swampy places, came alive, with a wild, sustained, passionate life of shrill, high, sweet piping. All the air was filled with it; the trees echoed it; the sky rang with it. They heard the voice of vivification, of birth emerging from death, of rapture, of hosannas to the spring. The song, almost unbearably joyous, did not rise and fall. It was sustained, steadfast, increasing in tone and intensity rather than in mere volume.

The children listened in awe. They stood in the midst of the surging, the bursting forth of life, and their hearts rose on wings of agonized joy. Now it was at their very feet, all about them in the air, a choral ecstasy that was taken up in every direction.

"Tree-toads," whispered Paul.

Frank did not answer. He knew now, though he had not known it before, that he had come for this, for this first paean to the spring. It had called to him in the dusty, chalky schoolroom. A message had been delivered to him as he sat at his desk while the teacher scrawled dull algebraic symbols on the blackboards. Pan, dressed in his green leaves, his eyes heavy with sleep, his gleaming hoofs tapping impatiently, had cried to him.

He could not bear it. His eyes filled with tears. He turned to Paul. Paul saw those tears, and suddenly his own eyes were wet. They moved closer together.

"Thank You—God," Frank said in himself, and he felt a convulsion of mingled pain and solemn elation and gratitude that God had called him here, to listen to the promise and the voice of spring.

A poem began to form in his mind, as he listened, as the piping penetrated to every cell of his mind and body. It would be part of the blank-verse poem he was writing now, a play-poem in three acts. He heard the measured majesty and flow of the poem, the lilting brightness of it.

On the way home, he told Paul of the poem. They lingered in the silent muddy lanes, while Frank repeated a few lines. Paul listened, his eyes on his friend's face. He was absorbed. It was as if he were hearing a voice that came from himself, which made articulate what he had always known but had never been able to express.

> "O strange and fearful world, where every morn
> Is full of solemn splendor and despair!
> Each breath we draw, each lift of hand and eye,
> Is filled with wonder and dark mystery.
> We live in marvels, question every hour
> By very living; hurl demands to gods
> In every heartbeat. And our smallest step
> Confounds the sage, refutes philosophy.
> Strange things, mysterious things, each filled with awe,
> Do by familiar presence lose their fear,
> Yet every one, if man but had the eye,
> Would smite him to the dust with hidden face.
> The gods are kind. So little is man endowed
> With power to see, with heart to beat with dread.

Our very childlike blindness is our shield
Against the unseen portents massed about."

"That's beautiful," said Paul, softly. "It is what I've always known, Frank, but I had no words for it."

Frank swaggered a little, tried to look modest. "Oh, it's not very good. I try and try, and then just squeeze some little squeal out, not what I had in mind." Now a sincere shadow of distress and longing touched his face. "I wonder if there is really any way a person could express it for what it actually is? Music, perhaps, only music. I wish I could play something. Words are so—so inadequate."

Paul did not answer. A shadow of suffering darkened his features. Then he said: "I hear it sometimes. But I can't bring it out on the violin. I've stopped taking lessons. Dad was annoyed. But I—I didn't dare go on. It was like"—he paused, and now he colored—"like a blasphemy, or something."

Frank's hand rose awkwardly from his side; he touched his friend's hand, and at that touch Paul's heart swelled with unendurable pain. And yet he was comforted.

They wandered down the silent lanes. Sometimes they saw a house, far back from the road, and heard a dog barking, or caught a glimpse of cattle in a wet meadow. They passed over a small wooden bridge that spanned a brown and rushing little stream. They could see the polished stones at the bottom, sparkling like laughter.

Then they heard the whistles from Bison, over the water, and knew it was time to go home. Depression came to them. They turned back.

They came to a wooden fence. Two little girls of their own age were perched on the wooden railing. Their heads were bare, and their yellow locks fluttered in the wind. They regarded Paul and Frank with inquisitive but wary friendliness, and their rosy faces dimpled coyly.

Paul gave them a glance, and his own face closed, became almost lividly malignant. But Frank slowed down, hesitated, came to a momentary halt.

"Hello," he said.

The girls giggled and blushed. One of them faltered: "Hello."

Frank was pleased at the sight of them. He stared at their roughened red hands, at their torn black stockings, at their broken, muddy shoes and poor clothing. He was filled with warm compassion and friendliness and understanding. This emotion had been growing in him during the past few years, so that he could not gaze upon others without a kind of sad tenderness, especially if they were harmless and intended no evil. For him the world was divided between the shy and the lonely, the frustrated and hopeless and yearning, and the vicious and cruel and heartless.

"Come on," muttered Paul. The light had gone from him, was replaced by uneasiness and aversion.

But Frank lingered. He said: "Do you live here?"

One of the girls nodded. She beamed at him. She teetered on the fence.

"It's nice to live here," Frank offered.

The girls gaped, astonished. They looked at each other. Then, simultaneously, they burst into laughter. They rocked on their perch. They regarded Frank with mocking and repudiating eyes, as if he had gone mad before them.

Paul tugged at his arm. "You see," he said harshly.

They walked away, followed by the hysterical laughter of the girls.

"You never learn," said Paul angrily. "You know you can't speak to people. 'It's nice to live here'! Do you think they knew what you meant? No! They could only laugh, like fools. That's because almost everybody is a fool, and you won't understand."

But Frank walked beside him, wrapped in sadness. He kept shaking his head. Then he spoke:

"It's terrible. They didn't know at all. And that's what's so terrible—not knowing."

Then, all at once, he thought of Jessica, and he said to himself: But Jessica would have known! He did not know why he thought this, or why he saw Jessica's face, but the thought was so vivid, and the memory of Jessica so over-poweringly strong, that he stopped and looked intensely at Paul.

"What's the matter?" asked the other boy.

But Frank shook his head and went on. He could not tell his friend, and he did not know why this was, either, but he only knew he could not.

CHAPTER 24

FRANK did not win the gold medal that spring for his essay. The subject chosen had been "Why We Owe So Much To Our Parents." Frank simply could not think what he owed to his parents. His life? They had given it to him accidentally. Duty? What duty did he owe them, who saw in him only a source of expense, however meagre? Love? They deserved no love. They excited only his apprehension, and, infrequently, his pity. Could he write an essay on the contemptuous pity he felt for his parents, for their increasing fears, their distrusts, their sullen suspicions, of everyone and everything?

He wrote, instead, his poem about the song of the treetoads in the white spring woods.

It happened just then that this teacher died, and another teacher was installed in her place, a fat elderly little woman who bore a remarkable resemblance to Queen Victoria. She was shrewd and humorous, intelligent and kind, and somewhat satirical. She, like Miss Emily Jones, was constantly on the alert for the unusual child, the child of promise as distinguished from the docile and well-mannered mediocrities who filled the other seats. It was her theory that the mediocrities exactly illustrated the words of a certain poet that such "licked the platter clean and died" and left behind them, as a legacy to the world, only a heap of offal. She could frankly see no reason for such lives, which she admitted were in the majority, though it was possible, she would say, that they form a sort of Greek chorus to the exploits of the hero.

Miss Lois Bendy, then, had not been in charge of Frank's class more than four days when she discovered him. She said to herself: "There is a very odd boy, indeed. Sometimes he looks hunted and surly." She saw that the other children despised him, and she was certain that this alone would indicate something interesting and to his credit. When she called upon him for recitations, he would rise slovenly to his feet, and announce, under his breath, that he didn't know. This would delight the other children, and Miss Bendy would listen to their laughter, her ears intensely alert. Yes, it was

165

most certain that this boy was unusual. Mediocrities and fools never laugh at their own kind.

When she had the compositions of the class first before her she knew at once. Frank had written a prose poem about the light that came in the schoolroom window, and how it changed, had a different substance, a different reality, each day, each week, each season.

Miss Bendy smiled to herself with satisfaction. She was never wrong. She asked Frank to remain after school that day. He looked at her, startled, and she saw him glance at another boy in the room, with uneasiness. She followed that glance. Ah, that Paul Hodge, that silent, impassive and frozen young fellow who was always correct, always ready for recitations, always punctual with his homework. What had these two in common? Then she recalled that she never saw one without the other, that they hovered, during recess, like unaware ghosts, on the edges of the other groups of children.

She said instinctively: "Never mind, Frank. I'll see you at noon. Then you won't be kept after school."

Later she questioned Frank Clair. She saw that it would be hard to obtain his confidence. She did not look at him while speaking about his composition. There was only one error, a misplaced comma. She said kindly: "Did you really write this, dear? It is wonderful. A grown man, an accomplished writer, might have written this. If you really do this sort of work, then you have a great future."

She looked up then, and he saw her tiny, smiling gray eyes full of satirical kindness and friendly humor. He stammered: "Yes, I—I wrote it, Miss—Bendy. I write lots of things, all the time. I—I've written a book, a play, in poetry." Now his long pale face flushed deeply. "If you want me to, I'll b-bring them to you."

He stared at her, and swallowed visibly. "I—I had a teacher once, Miss Jones. But I—I found out she was dead."

Miss Bendy found nothing irrelevant in this remark. She understood immediately. But she said cheerfully: "Oh, I knew Emily Jones. Such a fine woman! She was your teacher? How lucky for you! Yes, dear, bring me your book and your poems. I'd love to see them. Really, Frank, I'd love to see them."

He brought a huge batch the next day, wrapped in newspaper. She looked at the pages, and again she understood, but now there was rage in her. Some of the pages were sheets torn from the backs of books; some were toilet paper. Some were bags which had carefully been taken apart, and smoothed, and some were even fragments of wallpaper, on whose difficult surface the pencil writing was hardly discernible. Reverse sides of lesson papers had been utilized, and cardboard. There were very few sheets of ordinary tablet paper. But all the miscellaneous papers had been carefully cut to a conventional size, and all were neatly numbered.

She took the pathetic batch home with her that night. She intended to read for half an hour or so. At midnight she was still reading. Then she wrote a note to Maybelle.

Maybelle and Francis were thrown into consternation when they received this message, and they loudly and violently accused Frank of "being at it again," and "saying something." What it was that he was being "at" or what it was that he was "saying" Frank never understood. He only heard accusations, and his sense of guilt haunted him again.

The note had requested Maybelle to call at the school, at four o'clock the next day, if convenient. It asked that Frank should not be present, which heightened Maybelle's dark suspicions. "He's stolen something!" she screamed to Francis, while Frank, his back to the kitchen wall, turned white as death. "They'll have the police there! They'll put him in jail, and disgrace us! I wish to God he was dead!"

It was the first time she had delivered herself of such a wish, so fervently, so sincerely, and Frank felt a dreadful sinking in himself, a horror. He had vaguely believed that, in spite of the beatings and revilements, his parents loved him in their way. Now he knew that they hated him, that they wished the earth to close over him. Then, as he did thousands of times in the coming years, he asked himself: Why? In his manhood, the mystery baffled and enraged him. Had he truly been as vile and foul as the treatment his parents accorded him would indicate? The leaden pool of guilt in himself expanded so that it crept into every crevice and boundary of his soul, and he was never to free himself of it, not even to the end of his life.

He crept up to bed, and lay there, shuddering, awaiting the appearance of his father with the strap. But Francis did not come. He and Maybelle were now accusing each other of responsibility in the crimes of their son. They almost came to blows. In the midst of it, Frank went to the bathroom and vomited. Now, for the first time, he was aware of a murderously sharp pain in the region of his chest, so intense, so cutting and burning, that it took his breath. He crawled back to bed, and lay there, certain that he was dying, and glad of it.

The next day was a hell of anxiety and apprehension. He would look at Miss Bendy with a kind of terror. What was she about to say to his mother? She saw his glances, and a hard iron knot of anger formed in her chest. She had never seen Frank's parents, but she knew in some mysterious way.

At three o'clock, she patted his shoulder and said soothingly: "Your mother is coming, dear? Well, I have such a nice surprise for her. You run along now, with your little friend, Paul."

Frank and Paul went away together, and for the first time in his life Frank spoke fully and objectively about his parents to his friend. They sat on the stoop of Paul's house, and Frank, unable to restrain himself, poured out his bitterness, his disgust, his new hatred, his contempt, and his anxiety. Paul listened without speaking.

"I'd run away, if I were old enough," Frank said, knotting his fists and staring before him with an expression that a boy ought not to have worn. "I'd go away and never see them again—never. I'd pretend they were dead. They—they've made me feel dirty. I didn't mind the beatings so much, but they made me feel dirty." He looked at his hands, unknotted them, and stared at his palms. "I feel I'll never get my hands clean again. I feel dirty, inside."

Paul said gently, knowing horror in himself: "You're almost fifteen. You've only got to stand it for a few more years. You've stood it all this time. Then you can go away and pretend they are dead."

But Frank went on, as if he had not heard: "It never occurred to me that other parents weren't just like them. I— I thought it was natural, that all kids were beaten and treated like that. But now I see they aren't. I see how your father is, and other fathers. What have I done? I don't know. It must be something terrible, what I've done. I must be a—a terrible kind of person."

"You're not." Paul put his hand on his friend's arm and pressed it strongly. "Oh, Frank, you're not! You're wonderful. In some way, you're wonderful. Maybe that's it. They think the wonderfulness is criminal, or something, because you're not like them. You're not like everybody else, and that's why people, and your father and mother, hate you."

Frank turned his suffused eyes to Paul. Paul smiled, and the smile was tender. Frank tried to speak. Then, to his despair, he burst into tears. He bowed his head upon his knees and wept.

When Frank crept silently into the house at dinner-time, Maybelle greeted him in a peculiar voice. Her eyes shifted; her mouth sagged in an odd fashion. She said: "Go and wash yourself, Frankie. Tea's almost ready, and your father will be here soon." She hesitated. She went to him and roughly smoothed his hair. For the first time, his flesh crawled at her touch, and he backed away and shivered. But he was relieved at her tone, and washed his hands at the kitchen sink.

He was deeply curious about the interview that day. But he only saw Maybelle wink elaborately at Francis when the latter entered the house. He could not eat, though Maybelle urged him with a surprising anxiety. "Leave him alone," said Francis, with disgust. "If he wants to die, let him."

Maybelle said, with spirit: "That's a fine way to talk, I must say. He's got to eat, to keep up his strength. Look how thin he is, and he's so white. Almost green."

Frank went out after dinner, to wander through the dusky spring streets. Then he noticed that as he walked, if too fast, the pain would appear in his heart, catching his breath, numbing his body, causing him to lean against a tree for support until the spasm passed. He wondered why there was such a beating in his chest afterwards, such a sickness.

In the meantime, Maybelle was telling Francis of the interview with Miss Bendy. "She says he's a genius, Francis, a genius. She says he is a real poet, a real writer, and that he must have the best of education, and will make us proud." She looked at her husband with her somewhat protruding brown eyes, and waited.

"Rot!" said Francis angrily, rustling his newspaper. "Just a scheme to get him in some college and waste our money. They're always up to such schemes, these teachers. Genius! It's work for him, and damn soon, as soon as the damn Yankees will let him go to work. We need the money. He can get six or seven dollars a week in some factory, or something, and that's extra money in the bank. Don't tell me," he added, with choler, "that you've let that damned old maid come over you? He's a dreamer, that's what he is, a silly dreamer. He's got to wake up, him and his poems!"

But Maybelle was strangely silent. She played with the tableware and stared down at it emptily.

"It's not that he does well in school," continued Francis irately. "You know what his record is. And the other teachers detested him. You know that. That old woman's got some scheme up her sleeve, to make us spend money. D'ye know what college'd cost? Have you given it a thought? It would take all our savings! And I'm damned if I'm going to stay in this hole just so that young rotter can waste his time in college!" Now his meagre face flushed with rancor and fury. "College! That's the Yankees for you!"

Maybelle played with the tableware. "I wonder if she's right," she said, almost inaudibly. "She said he ought to have a chance, or something will be lost to the world. That's what she said, so help me."

Francis laughed furiously. "I can tell you what'd be lost! A wastrel, a fool! I never heard such blasted rot. If he's got anything in him, which I doubt, it'll come out without college. Work. Work, for him. He'll go to work next summer at anything he can get, and be damned to him."

Maybelle was again silent. A pinched expression came over her flabby features. She licked her lips. Then she said, in a dull voice: "I don't know, Francis. What if she's right? Think of all the money he could bring in as a writer—"

But Francis could no longer endure this nonsense. "Look here, you're the one who's been mithering me about going back to England! D'you want us to spend the money, just as things're in sight? You want to stay here in Yankeeland the rest of your life?"

CHAPTER 25

THE world changed, that August of 1914, and though its vast and terrible upheaval did not at first impinge upon the life of Frank Clair, it changed it nevertheless.

It was a warm and golden summer, full of sunshine and birds and peace, until that most appalling day in August. A neighbor of the Clairs, more affluent than most, had purchased an automobile, with a canvas top painted to resemble leather, and a lofty chassis of the purest, most vivid and most startling red. One understood that only the rich could possess such a wonder, and the appearance of an automobile in that neighborhood was an event that furnished envious, admiring or sneering conversation for many a day. Frank, incredibly, was once invited for a ride.

Automobiles were nothing new on the street. They had

been churning and roaring and smoking through the city
for years, and no one screamed "get a horse!" as once had
been the custom. But Frank had never ridden in a motorcar,
though he himself had often sung "In My Oldsmobile." This,
then, was actually an Oldsmobile, and he was actually being
invited for a ride. Stunned, disbelieving, for he had never
been intimate with any neighbor, he climbed into the vehicle's
high back seat, clutched the sides, and was borne, breathless,
through the streets at all of twenty miles an hour. The car
rolled smoothly, but not without some inner gruntings and uncertain squeals, and after a while Frank sat proudly, elated,
full of excitement, and surveyed the houses that passed so
rapidly.

That ride, more than the assassination of the Archduke of
Austria and his wife, had pertinence for him. The world had
writhed in a sudden and awful convulsion, and Frank dreamt
for days of his ride in the motorcar. The news in the papers
was less annoying to him than the new song, "On the Trail
of the Lonesome Pine," and he spent hours, not in brooding
alarm over the fact that England had declared war on Germany, but nursing his irritated reactions to the maudlin mel-
ody.

The Germans invaded Belgium, and Frank, on the urgings
of Paul Hodge, read *Pollyanna* and had another occasion for
wrath.

But finally the agitation of his parents, their passionate
devotion to the newspapers, reached his consciousness. England was threatened. Someone, "that dirty Kayser," had dared
to challenge her supremacy. Frank heard nothing else during
the dinners at his grandmother's house. Mr. Farley said nothing, but his eyes sparkled angrily. He hated Germans,
for the Germans in Bison had been sedulously stirring up animosity, suspicion and dangerous dislike against the Catholics
of the city. Indeed, so unremitting had been their activities
that the Catholics had been seriously alarmed, for more than
one child, emerging from his parochial school, had been set
upon by gangs and severely beaten. More than one priest,
walking in his yard at twilight, meditating, had been in-
jured by stones thrown by hoodlums. But still, Mr. Farley,
who fervently hated Germans, as only the Celt can hate the
Teuton, was annoyed by the fanatical outpourings of the
Clairs, mother, son and wife. "To hear 'em talk," he would
say, "you'd think nobody had a right to live but the English,
and that anyone who didn't like the English, and didn't think
they were God's chosen people, was a criminal or a fool."

Mr. Farley fervently prayed that the Germans would be defeated and destroyed, and fervently hoped that this would end the rising tide of hatred against Catholics in America. But he hoped, equally fervently, that England would first receive a good trouncing, enough to put the fear of God in her heart, and reduce some of her arrogance. He felt that England was quite strong enough to administer the coup de grace to "the Kayser," and was annoyed by Francis Clair's angry demand that America go to war with Germany immediately. "If she doesn't, you'll have the Heinies swarming all over the country," said Francis earnestly.

Mr. Farley felt certain that Americans were brave enough and strong enough to prevent such a disaster, and he said so. His manner was so abrupt that Francis, frightened, decided not to discuss the war in his employer's presence.

At home, the Clairs talked of nothing else but the war. When the first Zeppelin appeared over London, and dropped the first bomb, they flew about like chickens at the sight of a hawk.

Great excitement burst over America soon after the outbreak of the war. Teddy Roosevelt demanded "immediate action." Mr. Wilson timidly counselled patience. Congress heatedly discussed the situation.

Then the war, in September, bore in upon Frank.

The Germans of Bison went into action. (They were to display German flags on the very day that America declared war on Germany, in April, 1917.) In Bison, at least, they stirred up hatred for England and sympathy for Germany. They found listeners among the Poles, and among many of the Irish, who feared Germany less than they hated England. But fortunately the families of British descent were as yet in the majority, and the sedulous fomenting of the alien Teuton did not appreciably lower the anxiety and concern and affection for England in the city. Then the Italians, always friendly to England, who they had discovered was their only champion in the world, began to engage in street fights with the sullen Germans, and, contrary to expectations, often emerged the victors.

School Number 18 had a large quota of German-American children, who, though born in America, would and could never be part of her. American-born, they still used English with a taint of German phraseology and a slight but perceptible accent. Frank's life at school, never happy, never without persecution, soon became unbearable. He saw again, as once he had seen, that he must fight. As long as the German boys confined their activities to calling him "bloody, bloomin' Englishman" he ignored them. But when these oral activities threatened to quicken into physical assault, he made himself ready.

He did not have long to wait.

One gold and blue October day the hatred that followed him flared into violence. He and Paul Hodge had emerged from the school at quarter after three, confident that the streets would be empty of their persecutors, and discovered that a gang of five German-American boys was awaiting them. The boys were all hulking, surly-faced and porcine, their cropped heads thrust far forward on their necks, their clenched hands in their pockets. As always, the Teuton had resolved on an unfair fight. The five, it was arranged, were to attack the two boys en masse.

Frank and Paul halted, their way blocked by the others. All at once, though nothing had as yet been said and no overt act taken place, Frank's flesh prickled, the hair on the back of his head rose, and he turned cold. Paul, as always, was impassive. He eyed the German youths with aversion, unaware of the tension in the air.

Then one of the Germans spoke: "You dirty——! You dirty bloody, bloomin' Englishman!"

Frank said nothing. Paul shrugged. "Get out of our way," he said clearly, in his musical voice.

The Germans burst into a piggish roar of laughter. One of them imitated Paul's voice with startling accuracy. Paul flushed a dark unhealthy red. His fists clenched. But he made no move.

"We're gonna kick the——out of you," announced one of the Germans.

Frank stirred. He said, quietly: "One at a time, and I'll show you."

But the Germans naturally had no such intention. One at a time might possibly be beaten. Their hope lay in their weight, their numbers. They crouched forward, fists doubled, and moved towards Frank, who still made no move, either to advance or retreat.

Frank did not see Paul swiftly bend over, pull off his shoe, and hold it by the toe, behind him, as a weapon. The others did not see it either. As far as they were concerned, Paul was not in the fight. They detested him, but they ignored him. Their attention was all concentrated on the one boy they intended to injure as severely as possible. If Paul interfered, as they believed he would not, he would be eliminated at once. Nothing in his manner had ever indicated that he would display any belligerence.

There was one boy in the lead. Frank suddenly shot out his leg and caught him in the shins. With a howl, he doubled up and began to circle about the sidewalk, squealing with pain. He was now eliminated, at least temporarily, as an attacker.

The four remaining Germans, taken aback at this swift assault, hesitated. One stooped for a large stone, and held it ready. They rushed upon Frank.

He stuck out with his feet and his fists, bending his head, using it as a battering-ram. He used every means at his disposal in this unfair and vicious fight. He utilized his sharp elbows, the weight of his shoulder. But he was not overly strong, and now, in the desperate struggle, he felt again the paralyzing paroxysm in his chest. His arms, numbed, fell momentarily to his side, and he gasped aloud. One German used that moment to strike him full in the belly.

His nose had been punched, and the blood was running down his chin. His head was throbbing blindingly from the impact of the stone upon it. He could not see; there were sparks and blazes before his eyes. The pain in his heart had increased to an ominous agony.

Then he heard a sharp cry. Shaking his head free of the mists, he discovered that his attackers had fallen back. Paul was raging among them, wielding his shoe, a formidable weapon. He had stunned two of the boys, who backed away holding their heads. Another, whimpering, moved to the edge of the curb, rubbing his wrist. Paul had fallen upon the oldest and strongest, and was beating his head with the heel of his shoe with a kind of wild and obscene joy. Then, with something that sounded like an eldritch scream, with talon-like hands he grasped the boy and sank his teeth into the side of his neck.

A kind of horror seized the German. For a long moment he stood there, his mouth agape, his eyes popping. Then, desperately, he tried to free himself. His hands plucked helplessly at Paul's shoulders and arms. He began to scream, shaking his body from side to side, unavailingly.

Frank came to himself. The pain in his heart had subsided. He saw the shoe in Paul's hand, and he seized it. Paul relinquished it unconsciously. Frank went after the whimpering Germans who were holding their heads. He struck them again and again, as they retreated, and even when they turned and fled in disorder, he pursued them for half a block.

He returned to the one on the curb, who held his arms over his head and sobbed: "Don't do it, please. Don't do it. I didn't mean anything—it was only fun."

Frank kicked him vigorously and sent him sprawling into the gutter. He then turned his attention to the boy in whose neck Paul had fastened his ferocious teeth. He said: "Paul, let him go." And took hold of Paul's shoulder strongly.

Paul, who now began to shudder, obeyed. He drew away. His mouth was stained with blood. But his eyes, one wild greenish glare, were demented. His tremblings almost rocked him off his feet.

Frank struck the remaining German on the head with the shoe, followed the blow with a punch to the jaw. The boy fell prone on the sidewalk.

All this had taken place without an audience. It had lasted less than ten minutes.

Frank turned to Paul, who was panting and shaking and glaring down at the two fallen enemies. "That's enough. That'll teach them," he said with satisfaction.

Paul swung towards him. He saw Frank's bloody face. His mouth worked. He pulled out his neat white handkerchief and wiped the bleeding nose. "I could kill them," he said hoarsely. "Why didn't you leave me alone? I'd have killed him."

Frank smiled and took his friend's arm. "I guess it's enough. They won't bother us again. My pa says Germans are cowards. They only fight in packs. I don't think they'll ever attack us again."

His body swelled with gratitude and love. This had been no fight of Paul's, but Paul had flown to his defense. He linked his arm in Paul's and they went away together.

The news of the fight ran swiftly over the grapevine of the school. Frank was quite right. He and Paul were never attacked again.

CHAPTER 26

THIS was the last year of Frank Clair's boyhood, and in one respect at least it was the happiest.

Young manhood quickened all through him, and like a tide of exultation, the glory that was on the earth quickened also. The war was in its seventh month, and the world knew its own quickening of terror and foreboding. It knew also that an era was passing; it felt this passing instinctively. The depression of 1913-14 had lifted with the war in Europe, and American factories were roaring with the munitions of death. Americans, young, ardent, still undisillusioned, stared with sparkling eyes across the somber Atlantic, and hostility against Germany, especially in the Anglo-Saxon South, ran swift and violent in men's veins. When Germany announced that she had drawn a submarine zone about the British Isles, Mr. Wilson had issued his Note of Strict Accountability. On May 7th, the *Lusitania* went to her death, carrying with her hundreds of neutral American lives. In the meantime, there was grave trouble in Nicaragua. But there was, as yet, no real threat to the safety and peace of America.

The war was still unreal, insubstantial and unimportant to Frank, fifteen years old. He was discovering himself as a human being approaching maturity and manhood. The world, as a thing in itself, became imminent, a glorious dream of adventure into which he would soon step and distinguish himself.

One of his favorite haunts was the old Church of the Nativity on Albany Street. Nothing would induce Paul to enter that church, so Frank went alone, while Paul lingered outside, sourly, and waited for him.

One lovely May day, as he and Paul were passing it, Frank felt an urge to go into the church. Paul obdurately refused to enter, and went across the street to the little green park to wait. The church was dim, suffused with a soft lavender shadow, in which the sunlit windows were set like fiery and multi-colored jewels. Frank saw the statues, gleaming like snow in the gentle gloom. He saw the altar, with its flickering far light. He knew very little of Catholicism, but there was something here that thrilled and awed him, filled him with reverence. This church was not situated in a prosperous parish, yet beauty was here, noble and clothed in radiance. Frank would wander along the Stations of the Cross; he would pause before the altars to Mary and Joseph. He would see the arch of golden candles in the dusk. Sometimes, though not often, he would approach the great altar with its eternal light, and kneel on the red-carpeted steps before it and remain there for a long time, lost in formless meditation. Silence would surround him, broken only by a soft foot-fall, or the click of the beads of a worshipper in one of the shadowy pews.

It seemed a lovely thing, this open church which did not shut its doors after Sunday services, and then open them on the Sabbath to the smell of old carpet, mustiness and staleness. Here the church, and God, were always waiting, always ready with solace and meditation and gentleness.

In his earlier youth, Maybelle had sent him to a Baptist church not far from this Catholic church, but he had long abandoned attendance. On those Sundays, he would tuck his Testament under his arm, straighten his clothing, and, with a miserable sigh, start out for Sunday school. He would pass through endless, abandoned streets, where the houses lay in sunlight like sleeping tombs. A few "Chinese" glass ornaments would tinkle feebly in a faint breeze on deserted porches, and the trees would rustle slightly. The wooden doors of the church would yawn. The organ would groan rustily as the congregation entered; the choir would tune up in those childish and toneless hymns so peculiar to the Protestant service. The doors would close behind him, and all hope would be abandoned for two of the longest hours in recorded time, while a half-educated minister droned along tonelessly on a subject so far removed from God and reality as to resemble the drone of a fly on a windowpane.

Frank was to be bored many times in his life, but not so completely, so hopelessly, as he was bored in his own church. In all his experience of being bored by assininities and inanities, nothing ever surpassed the hours he spent in that church, and nothing ever afflicted him with such sheer torpidity and dullness and lifelessness. Occasionally, however, the minister enlivened the proceedings by furiously belaboring the Roman Catholic Church, and his attacks upon the "Scarlet Woman on the Seven Hills" would arouse the sleeping congregation to the first animation they had so far displayed. Even his philippics against "the demon rum," against men who swore and smoked and ladies who showed their ankles, against all who violated the holiness of the Sabbath, could not awaken such concentrated attention and joy. Then the faces would gleam with suppressed and ecstatic hatred; hands would tremble lustfully; mouths would part in rapturous smiles of delight.

Then Frank had discovered the Church of the Nativity, and he often attended High Mass when ostensibly he was safe in his own church. Here he discovered majesty, mystery, heroic music, virility and pageantry. The priest did not seem to have much to say that was superior to that of the minister, but his sermons were short, and the rest of the time was spent in moving and solemn loveliness and grandeur. He discovered that the Catholic Church offers to the beauty-starved and humble masses, the drudges of the dreadful factories and the dusty shops, a scene of splendor and passionate warmth and dynamic emotion.

He was beginning to understand these things, vaguely, but more completely as time passed, when he visited the Church of the Nativity. He felt them strongly on this warm May day, while Paul awaited him in the little park outside.

He saw a group of women lighting fat candles in little red glasses, and he went up to them and discovered, by an adroit whisper or two, that these candles burned in remembrance of the dead. He stood there, filled with a nameless emotion, watching the flickering of the crowded little flames.

He saw the spirits of the dead, their dull, clay-filled eyes struck by these small lights. He saw those eyes open, brighten, fill with tears, because they had been remembered, and their love had not been forgotten. By those lights, they took another step upward to the eternal sun, and the darkness receded about them.

He knew the dogma of hell. He thought of the souls in hell who would never see a light, who would never rise out of darkness and pain and lostness. It seemed to him that this was a most terrible thing. He glanced at candles waiting to be lit, and saw the coin-box beside them. He had no money. He waited until the women had drifted away and only the golden little flames lighted in remembrance were before him. Then he took several of the candles, lit them, and whispered: "For the souls in hell, to light their way." He was certain, with a profound and swelling certainty, that they saw these lights and took their first step back to God. And it seemed to him most appropriate that the lights set aflame for their guidance were stolen lights, and that by his sin he had saved them.

He had known compassion before in his life, but now this small act of compassion, like the sudden bursting forth of a flower, filled all the air about him with a passionate and unbearable fragrance. He knelt before the great altar and knew his deepest peace, and made his first vow to help in the rescuing of the lost and the mourning, the abandoned and the hopeless, the pain-filled and the blind and the despairing, the persecuted and the exploited, and those who knew neither the joy of God nor the love of men.

As he knelt, he looked at his fingers and whispered: "In my hand!" He felt there some mysterious touch, some dedication, some anointment, He knew this was so, beyond all reason and all words.

When he joined Paul, his first impulse was to tell him of this experience and of his compassion and love. But when he saw Paul's pale compressed face, saw the glance he gave some playing children, he fell into silence.

Later, when Paul left him, he hurried quickly to the great still house where he had met little Jessica. He looked through the gates at the deserted driveway. He wandered up and down the street near the low gray wall. He did not really expect to see the girl, but he hungered for something he could not explain. He only knew, vaguely but surely, that Jessica would have understood about the candles and the dead in hell, as Paul would not. He took the gates in his hands and shook them urgently. They were locked.

But he went away comforted. Some day, he would find Jessica again, and he would tell her things he could not tell Paul. There was some reason why he could not tell everything to his friend; there was some barrier which, in his innocence, he could not comprehend. But there would be no barrier between himself and Jessica. This he knew, though he did not know why.

Even when he no longer came back to the house, the comfort remained with him for a long time. Even when he believed, almost, that it had been a dream, he was still comforted and could wait with a kind of steadfast expectation. Even when the very house was lost to him, he had the consolation and the hope.

In June, Miss Bendy was delighted to inform Frank that he had not only distinguished himself in English and history, but had also attained a fair passing mark in civics, grammar and mathematics.

"I knew you could do it!" she exclaimed. "I knew you would remember what I had told you. I have tried, haven't I, Frank? I did teach you that it was almost as necessary for you to master other subjects as it was to pass in English and history. Yes! After all, education is not one-sided. A top-heavy structure must fall of its own weight. How can you be a writer if you know almost nothing else? A great writer must have knowledge of many things."

She looked at him solemnly, her fat, wrinkled little face alight. "And now you are being graduated! You are going to high school, and then to college. I do hope I may live long enough to say: 'That wonderful writer, he was a pupil of mine, and I had a little part in his success!' "

She smiled at him. Then she saw how dark his eyes had become, and how he looked at her. She asked quickly: "What is it, Frank?"

He stammered dully: "I'm not going to high school, Miss Bendy. I'm not going to college. My father says I must work."

She was aghast. "Oh, Frank! Surely you are mistaken! I talked with your mother, and she was quite impressed by the necessity of your getting a good education. I thought that was all settled."

He moved restlessly. "It isn't, Miss Bendy." His voice choked in his throat. It was some moments before he could speak. "I—I'm almost sixteen. My parents need the money. I—I suppose I can get books out of the library, and go on studying. I can get my working papers now, because I've graduated from the ninth grade." He paused. His voice failed, and he could not go on.

Miss Bendy twisted her plump fingers together, and her heart burned with fierce indignation and grief and hatred of Frank's parents.

She tried to keep her tone reasonable: "Frank, your parents don't need the money. I know. Your father is doing very well; I know Mr. Farley, his employer. Your father—he is getting forty dollars a week now. I've heard he is very saving. He could send you to college, Frank."

Frank said, through white, hard lips: "He won't, Miss Bendy. He wants to save everything, so we can go back to England after the war." He stared before him. "I don't want to go back to England. This is my country. I love it. I want to live and work and die here. This is my country."

"Of course it is, Frank." But Miss Bendy spoke with abstraction. I must watch my blood pressure, she told herself sternly. Then she said: "Shall I talk to your parents, dear? Perhaps I can persuade them."

But an expression of sheer fright filled his eyes. "No! They'd only blame me, Miss Bendy. I—I guess we'd better not talk about it any more."

He picked up his cap and turned away. She caught his arm. She held it, forced him to look at her. Then she spoke slowly but vehemently: "Frank, perhaps I shan't ever see you again. But I want you to remember this, all the days of your life. God has given you a great gift. You dare not throw it away. No, you dare not! It would be a most terrible sin. So, somehow, some way, you must get an education. Perhaps you can go to night school. Yes, you can go. It will be hard, almost heart-breaking. But you must go. It will take a long time, such an awfully long time. But it is worth it. Frank, look at me. It is worth it!"

He did not answer. And after a moment she released his arm and watched him walk away.

CHAPTER 27

In September, armed with his working papers, Frank found a job in a little factory on Ellicott Street, which paid him six dollars. He was to work six days a week, from half-past seven in the morning until six o'clock at night. His mother took five dollars and fifty cents from him, gave him his carfare, and packed his lunch. The other fifty cents belonged to him.

The factory printed and stapled little pamphlets to be wrapped about tubes of toothpaste. Frank's task was to stand at a large machine, scoop out masses of pamphlets, count them, staple them, and place them in cartons. He had no rest periods. His world was encompassed by that roaring and impersonal machine, and by the boxes, and by his aching arms, his tired feet, his stiff back, and sometimes by the tearing pain in his chest. He dared not stop for a moment, otherwise the crate into which the pamphlets fell would fill up and spill over, and the foreman would materialize like a demon with a flailing tongue and threats of dismissal.

But somehow he did not care. His mind was a poisoned wound, bleeding and throbbing. For his first, and, in some ways, his worst, grief had come to him, and he was all desolation and anguish.

Gordon Hodge had triumphantly won a scholarship in some college in a small city down-state. The Hodge family had packed their miserable belongings and had gone with the conquering son.

Frank never forgot the day he said good-bye to his first friend. He never, to the end of his life, fully recovered from that day, for it marked the hour when he stopped writing for many years.

If only there had come to him the slightest warning, only the faintest foreboding. But there was nothing, that hot

August night, that might have prepared him by hinting of the frantic sorrow to come.

He had been working in that factory for nearly two months. Each morning saw him racing in the cool damp dawn for the infrequent streetcars. Each noon saw him fall away from the machine, drenched with sweat, his knees and hands trembling, his heart beating painfully. Each evening saw him leave the factory on feet so weary that they felt as if turned to wood. He would reach home shortly before seven. Maybelle's chronic ill health, she assured her husband and son, now prevented her from completing the day's work. So it had become Frank's duty to wash up the "tea" dishes and straighten the kitchen. He was usually finished with his work by eight o'clock. Then he would race off, the sweat stiff and itching on his irritable skin, to meet Paul at his home.

This was the crown of his day, the evening rainbow after a storm of pain and misery. Adolescence, puberty, came late to him, so absorbed had his mind been in his writings, in his work, in the crowded and hurried days, in his dreams and hopes. The young girls he saw about him stirred him only faintly, still, and then as golden creatures awaiting him in the future. Not for him had been the pleasures of other young boys, the happy groups on warm, summer-filled verandahs, the community picnics, the meetings at drugstores for sodas, the visits to public dance halls, the parties in neighboring houses. His natural love for solitude, his lack of any spending money, his repudiation by others because of his shabby clothing and the unfriendliness of his parents toward their neighbors, had militated against even the slightest opportunity to enjoy the pleasures natural to his age. Also, in Paul Hodge, he had found the only contemporary to whom he could talk and who understood him. At once too mature and too immature, he was at home neither with the young nor with adults. A man in mind and emotion, he found the company of even those few youths willing to be friendly insipid and unproductive and tiresome. A child in body, he was ignored by those older than himself.

To his Jonathan, then, he hurried each evening. Only when he saw Paul did the accumulated wretchedness of the day recede. Then he was happy again, full of talk, eager, impetuous. Paul, of course, was not working. He spent his days in reading, in desultorily cleaning the miserable little cottage, in dreaming. When the two met they would look at each other in silence, their faces shining and smiling, then they would burst simultaneously into speech. They would sit on the stoop of the house, while the warm darkness fell about them and the arc light on the corner began to sputter and the dark trees murmured in the evening wind. And they would talk, or fall silent for a long time, content. Then, sometimes, they would go to the little corner store and Frank would buy two ice cream cones, and they would lick them blissfully until the last sweet drop was gone.

No, there had been no warning, nothing to hint of the coming calamity. On this August evening, Frank hurried as usual. The last of the evening sun lay in the high tops of the trees like a dying fire. The streets basked, fuming, in a blessed violet shadow. Every verandah creaked with rocking chairs, muttered with the exhausted hushed voices of those resting from the heat. Silent lightning fled and leaped in the east, but the evening star was rising, tranquil and silver, in a rosy western sky.

Frank wished to talk tonight of the evening courses he was to take in the night school that fall. He had discovered that he would miss the first class, because of the late hour when he would be free. He must have Paul's advice, he had decided. His coarse blue work shirt was damp under the arms and about the wilted, open collar. His shabby trousers clung to his legs. His feet were slabs of flame. But he was hardly aware of all this in his hurry.

The little house was blazing with gaslight. This, in itself, was strange, for Edward Hodge was extremely careful about wasting gas. Paul was waiting for him on the stoop. He rose slowly tonight, not with his usual quiet eagerness. Frank dropped down beside him and wiped his face with a dirty handkerchief. "Whew!" he exclaimed. "Was it hot today! I thought I'd cave in before six o'clock."

There was a splutter and a crackle in a nearby house, and a man's shrill and tearing voice emerged from a phonograph: "Come, Josephine, in my flying maching, and it's up we'll go, up we'll go—!"

Not to be outdone, a phonograph across the street implored some coy female not to use her eyes disastrously, "for they don't mean what they say!" A child screamed petulantly, an automobile chugged and honked down a neighboring street, a door banged, and shadows crossed and recrossed hot gaslighted windows. A man's angry voice sounded from a yard: "And if they think they're goin' to drag us into this war, they'd better guess again!" The street darkened, shadows falling like rain over the wan sidewalks and dusty asphalt.

the lightning leapt and shivered across the shining stars; the trees lifted their heads and murmured a deep question. Now there was a faint rumble of thunder, rising as if from the earth itself.

Frank watched the lightning; he felt the dry cool breeze on his cheek; he listened to the thunder. He said: "There might be a storm. I hope so."

He saw that Paul had not seated himself, and he suggested that his friend do so. "I've a lot to talk to you about," he said.

Paul said, and his voice was very low: "I want to talk to you, too."

There was something in his tone, hesitant, dull and reluctant, which caught Frank's sensitive ear. But still, he had no foreboding. He was only curious.

Paul sat down, not with his usual lithe ease, but with heaviness. He clasped his hands on his knees and stared before him.

"Two weeks ago we had news that Gordon had won a scholarship to a college in a little town down-state. We thought we might be able to get it transferred to a college here in town." He paused. His hands tightened about each other. "But we couldn't. Dad thought we might not, so nearly two weeks ago he went down there and got himself a job, just in case. You remember, he was away? I didn't tell you anything then, Frank, because I didn't want to believe it. I didn't want to make it come true, even in words. I—I thought it might turn out all right. But it didn't."

He stopped. He did not look at his friend, who had become deathly still.

"We have to go down there in a hurry. If Dad wants that job, he'll have to be there day after tomorrow. We are going on the five o'clock train. Tomorrow night."

Frank was to hear many calamitous words in his life, but few that struck him as mortally as these. They danced before him, outlined in the fire of acute agony. They were fists beating on his heart. They were blows that made him faint and numb. He felt something thick and dry and choking in his throat. A coldness ran down his hot arms and legs and ended in a pool of pain in his feet. His hands gripped the splintery wood of the steps on which he sat. He said: "No. You can't leave me." The dryness in his throat shut off his breath and he coughed.

Paul sighed. "Yes. We are going. Tomorrow."

The arc light spluttered fiercely and flooded sidewalk and tree with a vicious white blaze. One phonograph begged its honey to squeeze it tight. The thunder deepened its threat, and now a mist blew across the stars. The man in a neighboring yard raised his voice: "Why, if those Heinies ever tried to set foot on one inch of this country, we'd blast 'em off the earth in an hour! As my wife says, we didn't raise our boy to be a soldier, and we don't need soldiers. We need just our good ole American stren'th!"

Then, borne on the rising wind, came the far howl of a passing train, heart-breaking, full of lostness and desolation and grief. It was a cry that spoke of sorrow and despair, of an eternal farewell, of something too terrible to be borne. Frank listened to it; the sound entered his body, tore into his heart, and he suddenly put his hands over his ears, and crouched in motionless torment on the step.

Paul knew. He said gently: "It's just a train. We hear it every night."

Yes, they had heard it every night, but Frank would never again hear it except with sadness, with misery, with a wild desire for flight. Never again would he hear it without lifting his hands, as if to cover his ears, without shivering. Never again would it come to him without that dreadful pang of bereavement.

Finally he dropped his hands. There was nothing but the blaze of the arc light. He said: "I shan't see you again, then."

He would never dare play truant from that factory, for he would be dismissed. He dared not be dismissed.

"I guess it's better for you not to go to the station," said Paul. He waited. Frank could not speak. Paul went on: "I'll write. I'll write every day. We can write to each other."

Frank whispered: "You never told me. You ought to have told me before."

"But I didn't know, for sure. I didn't know until this afternoon."

Edward's voice came through the window: "Paul, son, you'd better finish your packing. We have a lot to do tomorrow, you remember."

Packing. Clothes folded into narrow boxes and bags. Clothes folded away with one's life. A lid closed down like a coffin lid.

"I don't know what I'll do," Frank whispered. "I don't know what I'll do!"

Paul murmured: "You'll be going to school at night. You'll be writing. And you'll be writing me letters. Then, when you have some money you can go down there to see me."

His voice was so quiet, so steady, that Frank felt a sudden

convulsive rage in himself. It meant so much less to Paul, this going, than it did to him! His own voice came, thick and stammering: "You—you don't care! It doesn't—mean—anything to you! You have your father and your brother, and your school. I—I have nothing!"

The raw anguish in his words made Paul wince. But he said, bitterly, wonderingly: "How do you know how I feel? How can you tell?"

Frank was silent. Paul put his hand hesitatingly on his friend's arm.

"You'll send me your poems and stories, won't you? We'll write every day."

Edward called through the window pleadingly: "Paul! Please come in at once!"

Gordon, from the depths of the house, shouted: "Come on in, you lazy wretch, and do your share of the work! If you think I'm going to put your dirty clothes in your bags you're wrong."

"Paul," pleaded Edward.

"Come in while I pack," urged Paul, rising.

Frank stood up. He shook his head. He could not speak again. He looked at Paul's face, blanched by the arc light. He looked as if he could not take his eyes away. His lips parted, but nothing left them. Then he stumbled down the steps and ran down the street. Paul watched him go. He called: "I'll write, first thing—"

Frank did not answer. His tall thin body disappeared in the dark shadows. Paul stood there a long time, watching the pit of darkness into which his friend had fled. Then he went into the house.

PART II

"It is not now as it hath been of yore;—
    Turn whereso'er I may,
    By night or day,
The things which I have seen I now can see no more.

"The rainbow comes and goes,
    And lovely is the rose;
    The moon doth with delight
Look round her when the heavens are bare;
    Waters on a starry night
    Are beautiful and fair;
    The sunshine is a glorious birth;
    But yet I know, where'er I go,
That there hath passed away a glory from the earth."
                            —*Wordsworth*

CHAPTER 28

LONG endless days. Silent, motionless days. The wheel of the seasons revolving, and always in grayness. Morning, noon, evening, night. Only paler or brighter shadows. Sounds approaching and receding, like meaningless tides under a dead moon. Faces appearing, falling away, and voices like the voices in a dream. Muteness heavy on the tongue, dryness in the throat, dimness in the eye, nightmare weight on arm and leg. Doors opening and shutting on endless corridors, and weariness a disease in the flesh.

"I don't know," Maybelle said with anxious complaint to Francis, when Frank had gone to bed. "He takes no interest. Have you seen his face, lately? He looks like a corpse. He seldom speaks. He never goes out wandering, the way he did when that Hodge lad was here. He never writes any more, though I've tried to encourage him, blessed if I haven't. It was better than nothing at all. He doesn't eat a thing; leaves everything mauled around on his plate. Broods."

Maybelle's natural maternal instinct was stirring feebly under her fears and chronic misery. Her newspaper spilled from her lap onto the floor. Francis was reading, but he glanced up irately, coughed deeply and hoarsely, took a sip of beer.

"Moons around like a love-sick calf," he said, with rancor. "Though I must say he brings his wages home regular. No complaint there. What about that going to night school that he yawped about so much last summer? Babbling Bill! Did he go? No! It was all talk, as usual. It's always just talk with him. And you wanted me to send him to college! I know him better than you do. Spoiled."

He coughed again, violently, his withered face turning scarlet with the effort. He looked furtively at his handkerchief when he drew it away from his lips. Clear as crystal, there. But everyone in this blasted city had catarrh or bronchitis. Worse than Manchester.

"You always spoiled him," Francis continued, and Maybelle, under the accusation, glanced sideways with coy melancholy and an affected meekness. "Books. Dreams. Poems. Be thankful he's forgotten the whole ruddy thing. He's bucking up. If you'll just leave him alone, all will be well. They grow gawky at that age. Like colts."

"I don't know," said Maybelle, in a sighing and petulant tone. "I've done my best. If I had it to do over again, I couldn't do better. Good food. Good bed. Cleanliness. Yet he looks like a ghost. Takes no interest."

"Rot. He's just growing up. Glad that Hodge lad went away. Bad influence. Always dreaming. Now he's buckled down, and be thankful for it."

Frank sat on the edge of the bed, under the flickering gasjet. Paul's last letter lay on his knee. He bent over it, and read it as he had read and reread it a dozen times that day.

"I don't like the high school here. Dad is worried about it, because they have very poor teachers. But Gordon likes his college. The country is beautiful. Dad and I take long walks. It's all hills, and it was wonderful last week when the trees were just coming out and we heard the tree-toads as you and I heard them that other spring. Remember? I try not to be discontented. Dad seems a lot happier here, and if the school were just as good as Lafayette, things would be all right. The people here had a Preparedness Day parade, and it was exciting. Dad says we are sure to get into the war, since Germany keeps right on sinking our ships. But I know he's worried about Gordon being taken by the Army, if we go to war. I saw pictures of the Preparedness Day parade in Bison, and it, the streets I mean, looked awfully familiar. There was the Teck Theatre on Court Street. Remember when you and I saved our money and went to a vaudeville show there, and could hardly see or hear anything, up in the gallery? But it was fun, anyway.

"Dad doesn't like his job. He gets two dollars less a week than he got in Bison. But he does look a whole lot happier. I suppose that's because Gordon won that scholarship. We all go on picnics on Sundays, when the weather is good. There's a view from the hill—"

Frank's eyes blurred. But he did not move. He stared down at the letter, and the precise and careful writing jumped and danced. He continued to read:

"In a lot of ways, I like this town better than Bison. It is quieter. There aren't so many people. Do you think you could come down and visit me this summer? There's a pretty good hotel near here, cheap—"

Francis' voice roared up the stairway, full of ire. "Turn off that blasted light! It's half-past eleven, and you've got to get up in the morning. Think we're millionaires?"

Frank reached up and turned off the gas. He sat in darkness, the letter on his knee. The early summer moon lay on the window-sills, filled the coarse lace of the curtains with threads of silver. Trees gave soft voice outside. A couple passed, laughing. A lake steamer bellowed, far out over distant waters. The trees spoke louder in the increasing stillness. Then a train rumbled at a distance, and its long, melancholy howl passed under the stars. Frank bent forward, as if in agony, and covered his ears with his hands. The letter slipped unnoticed to his feet and lay there, blanched by moonlight. But even through his covering hands, Frank could hear the train; he could hear it still, long after it had gone. He fell over sideways on the bed, and lay there, staring blindly into the moonlit darkness, his breath hardly stirring over his lips. He heard his parents go to bed. He heard their door shut, the complaining of the springs of their bed. He lay there a long time until, fully dressed, his feet trailing on the floor, he fell asleep.

"Of course," said Mr. Farley ("taking advantage," as Mrs. Clair grimly commented to herself), "it's none of my business. But I like the kid. Your grandson, I mean. I didn't like the look of him today. He's sixteen, isn't he?" Mr. Farley shook his head, and rocked slowly on the verandah. The street was awash with Sunday quiet and sunlight. "But he's too pale and thin, I'm thinking. He never was a hearty kid, but he's too tall for his age, and he looks sick. I gave Francis a bottle of iron pills for him last week."

Mrs. Clair embroidered vigorously. She said: "Growing. That's all. He always was a burden to his parents. He was never all there, I used to think. It surprises me that he's held his job in that factory. He gets seven dollars a week now, Francis says, and that's not to be sneered at. They need the money."

Mr. Farley gave her an impatient and contemptuous glance, which she did not see. I pay him forty a week now, he thought. And he's got most of what I've ever paid him in the bank. What for? What've they ever got out of living, those two? And they've killed something in that poor kid. The clothes he wears ain't fit for a dog, I'm thinking. I've seen beggars better dressed, and him working six days a week in that damn factory. Bright kid, too. You need only look at his eyes. Something there. But you can't expect these damn people to notice that! Doesn't look like their kid at all. Wish I could do something for him. He used to like to talk to me, but now he never says a word if he can help it. When I try to speak to him, he shies away. I don't like his face! I don't like the look in his eyes. Looks as if he lost somebody, as if somebody had died on him.

He said, aloud: "That kid ought to be in school, instead of working."

Mrs. Clair tightened her lips against her wrath, but she remembered in time that Mr. Farley was her son's employer and her own star boarder. Yet the creak of her rocker was a sharp protest.

"We don't pamper our children, as you do in America," she said, with hard condescension. "We believe in making them get out for themselves. Makes them independent. Puts them on their own bottoms. Every tub must stand on its own bottom. That's what we always teach our children at home. Young Francis is sixteen. He's a man. Besides, his parents need the money."

She arose with a stately sweep of her skirts. "Time for tea, I am afraid."

She sailed into the house and gave the screen door an emphatic slam. Her hair had turned a cold wintry white, but she was still as energetic and competent as ever. Mr. Farley said nothing, but continued to sit on the verandah. A car or two passed in a swirl of dust. Church bells rang a soft and melodious call to vespers. Mr. Farley sighed.

I'd like to do something for the kid, he thought. But it's no use talking to his father. He's money-mad. God damn it! I'd like to do something! Maybe I ought to make a novena for him. I'll have to ask Father Walsh if you can do that for a Protestant.

He stood up. If he hurried, he'd be in time for vespers. He hadn't made his confession for two weeks now. Funny thing, thinking of prayers for a Protestant kid, when he hadn't made his confession for two weeks! Couldn't expect God to listen to an unregenerate sinner.

A gramophone in a neighboring house began to shrill out: "I didn't raise my boy to be a soldier!" A child clattered down some stairs. The sky was golden in the west.

Well, thought Mr. Farley, grimly, maybe you didn't raise your boy to be a soldier, ma'am, but it looks pretty damn sure, now, that he'll be a soldier anyway!

CHAPTER 29

As PURE grief and shock slowly subsided from their acute crescendo, loneliness closed in about Frank Clair. Loneliness like a sound-proof glass wall through which he could gaze at others, see their gestures, catch distorted views of their faces, but hear no voice. He rumbled along in the groaning streetcars of Bison, and the people about him spoke in an alien language which he could not understand, and their eyes passed through him as if he were not there.

The sun had literally gone from him. There was only the glare of stage lights on crudely painted, two-dimensional back-drops. Desolation walked about him, echoing. For him, the city was dead. He wandered through familiar streets. He saw sunsets. He sat on benches at Front Park, and looked at the river. He saw the spring, the summer, the ruddy fall, the blazing blue winter. But glory had gone from it all, and wonder, and delight. He could not read. The spring of fancy, of color, of vitality, of exaltation and joy, had subsided into the wasteland of choking sand, and he had neither the desire nor the inspiration to write again. Numbed, silent, bereft and empty, he went to work, ate, slept, and felt nothing in himself but dejection and anguish. All about him lay a dead garden, in which a dry wind rustled, and dead grasses bent, and the withered flowers hung on their yellow stalks.

On a dewy lilac evening in April, he heard that America had declared war on Germany. He saw the bustle of excitement in the streets, the groups gathered on corners, passing papers from hand to hand. Somewhere there was the sound of an excited drum. The streetcars buzzed with comment and raised voices. But to him it was all a meaningless stir of idiocy, the unrelated, irrelevant sounds and voices of nightmare.

Maybelle said to him uneasily, one night: "Sonny, why don't you get a companion? I know you haven't been yourself since Paul went away. Isn't there anyone in the factory you could talk to? And bring home for tea? Some young chap your own age?"

He felt the hesitant concern in her voice, and he looked at her squarely as he had not looked at her for years. Her slightly protruding brown eyes were soft with anxiety. He smiled at her. The muscles of his face moved stiffly. He said: "There isn't anyone, Ma."

"But look around, Frankie! There're lads on this street. You could go to a show with them, or the beach." She hesitated again. "I could squeeze out a dollar or two. You don't go to the library any more. You don't read. Look at the papers! Aren't you interested in the war? If it keeps on, they'll take you."

He was touched. A hand had encountered his in the darkness, a calloused and uncertain hand. He thought: I guess she does care about me a little. He tried to smile again.

"I wouldn't care if I went into the Army."

The monstrous spiritual pain which had afflicted him during the first months of Paul's absence came back like the sudden stroke of a sword on his heart, and he felt the blazing impact again. He got up and left the table.

Francis had been afraid that his son might "get to know girls, and waste money." If Frank became like a lot of callow young lads, he might even marry and deprive his parents of wages. But Frank saw neither male nor female about him, only shadows.

"That Paul doesn't write to him often now," Maybelle complained. "It used to be every day or so. Now it's only twice a month, sometimes less. But it's not Paul's fault, I fancy. I found one of his letters. He asked Frankie why he didn't write."

"Moonstruck," commented Francis, sourly. "You'd think he'd take an interest. War going on, and the world in a turmoil. And he walks around like in a dream. And I thought he was bucking up! He'll never amount to anything. He's a failure. He'll just jog along at a daily wage. No ambition."

"I try to wake him up," said Maybelle miserably. "If he'd only eat. He's nearly seventeen, and he looks like a rail. No flesh. He might be going into a decline."

But Francis ended the conversation, as he ended all conversations that annoyed and bored him, by coughing violently. Now he did not look at his handkerchief, for once or twice he had tasted something salty on his tongue. He had his own troubles, God knew! And now his wife mithered him about a stupid lump of a lad who didn't know when he was well off. Some chaps had good sons, who had ambitions and saved money and were a pleasure to their parents. It was his bad luck that he had a dolt for a son who in two years had had an increase of only two dollars a week.

Now Francis began to tell Maybelle that after the war they would surely return to England. There were ten thousand dollars in the bank now. Two thousand pound! A fortune. Francis was beginning to feel a pressing sense of hurry, of anxiety, though he could not have told why. Maybelle became reasonably happy and full of anticipation. She talked to Frank about England. "Don't you remember our old home, lovey?" she urged. "Reddish Vale, and Sandy Lane? Our own land? Think how happy we'll be, home again!"

Her words penetrated to Frank's consciousness, but he experienced no reaction in himself. England. Why, England wasn't his home. This was his country. For the first time there was a faint and protesting stir in him. This was his country! He read the paper that night with a new interest. He saw photographs of Bison young men going to the station, marching in young and exultant ranks, led by a band. Why, he had heard that band that day, and everyone in the little factory had run out to see the passing of the young sacrifices to Moloch, to a world's stupidity and blindness and tardiness. But he had not gone out. He wished he had gone. And now, again for the first time, there was a dull aching in his atrophied heart, a feeble moving of congealed and sluggish blood.

What was the war about? Germany had invaded Belgium and France. The Kaiser threatened. Woodrow Wilson replied in sorrowful and measured tones. "The war to end war." "Make the world safe for democracy." What was it about? He thought of the children in the German schools, and a little tongue of fire licked his dull mind. It did not matter what the war was about; the Allies intended to kill as many Germans as possible. That was the only important fact, the only relevant and justifiable fact. To kill Germans. Power politics, aggressions, struggles, the clash of arms: these were nothing in the end, compared with the necessity to kill as many Germans as possible, men, women and children.

That night Maybelle again reiterated her plea that he "find a companion." It was silly, but the next morning he made himself look at his fellow-workers with interest and forced speculation. Many of them were young; they might soon be going to war. Now voices and faces had relevance. They rushed in upon him.

The operator of his machine sat high on a stool, moving levers and gears. She was a woman, not more than twenty-five. She had the peasant's thick features, but she also had an alert concentration about the eyes and mouth, and she did her work competently and swiftly. Frank looked up at her that morning and smiled. He said aloud: "Hello, Elsie."

She glanced down at him and gave him a wry grin. "Hello, deaf-mute," she responded. "Found your tongue? Why all the interest, all of a sudden? See me for the first time?"

"Yes," he replied, seriously. "I guess I do."

She scrutinized him critically. "I'm sure flattered. Say, you aren't a bad-looking kid, just kind of funny. Wish you was older. You could take me out."

She began to sing: "K-K-K-Katy, beautiful Katy!"

Frank, to his amazement (for he was not aware that he had ever heard the foolish song before), joined in:

"You're the only g-g-g-girl that I adore!"

"Listen to him, guys!" shouted Elsie, pleased, to her fellows nearby. "The dead's come to life!"

He ate his lunch that noon with several of the others. He sat beside Elsie, who felt that, in some way, she had something to do with his resurrection. He studied each face and each pair of worn, calloused hands carefully, and with objective interest.

There was the foreman, a short, fat little Hungarian, who had been christened Tom by his subordinates, though he had a much more complicated name. His face was as round and golden as an autumn moon, and he had tiny little twinkling eyes, sly, hard and humorous. He sat on a bench, a smelly, solid little keg of a man, and brought out for his friends small Hungarian cakes which his wife had made. What pastries! Frank ate one with appreciation and looked hungrily for another. Tom gave him another and eyed him curiously.

"I got a kid nineteen," he said, munching. "He'll be called up in the draft. Now, I'm a Hunky, and my country's fighting the Allies. But know what I said to the old woman last night? 'See here, Austria-Hungary ain't our country no more. Look what this country's done for us. Don't we own our own house? Ain't we got a bank account and enough to eat? Ain't folks been good to us?' That's what I said, and my boy —he's the one that got a scholarship to the University of Bison—he said: 'Pa, you're damn right. This is my country, and she's goin' to get all I got to give her. That's what.' "

A little frail girl, obviously consumptive, looked up eagerly: "They got these girls, now, in the Navy. Yeomanettes. Thought I'd join up. But me, I ain't got no education. They want girls that can pound a typewriter. But I can buy liberty bonds. I'm buying one—so much every week." She coughed hoarsely, and the others looked at her with sympathy.

The tall thin shipping clerk, a dour, red-faced man in his forties, munched his sandwiches and drank cold coffee. "Well, we get more money now, don't we? Heard we was to get a raise. He's gotta do it. All the folks're goin' in the war plants. Curtiss is yellin' for hands. Anybody kin get a job now for big money. Why, I heard they was payin' shippin' clerks thirty-five dollars a week down at Curtiss! My old woman says: 'What you workin' down there for, for twenty-two dollars a week?' Besides, it's patriotic."

Every face became thoughtful and reflective.

"Yep, big money goin' around now," admitted Tom. He cleared his throat. "Now this here bindery work: it ain't so important, to win the war. Wouldn't blame anybody who got more money in Curtiss. Jeez! Money's hard to get."

"Gotta make hay while the sun shines," observed Elsie wisely. "Me, I'm a good machine hand, and my sister's girl-friend says they're paying machine hands up to thirty dollars a week down at Curtiss. Maybe she's lyin'. Who ever heard of machine hands gettin' thirty dollars a week? It won't hurt to look around, though, and find out."

"Money's money," said Tom. "And I'd like to see some real jack. Gettin' old now. What'll I do when I can't work? I hear they got a union at Curtiss. Ought to have had unions long ago. Remember that kid that got his fingers chopped off in the machine two months ago? Well, that's all he got: two fingers chopped off. If we get our heads knocked off, it's too damn bad. Know what I read in the papers? That American workingmen are just like workers in India or China. No damages, no help, if they lose their legs or arms. There's that I.W.W. International Workers of the World, guess it is. Think we ought to have workman's compensation when we get our hands chopped off, or somethin'. Make the big guys pay. Now we just starve to death."

"Oh, that's them Roosians," said the shipping-clerk, with wise scorn. "I.W.W.!"

"You talk like a damn fool!" exclaimed Elsie. "What if it is Roosians? Does it make it any different who talks about us getting protection? Look at my dad. He worked for a com-pany that had a railroad in its back yard. He loaded crates. One of 'em slipped and mashed his foot. Just like a potato. Us kids was only little shavers; oldest twelve. Well, Dad got blood poison', and he died, and the old lady had to take in washin', and she got pneumonia. That was when I was four-teen. Did Dad get any money for his foot? No! No, Ma had to die, and leave the whole shebang of us. I had to leave school, and was I good at algebra! Might've got a job in an office and made some decent money. But no, I hadda go to work, and my brother Jim sold newspapers, and then he had to leave school, and just as soon as the other kids was fourteen, they left. If we'd had compensation, Ma wouldn't 'a' died, and we coulda gone right on at school, and things woulda been hunky-dory."

Her intelligent dark face twisted. She did not speak of the pretty little sister who had been forced into prostitution because she was not "bright" enough to hold a job as a bundle girl in a department store. Sweet little Mamie! Now she was in a charity hospital, dying, rotting away.

The others spoke of similar cases in their own families, or among their friends. Money. The terrible, driving, tragic need for money. Not money to save, "to hide in a hedge," but just money for bread, for safety, for a roof, for clothing, for medical care. Money for life. Money for the right to breathe, and to be a human being. Money for the protection of children. Money, money!

Frank listened. Money was no new refrain to him. But this was a different kind of money, a most frightful necessity. It was not money for the bank; not money to attain a certain goal. Money for existence! Money, blood, life, air, shelter! It was money that was the supreme difference between a man and a beast, and without money one was only a dog, an outcast, less than beef cattle.

Frank had seen poverty all his life, first in England, then in America. He had seen it in his own home on Albany Street. (But there was a difference in his own home: poverty there was self-willed. It was deliberate.) He had seen it, this dreadful poverty, in almost all the streets of Bison. He had smelled it, and it had smelt of that most appalling stench: fear in every house. Yet, it had not reached him, who had walked in rainbow dreams. He had always had enough to eat; he had always been sure of a bed. His clothing, though poor and patched and grotesque, had at least kept him warm and protected from the weather. No, it had not touched him, that skeleton hand, and its stench had not reached his nostrils with any insistent meaning.

Now he saw it as it was. The opaque cloud that had been over his eyes so long lifted, and he saw the faces of his fellow-workers, anxious, brooding, tired faces, dusty with the grit of fear. And now he was frightened and enraged. Why, they had nothing but their hands, and if their hands failed them, then they must starve! It was not to be borne.

The threat hovered like a dark mist over the city. It swirled in this dusty packing room. It haunted the machines. It stood like a ghost of ruin in every streetcar. There was no refuge from it.

He had seen so many dull faces in his life, beaten faces, crushed faces. They had vaguely, and with so much more reason than he knew then, depressed him. He had thought the thick patina over those faces the evidence of pure brutish stupidity, and had avoided them. But now he knew what it was. It was poverty, the frightful need for sufficient money; it was terror.

He felt no compassion, now, for these people about him. Compassion, like color and glory, exaltation and joy and mystery, had gone from him with the going of Paul Hodge. He felt only a grim fear and anxiety. Some way, somehow, he must have money! But how? He was receiving so very little. He could hardly support himself on it when his parents returned to England. (There was no question in his mind about returning. He would stay.) What was he to do? He would be as insecure as these when he was alone. He must make money!

"What you thinking about, kid?" asked Elsie, nudging him.

He started and looked up. "I—I was thinking about money," he confsesed.

She nodded grimly. "Don't we all! You know, I been working here a long time, but it never comes Saturday night that I don't get the chills. What if the pink slip's in my envelope? What'll I do? I still got a kid brother at school, and he's bright! I ain't got but fifty dollars saved. Never could seem to get enough together to save. Never made enough." She looked at her scarred and calloused hands and shook her head. "All these years of me working, and only fifty dollars to show! Do I buy nice clothes? I got only two camisoles to my name, and three pair stockings, one extra serge skirt, and one cotton blouse. That's all. What if I get sick? Say, I've been so sick my head nearly fell off some mornings. But do I stay off? You can bet your life I don't! My kid brother needs specs. I been saving fifty cents a week. Gotta have ten dollars. Know what I heard? In Germany, they got what they call sick and unemployment insurance. Think of it! You get thrown out of a job, and they pay you. You get sick, and you go to a free doctor. When you're old, you get a pension—"

"Oh—!" said the shipping clerk. "God damn lie, most

likely. Anyway, that's Germany. We're free an' independent Americans. That sounds like Roosians, anyway."

"Russia," said Frank, stiffly, "is under the Czars, and they're slaves, there. They have nothing at all."

"Well, anyways," said the shipping clerk, "there's Roosians here, stirrin' up trouble. I.W.W.! Want to make socialists outta us. Free, independent Americans!"

"Don't know anythin' about socialists," said Elsie, dryly. "But, by Jeez, I don't care what you call it, if I get money for my brother's specs, and I don't starve if I ain't got no job!"

"Now if any of yez should go down to Curtiss and get good jobs, I ain't goin' to blame you," said the foreman, clearing his throat with embarrassment. He grinned. "Why don't one of you go down and let me know? Maybe I'll do it myself!"

Money, I must have money! thought Frank. Not to save it, perhaps, but to use it, to build a fortress with it. He looked down at his patched and faded overalls, and for the first time he loathed his shabbiness, revolted against it with an intensity that almost nauseated him. If he had money, he could buy decent and respectable clothing. He could travel. He could see the world. He could go down and see Paul—

He thought of Paul's home and his father. Why hadn't he seen before in what dire and horrible poverty the Hodges had lived? Why hadn't it reached him, with understanding? Why hadn't he been sickened at it? I must have money, money, money! I must have it to get away from this ugliness, this stench of fear, this quagmire of hopelessness. I must have it to get away from these disgusting people!

He looked at the faces about him and hated them. They were his enemies, because they were poor, and had no hope; because they could do nothing but suffer, like dumb cattle before the whip of a driver. They had no guts! They had no strength. They complained, but their complaint was impotent and futile. They were ugly! They were detestable.

The bell rang and he went back to his machine.

Now, for the first time in nearly a year, he felt strength and vitality in himself, a passionate purpose, a purity of angry emotion. Elsie spoke to him from her high perch, but he ignored her. He must get away. There was a light again in the world, a vivid stark light, without beauty or gentleness.

CHAPTER 30

FRANK slipped away early the next morning. He was always up before his parents, for Maybelle no longer rose to prepare breakfast. Frank prepared his own, of shredded wheat and hot milk and tea, and Francis did the same. So he had no difficulty in dressing in his one good suit, tying his tie carefully, brushing his thick mop of chestnut hair, and shaving the few hair sprouts that occasionally made their appearance on his face. He polished his one good pair of shoes, gave himself a last brushing, assumed an expression of aggressive confidence, and caught a Niagara Street car for the Curtiss plant on Austin Street. He carried his work clothes inconspicuously in a paper bundle under his arm.

The streetcar rumbled, jerked, complained on its way. It was crowded with workmen in overalls and carrying dinner-pails. Their faces were drained and sweaty in the summer heat. Their feet were sprawled before them, listlessly. Frank averted his head. He felt the stimulating but deadly hatred for them in his heart. They were the threat! They were what he could be reduced to, because they had no money, no hope, no purpose! He looked at the passing streets, and saw their dinginess and grime. Clouds of chaff blew over cobbled walks. Garbage had been set out, and its stench drifted on the hot wind into the streetcar. Dirty children already played on filthy sidewalks. This was poverty. Why had he not seen it before? Why had he not hated it, as he hated these people who reflected the corrupted horror of its bitter blight? Poverty was a blight, and they were blighted by it.

They deserve it, he thought, grimly setting his young jaw. This is all they deserve! It is their ugliness and barrenness which creates their slums. They are at once the cause and the result of their ghastly existence. They have no intelligence. They have no desire to be other than what they are! Oh, my God, if only I could get away from them! But I will! I will, I will!

The personnel manager of the Curtiss Aeroplane Company had not arrived when Frank reached the plant. But workmen were already waiting for him on the benches in the office. In his mind, Frank was feverishly going over his qualifications. He knew how to type. He did not know "touch" typewriting, but he could type very fast. I've had three years of high school, he thought. They couldn't check up on it, so it doesn't matter about the lie. And, I'm eighteen. I look it, anyway. Besides, I'll be eighteen in November, so it's all right. And I'll go to night school this fall! I'll learn typing, touch typing, and shorthand. I'll learn bookkeeping. That is the first step. I won't stop there! I'll amount to something! I'll make money.

He looked about him. Where he had once put forth the antennae of his mind probing delicately into every face, where once he had felt compassion and tenderness, where once he had seen beauty and the wonder of life in every living thing, he now saw ugliness. He hated the workmen. He felt the powerful throbbing of determination and ambition in himself. Why, there was nothing he could not do! He had hands, but he had a brain, too, which distinguished him from these dull and brutish cattle about him. He turned his gaze back to them, and felt the force of his hatred like an irresistible battering-ram in himself, a swelling of strength.

The personnel manager was a kind and harried young man. He saw Frank before he saw the others. Why, there's a boy with intelligence and grit! he thought. Good-looking, too, in a queer kind of way. He called Frank to his desk and took down the falsified information on a small card. He heard Frank's quiet, controlled voice, which spoke so smoothly. "Three years high school. Typing. Majored in English. Good at figures. Clair, I think we can use you in the office. Twenty-two dollars a week to start. That all right? A boy with your background and ambition can go far. You say you've worked in the office of the Bison Wheat Elevators? No, we don't need references, I guess. Got to dispense with them these days."

Frank drew in a deep tight breath of relief. Twenty-two dollars a week. That was incredible. They'll not take all that away from me, he thought grimly of his parents. If they try it, I'll move. I'll give them ten dollars a week, that's all. Take it or leave it.

He carried a yellow card through the clattering and roaring factory. Someone was testing an airplane somewhere, and the shattering thunder of it assaulted his ears. He reached a small wooden office hastily thrown up in the very center of the factory. He presented his card to a Mr. Wilson, who looked pleased. He was seriously undermanned, and this looked like a boy who knew his business. He pointed to a typewriter.

"Look at all those bills of lading and requests for factory parts! Get down to work at once, kid. Clear up all you can."

There were young stenographers here, and girls working noisily on billing machines. Frank looked about him and smiled. The girls were clean, pretty and well-dressed, and they eyed him furtively. The men wore well-pressed suits and white shirts and ties. This was something like! he thought, in the phraseology of his parents. He had taken his first step away from ugliness, from the hideousness of work clothes, from the sodden and hopeless faces of the poor. Besides, his work began at nine, ended at five.

He made up for his lack of skill on the typewriter by sheer, persistent industry. By the time it was five o'clock he had almost reached the bottom of the pile. Mr. Wilson was delighted.

Frank reached home at half-past five, a full hour before his usual time of arrival. Maybelle was so dismayed that she did not at first notice his good clothing. "Have they sacked you?" she cried, in angry fear.

He sat down in the kitchen and coolly told her of his new job. At first she was incredulous and enraged, then awed. She sank into a kitchen chair, moistened her lips, blinked her eyes. "Twenty-two dollars a week," she murmured. "But it won't last." She was pale.

Francis returned home, and his first exclamation, after being told, was: "It's a damned lie! I don't believe it!"

He was less impressed than Maybelle. "I knew he couldn't stick at anything," he said furiously. "He's worked in that shop for only two years. But he'd never learn to keep his head down! That was all the trouble, never learning to keep his head down."

Frank stared at him fully, contemptuously. How clearly he saw his parents now, and despised them! "Why should I keep my head down? Why? I intend to lift my head up. I intend to keep it up."

"Talk. You were always a babbler. Babbling Bill! Big talk and little action. Well, you won't last there. You'll never last anywhere. You're a failure."

Frank clenched his fists. Now he was inspired by a really murderous hatred and rage against his father. All at once he seemed to expand, to grow larger, to overflow the narrow boundaries of the apprehension of his childhood. He said:

"All my life you've told me I was a failure. Keep on. I don't hear it or believe it."

Francis glared at him. He was accustomed to Frank's eye falling away from his. But now it did not. He felt his own smallness, suddenly, before this tall young boy. He gritted his teeth and blustered: "I'll give you a clout for your impudence! Liar, that's what you are. You were always a liar; couldn't rely on a word you said! Babbling Bill!" But he was little, he was small, and Frank was suddenly a man. Here was a stranger, no longer a child, but a man, and he had no power over him. "I'll clout you!" he repeated again savagely. "You weren't belted enough!"

Frank smiled, and that smile infuriated his father.

"Twenty-two dollars a week," murmured Maybelle uneasily. "That's a fortune, for a lad his age. Think of the money we can put in the bank."

Francis gnawed the corner of his mustache, and his eyes blinked reflectively. He muttered: "Eighteen dollars a week in the bank, at least. Extra. Two dollars a week for his clothes. Now he's in an office, damn it, he'll need some more clothes. A dollar for his carfare. That's twenty-one dollars. A dollar for him—"

"No," said Frank, quietly. "Not a dollar for me. Twelve dollars for me. Ten for you, for my board, my lunches."

"What are you talking about, you ruddy beggar!" screamed Francis, grasping the arms of his chair. "I'll knock you down—I'll—I'll—!"

"You'll do nothing," said Frank quietly. "I've made up my mind. So, I'm Babbling Bill, am I? This time I'm doing more than babble. You'll take ten dollars, or you'll get nothing. And don't think you can tell me I'm under age. I'll be eighteen in November, and my own master. I'll go away. You'll get nothing at all, and I mean it."

They sat there in their chairs, and they looked at each other, and it was Francis' eye that fell away.

"You've exploited me too long," said Frank softly. "I'm doing you a favor by staying here, by giving you anything. You gave me fifty cents a week of my hard-earned money. You didn't need it. You've got over ten thousand dollars in the bank. Now I'm on my own. And I'm going to stay on my own. You can talk about my being under age, and you being entitled to my money. You can threaten me with the police, as you did before. And I'll tell the police that you forced me to lie, to say I was sixteen, when I was only fifteen. I'll tell them how you sent a fifteen-year-old boy into a factory. I can talk, too."

"But ten dollars a week isn't enough," whimpered Maybelle, as Francis, choking with rage, could not speak. "Why, we got eight and a half dollars from you when you worked in the factory! This is only one dollar fifty cents more, that you want to pay us. Don't you think you owe us something for our years of work and effort and sacrifice for you?"

Frank stood up. He looked from his father to his mother. Then he spoke, and his words, though quiet, came in a stream of steady vitriol and hatred from his lips:

"I owe you nothing but pain, ridicule and abuse. That is what you gave me. I owe you a wretched childhood, and meanness, and fear. That is what you gave me. I owe you cruelty and undeserved beatings. I owe you the lack of a decent education. If it had been necessary, I would understand, and forgive, and do what I could. But it was not necessary! You made a laughing-stock of me, because you would not buy me clothing that wasn't clown clothing. You deprived me of the ordinary equipment for school, so I had to steal paper and pens, and even books. I owe you years of ill-health, because you wouldn't provide me with medical care. I owe you hatred, for you gave me hatred. You made me a liar; you made me dirty in my own sight. I owe you all this, and in return I offer you ten dollars a week."

Maybelle could only listen dumbly, making futile gestures with her little fat hands. Then tears came to her eyes. "To think I'd live to hear this from my own child!" she said at last. "Serpent's tooth. Sharper than a serpent's tooth. That's what Shakespeare says about an ungrateful child. I did my best. And only ingratitude in return." She turned to her husband for support. Francis' face was hideous with his fury, it was scarlet. He had thrust his tongue out between his lips, and his teeth were clenched on it. He looked mad.

Frank felt a last quiver of apprehension. It passed, never to return again. He said: "Shall I pack up and go?"

"You've got to give us eighteen dollars a week!" screamed Maybelle, beating her plump fists together.

"Ten. Shall I pack up and go?"

Francis found his tongue. He staggered to his feet, and brandished his fists. He fell upon his son. Frank deftly caught the flailing arms and pinned them down with one hand. He looked down into his father's eyes, and it was that look, hating, loathing, contemptuous, which halted Francis, rather than his son's grip.

"If you ever dare to touch me again," said Frank softly, "I'll knock you down. I know the law. I've done a little studying of it, myself. Assault and battery. Do you want to go to jail, Pa?"

He flung his father's arms aside, and brushed his palms together, as if ridding them of dirt. He stood up, lifted his chin. His parents were like small children before him. Francis' head barely came to his mouth and Maybelle's dusty crown reached only to his chin.

"Ten dollars. Think it over."

CHAPTER 31

IN SEPTEMBER, Frank's salary was increased to twenty-five dollars a week.

He was able to save seven dollars a week now. He looked at his bankbook and saw freedom. He studied the figures, not as his parents did theirs, with avarice, but with a fierce determination. It was not enough! He needed more money, a great deal more money, not ten thousand dollars, or twenty, or fifty, but an astronomical amount. He needed enough to free himself forever from the deathly touch of poverty, to hide himself forever from the faces of poverty, from its raucous voices and its drab habitations.

He took to haunting the streets of the rich again, not with pleasure in the beauty of the trees and the lawns and the gardens, as once he had done, but with envy and grim purpose. He saw nothing of the beauty. He saw the luxuriance there, the lavishness, the ease, the leisure, the security as of fortress walls. He saw the fine automobiles that rolled from driveways, and he imagined himself at the wheel. Now there was a devouring lust in him for wealth, wealth secured at any price, at any cost. If he thought of Paul Hodge now it was as one thinks of a dream, clothed in radiance and color, but, after all, only a dream. There was a callous growing over the memory of Paul, thick, impervious, scarred, but numb. He had not written to Paul for nearly six months.

One day in warm and golden September, Mr. Wilson tapped him on the shoulder. "Kid, there's a guy out here to see you, in a sailor suit. Says he knows you, and wants to talk to you. Go ahead; the work'll wait a few minutes."

Puzzled, Frank rose and went outside the wooden walls of the little office. His ears were immediately assaulted by the roar of an airplane. A sailor stood there, watching the testing of the motor. He turned and smiled. It was Paul.

Frank halted abruptly. For a moment all his blood rushed to his heart, and made him faint. Paul's figure became slanted, gray, dim. He felt Paul take his hand. He heard his voice. The factory fled away, and they were standing in spring woods again, listening to the shrill, sweet piping of the hosannas to life.

Then he was looking into Paul's face, and he could do nothing but look. They smiled at each other and could not speak. They only stood and smiled, and there was a thickness in Frank's throat. Their hands gripped together, and Paul was saying gently: "You've changed, Frank. My God, I'm glad to see you again! Why didn't you write to me?"

Frank said almost inaudibly: "It was no use. No use."

He cleared his throat and pointed speechlessly to Paul's uniform. Paul looked down at it. He colored. He said awkwardly: "It was the only thing to do. Dad gave his permission. After all, I'm almost eighteen." He paused. "I'm on my way to the Great Lakes Training Station. My train goes at six. I spoke to that man, and he said it would be all right for you to go out with me now, so we can have some time together before I leave."

The door opened, and Mr. Wilson grinned out. "Go on. It's O.K., boys. Good luck, sailor."

Frank was dizzy. He stood there, inert, and again looked at Paul. His friend was as tall as himself, and as thin as ever. His small pale face and delicate features had changed very little. His uniform gave him an elegance, a poise, which recalled the childish dignity of his earlier years.

Frank said: "They say the war will be over soon."

Paul was not baffled by this apparently irrelevant remark. Instead, he was touched. His hand brushed Frank's sleeve. "Shall we go out now?"

They went out into the warm blue and gold of the beautiful day. They walked down the vociferous and grimy street together, without speaking. Then Paul said: "Let's go down to The Front, shall we? We used to haunt the place once."

Frank was silent. Paul's greenish eyes studied his face, and his own darkened a little. A streetcar came rattling and swaying down the tracks. They went into the car together. It rumbled on down Niagara Street. They said nothing during the ride. Frank did not look at his friend. His profile was turned to him, and Paul studied it, and his pale mouth tightened in a depressed line.

They reached The Front. The river lay below them, blue-green, hurrying, sparkling. A boat was going down the Canal, blowing its whistles. The Canadian shore was a vivid green across the water. The sky arched over them, a pure and brilliant ultramarine, without a cloud. They sat down on a bench, and felt the warm bright wind on their faces.

Paul had never taken the initiative in speech. He could only wait now. He was heavy with despondency. This was not the Frank he remembered, this remote and restrained stranger with the hard jaw and the averted eyes, and the cold silence. Where was the old warmth, the old eagerness and ebullience, the old laughter and hasty, laughing speech? Where was the assurance he had always felt, the happy strength and hopefulness, the eye that saw so many mysterious and significant things?

Then Frank said: "What about your education?" There was a hard, almost sneering, note in his voice. He did not look at his friend.

Paul turned away. He gazed at the river. He said, in his light, neutral voice. "That can wait. But—but this can't."

Frank's mouth lifted slightly in a faint smile. "What can't wait?"

Paul looked down at his narrow quiet hands. He moved them a little. He said: "My country."

Did Frank shrug, ever so imperceptibly? Paul's lips tightened briefly. He went on: "I can give a year for what America means to me. I can give a year to—"

"Save democracy," interjected Frank.

Now Paul flushed. He lifted his head. He said, with dignity: "Yes."

He waited. Frank did not speak. Then Paul said: "Words can be used so often, so lightly, so—so meretriciously, so thoughtlessly, so banally, by politicians, by fools, by mouthers of easy phrases, that they can sound meaningless and absurd. But they don't lose their essential significance. They can be soiled by dirty and stupid hands, but underneath the grime they are still bright." He paused. He was not given to long speeches, but his heart was now beating in the strangest way, as if with indignation, or fear, or as if it was trying to communicate something to one who had turned blind and deaf. "But you know that. We often talked about it. Remember?"

Frank stared at the river.

"You know what I mean," continued Paul, helplessly. "Look: this is my country. I want to do something for her. This is the only way I can do it. It—it is all I have to give."

He waited again. Then he spoke desperately "What's the matter with you, Frank? You've changed. You don't look like your old self. What's wrong?"

Frank said: "Did you expect to find me a kid in knee-pants? Never mind. You've changed, too. Let's not talk about me. How are you? Did you know I'm damned glad to see you again?" He smiled now, and something in Paul's chest contracted with pain. It was like seeing the reflection of a well-remembered and beloved smile on the face of a cold stranger. It was like hearing a dead voice's inflection in the voice of someone he did not know. It was like catching the face of an alien, in an alien crowd, that recalled someone who had vanished, and who had been more than a brother.

"Are you glad to see me?" asked Paul quietly, and glanced away.

He felt Frank's hand on his shoulder. He was being shaken playfully. He did not know what made him speak out with quick sharpness: "Don't do that!"

Frank dropped his hand. He stared steadily at his friend's flushed face. Now it was the young Frank, disturbed, perplexed, volatile and hurt. But he was gone in a moment, almost before Paul had glimpsed him.

"I'm sorry. I had forgotten you were so touchy, Paul."

It isn't that, you know it isn't that! cried Paul to himself. What is it? What has happened to you? He could only say lamely: "Why don't you come with me? We could be together, as we were in the old days."

Frank's eyes became thoughtful and still. Then he said: "How about Gordon? Did he join up, too?"

Paul shrugged. "He couldn't. His eyes were too bad. He's studying for his Master's now. He has been promised a job as instructor in the University when he is finished. It means a lot to him, and to Dad."

How could he reach Frank? All that day, during the long ride, he had thought of nothing but his friend. How they would talk again, and laugh, and see the same things, and how eloquently Frank would interpret everything for him, so that once again he would have eyes and there would be beauty and significance and glory in the world! He felt as though he had been deprived of his sight, by one who could return it to him, deprived of hearing, by one who could lift cold dead hands from his ears.

Paul looked at the river. Now it was all shades of green and blue, full of vigor and vitality. But he could not feel it. The interpreter had gone away. He remembered his years of absence from his friend. He had lived in his memories. He had seen beautiful scenes, and he had talked them over in his mind with Frank. Frank would say this, of this incredible sunset. Frank would discern the meaning of a wheat field, a pale gilt under the moon. Frank would translate the sound of the river in winter. But Frank had gone, and the glory had passed away from the world with his going.

I was always only a mirror, his mirror, thought Paul. He made me see what he saw, made me hear what he heard. But now there is nothing left for me.

Frank was saying: "I'm getting twenty-five dollars a week. I'll be getting more. I've started to go to night school. When I've finished my high school course, I'm going to college."

Paul brightened; a faint warmth touched him. "That's what you said before! I'm glad. But haven't you gone before this? You said you were going."

Frank's flat cheeks became more flat. "No. I didn't have the time. I lost interest in everything after you went away. I was a fool, I suppose. I had no ambition. But now I have."

Paul was quiet for a long time. Then he asked softly: "What is your ambition?"

"Money. Only money." The words were tranquil, but Paul felt the iron behind them. He tried to laugh.

"Well, that's my idea, too. I've always wanted money. I hate to be poor. Not in the way that sounds, perhaps. But I wanted money so I could buy things. Books. Pictures. Is that what you mean, too?"

Frank turned his head and looked about him slowly, and Paul saw the hard line of his mouth. "No, that's not what I mean. I just want money. Because I hate. Because money is all there is."

Out of some insight, some anguished perception, Paul cried: "You are a coward!"

But Frank could not be aroused. Paul turned to him with a rare vehemence.

"What about your poetry? Your writing? What are you doing?"

Frank burst out laughing. "Oh, I've forgotten all that rot! I haven't written anything for years." He paused. He turned abruptly, to stare at his friend, and his blue eyes glittered briefly, reflectively. "What do you mean? There isn't any money in writing. Writers die in garrets." He waited. Paul did not answer. Frank repeated, almost urgently: "There isn't any money in writing, is there? Did you ever read of a writer making money?"

Paul replied listlessly: "Why, certainly there is money in it. You never thought of the money end of it before, did you? It never occurred to you." He sighed. "You wanted to do something for the world, you said. You wanted to give men something. That is what you said." He was silent a moment, then continued in that lifeless voice: "I read, only recently, that E. Phillips Oppenheim and Rex Beach and a few others have made hundreds of thousands of dollars. Is that what you want? Do you want to write books like theirs?"

But an odd excitement had come into Frank's face and eyes. He had turned on the bench. He was staring at Paul, almost crouching. He said: "If only I could write like them! I can! I will! I know I can still write! But I've got to go to school a long time first. I've got to learn. I don't really know anything!"

Paul gazed at him, speechlessly. Then Frank laughed, abruptly.

"Look who's talking about 'giving men something'! You never wanted to give anything. You used to say you hated almost everybody. Why this conversion to sweetness and light, all at once?"

Paul drew away from him. Then he said steadily: "I still don't like people. But you aren't—weren't—me. You had something else. You had something to give. I didn't. Maybe that's why I hated the world. I had nothing to give. You did. You had something priceless. Now you haven't." His pale green eyes dilated. "You've even taken away what you gave to me."

Frank began to speak, then his mouth closed in a derisive smile. "Don't tell me you are sentimental now!" he said at last. "You're like everyone else. You are quite willing to have money for yourself, and will do anything to get it, and think of nothing else. But you think 'those who serve the arts' should live a dedicated and a starving life. You want them to serve you, while you money-grub yourself. Why should they serve you? Why? Are you so valuable, so heroic, so worthwhile?"

Paul tightened his hands together. He turned away from Frank. He looked at the green line of the Canadian shore. "You made me see—all this—once. You gave me something which made the world tolerable for me. You made it—beautiful—for me. Now you've taken it away."

"Oh, hell!" and Frank contemptuously. "I don't know what you're talking about."

Paul's face had become completely dead and lifeless. He felt all the color draining away from the scene about him. It was dead, dusty, painted in gray, and there was a gray sick taste in his mouth. The world was a wasteland; it was full of ashes and soundlessness.

He stood up. "I'd forgotten. There are a couple of other people I wanted to see before I went away."

He looked down at Frank, and now his face was impassive, withdrawn, as frozen and rigid as it had been when Frank had first seen him. Frank was stunned by it and curiously shaken. He stood up.

Paul held out his hand, and after a moment Frank took it. It was an alien hand. It was the hand of a stranger who did not know him.

Paul walked away. Frank stood there and watched him go, as Paul had watched him go that terrible night so long in the past.

Then Frank, on one sudden and convulsive surge of pain, cried out: "Write to me! Don't forget to write to me!"

But Paul did not turn or answer.

He had parted from Paul like this once before, and he had been the one to go and not look back. But once he had gone down a long empty driveway, and had turned his head, and someone had waved to him, someone like a small pink cloud. He shook his head impatiently. It had been one of his dreams, of course, and it was a dream that had mingled, long ago, with his fantasy of the woman in the mauve rain among the lilacs.

CHAPTER 32

FRANK returned to the bench in a state of profound agitation. He sat and stared before him, blindly watching the play of light and shadow on the river. He had lately learned to smoke. He lit a cigarette, but it tasted bitter and acrid in his mouth. He held it, then, in his hand, until it burned down to ashes.

How could he have spoken so to Paul, for whom he had mourned so long? Why, that was Paul! It was his friend, and it was because of his friend that he had suffered so terribly; all the light had left the world with Paul's going. He could not, even now, think of that hot August night without depression and desolation.

The somberness and bereavement were there still, as dark and motionless and aching as ever. But they had enlarged themselves, diffused themselves. He mourned, as he sat on the bench in the waning sunlight. But it was no longer for Paul, and that seemed strange even to him. It had gone beyond Paul, had lost outline, embraced everything he saw and everything he touched and thought. It had begun on an August night. It now filled all the years. But it was not a sharp and personal grief. It was something he could not understand.

He thought: I ought to have asked him about himself. I ought to have talked. Just talked. Even if it had been hypocrisy, and I had not been there, really. I ought to have smiled and been pleasant and pretended. Pretended? Was it necessary for me to pretend?

Yes, he thought, with stern and suffering wonder, it would have been pretense.

Pretend with Paul! Pretend as with a stranger, for whom one cared nothing! He had dreamt of Paul's return, and the dreams had been rapture and despair and tears. And now Paul had returned. And—there had been nothing. Nothing had moved or stirred in him. Once or twice there had been a twinge of impatience, irritation, tiredness. And only once there had been a turning, a sighing, as if someone dead had moved in his grave for an instant. That had been when he had first seen Paul, there in the factory. But the dead had become dead again, and he had walked away with someone whom he did not know.

You can't go back, he thought. You can't go back to joy, or to summer days, or to remembrance. You can go back to grief. Yes, always, you can go back to grief. And, in some ways, it is a larger grief, a sorrow that has filled a fallow field with weeds and stones. You can go back to agony, but even then it is a different agony. It has become not one dead soldier, but a whole battlefield of pain.

There was a numbness and a weariness all through him. He looked at the shining river, and was mute. Yes, he was mute. It was his muteness which had so dismayed Paul. But I had nothing to say to him. Nothing at all! I never have anything to say to myself, either, any more.

Once he had sat on this very bench in a violet spring

twilight, with the trees dripping slow crystal drops all about him, and the murmur of the river below him. He had sat there and felt such exultation and such passion, and he had been filled with such love and tenderness! He had been alone, yet he had not really been alone. Not alone as he was now. He had looked at his hand, and had cried to himself: "In my hand! In my hand!" His empty palms lay on his knees now, and he stared down at them. They were empty. They were empty with a complete emptiness. And Paul had known. That is why he had not gone after Paul, had not called to him, and taken his arm. He could not go with such hands. They had had nothing to offer Paul, who had always come to him for life and meaning and insight and brightness.

He mourned, and his mourning was not for his friend. It was for himself and his emptiness and his desolation. He was impotent. He felt his impotence like a stifling in his chest.

He moved on the bench. I'm being sentimental, he thought. I've come awake now. I'm not a young, gibbering fool. I'm a man, and I have work to do—for myself.

The west was turning a delicate rose, the tint of a fresh petal in the morning. He looked at it. He watched it deepen. A flock of white gulls rose up from the river bank below, and blew against the sunset. He saw the rosiness on their wings; he heard their wild cries. The river turned a dark and brilliant blue. Beautiful, he thought, dully. But he did not feel it.

He could not look away. He had a habit, lately, of observing all lovely things intently, where once he had felt them and translated them into poetry and ecstasy. Now he only remembered them. He took the canvases of sunsets, of trees and skies and waters, and stored them in his memory. He knew now why he did so. He would write of them again, sometime, though it would be objectively, without feeling. But he would write of them, and the pictures he would re-create from his memory would bring him money.

This purpose must have been in his mind all the time, he thought, with surprise. It had been there, and he had not known it. It was a purpose without emotion, loveliness discerned without passion. Someday, he would even write about Paul, and it would be with understanding, with delicate discernment and deftness. But it would all be without tenderness and without love, without glory, without the sensation that for one instant even he had sensed the passing of God.

I have a lot to learn, he thought. I'm really ignorant. I've read a whole library, and I know nothing. I must learn, and as quickly as possible. What had Paul said? There was money in writing. But I must have known it all the time. It just never rose to my conscious mind before.

He sat there until the blazing orb of the sun sank into the far lake and the purple twilight came down. He saw it all with a clarity he had not known in his youth, for there had been a golden mist over everything, and there had been a quivering in his heart. Now it was as if a plane had shifted, ever so imperceptibly, and some deep dimension had flattened. All the colors were still there, and the outlines, but they were sharp and the light was just a little too stark. They were only static paintings of scenes he had once gazed at in their living reality, when the trees had been murmuring, and there had been the swell of actual life moving through them like wind. No matter how gifted the artist, his brush could produce only soundlessness, and the light on his trees and his landscapes and on the faces of his people was a motionless and depthless light. They remained, but the thing which the painter had seen, and had been unable to transfer fully to his canvas, was gone forever.

The gallery of his mind was filled with these static landscapes and portraits. But the emotion with which he had once seen them had departed, and had left only a voiceless grief, the very shadow, the very mist, of remembrance.

It was getting dark. The lamplighter was going his rounds. Yellow moons bloomed along The Front. There was a distant rumble, and Frank saw the round white light of a train approaching on the rails below. He tried to turn away. He could not. The train was now below him, and then suddenly he heard its wail, prolonged, despairing, melancholy. He listened to it. It echoed through every cell of his body, and it echoed in emptiness.

CHAPTER 33

THE train had gone, its last echo drowned in silence. Now there was only the rustling of the dry autumn trees, the wild smell of the dark river, the scent of autumn grass. A wind blew up from the flying waters below, and the trees complained restlessly. Frank sat and smoked one cigarette after another, until his mouth was parched. But his mind was racing, turning, examining, with a new cold excitement and plotting.

It's been so long since I've written anything, he thought. I might be out of practice, but it will come back. I'm like a pianist who has neglected his piano and must go back with stiff fingers and stiff mind. But I must go back. I can do it! I did it once, when I was a kid, and I can do it again. And for money! There was never anything so important as money.

He would return to school. He must see about that to-morrow. High school first, of course, and later, the evening sessions at the University of Bison. Years. That did not matter. If one was determined and had a goal, time passed, and became richer with the passing. "The race to the swift, and the battle to the strong." He felt a surge of power in himself, and exultation and grimness. What did it matter if it was not the old sweet and lovely power, the old rapture? This was new, and yet it was old. It was the passion of a man, not that of a dreaming child. What had the child desired? Beauty, compassion, service— Service to what? Frank rubbed his forehead and smiled unpleasantly. He could not remember what it was he had desired to serve. It had been a terrible and splendid thing—but he could not remember. Puling stuff! "The glory and the freshness of a dream." Wordsworth must have been approaching senility when he wrote that poem. There was a glory, and it was money. There was a freshness, and it was ambition. Everything else was rot.

While I go to school, I must write and practice. I must write. Of what? He knew nothing. He knew nothing at all of great cities, of exciting adventures, of strange places. Of these things writers wrote. What did he know, of what could he write? Whom did he know, whose life-story might be of enormous interest to the world? He knew nothing, he knew no one. If he wrote, he must write of insignificant things, of worthless and unimportant people. Who would be interested, for instance, in the story of his craven father, who knew nothing but fear and had wanted to be a great violinist and was now not even a "fiddler"? What sophisticated audience would be absorbed in Francis Clair's weekly, half-running errand to the bank, and his gloating over the bank-books, and the way he had once stopped abruptly on the sidewalk of an evening to listen to someone playing a violin in a dimly lighted house? Frank remembered that night. It was a summer evening, and it had been raining, and the trees dripped with a hushed and musical sound. The abandoned streets gleamed like black mirrors in the yellow gaslight, and no one stepped along the silent walks. He and his father had been on a "message" for Maybelle, but they had not spoken, for there was nothing they could say to each other. Then, as they passed that house, they had heard that violin, and Francis had stopped as suddenly as though someone had struck him in the chest and he could not move. Young Frank could smell the sweet scent of wet grass, and could feel a raindrop on his cheek, as it fell from the thick dark trees. The violin had accosted them like a strange and mysterious voice out of nowhere, a calling, a gentle urging, a sweetness beyond all sweetness, a yearning beyond all understanding.

"The Meditation—*Thais*," Francis whispered. Young Frank looked up at him. The lamplight lay on Francis' small and wizened face, and it lay on stark anguish, on frozen misery. And then, as young Frank still stared incredulous, he saw tears on his father's cheeks.

No, no one would be interested in such mean and little agony. Who would believe that a soul lived in the scurrying small body of an insignificant chemist, and that that soul could know torment, and strain after the voice of an angel? Now, if he, Frank, only knew a great musician, a composer! What a tale he could write of such a one, and with what pleasure and flattery—and money—would a writer of that tale be rewarded!

Who would pause to buy a book that told the story of Mr. Timothy Farley, his father's employer? Who would care that Mr. Farley was more interested in the state of his soul than in the state of his bank accounts? Mr. Farley had once been betrothed to a sweet girl in Ireland, and she had been drowned the day before their marriage. Mr. Farley had once told Frank that he could never look into water without seeing her white face floating in its greenness, and so he avoided river and lake forever.

Then there was Mr. Brislow, whose wife and four children had died in a railway accident. He had one daughter left, a girl of fourteen. Mr. Brislow had been another Francis Clair, careful, fearful, penurious and full of caution. But on receiving fifteen thousand dollars for the loss of his family, he had suddenly gone completely mad. He had quit his job in a tailoring establishment, and had taken his daughter upon a world cruise, outfitting the girl in the most lavish and stupendous wardrobe, and himself in every kind of tweed and broadcloth and sports clothing. Francis had asked him how long he expected the fifteen thousand dollars to last. "What do I care!" Mr. Brislow had cried in demented excitation. "I'll have lived, won't I? I shall have seen what I have always wanted to see! I'll know what it is to drink and sleep and eat when I wish, and do what I want to do, if only for a couple of years. What will it matter after that? This is blood money, see? My wife, that was Ethel, told me: 'Matt, if you'd only live, just once!' This is what she'd want me to do—live. Just once."

Who would care for Mr. Brislow, whose life had been like a small, tight little vegetable garden, which had now sprouted wild jungle foliage? Who would want to know what had released that worm-like soul, and what had sent those neat polished boots into strange and exotic places?

Then there was old Mr. Tom Sheridan, who had been crippled all his life, and who never left the meagre back yard behind the tiny shack in which he had lived. But old Tom was full of astounding stories of what he observed all about him. He found wonder in the industry of ants, delight in the garnering of the honey-bees, joy in the sight of a hummingbird, ecstasy in the flight of wild geese over his yard in the autumn, amazement in the heart of a dandelion. He found God in a blade of grass, the mystery of the flow of life in a leaf. He "talked" to the robins that hopped all about him. He knew Mrs. Robin and her mate, and declared that every bird had its own distinctive character. He quarreled with the blackbirds, who swore at him, and he had a dear friend, a crow, who sat on his knee and cursed at the other birds. Stupid old fool. What discerning reader in New York would want to know anything about Tom Sheridan and his imaginative follies in his shaggy back yard, which was a tangle of morning-glories and climbing roses?

Frank could see the readers for whom he wished to write and who would reward him. Languid, luxurious, elegant folk, who wanted tales of Machiavelli and the Borgias, of great musicians or singers or adventurers, of mighty historical figures and lost tropic isles, of France and its bordellos and bistros, of Germany with its castles and its gloomy forests and plains, of Russia with its endless steppes and dark rivers. They wanted stories of the stage and Spanish grandees, of people of their own kind who lived in New York amid the pale blue and lavender and yellow canyons of stone, who haunted the fine and exclusive restaurants and the rich exclusive homes of the "Four Hundred." What did he know of all this? Nothing. He knew that no amateur such as himself dared write the tales they demanded. They would laugh him to scorn. And he had nothing as yet to offer them but the Francis Clairs, the Mr. Brislows, the Tom Sheridans. What did they care for Bison, on its steep and rushing Niagara River, and what interest could they feel for the Lakes? People such as they ignored the very existence of the small townsfolk, who had nothing to offer the world but their ungrammatical philosophies, their ant-like lives, their petty and sorry hopes, their ignoble deaths.

I've got to learn. I've got to travel. I've got to know! he cried to himself, with angry but determined desperation. I don't have a minute to lose!

He heard the far chiming of church bells. He looked at his nickel watch and was conscious of hunger. His mother would wonder what had become of him, and she would nag endlessly when he returned. He was not as yet able to endure her nagging without nausea. Now he was chilly. He shivered. He heard the somber voice of the river below him, but the river itself was lost in the night.

He did not hear the soft footfall on the grass near him, but he felt the bench vibrate as someone sat down. He turned his head irritably, half rising as he did so. A girl was sitting near him, a girl in cheap flamboyant clothing, wearing a large black velvet hat with rose velvet facing. Her yellowish hair, he could see in the lamplight, was crimped and frizzed and bunched about a highly painted and impudent young face, and her thick lips were purple. She had pale blue eyes, wary, hard and knowing. She smiled at him, and the purple parted to show discolored teeth. The smile was coquettish. She could not have been more than a year or two older than himself.

"How ya, honey?" she asked, in a hoarse voice. "Nice evenin', huh? Lonesome?"

Her suit was a sickly pale gray, and she wore a red blouse with it, and a long string of pearls. Her stockings were of cheap, artificial silk, which gleamed, and her patent-leather pumps were cracked. She saw Frank's glance, and coyly lifted her skirt to show the rise of her calf. It was thin and scrawny. She smirked and blinked her pale eyelashes.

"Kinda by yerself, ain't you, hon?" she murmured. "Want company?"

A prostitute, thought Frank, with disgust. He suddenly remembered the sour and awkward warnings his father had given him. "Bad" diseases lying in wait for young fellows like himself. Rotten women who preyed on half-witted youths, and who gave themselves for two dollars. He wanted to get up and leave the girl, but something held him on the bench. He did not know what it was, but he remained and looked at her steadily and curiously.

"What do you want?" he asked.

"Why, nothin'," she answered. She studied him with her old eyes, and then smiled. "You ain't used to girls, are you? Never had a girl yet, did you?"

Frank felt heat in his cheeks, and anger. He was eighteen years old, but, as far as he could remember, his sex urges had been faint and muffled, held in abeyance by his father's disgusting tales. His life had been too circumscribed, too full, too busy, too desperate, for idle speculations, and in some way the smirking stories of his fellow-workers had slipped by his ears.

He was silent, still staring at the girl. With the writer's intuitive eye he saw all her cheapness. He saw her life. He saw her hunger and misery. But he saw them all objectively. That faint pain in himself, that faint stir: that could not be compassion, could it? He had got over compassion a long time ago. But some depression had taken hold of him, and held him on that bench.

Then he said: "Are you hungry? I thought I'd find a restaurant."

She had a stupid face, for all its cunning, but that face lighted up briefly, if cautiously. "Say, that's a swell idea! I'm kinda faint, myself. Where'd you want to go? By the way, my name's Myrtle."

Myrtle! Why did he see his father sharpening the carving knife just then, and see red roast beef on a platter before him? An ugly name. A grating, sharp, meanly smirking name! "Call me Myrt, honey," suggested the girl. "All my friends call me Myrt."

He winced. "My name's Frank," he said. The faint pain, the faint stir, became more imminent, clearer, and he clenched his teeth on it and tried to force it down. Then, all at once, he felt his loneliness, his tiredness. Any company was better than none. He refused to remember Paul Hodge. But what was he to do with this horrible girl? She exuded a nauseating cheap scent, reminiscent of vanilla. It had a smell of corruption. He stood up. "Let's eat," he said.

She stood up. The wobbling velvet hat came barely to his chin. He took her arm with instinctive courtesy. He felt its lean boniness under the sleazy gray wool. Again the stir, the pain, the depression. She smiled up at him archly. She tripped by his side as they walked towards Niagara Street. She laughed, and her laugh was the harsh, grating voice of a crow. She was too young to have such a voice. "How old are you—Myrt?" he asked.

"Nineteen," she answered blithely. "Older than you, huh?"

He shook his head. Nineteen. An old, sick, hungry woman. A piece of abandoned trash. Rubbish on a heap of other rubbish along the towpath. An empty tin can, rusting in the rain. A dirty rag floating on canal waters. A horror, a sickness, a deadness. A filthiness, a terror.

The extremely high heels clacked on the sidewalk beside him. The scent of vanilla and corruption came stronger to his nose. He averted his head. She was holding his arm. He could see the gloved hand on his sleeve. A cheap glove. Twenty-five cents. It was mended. Why didn't she work? The war-plants were crying desperately for help. The restaurants, the shops, were eager for any sort of labor. Yet she crept up upon park benches, and she smiled through purple lips, and she called strangers "hon."

"Got a job during the day, Myrt?" he said.

The hand slipped from his arm. She shook her head, eyed him warily. "Can't," she answered briefly. "Got—obligations. Yep, that's it, obligations."

She looked up at the September moon. "Now, ain't that pretty and romantic?" she asked hoarsely. "Say, I like a moon, don't you?" She began to hum a song: "By the light of the silvery moon!" The song was as horrid as her voice. Frank held himself taut until she had finished. Then she said, with animation: "There's a swell restaurant on Niagara Street, right near here. You can get anythin'. And cheap, too."

"Beer?" asked Frank.

She shook her head, lifted it, gave him a grotesquely prim look. "I don't drink. Nothin'. But you can have beer, if you want it."

He had never walked on the street with a girl before. It was a new experience, and an oddly uncomfortable one. He had to shorten his long stride to her short trippings. He felt her weight on his arm. All at once, he forgot that she was a prostitute. She was only a girl; what did one say to girls? In fact, what did one say to anyone? His only friend had been Paul Hodge, and now, even with Paul, he had had nothing to say. He fumbled in his mind.

"Think the war'll be over soon?" he asked.

She shook her head with exaggerated solemnity. "Nope. Not for three years. That's what the big guys, Wilson and Pershing, say. They ought to know. Three years more, of all that killin'." Her voice dropped, became low and curiously stifled. He looked down at her, vaguely surprised, for he had heard the echoes of emotion. Then she lifted her head gallantly and grinned widely. "Hell, you can't think of it. You hafta go on, don't you? No matter what happens. All the casualties ain't just in France."

He had seen so much of that spurious gallantry, that theatrical fortitude, that heroic facing-the-facts and keeping-the-chin-up of civilians. The war had touched him hardly at all. He neither cared about it nor speculated much upon it. He suspected that almost all civilians, with the exception of those intimately concerned, cared as little. Yet there had been that degrading gallantry, that lofty lifting of head, that setting of lips, among his fellow-workers. Now he had encountered it again in the person of a stinking little prostitute! Again he was angered. He said: "Have you a brother, or someone, in the war?"

The velvet hat was lifted high. "No," said the girl, loudly and emphatically. "Nobody."

Frank was silent. They were approaching a street corner. He felt an impulse to tip his hat and leave her abruptly.

"Nobody," repeated the girl, and now he was conscious again of her voice, hurried and more emphatic than ever. "I don't know nobody. Me, I'm all alone. I ain't got nobody."

"No father or mother, sister or brother?" Hell, what did it matter? In a moment he would walk off. He was not interested in her answer.

She was shaking her head almost vehemently. "Me, I'm an orphant."

She hastily added: "What about you, honey? Ain't you old enough for the draft?" She glanced up at him, and he saw the pale hardness of her eyes, and he thought: Why, she looks as if she hates me! This confused him, and he stammered: "No. I'm not old enough. I'm not eighteen yet."

The hardness melted away like ice. She stroked his arm. "Why, you're just a kid," she murmured tenderly. "I'm a granny compared with you. Yes, I am. I'll soon be twenty. I feel like a granny, near you." There was a wetness around her eyelids. "Maybe the war'll be over soon. Maybe. Maybe you won't have to go. I'd hate to see you go. Look, I read the papers. I try to find out what's it about. How'd we ever let the Germans get that way, in the first place? That's what I ask. We got eyes, ain't we? We see what they was doing, all the time, before the war, di'n't we? Whyn't we do somethin' about it before they made a war? Why, there was a feller in the newspapers that said the Germans was always trying to cook up wars, years and years back. So we know the Germans, don't we? We could see what they was doing, all the time. We coulda stopped it, before there was a war. We didn't, though. That's what makes me so damn mad I could puke. And now all them boys dyin'."

I could tell her something about geopolitics, thought Frank, with grim humor. But she wouldn't understand. And, of course, I don't know enough about it myself. He patted her hand. He was surprised to feel it trembling in its glove. "Never mind," he said. "Perhaps we'll learn after a while, about Germans."

"Maybe," she murmured. And now she sighed, deeply and heavily.

They had reached dirty and brawling Niagara Street, where Italian housewives sat on broken stoops and dirty Italian children raced and fought and screamed on the sidewalks, and the new electric street-lamps glared on asphalt and shabby, unpainted houses. A yellow "high-speed" trolley rolled and clattered along. Automobiles clanked and hooted. There was a fetid smell here, as of old fermented dough, and dirt and sweat. Saloons roared on the corners. There was a sudden stench of ham fat burning, and the fumes of beer.

"I know a rest'runt," Myrtle was saying. "Ain't much to look at. Ain't a Wop rest'runt, either. Good ole American food. Not fancy, and no serviettes. But good."

Frank forgot he had planned to desert her. He was hungry. And he felt an odd kindness for Myrtle, who did not matter, and whose ugly little life was an insult to the alleged dignity of man. She was leading him to the open door of a hideous small restaurant, where pies and cakes and cooked meats, completely encrusted with flies, stood in a window. Frank's acquaintance with restaurants was very limited. Sometimes, on Christmas, when Maybelle didn't "feel up to" cooking a holiday dinner, Francis would take his family to the Statler Restaurant in the Shelton Square Building, where a reasonably good and clean dinner could be had for sixty-five cents, including a tasty dessert. He had never been in a restaurant like this, narrow, hot, glaring, small, where gas mantles blazed overhead in an insufferable heat, and dirty tables, covered with dingy white oilcloth, awaited the casual diner. The place swarmed with flies, was permeated with the stench of old rancid grease, with the sweat of the few shirt-sleeved, brutal men who sat about at the tables accompanied by fat shapeless women with pig-like features. There was a brown linoleum on the floor, slippery and stained. A waitress or two drifted about, their white uniforms stained and too short, their frizzled hair clinging to wet red faces, their hands filthy. They carried platters of greasy hot meats and gray mashed potatoes and coffee, and when the smell hit Frank's nostrils, he lost his appetite. He had a momentary impulse to back out, to suggest the Statler Restaurant, but Myrtle was leading him blithely to a table, and he had to sit down.

Evidently she was known here. The men winked at her, their women glared, the waitresses smirked. "Hi, Myrt!" one of them called. Then the attention of the entire restaurant was turned upon Frank, who sat there miserably in his neat blue serge suit, his dark red tie, his polished laced boots. They saw his white collar, the white cuffs at his wrists. They saw the combed neatness of the chestnut waves on his head, his clean thin face, well-shaved, the features clear and hard and strong, and his blue, embarrassed eyes. Their interest quickened. This was a new kind of client for Myrtle. Where did she pick up that swell? Out of the University? Was Myrtle goin' to college now? They snickered, stared at Frank openly. But Myrtle, preening, was settling herself with "serviette" gestures, puffing up her frizzes of pale yellow hair, furtively dabbing her nose with white rice powder from a little bag, rearranging the red ruffles of her blouse. She ostentatiously ignored her former companions. She ceremoniously handed Frank the fly-spotted and greasy "menu," which was written out in pencil in illiterate English.

She said, in a mincing, artificial voice: "I kin recommend the roast beef. It's kinda good here. And the creamed peas, and the mashed potatoes. And they got razberry short-cake, too, tonight, with whip cream. Coffee's good, too. Best in town."

The gaslights spit and hissed; the heat seemed to increase. There was a swinging door at the rear, which, upon opening, emitted the bass roar of a Greek cook, and the overpowering effluvium of frying grease. Frank could see Myrtle more clearly in this glare of steaming light. Her fair hair had black roots; her lips were as purple as plums, and the homemade black velvet hat faced with rose-colored velveteen was obviously put together over a frame of uncertain cardboard. The brim had a wavy effect. The gray suit was spotted. There were many "Woolworth" bangles of greening yellow metal clattering about her wrists. The skin of her face was so overlaid with rice powder and thick red paint that it had a canvas-like appearance, through which sweat had made seams and cracks. Her features were small, even delicate, but so cunning, so stupid, that their delicacy was lost, and had become degradation.

It was impossible. He must leave this horror at once, this filthy little corruption! And then he saw her neck.

What a thin, young, vulnerable and pathetic neck, so childlike, so tender, so unbearable in its appeal. Frank could not look away. The painful stir which he had felt before now became intolerable in its immensity. Why, that was the neck of a little girl, a little hungry waif, an innocent and defenseless child! There was a rope of ten-cent pearls about it, twisted with black velvet, but this only enhanced its touching pathos. Frank wanted to stroke that neck, to cry out something, to turn away. The emotion in himself was new, or, rather, it was renewed. He had felt this way so often when he was younger, and he had hoped, and believed, that he was done with it. It had no crippling and softening place in his life any longer. It was a chasm in the road he had set out to walk. He must pass over it, no matter how difficult that might be. He set his teeth. He said: "I'll have what you have, Myrt." And he would not look at her neck again. His hands knotted into fists under the oilcoth.

CHAPTER 34

THE meat had a hot and acrid taste; the gravy was rancid. The mashed potatoes were soap-suds, solidified. The "creamed peas" tasted of soda and sour milk. The coffee was pure chicory, black and bitter, in which the alleged cream floated in semi-solid little wafers. Frank ate a mouthful or two, gagged, sat back to watch Myrtle devour the horrid mess with gusto and an almost ravenous appetite. When she saw him watching her, she assumed great daintiness, but let him glance away and she fell upon the mess like a starving wolf. She drank milk, three or four glasses of it, not with appetite and pleasure but with a kind of grim determination. "If you don't like it, why drink it?" he asked. Her eyes sidled away. "Gotta," she muttered.

Had she tuberculosis? She was scrawny, and her skin, where it was not caked with powder, had a bluish look. But there was no hectic tinge to it. Anaemic, then. But milk was not the thing for anaemia. Frank heard his mother's firm, dogmatic voice: "Iron! Blaud's pills. Iron." He wondered, with dry amusement, if he ought to buy a bottle of Blaud's pills for Myrtle.

While she ate, he studied the restaurant and its diners. This, then, was poverty. He had been surrounded by poor people all his life, laborers, mechanics, miserable artisans, washerwomen and teamsters. But never before had the poor so impinged upon him, and with such acute and stinging disgust. Had he been blinded by childish unawareness, or that sickening compassion of which he had once been a victim? He did not know. He only knew that when he looked upon these animal-like faces, these dirty shirts stained with sweat, these empty eyes and thick dull mouths, these cracked, soiled hands and black nails, he was filled with loathing and hatred. He heard the loud, empty guffaws all about him. He caught snatches of hoarse conversation. They sounded like the grunts, squeals, bellows, of animals. Could one honestly believe that these creatures belonged to the heroic human race, these women with flat, piggish features and frizzed hair, these men whose every glance was ox-like and blunted? Look at that man there, whose thick wet hair of an ugly tan shade grew far down on his forehead so that the peak almost met his scraggy eyebrows. The back of his head was as flat as though it had been pressed with a board. His neck was bull-like. His mouth was flabby, half-open, his nose was wide and bulging, and his eyes, tiny, porcine and lightless, kept staring at his fat companion's breast. Was this a man? Had this monster a soul? A soul!

"An' I said to him, I says, 'Why, you bastard, I coulda beat you ten to one at that bowlin' match if I hadn'ta had eight glasses of beer just afore!'" His female companion growled an affectionate affirmative. "Even if he was the foreman, I said it to him, right out, and the——hadda shut his trap."

"They gotta, these days," a short and enormously fat man at another table joined in. "We gottem on the run, these days. Gotta kiss our behinds, or out we walk. And where'll they git more hands? That's what I'd like to know. Yep, we gottem on the run. They gotta raise us ten cents more an hour, and cut down the work-week. That's what our union's gonna tell 'em next week. You guys oughta git yoursel's a union. Nothin' like it. The war's gonna last three years more, at least; that's what they tell us, and they gotta have us workin' for 'em, all the rich bastards."

His lady companion shook her head dolefully. "I heard different. The war'll soon be over," she said.

She was greeted by a chorus of angry hoots. "Shut yer trap!" "You're a damn fool, Maisie!" "Whadaya know, anyway? I got it straight it's gonna last three years! Hope so, anyways. Why, the Huns're stronger than ever!"

The others bellowed and squealed emphatically, nodding their heads. "War's gonna last! Maybe five years, if we're lucky."

Frank stared at them grimly, these creatures who dared believe they were his fellows. These men voted. They were the masses. They formed seventy-five percent of the population in all nations. These were the enemies of civilization.

Again, from out of his subconsciousness rose Miss Bendy's voice: "The world is full of lightless, dull and hidden souls, like moles, Frank. When you are older, and you travel, you'll find them everywhere, in every village and town and city, on every farm. You'll find these blind eyes and these clay-covered hearts, these thick grunting tongues and these paw-like hands. They are the Terror, Frank, and we must do something about them. But what?"

Frank stood up abruptly. "Are you finished, Myrtle?" he asked.

Myrtle started, hastily wiped her mouth on her soiled handkerchief, and rose.

Frank hurried ahead of her, his flesh crawling at the proximity of these beasts, these depravities. He stood on the gritty sidewalk outside, and looked at the dirty, noisy street clattering under its lamplight. Myrtle reached him, smiled brightly. "Well, guess we oughta go to my place, huh?" She looked up at him coyly, and simpered.

He said involuntarily, out of his disgust: "Myrtle, did you hear them, in there? They want the war to go on forever, just so they can make big wages in the war plants."

Her face changed, and now it was old and withdrawn, and her eyes shifted. "Yeh. I heard 'em. You'd wanta hate 'em, maybe? Maybe that's what you think, thinkin' about all the boys that're dyin'. But then you think, too: 'This is the first time they ever ate regular, and the first time they ever had a little cash in their pockets, and they could feel that they wasn't—wasn't—just horses. And they gotta place to live, for once, that they wouldn't be thrown out of, the first of the month.' That's what you gotta think. If you said to Johnny, back there: 'Say, you want the boys to die so that you can make forty dollars a week?' Johnny'd say no, damn fast, and maybe punch you in the jaw. They don't want the boys to die. They only want to eat."

She sighed. "It's kinda terrible, ain't it, that the only time they kin eat is when kids die?" She waited for him to speak, and then when he did not, she added: "I heard Lloyd shootin' off his mouth about tellin' his foreman off. It makes him feel kinda good that for once he's got the upper hand, and that he's a man, too."

Lloyd! Another one of the horrible names which the illiterates affect! Frank's first reaction was to the name, his second, to Myrtle's words. "A man!" Why did not some public benefactor rise up and teach these creatures that manhood was not implicit in telling one's foreman "off," but in self-respect and dignity, in an inner pride that set a human being on the high road to self-improvement? Instead, the newspapers pretended to find pathos in the American workingman's new and passionate penchant for silk shirts, and spoke with maudlin sentimentality of his delusion that "big" words, arrogant behavior and lavish spending meant that he had acquired importance. "They do not know," said one columnist with a sigh, "that wealthy and important men do not wear silk shirts or throw their money away recklessly." But there was no one to tell them this. Their monkey-like antics provoked tender smiles and foolish defenses from those who ought to have known better.

The glaring lamplight shone on dull passing faces, on little shifting eyes, on brutal, ape-like features, and Frank's disgust rose to hot rage. He had forgotten Myrtle; when she touched his arm, he shied from her as though struck.

"I live here," she simpered, pointing to a couple of dirty windows above a closed shop. Frank glanced up automatically. He saw filthy whitish curtains bellying out into the breezy night. There was a faint glimmer of lamplight behind them.

"I gotta ask you to wait a coupla minutes," said Myrtle. "Gotta straighten up things a little first. Then I'll yell down the stairs and you kin come up. O.K.?"

Frank was relieved. Once let the little horror out of his sight, and he would take to his heels. He hesitated. He looked down at her small painted face, and something was squeezed in him. He put his hand in his pocket. Then he withdrew it. He watched her as she opened the door on a black staircase, saw her flash him a provocative smile. and disappear. He heard her heels clacking on the wood, heard an upper door open. Somewhere an infant wailed, was hushed.

He stood on the street. A trolley crashed by, faces pressed against the lighted windows. A gusty wind blew up the street, filled with dust and chaff. A gramophone shrieked that a long, long trail was winding into a land of dreams. There was a distant thunder, a splintering noise, a clicking and a clacking. A bowling alley near-by. Next door, a saloon, through its swinging doors, emitted the stench of stale beer and a snatch of hoarse song. Two young soldiers, putteed and giggling, swaggered down the street, struck matches, lit cigarettes. One began to sing:

> "Over there, over there,
> Say a prayer, for the boys
> Over there—!"

The other said something obscene, and they both giggled like schoolgirls leaving the classroom. Frank watched them until they disappeared under the dusty trees. Now all the disgust and hatred slowly sank away from him, leaving a hollow emptiness behind, a kind of sickness. They were hardly older than himself, those boys. Surely he did not pity them for the threat of death that hung over them. He did not pity them for their youth, for he was young himself. The pity had no name.

"Say a prayer, for the boys, over there—" No, say a prayer for all the boys "over here," everywhere in the world. Say a prayer for youth eternally and inevitably betrayed, not by the world, but by its own dreams, by time, by mere living. If one could only die while one still believed—Believed what? He could not remember. What had he ever believed? There was a golden fog hanging between his present self and the child he had been, and he could not see through it.

Why was he standing here, aching like a fool from what cause he did not know? He had believed he was all finished with aching, with longing, with yearning. He looked at the black stairs up which Myrtle had disappeared. If he did not hurry, she would return, and he would be embarrassed, for he had no desire to accompany her to her room. He began to walk away. Then, impelled by what could only have been curiosity, he returned and crept silently up the stairway. He did not know why he did this. Was it to discover whether Myrtle had a previous customer, to sink himself in another scene of degradation? There was a dim light showing under the door at the head of the stairs. The door was not quite closed. He pushed it open slowly, and looked within.

In one swift glance he saw the wretched room, the tumbled bed, the littered dresser, the two wooden rocking-chairs. He saw the yellow gaslight hanging from a calcimined ceiling. There was another door opposite, near which stood a gross fat old woman, reminiscent of Mrs. Watson. She stood there, half-turned from Frank, her arms folded across an immense bosom. She began to speak sourly: "Well, you better get some money, that's all. I let you run a week. He'd better have some money, that's all. Hurry up. You can't keep a feller waitin' too long, and I got to get my sleep. I'll only keep the kid to twelve o'clock. Got to visit a frien' tonight."

Then Frank saw Myrtle near one of the windows. She was sitting on a stool, her back to him. She was nursing an infant. Her frail body was bent over the child in an arch of tenderness. Frank saw the full profile of her breast, against which the baby had pressed its eager, sucking lips. Myrtle still wore her hat. In her haste, she had not even removed her gray jacket. Her legs were bowed, to accommodate the weight of the child on her thighs. She crooned wordlessly.

The old woman snorted: "Don't see why you don't give the kid to an orphanage, or sumpin'. Get better raisin' than you can give it. An' you won't be tied down. You can git a job that pays regular wages."

Myrtle lifted her head sharply. Frank could see her profile, stark, terrified, full of rage. "I won't give my baby up! They'll adopt him out, and I won't never see him ag'in! This way I kin take care of him days, and support him nights! I won't give him up!"

The old woman shrugged. She chewed on a wad of gum indifferently. "Well, you do what you want. No use givin' advice to fools. That damn bastard shoulda married you before he went overseas and got himself kilt. You oughta had more sense."

Myrtle began to cry. "They sent him away too soon. We was goin' to git married. And then they sent him away." Suddenly she hugged the baby to her frantically, fiercely. "But I got Floyd! I got my baby, and his! And I'm gonna hang on to him!"

Again the harridan snorted. "Fine life you'll be givin' him. His mother a common whore."

"I ain't! I ain't!" cried Myrtle vehemently. "When I'm done nursin' him I'll git someone to take care of him regular, and

I'll work. I don't do this for money for my own self. I do it for Floyd! And I ain't a whore."

Tears ran down her cheeks. She wiped them away with the back of her hand, and sniffled like a child. The baby continued to suck contentedly. Myrtle sobbed.

"I had a good job in a rest'runt. I kin get it back, when I'm done nursin' him. But he needs me for another coupla months. Then I kin get help.".

Frank closed the door which he had opened. He stood in the darkness. He felt sweat on his forehead, felt it trickling down his back, for the stairway was very warm. He heard the dull sick beating of his heart. He put his hand in his pocket. He knew to the last bill what he had there. Fifteen dollars. He had intended to take the money to the bank tomorrow. He bent down cautiously and slipped the bills under the door. Then, holding his breath, he went down the stairway and into the street.

He had gone three blocks before he cursed himself for a fool. What had betrayed him once again into that weakening, that shameful, compassion? Fifteen dollars! Ten minutes ago he had been fifteen dollars nearer freedom, a strong full step. But he had stepped backward. For what? He berated himself the rest of the way home. Less than half an hour ago he had seen clearly and honestly. Now his sight had become murky, if only for a few moments, and he had joined the sentimental jackasses who encouraged the inferior in their bestial state.

What had he thought in his folly, there on the staircase? That Myrtle might stay in peace with her baby for one night, for two nights! But the third night? God damn it, he said to himself. What does it matter about the Myrtles and their horrible little "Floyds"! They were the weaklings, the rejected of life, the offal of humanity.

Engaged with furious thoughts, he was surprised to see that he had reached his home on Albany Street. Every window glowed with gaslight, and the shades, contrary to Maybelle's usual custom, were not drawn. In less stressful moments he would have paused to consider this extraordinary phenomenon. But now he felt only a revulsion against entering that hot, neat little house, there to be greeted by his mother's angry nagging about his absence.

The evening wind was dusty, and it carried with it the scent of drying horse manure and heated asphalt and cabbage. Somewhere, too, a housewife was making her winter supply of catsup, and now all the other odors were suddenly swamped in the fine rich scent of spices and stewing tomatoes. Frank was conscious that he was still hungry then. He heard the tall heavy elms near the sidewalk muttering to themselves. He hesitated.

Then he walked carefully to the rear of his home and entered the yard. Here it was dark and cooler. Francis had worked for many hard years in his garden of an evening and on his days off. He had borders of red and white roses along the wooden fence, a bed of mint and parsley and thyme, and another bed of his favorite flower, pansies. The grass, too, had been carefully tended, until it was thick plush under Frank's feet. In the very center of the yard stood the catalpa tree he had planted. When had he planted it? The golden fog between himself and his boyhood thinned, and through its wavering bright mist he saw himself as a child of—eight? Nine? Ten? He could not remember, but he did remember that it was Arbor Day, and each child at the school had been given a whip of a young tree for planting. He saw himself in full and splendid sunlight, his father beside him, the early spring wind in their faces, the sky above the color of a brilliant amethyst. Francis plunged the spade deep into the brown earth, in the very center of the yard. Frank saw earth thrown aside, full of writhing worms, their bodies red and wriggling. Now water was poured into the deep hole, and then Frank was allowed to set his tree in it. Francis carefully spread the roots. Frank took up the spade and tenderly threw the earth back onto those roots, and gently tamped it down. It was such a small tree. Planted, it was no higher than the little boy, just a whip, barren-branched, vulnerable and very young, bending in the wind.

And now it was very tall. Its trunk was thick and strong, as full of vitality as a youth. Its branches spread far above Frank's head; its long wide leaves murmured and were blown in a blur against the stars. In the spring, he remembered, it carried cones of sweet blossoms. It was strange that he remembered those blossoms, for he could not recall that he had seen them for the past few years since Paul Hodge had gone away.

He put his hand on the trunk of the tree. My tree. I planted it. It is part of myself. If it were not for me, this tree would not be here, full of leaves, living in the earth, straining to the sky. There would be no blossoms and no shade—but for me. Paul and I would examine it carefully in the spring to watch for the first buds. I would tell him when the blossoms were out. He would pluck a few, but they would always drift through his fingers. It is funny that I don't remember them blooming since I was fifteen years old. I will watch for them next year.

The tree whispered to him. When he had been a boy, he had imagined that the tree talked to him and told him stories and the strangest tales. He had heard actual whispered words, soft and deep. But he could not remember the stories now, and if the tree spoke, it spoke in a language forever alien to him, forever lost to him.

"Where do you go in the winter?" he had asked the tree. How old had he been then? Eleven? Twelve?

"The same place where you go, when you sleep," the tree had answered, rustling mysteriously. "The same place where I shall go, when I die, and where you will go, when you die."

"Where is that?" he had asked the tree, his young hands clasped about the bending trunk.

The tree had told him. It had been so clear and so satisfactory and so wonderful. But he had forgotten the answer. He could remember the question, but not the answer. How glorious the world had been then! So full of magic, of wonder, of complete and unquestioning awareness and understanding! Now the golden light had gone, and there was only bleak stark noon around him, the dull light of "common day."

For those few moments while he stood under the tree, he was young again, as he had once been young, and there was the faintest echo of the magic and wonder in his ears. He plucked a large cool leaf of the tree. How often he had held such leaves in his hands and had felt the dim mysterious pulsing in them, the faint leaping answer to his own pulse! Was he actually feeling it again? No. He tossed the leaf away. Kids have such damned imaginations!

Suddenly and reluctantly he thought of Paul Hodge. He would write to Paul. Somehow, he would have to explain his curious attitude. Would Paul understand?

Frank shrugged. He was conscious of tiredness and depression. He had forgotten Myrtle and the fifteen dollars. He went to the back door of the house.

He heard a deep and aching sobbing in the front room. He closed the door behind him and ran into the "parlor," which was also his parents' bedroom. Francis was lying on the bed, his face as white as death, the sheets drawn up to his chin, his eyes sunken and closed. Maybelle sat beside him, flanked on the other side by Mrs. Clair. Maybelle's apron covered her face. It was she who was sobbing. But Mrs. Clair was grimly silent and gray. She saw Frank as he entered.

"Where have you been, when we need you?" she asked,

sternly. "Your pa collapsed in the shop today. The doctor says it's consumption, and that he'll never be able to work again. A fine son you are, traipsing the street when your pa and ma need you!"

CHAPTER 35

FRANK was now face to face with the leaden image which was late November, 1918. He wrote to Paul Hodge, who was, apparently, still at the Great Lakes Training Station:

"I have written you five times, but you haven't replied once. Why? Well, I'll still go on writing, Paul. I know my letters don't rouse any echo, but I can't help it. I only want you to know—"

Know what? Frank stared at the typewriter keys, on which his hands rested, and then he looked out through the factory window at the lessened activity of the yard. It was his lunch hour. What did he want Paul to know? He could not remember. He added: "—that I think of you a lot. But you don't seem to reciprocate. You didn't even reply to the letter in which I told you that my father had died on October twenty-first."

Frank paused. Why should he think, just now, of the time when he could not attend the graduating exercises of the ninth grade of School Eighteen, which had been held at Lafayette High School? He knew only that he remembered he could not attend, for the reason that his parents had refused to buy him a blue serge suit, and had insisted that his old brown one, shabby and too small, was quite good enough for "Yankee nonsense." So he had not attended the exercises, and Miss Bendy had arranged to have his diploma sent to him. His heart burned with sick rage as he remembered.

Then the rage died away, however hard he tried to hold it. I am not really sorry, he thought, and he was empty and weak with depression.

"I think I told you my father had tuberculosis. The doctor had told him, in September, that he could never work again, or, at least, not for a long time. He was seriously ill, but he might have lived. He died of fear, in the end, and of the dread that his 'savings' would diminish. He wouldn't listen to the doctor. After his first hemorrhage, he insisted upon going back to his job. Then he collapsed. Two days later he died."

Frank's eye-sockets filled with a dark heaviness. He lit a cigarette. Suddenly, without any reason at all, he thought of his father's violin, lying in the cellar of the house on Albany Street, covered with mould and dust. An acute pain struck him in the chest. My old weakness, he thought, bearing down savagely on the pain until it left him. It was a different pain from the old one, in some way. He resumed his tapping on the keys in the deserted office:

"You will notice that I have a different address, and a pretty swell one, too, says he! My mother is now living with my grandmother, on Porter Avenue. They talk of returning to England in a year or two. I made the break with the family, for I can't stand my grandmother, and, of course, I won't go with them to England. After my father died, the doctor examined me for tuberculosis. No sign, thank heaven. But Ma has taken to coughing, apprehensively, though there's nothing wrong with her.

"Well, the war's over, and you'll probably be out of the Navy any day. Armistice Day was queer in Bison. I went downtown to see if there would be any celebration. Just a few kids with whistles, and a few adults wandering around, looking aimless. Didn't the end of the war mean anything to them? It didn't seem to. I know only that there was gloom around here, in this war plant. The war workers were very much depressed."

Frank's own depression and misery settled heavier upon him. The yard darkened, and a few flakes of snow drifted in the grayness. How he hated November, that leaden image with the legs and the arms melted together, and static! He went on:

"I suppose you will be returning to your father and Gordon. Couldn't you stop in Bison on the way home, and see me? Just let me know, and I'll be waiting. I have a nice room, at the address on the top of this letter.

"I've been going to night school at Hutchinson since September. My difficulty, as usual, is with mathematics. They tell me I must master it, or I'll never get my diploma, and couldn't go on to college. I've begun to think that the best way would be to take all the studies I need, and want, for my writing, then go to the University of Bison as a special student. That seems the only solution. They discovered, at Hutch, that I couldn't even grasp long division, and though

I learned enough mathematics to graduate from Eighteen, I've forgotten it all.

"I have a wonderful teacher in English, though, a Mr. Mason. Our first assignment was a composition, but I wrote a short poem in blank verse."

Again Frank paused, and he heard Robert Mason's gentle voice: "Remarkable. Excellent. But something is missing. I don't know just what. All the essentials are there: color, vitality, originality and vigor. You have a great talent, if we could only discover what is missing."

Frank frowned. "Missing!" Nothing was missing, nothing at all, except, perhaps, sentimentality. He ended the letter abruptly, put it into an envelope. His noon hour was over. The other office workers returned, talking and laughing. One was a young fellow with whom Frank had become rather friendly, a tall, stooped, smiling Southerner from Kentucky. He said: "Hi. Writin' ag'in?"

Frank sealed and stamped the envelope, dropped it into the mail basket. "Nothing important. Say, what're we going to do now, Tim? Did you get your notice, too?"

"Yep. I'm agoin' home, back to the hills. My three brothers say there's oil there. Only a dollar and a half a barrel now, but oil's flowin' like water. You ought to git in on it, like I told you. Come on back home with me. Why, sir, you kin make yo'self a barrel of cash!"

He really likes me, thought Frank, with faint surprise. He looked up at the tawny face, so slender and good-natured, at the pale blue eyes and the shock of tan-colored hair. He felt the easy manner, the mildness, of the other young man. As for himself, he was perfectly neutral with regard to Tim Cunningham. He neither liked nor disliked him. Something had atrophied in him. His responses to others were negative, indifferent. He hardly saw them. He congratulated himself on this "normal" attitude. He had learned to look at the world dispassionately, without much feeling.

"Maybe I will," he answered, suddenly bored with Tim's presence. Tim eyed him curiously. A funny cuss. A big, likely feller, though, with an "American" face. Not like these damn Hunkies and Germans and Wops one saw all around in this crazy city. He wasn't a "Yankee," either. Born in England. Tim warmed. The old friendship and affection of the Southerner for the Englishman shone in his eyes. Why, we're the same people, he thought. He put his hand on Frank's shoulder, pressed it, went to his desk.

Kentucky. Frank played with his pen. What had Mr. Mason told him? "You've got a lot to learn, Mr. Clair. A very great deal. Years and years of learning. But if you have faith in yourself, and learn, and travel a little, you can be a writer."

Frank had investigated the writing profession thoroughly. He had discovered that only a few could really make a living, writing. Only these few were truly professionals, receiving all the rewards. There were hundreds of others who wrote the many other books, which enjoyed so small a success, bringing to their authors sums ranging from fifteen hundred to twenty-five hundred dollars annually. A man couldn't do much on that. At the top, there were the shining prizes. But the top was a long way up. He wanted money much quicker than that. And there was no guarantee that he would reach the top eventually. Writing, in contrast to his younger efforts, had become a strain and a chore to him, a labor. Once, he had written with smooth and eager delight, the phrases rushing from his pen like liquid fire, entrancing even himself with their imagery, their power, their beauty. They had been like a pouring, a magic pot tipped to spill out the smooth, effortless gold. There had been wonder in the world then— now it was labor, a dull, mechanical labor. Something had happened to him, he felt a psychic exhaustion running down his legs and arms, draining away his strength, a prescience of failure.

Kentucky. "You kin make yo'self a barrel of cash."

If I could get a lot of money, he thought, I could really study, really travel. Then, when I was freed from the burden of making a living, I could get back that "missing something" Mason spoke about. It's just the anxiety of having to make a living that holds me back. Besides, I would see something of the country.

He had saved many of his earlier poems and short stories. They were crude, he had found, and amateurish. They were dreadfully overwritten. They were redundant with adjectives. They boiled with repetition. Yes, he was learning. He knew what was wrong. He could write much better than that now. But he knew secretly that he had lost something which he had once had: power, strength, exuberance, the magical ability to create a gleaming metaphor. He shrugged. Let him be free of the necessity of earning a living, and it would come back. Suddenly he said to himself, passionately: "It's got to come back! It must! It must!"

The vehemence of the thought startled him. It was like

some voice crying from dark and smothering depths in himself. It was a voice that had been choked for years.

Tim sauntered over to him, offered him a cigarette. He winked, bent over Frank, and whispered: "Say, those girls kinda liked us, the other night. Want to try it ag'in? They're safe, too, like I told you."

CHAPTER 36

FRANK lit another cigarette in the darkness, sat on the edge of the bed and smoked furiously. What was it Emerson had said? "Give no bounties, make equal law, secure life and property, and you need not give alms. Open the doors of opportunity to talent and virtue and they will do themselves justice, and property will not be in bad hands. In a free and just commonwealth, property rushes from the idle and imbecile to the industrious, brave and persevering."

He smiled grimly. I am industrious, he thought, I know I have bravery, and I can be persevering. Three spades with which to dig gold in a stony garden. There was something new in the world now, something ominous and suggestive of enervating influences, soft and weak. There were fools who were crying out that the stupid, the incompetent, and the craven had as much "right" to live as their betters, who possessed courage, and virtue and talent. Who gave them that right? Who were the fools who declared they had it? No man had the right to live who was not able to work and survive. The old iron adage of the Puritans came to his mind: "He who does not work shall not eat."

Frank nodded to himself. Yes. Emerson was right. The Puritans were right. He felt their rightness. But there was something missing, and it was in himself. There was a sum left out of the equation, and he knew it, and was angry again. He felt that "something" behind Emerson's somber words. Could it be that it was the same thing which Mr. Mason had said was "missing" in his writing? God-damn nonsense. Metaphysical.

He stood up and touched the switch on the wall, and light flooded his room. His thoughts paled away in the comforting glare, and he looked about his room with satisfaction. The last five years had brought a change to Linwood Avenue, in the first eight or ten blocks from the downtown section. Commercialism had caused the owners of many grand old houses to retreat towards the edges of the city. Those who had bought the abandoned houses had turned them into "private" rooming or boarding houses, and had demanded high rents for "superior accommodations." Frank's room in a house near North Street cost him ten dollars a week, with breakfast. But it was a handsome room, if small and old-fashioned. The ceilings were very high, and of molded plaster, and painted a soft old green, like the sides of a young apple. There was a faded Axminster rug on the floor, of good quality and of a reproduced Oriental pattern in dull reds, blues and greens. He looked at his furniture, and again was satisfied. They must be antiques, he thought, for his bureau was of old polished mahogany, with a rich grain, and a dimmed mirror.

He sat down in a rocker and smoked and stared before him. His gold watch, the only legacy from his father, showed that it was half-past ten. He would go out for his beer and his beef sandwich in a moment or two. In the meantime, he enjoyed his room.

Then he was uneasy. He had only another week or so of work at the Curtiss plant. Of course, he would soon secure another job, in spite of the rumors of growing unemployment now that the war had ended. He had been given notice in November, but here it was January, and he was still working. He worked well, he was intelligent and industrious. He had learned shorthand at night school, and male stenographers were in good demand. But he shrank a little from the depressing necessity of looking for another job, of fitting himself into another niche. Tim Cunningham had left in November, and had gone to "the hills." He was working with his brothers in the mountains, prospecting for oil, and apparently with significant success. "We made two hundred each last week," he had written Frank. "Why don't you come and get it, too? I reckon I must like you, to keep after you this way." His letters were marked Shortsville, Kentucky. It could not be found on the map, it must be a small country town.

Two hundred dollars in one week! That was almost as much as Frank had in the bank! He ground out his cigarette in a china dish. Two hundred dollars a week, he painfully calculated, was about eight hundred dollars a month. He calculated the sum for a year, two years, three. Why, he would be rich at the end of that time! But it would mean giving up night school. Hell, I can skip high school, he thought, and go on to college as a special student! Besides, I shall have seen the country.

He absently took out the heavy gold watch again and looked at its face. Quarter of eleven. He must go for his beer and sandwich at once, if he were to go at all. He stood up, went to the mirror, and straightened his tie. He saw his face. It was not the face of his boyhood.

He was a man now, almost six feet tall, with thin wide shoulders and long arms and legs. His suit fitted him well, and he had a fastidious air. He had been so untidy and gross when he had been a kid, he remembered. Now he cared for himself well. He reached out for the watch to return it to his pocket. It lay in his hand, and, curiously, it suddenly became heavy and pulsing, like a heart. He could not put it away. He stared down at it.

The golden smoothness of the case warmed in his hand. He heard its loud ticking. It was his father's heart, and he could feel the pulsations. Now the wild pain fanned out in him, and he clenched his teeth and bore down on it, despising himself.

The room faded from his sight. He was sitting beside his father's bed, the day before Francis had died.

His father's brief and spectacular illness had not impressed him very much. He was accustomed to his mother's whining about her health. Now, he decided, his father for once had taken the spotlight, and was sedulously playing in it. So, while he was at work, he did not think of Francis at all. Besides, it had been so long since he had given much thought to his parents.

The October day had been a yellow hard loveliness. Everything shone in that strong yellowness, was one with it, sunlight, trees, the light on passing faces, the light on the edges of brick buildings, along the curbs of the street, on the dusty windows of streetcars—everything had been plated with that brassy and metallic light. Everything, except the sky, burning and flaming overhead like an arch of deep aquamarine. It had no depths, that sky; it was a fixed arch, cunningly cut out of one enormous rounded gem, so blue that it was unreal. Frank, in the early evening, had left the Curtiss plant, and had missed a car or two, in order to see that sky and that goldenness before it all faded. And as he walked, seeing, but not feeling, enjoying, yet not participating, delighting without rapture, he remembered that it was on such an evening, while he wandered along the railroad tracks at the foot of Ferry Street, that he had seen that accident.

He had been fourteen then, and he was playing truant from school. He had had a lovely day. wandering, seeing, absorbing, dreaming. He had almost reached Ferry Street when he saw the little boy, scarcely ten, throwing a ball into the air and catching it. The little boy was shabby, and even though the day was not warm, he was barefoot. A son of a squatter on the towpath, a boy with hair as yellow and metallic as the late afternoon sun, with a face so pink and so dirty and so happy that it touched the heart to see it.

A train was coming around a slight bend, moaning like a legion of the damned as it approached the crossing. The boy was completely unaware of it as he played with his ball, and tossed it high in the air. It was a red ball, obviously new and possibly stolen. As the ball soared towards the sky, the boy leapt upward with it, eagerly, strainingly, arms flung up, small fingers spread out, bare feet and legs lifted like those of a young, flying Hermes, golden hair blown back like sharp wings. Frank could see his profile, pure and exalted, and he could sense the passionate urge to fly, to soar, with the ball, that filled the boy. He could feel, in the sensitive flesh of himself, something else as he watched the boy and the ball; he could feel the upward surging of all humanity in the boy's desire to ascend, to be weightless, to skim through the bright radiance of the air, to be done with flesh and death and ugliness and pain, to be lifted to the sun. He himself was only fourteen, yet he had felt a stab of anguish, of knowledge, and yet, of ecstasy, for that slender, impotent, but somehow glorious striving.

Again the ball was thrown up, again the boy leapt. But when the ball fell towards the earth again, a tiny globe of red, it missed the reaching hands. It fell to the ground, rolled foolishly down the slight incline to the tracks, fell between the glittering rails. The boy bounded after it. Frank, petrified, opened his mouth to cry out, but no sound came from a throat suddenly seized in iron hands. He had tried to take a running step towards the little boy, and then he was held there as if his whole body had turned to ice. He tried to close his eyes, but they were held open, inexorably, forced to see what they must see. It all happened in an instant or two. The engineer of the train put on the brakes desperately. There was a horrible squealing and groaning in the air, a grinding thunder, the scream of a whistle. But there was nothing that could be done. Like a giant monster sliding on its haunches in the dust, the engine by its very momentum was forced upon the stooping child. It was then that Frank could close his eyes.

He could never remember the next few minutes. He knew only that when he opened his swimming eyes a small crowd had gathered out of nowhere, shabby men in overalls and sweaters, crying women wringing their hands, curious, gaping children. There the train stood, beaded along the sides with the heads that craned from open windows. The engineer was standing on the tracks, sobbing loudly, harshly, while his fireman tried to console him. Male passengers were beginning to swing themselves off the train, and came running. The air was filled with exclamations, cries, calls, curses, so that it sounded like a jungle. And then a woman screamed, a fat, untidy little woman in a gingham dress, a woman who had run from a squatter's hut nearby. Frank could see the spirals of her black hair, her gypsy hair, her blank white face, as she joined the engineer and the morbid crowd which had gathered at the steaming head of the engine. He heard her scream, over and over, mad, demented, breathless screams. But the thing over which she was screaming, that bright soaring thing, made no sound at all, would never make it again.

His legs were trembling; he could feel trickles of sweat dripping down them. He turned away, wanting to run, to run forever, his inner vision imprinted with the memory of the ascending child against a blazing blue sky. But now the child did not return to earth. He soared away, was lost in the sun.

Frank's foot touched something, which rolled. In some inexplicable way, the ball had been tossed back onto the path, unhurt, red and untouched. He picked it up. It was as warm as flesh, as red as blood. It was innocent. It was printed all over with the small fingers of the boy who had held it, who would never toss it again. It palpitated in Frank's hand, burned into his skin. He carried it down to the Canal; he threw it into the water. He watched it bob a moment or two, then, filling up with water through an unsuspected hole, it slowly sank.

He did not know then that it was pure and uncorrupted compassion which he had felt. But he knew it on this October day, as he walked home through the golden light of the autumn evening. What a silly damned kid he had been! What a crazy kid! Mooning like a maudlin idiot over the death of a towpath brat, who, if he had lived, would have been a drunken, thieving sort like his squatter father, would, most probably, have ended his days in a prison or on the gallows. But he had stood there, watching the ball sink, weeping his idiotic, sentimental tears. The vision of the ascending child, pure and clean and eager against the sky, was blurred, was dimmed, was all but forgotten.

He said to himself this evening in October as he waited on the next corner for a streetcar: I had such imbecile heroic thoughts in those days when I was a kid! I could puke when I think of them. I was going to save the world; I was going to write idiot stories of such as that towpath brat. I was going to bring pity and love and joy and poetry to all other men! The outrageous, the impudent effrontery of me!

The mirror of his mind became as blurred as the mirror over his mother's sink, steamed over, marked, blotched, a hard sheet that reflected only a shadow in its depths.

He was remembering it all now, as he stood in his room on Linwood Avenue, with his dead father's gold watch in his hand. That October day so long ago, and the day his father had died, were inextricably fusing together, becoming one. Just as he had held the boy's ball, before throwing it into the Canal, he now held his father's watch, and just as he had imagined that the ball had pulsed, so, for a brief moment only, he imagined that the watch was pulsing.

His fingers became warm under the metal. He made a gesture to thrust it back into his pocket. But something held his hand, and he could only stand there and look down at the watch. Why—and now he was amused—it was almost the ball again, the ball of a nameless child who had aspired, had tried to ascend, had been stricken down, and had died!

He was back again in that "front room" on Albany Street, the bedroom of his parents.

The night had turned cool. The little gas-heater, with its "doughnuts" of smoldering clay, was burning high, throwing out a pleasant heat over the polished but worn brown linoleum. Maybelle's patched and darned "lace" curtains were snowy ripples against the drawn green blinds, stiff as paper, and as white. A settee of convoluted mahogany with a poison-green plush back seat, and a chair to match, had been added to the original bare furniture. Maybelle had bought this "set" in a secondhand store, and vigorous applications of "wash-leather" and rubbing cloths kept the wood in a brilliant shine. The brass bed was polished, too, until its narrow columns and twisted top resembled pure gold. In this bed, with its honeycomb white spread, lay Francis, high on plump white pillows (Maybelle's cherished pillows from England). The gaslight overhead had been turned low. Frank sat with his father while his mother slept. He was to awaken her at one o'clock in the morning, so that he might go to bed and she might resume her vigil until dawn. For now they knew that Francis could not live.

The light was too dim to furnish illumination for reading, so Frank was compelled to sit near the little gas-heater in a stiff rocking chair, from which point he faced the bed and could watch his father. He rocked restlessly, and the floor squeaked under the chair; the gaslight above hissed; the heater hissed and crackled. The October wind fumbled at the windows, and the curtains moved uneasily over the blinds. Francis seemed to be sleeping, though his breath was uneven and raucous, and occasionally he coughed dully.

It was a death's-head, there on the pillow, gray, hollow, splashed with heavy shadow, wizened and ghastly. The bald head, the tight, bulging forehead, were enormous over the dwindled features; they were whitish stone over a tiny countenance, which, as it sank towards dissolution, bore a ghostly resemblance to primordial and simian ancestry. Now, as humanity drained from it, preparing to depart forever, the remote and lost spectre of man's ancient beginnings manifested itself more and more clearly. Frank thought: Death is an ugly thing, but it is somehow mysterious. He was intrigued by the triumph of the forehead and the dome of the skull—the forehead and skull of man's ascent, which were not to be vanquished and dissolved, but remained inviolate and enduring long after the simian features below them were melted into clay. Like a monument, like a victorious tomb, the dome of the skull, full, polished, invulnerable, persisted through the ages, mute witness to the strange creature who had inhabited it, and it had grown steadily from the small ape head turned incuriously to the trees of the jungle, to that of a man dreaming of cities and conquered plains.

The gaslight flickered, the gas-heater hissed. Frank sat still in his chair, and for a few exultant moments he felt the flame and the passion of his boyhood, the exaltation, the ecstasy, the wonderment and awe. And he thought to himself, with what joy he did not realize: "I can still feel!"

And then he bore down on this imbecility, and thought of his school, and his ambitions, and of money, and flight forever from this room and all it implied. He looked about him and hated and rejected, and the vision passed.

Francis coughed heavily, devastatingly, and opened his sinking eyes. He saw his son on his chair, staring grimly into space. He saw his son's eyes, narrowed, hard, seeing nothing of the room or of his father, but something in himself. And

Francis saw something beyond this, too. He saw his son, this young man sitting there, his long legs crossed, his white collar stiff and shining, his tie knotted fastidiously, his strong slender hands gripping the arms of the chair. Something made Francis cry out: "Sonny!"

That nickname, so long abandoned, gave Frank something of a shock. He stared at his father, and he heard that nickname echoing to him from an earlier and kindlier childhood, from the green, daisy-embroidered fields of England, from the petrol-smelling whirl of the "dobby-horses," from the pantomime and the Christmas hearth of home. He heard that word and caught the freshness of hawthorn and water-cress, tasted peppermint sticks and Shrove Tuesday pancakes and heard the laughter of children eating potato chips while rain streamed outside. He heard it, and saw a young Francis holding his hand, as they walked through sunny Reddish Vale, while he listened to the story of Cinderella as his father related it.

"Sonny!" cried Francis, and Frank felt the warm kiss of his young mother, and heard his father's stiff awkward playing on the "fiddle." He saw his father's pathetic high boots on the deck of the "Baltic," saw the absurd cap and the thick black mustaches, the cane and the flash of alert blue eyes. And in that one instant Frank knew a passionate bitterness and bewilderment, and he tried to remember when his father had stopped calling him by that nickname. He could not remember, but the dolorousness of his boyhood had begun then, and the drab ugliness and despair of the life in America.

Trembling, he got up and went to his father's bed. His polished shoes clacked on the linoleum. He stood by the bed and looked down at Francis. Francis was gazing up at him urgently, his sunken mouth working under the gray mustaches. What was he trying to say? Frank bent over the bed. The mouth worked, but nothing came from it but a choked mumble, infinitely terrible in its incoherence.

Francis moved his right hand blindly on the counterpane. Something in Frank made him want to take that hand; he knew his father wished it. But he could not do it. He could not do it because something like a hard iron paralysis held him back voluntarily. Francis' hand became still. He looked at his son, and all his departing soul stared brilliantly from his eyes, as if he knew.

He whimpered. He whispered: "My fiddle."

"Yes, Pa." Frank's voice was cold and quiet. "It's in the

cellar. Do you want it?" He wants his fiddle, and he is dying! Something maudlin like this was to be expected, I suppose. He can't even die without making a gesture to attract sympathy!

There is no sympathy in me, he thought bitterly. There is no compassion for this ignoble life. There is only bitterness in remembering all those years. I can't forget.

And Francis lay there, watching, very still, silent, understanding. Desolation stood in his mute eyes, and terror, and hopelessness. The gaslight lay on a face of acute awareness never revealed in earlier and healthier life. It was the flaring up of the flame of a soul, expanding, shaking its damp wings in preparation for flight from this outworn chrysalis.

What words were there for this understanding, this awareness? They were not recorded in the language of any race. They were beyond words.

His fiddle, thought Frank. What would he want with his fiddle? He said: "Do you want me to bring your fiddle to you?"

Francis, not removing his urgent eyes from his son's face, moved his head faintly on the pillow in negation. He is trying to tell me something, thought Frank. Then he smiled contemptuously to himself at this sentimentality. What could this small mean creature tell him? What could he say?

He could not remember that Francis' eyes had ever been so brilliant, so blue, as this. Fever, of course. Fever and fear. Fear had always been his father's familiar. Frank drew a deep, slow breath, in his disgust.

He said, aloud, coldly: "Do you feel all right, Pa?"

Francis appeared not to have heard. How his eyes, dilated, enormous, stared from their caves of shadow! His lips were moving silently with what they could not say. Again his hand twitched, hopelessly, tragically. Frank saw this and averted his head.

"Do you want Ma?" he asked. He glanced at the alarm clock, which was ticking loudly on the square oak table near the window. It was almost one o'clock. It was time for him to awaken his mother and go to bed.

He watched his father. Then, after a long moment, Francis nodded. Frank went to the door. Francis watched him go. The blue burning of his eyes followed his son. The door opened, closed, behind the youth. But Francis' eyes continued to burn at its imperviousness, as if something in him had passed through it, following.

Maybelle, swollen, blotched and disheveled, lifted herself

from Frank's bed, groaning. She had covered herself neatly with his counterpane. Sighing, half-sobbing with exhaustion, she pushed back her graying mass of hair, and blinked in the sudden gaslight which her son had turned on. Her brown eyes were dead, lusterless. She asked: "How is he?"

"Awake. Better than last night."

Frank took off his coat and vest, hung them up on the nails on the wall, which served as his wardrobe. His mother began to cry. "That this should come to us!" she wept, wiping her nose and face on her rumpled apron. "Why did it happen?"

Frank removed his tie. He examined his collar critically, holding it to the light. He said indifferently: "Why shouldn't it happen to us? It happens every day."

Maybelle blew her nose. "No sympathy," she moaned. "You haven't any feelings, Frank. How can you be so calm when your pa is dying?"

He looked at her with a swift curiosity. All during his illness, Francis had bewailed the shrinking of his savings. Maybelle had not spoken, not once, of money. In a softer voice, Frank said: "Maybe he isn't dying. He seems much better tonight."

Holding her aching back, Maybelle went out of the room. Frank closed the door. He yawned. He went to bed. He lay there, then, not falling into his usual quick sleep. His father's eyes continued to stare at him, burning blue and unwinking in the darkness.

The October dawn was shattered by Maybelle's screams and cries, and even before Frank ran out into the front room he knew his father was dead.

He could put the watch back into his pocket now. It lay there like a weight. He had not remembered that it was so heavy. Suddenly he wanted to be rid of it. I'll sell it Saturday afternoon, he thought. I'll buy another one with the money.

He went briskly downstairs. He must hurry before the tavern closed. There were rumors of Prohibition. That was nonsense of course. Not to have a glass of beer when one wanted it! His father had been wrong: the Yankees weren't that damned stupid. He thought a moment, then added to himself: We aren't that stupid.

Linwood Avenue was infinitely quiet, dark and deserted, as Frank closed the door behind him. Scabs of black ice lingered on the shovelled sidewalks and blinked in the infrequent light of scattered electric lamps. Huge mounds of snow on the lawns and at the curbs were dirtily pitted and pock-marked.

The great melancholy houses on each side of the street appeared to have retreated even farther back on their snowy grounds; piazzas, jutting forward from the red-brick fronts, were like caves of shadow. An automobile went by with a melancholy sounding of a horn. A great white moon, hung over one roof, silvered the slates. The bare trees cracked in the silence, for the cold had strengthened during the last hours. Frank heard the rumbling of a streetcar as it swayed along on Main Street. He went up North Street to the tavern on Main.

The tavern, too, was deserted except for a yawning bartender preparing to close up, and one customer leaning heavily on the bar. One large globe of light hung from the ceiling. The place smelt of beer and stale sweat. Frank stood at the bar and ordered his beer. The bartender knew him. "A minute more, Frank, and you'da found us closed," he said. "Cold out, ain't it?" Frank nodded, drank his beer. The bartender rested his elbows on the bar, sighed wearily, ruffled up a fringe of hair around his bald head. He was a fat and shapeless man, of middle-age, with tiny kind eyes and a flabby face. He regarded Frank with sleepy friendliness.

"Couple of chippies in here 'bout an hour ago," the bartender confided. "Lookin' for business. Chased 'em out fast. Have to watch yourself, these days, with the Nosy Parkers tryin' to put over Prohibition. Well, the people won't stand for it, that's all. Funny thing about one of them girls," he resumed, in a livelier tone. "Kid only about sixteen, or maybe fifteen. One of them war generations, like the papers call 'em. Pretty as a pitcher, too, with her skirt hiked up almost to her knees, and a big Merry Widow hat. No, it was somethin' like a toadstool, I guess." He grinned. "Well. That kid walked in here with the older girl, swayin' her hips and chewin' gum, and actin' bold. Older girl wasn't no good; you could see that, but there was somethin' about the kid that kinda hurt me. Got one the same age myself. I said: 'Whyn't you go home, honey, and wash that paint off your mug, and go to school?' Know what she said: 'Ain't got no damned home, and Ma's out hustlin', herself.' " The bartender shook his head. " 'Brave new world,' that's what they said, in the papers, after the war. 'Brave new world' for who? There wasn't any 'brave new world' after the Spanish-American War, but I guess people just keep on foolin' themselves all the time. Don't seem to get it that if they want that kinda world they gotta make it, with their own hands, not wait for someone else to do it, sittin' back on their hams and just waitin'."

The bartender sighed again, and again ruffled up his fringe of hair. He said: "They blame the saloons. They blame the war. They blame everybody. But there ain't a goddam mother's son of 'em who looks in the mirror when he shaves, and says to hisself: "There's what's keepin' that 'brave new world' from comin'. There's the son of a bitch that's gummin' up the works. Get busy, brother, and throw your weight in. No, they don't do that." The bartender shook his head sadly.

"What are you doing, Tom, about that 'brave new world'?" asked Frank idly.

The bartender grinned sheepishly, rubbed his chin. "Me? I listen to their sad stories. A man's gotta have somebody to talk to, don't he, and let me tell you, kid, that's hard work, listenin'. Harder'n you think, maybe. I give 'em advice, when I ain't too rushed. I tell the gripers to go home to their wives, and play with the kids. I tell the veterans to stop whinin' about the Government not doin' right by 'em. I tell the boys to stop lookin' for soft snaps, and get down to hard work. I tell the silk-shirt fellers not to cash their Liberty Bonds, and to stop buyin' big cigars, and talkin' big about just changin' a twenty-dollar bill. I tell 'em all that hard times is on their way agin, right around the corner, and they'll be grubbin' for pennies instead of tossin' around dollars like they was big guys. I tell 'em the easy jobs are on the way out, and that there ain't anythin' less permanent than 'permanent prosperity.' Everybody's got to get down to hard work—that's what I tell every bastard that comes in."

"Do they listen?"

Tom considered ponderously, lifted himself from the bar, and scratched his head, pursing up his fat lips. "Well, sir, some do, some don't."

Frank smiled amiably and said: "Looks as if you are 'a force for good,' Tom." He paid for his beer, finished his beef sandwich. He heard the ring of the cash register.

Tom said, his back to Frank: "There's some that thinks the workin' fellers haven't any brains. They're just mules, they think. But you'd be surprised how much they think. The whole American people."

Frank's eyes narrowed as they stared at the fat, sweat-stained back of the bartender. He got up abruptly, said good-night, and walked out. The bartender watched him go, turning slowly on his heel. He looked at the last occupant of the bar, winked, and sighed. "That's a young feller that thinks he's got all the answers. He'll wake up some day. I hope. He could be a regular guy, if he'd just let hisself go. Hope he won't wake up too late. Didja notice his mug? Like it had a false-face on? Betcha his own is better, if he'd only show it."

CHAPTER 37

FRANK ate breakfast at eight-fifteen in Miss Woods' dining room. He looked forward to this meal, for then those who were least important had finished and gone, and the more "desirable" ate leisurely, or drank a last cup of good coffee. But Sunday mornings were the best of all.

Miss Woods' dining room was very pleasant, with old pan-elled walls of rich walnut. It was true that little sunlight entered here, for the red-brick houses on Linwood Avenue had been built in a dreary spirit by uninspired architects afraid of sun. Miss Woods' dining room was at the side, behind one of the parlors; its dimness gave it an aristocratic air, which was further enhanced by tall narrow windows discreetly clouded with lace curtains and thick velvet draperies of brown brocade to match the walnut panelling. The massive sideboard, with its mirror and pillared ends, the huge round table, glossy as heavy glass, and as ponderous, the old chairs upholstered in black leather, the serving table, with its bottom mirror and silver candlesticks, had belonged to Miss Woods' mother, and ugly and massive though it all was, the furniture was her great pride.

On winter mornings, the dining room was especially pleasant. An arrangement of electric candles, quite cleverly installed in the ancient gas chandelier above the table, shone down on pure white damask, bright silver, excellent Haviland china of a pale cream color with a border of tiny roses, and the coffee urn. Sometimes, on Sunday mornings, Miss Woods would light a log or two on the black marble hearth at the far end of the room, and the fire, combined with the rich smell of coffee, the crisp smoky sweetness of well-grilled bacon, the hunger-inspiring scent of hot rolls, made of the dining room the most welcome and beloved haven in the house.

Frank, as he came downstairs at nine o'clock this Sunday morning in early March, was pleased to see that Miss Woods had lighted the fire. He knew it was very cold outside, prob-

ably far below zero, for his windows had been blind with
white frost, and he had had to blow his warm breath against
it for quite some time before his finger could rub a hole in
it for a sight of the street. In the morning, the bedrooms were
somewhat chilly, and it was agreeable to see the fire and
smell the coffee and the bacon and the rolls. All the guests
were downstairs, waiting for the first course, prunes in cream.
The noise of the wind, hurled violently against the windows,
the shrieking in the chimneys, had awakened all of them unusually early this morning.

Miss Woods sat at the head of the table, a very stout little
woman, almost as broad as she was tall. But this grossness of
flesh, this expanse of breast and shoulder, this massiveness
of short arm, had the most peculiar effect of adding to her
innate aristocracy rather than diminishing it. She wore the
black silk of a widow, though she had never been a bride,
and as she was seventy-two years old and old-fashioned and
"proud of it," she never appeared without a wisp of white
lace on the top of her brilliantly white hair. Her small pudgy
features, her little gray eyes set in rolls of fat, ought to have
given a coarseness to her broad, thick face, but again, they
oddly gave refinement. There was an air about Miss Woods,
a solidity, a majestic zest, an intelligence and good sense,
which imparted to her some queenly attribute. Her speech
was pure and excellently phrased, for she was a woman of
considerable education; she enjoyed a joke and loved subtlety.
She was vain of her little white hands, which even in the
mornings were heavily ringed.

It was inexplicable how those fat little features of hers
could express, with mobility, the changes, the sorties and
dashes and summings-up of a very lively and astute mind.
Miss Woods had no illusions about the excellences of human
nature. But she was no cynic; she was too old for cynicism.
Nor was she comfortable and complacent about her fellow-
beings; she did not, in the least, think "the best of them."
She merely accepted them, with imperturbable good humor,
a little dryness of private comment, a quizzical if kindly
indifference. No one expected sympathy from Miss Woods;
she was no one's confidante. It was not that she was bored
by anyone; she was too interested in life for that, and too
intelligent. But she had evolved some philosophy of her own,
insisted upon preserving her own privacy, and discreetly demanded that others preserve theirs. She did not wish to be involved. To many of her guests, she must have appeared a
hard and insensible woman, even selfish, in her refusal to be

drawn into the maelstrom of another's troubles and griefs and anguishes, in her demand that life in her house take on the atmosphere of permanent pleasantness and agreeable calm and tranquillity.

At her right—and this was strange—sat a most unattractive young man. Miss Woods preferred comely people; they did not snare any unwary interest on her part. Moreover, they were pleasant to look upon, and she liked people who did not present a disagreeable aspect to her discriminating eye. But as Miss Woods never explained, or complained, or attempted to justify or rationalize her actions, no one dared question why Irving Schultz sat at her right hand and was the recipient of more sincere kindliness and interest than she had ever extended to any other guest. She had even gone to the length of giving a thumb-nail sketch of the young man to the other guests, after his first appearance at her table, and for the first time, and inexplicably, the others were astonished to hear the faintest echo of emotion in her well-bred voice.

Irving Schultz was the son of Alsatian immigrants. This much Miss Woods imparted. He had once lived on Plymouth Avenue, near Albany Street, so that though Frank was well acquainted with his background he was convinced that Miss Woods was not, and he derived a cynical amusement in wondering just what her reactions might be if she really knew. (Miss Woods knew.)

Irving's parentage was somewhat ambiguous. He never knew whether his father was Adrian Schultz, or his ostensible uncle, Rudolph Schultz, Adrian's brother. The family of father, uncle and rollicking wife and eight children had lived on Plymouth Avenue in a horrible shell of a house, next to a barn which contained Adrian's two draft horses. For Adrian was a teamster, working at odd intervals for local trucking concerns, while his horses, if not his children, waxed fat. Even the neighbors in that poorish neighborhood, none too particular themselves about the outer appearance of their raddled houses, or the condition of the interiors, found the Schultzes intolerable. It had been at least twenty years since the clapboards of the Schultz house had been painted, and the shingles of the broken roof curled in summer suns and wilted like cardboard under winter snows and rains. At least one third of the windows had holes stuffed with wads of newspaper and old rags. What few curtains there were were so filthy, so torn, so ragged and so limp, that they were scarcely more than rags themselves. The verandah in front was so full of broken gaps, so tilted, scarred, upheaved and shattered that negotiating it successfully in the dark ranked as a major triumph. Only Adrian and Rudolph, in their drunken interludes, could miraculously wind their way safely to the door, which sagged on its hinges. The grounds, front and back, were heaped with ash barrels, with soggy boxes and crates, with garbage of every description, with mounds of trash, sticks, stones and miscellany, including heaps of empty beer-bottles which apparently constituted the main liquid refreshment of the Schultzes. A dreadful stink hung over the grounds and the house, so that neighbors made an ostentatious point of holding their noses when passing, especially when Mrs. Schultz had contrived to find a safe spot on the verandah upon which to sit in a broken rocking-chair. When they did this, which was almost always, Mrs. Schultz, her arms comfortably folded across her breast, would lean forward to make a robust and obscene noise, to thumb her nose in an immemorial gesture, or to burst into strong and hearty laughter prefaced by a colorful oath.

No neighbor's child played with the Schultz children, for the latter were invariably filthy, barefoot from early spring to late fall, and ragged. They swarmed like squirrels over house and grounds, sometimes appearing on the precarious roof of the verandah, the younger children squatting there unconcernedly to give passersby a view which polite society had decreed must not be presented to the public eye. The children swore richly, picked their noses on the sidewalks, played dice on the verandah, fought, screamed, roared, yelled, in a constant bedlam, from dawn until almost midnight. As no screens ever guarded the windows, flies, swarms of them, came and went at their leisure. The interior of the house boasted no rugs at all, and was at least as foul as the exterior. The children slept anywhere, at any hour they desired, like pigs in a pen. There was no such thing as "a proper meal," as Maybelle called it.

To enliven these proceedings, Mrs. Schultz, Adrian and Rudolph generally chose Saturday night for a real set-to, accompanied by screams, threats, curses and blows. Adrian could be clearly heard roaring a demand at his wife, accompanied by the threat of death, that she sort out whose children were whose. Mrs. Schultz, a stout, short, very dark little woman of forty, and a lady of spirit, would advise him where he could go, and in a hurry. Once, when the demand became particularly urgent, she was heard to reply, in a very carrying voice: "How the hell should I know, you——bastard?"

Irving was the eldest of this ambiguous family, and was about a year or two older than Frank. Like all the other children, he was distinctly unattractive, being excessively tall, thin, stooping, dark, and possessed of his mother's large beaklike nose, little black eyes, swarthy skin, long pointed chin and thin mouth. Moreover, he had an untidy mass of black curling hair, almost Negroid in its crinkles. But Irving had always been the sole quiet member of the household, a silent, uncommunicative boy who unaccountably was brilliant at school whereas his brothers and sisters were hardly above the idiot class. He had always been one or two grades ahead of Frank Clair, but rumors of his exploits in mathematics, English and grammar had reached above and below him on the scholastic ladder. He had passed through Miss Bendy's hands, and she had given him all the warm encouragement at her disposal.

He had gone to high school, oblivious to the sneers of the other children at his patched torn clothing, his grimy hands, his Negroid hair, his enormous nose, his rags of handkerchiefs. Unlike Frank, he apparently was completely indifferent to the persecutions he suffered. He never fought, never spoke to his classmates, and his voice was heard only when he got up to recite, which he did with aplomb, gentlemanly poise, and eloquence. Not even Miss Bendy ever knew what he thought.

He had contrived to go to high school by the simple expedient of working all night in a local box factory. Upon graduation, he passed with the incredible average of one hundred percent in all his studies, and won a scholarship to the University of Bison.

He had, by then, advanced to the position of foreman in the box factory. By the time the war had broken out, wages had gone up, and Irving continued on the shift from midnight till eight in the morning. He went directly to the University, arrived home at four, slept for a few hours, rose and did his lessons, got himself a haphazard meal at one of the tables, and went off to work. By this time Frank had lost sight of him completely, and as Mrs. Schultz, Adrian and Rudolph had reached the comparative tranquillity of late middle-age, the Schultzes were no longer the bright and refreshing scandal they had been in the earlier years. Then in 1917 Mrs. Schultz had died of delirium tremens, and the family had vanished.

It was a shock to Frank to find Irving at the select home of Miss Woods. No sign of recognition, however, passed between them. Irving had nodded courteously, had continued to eat, for the two were introduced at the first breakfast Frank had enjoyed in the pleasant dining room.

Later, Frank was informed that Irving was in his third year at the University of Bison, that he was the most respected worker at the box factory, at a salary of fifty dollars a week, and that he rented the cheapest and least desirable room at the top of the house. Irving, said Miss Woods, was going to be a physician, a research worker in mental diseases, a "specialist"!

She displayed her favoritism only by allowing him to sit at her right hand, and by giving him, on occasion, a warm and almost maternal glance. She never asked him a question, understanding and respecting his queer dark silences, and was content, when she addressed a remark exclusively to him, with a quiet nod or a faint smile in return.

If she knew what he really was! Frank would think, with contempt.

Nothing passed between the two young men but the briefest of silent nods. Eventually, Frank ignored Irving's existence. It was Frank's firm opinion that sooner or later Irving would end up, as his parents had ended, in the gutter. Water could never rise higher than its source, as Francis had said. The sons of thieves, drunkards and degenerates must become thieves, drunkards and degenerates in their turn. Irving's pretensions were the grossest impudence.

Frank found it pleasanter to contemplate the other roomers.

There was the dried up little bachelor, Mr. Roberts, head bookkeeper at the Bethlehem Steel, and reputed to be quite "well-off." He was in his late sixties, a quiet, courteous old gentleman, with extremely old-fashioned ways, very polite, dimly friendly, and a great reader of Walter Pater, Aristotle, Locke, Berkeley and Hume. He and Miss Woods often engaged in edifying and spirited discussions of these worthies.

There was Miss Ethelinda Shaw, principal of a high school, a tall, lanky and very stylish woman of forty, with very advanced opinions and a very dogmatic manner. She was a suffragette, and she and Miss Woods, who was, astonishingly, also a suffragette, were almost intimate. Miss Shaw reminded Frank of a heron, and he disliked her very much, especially when she would turn her shrewd and scrutinizing schoolteacher eyes upon him. Then he felt like a truant, a misfit, and though he wore good clothing, Miss Shaw made him feel that he was attired in the scanty and patched garments of his boyhood.

Miss Shaw had only to turn the blank blaze of her spectacles upon him for him to wince. He was certain that she saw through him, which she did. He did not know that she was sorry for him.

Her assistant principal, a pale, buff-colored, shapeless little woman of forty-five, a Miss Ida Stengel, was also a roomer at Miss Woods'. In fact, she and Miss Shaw shared a large double-room, behind the star-boarder's room. Miss Stengel parroted all Miss Shaw's vigorous opinions, so that everyone considered her very tiresome with her unchanging, eager smile, and her fixed gaze at her superior. She even tried to affect Miss Shaw's smart clothing, with disastrous results, and Miss Shaw had only to say contemptuously: "Why, Ida!" to have the fat little woman shrink like a snail receiving a bath of vinegar.

Then there were the Crimmonses, husband and wife.

Frank might despise Irving, and ignore him, overlook Mr. Roberts as a tedious pedantic old fool, smile ingratiatingly at the formidable Miss Shaw and her companion and feel awkward in their presence. But he really feared none of them, with the exception of Mr. and Mrs. Crimmons. He was safe from all the others. But he was not safe from Mrs. Amy Crimmons.

For Mrs. Crimmons was one of the hated "knowing ones." She had "found out" about Frank Clair.

There was always that one, that two, or that three, wherever Frank went, who had only to look at him to "find him out." To find him out, in spite of that bitterly achieved look of normality, that specious, that lying, that false-face of a look! They could find him out, despite the carefully arranged features which—almost always—expressed the blankness and emptiness of the prevailing fashion, the vacant nothingness, the amiability or reticence or blandness or politeness. The commonness of the undistinguished, the faceless face of the multitudes of men who filled the earth. Yes, they would find him out, these sharp-eyed knowing ones, penetrate beneath his disguise, his eager pretense that he was one of them, was like them in speech, in dress, in averageness. They seemed to know, almost at once, that it was only a disguise, only something assumed in order that he might be accepted by them, admired by them in a brotherly spirit. And they knew, all the time, in some animal-like and instinctual way, that he was afraid of them and all that they were, and that he believed, shamefully, that they were superior to him, and had power to hurt him.

They were delighted when he truckled to them, when he sought to appease them, when he assumed their accents, their mannerisms. They had conquered the visible "difference" of him. And they rejected him always.

They were so sharp, these "normal" knowing ones. They were so clever, these parasites on the vines of life, these smug beetles in the heart of the living rose, these blighting lichens on the leaf, these strangling mosses on the trees. They were not harmless and ox-like, amiable and good-natured, as were their more stupid brothers and sisters. They were a potential danger to the world, for they had all the words of virtue, all the gestures of rectitude, the smooth plump cheeks of the self-indulged and the self-loving, the tight little smiles of the haters of men, the careful manners of the cruel, the tact and the superior phrases of the devourers, the serenity of the malevolent.

Even when Frank tried to discuss baseball games, football games, Gloria Swanson, Mary Pickford and Francis X. Bushman of the screen, or to express the conventional opinion about President Wilson, the knowing ones listened with vicious, half-smiling intentness, and then exchanged glances. They knew he lied, that he dissembled, and that his remarks, clothed as they were in the adjective-less, sterile speech of the familiar and accepted, were an assumed language through which he was attempting to reach and please them, and when he suffered shame at his conversation—cleansing, all-saving shame—he thought it was merely detestation of himself, that he had failed to reach and to please.

He never knew why Miss Woods watched him with curious sternness while he spoke to Mr. and Mrs. Crimmons, or why she answered him so curtly when he turned to her. He thought that it was because Miss Woods had found him out, too. But why did she then turn to Irving Schultz, who never tried to appease or to be accepted or to chatter in accepted manner, and smile at him so tenderly, and as if with relief?

Frank found these knowing ones to be female, more often than male. More often than not, they were women of low birth and inferior breeding, of lower middle-class heritage. However it is, men of a better class often married these well-bathed, these talcum-perfumed, these daintily apparelled vulgarians, these creatures who had a profound tenderness for themselves.

They even had countenances in common, these harpies, or,

at the least, identical facial expressions. Their skins were fresh; their hair shining, their chins childlike. Most of them had round faces, comfortable and lightly powdered, with little plump pursy mouths—the mouths of the eaters of great quantities of food. They usually had fat little snub noses, tiny, non-descript eyes glinting cunningly behind rimless glasses with gold nose-pieces. Their clothing was dowdy, if excellent; they liked frou-frou of lace foaming over fat bosoms, though sometimes they affected a severity of dress. Their hands were dimpled, with sharp-nailed little fingers, exquisitely clean and rosily polished by vigorous buffers. They were complacent and well-satisfied, ate daintily, enormously, and with much delicate care.

To Frank, they represented his first social step out of the pit of the poverty-stricken, the ignorant, the despicable and the hopeless, the stupid, with their soiled workmen's hands. They were his betters, from whom he craved acceptance. So it was that he catered to Mrs. Bennett Crimmons and to her husband, and wistfully prayed to become intimate with them.

Mr. Bennett Crimmons was a semi-prosperous supplier of office equipment to retail outlets. As dear Amy did not care for hotels, and he had known old Miss Woods from his earlier permanent residence in Bison, he and his wife usually stopped with her for the two or three months a year when he was in the city. These two were the only guests who ate all three meals with the elderly spinster. She, apparently, accepted them without mental reservations. They occupied the large front bedroom, nicely furnished, and as Mrs. Crimmons always brought with her a few pieces of good bric-a-brac, some heavily embroidered plump cushions, and some photographs of her two uncomely daughters and the latter's flat-faced children, not to mention a painted Japanese box holding a constant supply of bon-bons or little cakes, the room literally became theirs for the length of their stay. Mrs. Crimmons dominated her short stout husband, with his fringe of blond hair, his glasses like her own, his almost identical physical characteristics, his same atmosphere of frequent baths and talcum powder and passionate attention to dress and to food. He called her "Mother." She called him "Daddy."

But there was something about Mr. Crimmons, tenuous and uncertain though it was, that set him apart from the upholstered monster who was his proper and meticulous wife. He saw Frank as a well-dressed and quiet young man with a prepossessing face and good hands, well-spoken and polite. But then, he was a rather stupid man, and did not understand, immediately, that Frank wore a false-face, and that he was utterly impossible and suspect.

Frank no longer entered a room with the intent penetrating stare of his childhood, for, though he did not yet know it, he had lost the capacity for wonder and the intense interest in all things which had once made of the world a place of excitement and magic. He had lost all that; he had retained only his instinctive shrinking. So, when he entered the dining room this wild Sunday morning, he smiled tentatively and politely, and did not look with directness at anyone. But he had not entirely lost his acute sensitivity of perception, so that the glances turned upon him seemed to scrape some raw surface of his spirit. Without appearing to do so, he saw the dim vague smile of Mr. Roberts, to whom everyone was only a thin shadow, the swift, schoolteacherish blaze of Miss Shaw's glasses, the mild empty stare of Miss Stengel, the bent, bemused head of Irving Schultz, Miss Woods' bright cool nod, and Mr. Crimmons' affable smirk. He saw Mrs. Crimmons' elegant bridling, the stately inclination of her head, the polite lifting of the corners of her fat persimmon of a mouth. He saw Mrs. Crimmons more acutely than he saw anyone else. He sat at her left hand, and he took his place with a slight and awkward stumbling.

"Terrible day, isn't it?" he asked, through the old familiar stiffness of his throat. Everyone agreed. Mrs. Crimmons, daintily and sadistically dissecting her prunes, said nothing. Out of the corner of his eye, Frank could see with what cruel relish (as if the prunes could feel) she delicately tore out the hard bowels of the fruit and pushed them aside. When she pushed the dark flabby flesh into her mouth, he felt a momentary sickness and disgust. More than hearing it, he could sense the soft smacking of her lips, the rich enjoyment of her palate. He looked at the prunes in his own dish, and was revolted by them. But he ate them carefully. He could smell Mrs. Crimmons' talcum, her skin perfumed with Cashmere Bouquet soap. Something moved in him, which he could not recognize as honest hatred. He thought it resentment because Mrs. Crimmons patronizingly ignored him, as was her custom except when he addressed himself directly to her.

Mr. Roberts had been arguing sedately with Miss Woods about Darwin and Huxley. He had been claiming gently that Mr. Huxley's defense of Darwin had been in the nature of irony and satire and not truly sincere. Miss Woods had been defending Huxley from this craven calumny. They spoke as if both these eminent scholars and gentlemen were alive, as if the ancient argument were still current in the newspapers of the world.

Frank listened, as he awaited his cereal. Only recently, Mr. Mason, his teacher, had introduced him to both Darwin and Huxley, and it was with the freshness of discovery that he listened to the amiable discussion going on exclusively between Miss Woods and Mr. Roberts. He said, as Miss Woods paused to pour coffee: "I think you are right, Miss Woods. Huxley was sincere in his defense of Darwin. I've never heard that he was sarcastic." He paused. Miss Woods gave him a smile, as if she approved, not so much his words, but something else in himself. "Scientists," added Frank, "are usually without humor or even satire. They defend or they attack without lightness of any kind."

"Yes," said Miss Woods. She gave him his coffee with a curious glint in her eyes, as if she had caught a new glimpse of him. Frank, delighted at her kindness, took the coffee with some emotion. He did not see that Irving Schultz had lifted his dreaming head and was gazing at him intently.

Mrs. Crimmons laughed with dainty amusement. Miss Woods favored her with an inquiring glance. "Oh, please excuse me, Pollie," said Mrs. Crimmons, with some malicious meaning in her affected voice. "I'm not laughing at you, truly. But it does seem so—so—"

"Irrelevant," suggested Miss Woods, who was very subtle, and who now assumed a bland expression.

Mrs. Crimmons coughed in an aristocratic way. "Yes. Ir—elvunt," she agreed, without the slightest understanding of the word. "I mean, it don't seem a part of what's going on in the world today."

Frank's lean flat cheeks began to burn. But he was delighted at the mispronunciation of the borrowed word as it had come awkwardly from Mrs. Crimmons' refined lips. Parvenu! But he immediately crushed down the epithet and was angry with himself. He turned to Mrs. Crimmons attentively and with the utmost deference.

"I think you are right, in a way, Mrs. Crimmons," he said. "It isn't pertinent to the modern world. All that is dead and gone."

Mrs. Crimmons smirked, without looking at him. There was a kind of evil satisfaction in her at his capitulation, another mean triumph. But Miss Woods, with some tenuous sternness in her voice, said: "Nothing is without pertinence or without relevance. The past and the future and the present are all inextricable parts of a living whole."

Mrs. Crimmons understood not a single word of this, but she was clever enough to understand that the reproof had not been administered to her, but to that horrible young upstart, Frank Clair. Why, she did not know. She thought only that dear Pollie was putting the creature in his place, as he deserved, and this gave her further cause for complacency.

"Frankly," said Miss Shaw, in her strident and direct voice, "I'm not interested any longer in either Darwin or Huxley. What I want to know, without emotionalism or anything else, is when do women get the vote? Never before, in the history of the world, has it been so necessary that women be enfranchised. Men have made such a frightful botch of the world. Wars, religious, international and internecine. Massacres. Political anarchy. Governmental nefariousness, chicanery, treachery, and bungling. Look at our political attitude towards Russia."

They looked at him politely, and with confusion. It was evident that not even Miss Woods had caught the drift, and as for Mr. Roberts, he had retired silently to his contemplation of Darwin and Huxley as being more comprehensible and a great deal more worthy of the scholarly mind.

Miss Shaw shot a snapping and challenging look about the table. Miss Stengel murmured: "Look at our political attitude towards Russia." Miss Shaw glanced at her with irritation. "Don't be a parrot, Ida," she advised. "Use your own mind. That's the trouble with women. They allow others to do the thinking for them."

She challenged the company. "Has anyone any suggestion? Is there no one interested in the tremendous possibilities of women's participation in the world scene? Is there not sufficient imagination here to grasp the significance of emancipated womanhood—"

"Rampant," said Miss Woods, who could not resist a joke even in the face of her private convictions.

Mrs. Crimmons tittered. Miss Shaw flushed, and the glasses on her heron's nose almost exploded in the electric light overhead.

"I'm sorry, Ethelinda," said Miss Woods. "Well, I quite agree with you, to a certain extent. Women should vote, if only because they are mature human beings. But I doubt very much that 'participation in the world scene' by women would result in a new and rejuvenated, or even much more virtuous, world. Women, like men, are still afflicted by human nature, which our pastor calls Original Sin. When women vote, we'll have only an enlarged Republican or Democratic Party. The counting of noses will be that much more complicated and laborious. However, I want women to vote, and I'll fight for that right. It's the principle of the thing. I, myself, am mature, and, I think, as intelligent as most men, and have a mind of my own. I dislike being classed with children, criminals and idiots."

Miss Shaw, with restrained but passionate vehemence, brought her clenched fist down on the table, so that the near-by silver leapt. "Oh, Pollie! Such a short-sighted attitude! Surely you do not believe that men are as intimately involved in world affairs as are women? Men *like* war, I tell you. They *like* murder and rapine. It's in their very natures. But women have a stake in the world: their children, their homes, their peaceful lives. They hate war and murder. They instinctively hate crime and dirtiness and filthy politics—"

Miss Woods shook her large white head and smiled cynically. "My dear," she said, "women, in the majority, may hate war. I concede that. But they are just as susceptible to propaganda as men, and, in a measure, even more so, for they are emotional rather than reasonable, and—though I hate to confess it—they are more cruel haters. And as for women hating crime and dirtiness—" Again she shook her head, humorously. "My father used to say that for every fallen woman there is a fallen man. Unless history lies, many women have surpassed men in crime and viciousness. Virtue isn't the exclusive possession of women. I've known many virtuous men whose integrity could not be attacked successfully. And, I confess, I have known many more virtuous men than I have known virtuous women."

"Oh, Pollie! How can you say that!"

Miss Woods' smiling face became grave. "It is the truth, Ethelinda. I've known bad men, but few vicious ones. And, a most extraordinary thing: the most vicious women I have ever known have been chaste virgins or matrons. But perhaps when we speak of 'viciousness' we are not speaking of the same thing. There is a viciousness of the soul which is far worse than the viciousness of the body, and in that viciousness women far excel their brothers."

Miss Shaw, a valorous but innocent soul, mulled over that with confusion. She was still undaunted. Her glasses blinked rapidly. Miss Woods watched her with a faint hint of amused compassion. She leaned across Irving Schultz to pat Miss

Shaw's hand. "Never mind, dear. We agree on essentials, don't we?"

Miss Shaw said, lifting her heron's head valiantly: "Sometimes you do talk incomprehensibly, Pollie. I really don't know what you mean, sometimes."

"Good," said Miss Woods. "Keep your nice ingenuous heart, Ethelinda. It's so refreshing in a very naughty world."

She turned to Mrs. Crimmons. "More coffee, dear?"

"No, indeed, thank you," said Mrs. Crimmons archly, with a pointed glance at Frank's second cup. "I am so careful of my health, you know. A priceless possession."

Miss Woods smiled. "Excellent. We have to watch our health as we grow older, don't we? We haven't the resilience of youth. Ah, me."

Mrs. Crimmons looked at her sharply. Her fat smooth cheeks colored. Miss Woods' expression was all friendly blandness. Seeing nothing inimical in that big, bland old face, Mrs. Crimmons favored Frank with a sidelong and malicious glance, full of resentment. He felt the poisonous touch of her eyes, and was miserable. He said placatingly: "I know I shouldn't have more than one cup. But the coffee is so good "

Miss Woods' face changed. She said coldly: "Of course, you should have more than one cup, if you want it. What's youth for, anyway?"

Frank was bewildered, as always when Miss Woods spoke to him in that tone and gave him such a disdainful look. How had he offended her? He had not even succeeded in appeasing the harpy, Mrs. Crimmons.

The torn morning light outside the windows darkened. Now the gale, which had briefly subsided, assaulted the house with a hoarse roar like thunder. Everyone looked uneasily at the windows, whose curtains and draperies stirred and moved. It was impossible to see beyond the clouded glass. A wall of shivering whiteness stood there. The old house groaned; the electric candles overhead flickered, and from somewhere, even into that warm snug room, came a congealing breath.

"A terrible blizzard," commented Mr. Roberts, coming out of his contemplation. "Four feet of snow in less than twenty-four hours, and more to come, it seems."

A maid brought in a platter of fresh bacon, sizzling and spluttering hearteningly. Everyone helped himself to a fresh supply. The brown coffee, steaming, hissed into cups, as if each man and woman wished to prove that he and she were still "young." Miss Woods smiled, and filled a third cup for herself.

Mrs. Crimmons announced that she had received a special delivery letter from her daughter that morning. She simpered: "Dear Sally just *begs* me to come home for a few days. Of course, she and her husband, darling Billie, are taking such good care of our dear little house while we are away. Watching the pipes, and everything, and keeping up the furnace. But my dear children miss me and Mr. Crimmons so! They are married, and have children of their own, but they can't get along without their Mommy and Daddy! Sally's little Billie has had bronchitis. Such an intelligent little fellow! Not in school yet, but he can read and write as well as a ten-year-old. It's amazing. Isn't it amazing, Daddy?" she demanded of her husband, who had not participated in any of the conversation. As Mr. Crimmons had been devoting himself avariciously to the food, to the exclusion of everything else, he started, glanced at his wife, who favored him with a thin stare of her pale blue eyes, and stammered: "Eh? Yes, yes, of course. You're right, my dear."

Mrs. Crimmons accepted a fourth hot roll, and buttered it broodingly. Mr. Crimmons watched her with anxiety. Miss Woods' huge fat upper lip lifted almost imperceptibly. With amazing good fortune, Mr. Crimmons spoke relevantly: "Do you want to go home for a few days, Mother?"

She smiled with deep tenderness, placated. "I really don't know, dear. In this blizzard, and all. You know how trains are. And sometimes I think it is best for the children to get along without us, sometimes. They're so dependent. Even their husbands are dependent upon Mr. Crimmons' advice," she informed the rest of the table with plump pride. "You wouldn't believe it. Daddy must settle this and must settle that. He must decide upon a new automobile—they always get a new one every three years. The boys are doing so well, you know. Billie in the advertising business, and Mark in the wholesale grocery. Such fine, successful boys. But Daddy must decide everything for them. And the girls *insist* that I pick out every new piece of furniture, though they have wonderful taste of their own. When Sally wanted to have her sofa reupholstered —she paid four hundred dollars for it, the extravagant little girl!—I just put my foot down, and said: 'Now, honey, the new linen just wouldn't go with your drapes.' And there wasn't any argument about it at all. She just agreed, just as she always did, even when she was in braids and middy blouse, at school."

Frank was the only one who listened, for the other faces had grown politely blank. He saw a vision of three comfortable middle-class homes, with canaries at the windows between ruffled white curtains, with cars in garages set in well-kept back yards, with big sunny bedrooms furnished with quiet elaborateness, with kitchens equipped with enormous white iceboxes filled with crowding chickens and hams, with lawns bright green in the summer, with awnings shading polished windows, with gushing warmth issuing from steam radiators in the winter. He saw peace, security and contentment, solid middle-class safety and pleasant, dignified lives. He saw happy amiable traffic between the three smug houses, and heard the fat laughter of well-fed children. And this was exactly what Mrs. Crimmons intended to convey to her audience. Detroit was a long way off. It was not possible that anyone at this table would go so far as to investigate, and to discover that Sally and Susan and their husbands and children lived in two-family flats of five rooms each on a very shabby side-street, that the sums of money tossed off so nonchalantly by Mrs. Crimmons were lies, that Billie and Mark were respectively, a clerk in an advertising house and a shipping clerk in a wholesale grocery house, and that the Crimmonses themselves lived in a little rear cottage near their children, a cottage hardly more desirable than the tiny house on Albany Street, and not quite so clean.

She continued, this morning, to flourish, to smirk, to gloat, to smile with tender humor, as she rehearsed her family saga. And Frank listened avidly and with respect. Mrs. Crimmons felt this, and despised him even more. Her head arched higher from the depths of her fat warm bosom. It was then that she caught Irving Schultz' deep black eyes staring at her from behind his thick glasses. And what she saw chilled her, infuriated her.

It was seldom that Irving looked directly at anyone, and certainly rarely with that intense concentration. He said, with his eyes, to Mrs. Crimmons: "You are a fat old liar. You are not even a pathetic liar, for you are a malignant and stupid woman, with no charity in you. You are a poseuse, vulgar and cheap and pretentious."

It was strange that Mrs. Crimmons was so impressed and so infuriated by Irving's eyes. She had always ignored him. He never pretended to be other than he was, and he was not ashamed of what he had been. To Mrs. Crimmons, he was nothing at all, and she had often wondered why Miss Woods had permitted such a nonentity, such an ugly, unprepossessing young man, to so much as enter her house. She might despise Frank, for she had unerringly detected another pretender like herself, but at least she spoke to him at times.

She actually trembled. She felt shocked, right down to her fat, impervious heart. Suddenly she raised her voice with hard strenuousness, like a blow to beat down those steadfast black eyes:

"Daddy, I think perhaps I *will* go home for a few days, to our own darling house! And the children. Did I tell you that Sally wrote me that Mrs. Gregory St. John-Simmons was giving such a wonderful affair for a few select friends, and that she *insisted* that all of us attend?" She smirked, though a pulse beat heavily in her thick throat. She explained to everyone condescendingly: "I'm sure you've all heard of Mrs. Gregory St. John-Simmons. Connected with the Cadillac people? A wonderful house in the suburbs. Superb. And so very exclusive! Marion has been devoted to Sally since they were children, and *nothing* is complete unless Sally goes to every affair Marion gives."

Then Irving smiled strangely, faintly. He returned to his bacon.

Frank, with his acute perceptiveness, realized that Mrs. Crimmons was angered. He saw the vibration of her brown silk sleeve, the shaking of her fat little hand with its cruel nails. He felt, in some odd way, that her hostility was directed at Irving. A quick look assured him that it was, for she was glaring through her pince-nez at the top of his untidy mop of Negroid curls. Of course, a woman like Mrs. Crimmons would resent the presence of such as Irving Schultz. It was to be expected.

He looked at Irving himself and detested him. He did not know from what in himself had sprung this detestation. He knew only that now something burned in him, strong and agitated. For the first time in months, he spoke to the other young man, with a smile:

"How are the studies going, Irving?"

Very slowly, Irving lifted his head and gazed at Frank. Miss Woods laid down her fork. She did not move. She only listened.

Irving smiled, a queer, crooked smile, almost sad. "Very well, thank you. Frank," he added, meditatively.

Frank threw Mrs. Crimmons a protective and humorous glance. He said: "Mental diseases. For heaven's sake, why mental diseases? Why not anything else? Something tangible."

Irving said softly: "There's nothing more tangible than

a mind. It's the only real, tangible thing—Frank. My professor said yesterday that the external world is only the projection of the minds of mankind. Maybe he's metaphysical, or something, but I don't know. Do you remember, in school, that old question: If a tree fell in a forest where there was not a single ear, would there be any sound?"

Frank tried to speak. But something held him in a kind of enthrallment, as if he had heard a wonderful familiar voice which he had forgotten, a dear, a lovely, a noble voice, calling to him from across vast and ashen wastes. And something clutched him in a very paralysis of despairing grief, in a very desolation of loss, as he heard that voice. He could not utter a single sound. But the others stared at Irving in surprise. They could not recall that he had ever spoken as such length as this, and his voice was strange to them, a voice that was rough yet gentle, hoarse yet soft and compelling.

Irving, having spoken, looked at Frank and waited. And knew.

Behind his glasses, his eyes glowed. Come out, come out! they cried to him. Come out into the light where you belong. Where you lived, once. Come out!

Mrs. Crimmons tittered, arched her head. "Well, I only went to one of the best finishing-schools, of course, but I don't know what you're talking about, Mr. Schultz. Maybe I'm not so bright, so maybe you'd explain it." She tried to catch Miss Woods' eyes for a humorous and malicious exchange. But Miss Woods, gaze bent on the shining round silver of the coffeepot, was oddly absorbed in her contemplation. "Maybe I didn't go to the right school, after all, Mr. Schultz," continued Mrs. Crimmons in a voice corroded with amused hatred, "though my dear papa paid nearly two thousand a year for my education. Maybe I ought to have gone to the schools you did, Mr. Schultz, and had your background."

But Irving apparently did not hear. Come out, come out! said his eyes, imploringly. Come out, Frank, with me.

He said aloud, in his slow, strong but uncertain voice: "Would there be any sound if there wasn't an ear, and a mind behind the ear, to hear the noise of the tree falling— Frank? And if you go on with that, would there be any world of sound or sight, if there wasn't a—a comprehending —ear and eye to hear and see it? That's what my professor meant when he said that the human mind was the only real and tangible thing, and that only when it projected itself did the world become a reality."

Mrs. Crimmons tittered again. But no one heard her. There

was a brightening on Mr. Roberts' old faded face, an eagerness. Miss Shaw and Miss Stengel listened, their mouths partly
open. Mr. Crimmons had returned to his food. Miss Woods
smoothed the hot silver of the coffeepot with a meditative
forefinger. Frank sat motionless in his enthrallment, in his
deep pain.

Irving said softly: "That's why I am studying mental
diseases. If the minds of men are distorted and don't see
clearly and straightly, the world they project will be distorted,
and it will be a nightmare of wrong—angles—and delusions.
A nightmare. That's what it is now, you see. Just a nightmare. It's been getting that way a long time." He paused.
"You look through a warped piece of glass, and the world
you see is all out of perspective. We're all looking through
warped glass. What we see is the projection of our sick
minds. Remember what that old German philosopher called
man? 'The sick animal.' "

"The sick animal!" Yes, yes, it was true! Something was
moving, stirring, passionately in Frank. A sick world waiting for the healer, not of its misshapen body, but of the mind
within it which had given that body its distortion. A world
waiting for the healers, for the physician of the soul, for the
great writer, the great artist, the great prophet, who would
remove the warped glass from the ailing eye and allow that
eye to behold a world of beauty and compassion, of joy and
excitement, of love and peace and God!

Once, he, Frank Clair, had known this, had known it
with intense pity and love and clear sweet anguish. He saw
himself in the old Church of the Nativity, and the candle-
light on his fingers as he looked at them. They had seemed
to shine, as if some holy oil had been poured on them in
consecration. In memory, he felt the beating of his heart,
exultant, humble, terrified yet joyous.

The memory of that heart-beating became a dark pounding in his mind, an upheaval, a clamorous movement. Something was surging in him, a giant pain, a sorrow, a piercing
sweetness.

He heard a shrill rasping sound and started. Mrs. Crimmons had thrown herself with plump restraint against the
back of her chair, and was laughing viciously. "Oh dear me,
dear me!" she exclaimed. "Such intellectual talk! I never
heard the like, on a Sunday morning, just before church! And
from you, too, Mr. Schultz! Maybe it's your mind that's
sick, my dear boy. I've often thought it. Just kind of—of—
And is *that* the sort of thing they teach boys in school now?

That the whole world's sick, this nice, comfy world where everybody's happy now that the war's over?"

Frank heard her. He heard her dull and stupid hatred, raucous and venomous. He heard her smugness; he saw her twinkling fatness. He saw her cruelty and mediocrity, and knew her and her kind for what they were. The Enemy. So many of the Enemy, the liars and the poseurs, the sadistic and the mean—a whole evil, seething, maggoty world of them, like a foul and squirming hill blocking the bright road! His fists clenched. He turned to her abruptly, and his eyes were a still blue fire of rage and disgust.

"Shut up, you fool!" he cried. "You silly, wobbling fool! You babbling, lying idiot!"

He jumped up so suddenly, and with such vehemence, that his chair fell down behind him with a crash. Miss Stengel squealed. No one else moved or spoke. But Mrs. Crimmons, her mouth fallen open, was glaring at him incredulously. He saw that, and was exultant. He felt as if he had received a clean and shining baptism. He wanted to strike that well-fed, quivering face, that ugly personification of all the huge mediocrities in the world.

"You God-damned stupid old woman!" he exclaimed. "And that goes for all the rest of the world like you! You—you dirty killers!"

He went out of the room blindly, crashed up the stairs to his own room, slammed the door behind him. He heard his own breathing, harsh and strident, as if he had been running. The room swam in dark mists. He sat down abruptly on his bed, and then involuntarily he gripped his knees with his hands, in Francis' old gesture of uncontrollable emotion.

CHAPTER 38

Miss Woods, breathing stertorously, climbed up the stairs to the third floor. Her fat old thighs ached with the effort, and her great jowls were soon bedewed. She could feel her enormous flesh trying to burst through the armored stays she wore, and the thumping of her heart. None of this caused her any apprehension. She knew she was old, and she had no desire for youth. There was too much in her childhood and young womanhood which had been intolerably ugly and revolting, and she had known happiness only in her old age. She thought youth the most dreadful period of life, not pathetic, not amusing, except to obtuse and sentimental adults, not bright and gay, as the novelists believed, not filled with stars and shining marble towers and a light on silver seas.

"Trailing clouds of glory do we come—from God, who is our home." Miss Woods paused on the second landing to wipe her jowls, to adjust a lock of her white hair, to pull down her corsets. The storm-locked old house creaked and snapped in the late afternoon gloom of this Sunday. She could hear the hissing of the snow against the spectral windows, the onslaught of the wind against the walls. There was no other sound. The roomers were either asleep or reading. She had seen yellow light under doors.

She thought absently: March is always the worst month of the year in this climate. She opened her large fat mouth in order to steady her heart. She disliked pain, either in herself, or in others. It was a humiliation, a reminder that no matter how the mind might soar, or philosophize, or meditate, or dwell upon the possibility of God, the body could always drag it back, like a flying hawk on a string, to huddle on the offal heap which was flesh. There was the indignity, that the mounting soul, fixed upon the sun, must be tumbled from its ascension by a hive, a gallstone, an itchy ear, or, as her generation delicately put it, by "a call of nature." If there was a soul and it survived the decay of the mortifying flesh, how happy it must be when it was released and could flee not only the dark miseries of the world, but the secret ignominy of the body. The world was all wrong for mankind, because mankind could think. The world was all wrong for the young, because the young could remember a time before the soul had put on flesh.

Miss Woods, hearing rumblings in herself, patted her large, protuberant belly. "I'll be rid of you soon," she informed it, with satisfaction. "I don't know if I'll know anything about it, but at least I shan't be aware of you, you swollen humiliation."

On Sunday afternoons, though no one else in her house knew it, it was her custom to climb the stairs to visit Irving Schultz. There they would sit together, in the small room under the roof, with only the snow to see in the winter and the trees in summer.

She went up the last steep flight and knocked at the door at the top. She opened the door, and puffing, entered the little room.

Furnace heat did not penetrate up into this eyrie, but there was an adequate substitute in the way of a gas-heater, glowing redly and sturdily in a brick recess. It glowed and flickered cheerily in the dark-gray gloom under the pitched ceiling, which was further alleviated by a large lamp set on a wide cherry table, now serving as a desk for Irving Schultz. A few weeks after Irving's appearance in Miss Woods' house, she had placed one of her best Persian rugs on the polished floor, had hung rich yellow and green linen at the four tiny windows, had added an old comfortable rocker to the assembly consisting of a narrow tester bed, small, round pie-crust table at the bedside, a good lamp, and an extra old carved chair with a horsehair seat. Irving himself had built that large bookcase on the wall opposite the bed, and had expertly stained it mahogany and rubbed it down with wax. As a result, the room, this wild March afternoon, had a cosiness and dignity which made it more attractive than any of the other bedrooms.

Irving's study books were piled at one end of the cherry table. He had spread out his notebooks and was busily making notes from his texts. He glanced up when he saw Miss Woods, and rose with slow and awkward courtesy. Silently, and with only a smile, he drew the rocker closer to the gas-heater, and brought his own chair to stand opposite.

"I hope I'm not disturbing you, Irving," said Miss Woods. This was always the etiquette of her expected visit.

He answered, in formula: "Of course not. I was waiting for you, Miss Woods."

She sat down, groaning slightly. She rubbed her knees. The black silk hissed under her be-ringed hands. She beamed upon the young man. She glanced at the little windows, and saw the savage veils of snow surging against them. "Isn't this an appalling day?" she remarked. "I've lived seventy-two years in Bison, and I never get used to the winters."

Irving looked at the snow. "I like it," he said simply. "It— it sort of shuts me in. I feel safe in a storm, and happy."

He spoke with shy ease, for he and Miss Woods were fast, if secret, friends. He regarded her with affection, and she returned it. "I declare, Irving, you look more like Abe Lincoln every day," she said. "Well, how are the studies going?"

Now his dark and ugly face lighted up, almost with passion. "I can't get enough of them. I hate to sleep, because I have to leave my books. Does that sound kind of precious?" he added, with a dark color on his sunken cheeks.

"Nonsense," she replied, sturdily. "If you don't have a

passion for a thing you might as well let it go. Now me, I've always had a passion for living. That's why I expect to live to be a hundred," she went on, with a chuckle. "My father used to say that if a man had no passions he was more than half dead, and that a vice, if pursued vigorously enough, and with happy ardor, was more desirable than any of the milky virtues. He was a great drinker, but not a drunkard, and there was never a healthier or more charming man anywhere. You ought to have seen the cellar in this house when he was alive! He had the finest collection of brandies in the whole world, I do believe. That reminds me: how is the brandy? I don't remember whether we drank it all last Sunday."

Irving went to his dresser, a piece of furniture authentically a museum piece, which Miss Woods' great-grandmother had brought with her from England a hundred years ago, a present from her own grandmother. He opened a lower drawer and brought out a bottle of Napoleon and two little crystal glasses, carefully wrapped in tissue paper. He poured out the golden liquid while Miss Woods watched intently. Then they gave each other a silent, friendly toast, and sniffed, and drank. "Um," said Miss Woods, looking down lovingly at the glass in her hand. "That's nectar. That's divine elixir for the blood. A kind of transfusion from heaven. Didn't Omar Khayyam say something about forgiving God because he had devised alcohol to help man endure the sorrows He had invented for him? Yes, it was something like that. And there is this crowd of sour, misbegotten women trying to inflict Prohibition on us! Do you know, Irving, I think they'll succeed. Cranks find America quite a happy hunting ground. It's because the great majority of Americans unfortunately are the children and grandchildren of superstitious peasants, and haven't any wits. It's too bad. We ought to have Immigration Laws which will admit only the middle class, the upper middle class, to this country. We've got too many sub-humans here, and this is true even of our so-called 'old' Americans."

Irving smiled slightly, but said nothing.

Miss Woods narrowed her eyes at him shrewdly. "Now I'm not trying to offend you, Irving, God knows. You're just the lovely exception to the rule. But look at what we've been getting for the past seventy years or so! Misshapen peasants from the starving areas of Europe! Mental illiterates! Now they're talking about quotas. They'll limit the quantity of immigrants, which is partly good, but our flannel-headed legislators aren't doing anything about quality. A farm laborer has just as good a chance of coming here, and breeding steadily, as a professional man. Let's raise the quality, I say. Make no quota restrictions on teachers, professional men, artists, thinkers, writers, sound little business men. Let 'em come in, in droves, say I. Keep out the peasants, the nasty grubbers. It don't matter what country the better people come from: let 'em come, swarms of 'em, whether they're Italians or Germans, Swedes or Jews, Poles or Turks. Just so we get the best, and keep out the peasants. Just so we skim the cream of Europe and exclude the dregs. But that's beyond the comprehension of our law makers, who are just peasants and thick-headed bulls themselves."

She sipped the brandy appreciatively. "Ethelinda Shaw's a Prohibitionist. Rabid on the subject. That's because her soul's dried up, and she hates everybody, in spite of her passion for the suffragettes and her championing of what she calls 'the common people.' Have you noticed, Irving, that the champions of 'the common people' usually hate everybody? Dreary folk. Dangerous, too. Me, I love a few people, and I don't care a fig for the rest, but I don't hate them. Hate's bad for the digestion anyway."

She allowed Irving to add a little more brandy to her glass and smiled at him tenderly. "I suppose you don't hate anybody, eh?"

Amusement passed like a ripple of light over Irving's face. "I have a good digestion," he said.

"Um. Well, then. It's really very queer. I've noticed that kind of people in churches too—like Ethelinda. Every kind of face and nature. But they've got one strange thing in common: they hate people. I wonder why?"

Irving said, with a look at his books: "We have a new word for it, a word invented by a great German physician, Freud. He calls it 'compensation.' Those people feel guilty; they know what they really think and what they are. They know consciously or unconsciously, that they're—evil. They don't want the world to know; they don't want themselves to know, sometimes. So they interfere with all human activity."

He got up and lit an old pipe and puffed at it with reflection. "It's now suspected that the reformers, the ones who want to pass laws to prohibit this, or outlaw that, to 'protect' the working people, to overthrow the established Government, to change the face of things, to pass what they call 'good' laws, are vicious."

They sipped the brandy in companionable silence and listened to the storm groaning and lashing at the windows. Now the lamp and gas-heater grew brighter as the room steadily darkened. This was a cave under the eaves; rosy fingers moved over the sloping ceiling, with its pattern of nosegays. Miss Woods finally spoke again, somewhat restlessly and obscurely: "I don't like the feel of the world these days. Something is wrong, really wrong, Irving. The calamities prophesied when we entered the war: the end of capitalism and individual liberty, universal starvation and ruin, haven't materialized. Thank God for that. We still have a healthy capitalism, and we are still free, and we'll manage to help the rest of the world to live. Europe will rebuild itself, with our help. So the calamities haven't come, after all. But there is something else abroad, much worse. I don't know what it is. Something prowling, something which might ruin us, I am afraid. What is it, Irving?"

She spoke as to an equal, this seventy-two-year-old woman speaking to a youth hardly twenty-two, and she spoke urgently.

He answered soberly: "I think we're sick. Of course, I don't know what the world was like when you were young—"

"Well, I do, my dear. It was a hard world, but a robust one. Nobody expected to eat, who didn't work. And everyone worked, it seems to me, in America even the very rich. I don't quite remember what it was for which they worked, but they were very enthusiastic about it, and not dreary the way they are now. I believe they felt they had something to work for, rich and poor alike. They don't now. There is a kind of godlessness now—" She put down her glass and wiped her lips. "I didn't believe, with everyone else, that a noble era would ensue after the war, when everybody would love his neighbor and there would be a new spiritual revelation. But I did think we'd learn our lesson, that if there was only one God there was only one world of men. Poor Mr. Wilson knows that. But he's doomed to fail, and that's what is so terrible. Perhaps I'm getting old, but I feel that if we don't learn this now, and act upon our knowledge, we are going to see such frightful things, in ten, or twenty, or thirty years— Godlessness, that's it. A sick world."

"Yes," said Irving Schulz. He looked at Miss Woods, and even in the dimness of the room she could see how his face had become intense and alive and passionate. "That is what Dr. Pembroke said when he spoke to us just after the war ended. He said that we've tried to find in ourselves a solution for all our problems, like a snail trying to find a world within its narrow shell, and only winding itself farther into its own convolutions. He said there was something else outside the shell, and we must find it. We must have a larger conception of ourselves than mere animalism and materialism, a belief that there is something significant in mankind, though, of course, that might sound ridiculous and metaphysical to those who call themselves sophisticated."

"Or those who might find it agreeable, or profitable, to set every man against his neighbor," added Miss Woods grimly.

Again there was silence between them, and now Irving appeared uneasy and awkward, engrossed in his thoughts. He said hesitatingly: "I'm sorry about breakfast today, Miss Woods. I'm afraid I stirred up something, somehow. You see," and his voice became lower, "I wouldn't want you to hold it against Frank Clair the way he jumped down Mrs. Crimmons' throat." He looked at Miss Woods appealingly, remembering her summary dismissal of those who disturbed the placidity of her home. "I knew Frank years ago. Just a little, but it was enough. He—he was miserable. I used to watch him, though we hardly ever spoke. I don't think he has much self-control."

Miss Woods was silent, watching him inscrutably.

He still pleaded with her, knotting his dark, heavily knuckled hands together.

"I know how you feel about keeping everything here pleasant and impersonal. I don't know how to say it, Miss Woods, but I was glad when he spoke that way to that woman. I hoped he would say or do something. I suppose you can't understand that. But, you see, I know Frank Clair. Yes, I was very glad."

Miss Woods said quietly: "I knew you knew him. He told me when he first came here."

Irving sat up eagerly. "He did? Well, I'm glad of that, too."

He searched her great white face in the lamplight. Then he sighed. "I see," he said, with sadness.

Then he added: "But I'm still glad. It's very hard to put into words. But Frank used to write poetry and stories at school. My old teacher, Miss Bendy, would show them to me sometimes. Then he left school to go to work. It wasn't that his parents were so poor—like mine. But he was sent to work, and I lost sight of him, and didn't see him again until he came here. I saw immediately that he'd changed. It was—it was kind of terrible to me, Miss Woods. He's younger than I am, but now he seems old, and sick and tired. Something must have happened to him. I couldn't ask him, of course, because we'd never been more than just acquaintances." Irving's face had colored painfully. "I know I'm not making myself clear. It's something I haven't words for. So you couldn't be expected to understand why I was glad he flared out like that, so savagely—"

"Yes," said Miss Woods, "I think I understand." She paused. "That is why I am going to give the Crimmonses their notice tomorrow. I never did like that woman, but I was sorry for her husband. He's a fool."

Irving regarded her incredulously and with joy. "You mean that, after all that, you will let Frank stay, and make the others go?"

"Of course," said Miss Woods briskly. "After all, it would be embarrassing for Frank if they stayed, wouldn't it?" She smiled at Irving with deep humor and tenderness. "I was getting just a little tired of Frank lately. I'm afraid if he hadn't spoken up, I'd have told him to go. And, as you say, my dear, that is a thing I haven't words for, either."

She stood up, and he rose with her. She smoothed her black silk frankly over her great breasts and belly. "I hope, after this, that you boys may be friends. It will be very good for both of you, especially for Frank. He needs you, Irving. He really does. He hasn't a single friend in the world. He isn't like you; you have something more important than friends. But he hasn't anything, poor child."

CHAPTER 39

FRANK let himself out into the storm, for his room had become intolerable to him in its small quiet. He had planned to study that afternoon, to work, to write the "composition" Mr. Mason had assigned to him. In the morning, he had anticipated that afternoon with pleasure. But as he sat in his room, on his bed, seething, his heart pounding with excitement and rage, he knew that it would be impossible to control himself and to devote himself to orderly work. He would go out. Perhaps, a little later, he would visit his grandmother and his mother, and have "tea" with them.

It came to him, with overwhelming bitterness, that he must resort to this call at the Porter Avenue rooming-house if he was to have any contact of any kind with human beings. He had stood up and looked about his room, and then for the first time he had realized his loneliness, his utter isolation, his lack of contact with his fellowmen. It had been years since he had felt this loneliness, and, strangely, while he experienced a kind of choking desolation, he was also enlivened by it. Always, since the going of Paul Hodge, he had lived in a narrow world of his own, where his own breath, the sound of his own heart, had been enough for him. But something had exploded into that tiny shell of a world, scattering the fragments, leaving him exposed. He was not certain whether this exposure was pleasurable or disagreeable. He only knew that he was oddly excited and restless now, and that he could not remain in his room. Also, he was, as yet, afraid to think. He was afraid to think of the consequences of his inexplicable outburst of the morning, and he did not want, just now, to examine the reasons for it. He took care that no one heard him slip out of the house, for he shrank from encountering Miss Woods, who was already on her way downstairs to talk to him.

Snow and wind poured down from a purplish sky, and engulfed him. Linwood Avenue was completely deserted. A smooth river of whiteness stretched from curb to curb; the street lamps were capped with snow; the cold icy mounds along the sidewalks had become miniature mountains of purity. Zero cold struck at Frank's cheeks, nose and chin, and he turned up his collar and huddled in the frail warmth of his coat. He pulled down his hat, which soon became a wreath of heavy white. He plowed on, thankful for his buckled "arctics," the woolen gloves on his hands. The snow reached to his knees; soon he was panting. But in spite of his struggles against the wind and blizzard, he did not grow warmer. Rather, the cold began to penetrate through the wool over his knees, and found every crevice in his clothing.

It was too early for tea at his grandmother's, and he had had no dinner. He would walk for a while, then go to West Utica Street and eat a good meal at Louis'. That was the pleasure he always reserved for himself on Sunday. But it was still too early. He went on down Linwood Avenue, fighting the storm. Every house was plastered with patches of white; every window sill was heaped with it. Sometimes he could not see the houses for the snow, and he was plowing through a wilderness of wild gale and white snowstorm which cut his flesh. He walked on for fifteen minutes, and encountered no one, not even a vehicle, though occasionally he could hear the streetcars on Main Street groaning in muffled struggle as they fought their way down the heaped tracks.

Occasionally he glimpsed a yellow rectangle through the swirling dark-and-white, and knew it for a lighted window. The great elms over his head cascaded avalanches of snow above and over him, and creaked with the cold. Their trunks, too, were swathed in bitter whiteness.

There was no sound, only that savage howling which roared down from the sky. Frank went on, breathing more painfully, a flap of his collar pulled over his breathless lips so that he might not be stifled.

All at once, he felt a sudden upward surge of his heart, a sudden immense joy. He stopped abruptly, in order to feel it, in order not to miss this intense flow in himself. It brought such elation to him, such excitement. He had not felt like this since he had been fifteen years old, and the world had floated in colored dreams. Now all loneliness and anxiety left him, and he was warmed by a nameless fire of exultation, an expectation, a passionate release.

What had so suddenly released him from his grim misery and loneliness? What finger had torn the iron ring about his heart? He stood and thought, and he did not see or feel the storm. What had brought the old sweet tide to him again, flowing in from the darkness of the past four years? That old sweet tide of trembling promise and anticipation, of strength and power and tenderness! That old mysterious sense of communication with enormous things outside himself! Staggering a little under the weight of the wind, he moved to the trunk of a great elm and leaned against it, closing his eyes.

He remembered now that he had first sensed the movement of the incoming tide when he had listened to Irving Schultz. When he had stood up, and had shouted at Mrs. Crimmons, the tide had increased in strength and motion. It had lapped his feet and had given him that restlessness in his room, his desire to escape. He knew it now. And as the knowledge came to him, so the sense of courage and of faith and old joy grew stronger in him. He was still enormously confused, and there was an aching in his head. He could not understand. But all at once he saw that some profound conflict had been taking place in him these past years. If he waited only a few moments longer, he would know what that conflict was, and he would be free of it.

The roar of the wind became in his ears the thunder of a huge struck harp resounding with primordial music. The music faded, retreated, swept over him. The blizzard was lessening; now he could see the black shapes of houses. Suddenly they were no longer mere houses; they were emotions projected to him over the white banks of snow. They had a separate being, separate personalities, and he stared at them, blinking the flakes from his eyes. Why, he had felt this way when he was a kid, and he had forgotten!

There was a thick and crowding exultation in his throat, a pounding in his chest. He was remembering; he was re-experiencing. He stared at the houses, at the shrouded trees, and felt their individual and distinct beings in his own body, which was no longer aware of the cold.

There had been a time, he remembered, when all things, whether a teacup or a chair, a fork or a table, a curtain or a bed, a tree or a cloud, a blade of grass or a stairway—all things, in fact on which his eye had rested even momentarily—had possessed, for him, an *emotion*, an actual personality of *being*. It was not so much their texture, their appearance, their reality in time or place, their color or the lack of it, which had so impinged on his consciousness. Rather, it was their intense projection of themselves into his own consciousness, an individual projection, acute and sentient, personal and intense, which had always so enthralled him. And he had forgotten this joy, this glorious participation in all visible matter, his instinctive, childish knowledge that all objects, in becoming form, had become life!

Now he remembered that once a spoon or a glass of water had not been, as they were to others, merely insensate objects. Perhaps, in his boyhood (and this he now believed) he had unconsciously endowed all things with the magical intensity of his own imagination, childish and fundamental, just as primitive peoples had endowed trees, rocks, waters, with personal spirits, beautiful or malign, dull or poignant. (But again, perhaps the eye and the heart of childhood were more keen, more discerning, than the cataract-covered vision and the scarred sensitivities of manhood.)

However it had been, the object's beauty or ugliness, smoothness or roughness, had inspired liking or hatred in him, as a personality in itself, without reference to what it actually *was*. It had been an individual to him, endowed with a distinct if vague consciousness. When an object had broken in a careless hand, whether it was a lamp or a drinking-glass, a dish or a plate, he had felt loss in himself, a physical hurt. Something which had existed had died, been destroyed. Once Maybelle had accidentally smashed a teacup. The teacup had mysteriously been his friend, for it had been a jolly creature, wide and round, with a foolish curved handle. It was in no way distinguished: in fact, Maybelle had bought it in a cheap store, and she possessed better cups which she had brought from England. But it had been Frank's friend from the moment he had seen it, and he had loved it for its individual being, the emotion it had imparted to him.

He remembered that he had particularly hated a pair of draperies of his mother's. They were of red cotton, and red had always been his favorite color, so it was not the hue by which he was repelled. But he had thought the curtains arrogant and of a rough temper, and they, quite acutely, had not liked the little boy. He had felt their dislike, just as he had felt the dislike certain doors had for him. His father's footstool had resented him, while one of Francis' pipes had liked him in a stolid fashion. A certain house on Normal Avenue hated him, though it was not unlike the others on the street. He literally had believed that when he came down the street the house gathered its dormer windows together like clenched fists and threatened him over the frowning roof of the verandah. Its steps sneered at him openly.

Wistaria vines on his grandmother's porch had liked him, and had nodded their purple heads at him in greeting, but the sidewalk in front of her house was his enemy. It was not so much that its cracks and depressions formed a snarling face as the fact that its very surface, gravelled, gray-colored and slightly tilted, appeared to project to him a malefic emotion of its own, whereas its brother and adjoining sections, almost identical, only stared at him blankly.

He remembered, as he huddled in his coat against the lessening wind, that a certain picket fence was smug and knowing, and grinned at him in a cunning way. But a small fir tree on a dusty lawn had stared at him wistfully, so that he had never passed it without touching it furtively with a tender hand. When he would go on, he knew that it watched him go, like a little forlorn dog, untended and homeless. Its look and sadness hurt him.

His mother had had a bowl of cheap glass, multicolored, which she had bought for twenty-five cents. The prevailing color was a kind of gelid brown, flecked with yellow, russet-red and dull amber. There it had been, on the kitchen table, so ugly, yet satisfied with itself, as if it were a lustre bowl of great price! Frank had detested it. When he was alone, he would lean over it and mutter through his teeth: "You're only a cheap old bowl, and just pretending you're so darn much!" But the bowl would glisten complacently, and ignore him, or maybe it would flash a little in the sunlight, as if it shrugged nastily and thought his opinion too unimportant for consideration.

Absorbed in his memories, absorbed in his renewed prescience and awareness, Frank stood in the snow, his back against the tree. He thought: I am alive! I'm really alive. I didn't know I was dead, all these years.

He felt his enormous loneliness, and it was like a benediction. He felt his loneliness, and his oneness with everything in and about him, so that the loneliness was participation. And then he saw that the storm had abruptly stopped, was passing. The sky overhead was still ashen-purple, but only a few desultory flakes of snow fell from it. The groaning in the trees had subsided to a restless mutter.

He looked at the west, as he had looked when he had been a child, and felt a sudden wild lifting in himself. The wrack of clouds was leaving the western heavens, racing before some high, unfelt wind. And now these heavens were a clear pale blue, cold and limitless. Frank's attention was caught and held by a curious cloud formation, such as he had never seen before. A great pillar of cloud, seemingly having its heavy base on the earth, rose like a shaft of white stone against the blue sky, smooth, vast, tapering, a veritable monument, crowned with gold. He could not believe it was real, fashioned as it was by the giant hands of the wind, a "Cleopatra's needle" of vapor, possessing the quality and the sculpture of marble.

He saw it, and then he knew again, after so many years, that sweet, mystic anticipation, falling like sudden swift light on the spirit, that moment of glory when the heart expects, prays, urges, that something will be revealed, will descend, will expand, emerge from the invisible into the visible, will surely—surely—soar, leap, into all-embracing, all-explaining, beautiful reality, will become a pure, ecstatic joy, a revelation known by the soul from a hundred millennia before, and demanded by the body, which still did not know. That tranquil yet rapturous anticipation! That knowledge, guessed, previously known, half-forgotten, daily becoming less remembered, suddenly on the verge of being, complete and seen and shining, as once it had been remembered!

He watched and waited, alone there in the cold desert of Linwood Avenue. The tower of whiteness crowned with gold stood there, an awesome monument to what he instinctively knew existed. Then, moment by moment, it dissolved, drifted, expanded into mist, became a mound of nothingness, began to drift away.

He knew the sick spiritual disappointment then, as he had known it a thousand times before, the grief, the loss and the universal desolation, the darkness of mind because of the passing of what had almost been revealed, and then had not been revealed.

But he was not left empty. The exultation was still there, quieter now, yet luminously shining, as if, though the glory had passed, its memory remained as a sweet consolation and solemn promise.

He went on down the street. He looked at his father's watch, which he had not sold after all. It was three o'clock. He would eat his dinner at Louis', then go to see his mother and grandmother. All at once he wanted to see Mr. Farley, to talk to him.

CHAPTER 40

Louis' Restaurant was almost completely empty, snow was heaped outside nearly to the wide glass windows, the interior warm yet possessing a curious frontier quality because of the weather. Frank stamped his feet, felt the warmth flowing over his numbed flesh. He smiled at the headwaiter, who came to meet him eagerly. He took Frank's coat, shook it free from a shower of snow, hung it up. He remarked on the passing of the storm, and gave Frank his favorite table to one side.

Frank looked about him, still excited. Now the walls of the restaurant were no longer just walls, but friendly personalities who were glad to see him. Now the round white tables were jocund and placid, the chairs, with their chintz covers, stout little young persons waiting for friends. The plate of bread and rolls on his own table was crustily amiable, and the silverware winked at him in a holiday mood. Even the menu in his hand was intimate, and he felt its texture with pleasure.

He saw the few diners, the shaded lights overhead, the gray blankness of the windows, and felt the carpet under his feet, the menu in his hand, the fit of his collar and tie. Everything had a depth, three dimensions, a patina, a color.

Only last week he had sat in a photograph, flat, without depth, without meaning. Now everything was significant, a pattern, projecting its personality, absorbing his own personality in return, fusing them together to give him this sense of participation and joyous reality.

His excitement, as he ate, became enhanced rather than lessened. His mind teemed. A dozen plots for novels raced through his imagination. Nothing was too worthless, too insignificant, nothing too small, to demand projection through the written word. That old waiter, now; his life story might be profound. That elderly couple, moderately well-dressed, munching, smiling at each other, had dignity, and any tale of their lives would have deep meaning and drama. The young woman cashier at the desk, with her buns and rolls of taffy-colored hair, her cascades of ruffles at wrist and throat, could probably give him material for a dozen short stories. Every human being, those passing by the windows, the cook and his assistants in the kitchen, were individual human souls of tragedy and purport and importance. Through them breathed an intense purpose; their lives were part of a great whole, mystical and complete.

His awareness became an almost overpowering emotion. He was conscious that he was no longer afraid, no longer anxious and tense. He thought briefly of the morning's débâcle, and smiled to himself. If Miss Woods told him to leave, he would be sorry, of course, but the matter would be unimportant. There were dozens of other rooming houses; hers was not unique. Besides, he had told that old hag off, and that was an immense satisfaction. He wondered why he had ever catered to her, tried to please her. Mortification made his face hot, but this, curiously, only excited him further.

As for his job, if it vanished in a week or two, as it most probably would, there were other jobs. Even jobs did not matter. He had recovered something priceless: the ability to think and feel. All at once he was impatient to go back to his room and begin to write. Now the thought of writing was a joy. Words, phrases, sentences, full of color and vitality, rushed through his imagination in a burning stream.

He thought of Irving Schultz, and he said to himself: I'll talk to Irving. How could I have missed it, that he is great and heroic? Perhaps he'll be my friend. I can talk to him! He'll understand what I am saying.

I am free, he thought, and the very sound of the words

in his mind held him hushed and taut, as if he had come upon a miracle.

I'll write to Paul. I'll write in such a way that he can't fail to understand. Maybe I'll get a job near him, and we can be together again. Yes, yes, everything is possible now!

The golden river of his thoughts became a teeming flood, overflowing cold dark banks with its exuberant currents and swelling streams. He saw them brightening under a golden sky, until heaven and earth lay before him, flowing together in an ineffable glory. He heard voices in the light, singing, calling voices, and each had a story to tell. The waiter laid his favorite dessert on the table—bread pudding with a rich sauce—but he held his spoon suspended over it while he stared before him, his eyes heavy with entrancement. He saw marble stairs rising swiftly out of the golden river of his imagination, and he mounted them. Voices and light became one, and now they had a single tale to relate, a novel which moved, like music, from chord to chord, as in a symphony. He had it now! It was beautiful; it was rounded; there was no part which was not perfect. Step by gold-splashed marble step, he rose, and each step was a part of his story.

He would write of the physician who had been one of Christ's disciples, Luke, the subtle Greek, the man who had come from nothing into immortality. Behind him, white porticoes in a violet mist, voices raised in lofty dialectics, a world sinking into insignificance, becoming a desert of words in which everything was sterile. Luke, a young man, yes, most certainly, a young man, dark-faced, faintly smiling, learned, full of the gestures of decadence and attenuation, an elegant young man who told nothing about himself, but whose eyes hinted at cynicism and despair. His hands would be the hands of a physician, strong yet calm, but now empty. Had he seen Rome? Yes, of course, he had seen Rome, and all its splendor, and he knew now that it had been a disintegrating splendor like murals painted on crumbling walls. Where had he encountered that young Jew who, by a glance of his eye, could melt men's souls and re-impart to them a knowledge they had forgotten? He, Frank, must reread his Bible. But, if he remembered rightly, the story of Luke was dim, untold. Yet he knew! He knew it in his heart; he knew Luke as if he were Frank Clair's own flesh and thought.

What had he thought when he had first seen that young Jew, so travel-stained, so ragged, so tired, and yet with such incandescent flesh? What did he think, this Grecian Luke, when he had first listened to the words that had convulsed a world of decadent lost men, despairing and stricken with every ill of the spirit? Now Frank saw that world; its sounds and its tumult were in his ears. Out of that chaos of pride and lust, slavery and death, banners and fury and grandeur, conquest and majesty, out of that Roman universe of triumph and ostentation and power, Luke had wandered to this sandy and barren Jerusalem, which was filled with hopeless but unconquered Jews. Had Luke been a slave who had fled the Roman world, and sought hiding here, beneath these dusty palms, along the shores of this dead sea, within these noisy and fetid streets? Had he thought to find a new philosophy among these red rocks, these scorpion-filled paths? Luke, the sophisticated and elegant Greek, tired as only a man of thought and learning can be tired when he is sick of his world: what had come to him when he had seen the miserable Jewish rabble congregating about this even more miserable young Jew whose voice was like a trumpet suddenly raised amid hubbub? At what moment had the rabble parted, so that the young Jew could be seen clearly by Luke, who had halted, idly and wearily, on their outskirts? Had Jesus spoken then? Had He smiled? Had He known instantly that this alien Greek must be His? Had He called, lifted His hand? Or had that look been enough to enslave, to awaken, that poetic and polished soul, so dusty and sickened? What had transpired when their eyes met, grave and smiling?

Meaning, tremendous, shaking, powerful, must have flashed between them. Luke had known! He had stood there under the blazing cataract of light which had poured down from the heavens upon this red and fruitless earth, and he had known. He stood as if he would never move again, for he had seen God. Had he bent, in a gesture of ceremony, and removed his worn sandals, as Moses had removed his shoes, knowing this was holy ground? Yes, Frank could see him do that, bending his flat scholar's body, extending his thin and graceful hand, his austere profile darkening with his own shadow. And then he had stood, simply and with dignity, his bare feet in the dust, his eyes gazing upon Jesus with pride and humility, with understanding and peace and joy. All his shallow philosophy, his epigrammatic wisdom, his artistry and weary decadence, had become as nothing, a corruption which he had shed with his sandals.

All at once, Frank could not wait to be back in his room, writing this wondrous tale. But perhaps this ought to be a play! Frank, in the very act of rising, fell back in his chair.

A play in three acts, six scenes, written in fervent and stately blank verse. There was Luke, talking idly with a group of bearded Jewish elders, near the steps of the threatened temple. The elders listened courteously, and with curious attention, but with impatience. Behind them, in the hot scarlet sunset, rose the temple, and throngs passed with laden asses, and women with striped headdresses of yellow and white, blue and red. Luke stood there, smiling faintly and with superior indulgence as he said:

> "If men were in this hour to lose their sight,
> All beauty and all life would cease to be.
> In man's small iris, vague, confused and dim,
> Are held the gods, all wisdom, and the suns."

Frank could see the elders shaking their old heads and lifting their faces with dignity as they denied. One spoke of the objectivity of God, in rebuttal, spoke of great and shining universes which man had never seen and which existed apart from him. Measure after measure flowed through Frank's mind; he listened to them enthralled. How could he ever put down on paper the beauty and majesty of these words? He must hurry, hurry back to his room and try to capture even a faint echo of them!

He stood up. The waiter came hurrying with the bill. Frank glanced at him, then paused. What had happened to his eyes? Had they recovered from a strange myopia, that the waiter's face should now be so clear and vivid, so minutely etched with old wrinkles? This waiter was an old familiar; he knew Frank by name. He had talked often, and haltingly, to this frequent customer. Yet Frank, with a kind of wonder, could not remember a single conversation, a single phrase. Why?

Feeling everything so imminent upon him now, so acute and sentient and meaningful, Frank said: "How is your family, Giovanni?" Giovanni! It was no longer a name; it was a person, a living creature, a man, flesh of his flesh, a brother with members like his own, with his own heart and his own sensations!

Had Giovanni a "family?" Frank could not remember, but he had a faint impression that during their conversations a family must have been mentioned. He watched Giovanni closely to see if the old man would show signs of bewilderment. But Giovanni smiled radiantly. He stood, with the tray of empty dishes on his arm, and his wizened face softened, and became tender. "Maria Pia is happy now," he said.

Maria Pia. Who was Maria Pia? The name had a familiar sound, but it brought no recognition to Frank, and he was ashamed. Giovanni must have talked often of Maria Pia and he had not listened! Shameful, shallow, degrading thought, that one could, at any time, be so insensible to a fellowman! He made his face interested, and again felt his shame.

"What is Maria Pia doing now?" he asked.

"She is dancing again." Giovanni's eyes shone with liquid and simple joy. Their corners had moistened; those were tears, there, in the tired old eyes, but they were tears of happiness.

"Good." Frank's voice was cautious, tentative. In a moment, now, he would know all about Maria Pia, whoever she was. He waited.

The waiter laid soiled silverware on his tray. His hand, veined and dark, trembled uncontrollably. But the light was still on his face. He murmured: "After all this time, she is dancing with the angels. Her mama and me: we're very happy now."

He went away, walking gingerly but quickly, on his aching waiter's feet. Frank stared after him, feeling a sense of complete loss and frustration. A tale had been told him. He knew the end, but not the beginning. He would never know. There had been a drama, stark, tremendous with pain and suffering, but because he had been blind and deaf, and there had been a shell over his heart, he would never know. He put his usual fifty-cent tip on the table, then impulsively added more silver.

Maria Pia, Giovanni's daughter? A young sister? Had she danced once, then been stricken down? Giovanni had told him; Frank knew that. He went out into the somber gray of the early twilight, restless and unfulfilled. The last pages, stained with tears, were in his hand. The first were lost. Good-bye, Maria Pia, he said humbly.

How much every man lost by not knowing, or loving, or caring for, his neighbor! How empty, how impoverished his life must become, if his eyes were always turned inward upon his own greed, his own selfishness, his own insignificance! When one did not see other men, one did not see God. One saw only emptiness, a dry fountain in a wilderness of bleached boulders and stone, a dead garden full of blowing straw and the skeletons of blasted trees. One became stone himself, a pillar of salt, a being without beginning and without end.

Frank felt a thickness in his throat, and a hate for himself. Forgive me, he said. Forgive me for my obtuseness and my selfish pain, for my self-dramatization and sterility. If there is a hell, he thought, it will be filled with the bitter waters of self-seeking and egotism, and the foot will be bruised by stony earth.

He would go to his grandmother's. He would look at his mother with eyes of new understanding. He would talk to Mr. Farley. Then he would go home and write, write as he had not written in years. The sonorous cadences of the tale of Luke were sounding louder and louder in his ears with exultation.

CHAPTER 41

THE STORM had definitely abated. Main Street, however, was still deserted, except for an occasional scurrying man or woman looking for shelter, for the air that struck Frank's cheeks was like the blades of icy knives. A streetcar rocked by, its windows almost obliterated by snow, its roof steaming. Frank crossed Main Street, and as he did so, pale street lamps bloomed mistily in the twilight. He would take the West Utica car to Niagara Street, and arrive at his grandmother's in plenty of time for tea.

He was the only one waiting for the West Utica car. There was no shelter in which he could huddle away from the flaying cold. He kicked a place in the deep snow in which to stand, and its essence seeped in through his arctics and numbed his feet. Though the worst of the gale had passed, the snow hissed uneasily as currents of wind lashed it, and clouds of thin and scalding whiteness blew into the gray air.

He thought of Kentucky. Tim Cunningham had recently written of the spring warmth in the valleys, the fruit blossoms which were making of the hills great mounds of pink and white, of the dogwood soon to be scenting the woods, of the greening fields. He had written with the simple poetry of the countryman, and he compared the Southern climate with the nefarious cold and deadly winters of the North. Frank had a vision of great white houses set on lush knolls, of "Kentucky colonels" sipping their juleps, of stately dignity and golden sun and the songs of Negro workers in the fields.

All at once he yearned for warmth and pleasantness, for the theatrical South he had imagined from the reading of sentimental novels and from the words of Southerners themselves. How agreeable it would be to work during the day in oil fields, and at night on his poetic novel of Luke! He and Tim, perhaps, would have a vine-wreathed cottage in the woods, where only the moon lightened the darkness, and the whippoorwills sang to the night. He saw himself at a plain table, under a lamp, writing hour by hour while Tim slept or read, and the moonlight mingled with the lamplight, and the fragrance of earth and flowers and trees drifted to him through bowered French windows.

Frank knew that in spite of the universal hope that the war would be renewed and the factories roar again, the Curtiss plant was shutting down, day by day. Any day now he would be out of a job. Why wait? He would write to Tim Cunningham tonight and tell him that in April, or in May at the latest, he would join him in Benton, Kentucky.

Coming like a white, prehistoric monster out of the gloom of the encompassing winter, the West Utica streetcar groaned towards Main Street and Frank. He entered the car; he was the only passenger. The windows were thick and white with frost. He was encased in an airless chamber of freezing cold, in which his breath rose in clouds. He clung to his seat as the car rocked down the ice-filled tracks. The uncertain lights overhead blinked, went out momentarily, as the pole struck crystallized switches. The car rolled on, through empty and gusty streets. But Frank's mind was busy with exciting dreams, and though his flesh chilled and numbed, he did not feel it.

When the car reached Niagara Street, he was still the sole passenger. Stiff and almost unfeeling, he left the car. He would have to walk to his grandmother's, for it was hopeless to expect another streetcar in this wilderness of snow. Shivering, he started to walk down Niagara Street. He passed Albany Street, where once he had lived and where his father had died.

All at once, he wanted to see his catalpa tree, standing stiff and black and expectant, in the yard. He wanted to see it, then he would write to Paul Hodge of it; he would examine a branch, to see if the buds had as yet become tender, and if they were swelling. He would touch the trunk, and tell it what was now in his heart, and it would listen, dull and sleeping though it was, and understand and be glad.

Doubtless a new family lived in that house now. Well, it

was dark, and the blizzard had engulfed all life. No one would see him go into the yard to visit his friend. He would stay only long enough to tell the tree, and would go away, enriched and comforted. The tree he had planted so many years ago, and which, like himself, would soon flower and fill the air with richness and leaves! The sap was rising in it, irresistibly, hopefully, steadfast in the empirical knowledge that spring was coming, and that though it was still locked in ice and snow, ever-powerful life was tingling in every branch.

He stood a moment on the corner of Niagara and Albany Streets. He hesitated. He did not understand this sudden reluctance which came to him like a warning voice. He argued to himself: It will take only a few extra minutes. But the reluctance sharpened in him insistently. Now it was like hands on his shoulders, urging him to continue on down Niagara Street. But why? Only a few moments, and then he would go on. He felt the tree waiting for him wistfully, stirring in its sleep. He went resolutely down Albany Street, still arguing vaguely with himself.

The little old white house was still there, as he remembered it. Lights were in its windows. He paused to look. Surely his parents were in that room, toasting themselves before the heater, and there would be a smell of roasting chicken in the kitchen. He had only to put his hand on the knob of the door, to open it, to hear Francis' irritable voice: "Shut that damned door! You're letting in the cold."

But there was a look of strangeness over the house, as if it had withdrawn from him. Strangers were there now. That was not the window through which he had looked at snow, at trees, at greening lawn. He had never stood on that doorstep. Something ineluctable had happened to the house; it had withdrawn to another plane unfamiliar to him. It resembled only slightly the house he had known, as one human being might wear, for a brief instant, the smile of someone well known, use a familiar gesture. Something had shifted; the very clapboards, the very cellar door, the very shape of the windows, denied that he had known them. Something in time and space had gone on, part of him, but not part of what he now saw.

There was an eeriness about the dark street with its flickering lamplights. He looked at the surrounding houses. He glanced down the street. He saw the shop on the corner, Vincent's, where he had sipped, in ecstasy, a rare soda, or had stared in at the windows at the advertisement for lollypops, with their offered multiple flavors. The faint light which shone out on the street was not the light he had remembered. Only six months had passed, but the world he had known had gone on with him. This was another world. Across the street lived the Campbells; that house with the yellow porch was the home of the Flahertys. Old widowed Mrs. Berger lived in that brown cottage. They had not gone. But had they? If he should knock on their doors, would familiar faces stare out at him? Or would the faces of strangers wait, questioningly, for his first words?

Again, as he stood in the drift of snow, he felt the urgency not to see his tree, to turn back. The tree you knew is not there now. You have the tree in your heart. It will flourish there forever, forever blossoming, forever alive. You have the tree with you; it is yours, never to be uprooted. Turn away; go on. You cannot come back, for you come back to what you have never known. What you have known is always with you.

Frank stamped his feet impatiently, shrugging off the ancient wisdom to which he had been listening. He plowed through the drifts towards the rear of the little house. His feet crunched hard and crackling snow. As the lamplight struck his back his shadow fell before him, distorted and twisted. He thought, as if in an enchantment: That shadow belongs here. It lives on this street, this gangling and mysterious thing. It lives in this house. It owns the tree. I have no right here.

Cautiously, so as not to disturb the mysterious creatures behind the lighted windows, he reached the rear of the house.

The moon broke through a wrack of clouds, pure spectral light on a waste of alabaster. Frank saw the picket fence, almost obliterated by snow. He saw the roof of the chicken coop on the other side. He saw chimneys of neighboring houses steaming in the moonlight, and the steam turned to frail silver. He saw gleams of light from back windows. He felt the silence and the solitary, frozen immobility of the night.

But he did not see his tree. His tree was gone. There was not even a black and wounded stump on the smooth deep marble of the yard. There was nothing at all.

He stood there, and everything became very still in him, as if his heart and his blood had stopped. Always, powerful emotion had been late in coming to him; always, he had at first been stunned as if, so to speak, lightning had struck him, and thunder delayed its reverberation. So he felt nothing as he looked at the sparkling drift where his tree had stood. He said to himself: They have cut it down. And the thought had a kind of smooth impersonality and indifference in his mind.

They have cut it down, he said to himself, as he stood there, a tall, dark thin shadow under the moon, his hands thrust deep in his pockets, the snow rising high above his ankles. Someone in the little house where he had lived lit the kitchen light, and a narrow golden flood gushed out onto the snow. Automatically, Frank stepped a few paces to one side, where the light would not strike him. But, in his stepping, he did not move his eyes from the place where his tree had stood.

And then he turned to go. Desolate, forsaken, he looked back. There was the ghostly drift where his tree had stood. Now he was aware of the emptiness, of cruel sorrow and fury. Surely, surely, his tree had stood there only a moment ago, and then the ax had been laid to its trunk, and it had fallen into nothingness and had disappeared. He ran to the drift. He stood in it, feeling desperately with his feet. There was no stump. But all at once he sensed the roots in the ground, deep within the ground, as one senses the dead under a grave. The roots were still there, rotting as the dead rot.

The roots tried to reach him, like the hands of the blind, imploring his pity and his help, conscious of his love as they died. He felt their reaching, their bewilderment. Spring was coming. There would be sap in the roots, still, but it would be a sap stifled and blocked. There was nothing in the airy world above to which it could rise. Hour by hour, the roots were dying, baffled, trying to understand how they had been betrayed, and why the hand which had planted them had allowed this thing to be done.

Frank could feel his own blood seeping down to the roots, mingling with them. He felt their blind call. Without knowing what he was doing, he knelt in the snow and frantically threw it aside. His gloved hands plowed deeper and deeper; he heard a loud rustling in his ears, and did not know it was his breath.

His hands struck black hard earth. He felt over it. There was nothing. But he pressed the wet gloved palms of his hands strongly on its roughness. Something pulsed under them. Like a failing heart. He felt the life of the roots, their young strongness. And then, as if they acknowledged him with a last expiring sigh, their pulsing dwindled, was gone.

He got slowly to his feet, and looked down at the grave of his tree. His sorrow was an unbearable sickness in him. And then rage came, wild and terrible. Why had this tree been done to death? Who had dared do this to a being so beautiful and so living? Man was an evil, dirty creature, an animal, an obscenity. Without compunction, without thought, he could destroy a harmless and lovely thing, and not care. Frank saw his tree carted away, thrown upon some rubbish heap. Perhaps its leaves had been bright with autumn when this was done. He saw those leaves, fading slowly, drooping, falling. Why hadn't he known?

Somewhere there was a rough noise as a door opened. A man's hoarse voice shouted out, "What the hell you think you're doin' out there?"

Frank, trembling and weak, turned to see the huge bulk of a man plowing towards him in the snow. The moon came out again, and he saw under a bald dome a great and bristling face, the face of an uncouth laborer. The man approached him, half crouching, an ape which had ravished a nymph. The moonlight was so vivid that Frank could see the beetling eyes, glittering savagely and with suspicion.

He said, in a faint choked voice: "Where is my tree? The tree I planted?"

The man stopped abruptly and stared. He looked at the narrow black hole in the snow; he looked back to Frank. "You crazy?" he rumbled. "You mean that tree that stood there? I cut it down so the kids could have a baseball diamond, that's why. What you mean, comin' here?"

Frank did not know that he had clenched his wet fists; he did not know that he had taken a step towards this dread horror, this personification of a world he now hated. He saw that the ape was retreating, slowly, warily. He followed it. He said very softly: "I planted that tree. I watched it grow. It was mine. You've killed it."

"You crazy," said the ape, finally stopping in its backward retreat. "You lived here, 'fore we came? Well, what of it? The kids wanted to play baseball, so I cut the damn thing down. Who the hell cares, you crazy son of a bitch? Get out o' here, or I'll call the cops."

He raised his voice to a shout, not daring to look away from Frank, whose face he saw clearly in the moonlight: "Grace, call the cops! Got a crazy bastard out here! Tryin' to break in the house!"

A coarse female shriek sounded from the house. Frank was not aware of moving, but automatically his arm shot out from his shoulder, the clenched fist like a wet stone at the end of it. He felt it strike flesh and bone, and he heard a meaty and crunching sound. He saw the ape fall backward into the snow, arms and legs flailing. Still without full consciousness, he kicked the creature in the side several times. Then he ran, stumbling in the deep drifts.

CHAPTER 42

HE SAT again in the West Utica streetcar, huddled in his seat. Again he was the sole passenger in that heaving and rocking vehicle whose windows were thick with frost-ferns. He sat, almost crouched, like a man in pain, hands thrust deep in his pockets, collar up about his ears, hat pulled down. He listened to, and felt, the crunching and grinding of the wheels; he swayed back and forth, and from side to side. The clattering noise, flat and raucous, echoed in his flesh. One of his fists ached; he knew the hand to be bruised. He moved his hand in the glove, and was pleased by the smarting of the scraped skin.

He looked about him dully. Everything was without perspective, like a photograph. He sensed the walls of the car, the coated windows, the flickering light on the ceiling. He saw them, but they were flattened and meaningless. Somewhere, far off in space, there was a pain, a pain like nausea. He did not think of the tree. The tree was gone; it was no longer part of him. He knew only his hatred.

The car swayed, and his body swayed with it; he was thrown back against the seat. The pain quickened and throbbed. He saw the motorman at the controls; the man was whistling through his teeth, jangling his bell ferociously. He hated the motorman. He hated the broad squat shoulders, the red ears, the silly uniform cap, the way his hand tugged at the bell-rope. He was an animal, like all the rest of them, a forked animal in old blue serge, a monstrosity, a meaninglessness.

The car grunted to a stop. A very old woman climbed aboard painfully. She was dressed in an ancient black coat, down to her thick, bent ankles. Big black buttons twinkled in the yellow light. She wore a shapeless bunch of felt on her head; her hair, gray and stringy, flattened itself on her wrinkled forehead and fallen cheeks. She tottered down the aisle, found a seat, and sank onto it.

Frank looked at her. He hated her. He resented it savagely

that she breathed, this misshapen, dirty, ugly parody of humanity. Her watery blue eyes blinked behind steel-framed glasses. She pursed up her toothless mouth, and appeared to be chewing. Vacantly, she stared about her. Her wizened lips moved from side to side, then up and down, as if munching. She rubbed her cheek with her mittened hand; it trembled. She dropped it aimlessly, and chewed and munched again.

Frank held himself tight against the back of his seat. He must not get up and kick her! They arrested people for that. How could he explain to the police: She was horrible-looking; she was old and hideous; she had no mind, no feeling! She was not even alive. She made me sick, so I had to hit her.

The watery, almost sightless eyes turned toward him. The munching and chewing stopped. He looked at her. She shrank back. She mumbled something, a faint animal sound. Then she got up and moved back a few seats. Her mumbling grew louder. Now her sunken face became cunning and vaguely frightened. "What you lookin' at, anyways?" she quavered to Frank's back.

He must press harder against the seat. He must hold himself still. The motorman jangled the bell. and Frank's teeth clenched. Again the car stopped. A pale shabby woman of about thirty lumbered aboard, skirts dragging against her old buttoned boots. She carried a pallid child in her arms; the little four-year-old girl's face was stained with dirt and dried tears. Frank watched them pass him. Filthy animals! They ate and excreted as did all other animals, and slept and snored and lived in their vile slums. But they had none of the wild beauty and grace of the furry creatures in the woods, the feathered creatures in the trees. They had not even the excuse of comeliness for their existence. Why was it not possible to kill them, to have done with them, to preserve the food they devoured for men who were truly alive and had a reason for living? It was an evil thing that they had been born; they became harmless only when they died. Between birth and death they were an affront to heaven.

The nauseous pain deepened in him. Now he was truly sick. He pressed his lips against an involuntary retching. Everywhere he glanced he saw only ugliness, senseless motion, repulsive sights. Everything was foreshortened, dim, superficial. How had he forgotten, for a brief few hours that day, how unsightly and foul the whole world was, how offensive to the eye? How stinking!

The child squalled behind him. He shivered with his hatred

and disgust. The old woman was still mumbling. Now his hatred and disgust turned savagely upon himself. What a sentimental half-wit he was! Only a few hours ago he had felt a silly shining in himself, had believed he had discerned a meaning, a pathetic yet heroic pattern, in such creatures as these. He had ached and throbbed with a loathsome compassion; he had wallowed in languishing romanticism. Maria Pia! Giovanni! The old woman and the young drab woman, the squalling child! Beasts and dogs, in the deformed image of angels. Drooling laws permitted them to live. In a better and more realistic society they would not have been permitted to be born, or, born, they would have been destroyed and decently hidden from sight under the earth.

He wanted to be home, in his handsome quiet room, with the lamplight glowing on his old bed, with his books about him. He wanted to shut out all this ugliness and forget it.

Suddenly he was sharply frightened. He remembered Miss Woods, and the uproar at the table this morning. What would Miss Woods have to say to him when she heard him come in? Would she give him his notice? Fool! What had he done, and for what? For a pimpled, sallow-faced idiot who could not claim an exact paternity? For a slum rat with pretensions to being a man? He had jeopardized his quiet retreat, his pleasant life, for an Irving Schultz. He had insulted a respectable woman, and thrown a fire-lit room into embarrassed confusion. If he received his notice, it would not be more then he deserved. Now he began to breathe more quickly in his furious anxiety. He glanced at his watch. It was after eight. Miss Woods would be in her "parlor." He would go to her at once, humbly apologizing, and he would go to Mrs. Crimmons, begging her pardon for his unjustified and insane insults. Perhaps, then, Miss Woods would permit him to remain. Perhaps he would not be driven out of her house. If only he hurried.

He blew on the window, rubbed a hole in the frost. He would soon reach Linwood Avenue. He cursed himself for the imbecile he had been that morning. He yearned for his now threatened security and tranquil quiet. If only it was not too late! Why had he endangered himself so? What had made him stand up and shout at poor Mrs. Crimmons? What had there been in that slum rat's face and eyes to induce him to injure himself in that disgraceful fashion? Babbling Bill! His father had been right, after all: he was a dreamer, a talker, an empty silliness. After all these years of effort, he had allowed a nameless something to ruin him. After all these years of struggling for normality, for respectability, for smooth averageness, he had permitted some delirious emotion to deface all the painful remodeling he had done to himself. He could not even remember the emotion, but he knew it was shameful. His face burned with misery and humiliation.

He stood up and tugged at the bell-rope. He ran to the door. The old woman and the young one watched him go. The child squalled and struggled in her mother's thin arms. The door closed after Frank; the car churned on without him.

The old woman blew her nose on a dirty rag and mumbled: "See that feller just got off? Looked kind of dippy to me, or drunk, or somethin'. Looked at me, he did, like he wanted to kill me. And I never saw him before in my life! Must be drunk."

Frank plowed and stumbled through the snow to his rooming-house. His body felt hot all over, yet shivering. Blundering, maudlin idiot! If only it was not too late! He would talk to Miss Woods immediately, then go to Mrs. Crimmons and apologize. If only he had persuasive powers! But he had no natural graces, no cajoling ways. Feverishly he rehearsed: "Miss Woods, I'm terribly sorry. I don't know what got into me." No, that expression was English. He had worked so hard on himself to eliminate any Britishisms which he had acquired from his parents and which seemed to annoy Americans.

"Miss Woods, I'm terribly sorry about this morning. Do you think Mrs. Crimmons would accept my apologies?" That was better. It had dignity. It placed him on a man-to-man basis with Miss Woods. He saw her large bland face before him, and hated her. I hate everything, he thought savagely. I'm sick of everything.

He stamped his feet in the winter vestibule to rid them of snow. He saw that his trousers were wet far above the knee; snow had seeped in at the top of his arctics; there was a wretched area of cold between his shoulder-blades, as if a large icy hand were pressing there. Now he was shivering quite violently; he drew a deep breath. Immediately something stabbed him viciously in the right side. He held his breath, then slowly exhaled, frightened. He ought not to have run through the snow.

He glanced through the velvet portieres of the parlor doorway. Miss Woods was sitting before the fire, surrounded by somber family heirlooms. Her cat slept at her feet. She herself was reading. She put down her book calmly when Frank entered, and looked at him steadily, without speaking. He could read neither animosity nor kindness in her eyes. She merely waited. Why didn't she speak? She usually greeted him pleasantly. But it was evident to him, even in his confused mental state of anxiety, that she was waiting for something. He was relieved; she was expecting him to say what he must say. He spoke his rehearsed speech hurriedly: "Miss Woods, I'm terribly sorry about this morning. Do you think Mrs. Crimmons would accept my apologies?"

Her face seemed to move towards him across the faded carpet, and he could see her eyes, very intent now, very piercing. She did not smile; her expression was closed and inscrutable. Then she said very slowly: "You are really sorry?"

He could see her almost as though he had brought her into sharp near focus with a telescope. Everything around him had become too clear, too vivid. But he was greatly relieved, for he had expected her first words to be stern and forbidding. However, she only watched him, and appeared to wait intently for his reply.

He said eagerly: "Yes. I'm awfully sorry. You see—"

She turned her head away from him then, and he saw her big pudgy profile against the firelight. She looked down at her be-ringed hands meditatively. Then she said: "Yes, I see."

She sighed; her great bosom heaved, as if with some deep regret. Still not turning to him, she continued: "I'm sorry too, Mr. Clair. But you will understand, I know. I can't have violent controversies in my house. Mr. and Mrs. Crimmons are old—acquaintances of mine, and have been coming here for years. It would be awkward for them if you remained, would it not?"

His heart sank. He felt the cold wetness of his clothing clinging to his shivering legs; the icy hand pressed deeper into his back. There was a faint sensation as of shock in the pit of his stomach. He stammered, as he had not stammered for years: "I—I think I could—apologize to Mrs. Crimmons, and it would be all right—"

She shook her head. Now she turned completely away from him, so that he saw only her mass of white hair and her heavy shoulders. "I think it would be better for everyone, and for you, too, if you gave up your room a week from tomorrow. I really think so."

Mortification, rage and disappointment flooded over him. In that queer clarity which filled the room he could see every line in the face of that old woman, and the way the black silk shimmered on her shoulders and encased her arms like a dark sheath. Everything in the room became inimical to him, repudiating him, withdrawing from him. He was a stranger; he had never lived here, or spent one night here.

"Please, won't you—change—your mind, Miss Woods?" he stammered, pleadingly. "I—I like it here. In a way, it's been the only home I ever had—"

He hated her with profound malignance, because of his humiliation.

She said, almost inaudibly: "I'm sorry. I don't think you'll ever have a home, Mr. Clair, until you find out about yourself. I'm very sorry for you. Truly I am. But perhaps one of these days you'll understand what I am talking about now. I must ask you to excuse me. I can't change my mind, so please don't ask me."

The hateful, vicious old bitch! The fat and avaricious old harridan! She had allowed him to debase himself, enjoying every moment of it. He wanted to pummel her head with his fists. He wanted to kick her as he had kicked that ape, in the yard on Albany Street. But she was speaking again: "If I were you, I'd take a hot bath immediately. You are wet all over. And now, good night, Mr. Clair."

He went up the stairs, which swam before his eyes. He had to stop on the first landing to catch his breath, and again the hot knife stabbed his side. Now he was shivering so strongly that he had to hold on to the banister to keep from falling. The warmth and quiet and dimness of the old house were all about him, but it was a withdrawn pleasantness, which was going on without him. He saw lights under doors, heard a slight laugh, a cough, the rustle of a newspaper. A week from tomorrow he would be gone; the house and its fortunate inhabitants would have smugly forgotten him. He heard the old clock chiming in the parlor; a tall mirror on the wall before him glimmered, showing his ghost of a face. The wind was rising again; it was flowing about the stalwart eaves, gushing over the roof which would soon no longer be his cherished shelter. He would no longer have access to those fine books in Miss Woods' den, nor would he be permitted to sit there in the depths of the old red-leather chair, enjoying the privilege only lately given him. He would not hear that melodious chiming again, nor linger in the dining room over warm winter breakfasts. Grief stung his eyes. This was his home; he was being evicted from it. Now he was exposed again, stripped naked, homeless.

His room, at the end of the hall, was, all at once, too far. When he opened the door the furniture, the rugs, the old rich draperies, no longer welcomed him. He turned on the lamp by the bedside. It shone coldly on the white bed, which resembled a sheet of snow. He could feel the warmth on his skin, but it did not penetrate into his flesh. The pain was sharper, now, in his side, and came and went with his slow and careful breathing.

He did not take off his soaking coat. With a kind of deep wonder, he thought: "Why, I'm sick! I can't stay here. Something's happened to me."

CHAPTER 43

MAY FOAMED, a tide of flowering shrub and tree and plant, on every street, in every yard. Lilacs bent in plumes of poignant white and purple over broken fences; syringia shrubs were banks of snow against porches and verandahs. Forsaken back yards became beautiful with the rosy blooms of gnarled apple trees; elms dropped their showers of brown seed upon the earth; the young maple's leaves were tipped with gold. Spring had tossed her pale green garments on every branch. Now the streets, at twilight, rang with soft echoes, and mauve shadows lengthened over brightening lawns. The city was embowered in fragrance, in sweetness under wide and gentle skies, though the air remained cool, and the wind, blowing from the lakes, still retained the sharp edge of churning ice.

Frank Clair, wrapped in heavy coats, with an old blanket about his legs, sat on his grandmother's verandah and looked silently at the street beyond the little lawn. He could smell lilacs, the freshness of new grass. Long beams of sun fell across his thin white hands with their strong knuckles. His hands lay on his coat, still, flaccid. He heard church bells ringing with a new spring clarity; several family groups passed, hurrying to worship. His eyes followed them indifferently, blankly, then turned away as if vaguely sickened. There was none of the new strength of the convalescent in him, none of the reborn hope. He sat there motionless, feeling the warmth of the sun on his hands, not caring, hardly feeling. The fresh wind blew a lock of his dark chestnut hair over his forehead. He did not push it back; it moved, lifted and blew across his eyes, and he did not shake his head to rid himself of it. His strong thin features appeared to fill his emaciated face; his lips were almost as white as his cheeks, and his eyes moved too slowly in their pits of dark shadow.

Maybelle passed the screen door and peered out at him furtively. She saw him in profile; she saw how still he sat. She remembered his young quickness and restlessness. This was not like Frank, she thought with anxious petulance. It was more than she could put up with, after everything, to have him just sit there, day after day, seldom speaking, then only sluggishly, "showing no interest," eating when querulously prodded, not responding when it was hinted to him that the doctor said he was well, and that he could soon look for a job.

And me so fagged out, thought Maybelle, and been through so much. No one sympathized with her. And me a widow, her wretched thoughts continued, with nowhere to turn, and not even a place of my own. Among strangers. It was little enough for her son to do, to "show some interest," and think about bestirring himself and getting a new job, and bringing in a bit of money. That doctor said to "give him time," that he had had a bad bout with that Spanish flu, and that he was still a little weak. But he was pampering himself now, just sitting on the verandah on days like this, or sitting in his room in the attic when it rained. Never offered to help about the house. What if he did pay the doctor promptly, and was now giving his grandmother ten dollars a week for his lodgings? It wasn't as if he were a proper lodger, with no responsibilities. After all, his mother had nursed him through "three weeks of hell," and he had given her no thanks—not a word of gratitude. Nor had Mrs. Clair offered to relieve her of her tasks about the house, even when she had had to sit up for three nights the first week, when Frank had had pneumonia. It was hard; it was very hard. He had just lain there, cosy under his blankets, with a really good color in his cheeks, and he had not looked at her. What had he said? Just a lot of rot about a tree, and swearing like a navvy, and crying like a baby, a big lad like that! Never showed her any sympathy for what she had to do, carrying his slops, and wiping up the floor when he vomited. Even when she dozed a few times in her chair, he had just talked and screamed and sworn, babbling like daft, and not giving her a minute's rest. It was a fine thing, just, for the doctor to talk about nurses, but who had money for nurses? She, Maybelle, had "given it to him" when he had suggested a hospital. "Hospitals were full of quacks; 'kill 'em quick,' is their motto!" she had replied to him, and he had gone off with his tail between his legs. Yankees!

No one had any sympathy for her, neither "the old devil" nor her son, and as for that doctor, he'd never dare show his face to *her* again. Maybelle's brown eyes flashed vindictively as she looked out at Frank. Coddling himself there, when he could be bringing in some money. What if he never bestirred himself, she thought, frightened. What would "the old devil" say? Mrs. Clair was hinting in no uncertain terms that it was about time he took interest and looked about him for something to do. What when his money was gone? He had only two hundred dollars left. Somebody must tell him to brace up, to be a man, to get back on his own bottom.

Frank began to cough suddenly, hoarsely and with violence. He was racked with the spasm, bending his head over the arm of the chair, his whole thin body shaking. What if he got consumption, now, like his father? Maybelle was filled with enraged terror. If he did, it was off to a charity hospital for him, mark her words! Her, a poor widow, at the mercy of strangers, in Yankeeland, with no place to go, with not even a stick of her own furniture and people expecting her to take care of "him."

Frank, in the act of raising himself from his bent position, glanced at the screen door. He's seen me! thought Maybelle, with mingled anger and relief. He's putting it on, for sympathy. Wants to coddle himself. Putting it on.

He had shown enough spirit, he had, when she had opened his letters. Came down on her, brutal. Why, she had always opened all letters that came to "the house," whether they were poor Francis' or her son's. How he had carried on! And refused to talk to her about what she had read in the letter, about that stranger asking how to come to Kentucky. Yes, he could be strong enough to carry on, when his poor old mother opened his letters, and he had looked at her vicious. After all her work, and no sympathy. And now he was coughing so that she wouldn't have a proper talk with him about getting out and getting a job. Well, she'd show him, that she would!

She pushed open the screen door and stepped heavily onto the verandah, her double chin set belligerently, her eyes sparkling with indignation and malice. The fresh May wind ruffled her untidy masses of hair, which were more gray now than auburn. She rolled her stout arms up in her apron, and marched to her son with a purposeful tread. No nonsense now. She'd put up with enough.

Frank did not turn toward her. He was staring blankly at the street again.

"Look you here," she said roughly. "It's time you thought about me for a change. There's nothing wrong with you now, do you hear me? Tomorrow's Monday. You'll get out and look for a job, and quick about it. I'm tired of you hanging about, and her after me all the time, asking me when you're going to lift yourself and do something for your mother."

Frank did not reply immediately. His hands were almost transparent in the sunlight. She could see his jawbone under his white skin, the pits about his nostrils. Then, just as she opened her mouth to continue her angry demands, he said quietly: "I'm getting out. In a few days."

"Tomorrow," said Maybelle, with loud firmness.

Frank said: "I'll go and get my ticket."

Eyes bulging with bewilderment, Maybelle stared at him.

"I'm going to Kentucky," continued Frank. His voice had a curious hollowness since he had been ill. "I talked to the doctor on the telephone yesterday, and he said a warmer climate and a change would do me good."

"You'll do nothing of the kind!" cried Maybelle furiously. "After all I've done for you, night after night, with never a word of gratitude from you! You'll get a job, and you'll bring the money in—"

She pulled her hands out from under the apron, and, knotting them into fists, pummelled them together, as if his head were between them. "I'll give it to you, if you talk that way!" she continued. "You owe me something."

"I'll give you fifty dollars," said Frank indifferently, his eyes following the slow passing of a dog. "The doctor's paid, and I don't owe Grandma anything."

"I'll *give* you 'fifty dollars'!" exclaimed Maybelle, outraged. "You cheeky devil. Who do you think you are, talking to me like that, and me slaving over you when you had that bad cold you got from tramping around among strangers, me emptying your dirt, and you carrying on demented like about a tree, or something! You're daft. You're a failure. Babbling Bill, like your poor father used to say. Well, I can tell you you're not going to hang around here, putting it on, and me working day and night—"

A stout gray old man was turning in towards the verandah. He looked at Frank quickly, then smiled amiably at Maybelle, who was panting.

He stepped up on the verandah, removed his old brown felt hat, and fanned himself genially. "A lovely day, isn't it?" he commented. "Nice to be sitting out here, I'm thinking. You look good to me, Frank. Almost as good as new."

"That's just what I told him, Mr. Farley!" exclaimed Maybelle, with a vigorous nod. "You give it to him. Give him a proper talking to, about what he owes his mother."

Mr. Farley sat down on the verandah railing, his fat brown thighs spreading comfortably. He still smiled, but his eyes were thoughtful. He waited.

"I've just been telling him he's got to get out and get a job, and bring some money in," continued Maybelle irately. "He went off among strangers when his poor pa died, though he was offered a good home here, with his mother and grandmother. But no, off he went, and look what he came to, after I pleaded and pleaded with him that his proper place was with his family. But strangers was better than us, until he came down with something."

Mr. Farley looked down at his wide polished boots. He remembered the night that Frank had come to this house, wet, shaking uncontrollably, his eyes already wild and dim with fever. He had come to his mother instinctively, as a sick animal crawls into an old familiar cave to die. Mr. Farley doubted that reason had had anything to do with Frank's coming. He had acted blindly, out of his instincts, when, if he had thought only a moment, he would not have come.

Mr. Farley also remembered that he had nursed Frank for the three weeks he had been in bed, with the exception of the few nights when Maybelle had "sat up." He had found Frank abandoned, delirious. In fact, it had been Frank's discordant ravings which had brought the tired old man up the stairs to the miserable attic room. He had listened to them for hours; he had heard no footstep above him, no soothing voice. He had gone up, to find Frank uncovered, struggling to get out of bed. Mr. Farley did not like to remember that night. He remained with Frank until morning, and then had gone quietly away, carrying with him his own sponge and bowl of water, with which he had bathed that burning flesh. But he had left Frank asleep and quiet.

Night after night, thereafter, he had crept noiselessly up the stairs, bringing his bowl, his sponge and his own towels, holding cool water to the parched lips, murmuring gently, praying, saying his beads with simple faith. No one knew of those weeks of patient and tender nursing, except himself and Frank. No one knew that it was he who had given Frank his medicines, and had brought him hot milk when he could finally swallow, and ice cream from his shop, concealed under his coat. Maybelle, "fagged out," had left her son each night at eight, and had gone to her own room and bed, where, though she always claimed she "never closed her eyes," she slept the sound sleep of the just. She labored under the bland misapprehension that Frank doctored himself and slept comfortably during the night, and that his recovery was entirely due to her.

Mr. Farley said mildly, for he was a gentle and patient man and an understanding one: "Well, he'll surprise you one of these days, Mrs. Clair, and find himself a good job. He's just getting better now, aren't you, Frank?"

Frank looked at him steadily and smiled a little.

"Nonsense," said Maybelle roundly. "He's jolly well enough now to find a job and bring a bit of money in. You've got to give him a proper talking to. He needs a man to stop his cheek. And now he's talking about going to Kentucky!"

Mr. Farley raised his reddish eyebrows. "Is that so?" he murmured mendaciously, for Frank had already discussed the matter with him. "Well, we'll have to talk about it, shan't we?"

"Do!" said Maybelle, nodding and throwing her son a satisfied glare from her protuberant eyes. "Perhaps he'll listen to you." She went back into the house, and slammed the screen door after her.

There was silence on the verandah after she had gone. Mr. Farley continued to fan himself nonchalantly with his hat, and regarded the street and the passersby with that amiable and affectionate expression of understanding which had often infuriated Frank. But now little disturbed the young man; nothing broke through his apathy. Sights, sounds, scenes, voices, movements: all approached the extreme periphery of his consciousness but penetrated no farther. Only Mr. Farley, ignorant, unlettered, simple and pious Mr. Farley, understood that Frank's spirit was in extreme abeyance, that he had reached a dangerous point of negation and mental lassitude.

Frank, in his delirium, had raved of a tree. Mr. Farley had gathered that the tree had been cut down. What tree, and why? What did that tree represent to Frank? He had known Frank to be sensitive and too vulnerable to environment, but he had also recognized a kind of hard ruthlessness in him and an absence of sentimentality. Mr. Farley, being human, was curious, and being kind and generous, was anxious. There was more to this tree business than met his eye.

Now Mr. Farley, apparently engaged only in pleasant contemplation of the street, was wondering about that tree. Intuitively, then, he understood that the tree must have something to do with Frank's inertia, his prolonged silences, his emptiness of eye.

Mr. Farley got up and closed the door behind the screen door. He chuckled as he returned to Frank. "Guess we ought to have that 'proper' talk your ma spoke about," he said.

Frank gave no indication that he had heard. Mr. Farley offered him a cigarette from his battered pack, lit the cigarette for the young man, and one for himself. The smoke curled upward in the brisk mild air. Mr. Farley said: "Two hundred won't be enough for Kentucky, Frank. Guess you'd better let me lend you another couple of hundred. You don't want to get down there, broke. Oh, I remember the letters you showed me from that young feller, but young fellers get enthusiastic, and the first thing you know, you're broke and a million miles from home. Not so good."

Frank shook his head. "Thanks. No." He smiled. "I'm giving my mother fifty. That'll leave me one hundred and fifty. It'll be enough. I'm going to live with Tim Cunningham anyway. He has a big tent all to himself, in the mountains."

Mr. Farley, artlessly, had a vision of snow-capped peaks and deep green valleys, of clear bright air and health, of pine-scented winds and peace. It would be good for Frank. Pull him out of this. Didn't the doctor talk ominously of incipient tuberculosis? Nothing like the mountains for that! Mr. Farley's vision of the Kentucky mountains was only slightly less incorrect than Frank's own.

"When do you think you'll leave?" asked Mr. Farley.

"Tuesday, at the latest."

Mr. Farley frowned. "Sure you can make it? You had a bad time, remember. Kinda weak yet, ain't you?"

Frank's jawbone, so sharp beneath his white skin now, stood out clearly. "I'll make it. It's all right." He paused. "I never thanked you, 'proper,' for what you've done for me. I've been wondering why you did it."

Mr. Farley, amazed, stared at him. "You wonder why? Why, Frank, when you talk that way, you make me wonder about you. I thought you knew things better than that. Or, maybe you've forgotten. Maybe you've forgotten what you knew when you were a kid."

He waited, but Frank did not answer. Mr. Farley was greatly perturbed. He had touched the periphery of Frank's being, and had felt something smooth and hard and cold and unresponsive. Now he was frightened. He leaned towards the young man and said urgently: "You got to tell me, Frank, that you didn't mean to insult me. You got to tell me that you were just talking—"

Frank answered with his old quickness: "For God's sake, Mr. Farley, insulting you is the last thing in my mind! I was just wondering, that's all, why you bothered. After all, I'm nothing to you."

Mr. Farley could only look at him with such misery that Frank felt an uneasy stirring in himself. He quelled the stirring immediately, and smiled with blandness. "Well. I'm truly grateful—and, of course, I understand. I'll try to make it up to you some day. When Tim's wells come in, I'll come back a millionaire." He laughed, then went into another spasm of coughing. Mr. Farley gently withdrew the cigarette from the thin white fingers and threw it away.

"You got to promise me," he said, a little hoarsely, "that you'll let me know if you need any money. I couldn't rest easy if I thought you was broke down there."

Frank nodded. Now, after the cough, the lassitude in him was too overpowering.

"You'll go on writing, won't you, Frank? You got it in you."

Frank rubbed the palm of one hand over the back of the other. Writing? He'd never write again. That was gone forever. He knew it, with complete finality. The ability to write had gone from him with the tree. Where the fever and the bright brilliance had been was only an emptiness, a stillness, dead and filled with stones. He knew. Several times during the past week or so he had tried to write. He had tried to write the poetic drama of Luke. He remembered how he had sat at the table in his room under the eaves, and had put his pen to the paper. But the pen had remained there, its point pressed down on the whiteness. Nothing had come. The dark emptiness in him had spread. Finally he had forced himself to write: "Luke stood before—in front of—the temple, and the elders—the Jewish elders—" Then the sickness had come on him, the horrible nausea and collapse, and he had torn up the paper and had thrown the pen on the floor. There was nothing now. There was only this sick nothingness, this turning away, this horrible flattening of perspective, this draining away of color, this flaccid despair, this complete undesire. Writing! A huge contempt for himself had struck him like a stunning blow. He was nothing at all. Whatever he had had in the past had been an egotistic delusion, a child's daydreaming, a complete and shameful conceit.

A failure. That was what he was. His parents had called him a failure; his teachers had despised him; his schoolmates had ridiculed him. Miss Woods had rejected him with scorn. They knew him! Now he knew himself, accepted himself as others saw him. A failure. He had wasted years in his delusions, when he might have been laying the groundwork for a solid future. Bitterly, he looked at himself as in a mirror, and his self-hatred was like the taste of gall in his mouth.

Frank said listlessly: "I'll think about it when I'm stronger, Mr. Farley." He had learned so quickly how to turn aside from the smallest issue, whereas before he had attacked vigorously. Now he wished only to escape the slightest controversy.

No, he had nothing left, except his desire for money. That was more powerful than ever. Someway, somehow, he must have money, a lot of it, countless thousands of it. There was just one way: the oil fields of Kentucky.

Mr. Farley saw Frank's thin and prominent profile, so tense now, so grimly set. He saw the transparent pallor, the dark caves under the narrowed blue eyes. He thought: My God, the poor kid!

He added rapidly, in his mind, with humility and pleading: "Holy Mary, Mother of God, pray for us sinners now, and in the hour of our death—amen—please, Holy Mother, Tower of Ivory, Refuge of Sinners, you got to help this kid— I don't know why, but he's just like my own kid, though you know I haven't any—he's in pain, dear Blessed Mother, and he needs help—he's just like he was your own Son, on his own cross, now, only he hasn't got no faith to help him, and he doesn't know about you—and he's down in the pit of himself, fighting there, without no hope—you got to help him— Hail Mary, full of grace, the Lord is with thee—blessed art thou among women, and blessed is the fruit of thy womb, Jesus—I'll make a novena—I'll—"

Even—before—I could write, Frank thought. Even before that damned Sunday, out in the snow. It was hard, but I could write. I could grind out fairly creditable compositions, and even poetry. I could do a workmanlike job. Mason said so. He said I practically had genius. But now I can't write a thing coherently. There is nothing in my mind, nothing. And I don't want anything. I want only money.

He said aloud: "Everything's got to wait until I make some money. I want to send my mother some."

Mr. Farley, coming out of the daze of his fervent prayers, replied: "Your ma said she and your grandmother're going back to England. Maybe next summer."

"Yes."

The dinner bell clamored out into the Sunday quiet. Frank stirred. Desperately, Mr. Farley decided he must make haste. He remembered that Maybelle had some twelve thousand dollars now. He had given her a thousand dollars after Francis' death, and, in explanation, he had mumbled something about "a kind of insurance he carried for his people." Maybelle did not demur, nor question this entirely fallacious statement. He wished now that he had given the money to Frank, with the lie that Francis had left the "insurance" to his son.

But there was something more important to be said. The boy was going away. He must not be allowed to go away like this, embittered, inert, turning aside from any kindness as if he could not bear it, swamped in undesire and despair. Mr. Farley cleared his throat, and slipped down from the porch railing. His words came in a rush, incoherently:

"Look, Frank, maybe I shan't see you again, after tomorrow. You've kind of been like a son to me, y'know. I've kind of had you on my mind, ever since you were a little shaver, when you and your ma and pa used to come here every Sunday for dinner. You got great stuff in you, Frank. You got to believe that, see? You mustn't ever forget it. And—you've got to forget lots of—other things."

Frank raised his eyes to his old friend with a faint curiosity. "What must I forget?" he asked, in a tone that humored the vagaries of elderly folk.

Mr. Farley turned crimson. He rubbed the top of his head, and sweated a little. "Well. Maybe you think I'm pokin' my nose where it don't belong. Maybe I am, at that. But you're kind of like my own kid, if I ever had any. See what I mean? Well. Well, maybe you've had a hard sort of life, and things didn't go right with you. I was a kid once, and it's a funny thing, but what happens to you when you're a kid kind of leaves a mark on you, more than it does when you grow up and know all about everything. Folks that're not so good to a kid when he's young—he remembers that, and if he ain't got strength of mind, and a little bit of understanding, he can let those folks ruin the rest of his life, just remembering about them."

Frank's thin face had become slowly narrowed and intent, yet it remained closed as stone. But he listened, not looking away from Mr. Farley.

"Now, take me," said Mr. Farley, cursing himself for his inarticulateness, and praying for just a little eloquence: "Take me. I come from Ireland when I was just a shaver of thirteen. Come to an uncle and aunt, and they put me to work right away. That was in Detroit. They took all my wages, and didn't send me to school, and I had to sleep in an attic. And it was damned cold in the winter, too. Well, I hated 'em, and I hated their kids, all six of 'em. My uncle drank all the time, and my aunt took in washin'. They didn't give me any sort of kindness at all; I worked in a factory, and brought home my wages, and I saw about ten cents of it a week, and I was making five dollars. So I'd lie up there in my room, and just hate, sometimes, until it was time to get up. Then maybe my Uncle Pat would knock me over the head, just out of mean temper, or my aunt would clout me with the end of her broom. That made me hate 'em even worse. I kind of got so I enjoyed hating them."

Frank smiled, and the smile wasn't pleasant. But he still listened. Mr. Farley cleared his throat and continued earnestly:

"Well, it could of ruined my life, just hating them and thinking up ways to get even. And then the old priest of our church had a talk with me. He showed me how Uncle Pat had a game knee that pained him all the time; he explained that Uncle Pat had been a fine broth of an ambitious lad in the old country, and had come here full of hopes. But he had only his muscles and his two hands, and like Rockefeller says, a man's worth only a dollar a day from the neck down. Uncle Pat didn't have no education, and no time to get it, because he brought a bride with him, and the kids come one after another. Uncle Pat worked for a brewery feller, and drove his wagons. One dollar a day, and the kids never stoppin' comin'. And there was Aunt Bridget; prettiest girl in Cork, they said. Could have done better than Uncle Pat, but it was love, or something. They come here, going to conquer the whole world. One dollar a day, then, for Uncle Pat, and Aunt Bridget takin' in washin', between kids. Maybe she'd been pretty. She was an old hag when I first saw her here, and she not thirty, with most of her teeth gone, and no money for a plate.

"Both of 'em were sick, hopeless and tired, pulled down by babies, and nothin' to hope for. Maybe there wasn't no excuse for them to treat me like that, you might say. But they couldn't help it, the old priest told me. It wasn't that they was naturally mean and bad. They wasn't no worse than other human critters, I'm thinking. But they needed my money, and so they took it. There was no way out for 'em, out of what they'd gotten into. They just hit out at anythin' they saw, and I was a big husky lad, and could take it. They hit out, like a dog, when he gets run over, starts bitin' every hand that comes near him, even the hand of his master."

Frank stood up. Mr. Farley, puffing, bent and helped him untangle the blankets from his legs. Frank stood in the sunlight near the edge of the porch, and the bright light seemed to go through his white and transparent flesh. He did not look at Mr. Farley now.

Mr. Farley put his hand on the bony shoulder and smiled feebly up into Frank's face. "You'll remember that, won't you, Frankie? I'd like to think you'd remember it. Look, Frankie," he continued desperately, "think of it like this. The minute you feel sorry for someone you think's hurt you, then you're saved. And before you feel sorry, you got to understand first. It just takes a little doing, and then you understand, and then you're sorry, and then you're saved. And you're free, too."

He waited. Frank did not move. He only stared at the warm quiet street.

Mr. Farley, sweating more profusely than ever, went on: "There's all kinds of people in the world. You don't have to love 'em. You see bad and good, mean and nice, kind and cruel, stupid and bright. You see hundreds of different faces. It's more than human nature to expect any feller to go around, lovin' every son of a bitch in the world; there's some you just got to avoid, and steer clear of. But there's one thing you can do for everybody. You can feel sorry for them. See? And why? Just because we was born, that's why. Life ain't easy for anybody, good or bad. It's just bein' born we ought to be sorry for."

He walked to the door with Frank and stammered as he opened it, staring almost passionately at the young man: "Charity. That's it. That's what Our Lord says was more important than faith or hope. Just charity. See?"

"Yes," said Frank politely. "I see. Thank you."

They went into the cool dark cave which was the dank hall of the house. The "guests" were filing timidly and pallidly down the oaken staircase. They nodded to Mr. Farley and Frank, then slunk or slithered towards the back dining room. Mr. Farley watched them go.

"God help you," he murmured. "May God help you."

CHAPTER 44

MUCH of Frank's lassitude and apathy lifted as the train approached Cincinnati, though the gritty day coach this late May day became increasingly hot and fetid with the sweat of the passengers. He had never been far from home before. Now, as he passed through towns and villages, and saw a portion of America for the first time, a normal human curiosity and interest awoke in him, he forgot his physical weakness, and his dark and heavy despair subsided in considerable measure.

With Bison behind him, he began to wonder about Kentucky, and the romantic notions of the North with regard to the South recurred to him. Tim Cunningham had written him of the huge and comfortable tent in which he lived. Frank saw gracious blue-grass meadows surrounded by great and lofty mountains, majestic white-pillared homes scattered about in bowers of blooming trees and brilliant gardens, stately and distinguished families gathered on purple-shadowed piazzas in the cool of the day, and beautiful Southern towns filled with easy and happy folk. A little excitement was aroused in him. He found that he could eat the dry sandwiches and could drink the strong hot coffee, sold on the train, with some return of youthful appetite. He went back into the steaming smoker for a cigarette, just before the train pulled into Cincinnati.

Had he taken this journey some months earlier, his reactions to the passengers in the day coach would have been milder and more tolerant. But now he had nothing but hatred and sick revulsion for them. He feasted on his hatred. The dirty children who squalled and swarmed and ate oranges and bananas, and filled the coaches with acrid smells, and dirty and slatternly women, the shirt-sleeved and work-stained men, to him were all symbols of what he must escape at any cost. He went to the smoker frequently, where he had to be afflicted by the presence of male passengers only, and where he could avoid the sight and sound of the filthy children and animal-faced women of the working class. When, at certain stations, the Pullman passengers had alighted on the platform for a brief leg-stretching, Frank had stared at them through his dusty window and had thought: I am one of you, though I am here in this coach. And some day you will know me and recognize me, and receive me in your cool and pleasant houses, and be proud of my presence.

When he thought these things, he was stimulated and became so restless that he could hardly endure the confining walls of the coach. So he would get up and go into the smoker, until he was too excited to remain there, and would return to his own coach. He had slept on the train all night, upright on the uncomfortable green plush seat which reeked of dust and grit and smoke, but, to his surprise, he was not exhausted. His heart was beating faster; his weakness was disappearing, and he coughed hardly at all.

Though the windows were open, it was not possible to see distinctly in the smoker. Smoke poured in from the engine, accompanied by stinging soot, and smoke poured out from the pipes and cigarettes of the passengers. Every man was in his shirt-sleeves; almost everyone had taken off his stiff high collar and tie, and pale throats glistened with sweat. Newspapers were scattered about. There were many demobilized soldiers, playing dice and poker, and drinking strictly prohibition gin and whiskey with open gusto. Civilians watched the games in progress, cheering or making rude derisive noises. The coach was filthy and pervaded with various stenches, but it was a rough male atmosphere.

He sat down beside a quiet passenger who was reading a book. Frank did not look at the man. He lit a cigarette and stared beyond his seat-mate at the smoky suburbs of Cincinnati. Then his eye fell on the book: *Folklore and Culture of Rural America.* Surprised, he glanced up at the reader and discovered an old Evening Sessions classmate, Jim Watson, a mulatto.

Jim Watson, a tall, silent, young Negro, was a mill-hand. He rarely spoke, his smile was whitely brilliant, and he had gentle brown eyes and a grave, courteous manner full of dignity and self-respect. Some few of the students had been contemptuous of Jim Watson. He had freely admitted that he had not gone beyond the second grade in grammar school, never having attended any high school whatsoever, but he had admitted all this as if it were only a casual and insignificant matter. No one knew exactly why he was attending the Evening Sessions. It would always be impossible for him to obtain a degree, no matter how distinguished his record, and distinguished it was. He was taking six subjects, including French and German and Music Appreciation, a prodigious feat, but he had not entered the college through the narrow gate of any high school. Therefore, though he was always at the head of his class, and though his papers were miracles of neatness, mental clarity, logic and intelligence, a degree would always be denied him. His poetry had aroused Mr. Mason's genuine and passionate enthusiasm, for it was superbly simple and almost perfect, and written in the unaffected language of America. Some of it, he had confessed to Mr. Mason, had been written expressly for the purpose of setting it to music. Jim intended to do this, eventually, another thing which much amused certain of his fellow students.

Frank, whose reactions to people had long ago been blunted, had been entirely indifferent to Jim Watson. He was only a dark-skinned nonentity in a room full of nonentities. Frank had experienced impatience and jealousy when Mr. Mason had read some of Jim's poetry and compositions aloud to the class. Frank thought them banal and without significance. However, reared as he had been in a British atmosphere and in an unrelentingly British home, he had not acquired much of the racial and religious prejudice which was so rampant in America. Even his father, Francis, who had the Englishman's contempt for the Irish (similar to the Southerner's contempt for the Negro), had rarely uttered a word of prejudice in his house, and Maybelle had never been known to express anything but a diffused antagonism to "Yankeeland," and that solely because America was not England. So Frank had listened to expressions of racial and religious hatred in his schools, in the offices in which he had worked, and among his few acquaintances, without responding to them with anything but boredom and indifference. It was not that he was immune to reasonless passions, but it seemed silly to him, as an American of English stock, to condemn a man because of his race or color. He had discovered, too, that the more intelligent and gently bred a man, the less prejudice he harbored against men of other races and creeds, and he had come to the conclusion, not entirely fallacious, that such prejudice was part of the general depravity of the ignorant and mentally inferior. Those of his office mates who had come from respectable middle-class families, and could boast at least a high-school education, merely smiled at raucous ejaculations of hatred, but those who had risen from a laboring background were viciously insistent upon their superiority to Negroes, Catholics, Jews, Poles, Italians, and all "foreigners" in general. Therefore, to have succumbed to the stupid and unlettered prejudice so ominously prevalent in America would have marked Frank, in his own mind, as a member of a class he despised with overwhelming passion.

So it was that Frank's indifference and even dislike for Jim Watson had not stemmed from any racial aversion, but rather from his increasing indifference to all humanity and from his jealousy. His first impulse was to get up and leave the seat. But just as he made the first motion, Jim glanced at him and smiled with a radiant flash of his white teeth.

"Why, hello, Frank!" he exclaimed, surprised. "What're you doing here, going down South?"

Sullenly, Frank subsided on his seat. "I'm going to Kentucky," he answered, curtly. "Where are you going?"

"Farther South. Tennessee. I came from there, you know, when I was fifteen years old." Jim's soft voice was rich with inflections, and had a sonorous quality which Frank had unwillingly liked.

"Going to live there now?" asked Frank indifferently, already bored.

"No." The word was low and vibrant, and, vaguely aroused, Frank looked at Jim with more interest. "No, Frank. Never again. I'm just going back to get—material."

"Material? For what?" Now Frank's curiosity became stronger, though more derisive.

Jim hesitated. He looked down at the book on his lap. Then, as if he had persuaded himself that it was humiliating to have hesitated at all, he said simply: "I want to write songs, the words and music both. I can do it. I intend to stay down South for a few years, and refresh my memory. I want to listen to the songs of the Negro cotton-pickers and farm hands, and to adapt them. Their songs are wonderful!" The gentle brown eyes glowed eagerly as they stared at Frank, became radiant with dreams. "They're—melancholy, and —and—haunting. They're an expression of the black American's—soul. They're part of America, and all Americans ought to know them. You see," and he spoke more slowly, as if to find the perfect words with which to embody his thoughts—"you see, Frank, there's a quality in the black American's songs, a mixture of despair, lightheartedness, gaiety, misery and fatalism, which can't be found in the songs of any other racial group. And yet—and yet—they sort of make—articulate—the feelings of every man. Universal, as Mr. Mason says."

Frank said nothing. Then, after Jim had waited for a few moments, Frank spoke: "I don't know very much about Negro songs. I suppose I'll hear them down in Kentucky. I'll remember what you said."

Jim replied gently: "Kentucky. Whereabout in Kentucky?"

"In Lawrence and Johnson Counties, I think."

Jim shook his head. "You won't find many Negroes in the mountains. And there aren't many of them in the mountain villages and towns. Where you're going, is almost like the North, in some ways."

Frank was disappointed and annoyed. "I don't know."

He began to think of Jim Watson's presumption. The mill-hand setting himself up as a song-writer! It was as presumptuous as his own past dreams, his own folly. Remembering those dreams and the folly, Frank was resentful and contemptuous. He said: "Jim, I hate to depress you, but I think you're on the wrong track. Nobody wants songs like yours. You're wasting your time. I know. Just as I wasted my time in the Evening Sessions."

Jim glanced at him quickly and piercingly: "You think that? Why, that's terrible! Mr. Mason said you were a potential genius, Frank. You don't believe it?"

"No, I don't." Frank's voice was flat and bitter. "Mr. Mason was a pedantic fool. He thought every scribbler in his class was a Dickens or a Brontë or a Tolstoi. Something ought to be done to men like Mason. They give tyros and mediocre idiots wrong ambitions, and keep them forever from achieving small successes. I'm glad I came down to earth, myself."

"You mean," asked Jim, in a low voice, "that you're not going to write any more? That you've given up?"

The phrase made Frank furious. "Oh, don't be a fool! I didn't 'give up' anything but silliness and a pack of foolish dreams. I didn't have anything else, when you come down to it, so I didn't 'give up' anything at all!"

Jim was silent. He turned his head and gazed through the dusty window for a long time. The demobilized soldiers were shouting at each other above the clamor of the engine. Smoke belched into the coach. The heat and sunlight became more intense. Frank was conscious of nausea as the coach swayed and jolted. He leaned back and closed his eyes, swallowing the salt liquid that welled into his mouth. He was frightened, and fought his fright. Again, he was exhausted and sick, overwhelmed with gray misery and hopelessness. Apparently he had not completely recovered from his illness, after all. He felt weakness creeping like water all over his body, cold and penetrating water. He shivered a little, in spite of the heat. Restlessness and torpor simultaneously overcame him. His head throbbed. Now, behind his closed lids, there was a prickling and a burning, and something ached and twisted in his chest, like the memory of a wretched grief. What did it matter where he went, whether he did or did not go? What did anything matter? The world retreated from him like a livid tide, and the shingle was strewn with stones. Should he get off at the next stop? Should he go on? What did it matter? If only I could die, he thought. But he knew that he lacked the will to die, just as he lacked the will to live. If only there were some way to forget—what? He could not remember what it was that he wanted forgotten. He knew only that somewhere in him was a great and deathly sickness, but whether it was of the body or the mind he did not know.

He felt his hot palms sweating against the gritty green plush; he felt the painful rolling of his head. Every jolt of the coach wrenched every bone in his body, and went beyond his body. The heat beat against his flesh, yet he was cold. The noise in the coach became a distant vague clamor. He was no longer conscious of the young man beside him. Now images formed and floated against the red and burning background of his closed eyelids, sick wanton images, grotesque faces, visions of pain without surcease, dark lakes surrounded by blazing scarlet mountains, flashes of black lightning, crimson abysses palpitating with anguish.

Something stirred and pushed against his knee. He opened swimming eyes to a roar of heat and noise. Jim was getting up, carrying his heavy book under his arm. "Got to get back to the Jim Crow coaches, Frank," he said.

Frank sat up, blinking. "Jim Crow coaches?" He had heard the phrase, and now he remembered, and he frowned. He let Jim pass him, saw the young Negro pulling his bags from the rack. And now he felt shame and mortification and anger.

"We're in Kentucky, you see," said Jim, in a pleasant and casual voice.

He picked up his bags. Several other Negroes were rising from their seats. Frank glanced at them furtively. Now he was alive, aching in every cell with humiliation.

"Good-bye, Frank," said Jim, standing in the aisle. He hesitated. There was no resentment in his handsome dark face. He bent over Frank, and spoke softly: "Frank, you mustn't give up. I—I've been watching you, for about an hour. You can't give up, Frank. You—you won't live, if you do." He paused. "I'm terribly sorry. You said you didn't give up anything. But you did, see? And you know it. Good-bye."

Frank did not answer. With a blaze and a rush, swelling and rolling, life came back to him as his humiliation and shame became stronger. Now he burned with a pure and vivid anger as he watched Jim and the other Negroes leave the coach. Sight and sound became vivid, immediate. The coach, which before had been only a colored photograph, flat and meaningless, lengthened into dimension. Every wall, every seat, every swaying bag on the racks, had a meaning, a being. The faces of the young soldiers rounded, became the embodiment of something living and significant. The hot white clouds floating in an incandescent sky shaped themselves into forms of purport.

"Mind if I sit here?" The droning voice broke into Frank's dream, and he started into wakefulness. He saw the man who was pressing against his knees, a lanky red-faced man with dull and brutal features. The man was dressed in denim overalls, rank with the odor of manure, and over his blue work shirt he wore a denim jacket with metal buttons. A broad-brimmed dusty hat was pulled low over mean and crafty eyes, and his grin revealed broken and yellowed teeth. He sat down beside Frank, pulled out a hunk of tobacco, bit into it, and began to chew.

The dream retreated. Frank clenched his fists. Again he felt hatred, but not the same hatred as before. Now it was the familiar hatred of disgust and revulsion. Slowly, everything flattened, darkened, paled. Frank pulled away from his chewing companion. Again, he was exhausted, desolate, full of misery. The dream was lost. Moment by moment it became nothing, and moment by moment it was forgotten.

CHAPTER 45

PAINTSVILLE, KENTUCKY, in the hot and glaring light of early morning.

Never had Frank Clair imagined, or experienced, such relentless heat, such blazing heat. Never had he seen anything so dismal and so foreign as this little town. Its very facelessness, its very lack of character, depressed him. His parents had told him that every English hamlet, town and city had its individuality, its distinguishing peculiarities of architecture and streets. His wide reading had taught him that every Continental city was distinct from its sister cities.

Now he was seeing his first small American town, ugly, characterless, bleak. He had gathered, from Tim Cunningham's letters, that Paintsville was, in a way, a "settlement," a frontier hamlet. "The jumping-off place" of the mountains. It had none of the raw and colorful frontier quality of Western towns, as vividly depicted in the moving pictures. It had a hideous little clapboard Methodist church, one perceptible street or two, lined with wooden houses, a "hotel" built of wood, with a gabled roof, a series of cheap-jack "general stores," a tiny depot, and hot, broken pavements. Even the few trees, dusty, browned by early summer heat, had no freshness, and none of the vigorous green of Northern trees.

A few buggies, shabby and battered, were hitched before the general stores. Women, in long, chemise-like gingham dresses reminiscent of nightgowns, reaching to bare ankles and feet, and wearing checked pink or blue gingham sunbonnets, moved along the burning pavements, "totin'" dirty babies on their arms. Yellow curs slunk behind them. Husbands, in overalls and denim shirts, barefooted and wearing battered felt or wide straw hats, chewed and conversed listlessly along the curbs. Frank stared at them curiously. These were certainly not the "Southerners" he had imagined. These, then, must be the "white trash" spoken of by Tim Cunningham and various novelists. But they were not picturesque. They were merely ugly, quite dirty, with faces that, to Frank, accustomed as he was to the more colorful faces of Italians and Poles and Slavs to be seen in Bison, were very odd and alien.

Most of the men were of an incredible height. Six feet was only average. But they were like weeds, unbelievably thin and lanky. When they walked, they loped and sidled like stringy saplings suddenly given animation. The women were smaller, with peaked dull faces, blank empty eyes and dun-colored hair. It was apparent that most of them were sickly. They coughed and spat copiously. The children were obviously suffering from pellagra, for they had pinched pale faces and swollen bellies, and their legs were misshapen and knock-kneed. One and all were barefoot. It was obvious that most of them were farmers from the nearby countryside, for the better-dressed and leather-shod townsfolk had a plumpness and healthfulness of appearance not to be found among the country folk.

Paintsville was in the foothills. Beyond the hideous little town Frank could see the dark rolling hills, flattened of top and gentle of slope. Frank was greatly disappointed; his dreams of immense and stony mountains, crowned with brilliant snow, were fading. But, he thought bitterly, that comes of my ignorance. I ought to have known that such mountains can't be found this side of the Rockies.

The listless voices echoed in the glaring heat and light. Horses stamped, and clouds of dust arose. Doors of the "general stores" banged. Flies buzzed everywhere. There was a strong stench of manure. The miserable town buildings cast no shadows as a refuge for the strollers and the "jawers" along the littered curbs. The sky shone pitilessly, white with heat and brazen sun.

Frank, carrying his coat and his big cardboard suitcase, walked to a blacksmith shop, as directed by Tim Cunningham. Iron clanged on iron. The smith, a refreshingly vigorous man, swung his hammer on the anvil. He had a great bearded face, sensual and strong, and Frank thought of a village character in Shakespeare's plays. He favored Frank with a wide grin which revealed broken teeth stained with tobacco juice, and he wiped his brown forehead with his bare forearm. "Whut kin I do for you, sir?" he asked, courteously, after he had spat a gob of tobacco onto a casual pile of manure near the broad doorway. The stink and heat of the shop almost overpowered Frank, who drew in his nostrils and tried to breathe lightly.

But Frank liked the man. He heard his own English accent in the other's rude voice, and he was suddenly pleased. How sedulously, in foreign Bison, he had tried to eliminate his accent, and with what awkward care and self-consciousness! How afraid he had been to speak much at school, to the children of Germans and Italians and other aliens, for fear of their ridicule! Now he could speak without nervousness, and would not be found strange and suspect. The smith spoke, and it was the true voice of America, overlaid slightly with a drone and a languor. The smith, well-fed and mighty of muscle, was, like himself, of pure English stock, the glaring light of his fire reddening his swarthy cheeks, his short curly beard and longish curly black hair. There was no decadence in him, no depravity, such as appeared on the faces of the lounging farm folk on the streets.

Frank set down his suitcase. He spoke slowly but freely: "I was supposed to meet a wagon, or something, near here. To take me 'down on Benton.' Do you know anything about it?"

The smith squinted, laid down his hammer. He pulled a slab of tobacco out of his overall pocket, and offered it to Frank, who declined politely. The smith sank his teeth into the tobacco, and thoughtfully chewed, as he eyed Frank in a friendly manner. Then he left his anvil, affectionately smacked the rump of a mule near the door, and came up to Frank, staring at him with childlike candor.

"Whut your name, sir?" he asked apologetically.

"Frank Clair. I'm a friend of Tim Cunningham's. Do you know him?"

The smith studied the young man carefully. Frank could smell his rank sweat, but it did not offend him, for it was the very emanation of health and virility. He was puzzled, however, by the close scrutiny of the smith, and the way the latter's eyes squinted at him cautiously.

"Yessir, I knows Tim Cunningham. You say yore name's Frank Clair?"

Frank became uneasy, for there was a sudden watchfulness, an alertness, about the smith. "Yes, that's my name."

"Whar you frum, sir?" asked the smith, with more apology in his lusty voice.

Frank frowned. "From Bison. Up North. What's the matter, anyway?"

But the smith stared at him almost cunningly, and was silent. Then slowly, he grinned. He smote Frank heavily on the shoulder. "Reckon yo is the feller Tim spoke about," he said, and burst into laughter. "Pardon me, sir, but we uns got to be careful. Revenooers comin' in all the time. You ain't a revenooer, eh?"

Bewildered, Frank considered. Then his face cleared. "Revenue agents." He shook his head. The smith grinned wider. He reached behind him, pulled a bottle from his rear pocket, and extended it largely to Frank, who took it uncertainly. "Have yoreself a drink, sir," invited the smith. "Applejack."

He watched while Frank fastidiously wiped the neck of the grimy bottle and tilted it to his lips. The pungent and burning liquid, golden as sunlight, almost choked the young man. The smith was heartily amused, and bent backwards to laugh. "My brother made it," he informed Frank, when the latter could get his breath. "Cain't find no better anywheres in the mountings."

Now that friendship was on a warm footing, the smith expanded. The mule team was expected momentarily. "Roads still bad," said the smith. "Cain't get the lazy sonsabitches to do nothin' hereabouts to fill in the holes. Just want to jaw around in town."

He invited Frank to sit on a bench near the door. He refreshed himself frequently with his bottle as he talked. The mule stamped restlessly. A wagon rolled by on the cobbled street. Sunlight, unbearably brilliant, poured into the dark, firelit smithy. Beyond the door, Frank could see the shapes of the somber "mountings."

He learned that the smith had a farm "down on Benton," some twenty-five miles away. According to the profane smith, it was a "no-account" bit of land. But oil had been discovered on it by Tim Cunningham and his brothers, and was now bringing in three hundred barrels a day. Frank calculated laboriously. Three hundred and fifty dollars a day! Why, then, he asked the smith, did the latter work here? Where would a man go? the smith inquired artlessly. Louisville? He, the smith, didn't "hold with" the city. Didn't like it, no sir. This was a purty country, and he'd lived here, man and boy, for forty years. Cities were godless, runnin' around with wimmen, and drinkin' on Sundays, and card-playin', and what all. Theatres, too. The smith shook his head. He could, Frank thought, conceive of nothing beyond his mountain horizon and his bare and simple life. What did he do with his money? Put it right here, in the bank, replied the smith emphatically. What all did a man do with money besides putting it in the bank? It was obvious that he had no knowledge of the "sittlements," as he designated the outside world, and that he didn't "hold with" long journeys on the "steam-cars." When Frank spoke of automobiles, the smith again shook his head. Nothin' better than a team of good hosses, and he had that team. He lived in a three-room log cabin up the road, and it was big enough for himself, his wife and two daughters. One of the girls, "bright as a button," was going to Berea College, and she would then teach in Paintsville. The other girl was about to marry a farmer who owned fifty acres of good bottom land. Money as a thing in itself meant nothing to the smith. There was nothing he wanted, and, as he naïvely said, what more *could* a man want? More wimmen? Wimmen were a sight of trouble, and his old woman was good enough, or bad enough, for him. Besides, he was an old man now, goin' on forty-one, and nothin' but devilment came of a man forgettin' his age. Books? Well, he couldn't read a word, thank God, with all the sin there was in books.

Frank thought of that three hundred and fifty dollars going daily into the bank, to lie there uselessly. He thought of the freedom and the peace such money would bring to him; he thought of the ninety dollars in his own pocket, all that he had in the world. The smith looked at him with his innocent black eyes, shining so brightly in the firelight, and he wondered why this thin young man had such a dark sour face. Reckon the applejack ain't sittin' well on his stommick.

Frank was so lost in his bitter resentments and musings that he was not aware that someone was entering the smithy until he heard the smith's jovial greeting. A tall thin young man stood there, dressed neatly in a dark "city" suit and black leggings, and wearing a broad-brimmed black felt hat. He moved into the smithy with such an air of quiet elegance and dignity that Frank's attention was caught.

"Howdy, Parson!" cried the smith, rubbing his hands on his leather apron. "Purty day, ain't it? Yore mule's shod and ready. He's an orn'ry critter."

One of those "circuit riders," I suppose, thought Frank, a travelling evangelical minister of whom he had read in some forgotten tale of the Southern mountains. He half turned away with disdain when his attention was again arrested by the sound of the young man's pleasant Western voice:

"Thanks, Little Les," he said. He slapped his waiting mule affectionately with the flat of his hand. The intelligent animal nuzzled him. "He isn't ornery, are you, Boss? He just happens to be bright. Maybe it's the same thing in the long run. Eh, Boss?"

The smith, "Little Les," himself, the "parson," the "bright" mule, the dark rounded shapes of the mountains outside, the heat, the brilliant sunlight, the alien sounds and smells and forms all about him, struck Frank even more acutely now. His perception, which had become so dim and faint and superficial, sharpened. But as everything rushed in upon him, he became deeply depressed and disoriented, and something like a dull nostalgia made him ache briefly.

Genial comments about the mule passed between Little Les and the "parson." Frank listened. The accents in those voices no longer pleased him with their familiarity. He stood, withdrawn, covered with his depression as with a cloud. He had acquired this ability to efface himself, so that, in this withdrawing of his personality, this impositon of a blank neutrality upon his body and his mind, he no longer seemed present. So it was that when Little Les, turning from the "parson," became aware of him, the smith actually started. "Eh!" he exclaimed. Then he grinned. "Reckon you'll have the parson along when you go, Frank," he added. He explained to the other young man: "Feller from the sittlements going down on Benton with Tim Cunningham. Name of Frank Clair. Shake hands with the parson, Frank."

The "parson" appeared surprised at seeing Frank, but he extended his hand with friendly candor. Frank, desperately uncomfortable, took that hand. He felt the warm grip of the hard and slender fingers, and in spite of himself, he could not help returning the other's quiet, open smile.

"Going down on Benton with the oil outfit?" asked the "parson." "Well, we'll be seeing a lot of you. I'm Doctor Wade O'Leary, from Salt Lake City, Utah. A medical doctor, not just a theologian." His smile was warmer, and Frank's tension relaxed gratefully. He knows I'm not an ignoramus, he thought. He hardly stammered when he replied:

"Dr. O'Leary? You're a minister, too?"

"Yes. Church of the Latter Day Saints. Some people call us 'Mormons.' I'm really a missionary, with my brother, Peter, to the Kentucky mountaineers. We've managed to build a little school for the children, where my brother teaches. He takes care of their minds, and I take care of their bodies. And sometimes their souls, when they need it." Dr. O'Leary laughed lightly, gave Frank's hand a final sincere grip, and released him. "Best of all, though, we've managed to set up a small hospital for the poor women. You'll find the mountains very educational. Where have you come from, now? You aren't a Southerner?"

"No. I'm from Bison, New York."

"Oh." Dr. O'Leary's expression became thoughtful as he studied Frank. Frank, in his turn, studied the doctor. What he saw pleased and released him still more. Wade O'Leary had an extremely tanned and slender face, the face of an alert and yet reflective scholar, all fine angles and strong, delicate planes. It was evident that he had what Maybelle called "good blood." His eyes, set deeply in wide, bony sockets, had a steadfast brown brightness under very heavy black brows. His nose, somewhat aquiline and sharp, gave a hawk-like vigilance to his face, a still and prideful poise, which was yet paradoxically gentle and considerate. His thin and flexible mouth was also paradoxical, for though the lines of it were extremely firm they were also mobile and quick, and his smile flashed easily and subtly, as if denying the determined jaw beneath. He had taken off his hat, and Frank saw the thin and sculptured contour of his small head, with its patrician length and fineness and smooth black hair.

"You're a long way from home," remarked Wade. "You know Tim Cunningham well? He's a nice fellow. I know his brothers, too. I saw them last about a month ago, before I went back home for the typhoid serum. There's been a lot of typhoid down on Benton. I also brought some smallpox vaccine. If you haven't been vaccinated recently, you'd better let me do it for you when we reach Benton. Ten cases of it, before I went back to Salt Lake City. Hope no more of it has broken out in the meantime."

"Haven't they got any other doctors there?" asked Frank apprehensively.

Wade shook his head. "Only a very old man, who is by way of being a kind of witch doctor. I doubt very much if he ever had any medical education whatsoever. He brews potions and gives cathartics for everything from smallpox to puerperal fever. I'm the only religious advisor down on Benton, too, except for a Holy Roller expert who makes a whirlwind visit every summer and disrupts what I've been trying to do for years. But he does add drama to their poor, miserable lives, and I don't suppose I ought to begrudge it." He paused and smiled slightly. "You'll find it another world—Frank. I hope it'll interest you."

Frank, in fact, was more than a little alarmed. He had not thought of Benton as a place in dire need of missionaries and vaccines, of fine devoted men who wished to dedicate their lives to a people and a community which ominously suggested a leper colony. When he had thought of Benton, he had believed it to be a small country town in whose outskirts oil had been discovered.

Wade O'Leary was speaking in a grave voice: "You'll learn a lot about the country, Frank. And I've found out that whatever a man learns is valuable, though he might not think so at the time."

"I didn't—come to learn," Frank could not help saying bitterly. "I came to make money."

"I see," said Wade thoughtfully. He pulled a pipe from his pocket, filled it with tobacco. He lit the pipe. He did all this without taking his eyes from Frank. Then he went on: "I hear that Tim Cunningham is making a lot of money, considering everything. Hope you make it, too."

The smith cackled nearby. "Cain't help it, seems like," he contributed.

"Staying with Tim?" asked Wade.

"I suppose so." Frank's depression thickened his voice life-lessly. "Though perhaps I can get room and board—in some small hotel?"

Wade smiled. "There aren't any hotels," he said. "There isn't even a rooming house." He paused. "Perhaps you'd better go home, Frank. I'm afraid you don't know just where you're going."

There was a rumbling on the cobbles outside, and a flat wagon filled with straw, and drawn by four dusty mules, drew up at the door.

"There's your—conveyance," said Wade. He turned to the smith. "Holes filled in yet, Little Les?"

The smith chuckled and shook his head. "No-account sons-abitches," he said jovially. "Ain't done a lick of work since the spring rains. Feller blew up last week, with his truck, carryin' the 'soup' in to Benton. Just made a bigger hole in the road." He laughed uproariously, slapped his leathery thighs.

Wade explained to Frank: "The 'soup' is the nitroglycerin they use to blow the wells. I've expected an accident for a long time over these roads. No place for automobiles. The poor man ought to have known better. I've been telling them not to try to make it with trucks, but to use the wagons all the time. But it's twenty-five miles away, and it takes at least twelve hours by wagon."

"Two miles an hour!" exclaimed Frank, in incredulous dismay.

Wade nodded. He examined the saddle and straps on his mule "You'll see for yourself. Well, are we all ready?"

He picked up a thick square black bag from the floor, expertly fastened it to his saddle. He led his mule outside, and engaged in conversation with the bearded man who sat in the bottom of the straw-filled wagon. Frank followed slowly, blinking in the hot and blinding sunlight. Sweat burst out all over him in great huge drops, instantaneously, and he saw the sky, white now, incandescent as pure flame. The cobbles danced before his swimming eyes; a shimmering wave hung over the bleak street. Voices, muted, overpowered with heat, came like faint hollow echoes from doorways. The mules twitched their tails, turned their malicious and intelligent eyes upon Frank, shook the dust from their flanks. Beyond the town, the mountains were coiled like the dark backs of great serpents.

He was introduced to Ben Calloway, the bearded driver of

the mule teams, who studied him solemnly, spat out a mighty cud of tobacco, and offered him a dirty and calloused hand. "Name of Frank Clair?" he repeated, after Wade O'Leary had mentioned the name. "Bin expectin' you. Got yore victuals?"

Farnk was silent, bewildered. Dr. O'Leary, who had sprung into his saddle, patted his black bag. "I've got enough for the two of us, Ben, and maybe I can spare you a chicken leg or so, for yourself. And Little Les gave me a big bottle of applejack. We shan't starve."

Gingerly, miserably, Frank climbed with awkwardness into the wagon, after first boosting his black cardboard suitcase onto the straw. He wondered why there were no planks to sit upon, but he found out very shortly that a seat of any kind would have been most impractical.

He removed his coat, tie, and hat, and laid them apprehensively on the yellow straw. He rolled up his shirt sleeves, and felt the play of the burning sun on his pale flesh. Well, that wasn't too bad, if he didn't get sunstroke. Little Les waved cheerily from his smithy, shouted a profane warning about the holes, hoped they wouldn't meet a feller with any "soup," and retired into the hot dark cave of the shop. Ben slapped the reins on the mules' backs, struck them smartly with a cowhide whip, and the wagon lurched on over the cobbles. Dr. O'Leary cantered beside the wagon, smiled down at Frank, and offered him a cigarette.

Apathetic women on the streets and on the high verandahs of the old houses stared at them as they rumbled by. The straw pierced Frank's socks, above his boots; it gave off a dusty cloud of chaff which made him sneeze. The sun struck him like hammers on a flaming anvil. The mountains coiled closer, and then the wagon rolled out of the town onto a dusty ragged road the color of new copper. Trees, covered with a fine patina also the color of copper, hung spindly and lifeless over the road, casting impotent thin shadows. The narrow land at the foot of the hills was overgrown with tall brown grass and patches of red and yellow wild flowers. Over it all blazed the murderous sun, which burned the earth and filled the lungs with hot air.

Now the town was behind them, hidden in a fold of the hills, and there was nothing to be seen but the occasional dried bed of a "branch" between the mountains, a clump of half-dead firs, and the sick straggling of second-growth timber. Frank was forced to replace his hat, to protect his head. He pulled up the legs of his trousers, partly to protect them

from the straw, and partly because he believed such a sun
ought to have curative powers. Sweat rolled down from his
forehead, along the arch of his nose, settled in driblets at the
corners of his mouth. He felt his shirt sticking to his back.
Wade O'Leary cantered easily nearby, and Frank was grateful. He knew that the doctor could outdistance the lurching
wagon without any difficulty, yet he remained with his new
acquaintance.

A mile from Paintsville, Frank began to concede the wisdom of the straw on the floor of the wagon, for, at every
twenty or thirty feet, the wooden wheels encountered huge
holes, half the depth of a grave. Ben Calloway crouched
on the straw, wielding his whip over the backs of the struggling mules. He negotiated most of the holes successfully,
skirting the edges so that the wagon tilted at a thirty degree
angle only, and Frank was able to hold his seat on the straw
by merely gripping the shallow edge of the vehicle. But sometimes two holes appeared only three feet apart, the deep bottoms still caked with a half-dried mud, and the wagon stood
up on end or dived unexpectedly, while the lead mules appeared to totter overhead or to disappear into a pit. Then
Frank had all he could do to remain in the wagon, apparently standing on his head one moment or gazing down the
steep slant of his legs the next. He finally decided that a half-
supine position imposed less wear and tear on his body than
did an attempt to sit upright. The chaff of the straw began to
cling to his wet flesh, where it gave off a musty smell.

Only the blazing silence of dark hill and bleached gravelly
earth lay about them, broken occasionally by Ben's masterful
oaths directed at the mules, the panting of the lathered animals, or the singing of hungry insects which gathered in
clouds over their backs or swooped down to drink the sweat
of the men. Sometimes Wade reached down to grasp the bri-
dles of the lead mules, and, with words of low encouragement
and the strength of his hand, helped them to struggle out of a
pit. The mules were not docile creatures, like horses, and had
none of the horse's bewildered acceptance of fate. Frank felt
their disgust and resentment, and he was quite convinced that
they swore to one another as they commented on the journey. He could see their tall dusty ears, their distended nostrils, their bared teeth. In spite of his own misery, he was
amused, and interested. These were persons, cynical and corrupt, leathery and wry, who had a very poor opinion of the
man-creatures they pulled, and a low prejudice against the
sleeker mule which Dr. O'Leary rode. Apparently they in-

sulted the latter animal copiously, for he would prick up his ears contemptuously, toss his head, and ignore his companions in an elaborate manner which it was impossible not to detect.

"Orn'ry cusses," commented Ben. "I hate mules. Goddam critters, anyway. But got more brains than hosses. They thinks. Yessir, they do. Got to hold 'em steady; allus up to tricks, mean tricks. Hey, Wade, break out that applejack, will you?"

"In this heat?" asked Wade. But he "broke out" the applejack, and handed the thick bottle to Ben, who drank of it deeply. Frank shook his head when it was offered to him. He had a dull headache from the sun and the applejack he had drunk in the smithy. Now the whole barren and deserted countryside began to swim before his eyes. Wade tried to talk to him, but his wretchedness made it too much of an effort to answer. He lay in the straw and suffered, while his suitcase bounded against his legs and his wet clothing clung to the straw.

He must have slept, in his misery, for after a while he became aware that the motion of the wagon had stopped. He sat up, dizzily, with an enormous effort. He was nauseated and violently thirsty. He saw his bare arms, burned to a bright and painful red. His legs, between his rolled-up trousers and his dusty socks, were also scarlet, and itched and smarted.

The wagon had been pulled under a clump of trees off the broken and pitted road. Here the shade was a thick and inky black, a patch of grateful shelter in a stricken and fuming land. Nearby, Frank heard the trickle of water, ineffably delightful to the ear. Ben had alighted; he was tying up the mules, whose hides were flecked with foam. Their animal panting was loud in the bright and steaming silence. Dr. O'Leary had tied up his own mule, a careful distance from its mates, and he had produced a small white cloth upon which he was laying out his "victuals."

Frank, whose head was swimming ominously, climbed over the side of the wagon. The ground swayed under his feet. He half-staggered under the trees, and sat down abruptly. Wade glanced at him with a smile. "We're going to eat now," he said. His dark "city" clothing was still neat and elegant, and his smooth narrow head was unruffled. "Here," he said, with concern, "you're burned up. We'll have to do something about that." He opened his bag, and brought out a jar of white ointment. "Put this on that sunburn, or you'll be sick." Frank, speechless with suffering, accepted the jar, but did not have the strength to open it. Wade, giving him a quick glance, knelt beside him and lavishly anointed the smarting areas of sunburn. Frank watched him, too spent even to express gratitude. But the ointment had a cool and soothing effect. Frank watched the doctor, and then, in spite of his misery, he felt a slow and gathering warmth in his heart, a kind of strong devotion, at the sight of those lean brown hands ministering to him. Ben, having filled a pail with spring water, watched with interest. "City folks," he said with kind scorn. And spat.

Wade produced a tin cup, filled it with the icy water, and offered it to Frank, now well buttered with the oily ointment. He poured a good half-teaspoonful of salt into Frank's hand, and directed him to swallow it with the water. "You'll feel better soon," he said encouragingly, rising and brushing dead grass from his knees. He put away his ointment, proceeded to lay out cold fried chicken, slices of cornbread and chunks of fried "sow-belly," half of a pie, cut in wedges, and a half dozen oranges. Frank closed his eyes in a spasm of nausea, and leaned against the hard trunk of a tree. He could not endure the brilliant light on the empty earth and the burning hills.

But very shortly he began to feel revived; the sunburn's throbbing subsided. He accepted the leg of a very good chicken, and even a "swig" of applejack. But he could not stand the cornbread or the sow-belly. The pie, however, was good, though he realized incredulously that it, too, was fried. The orange juice was fresh and grateful in his mouth. He ate slowly, only half listening to the affectionate banter between Ben and Wade O'Leary, who ate with frank hunger. Now he could look, with careful squinting, at the incandescent countryside.

So, this was Kentucky, this raw and blighted land, this brassy and simmering earth, these somber mountains. Far up on a hill he saw his first log cabin, and now he heard the echo of fowl and the acid bark of a dog. A dry breeze rattled the dusty leaves of the trees. Gulfs of silence fumed everywhere.

CHAPTER 46

BEN and Wade sprawled out on the thick dead grass and dozed. But Frank leaned against his tree and gave himself up to his wretched thoughts and to the silence. The shade of the trees became narrower. He looked at his watch. It was past one o'clock. He had no idea how many miles had been covered since morning, but he suspected they were few. He heard the mules switching their tails as they drowsed, their heads bent. Now even the distant chickens and the dogs were silent. The sky was unbearably bright and bleached.

How was he going to endure the rest of the journey, through all that heat and sun? Where was he going, and why? He wiped his face with his damp soiled handkerchief. His body ached with exhaustion; his flesh felt bruised. He looked at his companions, who slept with their hats over their faces. He saw Ben's great and massive body, his muscular brown arms folded under his head. But Dr. O'Leary had managed to retain his neatness and elegance. Even his black leggings were only a little dusty. Suddenly Frank was reminded of his father's pathetic black leggings, and he was sick with his depression.

Kentucky and mules and heat and brazen silence; Kentucky and a Mormon minister and a mountaineer. Frank became dazedly disoriented. He could not believe he was actually in this place, huddled in a narrowing shade, a refugee from heat and strangeness. He allowed his ever-growing homesickness to flow over him. Bison, in retrospect, was a green pool of shadow, civilization. Now Frank cursed himself for coming. He knew, completely, that he would gain nothing, that he had condemned himself to exile and imprisonment in these mountains. He had already given Ben ten of his hoarded ninety dollars. Another ten would take him back to Paintsville tomorrow. Thirty-five dollars, or more, to get him back to Bison. Forty-five dollars left, if he were lucky, to begin again in Bison. It was not enough. Somehow, he must remain here until he had at least one hundred dollars, clear. How long would that be?

Dr. O'Leary was stirring, stretching himself with satisfaction. He sat up, yawned, and smiled at Frank. "You didn't sleep? Well, you napped in the wagon. Feel better now?"

Frank was silent, twisting long sheaves of grass between his trembling fingers.

He muttered dully: "I shouldn't have come. I was a fool."

Dr. O'Leary still smiled, but his eyes rested on Frank meditatively. "You know," he said at last, "I have a theory. I don't think any of us have much choice about where we'll go or what we'll do. The choice rests only in our individual reactions to where we find ourselves. Perhaps you couldn't have helped coming here. But you can help how you manage your environment, and how you control your own thoughts, and how you will act. A man, I believe, either gains or loses by his experiences, and the choice rests with himself."

Frank did not answer. He pulled at the grass.

"How old are you, Frank?" asked Wade gently.

"Almost twenty."

"Twenty," repeated Wade, with reflection. "Well, you're a man, now. What did you do at home, in Bison?"

"I—I was a stenographer." Frank's reply was curt and clipped, and he turned away.

"A stenographer. I didn't mean that, exactly. I meant, what did you really do?"

Frank looked at him. Wade's brown eyes were steadfast and very kind, and so Frank answered him quickly and involuntarily. and with unconscious bitterness: "I—I thought I was—a writer! I used to write—I've written all my life, since I first learned to put words down on paper."

"And now you don't write?"

Frank's pale mouth tightened with such an expression that Wade's brows drew together in concern. "No, I don't write. I never could, really. It was just a stupid idea I had when I was a kid. It wasn't anything at all; I just dreamt it was."

"How do you know?" asked Wade softly.

Frank opened his mouth, then shut it again. Then, after Wade had waited for quite a while, Frank began to speak in a dull slow voice: "I know. I have no education. Everything I know—I got from books I borrowed from the library. What can a man do without an education? I went to night school, after my day's work. I saw how hopeless it was. I found it impossible to learn anything, except English and composition. I had a mass of irrelevant knowledge. The more I learned, the more I knew how ignorant I was. I had read hundreds of history books, and I—I thought I had the— *feeling*—of history, but when it came to actual application—

I mean, I couldn't remember dates and events, in sequence, and so I failed my examinations. Then, any kind of mathematics was beyond me. I was a failure, all around."

He paused. Wade waited, then said: "And then?"

Frank glanced at him with bitter surprise. "'And then' what?" He was already ashamed of having spoken.

"I mean," said Wade. with great gentleness, "what made you think you were a 'failure'?"

"I knew," replied Frank sullenly. He exclaimed: "You're laughing at me, because you think I am presumptuous! Because I know nothing!"

Wade lit his pipe, blew out his match, threw the match from him and watched its spirals in the shining air before it fell into the grass.

He said meditatively: "I am thinking of what Machiavelli said: 'Let no one fear not to be able to accomplish what others have done, for all men are born and live and die in the same way, and therefore resemble each other.'"

Frank stared at him, then in a grim voice he said: "Machiavelli." He laughed shortly. Then he was silent, his face tight and closed. After a while, he said: "If Machiavelli said that, he was a fool, too. I can't accomplish anything. My parents were right, from the start. I'm a failure. I hate them, but they were right."

"Why were they right? Why do you believe them?"

Frank turned on him with unexpected vehemence and anger: "I didn't believe they were right until just recently! Then I knew. I had to waste all those years before I knew."

Wade scratched his ankle, slowly, and gazed off at a coil of mountain. He said: "A man isn't lost until he begins to accept what others think of him as the truth about himself, whether what they think is worse or better than his real self. If he is better, then he is forever defeated. If he is worse, then he will die struggling to live up to their exalted opinion. I don't know which is more evil for the man. At any rate, when he completely accepts the opinion of others about himself, then he is no longer an individual. He is only a projection of the minds of others, and has no real existence of his own." Frank listened and his thoughts, newly released, leapt along Wade's words as a man leaps along stones. "I see what you mean. But it isn't true about me. I—I reached my conclusion about myself from finally knowing about myself."

"You could be wrong," remarked Wade mildly. "What did you write about?" he added abruptly.

Though he hated himself for it, Frank found himself answering: "I wrote poems, first, then stories, then novels. I remember them. They were amateurish and ridiculous. And full of anachronisms and stupidities and ignorance. I—I always had to detour when I needed actual knowledge, because I didn't know." He paused a moment, then cried angrily: "I know what I'm talking about! It was hopeless for me. Now it's behind me. I'm going on from there. I'm going to get money somehow, so I won't have to live among the sort of people I despise."

"What sort of people?"

"The poor. The dirty. The stupid and wretched. What they call 'the masses.' I hate them. I'm—afraid of them." He stopped, and repeated as if in wonder: "Yes, that's it. I'm afraid of them!"

Wade did not make any remark. He puffed contentedly on his pipe, gazing before him. Frank was drawn out of his miserable self-absorption as he looked at the other young man. There was something so calm, so quiet, about Wade O'Leary, so gentle and contained, yet strong. Frank said, with somber curiosity: "Why do you bother about them yourself, you a doctor and minister? Why do you waste your time in these mountains with these horrible people?"

"Because," said Wade, "I'm sorry for them. They need help. You'll see for yourself. And someone has to help them. There was no use waiting for the other fellow to do it. It was there, that need. So, we came out here, my brother and I."

"What if they do need help?" cried Frank excitedly. "If a man needs help, it is because he hasn't the brains to help himself, and why should others do the job he ought to have done, or lacks the intelligence to do?"

"In other words," said Wade, smiling a little, " 'am I my brother's keeper'? Yes, I think I am. When a man is drowning, or starving, I'm not interested in asking how he got in that position. I try to pull him out, or I feed him. That's all."

He added, very quietly: "Some day you'll know it, completely, and then you'll write again, better than you could ever believe."

Frank bit back his contemptuous and bitter words. His wretchedness was like a sickness in him.

"You don't really want money," said Wade thoughtfully. "You just think you do."

"You talk that way," said Frank malevolently, "because you are a minister. Ministers are full of loving kindness. They don't understand. They're usually poor, and they have been taught to despise money."

Wade smiled again. "I'm not poor, really. My father is quite a rich man, in Salt Lake City. But he never thought money important. You'd probably say that is because he never needed it. Perhaps you're right; I don't know. My brother Peter and myself had everything we wanted. But we needed something more valuable. That is why we came here. We've found it."

"You probably have what they call 'faith,'" said Frank, with hard loathing. "What is your faith, anyway? What is Mormonism?"

Wade laughed. "That is a long subject. I have books, down on Benton, and you may read them if you wish. But Peter and I don't try to proselytize, in the accepted meaning of the word. We aren't evangelists. We don't believe we have the 'only true faith.' How can anyone really believe that? Do you remember what Samuel Butler wrote: 'It has been said that all sensible men are of the same religion, and that no sensible man ever says what that religion is.'"

Frank felt a curious excitation in himself, and he perceived, unconsciously, that the flat and burning countryside had acquired depth and meaning and perspective. This, in itself, excited him as it had always excited him.

"But you think what you believe is the 'truth'?"

"Yes, it is the truth. For me," answered Wade gravely. "But I do not believe it is the truth for all men. There is no such thing as the absolute truth, of course. Truth, like everything else, is relative. But that does not change its intrinsic nature, nor give it falseness."

He leaned back on his elbow and smiled humorously at Frank. "That is why I am trying to tell you that the 'truth' about yourself is not in others' opinions. Nor, perhaps, is the 'truth' in yourself. You'll have to find it in your own way."

But the dreariness had fallen on Frank again, and again the landscape had flattened, become a blazing phonograph. With it, came that utter desolation of spirit with which he was now so familiar, that utter undesire for anything and weariness with all things.

Ben Calloway groaned, turned over, cursed, sat up.

"Well, boys," he said, yawning, "reckon we ought to be on our way."

CHAPTER 47

"KATYDID-DID-DID-DID!" came the thin high shrieking from the dark woods. "Whippoorwill!" mourned a chorus of other voices. The black foliage was splashed with moonlight, which could not pierce to the earth and brush below. An owl cried to the night, answered by raucous screams in rapid succession. Autumn scented the air with smoke and spice; the moon hung, a golden bowl, in a black sky, and gilded the tops of the low and somber hills.

Frank, sitting at the bare wooden table in the tent, listened to the voices in the darkness and to the snores of Ira Cunningham behind him on the cot. The kerosene lamp cast a pool of pale yellow light on the table, and on Frank's book, a battered and ancient copy of one of Lord Lytton's novels.

The tent was about sixteen feet square, with a wooden wall some four feet high, surmounted by another wall of screening which reached to the canvas roof. A thick iron pole supported that roof, and in the gusts of wind its fly now rose and fell and flapped the under canvas. The tent was set in a circle of thick oaks, maples and locust trees on the edge of the straggling woods, where squirrels and other animals rustled and quarrelled by day, and birds shrieked, moaned and cried, by night. Facing a long and casual clearing, the tent looked at plantings of tobacco and corn, now yellow in the moonlight, as they sloped down to a small and narrow valley. Frank could see the fire of the oil-well in the valley, now in the process of being drilled, and when a quick shadow passed before it he knew the shadow to be Tim Cunningham, his brother Ike, or one of their mountaineer helpers. Sometimes, when the constant pounding of the machinery was stilled momentarily, a faint voice reached him. But otherwise the beating and pulsing competed with the birds and the animals for the honor of shattering the silence.

The woods wound up to the hilltops, behind the tent. Here could be found blackberries and raspberries, trailing and poisonous vines, snakes and clumps of vivid wild flowers. But now everything was lost in the impenetrable night, with only the moonlight and the leaping red flame of the fire below, to give visibility to the wild scene.

The tent was furnished with two Army cots, covered with brown Army blankets, where Frank Clair and Ira Cunningham slept after their "shift," which ended at midnight, and where Tom and Ike Cunningham slept by day; an oil stove where they did their rugged cooking, two wooden benches, and one large ancient trunk. The screened walls were festooned with work clothes hung on nails. The wooden floor was never cleaned, and great, gritty, oil spots decorated it at random. Everywhere, too, were boxes of foodstuffs, sent by oxcart over the roads, from Sears, Roebuck, in Chicago: powdered milk, cans of meat and fish, bags of sugar, coffee, smoked bacon, a ham or two wrapped in burlap, cans of baked beans and soups, hard cookies, and salt. The one general store "up on Benton" (as distinguished from "down on Benton") supplied them with other necessities from its meagre shelves, and there were always "salat" greens to be dug in the woods and in open places, not to mention the sour wild apples and the berries, the squirrels, quail and 'possum to be brought down by the Cunningham guns. Sometimes the general store could supply them with oranges or bananas and "store bread," also brought in by oxcart, and sometimes a farmer down on Benton could give them cheese and butter.

Among the furnishings were a number of iron skillets, one large iron pot for boiling the "salat" greens and salt pork (a hideous concoction to Frank, who had had romantic notions of "pot likker"), and a miscellaneous collection of always-dirty thick pottery and steel cutlery. The young men washed their oily clothing occasionally in the great wooden tub standing outside on a pile of stones, with water dragged laboriously up the hill from the artesian well sunk in the valley. As the washing was as sketchy as their housekeeping, and done in the iron-hard water from the well with cakes of mountain-made greasy soap, the clothing was always stiff with oil and dirt. Only dire thirst could bring Frank to drink of the well water, in spite of its vaunted purity and coldness, for, when it had stood an hour or so in its pails in the heat, it turned quite brown, and left a rusty rim at the water line. It smelled, too, of sulphur, which reminded Frank of the mountain privies or of rotten eggs. (There was no privy near the tent, but the woods and bushes served the purpose.)

Frank could smell the water now, as he sat at the table, bent over his book in the lamplight. He could smell the sweat curdled in the work-clothes along the walls, and the robust and virile Ira Cunningham, snoring on his tumbled cot in the shadow along the farther wall, exuded an acrid scent of his own. Then there was a pervading stink of annoyed skunk in the cool autumn air, and the odor of decaying vegetation. Sometimes, when the wind blew towards the tent, Frank could catch the stench of oil, pungent and choking, and the effluvium of gas released from deep in the earth. The Cunninghams had discovered oil near the well they were now drilling, and Frank could hear the low pounding of the pumps which filled the pipeline joining other wells in the vicinity. Thumpada-thump, said the pump; beat-dull-beat, answered the machinery of the well now in the process of being drilled. The fire flared and sank in the valley below; the katydids shrieked, the whippoorwills mourned, the owls hooted and cried dolorously. And overhead, the moon poured down upon the woods and fields its cataract of warm gold.

Frank was exhausted; he closed his eyes, and propped his head on his fists. He could feel nothing but his loneliness, his strangeness, his despair, and the sticky fabric of the blue shirt which clung to his back. It was not the work which so exhausted him, though he labored from noon until midnight every day, even on Sundays. In fact, he found release in tending the fire, in standing over the well and watching a new bit strike into the earth, in observing how the gray molten stone gushed up and poured out onto the green grass. But the Cunninghams struck dry wells more often than not, and even the few oil wells they successfully drilled produced poor surface oil, or a scant quantity. Frank had found out that the big wells had been struck when the Cunninghams had worked for other oil men. When they had gone into business on their own, their luck had incontinently changed.

But there was always the very good chance that the next well, or the next, would enrich them all, including Frank, whom they paid three dollars a day for his work. Frank marvelled at their gay enthusiasm, their unquenchable optimism, the bright sense of adventure which filled their every waking hour. Life itself, with its promise of a rich tomorrow, or just with its promise of a good drunk and a pretty wench, or, perhaps a rousing fight with other oilmen, a hunt in the woods, or a sound sleep, was sufficient. The riches for which they drilled without any abatement of hope were only happy afterthoughts, which, if they came true, would delight them. In the meantime, they were enjoying themselves vastly; simple, pleasant, laughing young animals who found Frank somewhat hard to understand, in spite of their easy liking for him.

They could not understand his grim obsession for money, his terrible disappointment when the well struck nothing but water, his despair when the bit was finally hauled up on its ropes, and the machinery moved to a more promising spot. He was having a good time, wasn't he? He drank with them, and sometimes, on Sundays, they could hire a couple of mules and he would ride with them over the mountains, down or up on Benton, or would visit, with them, a certain distant cabin where lived two amiable young sisters and their senile grandmother, who smoked a pipe in the sun. They had taught him to shoot, and were happily amazed and congratulatory when he brought down squirrels and birds and 'possum with the best of them. They would stare, surprised, when, turning to talk to him in the green, sun-spangled depths of the woods, they caught a sudden expression of misery or pain or exhaustion on his face.

"What are the chances for this new well?" he would ask them, white-lipped and intent. They would stare at him wonderingly, and then, shrugging, would say: "Pretty good. Maybe. Goin' up the hills to the girls tomorrow?"

Well, he was city folks, and a Yankee, too, poor critter. He worked like a dawg—for money. Not for enjoyment, not for today. Even after he had had a toss or two in the hay with the Crawford girls, he would rejoin them with a tense dark face, silent and unspeaking. It wasn't nat'ral. Well, city folks—

They jeered at him affectionately when he bought money-orders, in the Benton post-office, to be sent to Sears, Roebuck for books, along with the orders for victuals and other supplies. They laughed at him when he walked the three miles to Benton every week for the pile of magazines for which he had subscribed, or when the oxcart delivered the boxes of books tumbled among the hams and the sugar and the bacon. Sometimes they would leave him for their excursions in the woods or the hills, and wonder what he found so absorbing in the literature strewn about him as he lay in the shade of the great locust tree near the tent.

But they liked him. He was quiet and cooperative; he never shirked. He had developed the ability to make an excellent rabbit or squirrel stew, with green peppers and tomatoes bought from a local farmer, and little round potatoes and onions. He had learned to bake corn pone, too, though he obviously hated it, and when he experimented with yeast and flour and lard, and produced exquisite bread, baked in the tin oven put over the oil burners of the stove, they enthusi-

astically declared that never ag'in would they eat the "store
bread" brought in twice a week from Paintsville. They
balked at his "salats" of fresh, uncooked greens mixed with
hard-boilded eggs, vinegar and oil, but ate them politely on
his insistence that they would get scurvy if they refused. In
consequence, they eyed darkly the "medical book" which he
had bought by mail-order from Sears, Roebuck, and direly
threatened among themselves to "burn it one of these days."
But no one could "cook up" a better dried pea soup than he,
and his beans, baked with molasses and salt pork and mus-
tard, aroused their wild enthusiasm. He acquired the art of
making "clabber biscuit," too, rounds of tender white dough
baked to a golden perfection, real Southern biscuit. Then he
could fry chicken as could no one else. The Cunninghams,
who had laughed at the cook-book bought from Sears, Roebuck, now regarded it with the reverence a true Southerner
bestows on the Bible. Even when Frank produced strange
and alien dishes, to be approached with caution and suspicion, the Cunninghams remained to praise them and groan-
ingly to rub distended bellies. Frank was wonderful; they
loved him. They did not know that he had learned to cook
in self-defense, that he had found repulsive and inedible the
usual Southern dishes of fried sow-belly, corn pone, "salat"
greens cooked to oily black limpness with fat, and greasy
fried pies. He had had to learn to cook, or starve to death.
He preferred the first.

Besides the cooking, Frank managed to put in at least four
hours on the wells. His obsession for money would allow
nothing else. He saw how easily he could be assigned to the
permanent job of full cook for the outfit at three dollars a day and probably no share of any possible riches. When
he worked at least part of his usual shift, he retained his
position as co-prospector, and would have his one-fourth
stake. Though the Cunninghams had passionately told him
he would have that stake anyway, he preferred not to trust
too much in human nature.

Often he would go for days without thinking. But the
nights were the worst. Then, in the silence, his despair and
anguish would return; as they had returned, this autumn
night, with the book on the table before him.

How was it possible to endure this life much longer, in
these frightful hills, among these dreadful people? He knew
to the dollar how much he had tucked away amid the
tumbled clothing, his own and the Cunninghams', in the
ancient Saratoga trunk. Four hundred dollars for five months'

work. Little more than a thousand dollars, if he remained until next summer, unless a rich well were struck. He doubted this, and began to hate the laughing exuberance of the Cunninghams, who found dry or watery wells hilarious.

He thought of the inhabitants of this lonely and illiterate semi-hamlet in the hills, and shuddered with disgust and loathing. Benton boasted no highway save an irregular, mule-flattened road which wound through the mountains to Paintsville, twenty-five miles away.

Benton itself boasted some nine hundred souls, all living in gray log cabins in which they, and their ancestors for scores of years, had been born. It boasted, too, a "crick," which, with its "branches," partially dried up in the summer. No one repaired its single road, which was impassable in the fall and spring. Here and there a more prosperous ex-farmer had built himself a clapboard house, with an inside pump, and once or twice, in the outlying regions, an old small house of gray stone could be found. The one street, at its center, served the post-office and general store, a smithy, a saddle shop, and a drugstore newly competing with the general store. At the far end stood a tiny white church with a pointed steeple and no cross, a Baptist church, visited every summer by the circuit-rider. Sun-baked, arid, dirty and muddy, Benton was hardly a village. The local doctor and his ancient wife occupied the lone stone cottage opposite the church. The O'Leary brothers had built a little schoolhouse beyond the church, and had hopefully painted it red. It consisted of half a dozen backless benches, a blackboard, a large black stove, and a table for the teacher: Peter O'Leary, himself. The O'Learys lived in a tent, similar to the tent of the Cunninghams, on a hillside a half mile from the village.

For miles around little farming was done. The eroded earth opened in yellow yawns on the hillsides and in the valley. No one practised contour farming, though the O'Learys had painfully taught this for a number of years. So that little sustenance could now be obtained from the land in Benton's immediate vicinity.

Benton huddled in its narrow valley, treeless, blazing with raw sunlight, between the dour brush-covered hills. It had huddled there, lost for generations, until some intrepid oil-man had drilled the first well in the community. Now the oilmen, practically all natives of Kentucky or Tennessee or Oklahoma, had given some life to this drab and arid little spot in the mountains, and had brought with them a few civilized manners, decent food, and raucous immorality. Most of them were young men, with leggings and riding trousers, lusty and noisy, cigarette-smoking and singing, drinkers and lechers, fighters and cheaters, buying up options on land for a few pennies, and, some of them, becoming rich in the process. They lived in tents or abandoned log cabins in the mountains, and descended to Benton in small riotous groups on Saturday nights and Sundays. Some of them lived "down on Benton," to the east and some "up on Benton," to the west. They had imported good mules and sturdy horses for their own use, and generously allowed their mares congress with the local jackasses, the resulting mule offspring reverting for a small sum to the owner of the jackass.

It was not these that were loathsome to Frank, for some of the oilmen had more than average education and subscribed to periodicals. It was the natives who were repulsive to the young man, the women with their long shapeless gingham dresses, trailing dirty bare feet, their blank faces hidden in gingham sunbonnets of blue or pink check, their scrawny offspring with scrofula or deformed legs, their men, incredibly narrow of shoulder, many of them bearded and barefooted. Quite a number had become wealthy, but this had not alleviated their horrible poverty and disease and ignorance. The money went to "the bank" in the "settlements," via the oilmen, though Frank shrewdly suspected that "the bank" was the oilmen's pockets. If so, this did no harm. The natives would not have used it in any event; money had a cabalistic quality for those who had seen so little of it in their lifetime. The oilmen were lavish with occasional five-dollar bills, or, more often, with great cartwheels of silver. The silver money meant more to the natives than the green bills, possibly because of its enduring substance. They spent the money on whisky or applejack on Saturdays, and once in a while bought "store bread" or white flour or the strange yellow oranges and bananas they had never seen before.

Few of them bothered to raise gardens, though occasionally a straggling bed of onions, tomatoes, peppers, corn or tobacco or potatoes, could be seen struggling up, entirely uncultivated, in the rear of the log cabins. Here, on rare occasions, the tubercular and pallid women and children worked languidly, thence to retire to the interiors of their dark and squalid cabins.

Dogs, of course, were numerous, snarling yellow curs half-starved and mangy. Every family had a chicken coop or two, the fowl being allowed to pick up whatever sustenance could be found in the sweltering gardens or around the privies. Flies swarmed everywhere, great clouds of them.

The circuit riders, mountaineers themselves, were wise in their generation and wise in the ways of their people. They decried "sin," which apparently consisted of such vague things as "coveting your neighbor's wife," "desecrating the Sabbath" and "worshipping Mammon," but they avoided the subject of murder and unlawful whisky-making and promiscuous fornication among the young folk. These were picayune matters. The services of the circuit riders were necessary only for occasional marriages and baptisms, prayers for the dead, who might have passed away some ten months ago, and for exciting the natives to religious frenzies and madnesses and rollings on the wooden floor of the church. The fact that murders were usually of greater frequency after these excursions into dementia was of no concern to the circuit riders, who carried guns of their own strapped to the saddles of their mules.

The O'Leary brothers had built their little red schoolhouse under the scornful noses of the illiterate circuit riders and the derisive natives of Benton. They held their religious services in the schoolhouse or out under the trees which surrounded it. They made few converts, for they did little proselytizing, content to struggle desperately to bring books and learning to the children, alleviation of pain and disease to the men and women, and comfort to the dying in these hills. Quite often they brought patients to their own tent, for nursing. They tried to bring new agricultural methods to the farmers. They worked patiently and stubbornly for years, until the natives apathetically accepted them and turned to them for medicines and consolation in the dreary winter months when no circuit rider dared brave the hole-filled road. But it was unthinkable that they should ask Wade O'Leary to marry them. He was a Mormon; he believed in many wives, which was against the Bible. Where they had secured this erroneous information remained an eternal mystery to the O'Learys, though they suspected the circuit riders.

Wade had had a bitter enemy in old Dr. Jim Ward, who was firmly entrenched in Benton, and himself a native. He had at first tried to conciliate the old man, to make himself an ally of his colleague in the fight against disease and death. But Dr. Jim, who had "studied" for two years under a "doctor" as ignorant and benighted as himself, who had never subscribed to a medical journal, and whose knowledge smacked of the medieval, resented the newcomer with his "newfangled notions," his medical books, and his education. Dr. Jim had never seen a microscope and "didn't hold with 'em," regarded germs as some dark machination of the "city folks," had never seen or used a forceps in delivery of an anguished woman, was unaware of puerperal fever though one-third of his patients had died of it, and used herbs he gathered himself for anything from a boil to diphtheria. Dysentery was dosed with castor oil, as was typhoid fever; poultices of bread and hot milk were his panacea for smallpox; septicemia got the same treatment. He called appendicitis "sickness of the blind bowel," and advised hot stones on a tortured abdomen, with fatal results. He labeled tuberculosis "weakness of the lungs," and called for large wrappings against the sun, and a brew of dandelion roots. He surrounded himself with potent mystery, which impressed his ignorant patients. This mystery prevented many of them from consulting Wade O'Leary, with his instruments, his test tubes, his sputum tests, his "needle" and serums, and his well-stocked medical supplies. It was not until Wade had learned to make strange gestures, to mutter odd things under his breath, to put on dark glasses and assume an air of portent that he acquired any patients at all.

Frank often saw the O'Learys on their mules, riding up the mountain sides, or on mercy bent in Benton. Peter O'Leary was taller and more muscular than his brother, Wade, and was in comparison almost a giant. He had a fair, sunburned young face, pugnacious yet kind, and a shock of untidy yellow hair. All his features had an earthy bluntness and healthy masculinity. He ambled when he walked, which was a gait more familiar to the mountain folk than Wade's smooth, gentlemanly tread. He had a strong young voice, and had learned to swear obscenely and robustly at the natives when he collared their children for "book-l'arnin'." Wade might be regarded with awe, respect and devotion; the mountaineers loved Peter O'Leary, for he drank with the best of them, was a far better shot than his brother, and could "sw'ar like a sonofabitch." Frank learned early of the strong love between the brothers, the deep understanding and fidelity.

Wade brought books to Frank, who never found enough to read. At first, Frank had been more than glad to see him. But finally Wade, to his distress, saw that some somber misery had made Frank begin to avoid him. Moreover, the last few wells had been drilled farther and farther away from

Benton. The last well was some four miles distant, and Wade rarely came "up on Benton."

Frank, huddling over his book in the lamplight, suddenly remembered what Wade O'Leary had said to him on the last occasion when they had met awkwardly on the mud road in the village: "You haven't found anything of interest among these poor people? Haven't you talked to them?" Frank remembered Wade's grave and thoughtful eyes, narrowed in wonder, the slight rebuke and disappointment in his voice, and he burned with sick resentment. "I thought you might find material to write about—"

What interest could one take in these horrible caricatures of humanity, these whining-voiced imbeciles, these diseased and sub-human wretches? Frank, long ago, had ceased to feel fellowship with these men who spoke with the familiar English accent; they were no longer his people, his fellows in race and blood. He resented the English and Scottish and Irish names they bore; it was an insult for these depravities to bear those names. He found himself thinking nostalgically of the Italians, the Germans, the Slovaks, and even the Poles, of Bison.

"But they, without any fault of their own, have not advanced beyond the pioneer days their ancestors knew," Wade had protested. "Can't you find that interesting enough in itself, that you see folk right out of the pages of old Western history, not a step beyond the prairie schooners that brought them here and abandoned them? You don't have to imagine those far-away people of a century or more ago."

He had added: "I'm disappointed in you, Frank. Come to our tent, soon, and help me administer typhoid serum to them, and smallpox vaccine. I'll teach you; it's simple, and I know you will learn quickly. I need every extra pair of hands I can get. Then you'll have a chance to get close to these people, and to understand them. I want you to understand them. They'll learn to trust you, and to have affection for you, and you'll see them as they really are, so damned pathetic and human and simple."

But, of course, Frank had not gone. And he had taken care to avoid Wade O'Leary thereafter.

The despair he had known in Bison was happiness to the despair he was now experiencing, for he was completely disoriented.

Louder, fiercer, more primordial, more shrill and savage, came the wild and alien voices of the night to Frank Clair's ears. He pressed his clenched fists to his mouth, and stared through the dark screen of the tent at the now black and formless night, which was pierced only by the thin red tongue of the leaping fire. And it came to him, inexorably, that more terrible than anything else to a man are the strange voices he hears in a land which is not his own, in which he has not spent his boyhood and the flowing years of his youth.

The voices cried to the night, and the night answered, and all those who had been born in this place understood both the voices and the night. A sleeper turned, half awakened, became conscious, and heard the chorus and the deep answer, and smiled because he knew what they communicated to each other. Their words were his flesh; the message was given to him; he was one with the night which received the message, and one with the creatures who sang it. He was one with this earth, and the voices which had attended his coming would be the voices he would hear at his death.

Frank thought of Bison. This was late October. Perhaps the first swift dazzle of snow had already fallen; the trees would be bare and black against a blazing sky of chill Northern stars. Leaves would be whispering dryly in the gutters, would rustle down from eaves before the wind. Chimneys would be flowing out their frail silver under a great pallid moon. The shop windows along Grant and Ferry Streets would glisten in the lamplight, and show the big golden heads of the pumpkins crowding against them. Now Frank could smell the midnight dust in the streets; he could strain his ears and hear the lonely rumble of a late streetcar and the thrumming of telephone wires which vibrated in the cold breeze. A footstep would echo somewhere; the lamp lights would be blinking; the crowding wooden houses would sleep under the moon, their verandahs steeped in shadow. These were the things of his home, his city.

When he had left Bison he had expressed the bitter hope that he would never see the city again, never so long as he lived. When, only a few days ago, he had received a letter from his mother, in which she had said that "bookings" had already been made for herself and Mrs. Clair for England the following March, he had felt nothing at all. Yet now he sat, staring out at the alien night and listening to the terrible alien voices, and he was sick with his longing and nostalgia.

He thought: But I was not happy there. I was wretched and desperate. No matter, whispered his new knowledge, it was your home. It was the one spot of earth where you had known the dearest happiness and companionship, where you had felt your strongest ecstasies and had dreamt your noblest and sweetest dreams. In Bison was the grave of those ecstasies and those dreams. But even a grave can be more precious than a land in which there is no grave at all. Even men who are not of your race, but who were the familiars of your childhood, are more beloved than men of your blood if they be strangers. Frank thought of the Italian sections along the streets which touched at the Front, and he smelled the sour smell of yeast, of heat and dust and garlic, and the remembered smell was rich to his nostrils. He saw the neat little houses of the Bison Germans, which looked always as though freshly scrubbed with hot water and suds, and he loved them. He saw the broad square faces of the pale Poles, and heard their hoarse Slavic voices, and, though he could not understand a single word, those voices were more his own than the voices of these mountain men, who spoke in the accents of his own race.

Now, for the first time, he understood the tearing homesickness which his mother had endured all these years, and he felt a pang of pity for her. He thought of his father, and knew why he had saved so desperately, and so cruelly, why he had sacrificed his life for the dream of home. Why, thought Frank, with a strong and soaring wonder, that is the reason I, too, am saving! I never knew it before!

He thought of the money hidden away in the trunk, and he swung around on the bench and stared at the scarred exterior of it. There lay his ransom. He must add to it quickly, so that he might go home. He stood up abruptly. He heard the thumping of the bit, the dull beat of the pumps which were carrying away the thin trickle of oil from the neighboring well. This well produced only fifteen barrels of oil a day; his share was only three dollars above the three dollars he was receiving daily for his work. But perhaps the new well would "come in," and he would be free. Free to go home.

Ira Cunningham rolled in his blankets, and snorted in his dreams. The lamp flickered. Frank carefully opened the screen door, crept down the three wooden steps to the ground. He went towards the new well and the shadows that moved before and around the fire.

When he tried to recall the individual Cunninghams, he was exasperated that he could not do so. Tim Cunningham, tall, sunburned and tan-colored of hair, with a broad lazy grin and a slow, languid voice, was to remain vaguely in his memory. Ike was a somewhat smaller and thinner edition of

Tim, and Ira was of medium height and somewhat fatter than Ike. But their faces were to be forever lost, merged and melted together, so that they were one with the thousands of other faceless men he encountered in his lifetime. This seemed to him the supreme horror, that mankind, distinguished from the other beasts by a dim and flickering awareness of life and alleged to be just a little below the angels, had no real identity as individuals, no strong projection of personality, no intensity of being.

When he was reminded, by Wade O'Leary, of the great poets, philosophers, saints, scientists and artists that the world of humanity had produced, he declared with a swift rush of pain: "It is these who highlight the enormous stupidity and bestiality of all other men, who throw into relief the brute forms and brute features of mankind. It is not a paradox that men kill their singers and their heroes, their saviors and their saints; it is not even an evil or mysterious thing that they do. They act merely in self-defense, out of the depths of their animal logic."

Frank could not remember that any of the Cunninghams had a distinct personality, a sharp individuality. He could not remember whether or not he had liked or disliked them. Their emotions were shallow ripples on a shallow stream; they were happily and healthily merely laughing animals. So it was that when he approached the fire and was greeted with some surprise by Tim and Ira Cunningham, he experienced no contact of mind or personality with either of them, nor could he ever remember the names of the two mountaineer helpers who assisted them at the well.

"How is the well coming?" he asked Tim, or perhaps it was Ira.

"Just dandy," replied Ira's voice, or perhaps it was Tim's.

Frank broodingly watched the ropes rising and falling in the firelight. One of the helpers was hammering a red-hot bit which had just been removed from the fire. Then a shadow emerged from behind the machinery, and Frank saw the face and dark elegant figure of Wade O'Leary.

He stared at Wade, and felt his face flushing. He nodded his head in reply to Wade's casual greeting.

"Looks as if you might have luck this time," said Wade, drawing nearer to Frank. Frank scowled. Wade seemed always to hear a man's thoughts. He turned away; he took a few steps back towards the tent. Wade followed him easily. His voice was calm: "I wanted to see you. I came by here just to see you. I delivered the Hawthorne girl, up over the mountain, of another baby—poor thing. Wonder who the father is this time?"

Frank shrugged. He felt in himself the old nausea, the old undesire and weariness, which were always enhanced when he saw Wade O'Leary.

"What did you want to see me about?" he asked sullenly.

"Some books from a friend of mine who lives on the other side of the mountains, five miles away—and some magazines."

"Another Life of Christ or Mountain Life or a batch of Gospel Trumpets, I suppose?"

Wade laughed a little. "No. Six modern novels, and the four latest issues of the *Saturday Evening Post*, The five latest issues of the New York *Times*, two *Atlantic Monthlies*, three *Harper's Magazines*, and I don't know how many copies of the *Literary Digest*. All up to date. I've got them on my mule. Wait, I'll get them and we'll take them to the tent."

Frank waited, extremely surprised and embarrassed. Wade went back to his tethered mule, swung down a large pack of books and magazines. He gave them to Frank and smiled humorously. "I'd like you to meet my friend," he said, watching Frank incredulously examine the pack.

"You mean that one of these hill-billies really reads and buys these things?" Frank regarded him with cold disbelief. "Or maybe he's a Mormon missionary, too."

"No. He's a Gentile Kentucky mountaineer all right. He lives not far from other friends of mine, who are like him. I want you to meet them. Tomorrow's Sunday. I'll bring a good sound mare for you. Is nine o'clock too early?"

Frank's sullenness returned. "I don't like horses. I don't like the mountains. I despise these people, and their log cabins, and their dirt—"

Wade retained his good humor. "My friends don't live in log cabins, and they aren't dirty, and they haven't got tuberculosis, syphilis, smallpox or typhoid fever, and they don't swarm with children and mangy curs. I have a feeling you'll like them. You might think they are—different."

Frank sighed impatiently. "All right. And thanks for the books. I found an old torn copy of one of Lord Lytton's novels somewhere, and I've been reading it over and over because I haven't anything else and my next shipment of books and magazines isn't due for two weeks. All right. I'll go."

He turned away, and Wade watched him disappear into the tent.

CHAPTER 18

THE morning was a newly minted copper penny, hard, clear, and warm. Close coppery hills, their tops sharp and burning, swelled to a sky the color of an aquamarine. The narrow little valleys between them had hidden themselves in wisps of milky mist, so that any individual characteristics were lost, and each valley, each range of hills, was identical. Dried grass scented the dazzling air, and odors of pennyroyal, pungent woods' herbs and crisp leaves filled the brief gusts of warm wind. Over all lay a shining silence, broken only by the scuttlings of rabbits, squirrels and quail in the brush, and an occasional sweet and piercing note from a bird.

Frank Clair and Wade O'Leary rode over the hills, Wade on his faithful and whimsical mule, and Frank on the borrowed mare. The mare and the mule were great coy friends, and nuzzled each other when the young men paused on a hilltop to look at the earth waves that rose and fell all about them. Frank's dark and heavy depression had lifted a little this morning, but was replaced by a strong restlessness almost as hard to bear. As each winding little valley came into view, he felt a curious excitement, as if about to come upon something satisfying and rich and strange, and then when he saw the isolated log cabins perched on the hillsides or huddling in the bottom lands, he experienced a sharp, sick disappointment. When he had been a child, he had ranged all over Bison and its surroundings, and along the Canadian border, looking for a magical spot, a little island of dreams, and though he never found either, the hope had persisted in him that he had only to search a bit farther, or turn that clump of trees, or run across that meadow, and he would come upon enchantment. He had forgotten that childish searching for wonderland, but he had not forgotten the emotion of it, and finding only log cabins, or empty valleys, or dark broken woods, his frustration was, to him, inexplicably poignant.

However, he tried to conceal this and to be amiable to Wade O'Leary, whom he surlily and secretly loved. All his life he had searched for an ear, he had found and lost it in

350

Paul Hodge, and now here was another man to whom he could speak and by whom he could be understood. It heightened, rather than decreased, his pain that he had found this man in surroundings and in a country that made a mockery of his discovery. The thing was too subtle for any words, and though he longed to tell Wade of it he was afraid that he would not be understood.

As if he understood, Wade hardly spoke at all. He rode his mule as though riding a majestic charger, lightly springing to the top of each hill, gracefully sitting his saddle at each steep descent. His dark lean face was reflective and quiet, his head held proudly. Tied to his saddle, as always, was his black bag of mercy. He wore his black broadcloth with elegance; dust never seemed to gather on it. Frank envied and admired this impeccable grooming, for his own "Sunday" suit had already gathered a sifting brown patina, and he was sweating profusely.

They reached another hilltop, and now they found a singing little spring of cold fresh water. They dismounted, and lying flat on the green border, they drank, and were refreshed. They sat down and smoked and rested a little. They saw about them the burnished tops of other mountains; it was cool and dim under these clustering trees. Then Frank said involuntarily: "I keep thinking that each time we reach the top of another hill, we'll—we'll—find something—different down below." Then he colored hotly, and was mortified at this betrayal by his tongue.

But Wade nodded seriously. "I know. I think, in a way, we all hope that." He turned on his elbow and regarded Frank with prolonged interest. "Most of us never find it. But I think you will, one of these days."

"No," said Frank. He looked at the cigarette in his hand. "No."

He must run away from his own betrayal, and so he said, stammering as he always did when embarrassed or confused: "You have a lot of friends here, haven't you? You seem to know everybody." His voice was filled with the sullen sarcasm which concealed his lonely and bitter envy. "I never had any friends."

Wade did not smile. He was very serious and thoughtful. "Friends? I? No, I don't think so; I can't think of one real friend I have." Now he smiled when he saw Frank's incredulity and wary suspicion. "And, come to think of it, I don't believe any of us has a friend, in the meaning we give to the word. I knew a man in Salt Lake City who always bragged about the many friends he had; he hoarded and gathered them as some people do money, and he counted them over and over. That was his hobby, his joy and his pride. And he didn't gather these friends just for some advantage, financial or social. He was only an ordinary and ingenuous man, who collected friends as others collect stamps or first editions or antique china or butterflies. And he would parade his friends, gathering them around him as a beggar gathers his rags or a woman pulls her furs around her on a very cold night. And for the same reason, probably."

He paused, then continued meditatively: "Yes, he was very pathetic, the poor man."

Frank waited, but Wade did not speak again, so Frank said sardonically: "Then he got sick, or lost his business, or his money, and then he found out he didn't have a friend in the world, after all."

Wade shook his head. "No, nothing like that. He just went on collecting 'friends' and never found out, to the day of his death, that no one has a friend, and that friendship is an ideal which is rarely or ever attained. Just as the hero ideal, the savior ideal, the love ideal, is hardly, if ever, realized, and because of that becomes part of the heroic fairy tales which men tell themselves to make life more bearable. The friendship ideal is a lovely and glorious one, and it is quite enough if we try to approximate it occasionally, and to pretend, if only for one little hour, that we have found it. But we oughtn't to deceive ourselves that it's really attainable. That's dangerous."

"That doesn't—disgust you, or—or—make you feel wretched, thinking that?" Frank asked sullenly.

Wade gave him a quick glance of gentle understanding and pity. Then he said, with deep, kind comprehension: "No. Because I was never an idealist. Like you."

Thunderstruck and angered, Frank watched Wade rise to his feet, and fastidiously brush blades of dried grass from his clothing. But he did not get up himself. He merely glared at the other man.

"Me? An idealist?" he spluttered.

Wade tightened the straps on his mule and looked over his shoulder to smile at Frank. "Oh, yes you are! I knew it the first time I saw you. I think it's fine. I want you to keep on being an idealist. I don't suppose you can help it, anyway. And I know you've got to let your idealism have its way with you, and not let it get all dirtied up by your contacts with other men. And they can sure dirty it up for you, and that'll be very bad for you and for those you can help. There's nothing more dangerous than a potential savior turned realist by getting too close to the world of men."

Frank climbed back on his mare, humiliated and insulted, as though Wade had come upon him naked and had made a ribald remark about him.

They did not ride together now. Frank hung back a little, sullenly. They rode down a hill and came suddenly upon a large log cabin set in a grove of high pines. The grounds of the cabin were neat; rows of well-tended flowers surrounded the stoop, which held several rocking chairs. The hillside below had been farmed in accordance with Wade's ideals of contour farming, and the curving rows of corn and tobacco were green and gold in the hot sunlight. A great burly man with a beard sat on the stoop, mending harness, and a "hound-dawg" rose up to greet the newcomers with a friendly bark. Behind the house stood a large gray barn and a barnyard full of fowl.

The bearded man, brown and bare of arm, got up genially and grinned and waved. "Howdy," he said. He gave Frank a curious look, then, when introduced to the young man, he shook hands heartily. "Shore glad to see you, Parson," he said to Wade, as the two young men dismounted. "Bin a sight of time since you came 'round this way."

"Well, I cover a lot of territory, Eli," said Wade. "Did you miss me?"

Eli Gratwick chuckled. "Yep. Seems like I never git to see you 'cept when there's a funeral." He turned to Frank. "Parson here buried my ole woman a year come spring. Best damn funeral spiel I ever heard!"

"So you're a Mormon too?" said Frank politely if listlessly. He bent and patted the head of the dog.

"No, Eli's an unregenerate Gentile," replied Wade, laughing. He saw Frank's stare. "We call people who aren't members of our Church Gentiles," he explained. He looked at Eli Gratwick, who was a great brown giant of a man, with the peasant's broad and amiable face and twinkling eyes. "How is Bobby? Bobby's Eli's son, away at college," he added, to Frank.

Eli's face brightened, softened, became noble with love and shyness. "Why, the ole sonofabitch's just fine," he said. "Comin' home full of danged new idees, too. Got hisself a job as deputy sheriff, and is goin' to set hisself up in Paintsville." He suddenly roared with herculean laughter, so that the hills echoed with it and the dog barked in excitement.

"Better not git after these here moonshiners hereabouts!" he cried. "But Bobby's got sense, like his ole man. I hope. Comin' home in the spring, he says. Got hisself a gal back in the hills, like I tole you. Ole Saunders' gal, and though I don't hold with Ole Saunders' heathen idees, which ain't Christian, the gal's right purty and clever. She got idees too, from Berea."

Wade explained to Frank: "Isaac Saunders is one of my friends whom we're going to see today. His daughter, Betty, is a lovely girl, and I believe she is going to teach in Paintsville this fall, where Bobby is going to work, too."

Eli invited them into his bachelor's cabin. The interior was spacious and very cool, the pine floor was scrubbed to a milky whiteness, the bare table equally pure and smooth, and rush-bottom chairs were set about at neat intervals along the walls, which were freshly papered with the inevitable pages from the Sears, Roebuck catalogues. There was a great, rough stone fireplace against the farther wall, on whose hearth there smoldered chunks of the soft cannel coal of the vicinity. A blackened kettle steamed over it, and above the fire, on the wall, were hung four excellent Winchester rifles. Sunlight gleamed through the well-washed but uncurtained windows, and in one corner of the large room was a newly made "pallet" where Eli slept. Frank saw a shelf of white crockery arranged in symmetrical rows on another wall, and below them were hung several iron pots and skillets.

He was familiar with the interiors of mountain cabins, but the cleanliness was unfamiliar, and he was pleased. He and Wade accepted Eli's invitation to "set," and Eli clumped into a little pantry off the room. He soon appeared with a pitcher of fresh "sweet" milk, a plate of biscuits and a jar of wild-strawberry jam. He laid these down on the table, went into the pantry again, and brought forth a platter of thinly sliced and hickory-smoked pink ham.

Frank was at first distrustful of this mountain hospitality, but when he saw the gleaming glasses which Eli produced, and the shining aspect of the steel cutlery, he was appeased. He ate with real relish and pleasure, while Wade and Eli renewed their friendship and exchanged mutual jokes which were mysterious to Frank. It was clear that Eli had a tremendous fondness for Wade, which was evidenced by the jovial, profane and obscene epithets which he lavished on him. Once or twice he reached over and rested his mighty brown paw on Wade's impeccable knee, and beamed at him.

Frank, as usual, retired into the background, and appeared to have been forgotten by the two friends.

Then Wade apparently remembered his companion. He said to Eli: "Show Frank the photograph Bobby sent you from college. I want him to see a fine boy."

Blushing, beaming like the sun, Eli got up, lumbered to his pallet, and from somewhere under its blankets he brought out a folder of rough white cardboard which he proudly presented to Frank. "Ain't much to look at, the old sonofabitch," he said, his voice rough with love. "Got a face like a sick hawg. But he's my boy."

Frank politely opened the folder, and was surprised. The photograph showed a young man not more than twenty-one years old, and the head was the head of a scholar or a saint, thin, long and finely formed, covered with a silky cap of very fair and faintly waved hair. The features below were delicate yet strongly marked, beautifully clear and sharp, yet bearing too serious an expression, too much intensity, which gave them an almost fanatical look in spite of their great intelligence. Frank saw the eyes of the young man, overly large and light and gleaming, too vulnerable and too piercing. All in all, it was the face of a dedicated martyr ruthless in righteousness, overwhelmingly sensitive and pure, without humor or tolerance or tenderness.

It was hard to believe that this young man was the son of the burly brown peasant who hovered over Frank with a fatuous expression.

"Why, it's—it's—a fine face," stammered Frank incredulously.

Eli took the folder from him, and held it in his giant's hands. He almost drooled over it. He closed the folder reverently. Ole sonofabitch," he said, and his voice trembled. He put the folder away in his pallet, and patted the blankets down on it as one pats the covers over an adored child at night.

"Tell Bobby I want to see him when he comes home," said Wade, rising. "Maybe he'll let me marry him and Betty."

Eli scowled formidably. "Ain't no danged parson goin' to marry 'em but you!" he exclaimed. "Break the ole sonofabitch's head, if he picks out any danged circuit rider for it!"

As he and Wade resumed their riding over the hills Frank could not forget the brilliant and fanatical eyes of young Robert Gratwick. He brooded on that face, on the proud and delicate poise of the head. Finally he spoke: "Wade, how did such a face ever get into these mountains? Eli is only an illiterate peasant. His son doesn't resemble him at all. How did it happen that he had ambition enough, here in the hills, to want an education, or know anything about schools?"

Wade was silent a few moments, then he said: "Maybe you don't understand about these mountain folks. Most of them, I admit, were irresponsibles and dullards and incompetents when they lived in the East. They couldn't cope with life there, or hold their meagre own among more aggressive and ambitious and intelligent people. They'd heard something about the West, and thought they'd find easy pickings there, where they wouldn't have to work very much. So they set out. But they didn't have the energy or imagination to go beyond these mountains. They stayed.

"Still, a few among them were of good blood and breeding, ne'er-do-wells, probably, and shiftless. Yet men of family, notwithstanding. Then, some of them had wives of superior breeding, who could not leave their husbands, so they settled down and raised broods of children, mixtures of bad blood and good. In time, the bad blood won out, but occasionally, as in the case of Robert Gratwick, the good comes back in another generation."

He paused, spurred his mule up a slope, then went on: "I knew Bobby's mother for a year or two before she died. She looked exactly like Bobby. She was totally illiterate, but still she was a woman of delicacy and refinement. She knew nothing of schools, but she wanted Bobby to have 'book-learning.' Eli worshipped her, which is unusual among mountain men. He had a reverence for education, too. Cannel coal was found on his farm, to the east, and so he had a little money. He loved Bobby, just as he loved his wife, and so Bobby went away to school."

Frank said: "Bobby has a fanatical face. He looks like a disagreeable customer, narrow-minded and intolerant."

Wade sighed. "His mother was what we call a religious fanatic. It isn't that she was exposed more than any other mountain woman to the ranting circuit riders with their illiterate screamings and their religious frenzies. But she had the kind of mind, too delicate and finely balanced to withstand frenzies and madnesses. Then, about a year ago, she went completely out of her head, said she saw the 'wrath of God' on a mountain top one night, and killed herself by throwing herself over a cliff."

He went on, more angrily and rapidly than Frank had ever heard him: "More dangerous and more wicked than any so-called 'atheism' is a madness about religion, any religion at all! There is something obscene in complete religious dedication and devotion. I've travelled all over the South, and have seen the horrible intolerances and hatreds and ugliness which unbridled religious madness can inspire in people. I've seen Catholic churches desecrated, Jewish synagogues wrecked, schoolhouses burned, all in the name of ignorant religious dementia. Only education can do anything about it, and it will take generations to dilute the poison. Why don't the enlightened ministers and priests of other parts of the country come to the South, and work here, in a real vineyard full of snakes and lynchers and disease? Why have they left this beautiful country in the hands of illiterate demagogues and circuit riders and uneducated 'ministers of the Gospel'? The educated and aristocratic Southerners laugh and call their brothers 'white trash.' They think their religious frenzies and shouting revivals are too quaint and amusing. They don't understand, and the rest of the country doesn't understand, that here waits half a nation of partially illiterate and heathenish people ripe for any liar or rogue to arouse them to a murdering madness. In the name of the Bible, by God!"

He turned in his saddle and looked at Frank with a dark and kindling face full of angry disgust and furious fear. "Have you heard about the Ku Klux Klan? Well, it's riding again, against Catholics, Jews and Negroes. The educated Southerners laugh at it and tolerate it. They think it picturesque, some of them, even when they denounce it. I tell you it's not amusing or picturesque. It's hideously dangerous. It reveals the diseased minds behind it, the illiterate, uninformed, blind and hating minds. Perhaps the South will put it down, as it is attempting to do just now, according to the papers I get. But it'll wait, like an obscene beast in some slimy jungle. It'll wait for the hour to do murder in the name of the 'Protestant' Bible, or white supremacy, or something. It's a symptom of what's wrong with the South, and perhaps with all of America, perhaps with the whole world!"

Frank stared, confused. Then, as he listened, and as he saw Wade's aroused face, he felt a thrill, a tingle, as though blood were beginning to force its way through numbed tissue and squeezed veins.

Wade struck his mule vehemently on the neck, so that the startled animal jumped forward a pace or two. Then Wade contritely patted the slapped neck and went on, looking at Frank urgently: "You think I'm exaggerating. I don't think they even know what they hate; they just hate, and they'll find something! And then sometimes I think it isn't just the South; it's everywhere, that hatred of man for his fellowman. Last summer I went to Europe—"

He sighed despairingly. "I don't know. Sometimes I think it's hopeless. There aren't enough of us who seem to care anything about it or even see it. There's a kind of fatalism in men of good will. They think the work is too vast. They think stupidity and hate and ignorance are too fundamental a part of human nature for anyone to do anything about it. They form a little cloister of their own, and preach to one another, instead of going out into the hot vineyards and waste places where the rest of the world lives. But I tell you that men of good will could save the whole world, if they tried! If only they got together and worked as a body!"

They rode on together, in a sudden silence. Frank looked at the mountains; then it seemed to him that they enlarged, gathered substance, became significant. The sensation was tenuous; he thought: Each time it comes, it isn't as intense. I wish I could feel—I wish I could care.

After a while Wade said: "But I was talking about Lizzie Gratwick. She'd tried, poor soul, to infect Bobby. But he was indifferent to her religious dementia, and wasn't tainted by it. However, he retained its emotion, shall we say, for lack of a better word. He was all out for 'righteousness.' I distrust his enthusiasm, which is part of his intolerance. I distrust all enthusiastic men, I'm sorry to say, unless they are great men. But great men are rarely enthusiastic, and that, perhaps, is the trouble. Bobby's idea of 'enlightening' his people is to make them atheistic Puritans, completely lawabiding and rigorous, poor boy!"

He sighed. "I'm afraid I'm not very clear. Well. There it is."

"I gather you don't like Bobby," said Frank wryly.

Wade laughed shortly. "I don't like his kind of mind, whether it is religious or atheistic. When you boil it down, it is the same thing."

"And Bobby doesn't like you?"

Wade considered. "Frankly, I don't think Bobby likes anybody. I don't think he even sees anybody, in an objective way. I only hope that marrying Betty will soften and broaden his outlook. But I'm afraid, just now, after hearing that he's become a deputy sheriff in Paintsville. It's just the sort of thing he'd do!"

CHAPTER 49

THEY began to climb the slope of a high hill. The heat of the day had become more intense, though it was almost November. The sky had whitened; it fumed, and the hills had turned darker yet more vivid.

Frank thought: Why does Wade talk to me this way? He talks to me as a teacher talks to a student. He "shows me things." Why? Why should he bother? What is he trying to do? What has he in mind about me? And why does he think I'd care, anyway? Why has he brought me out here today? He isn't a man to waste time on just an excursion. He has something definite in mind, and he thinks, or hopes, I'll understand.

They reached the brow of the hill. Wade reined in his mule and pointed below. Far down lay a valley broader than the others, a green and smiling valley floating in a frail mist. It was dominated by a farmhouse which was so foreign to the log cabins in other sections that Frank was amazed. He saw the big white house with its minute green shutters, its red roof, its chimney with its plume of smoke. He saw the great barns, the red silo, the neat, white-fenced lawns, the well-tended barnyards, the patterned fields and meadows with their toy Holstein cattle browsing in the heat of the day. He saw clumps of mighty oaks and elms bordering the meadows, casting blue shadows on the warm greenness of the earth.

"Sherry Hempstead lives there," said Wade. "He is a very prosperous farmer. Besides, he owns a large tract of land near Benton, where the best wells have been found. I want you to know Sherry." He paused and looked at Frank meditatively.

"A Mormon?"

"No. A Gentile." Wade smiled. "But a good friend of mine, as far as friends go. We have a lot in common, and he is generous with the 'victuals' when I want them for the half starved people around Benton. He laughs at me, but he gives, out of his liking for me, for he has only contempt for the others. He is a very intelligent, shrewd man, hard as nails, and completely ruthless, and he has considerable education, most of which he acquired himself."

Wade paused. There was something peculiar in his manner, and, puzzled, Frank looked down at the farm and its wonderful green, brown, red and yellow fields. He did not know how it was, but suddenly he thought the serene and shining scene below had acquired a sinister air, something fateful and secret and foreboding. He shrugged off the impression and waited for Wade to go on, as he was evidently about to do.

"Sherry is about fifty. He has no children, but he has a wife. She is a very lovely lady, and was educated in an Eastern college. Her father owned that farm, and it passed to Sherry, who had considerable money even then, when he married Mary Wilcox. Mary is about forty-five." He paused again.

"How can she stand being so isolated?" asked Frank.

Wade abstractedly stroked his mule's neck. "She couldn't stand it. But she stands it now." His manner and voice were more peculiar than ever. He went on: "There is a strange story about Sherry and Mary. They say she liked him when she married him. Of course, I didn't know them when they were young. They must have got along all right. Then, one day, a minister began to ride through the hills. From what I heard from the contemptuous mountaineers, he was an 'eddicated' young fellow from Louisville, and he thought he'd do something for the people here. The story is that he and Mary fell in love and eloped."

And again Wade paused. "I don't know. I can only tell you the story, which is that Sherry went after them. They say that after riding two days, with three of his farm hands—mind you—they found Mary half-dead in the bottom of an old abandoned well, somewhere in the mountains. The farm hands who were with Sherry testified later that that was how it was, and nothing more. The young minister had vanished—they said. There was only Mary, in the well. No one ever saw the minister again. There was some curiosity about it in the cities, for the boy came of a somewhat rich and prominent family in Louisville, and they didn't let the matter rest. They sent swarms of deputies through the hills, questioning everybody, and most of all questioning Sherry and the farm hands. But no one ever saw the minister again."

"Well?" demanded Frank when Wade paused again. "What happened to Mary?"

Wade flapped his reins. "Sherry brought her back. He apparently forgave her. But she was out of her mind, stark, raving mad. He had to put her in a private sanitorium in one of the cities, they say. She was there for three years. Then she was discharged as cured. Sherry brought her home. They live together now, and the story's almost forgotten. I met both of them about three years ago. Mary is still beautiful, and one of the gentlest, sweetest women I ever met."

"Didn't she ever tell anybody what happened?"

"If she did," said Wade slowly, "I never heard of it. I don't think so. Perhaps she's forgotten, herself."

They began to ride down the steep slope, Frank slightly in the rear, the mule and the mare sliding cautiously down the stone-strewn earth, tearing up little clods of grass with their hoofs. Clouds of yellow dust followed them. Then Frank rode abreast of Wade, and said: "But look here, could they believe the farm hands? Maybe Sherry bribed them—What happened to them?"

"Now," said Wade reflectively, with a glance at the farmhouse rising to meet them, "that's a strange thing. A series of coincidences, I suppose. But one was killed when the tree he was felling toppled the wrong way. Another was kicked to death by one of Sherry's mules, an ornery cuss. Another was poisoned by spoiled meat; I suppose we'd call it ptomaine poisoning. That was before my time. I only know the reports."

"And it all happened on Sherry's property?"

"Yes." Wade's voice was a little tight. "On Sherry's property, and all within six months after they had found Mary." He rode on quickly, halted, slowed down, spoke without turning his head. "You'll like Sherry. He's much respected in this county. I like him. Very much. It's tragic. He's devoted to Mary, and always has been, and he's spent a fortune curing her."

"But what do the mountaineers think of the whole thing, and the deaths of the farm hands?"

"After twenty years, they still think Mary's a bad woman, but they never see her. She never leaves the farm, and hasn't since she was brought home. The farm hands? Well, the folks say the farm is 'hexed,' that there is a 'curse' on it, for some reason, probably from Mary's 'sin.' Sherry couldn't get hands if he didn't pay enormous wages. Pay for hands is about one dollar a day hereabouts; Sherry pays three, with board. But none of the men will sleep on the place."

Frank, annoyed at Wade's curious new reticence, said bluntly: "I think your friend murdered the minister, had his farm hands bury the corpse, and bribed them to keep their mouths shut. Then, afraid that someday they might talk, he killed them, one by one. I think Mary saw her lover murdered and buried, threw herself down the well, and went out of her mind. That's what I think. And I think it's rotten that the scoundrel isn't arrested and hanged."

"Wait until you see Sherry," said Wade quietly. He went on, after a moment: "The strange thing is Ronald Truesdale turned out to have been an old friend of Sherry's. He offered a reward to anyone finding a trace of Ronald, and it was a big reward. The mountaineers combed the hills for miles around, and they have woodsmen's eyes, and they'd have found any trace of a hasty grave."

"Well, what do *you* think?" demanded Frank challengingly.

"I have a theory." said Wade in a low and troubled tone. "It might be that Ronald Truesdale repented, or something, when he and Mary had been riding for two days over the mountains. It might be that he threw Mary into the well, and believing her dead, ran away and changed his identity, and still sentimentally repentant, or thinking he was a murderer, hid himself in a distant city."

Frank was silent a few minutes. "But you don't believe that, do you?"

Wade did not reply. He just rode on and Frank followed, seething with irritation.

The farmhouse lay before them now, in the center of the valley, serene, placid and peaceful, the lawns and the fields fat and rich in the cataract of sunlight. Dogs raced out to meet them, barking happily. Field hands lifted their heads and stared. The barking of the dogs echoed from hill to hill in the warm silence, and somewhere a man called, a horse neighed, chickens clucked. The windows of the large white house glanced brightly in the sun, and the chimney fumed gently. A curious flock of guinea fowl, gray, spotted with white, rushed to the white picket fence with calls of "pitty-querk, pitty-querk!" The sunlight made the silo a tall pillar of flame.

There was a low deep piazza around the front of the house, filled with potted ferns and other plants, and comfortable rocking chairs. A man rose slowly from one of the chairs as Wade and Frank hitched their animals to a post, and when he recognized Wade, the man came quickly down the three low steps, shouting merrily and waving his hand. "Wade! You old son-of-a-gun, you! Howdy! Where've you been, anyway?"

With distrust, Frank watched the man approach. But no one could have resembled a "murderer" less than did Sherry

Hempstead. He was a tall and handsome man of some fifty years, broad, agile and swift of step, with a mass of thick white hair above a very wide brown forehead and square brown face. Here was no peasant, but a man of excellent blood, virile and alert, intelligent and pleasant of expression, with a broad strong nose, a humorous smiling mouth filled with fine white teeth, a square jaw and the merriest, brightest blue eyes Frank had ever seen. Everything about him was hearty and bluff, shrewd and quick, and the handgrasp he gave Frank was firm and warm and steady. He did not wear the usual garb of the mountains, galluses, blue shirt and brass-buttoned "jeans." His shirt was white and starched, open at the neckline to show his pillar of a brown throat; his trousers were of a soft gray flannel, and he wore brown oxfords, well-polished. He had acknowledged the introduction to Frank with grave and friendly courtesy, and the steadfast manner in which he fixed his blue eyes upon the stranger was very reassuring and agreeable. Here, then, was the real Southerner, polite, hospitable and kind. "Any friend of Wade's a friend of mine," he said sincerely, and smiled his charming smile.

Yet, thought Frank uncertainly, he was probably a murderer.

Sherry invited them into the house, his arm strongly wrapped around Wade's shoulder, his loud but musical voice affectionately abusing the young minister for his long neglect. Frank was extremely surprised, for the house was beautifully, if quietly, furnished. The hall, with polished wood floor and polished panelled walls, was gracious and dignified, and an ancient grandfather clock chimed melodiously in the cool blue quiet. A white stairway floated and coiled to a second floor, and it was so exquisitely and airily wrought and carved that it seemed formed of snow held a moment before falling. Doors opened off the hall, and Sherry led his guests into a parlor, where the gleaming floor was covered with small Persian rugs, and a white marble fireplace was surmounted by a glittering crystal candelabrum very elaborately chased, and filled with white candles. On each side was a cloisonné bowl, cobalt blue and mounted on carved wooden legs, and the walls echoed the same color in a softer tone. One wall was given up to walnut shelves filled with books, scores of books in fine leather, and many in dust jackets signifying their newness. Frank saw the furniture, all precious antiques, well restored: a Queen Anne sofa, several small carved chairs in damask, blue and coral and rose and red, a number of Duncan

Phyfe round mahogany tables with brass feet, and, on the walls, one or two fine old landscapes and portraits. Here too was a novelty: brocade draperies repeating the colors of the chairs and tied back with tassels. Really wonderful lamps, globe-shaped and painted, or sparkling with prisms, stood about on the tables.

Frank could not believe his eyes. He sat down, completely confused by Sherry's cordial and friendly invitation. He listened as Wade and Sherry exchanged badinage and affectionate insults, and he was reluctantly charmed by Sherry's mellifluous and silken voice. He was more than charmed by the elegance and grace of the large parlor and its furnishings, and his cramped and miserable spirit involuntarily relaxed. Here was the room and the house of which he had dreamed all his life, set in smiling fields, with burnished hills shutting it away from an ugly world and enclosing it in a gleaming circle of sunny silence and peace.

Sherry called, and a moment later a mountain girl in a clean blue dress and white apron, with her pretty feet innocently bare, scurried into the room. "Fix up a couple of glasses, Sal," said Sherry, "three of 'em. And don't spare the whiskey." He waved her away and resumed his eager and affectionate conversation with Wade. As in the cabin home of Eli Gratwick, Frank was momentarily forgotten. He got up inconspicuously and examined the books. He found everything from Plato to Santayana, from Shakespeare to Galsworthy, from Dickens to Gene Stratton Porter, Harold Bell Wright and Michael Arlen. He opened a few books furtively, and saw that they had been read, for the corners were turned down and there was scribbling on some of the margins in a bold masculine hand. But the house had belonged to Mary's father, and this man probably did not read. Frank glanced around and saw several books scattered on a low bright table, and several magazines ranging from the *Literary Digest* to *The Country Gentleman*, and a newspaper, the Louisville *Times*, dated a few days back.

Frank sat down and listened to the talk between Wade O'Leary and Sherry Hempstead. Sherry dominated the conversation, and it was evident that he was starved for intelligent talk and companionship. After his first bluff but sincere personalities, he had launched into a discussion of national politics, and the past war. He spoke with verve and energy, with imagination and fire, and it was more than evident that he was well informed. As he spoke, using his hands in a lively fashion to emphasize his words, his brilliant blue eyes flashed and sparkled and glittered. Wade leaned back in his chair, indolently graceful and intent.

"Why, any sensible man could see from the beginning that Wilson could only fail!" he exclaimed vigorously. "That's the trouble with idealists; they transfer their own virtues and dreams to other men and think everybody thinks the way they do and wants the same things. This is the way the poor damfools reason: Peace, justice, brotherhood and kindness are good things, aren't they? Well, everybody wants good things, doesn't he? The idealists are good men, and they don't hate anybody, and they want mercy and tolerance and understanding between nations. They figure everybody is like them, and so, if everybody wants the fatherhood of God and the brotherhood of man on earth, why, it'll just have to come, won't it? What they don't know is that for every idealist, and every good man, there are millions of other men who don't give a good God-damn for anyone, and are just hell-bent on hatin' and grabbin' and murderin' and fillin' their own pockets." He laughed robustly and shook his head with its mane of glistening snow-white hair.

"But one good man in Sodom could have saved the city," murmured Wade, smiling.

"Well, damn it, there isn't one good man in the whole world then," said Sherry, laughing again. "You'll see. Everything's festering. Wait a few years, and all hell will break loose. Why? Because nobody really wants peace, or justice, or brotherhood, except idealists like Wilson. And there aren't enough people like him anywhere to avert what's inevitable."

"Then you think the League of Nations will fizzle out?"

"I know it will," replied Sherry sturdily. "Now, I'm not against it. Anybody but a damfool would be for it. But the world's full of damfools, and so the League hasn't a chance."

He stared at Wade, whose face had become somber and grim. "Hey!" he said, giving the younger man a benevolent slap on the knee. "Don't look like that. It ain't that serious. What do you care? But you do, I suppose. Yes, I suppose you do. Lord, boy, the world ain't worth it, believe me. Don't you go and addle your brains about it, and go a-grievin' up and down the country tryin' to reform anybody. We've got Original Sin in us, all of us, and you'd best leave us alone to simmer in our own juices. What can you do, anyways?"

"I don't like you to 'simmer in your own juices,' " said Wade, with a hard note in his voice, though he smiled. "Too many of us have that attitude."

Sherry slapped Wade's knee again, and his eyes, for all their smiling, were softened with pity. "Go back where you come from, Wade. Marry up with some nice girl, back home. Practice your medicine, and let the rest of the world wag itself to hell. It'll do it, anyways, believe me. Do you know something? Calvary was a big mistake."

"One Man died on Calvary, so that the rest of us shouldn't die on a million other Calvarys," said Wade.

"But we will, just the same! And you can't stop it—or Wilson, or anybody else. We're hell-bent for Calvarys, all of us, with the devil poundin' in the nails. At our own request."

"Well," said Wade grimly, "we've got to teach the rest of mankind that if it won't accept peace and justice and friendship among nations, it'll die in a welter of blood and leave the earth to the more sensible animals. We'll live together, or we'll die together, tomorrow, or next year, or ten, or fifty years from now."

Frank listened to the argument with interest and felt some sympathy for Wade. He was surprised at Sherry's speech, wavering as it did between the periods of the scholar and the simplicity and bad grammar of the countryman. He thought the last a complete affectation, a kind of self-conscious homeliness, and he was not entirely wrong.

"You can't do anything about it," persisted Sherry Hempstead. "Looky here, Wade, why don't you get yourself a farm somewheres? Not in this God-forsaken country, but back home in Utah, or maybe somewheres else. Remember what ole William Penn said: 'The country is both the philosopher's garden and library, in which he reads and contemplates the power, wisdom, and goodness of God.' Git around and dig in your garden, and ride over your farm, and, maybe, build a big wall around your house. Then forget the rest of the world. You can't help it. No use making yourself miserable a-whinin' over the rest of us."

But Wade sat in dark and depressed thought, and Frank, who had seen his friend as cool and dispassionate, tolerant and extremely poised, was surprised. Then Wade, stirring as if he were overpoweringly weary, said: "You talk like Cain, Sherry."

"Sure, sure! Know what? Cain was a sensible man, and opinion's been kind of hard on him. If he hadn't knocked Abel on the head, sure as you're livin' someone else would have, the milky-blooded damfool a-worryin' about God and doin' good! Looky, I just read somethin' this mornin' what Stephen Crane wrote:

"A man said to the universe,
'Sir, I exist!'
'However,' replied the universe,
'The fact has not created in me
A sense of obligation.' "

Wade laughed in spite of himself and shook his head.
Sherry listened to him, gratified that he had aroused his friend
from his misery.

A woman entered the room with a silver tray on which
stood three tall glasses. But it was not Sal, the servant. It was
a tall and slender woman in early middle age, with a pale
and beautifully carved face and a mass of bright blonde hair
rolled and braided on the top of her small head. She wore an
exquisitely fitted dress of blue linen, severe of line, which
set off her slender and youthful figure, and no jewelry but a
broad golden wedding ring. She moved gracefully and smiled
at Wade with a sudden shining pleasure. "Wade!" she exclaimed, putting down the tray as the men rose, led by Sherry.
"How glad I am to see you!" She held out her slim white
hand, and when Wade took it, she pressed her other hand
on top of his in a gesture of fervent affection.

"And I'm glad to see you too, Mary," replied Wade. "I
wanted to come sooner but there was an outbreak of typhoid, and I was very busy." He indicated Frank. "This is
Frank Clair, Mary, from the North. One of the oilmen and a
friend of mine."

She turned to Frank graciously, and he saw her pale composed beauty and her great light-brown eyes under golden
lashes and brows. He had never seen sweeter or softer eyes,
nor eyes so radiant and tender. Yet, in a curious way, they
seemed blind to him, unseeing, dimly unaware and un-
focussed. His first pleasure became discomfort, especially
when he felt the coldness of her smooth hand and the bone-
lessness of her fingers. Then, it was not normal for a woman
of her age to appear so youthful, so untouched. Her face
and skin might have been those of a woman in her middle
twenties, unlined and serene as of one newly dead in youth,
arrested in the very act of blooming.

Involuntarily, as he held Mary's hand, Frank glanced at
Sherry. Sherry was looking at his wife with a smiling but
passionate hunger and a profound intensity. He seemed to
be watching her every act, and to be too alert, inexplicably
ready for emergency. Yet nothing could have been more
poised than Mary Hempstead, more gracious, more tran-

quil. Her voice was lovely, soft with the true Southern accent, unhurried and very sweet.

It was Sherry who held a chair for her, who touched her hand, who smiled down into her eyes, who went for a glass of wine for her. He pulled up his own chair beside hers, and she gave him an unruffled and grateful smile. Then she sat with her slim silken ankles crossed, her hands folded in her lap, and regarded all of them with illuminated eyes, impartially polite and pleased. And Sherry, as if temporarily oblivious of everyone else, sat gazing at his wife, watching her every motion with unconcealed devotion.

It was his imagination, of course, but all at once Frank found it difficult to breathe in that beautiful room in the center of which sat that lovely and serene woman. Surely it was his imagination which cast a faint and sinister light on the windows and gave everything an almost imperceptibly livid shadow.

Sherry leaned towards his wife, draped his arm over the back of her chair, and again she rewarded him with her bland and unseeing smile. Sherry now insisted that Wade tell him of affairs "up on Benton," and his own experiences in checking the typhoid epidemic. Wade's voice appeared to please Sherry by its very sound, but he also had the isolated man's interest in the smallest event of the countryside. He roared with delight at the account of the feud between two rival moonshiners, wanted to know of every new well drilled, asked about mutual friends. And Mary listened, turning her great pale brown eyes from one speaker to another, and sometimes giving Frank an engaging and friendly smile. She was the very picture of a feminine, adored and pampered wife, content to bask in her husband's love, and to contribute nothing to the conversation, though sometimes, when Sherry spoke, she would glance at him with an eager, fond approval.

Later, on Sherry's invitation, Wade and Frank went out to inspect the ripening tobacco fields and the horses in the barns, that had been brought in from the heat of the day. Sherry was proud of his horses. He was entering one coal-black filly in the races this year. The barns smelt of leather and horse and were meticulously clean. Frank's interest in horses was not overpowering; to him, a horse was a horse, a not very intelligent animal with a flare for idiot malice and an appetite for oats. But Wade was genuinely absorbed and walked about from stall to stall, stroking the stupid beasts and allowing them to nuzzle his hand.

Sherry strode through his fields, talking incomprehensibly, to Frank, about tobacco and the mosaic disease, what he was doing to combat it, and what price he expected to get. His voice and his manner were genial and bluff; he was the typical gentleman farmer, full of vigor and health. Frank thought of the silent smiling woman in the room they had left, and wondered if she would be waiting, not stirring from her chair, when they got back to the house. She was. She sat there, still smiling faintly, lost in a strange cloud of dreams. Frank was actually startled when she gave evidence of seeing them, and invited Wade and himself to dinner.

Frank was now so uncomfortable and ill-at-ease that he felt great relief when Wade politely expressed his regrets and explained that he and Frank were expected to dine with Isaac Saunders. This amused Sherry, who made a few ribald remarks about the other man, which Wade fended off lightly. But Mary smiled her unchanging smile, and did not press her guests to remain. Frank had the impression that she was not even aware that she had given the invitation. She rose and shook hands with the two young men and graciously urged them to come again soon. There was no change of any kind in her charming and sightless expression.

Sherry put his arm about her, and she leaned against him lightly. They both followed Frank and Wade to the door and watched them go down the flagged path to the gate, where they mounted their animals, took up their reins.

Now a terrible thing happened. Mary suddenly broke loose from her husband, ran down the steps of the porch, hurled herself headlong towards them. Then, as if struck by lightning, by some frightful paralyzing horror, she stood on the path and flung up her arms. Petrified, Frank could see her beautiful face, transfixed, distorted, her rolling eyes, her pulled and twisted mouth. She began to scream, beating the palms of her upraised hands together. Sherry reached her in what seemed one bound and tried to take her in his arms. But she jumped away from him, sideways, not taking her eyes from Wade, who sat motionless and pale on his horse.

"Ronald!" screamed the poor, distraught woman, and her voice was a high and piercing wail, horrible to hear. "Ronald! My darling, darling, darling! O God, don't do that to Ronald! O God, God, God! Have mercy! Ronald!"

Her eyes glared madly, hopelessly, terribly, upon Wade. Sherry tried again to seize her, and she sprang backwards from him with a wild shriek of horror, cringing double, folding her arms on her breast, huddling together as if shrinking away from death itself. She backed away, and Sherry followed her, murmuring soothing and urgent words, trying to fix her with his compelling eyes. He was white; even from that distance Frank could see how he was shaking. He held out his arms to Mary, imploring her, and followed her retreat, not hastily, but matching her own progress. Then she stopped, huddled over, moaning in an appalling voice, as if overcome with an unbearable grief and despair. Sherry lifted her in his arms; her golden head fell on his shoulder; her white arms trailing under his own. He carried her into the house, and to the last they could see his cheek pressed on her hair, and the tenderness in his whole body, and could hear, until the door closed inexorably behind the last flutter of blue dress and trailing hand, her shocking cries and his comforting words of compassion and love.

Stunned by the tragedy, Frank, unbelievingly, watched Wade canter off towards the hills. It was not until Wade was about two hundred feet away that Frank followed, caught up with him. He said almost angrily: "Good God, aren't you going into that house to try to do something for that poor woman?"

Wade answered quietly, without turning his head: "Sherry knows what to do. She has these attacks—sometimes. Not very often, but sometimes."

"That murderer! You can see it now! He won't do anything for her; he'll just shut her up. He's afraid!"

"You don't know, Frank," said Wade, turning in his saddle to show his tight pale face. "You can't call Sherry that. You don't know. No one knows. I don't think anyone ever will know."

"She called you Ronald."

"Ronald," said Wade, almost inaudibly, "must have been a thin dark man, like myself. Then, he, too, was a minister." He sighed. "It happened so long ago, twenty years or more. It's been hard on Sherry."

Now his eyes were narrowed, somber. Frank said resentfully: "Why did you take me there? It's been a hideous experience."

Wade smiled briefly, without amusement. "You're awfully young, Frank. You don't know anything about life, do you? I thought it might be a little education."

"Education! Worst of all," continued Frank naïvely, "I don't suppose I'll ever know the truth, either!"

"That's what I mean." Wade's tone and smile were affectionate. "It's not ever knowing the real truth about anything that educates a man."

The farm and its gentle land, basking in sunlight, lay behind them. As they climbed the hill it retreated, became smaller, a haven of peace and contentment in the valley.

CHAPTER 50

FRANK, after that distracting scene, was in no mood to make another call, and with considerable exasperation he asked: "What freak do we see now?"

Wade gave him a bright glance. "The one truly Christian gentleman I have ever known."

"O God!" cried Frank wrathfully.

In a considering voice, Wade added: "He worships Aphrodite."

"What!"

Wade nodded blithely. "That's right. Aphrodite, Isis, Mary, Astarte—and I don't mean symbolically, or in an 'art' sense. I mean it literally."

Frank reined in his mare abruptly and pushed back his hat from his sweating forehead. He glared at Wade's back, stupefied. "Are you serious? Or am I in a nightmare?"

"I'm serious, and you're awake." Wade halted, also, and laughed. He filled his pipe leisurely, and seemed to contemplate the brightening hills with objective pleasure. "Isaac Saunders, so I understand, was once an idealist. Like you. And like all idealists, he had a fixation on perfection. He had formed, in his own mind, an inflexible pattern for God. From what he had told me himself, he was probably a complete devotee and mystic. But I'm a little ahead of my story. Isaac Saunders isn't a native of these mountains. In fact, he's a Virginian, not a Kentuckian, and he was educated at Princeton, and then in Europe. Don't look surprised. You'll find lots of strange people here—"

"You think so?" said Frank, with heavy irony.

Wade ignored the remark. "Like so many of the fine aristocrats of the South, he was an Episcopalian, but when he was in Europe he played with the idea of becoming a Roman Catholic. He was a man in search of the perfect religion to clothe the perfect God. But none fitted his idea of perfection. He just went on from country to country, all over the world. It was only after many years that he began to have serious doubts that God was perfect. For by that time Isaac, the idealist, had begun to discover the misery of man.

"Up to that time he hadn't seen mankind at all. Humanity was just a shadow lying far below the shining perfection of God. Now he saw the multitudes of mankind, suffering, dying, despairing, and his tender idealist's soul was at first stunned, then appalled, then tortured to the point of insanity. Now, if he had been a practical and reasonable man, he would have joined some merciful group of missionaries, or something, and set himself to alleviate some of the wretchedness he saw. But no, not Isaac. He saw the wretchedness, and hated God. He didn't lose his belief that God existed—Oh, no. He didn't become an atheist, as some idealists do when they find out what the world is. He told himself that man had a lot to forgive God, for making a world of such anguish and helpless pain and innocent death. But Isaac Saunders wasn't going to forgive God. He was just going to be his enemy."

"You make him sound ridiculous," said Frank, as they went on, slowly. For some reason his face had begun to burn, and he was embarrassed and resentful.

Wade suddenly became grave. A sharp blue shadow cut diagonally across his face, and in it, under the brim of his hat, his dark eyes shone. "God forbid! I happen to know what agonies he must have suffered. He told me, a little. Well, anyway, it wasn't possible for Isaac to go back to Richmond now and live smugly. He had seen too much, and he was too tormented. He couldn't stand it any longer. He found these mountains, and retired into them like a hermit who wants to spend the rest of his life contemplating God and adoring Him. Only he wanted to contemplate God and hate Him.

"Sometime, in between his travels, he had taken time off to marry a fine young Richmond girl, about twenty years younger than himself. He was in India, agonizing over the natives, when his wife died in childbirth, leaving him a daughter. He brought the child with him, when he came here, eighteen years ago, and a Negro couple who are still with him, and are the only Negroes in these mountains."

"I know!" said Frank disagreeably. "I know the rest. Our Isaac had to worship something, so he picks out Venus or Aphrodite, or what you will. He must be insane."

Wade rode on in silence for a few minutes, until they reached the brow of another hill. He pulled in his mule, and pointed below.

Here there was a soft deep fold in the hills, hardly a valley. In it, as if hiding, or nestling, stood a little white house of clapboards with a stone chimney. Over it towered pines and locust trees and elms, so that only glimpses of its clean white-ness could be seen between their crowding trunks. Before it, and behind it, burst a riotous mass of color: hollyhocks, enor-mous daisies, salvia, zinnias and cannas, mingling together, exploding upwards in splashes of brilliance, racing one an-other towards the sun. It was a tiny house of enchantment, lying there between the hills, lost and dreaming in color and sunshine.

Frank, though charmed, was also disappointed. He had half expected something on the order of Sherry's house, or a reproduction (Mr. Saunders being a rich Virginian) of a "Southern mansion." But this house, it was apparent, con-tained barely five or six small rooms, unpretentious and quiet.

Wade was speaking again: "I met Isaac three years ago. He was then just completing his new theology. I didn't tell you that in his youth he was quite a student of Greek mythology. Now he resurrected Isis, Astarte, Venus—the mother princi-ple, the smiling, gentle, lovely female Spirit of the universe. Somehow, he had convinced himself that God, being male, could quite logically be the murderer and torturer of man-kind, for, according to the Old Testament, did He not love blood and sacrifice and the clash of armies? Had He not in-vented hell and the lake of burning fire? You see, poor Isaac had a broad swath of Fundamentalism in him, in spite of his Episcopalian background. It was quite logical, in a way, that such a shy and gentle and tender man should come to love the idealized woman, the goddess, for such men as he are en-dowed with many feminine characteristics. The war almost killed him; I thought for a time he would go out of his mind.

"So now Isaac worships the Female principle in the uni-verse, the compassionate and grieving and forgiving and merciful goddess. He is also a devotee of Mary, who he claims was called Isis or Astarte, Venus or Aphrodite, ages before the male God became of any importance. It is his be-lief that the Female is the enemy of the male God, the Spirit of eternal light and good as opposed to the ravening Spirit who tortures men and permits wars and other horrors."

"And you didn't try to introduce the Church of Latter Day Saints to him, I suppose?" asked Frank sardonically.

But Wade said, in a gentle voice: "No. Why should I? What is the purpose of religion? To make man happy and content and hopeful. Isaac's new religion does all that for him, so for him it is right. It doesn't matter what name a man attaches to the Almighty, just so long as he is aware of the Almighty. Isn't there a legend somewhere that no one knows the name of God, not even the archangels? What does it matter, then, what name man gives to Him? He remains."

The little house rose up to meet them as they rode slowly down the hill. Washed in magic and brightness and radiance, lapped about in silence, it took on a fairy quality for Frank. They could see the windows glittering between the trees, now, and the little white door at the front of the house.

"I've told you that Isaac has quite a lot of money," said Wade, lowering his voice. "He paid for our schoolhouse. He is going to build us a hospital. He spends almost all his income on charities, hospitals, orphan asylums, peace societies, missions of all kinds, Catholic, Protestant, Jewish, Mormon —anything. Priests and nuns in leper colonies pray for him. Christian missionaries in India, China and Japan write him regularly, blessing him. He isn't concerned with their religions. He is concerned only in their lightening of human misery and pain. He aches for humanity. He loves mankind. He lives as modestly and frugally as he can. I believe he begrudges every morsel of bread he eats."

They were almost on a level with the house now. It lay as if deserted in the shining silence. The trees were shedding their leaves; faint rustling heaps of russet and gold and crimson had piled themselves on the tiny green lawns. The flowers were clouds of bloom foaming against the white walls. There was no sound of any human life, nor any sound of cattle or fowl. If they were there at all, they, too, dreamed in radiance.

Wade was alighting from his mule, and he was whistling clearly and shrilly. The mountains echoed back the sound, repeating it over and over. There was a faint stir within the house, and a small and delicate man appeared in the doorway, holding a book in his hand. He cried: "Wade! Well, well, so you've come at last! Come in, come in!"

Whatever Frank had expected, he had not expected anything so normal as Isaac Saunders, though perhaps his neat black serge suit, his white shirt, high stiff collar, black string tie and neatly polished black boots were hardly normal for the mountains. There was nothing countrified about Isaac. Isaac might have been a Virginia banker or business man, ready to step into his limousine for a quiet day among lowvoiced colleagues. His small pale face, thin and fragile of bone, his clipped black mustache and neat gray hair, his white hands, his shy but steadfast brown eyes, all proclaimed the city man of aristocratic tradition and background. His voice, too, was almost sweet in its tones, and extremely gentle and soft. When introduced to Frank, he did not stare openly as Sherry had stared, but considerately averted his eyes, shook hands warmly but with reserve, and bowed a little stiffly. There was much that was old-fashioned about him. He said with dignity: "Welcome. Welcome, sir."

"What a happy interruption you are, my boy!" he said to Wade, as he opened the door. "I have been at my desk since dawn, and now the sunlight hurts my eyes. The shipment of food and blankets you wished arrived a few days ago. And I have a check for you."

Never had Frank seen so gleaming an interior, so darkly sparkling, so cool and spacious. The walls were of smooth wood stained walnut; the old wide-planked floors had been polished until they were dim mirrors. Pieces of furniture were few. Frank saw a bare planked table, shining with a dark old patina, and holding an oil lamp and a huge bowl of blazing zinnias. The wide window-seat held bowls and heaps of books. One wall was given over entirely to volumes of all sorts, many of them in precious old leathers tooled in gold. The chairs were mountain-made, rush-bottomed, straight and severe, but lovingly fashioned, stained dark, and polished. There were no rugs, no ornaments but the flowers. The casement curtains at the low old windows were of cream-colored cotton, pushed far back to admit the warm autumn air. The stone fireplace glimmered with a fading fire, and over this fireplace hung a single portrait, that of a beautiful young woman with a dreaming face, clad in white with silver ribbons binding her breast, a crown of pale lilies on her drifting, golden hair. Under this portrait stood a small silver candelabrum, where candles were dimly burning.

The portrait was exquisitely done, and the lovely face shone like a moon in the blue clear light. Frank guessed that it represented no living woman, but a composite of what Wade had called the Female Principle of the universe. He was fascinated by the portrait; he drew near it, and looked into the tender blue eyes, so shining and level, so pure and so kind. He thought of Mr. Farley, who adored the Blessed Virgin, and he thought the sentiment a beautiful one, this adoration of the Mother, the Compassionate, the All-wise, the Merciful, Genetrix of God and men, the Female who knew birth pangs and sorrow, the agony of mankind and the suffering of children.

With the ceremonious courtesy and sincere politeness of

the aristocratic Southerner, Isaac Saunders saw to the comfort of his guests. He went into the kitchen and conducted a fat, middle-aged Negress into the room. "Randy, our guests are here. And you may serve our dinner, if you please," he said to the beaming woman.

He spoke to her as to a dear friend, and she gave him a warm glance of affection before leaving the room. Then he sat down near Wade and gazed at him fondly.

"You must tell me everything," he said, giving Wade his deep attention. "I want, particularly, to know of what you have been thinking, rather than what you have been doing." He looked at Frank apologetically. "It has been so long since I have seen Wade, Mr. Clair."

His pale pointed face and glowing eyes aroused respect and admiration in Frank. He sat on the edge of his chair, his hands planted on his knees, and every angle of his slight body was patrician. How strange to find such a man in these barbarous and abandoned mountains! It was incredible. Frank leaned against the straight back of his chair and listened to the curious conversation now going on between the two old friends.

Wade told Mr. Saunders of his belief that the safety and peace of the world depended on international law powerfully enforced, stringently administered. Mr. Saunders, his head bent courteously, listened intently to every word. Then he got up and trotted across the bare polished floor to his bookcase, returning with a volume through which he thumbed rapidly. He began to read from Spengler:

"'But a law consisting merely of a series of figures read off an instrument' (or a law of words written on smooth paper) 'cannot even as an intellectual operation be completely effective in this pure state.'

"Wade, before the law must be the desire. Before the desire, must be the thoughtful conviction of men. Before the conviction, must be the emotion, a love of justice and mercy. A group of idealistic men may, as they sit in conclave in Geneva, pass a thousand international laws to safeguard the world, but unless the whole of mankind feels in itself a hatred for war and injustice and cruelty, the laws are impotent. The cornerstone of all law is man's heart. Without that cornerstone, the whole arch must collapse into a heap of rubble."

Wade sighed. "But it is impossible to teach the millions of men all over the world that hatred is their own death."

"Wade, as the Chinese say, a thousand-mile journey is begun with the first step. I grant you that it will take many generations to enlighten all mankind. But this very minute is not too soon to begin. First of all, we must teach each child in every school that any religion which teaches hatred of another religion, or intolerance, is his enemy, and that any government which extolls its own people above all others, its political system as the best, is a band of murderers. The world was created for man; if man dies, there will be no world."

He saw Wade's dark smile, and again hastily thumbed through his book. "You smile at my anthropomorphic notions. But listen to this: 'We are presumptuous and no less in supposing that we can ever set up "The Truth" in the place of anthropomorphic conceptions, for no other conceptions but these exist at all.' Man's eye and man's ear project a dream into reality, Wade. Without man, there is not even a dream. The universe would cease to exist."

Frank thought suddenly of Irving Schultz, and he did not know why there was such an acute and immediate pain in him.

He broke into the conversation, with a loud stammer: "Mr. Saunders. I—I have a friend, back—home. He says that man is the only reality, and that he gives substance to nothingness, and—and—being to—God." He saw Wade's quizzical eyes, and flushed and despised himself. Then he saw Mr. Saunders' shining intentness, and went on: "I—I mean that without man's awareness of God, God Himself would have no existence. No. Perhaps I don't have that right, or something—"

Mr. Saunders smiled gently and eagerly. "I think you have. Words aren't adequate, are they? But you mean that when man is aware of—the Divine Principle, then that Divine Principle becomes a reality, and potent?"

Frank nodded, his face still burning.

Mr. Saunders tented his delicate fingers, and seemed to lose himself in contemplation. Then he said softly: "When man becomes aware of his awareness of the Divine Principle, then he becomes aware that other men are part of himself. How can a man hate others, then? He can only love them, as participants in his own life. But first of all must come man's complete awareness of the Divine Principle."

Peace and sweetness seemed to stand in the room like pure water, unruffled and tranquil. But Frank was already ashamed of his own words, and he drew back inside himself as a snail draws back into darkness under a leaf. What a fool Wade must think him! He did not see Wade's surprised and satisfied expression or his secret smile of content.

They rode home together in the purple haze that hung over the mountains. They hardly spoke. They paused for a long time to watch the sunset flaming above the hills. Streamers of long magenta fire were blown out against a sky of the deepest and most translucent turquoise. The hills crouched in dark and formless ridges, like the backs of enormous slumbering animals.

After such a day, it was a relief to Frank to return to the raucous company of the Cunninghams, to sit with them on the steps of the tent in the twilight, and to listen to Ira's strumming on a guitar and his singing of spirituals. He told himself that he had participated in a grotesque dream, and he turned away from the memory of the Hempsteads and of Isaac Saunders with aversion. He felt that Wade had inflicted this lonely disorientation upon him impertinently. I could go insane, myself, thinking of those people, he thought resentfully. A murderer, a demented woman, and a worshipper of Aphrodite! These had no part in the real raw world of Benton, the oil wells, the happy moronic company of the Cunninghams. Ira was singing:

> "In the evening, by the moonlight,
> You can hear those banjos ringing!"

The last of the whippoorwills called in the dark woods. The katydids shrilled. The autumn moon rose in yellow splendor over the trees. Frank sat, wrapped about in silence, and knew again that dreadful loneliness and abandonment of his childhood.

CHAPTER 51

WITH the coming of winter, the Cunninghams and Frank moved down into the valley, and set up housekeeping in an ancient and abandoned log cabin. The Cunninghams would have been content to see their cots anywhere, and to have lived in happy unawareness of the hoary filth and grime all about them. But Frank, to their amusement, began to scrub and clean, to bleach the splintered plank floors with lye, to paper the rough wood walls with pages from the Sears, Roebuck catalogues. Somehow, he managed to get glass and to putty it into the empty window-frames. He cut out large rectangles of black oilcloth, purchased from Sears, Roebuck, and placed them over the cots, so that they gave a grotesque formality to the large dark room. For some reason, Frank could not endure the sight of tumbled brown blankets and striped ticking, and the oilcloth inhibited the happy Cunninghams from messing up their beds. They were too lazy to remove the oilcloth during the day, or perhaps they were too polite. For the sake of his cooking, and because, in spite of his sullen silences and heavy despondencies, they liked him, they had learned to humor Frank.

Frank built a long wooden table, which he bleached spotlessly white; he also fashioned long benches, which he arranged around the table, refectory-wise. Procuring more odd lumber, he hammered a rude food "safe" into being, and painted it walnut. He even went so far as to order some cheap rag rugs from Sears, Roebuck, and he put up a shelf for his books. Then he bought a bright kerosene lamp, and paid a "soup-driver" to bring in the necessary fluid from the "settlements."

The Cunninghams were proud of him. It was pleasant to come in out of the raw winter rain, to hang up wet clothing under Frank's stern eye, and sit down by the fireplace and have a heartening drink while Frank placed steaming bowls of exotic canned food on the table. He had even ordered several cans of whale meat, which looked like "cow-beef" and had a faint fishy odor. But this was not a success with the Cunninghams, who had trustingly sampled the stewed dish. They thought Frank had gone a little too far this time, and their simple eyes were reproachful. Their ideal standard meal, morning, noon and night, consisted of fried bacon, fried potatoes, corn pone and butter, apple butter, coffee and fried pie. Frank played themes on these dishes, to his friends' delight.

He was forced to content himself with the bare shining cleanliness all about him, and with the loads of books arriving haphazardly from Chicago and from Wade O'Leary. He read with increasing passion and avarice: biography, history, new fiction, old classics, poetry, and religious works which the catalogue had piously declared were the "fruits" of "old masters." When better fare was lacking, Frank was often reduced to reading such things. But he made the acquaintance of *Quo Vadis* and *Ben Hur* and of Tolstoi's *War and Peace*, among other things. He memorized great poetry. He read and reread the complete works of Shakespeare, with which Wade had presented him, and much of the stately grandeur of the poetry remained with him. His hunger being catholic, he could read Tennyson and Keats with equal pleasure, Hall Caine and Walter Scott, Thackeray and Mrs. Humphry Ward. He thirsted after the printed word, and when he had nothing else, he even read *The Gospel Trumpet*, which could always be obtained from the wife of the foreman of the more prosperous wells. This lady lived in a neat converted railroad car—how such a thing could have been hauled into the hills remained an eternal mystery.

Then, for Christmas, Wade gave him *The Golden Bough*, complete and unabridged, and Frank, engrossed and enchanted, became acquainted with the world's multitudinous living and dead religions. Peter O'Leary, less exotic of mind, kept Frank supplied with every known magazine, then artlessly added some "Mormon" literature.

The cold wet winter had set in relentlessly. The Cunninghams, lovers of the sun, would have contentedly abandoned all well-drilling until March, but Frank, like an inexorable conscience, kept them at their work. The last well had produced a dribble of eight meagre barrels a day, and only Frank's insistence and his letters of honeyed persuasion to the Indian Pipe Line Company had added this well to the local flood.

The work on the new well proceeded with desultory languor, and only quickened on Frank's "shift." The Cunninghams complained plaintively among themselves. God, did that Yankee think of nothing but work and money? Here it was winter, and sensible men lounged and drank and slept through gray dreary months. But not Frank. And, alas, not the Cunninghams. They had another reason for uneasiness, but this they prudently kept from Frank. They were running out of money. If the new well did not come in generously, they were finished as private prospectors. They would be reduced to hiring themselves out to more prosperous companies in the hills. They talked among themselves of going down south, in the vicinity of Bowling Green, where, it was rumored, a hundred-barrel-a-day well was sneered at loftily. Had Frank been "regular," they complained to each other, they'd have told him the situation. Moreover, Ira hinted, he had about fifteen hundred dollars stowed away, and if he had been a Southerner instead of a damned Yankee, it would have been an easy matter to persuade him to "lend" his cache to his friends. After all, they were all in it together, weren't they? They did not ask him.

The gray heavy rain came down day after day. Sometimes it was speckled with wet snow. Frank, looking through the small dark windows, thought of the blazing whiteness of a Bison winter, the clean and dazzling air, the cold and sterile smell of Lake winds, the pale virgin sun in an arch of white and blinding sky. He thought of the decorous neat streets, the curbs heaped with mounds of snow. He heard the jingling of sleigh bells, and saw the vapor of his own breath in the sunlight. None of all this was here, only the dull lightless rain, the boiling gray sky, the dun-colored hills drenched and mouldering, and, within, the bare cabin room with the black cots and the fire. Nostalgia sickened him. The Cunninghams had contemptuously dismissed the North as "not really America," but Frank, looking at all this rain and desolation, felt that he was in an alien land, and that America lay, cold and shining, brawny and strong and vigorous, beyond the Mason and Dixon line. A kind of sweet and urgent patriotism came to him, a passion for America, such as he had never felt before.

The leaden rain of February passed into the leaden rain of March. Here was no burst of the wild cold greenness of a Northern spring, but only a slight, imperceptible rise of sluggish temperature, and a very slight slackening of rain. Spring brought no urge of anticipation, no eagerness for life and joy and movement. But it did bring a letter from Maybelle:

"Your grandma and I are leaving on April 3rd for home, at last. On the White Star Line, thank God. Home at last, after all my prayers. We're going to Manchester, where your grandma will open a new lodging house, in dear old England. Had you been a proper son, you'd be going with us now, to your native land. But no, you stick down there in Kentucky, where there's nothing. Don't you ever long for home? We thought you'd come back to Bison and say good-bye to us, at least. But no. Well, take care of yourself, Frankie, and write often. I'll write you when I get home, and perhaps you'll run over, yourself, one of these days. You say you are making money, and saving it, and though I was sorry you sent me so little money from time to time, I'm thankful you try to save. Maybe it's all for the best. If only Pa was going with us. That's our sorrow. Well, you can't have everything, I suppose. I'm giving you this citizen certificate which Pa took out when you were twelve years old. I don't need it. Your name's on it, and perhaps you'll want it."

The letter aroused in Frank no emotion at all. But he looked at the naturalization certificate with intense feeling. He had never seen it before. There was his name! He had known long ago that he was a citizen of the United States, but now he had the actual paper in his hands, and for some reason it was beautiful to him. He folded it up, unfolded it, read it again, smoothed it out with his calloused fingers, and held it tightly. Then he placed it in the cotton bag with his money in the trunk, and closed the lid carefully and slowly. Never before had he said to himself: "I am an American!"

For days, he was almost contented and happy. He even sang with the Cunninghams. They were Americans. But so was he! They had been born in this country. They could not feel the lift of heart, the airiness, the sensation of liberty and pride which he now felt. He pitied them, who had only been born here and knew nothing of the true exultation in citizenship.

Once, to his utmost startled amazement, he heard himself thinking: "Some day I shall write of America!" Utterly shaken by the thought, he stood over the stove where he was making a soup, and stared into space. Why had he thought that? He would never write again; he knew it. Yet that absurd idea had come to him, flushed with light, triumphant and strong. He shook his head and stirred the soup, but the singing splendor of his thought remained with him, like a strain of music blowing through the corridors of his mind, and would not be shouted away.

One day Tim Cunningham went "down on Benton" for coffee and salt and gasoline, and returned with a bag of books and a letter from Wade O'Leary. The letter was brief and curt and hard, and began without salutation:

"You must have heard that typhoid has broken out again down here, in spite of our efforts to induce the people to boil all suspected water. Then there are several smallpox cases hereabouts. Peter and I are working ourselves to death, and we need intelligent help. I am demanding, not asking you, to give us a little time and help us administer typhoid serum and vaccinate our patients. I can use you for a few days. I hear from Tim that work on the well has stopped until you can get some new supplies. If you have any sense of decency and any feeling of friendship for me, in God's name, come in and help us! In the meantime, I'm sending you a bottle of iodine. If you aren't sure of your water, add a drop of iodine to each glass, let it stand half an hour before drinking it. I'll be expecting you."

Frank flushed with anger at this note, and tossed it into the fire. He was infuriated with Wade for this impudence. So he was going to demand payment for his books and magazines, was he? The hell with him and his mountain cattle! Let the dogs die in their moldy hills. They had no right to live anyway.

Later he thought: I'll send him a little money for his damned serums. Alone in the cabin, he opened the trunk, got out his bag. He withdrew several bills reluctantly. Then he saw the crisp folded naturalization certificate, unfolded it, and reread it.

CHAPTER 52

"First," said Wade through pale drawn lips, "you scrub the arm like this, with soap and hot water. Scrub hard. Then you dab on this alcohol with this sterile cotton. Then you take this needle and scratch. Three or four little scratches, so you draw a little blood. Then you squeeze this vaccine onto the scratches. Take this gauze, then, and make a light bandage, and tell the poor fools not to take it off for any reason."

Wade's face was gray with exhaustion. The hills were full of sick and dying and terrified people. Moreover, the women had improved on this occasion to have a spate of babies, and there was much pneumonia. The O'Learys had taken possession of the half-finished little hospital which was being built by Isaac Saunders, and had set up their first-aid station in an interior which smelled of new pine and resin. Each delivery of mail and books also brought in fresh serums and vaccine and medical supplies. The mountains were in a desperate state, but the people obstinately and vacantly refused to boil their water or to clean their sodden and stinking privies. They wailed for the circuit riders, who could "pray" away this visitation, and while they accepted Wade's profane administrations, they did so listlessly and with fear. They trusted him, and if he wished to expose them to the "blood-pizen" with his needles and his bandages, well, he had queer ways of amusing himself. They submitted out of affection.

He and Peter were handy with babies, and saved many of them from "the fits." Let him go around with his new-fangled "idees"; with his needles he brought blankets and canned milk, and Peter brought his banjo to entertain the sprawling children. They saw no connection between their sicknesses and their murky wells, and Peter and Wade often found children playing at the bedside of a father or mother dying of smallpox.

The O'Learys had set up their cots and cooking equipment in the back room in the little hospital. They had ordered cots for the hospital, at Mr. Saunders' expense, and these began to fill the one narrow ward. Men, women and children *in extremis*, or unconscious, were brought here on hastily contrived stretchers, accompanied by relatives who docilely nursed them under Wade's direction. Another room was the laboratory, where the serums and vaccines were administered ruthlessly and speedily. Day after day, lines of fathers and mothers and children and old people stood shivering in the rain, waiting for their terrified turns.

The rain came down, the lines expanded and dwindled and whined. It was warm in the ward, and Peter patrolled it vigilantly, forcing the mountain nurses to wash their hands frequently, pausing to take a temperature and give medicines. The bare blank walls, still unplastered and unfinished, gleamed damply in the lamplight. The groans and whimpers of adults and children blurred together in one vast, hushed chord of pain and fear.

But Frank's place was with Wade, who initiated him into the simple procedure of scratching arms and forcing the greenish smallpox vaccine into the scratches, of plunging a hypodermic syringe full of typhoid serum into quivering and shrinking arms, scrawny with malnutrition. There was no time to wash the whole arm. Frank was disgusted at the pale patch which his washing produced in the area of soiled skin, and while he did his work expertly, he upbraided the mountaineers for their filth. They submitted to him sullenly, turning their fearful eyes in a childlike imploring towards Wade, who smiled at them sympathetically. The women huddled in their damp shawls, their cotton skirts trailing over broken boots borrowed from husbands or sons, their heads bent in their ubiquitous gingham sunbonnets. The men displayed more bravado, commenting lewdly on the proceedings, and watching Frank with dislike. They snapped their galluses, chewed tobacco, shrugged, but carefully spat into sand-filled boxes provided by the O'Learys. The children wailed at their mothers' skirts, or hung sleepily over their fathers' arms. Frank saw their pinched and pallid faces, the dead dumb eyes of the women, the gaunt unshaven faces of the men, and hated them. There was no end to them. They came on mules and on foot, steaming in the warmth of the little room, smelling to high heaven of manure, rancid grease and dirt. Every hour or so, Frank would scrape away the red mountain sludge from the floors, and throw a pail of hot water, heavily disinfected, over the bare wood.

But Wade, in spite of his sinking exhaustion, spoke to the people with gentleness, friendship and compassion. He joked with them. He patted the children's cheeks or heads. He had a huge box of lollipops for the youngsters, and promised each child a dainty if he did not "holler." The wan faces of the women brightened with smiles; the men looked at Wade with sheepish love. The quick heavy footsteps of Peter O'Leary could be heard marching to and fro in the ward beyond the shut door, and sometimes he sang to console a weeping child or a moaning woman.

Nothing could induce Frank to go into the ward. He stood, grim hour after grim hour, washing arms, scratching, injecting, filling and emptying syringes, cursing the people under his breath, and glancing with dark wonder at Wade. There was no time for conversation. There was time only for administering the vaccines and the serums, for washing floors, for cooking hasty meals in the half-finished kitchen. Where the hell did all these people come from anyway? What magic did Wade possess which had brought them here, against all their illiterate and superstitious convictions? Frank knew that Wade was working against time. Once the circuit riders rode through these hills, the people would no longer come for preventive treatment. Almost any day, now, the psalm-shouting and bellowing riders would arrive, and the laboratory would be empty. Every hour was precious. The army of science and enlightenment would soon be dispersed in the dusty uproar of the Bible-screamers, the gospel-thumpers, and the pounding hoofs of darkness and ignorance. It was hopeless. Why preserve the lives of these wretches?

Wash, scrub; scratch and clutch at shrinking arms; squeeze out the vaccine, bandage, roll down the sleeve, exhort sternly, dismiss. Hour after exhausting hour. Plunge in the syringe, ignore the shrieks, withdraw the syringe. Sterilize needles in the bath of water on the fuming oil stove. Bring out fresh supplies of cotton-batting, bandages.

This had gone on for days, days without end. There were interludes when Frank threw himself on his cot, which was near Wade's, and slept briefly and soddenly. Then up again, to cook the quick hasty meal, wash and scrub his own hands, and return to the laboratory, where Wade, shirt-sleeved and covered with damp sweat, turned whiter by the hour and smiled constantly. Sometimes Frank was alone with the people, who stared at him blankly or with hostility, feeling his antagonism and disgust for them. Wade, catching an hour's feverish sleep on his cot behind the door, would hear Frank's angry curses, the cries of the children, the oaths of the men. But Frank was a good and tireless assistant, and Wade would close his eyes, sighing, and sink into a nightmare of weary sleep, thanking God for even this angry and resistant helper.

"I only do it for you, damn you!" Frank said to him once, and Wade had laughed. "I don't want to see you and Peter die on your feet. I like to get your books too much."

The rain still poured incessantly. Now there was a sickly warmth to the spring air. The mules bellowed as they stood in muddy puddles, awaiting their owners. The Benton road flowed in reddish mud and water, the cabins streaming with gray moisture while the purplish hills slowly turned green. The "branch" that ran below Benton showed mottled blotches of yellow, purple and red on its rushing surface, for there was oil from the hills mixed with the water.

Any day now the circuit riders would be here, to set up their Gospel workshop in the raddled little church near the general store. The mountain folk still streamed into Benton, as if they, too, felt the cold wind of death and superstition on their necks. They came, out of simple gratitude to Wade, and affection for him, and out of a bemused faith in his "idees." Certainly, something had halted the smallpox in its evil tracks; certainly, the fever was dwindling. But it was still a race, and Frank knew it.

As each day passed, and the circuit riders did not come galloping into Benton on their wild mules, Frank was filled with excitement. Another life saved, another child's eyesight or features snatched from smallpox disfigurement and mutilation. Now the sight of the children softened him a little; they were so bewildered, so pallid, so trusting. He was surprised when they smiled at him, for he had not been aware that he had smiled at them first. When he saw that his own hands had become unusually white and thin, he could not tell why he felt exultation and pride. When he saw his face in the patch of mirror near the door, and observed how his cheeks had fallen in, giving him a gaunt and haggard expression, he was not alarmed. There was something good, something excellent, in this fight against death and ignorance. However unworthy the objects, he added mentally.

It was good to fight with Wade. Though he knew with the deepest conviction that never again would he trust another man as he had trusted Paul Hodge, that never again would he have an alter ego to whom he could speak or not speak and be utterly understood, he trusted and loved Wade O'Leary with what was left of his childhood's faith and unthinking devotion. His tongue was forever inhibited from completely revealing his secret mind, but it revealed as much as it would ever be possible for him to reveal to the other man.

Frank had only one puzzled regret: he knew that Peter O'Leary did not like him particularly, and he was sorry. For he liked Peter very much.

Once, in a momentary lull of mountaineers, Frank said to Wade: "Your brother doesn't like me."

Wade put down a container of serum, looked long and seriously at Frank, then said gently: "No. No. You don't understand Peter." He paused, then came closer to confidences than he would ever come again: "Peter's engaged to a very nice girl in Salt Lake City, a girl of good family and education and background. She—" Wade hesitated, then went on, trying to lighten the cloudiness on Frank's face, "she is just like him. They'll never expect too much from each other."

"Peter seems intimate and close enough with every one except me!" said Frank angrily, his fair skin darkening with humiliation.

"Perhaps it is because no one else gets that close to—to either of us," answered Wade, rather ambiguously.

Out of his loneliness and the barrenness of his life, Frank suddenly decided, one morning, that he would not stay here much longer. Jealousy began to torment him. In spite of Wade's affection and concern for him, he felt his friendlessness. Frank must have all, or he would have nothing. He did not know this yet. He did not know that he must always run from the kind of friendship that could not deepen into love. For he must either love or hate. For him, there was no middle ground. He must either trust completely, opening wide all the doors of his mind and his heart, or he must never trust at all, and keep the doors barred and locked and guarded.

A change took place in him, a kind of retreat, as if preparing for absence. Wade saw this and was helpless. He could do nothing more for Frank. For he, Wade O'Leary, was not capable of giving more than he had already given.

CHAPTER 53

THERE came a Sunday when the little hospital was quiet, except for the hospital sounds in the ward. No mountaineers waited docilely at the door of the laboratory. Frank woke from a long sound sleep to see that a golden day had come, a day all soft warm gilt, moist and shimmering. He went outside in the quivering sunlight, to see that, overnight, the hills had turned an intense green under a gentle blue sky. Even Benton appeared less raw, its rows of little wood houses and log cabins picturesque in the shimmering light. The great trees, which had been empty hardly a day ago, now were fountains of pure emerald green, swaying in a murmurous wind. Frank sniffed appreciatively, and smelled the rich pungent breath of the awakened earth. Then he heard the vehement sound of clanging church bells. So the circuit riders had arrived, and there would be few mountaineers to whom to administer serums and vaccines.

Frank stretched, felt the stiff weariness in his body. But he was elated at the sunshine and at the memory of work well and grimly done. He saw no one about; he sat down on the wooden step of the hospital and smoked a cigarette. He had learned to "roll his own" expertly. He felt the sun on his shoulders and head and new courage in himself. The wind rose a little, blowing into his face sweetly.

In a few minutes he would go into the kitchen of the hospital and begin to prepare breakfast before the arrival of the mountain women who cooked for the patients. A ham had arrived yesterday, and there was newly ground coffee and a bowl of fresh eggs. A farmer would soon bring some rich milk. Wade, apparently, was still asleep.

Then Frank heard his friend's booted footsteps, and Wade pushed open the door, yawning. He sat down beside Frank, rubbed his eyes, yawned again. Frank rolled a cigarette for him, and the two young men sat in weary and contented silence, staring up the road towards the church. Now they saw a few bent and bedraggled figures moving towards the open door of the church, and the bells clanged more excitedly.

"Well," said Wade, "the enemy has arrived. But we have won the fight." He had not yet shaved; his dark beard made his pale face almost white in the sun. "I suppose you'll be going back into the hills now, Frank."

"Yes. I've got to see what the boys are doing. When I'm out of their sight they lie down on the job. Funny none of them ever came down to see me."

Wade smoked, then stared thoughtfully at the tip of his cigarette. "Why don't you go home now, Frank? Somehow, I don't think the Cunninghams will ever make your fortune. They are too—too easy, perhaps. Besides, I think you've learned enough about the mountains and these people."

"I didn't come to learn," Frank reminded him, coldly. "I came to make money."

Wade raised an eyebrow. "I'm sorry. But I don't think you'll make it here. I don't think you'll ever make it by any sudden swift stroke of fortune. You aren't the kind. Go home. Work. Learn. Study. Start to write again."

Frank made an impatient gesture. Now he was all uneasiness. He stood up. "I'll get breakfast. Then I'll go back to the cabin. The boys ought to have the well going in full swing again, if they haven't decided to hibernate. They showed symptoms of it just before I left."

Wade was silent. He looked up at his friend, saw his pale emaciation. His dark chestnut hair had not been cut for a long time, and it had grown thickly above his ears and even down his neck. There were hollows under his blue eyes, his nose had sharpened, and it seemed that he had aged. Wade said: "You look like the devil. Go back there and sleep for three days. I don't want to thank you," he added, with a smile.

Frank wanted to say impulsively: "I did it for you, damn you! Just for you!" But he held back the words. He did not want to see the kind aloofness in Wade's eyes again, the reserved embarrassment. So he merely reached down and pushed Wade's shoulder in affectionate roughness.

They were joined a moment later by Peter, tousled, warm and yawning. He stood near them, his denim trousers pushed into hip boots, his blue shirt open at the throat, his blond hair grown too long, and a golden fuzz on his broad and healthy face. Unlike Wade, he always wore a broad leather belt with a revolver stuck in it. The belt sagged at his lean waist. He had all the appearance of a brawny adventurer, and little drops of moisture were always collecting on his pink skin, no matter what the weather. Frank could not repress his natural admiration for Peter, and he greeted him with pleasure.

Peter waved his hand at the church. "So, they're here, eh? But we got in our licks first, didn't we? Let them rave of hell-fire now; the folks are full of antitoxins, anyway. Wish there was an antitoxin for Bible-madness."

"Wish we could discover an antitoxin or vaccine for all the sins of the world," said Wade, half seriously.

"Then you'd have a damn dull world!" exclaimed Peter vigorously. He accepted a cigarette from Frank. His manner was warmer this morning. "Say, Frank, you did a grand job for us. I can tell you now that I couldn't believe it when I first saw you in there, scratching and stabbing like all hell."

"Why not?"

"Well, you didn't seem the kind." He smiled at Frank with high good humor. But he stood close to Wade's shoulder.

Frank's mouth tightened. "You shouldn't be so hasty in your judgments," he said. "How can you tell about anybody?"

He went into the kitchen and started breakfast. He could see the top of Peter's fair head through the screen of the door. He heard Wade's low voice and Peter's quick, rough answer. But he could not hear the words. He was depressed and uneasy, and decided that he hated Peter, who would never accept him.

Later, at breakfast, Wade informed him that Peter was leaving in May for Salt Lake City, and his marriage. "Pete won't be coming back, but I am going to stay until we are replaced by our Church. We've been here a long time now and are going to be recalled."

"What will happen to this community?" asked Frank, sick at the thought of never seeing his friend again.

"Oh, the Church will send out competent men. The missionary society is very active."

Wade and Peter began to talk with nostalgic pleasure of their home and their family. They forgot Frank. He accepted this grimly. He was nothing to them. They would remember him with gratitude and with pleasant words, and then they would think of him less and less until his very name was forgotten. He was only part of Benton, only a small part of the struggling years in this desolate place. But he would never forget them. When he was middle-aged, or very old, he would remember Wade's dark lean face and Peter's sunlike smile and pink moist skin. That was, he thought, because I have never had anything, really, and they have always been rich in everything.

They were forgetting him now. They talked about their father and their mother, the farm a cousin had purchased. They talked about the women they loved, and to whom they would soon return. They talked about the members of their Church and their old friends. Frank envisioned their home life, contented, agreeable, upper middle-class and satisfying. More and more, Frank felt his homelessness and friendlessness. He would return to Bison eventually, but there would be no one there who cared to see him or wanted him. While he struggled for a bare existence in hopeless insecurity, these two young men would advance in material wealth and in the respect and affection of their home community, married to pretty, serene women, and bringing up happy, healthy children in the love of God and in the safety of peace and adequate money. In their hearts, they had already left Benton. Their quiet eyes were turned west, and the light of a western sun shone on their faces. Let me go with you! Let me be with you always! cried Frank's lonely heart. But the two brothers were laughing over a family joke.

Later, Wade lent him his own mule for his return to the hills. "One of the boys can bring it back tomorrow when he comes for supplies," he said.

Frank rode into the hills, winding carefully around holes in the mud roads. As he left Benton, the wind grew cooler and fresher, and the smell of pine was almost overpowering. The hills rose before him, fell behind him, in green and shining silence. Occasionally, he saw oil wells, pumping steadily, but no living creature. Here and there, in the fold of a valley, lay a log cabin or a tiny gray farmhouse, but insofar as Frank could see, they were abandoned. The sun grew warmer on his shoulders and head; leaves rustled in the wind. The red mountain mud stuck to the hoofs of the mule and they came up with a sucking sound. Occasionally a bird called, and another answered.

After an hour, he saw the familiar little cleft and the log cabin where he lived with the Cunninghams. No smoke rose from the chimney. He saw the beams of the oil well nearby, but no one was near it. Damn their souls! They were probably still asleep in the cabin, which they had most likely turned into a shambles.

It was a lost land, and the gray logs of the cabin reminded Frank of an old man sleeping in the sun. He hitched the mule to one of the posts which supported the roof of the "stoop," and clattered on the planks to the door. He made an unnecessary noise, as if attempting to start life in all this golden silence.

The rough door was closed, and Frank impatiently pushed it open with a loud creaking. He called out: "What the hell! Are you still asleep?"

No one answered. He stood on the threshold of the dark room, stupefied and incredulous. The cots were tumbled; the floor was filthy, covered with grease spots, mud and old magazines. The stove stood in black and rusty abandonment. Broken dishes were scattered near it, and on its top lay a cold skillet half filled with dirty grease. The guns were gone from above the mantelpiece, and the hearth below was filled with trash. There was no sign of any clothing but his own, hung on pegs near the windows. The ancient battered trunk stood in its corner, and on its lid had been tossed a heap of rags and a couple of coffee-stained cups.

It took Frank only an instant to realize that the Cunninghams had fled and were not coming back. There was a furtive air in the smelly cabin, a secretiveness in the dusty corners. Frank, his heart beating wildly, ran to the trunk. His trembling fingers could hardly open the lid. Then he caught his breath with passionate relief. His "city" clothing was still there and his bag of money. He snatched up the latter, and then he felt sick. It was very light. He tore upon the string; a few bills tumbled out, and his father's naturalization certificate. There was also a folded slip of yellow paper. Now his hands were shaking violently. He blinked his eyes, which had acquired a misty film. He unfolded the paper, held it to the light, and read:

"Don't be mad, Frank. But there isn't any oil in these goddamn hills, and we've run out of money. No use staying here. We made up our minds. We heard from some friends that there's lots of oil around Bowling Green, and so we're going there. Reckon we ought to have told you about it, but there wasn't time. So we borrowed your money to set ourselves up in Bowling Green, where there's lots of money to be made, and we've left you one hundred dollars so you can come down there to us, when you get back here. When you come to Bowling Green, get in touch with Si Bellowes. Everybody knows him down there. He'll tell you where we've set up. We'll be waiting for you. P.S. Maybe this is a rotten trick, but you was busy down there with Wade O'Leary, and we're only borrowing the money. We'll pay you six per cent on it. Come on down. You can really make a fortune around Bowling Green. It's a real oil town, not like this son of a bitch of a hole."

CHAPTER 54

WADE READ the note, and his expression darkened with trouble. He looked at Frank's young and frenzied face, at the suffused eyes and mouth shaking with rage and terror.

"Well! That's a damned shame," said Peter. "I always had an idea they were no-account fellers, but I never thought they'd do anything like this."

"What shall I do? What shall I do?" stammered Frank, in despair. He actually wrung his hands, then clenched them. "My money! I've worked a year for that money. It—it— isn't right, for them to get away with this! What can I do? Can I have them arrested? I want to see the bastards in jail. I want my money!"

He was frantic. He looked desperately at Wade, who still did not speak, then turned to Peter. Instinctively, he felt warm indignation and anger in the younger brother, and he caught Peter by the arm. "Can't I stop them? Isn't there any police? What about the sheriff?"

The three were standing outside the hospital in the noon sunshine. Frank had raced down to Benton again, whipping Wade's philosophical mule frenziedly. His shouts had brought the brothers outside. They saw he was almost beside himself.

"Let's talk this over," said Peter, and there was more personal warmth in his bluff voice than Frank had ever heard before. He glanced at his brother, whose black brows were drawn together. "No use getting too excited just now. You say the cabin looks as if they hadn't been there for about two weeks? You came down here about three weeks ago, wasn't it? They must have taken advantage of the chance to skip out with your money. Wade, what about the sheriff, or the police in Paintsville?"

Wade pushed back his soft black hat from his forehead. "You can't exactly accuse them of stealing, in a legal sense,

I'm afraid. Frank was their partner. The brothers pooled all their money, and I suppose you could say that a partner should do the same. I don't know; I'm not a lawyer. They've told you where they are going, and how to get in touch with them, Frank. Morally, I suppose, you could call them thieves. The point is that we must find out whether they are in Bowling Green. If they are, they didn't really steal the money—technically; though I suppose the police would be interested. But if they are not in Bowling Green, then you can prosecute them."

He was alarmed at Frank's gray face and twitching mouth, at the wild glare in his raging eyes. He turned abruptly, after a glance at Peter, went into the laboratory and returned with a glass of water and a white capsule. He held them out to Frank, but the young man struck the glass from Wade's hand.

"My money!" he cried brokenly, turning from one man to the other. "My fifteen hundred dollars! I worked for it in this cursed place, tearing my damn guts out! I—I wasn't alive here! I just worked, so I could get out! And now it's gone, and you say it isn't—isn't—stealing!" His voice dwindled, and he began to tremble violently. "Fifteen hundred dollars doesn't mean anything to you. To me, it was my life!"

He was young, and they saw that in his anguish he was about to burst nnto tears.

"Wait a minute, please," said Wade gently. He glanced at Peter again. "We haven't much cash on hand, Frank. How much have you, Peter? Fifty dollars. I have about that, too. Look here, Frank, we'll—lend—you this hundred dollars. Go down to Paintsville and see the sheriff there. The fellow here isn't any good; he's drunk on moonshine all the time. Stay in Paintsville until they can find the Cunninghams in Bowling Green. Now try to calm yourself. I have a feeling you'll get the money back—"

He pushed the small roll of bills into Frank's hand. Frank stood there and stared at them dumbly. He tried to speak. Peter put his hand on his shoulder.

"I know it's rotten, Frank. But, as Wade says, I guess you'll find the Cunninghams. Whether they have any money left or not, I don't know. Equipment costs money, and they've already spent it, probably. But you can take a lien on the machinery, or something, and force them to pay you back bit by bit. Maybe he'd better do down to Bowling Green and not wait in Paintsville?" he added, to Wade.

Wade nodded. He took Frank's arm in his firm hand.

"You'd better not go back to the cabin, except for your clothes. I'll send one of the boys up for them. You stay here with us for a couple of days. There's a telephone in the general store, and I'll call the police in Bowling Green tomorrow. In the meantime, you'd better try to calm down. You've had enough, I think. We'll see what the chief of police in Bowling Green says."

"That's right!" exclaimed Peter. "You can't do anything until tomorrow. I've got some hot coffee on the stove, and you'd better have some."

The agonized tears were choking Frank. He pushed the money into his shirt pocket. He fumbled, his hands shaking. "You don't know what that money meant to me!" he said, over and over, in a breaking voice. "How can I go anywhere, get away from here, without it!" He could hardly see, and his words were full of hate. "This damned, stinking hole! I'm a prisoner here! I'll never escape; I'll go insane!"

"We'll see what the Bowling Green police say tomorrow," repeated Wade compassionately. He hesitated. "Look here, maybe you'd better go home in a couple of days. We can give you our personal check. Then, when the Cunninghams repay you, you can repay us. How would that be?"

"But—but they may have skipped the country!" Frank stammered. His painful breathing was slower, however, and his voice was quieter. "Then I'd just owe you the money, and it would take me years to repay you."

Wade shrugged and smiled. "We can wait. How about that coffee, Pete?"

They heard a hail and paused on the steps of the hospital. A young man, neatly dressed in brown tweeds and brown leggings, and riding a handsome mare, galloped up, raising a cloud of golden dust. He swung himself down from the horse, and with outstretched hands ran up to Wade. "Hi! How are you, Wade! And Peter? Gosh, am I glad to see you two!"

"Bobby!" exclaimed Wade with pleasure, grasping the young man's hand. "When did you get back here?"

"I've been home for a week, but I couldn't come down on Benton before. How about riding back with me, both of you, and eating with Dad and me today? I've got a million things to tell you."

Still holding the stranger's hand, Wade turned to Frank, to whose ashen face a little color was returning. "Frank, this is Bobby Gratwick. You remember we visited his father last October?"

"How do you do," Frank stammered, still trembling

slightly. He recognized Bobby Gratwick from the photograph he had seen in the elder Gratwick's cabin. His cold damp hand was grasped by a thin dry one, equally cold. After a very fleeting glance Bobby indifferently released him. His attention was all focussed on Wade. He had the mountaineer's high light voice, but not his drawl; he spoke excitedly, almost in a feminine manner.

Frank was beginning to feel a reaction from his desperate emotions. He felt sick and weak, and wanted to sit down. The O'Learys had momentarily forgotten him and his embarrassing problem and were engrossed in laughing and in talking to Bobby Gratwick. Frank felt a violent dislike for Bobby, which probably sprang from his unwelcome intrusion upon the scene. He hated the pale and mobile face, the soft mop of fair hair, the intense blue eyes and too flexible mouth. It was a God-damn girl's face! Too pretty for—words! Why the hell did he have to come now? He and his leggings and his sleek mare and his monopolization of the O'Learys! Frank felt a hot and unreasonable hatred for the O'Learys, who had temporarily abandoned him, and his old resentment against Peter and his slighter and newer resentment against Wade, came back in full force. They could so easily forget him, and turn to this elegant girlish creature; perhaps they were glad of the interruption. Perhaps they were hoping Frank had forgotten the offer of the check. There was no one a fellow could trust or turn to for help. Frank's shaken youth, wounded and desperate, made him glare at Bobby Gratwick and want to kick him savagely. It made him want to kick Wade and Peter, also, and curse them, because they had shut him out and were so engrossed with their old friend.

Fuming, sick, and with an aching head, Frank hovered in the background. His stomach was heaving; he swallowed hard, to keep from vomiting. And the light eager voice went on and on, accompanied by bursts of laughter from the O'Leary brothers. Jealousy tormented Frank. Then, after something the girlish fool had said, he heard Wade give a sharp exclamation. Now there was no laughter. Frank stared at Bob Gratwick, and saw that the smiling face had become pale and tight and hard.

"Yes, you heard me right, Wade. That's what I've been doing. The warrants were served on Big Les and his sons yesterday, and I'm after all the other moonshiners, too. Why do you look like that? Law is law, isn't it? It isn't a matter of 'revenue agents' any more. We have Prohibition in the country, and the sooner these hill-billies learn that, the better for them."

He waited for a comment, but Wade and Peter, after glancing at each other, stared at Bob somberly. He went on angrily: "I'm a deputy sheriff! That's my duty."

Then Wade spoke in a tone Frank had never heard from him before: "You've made it your duty, Bob. It isn't duty, in a way. You're just so damned righteous. That's what makes it wrong—"

"Now, you're not 'talkin' clever,'" said Bob's precise voice, reverting to the mountain idiom. "Law is law. I took my oath, and I'm going to live up to it."

Wade's tone was even tighter: "Bob, you've always hated your own people, haven't you? I don't know why; maybe you don't either. Your father's a mountain man, and he's always —worshipped you. Perhaps you don't like your father? You don't need to answer. I'm just trying to find out what makes you tick, Bob. Maybe you're just a righteous bastard, with a talent for interference in the lives of others. Now," and he raised his hand, "you don't have to try to justify yourself with me. But let's be sensible, for this is very serious. Your people have made whisky for generations, here in the mountains. It's in their blood; they consider it their supreme right, part of their life. You know that as well as I do. They've fought revenue agents since the first agent was sent into these hills. They considered an agent worse than a mere law officer. He was infringing on their lives, liberties and pursuit of happiness. They're free men; they wouldn't have a 'foreigner' dictate to them. That was their code of freedom, and they fought for it—"

"You're evading the issue!" cried Bob, irritated and flushed. "I'm not going to answer your ridiculous accusations about me hating my—these—people, and my father. My father! That's really absurd, Wade. The issue, now, is that I'm a deputy sheriff, of this county, and that we now have national prohibition, and I'm going to enforce the law!"

"And you've sent Big Les and his sons to jail—mountaineers who will die if they are deprived even for a little while of their freedom! You've sent them to jail, because they made whisky, as their fathers made it, and their grandfathers and their great-great-grandfathers before them."

"Don't you believe in the law of the United States of America!" exclaimed Bob, outraged. His fair skin had flushed dark.

"Law, hell!" interposed Peter, with loud rudeness. "You

aren't interested in law, and you know it, even though you try to kid yourself! You're interested in satisfying your malice, though I suppose you've told yourself that you are just a fine, upstanding law officer!"

"You can't talk to me that way!" Bob's face had suddenly drained itself of color.

Wade took a step toward him and spoke more quietly: "Bob, what does your father say about this?"

Bob's jawbone tightened, but he did not look away from Wade: "He feels, wrongly, as you do." Then his voice quickened, almost imploringly: "Wade, that's why I wanted you to come back with me and talk to him. He—he's an ignorant old man, and he's illiterate, and he doesn't understand. You do. You know very well that you Mormons don't approve of alcohol. I thought you'd help me," he added, with young helplessness. "I don't understand you, Wade."

"I'm not talking of law now, Bob," said Wade, almost gently, as to a child. "I'm talking of human psychology, of mountain psychology. Your people won't think of you as an officer of the law upholding your oath. They'll see you as a man who dares to infringe on their old proud rights."

"There are no 'rights' above the law," said Bob steadily.

Wade sighed. "I hate to hear anyone say that," he said. "When a man believes that, he has lost his freedom, his Americanism. He is ripe for autocracy. What is law? In a democracy, an edict passed by the majority. But the majority is not always right. It is up to good men, everywhere, to examine every law before it is passed, and if it is a bad law, passed by ignorant or vicious men in the name of the majority, then the men of good will should set out to abrogate it, in the name of liberty and honor."

"That is unconstitutional," protested Bob Gratwick, "and you know it. That's bolshevism."

"I see you read the timid newspapers," said Wade. "Look here, Bob, there's a moral law and a legal one. They aren't necessarily the same. But perhaps you'll learn that some day." He paused. "This is very serious."

"If I were you, I'd make for the wide open country, or the towns, as fast as you can ride," said Peter, with grim humor. "The men here are pretty good with a gun."

Bob lifted his chin proudly. "I'm not afraid of these illiterate pigs," he said. Now his voice became hard, almost vicious, and his eyes flashed. "It's about time someone put the fear of God into them."

"I thought so," said Wade somberly.

Frank had listened to this conversation with great interest, momentarily forgetting his own troubles. His dislike for Bob Gratwick became intense. The self-righteous bastard! What was behind his lofty talk? Hate? Most probably. Whom, and why, did he hate?

Peter was slapping his holster with loud ostentation. Bob heard it, finally, and swung on him almost savagely. "What are you trying to do? Frighten me? No one can frighten me, so stop rattling that thing, I tell you!"

Wade put his hand on his brother's arm, but looked at Bob: "What does Betty Saunders say about this, Bobby?"

Bob Gratwick hesitated. "She is teaching school in Paintsville. She never asks questions. She knows that duty is duty."

"Does she know that you came up here deliberately to injure and imprison her people, and that you volunteered because you know their ways so well, and where they hide their miserable stills?"

They were all so engrossed that no one except Frank heard the muffled sound of hoofs approaching. He was the first to look up and see a group of three horsemen, mountaineers with strong beards and harsh faces. They held their rifles in their hands, and their eyes were murderous, glinting in the sweet sunshine.

CHAPTER 55

FRANK'S first emotion, as he saw the mountaineers, was revulsion mixed with detestation. He never saw any of them without this first wincing of disgust. The snuff-rubbing, dirty, tobacco-chewing and illiterate swine! He could smell them as they sat above him; he could see their stained blue overalls with the brass buttons and galluses, the sweat-reeking shirts, the battered straw hats, the manure-caked boots. He recognized them. He had poured typhoid serum into them; he had rubbed smallpox vaccine into their scrawny but muscular arms. And he had wished, while doing so, that it were cyanide or tetanus germs.

Frank could not keep back his loathing as he shouted to them: "What do you want?" They had probably just come from their battered little church down the road, where, even now, he could hear the obscene yowling of the congregation. He had attended one session, a week ago, on the occasion of the circuit rider's first "service." He had sat there on the dirty wooden bench, in the midst of the sun-bonneted women and the squawling children and the denim-shirted men. The circuit rider, a lanky, gaunt-faced man in dusty clothing, had stood in the wooden pulpit, and had cried out: "In my Father's house are many mansions! In my Father's house are many mansions! Mansions! God! My Father's house! Mansions! Mansions! Mansions! I wouldn't tell you if 'tweren't true! True! Mansions." That was all. No "proper" singing, no prayer books, no ceremony, no sermon, only that howling, demented and insane and incoherent, in the bare-planked, stinking little church, while the congregation began to sway rhythmically and to mutter. Then, to Frank's utter stupefaction, the men and women suddenly went mad. They leapt to their feet, jumping up and down, throwing themselves upon the floor, rolling into the benches and scattering them, embracing one another in their prone positions, biting one another, screeching, howling, shrieking, while the circuit rider cavorted and screamed in his pulpit. Frank had fled in complete consternation, climbing over benches, fearful that some rabid worshipper might bite him in the ankle or calf, or catch him and roll him over and over in the tangled heap of them. He had stood outside, trembling and shuddering, listening to the inhuman chorus inside, hearing the banging of benches and the thresh of flailing arms and the screeching of the "minister."

When he had related the episode to Wade, the latter had been calm. "The oldest, the most primitive manifestation of religious ecstasy," he had said. "Don't look so horrified, Frank. You can see this in the African jungles, in the Indian dances. It is a strange phenomenon, I admit, but it has its interesting side. These people call it 'bein' taken over by the Spirit.' Poor things."

But Frank's loathing had not abated. He had not found this religious madness either "quaint" or "interesting." He had found in it something terrible and revolting. And now, as he looked up at the mountaineers, fresh from their yowling and their biting, he wished that his eyes could blast them into the earth.

At his demand, Peter and Wade and Bob Gratwick swung about. Then, it was as if they had been struck into petrified immobility. Frank waited for Wade to speak to the horsemen, to smile and greet them. But Wade stood rigid. His brother took a single step to his side. It was curious, but all at once Frank saw that the two brothers had interposed themselves between the mountaineers and Bob Gratwick. It was done almost without movement.

Then Wade said, quietly and easily, his voice strangely loud in the mountain quiet: "Howdy, Hank. Howdy, Eli, Jeremiah."

Bob Gratwick had turned white as death; he had shrunk in his fine clothing. But he did not move. He turned his pale face towards the mountaineers, and stood in silence behind the O'Leary brothers. He had given a single glance at the hospital, and had apparently abandoned his idea of flight as hopeless, some fifteen feet lay between him and safety.

Frank stared at them all, incredulously. Something in the air caused his flesh to prickle. He smelled urgent, stark danger. He looked at Wade. He looked at Peter. Peter had, imperceptibly, unfastened the flap of his holster; his hand lay on the butt of the revolver, and though he appeared at ease, there was something intent and watchful about him.

The mountaineers sat their horses in grim silence. They looked only at Bob Gratwick. Frank could see their faces, tight, gaunt and ferocious. The yowling in the church rose to an unbearable crescendo. Beyond the mountaineers the mountains showed green against the soft and radiant sky, and three geese, a gander, goose and gosling, lumbered down the road in dignified single file. The three stores across the road reflected the sunlight on their dusty windows. There was no one else about but these men on horseback, Frank, the O'Learys and Bob Gratwick.

Frank had known petty violence in his life, but never before had he felt this wild violence which lay all about him and the others. He could not believe it. What was the intention of these primitive creatures on horseback? It must be something serious. Wade's dark face was closed and stern; Peter's friendly expression was gone, and had been replaced by something locked and hard. Bob Gratwick stood behind his friends like a condemned man.

As the mountaineers did not answer him or look away from Bob, Wade said: "How is your Missus, Eli? How's the baby? Got over his fits?"

The mountaineers, who had not moved but had sat like statues for the past few minutes, now glanced at one another. The man, Eli, cleared his throat, and clenched his hand on the rifle which lay across his saddle. The other men repeated his gesture. Eli said: "The Missus is all right, Parson, but tard. Kid's doin' well. Thanks to you." He paused, then resumed in a growling tone: "Don't aim to have no trouble with you, Parson. Hope we ain't a-goin' to have it. Ain't that right, boys?"

His friends mumbled an affirmative.

Then Peter spoke: "Why aren't you boys in church? Hear there's a high old time back there."

The men shifted their rifles, lifted them simultaneously. Frank had never looked into the muzzle of a rifle before, and he found the sight unpleasant. Eli said: "Parson, we'd be a sight pleased if you and yore friends would kindly step aside. We got business with that pole-cat behind you."

Peter's hand moved slightly on his revolver. Frank saw that he had gripped the butt. But Wade was speaking with great quietness: "Look here, boys, none of us want trouble. This is our hospital, and there're a lot of your sick friends in there. Why don't you go home, and forget about this? If there is anything I can do to straighten things out—"

Frank caught a pent note in Wade's voice, a strong determination. He had fixed his dark eyes on the men whom he had rescued from death, whose friend he had been, whose wives he had delivered, and whose children he had saved from desperate diseases. He said: "You've always been my friends, and I have been yours. I've never asked anything of you except to let me help you. You've begged me, time and time again, to let you do me a favor. I've never taken you up on it. I am going to, now. Go home. Forget about this."

The men looked at him from their height, and their stern faces changed into a strange expression of regret and affection. Jeremiah said, his voice almost soft: "Parson, we uns know what you've did for us. We ain't denyin' it. You're our folks. You, and yore brother. We don't aim to have trouble with you. If you want our hides, we uns'd give 'em. You know that. But we ain't a-goin' to stop doin' what we got to do. You ain't got no part in it. You don't belong in these here mountings. And we aim to blast that pole-cat to hell!"

Bob Gratwick stirred. His fists clenched at his sides, and he gave the mountaineers a glance of complete loathing and detestation. His blue eyes flashed in the sunlight. "Can't you see what they want, Wade? They intend to shoot me down. I'm just an unarmed man, one to three, but I'm dangerous, and these brave men are afraid of me."

Peter said roughly: "Shut up, you damn fool." He looked up at the mountaineers, and grinned. "Oh, go on home, you half-wits," he said, humorously. "Bob's a jackass, and now

I'll guarantee that he'll get out of these mountains and stay away. How's that?"

Eli listened and gazed at him with a kind of primitive dignity. "Peter, it ain't no use a-arguin'. You don't understand. I kin see that. He's done somethin' bad to all us mounting folks. He's a mounting man hisself, and he took some of us down to the sittlements and put us in town jails. You don't think that's too bad. You don't know nothin' about it. There ain't words for it."

Wade said quietly: "I know. You've been wronged by Bob Gratwick. But you've got to think of yourselves. You see this hospital? The father of the girl Bob's marrying gave it to you. Jeremiah, your wife was in this hospital for nearly a month. We saved her life. If it hadn't been for Isaac Saunders, your wife would be dead now. Think of Isaac Saunders, and what he has done for you. Eli, your seed corn came from Isaac Saunders. You'd have starved to death without it. Hank, you had appendicitis last summer. Isaac Saunders paid for the instruments in our hospital which saved your life, and the horse you now sit on came from him. Bob's a fool. We all know that. But you must remember Isaac, who is your friend."

"He ain't our friend!" cried Eli with an oath. "He worships heathen gods! That's what our parson down yonder says! You kin talk yore sweet talk, Parson, but it ain't a-goin' to do any good!"

Now, at last, Frank saw anger and disgust in Wade's eyes. "Why, you damn fools!" he exclaimed. "So, you've got that in your heads, too? I might have known."

Peter put his hand on his brother's arm. "Wait a minute, Wade," he began. But Eli shouted madly: "Heathen gods, that's what our parson says! A-worshippin' wimmen back there in the hills! 'Tain't Christian! We uns be Christians, and after we git rid of this rat, we're a-goin' to run Isaac clear from here to Louisville! He got this bastard to put our friends in the town jail—"

Frank saw the wild and brutal faces above him, and he was frightened. He was standing apart from the group formed by the O'Learys and Bob Gratwick. Suppose he just backed away, nonchalantly, towards the corner of the hospital, and ran for it? Then he looked at Wade O'Leary, standing so dark and slender and elegant in the sunshine, completely unafraid, fiery with indignation and anger, and almost without volition he moved closer to the brothers. He was standing beside

Peter now, Peter the easy and bluff and blond, and he saw Peter's tense white fingers on the revolver.

"We uns don't want trouble," said Jeremiah savagely. "You don't know the code o' the hills, Parson. You be just Mormons. We bin good to you, and let you stay, even if you-all ain't Christians, you and yore brother. We don't aim to let you pizen our kids' minds no more, if you make things bad for us. So git along and mind yore own business."

Frank's fingers grasped Peter's hand. Peter did not turn to him, nor did he look away from the mountaineers. But his fingers were like iron on his revolver and resisted Frank's frantic efforts.

Wade, so pale now that he was livid, said: "If you kill this man, I'll see to it personally that you all hang. I warn you. You'll hang."

Jeremiah lifted his rifle and swung it upon the young Mormon minister. But Eli raised his hand and dashed down the muzzle. He did it abstractedly. "Hold yore hosses, Jeremiah. We ain't got no quarrel with the Parson. He cain't do nothin' to us. We got the sheriff with we uns. Sheriff's own boy's down in the town jail."

Then Bob Gratwick spoke with contempt: "Wade, don't get into this. They want to kill me. If you try to stop them, they'll kill you and Peter too. I'm not worth it. Why don't you and Peter go on into the hospital and shut the door? Look here, you," and he looked at the mountaineers over the O'Learys' heads, "I'll go into the hills with you, far into the hills, and you can do your dirty work there."

The mountaineers stared at him, then Eli spat. "Suits us," he said. "Let's git a-goin'."

"No!" cried Wade, and he and Peter backed closer to Bob. "There'll be no murder today. I'll give you men five minutes to clear out of here, or it'll be the worse for you."

Frank became aware, for the first time, that a group of blowzy women and dirty men had emerged from the church and were standing at a safe and craven distance from the hospital, watching avidly like wolves. He lifted his arm to them and beckoned frantically. Some saw him; they averted their heads and slunk behind their comrades. Then they all stood in silence, vultures who awaited the kill.

The horsemen studied the group of three valiant men below them. Bob Gratwick was shorter than his friends. They could not shoot over the heads of the O'Learys without injuring them. They glanced at one another. They looked tired but resolute. "Parson," said Eli wearily, "we didn't aim to do

this, but yore as orn'ry as a mule." And then, with heavy
deliberation, he raised his rifle and pointed it at Wade. There
was a spurt of blue flame, blinding, then a roar.

Instantaneously, it seemed, a crashing volley followed, and
the mountains threw back a series of resounding echoes.
Frank staggered back, wild with terror, stunned by the flashes
and the deafening noise, choking on the acrid gunpowder.
His ears rang; his eyes were filled with a blue and
floating cloud. He thought: They're going to shoot us all
down.

Then the cloud thinned; he heard the beating of hoofs and
a cry. The sun struck his streaming eyes. As in a dream, he
saw the mountaineers galloping off towards the hills. He
saw the sunlight on the store windows, the huddling group of
men and women across the road. He was alive. He had not
been hurt. He looked about him for the O'Learys, and then
he cried aloud.

Wade and Bob Gratwick sprawled side by side in the yellow dust near the hospital. Bob's face had been completely
obliterated; where his features had been was a smashed and
bloody pulp, surmounted by his pale mass of hair. Wade lay
in deathly silence, his eyes closed, his face gray and wizened.
Peter knelt beside him, his hands pressed against his brother's
chest, blood oozing through his fingers. He was saying over
and over, in quiet urgency: "Wade. Wade. Speak to me—"

Frank saw the death that lay at his feet. His eyes, sickened
and aghast, turned away from Bob Gratwick. He looked at
Wade, saw a trickle of blood creeping from between the
stern and livid lips. Then he sprang at Peter. He tore the
revolver from its holster. He swung about, panting, clenching
his teeth on his nausea and mad rage. The mountaineers
were some distance from him now, approaching the steep
slope to the hills. He had never held a revolver in his hand
before, but he felt the trigger against his sweating finger. He
lifted the gun, and instinctively sighted along it, as though it
were a rifle. The backs of the fleeing mountaineers danced
before him, like the horrible figures in a grotesque dream. His
knees shook, and he tightened them, made them rigid. He
pulled the trigger, and felt the powerful recoil of the gun all
through his body as he staggered sideways. He heard nothing
of the roar in this nightmare of horror and madness, but he
tasted the burning powder on his lips, felt it fill his eyes.

Thoughts rushed through his dazed mind: It isn't real. It's
a dream. It hasn't happened. His nausea was a huge salty mass
in his throat and chest. He shook his head, and peered about

him, stunned and incredulous. It seemed to him that a thousand long years had passed, that an era had come and gone, that he would awake on a roar of blinding sound, and daylight, and awareness.

Yet, only a moment or two had vanished into nothingness. He shook his heavy head over and over, and in the shifting and tilting nightmare he saw that the horsemen had stopped abruptly. Eli, who was riding between his two companions, had fallen over his saddle, and in that clear and dazzling light Frank could see that the back of his blue shirt was running with a red stream. Hank and Jeremiah were holding his horse, supporting him so that he did not fall from his saddle. Hank looked back, and cursed aloud, his voice echoing from the hills. But neither he nor Jeremiah responded to Frank's shot with a volley. They held Eli tenderly, and slowly rode off with him up the side of the mountain. The gaping crowd of men and women drifted off, vanishing as quietly and furtively as animals do. The sunlight poured down, and in the hospital there arose a few calls and querulous demands from the patients.

Peter had lifted his brother upon his bent knee, one big hand still pressed urgently against the shattered chest. Frank ran to him, knelt beside him, and sobbed. Peter, white as a ghost, threw him a brief glance. It was as if he had seen or heard nothing at all. He said very quietly: "Help me carry him inside, Frank."

Benton was very quiet. No one walked down that road of death that day. Only the gander, the goose and the gosling paraded in single file towards the "branch." Even the church and the stores had a subdued and furtive look, as if they had withdrawn themselves.

Evening came, and the mountains floated in a tender lilac mist, and a soft wind blew up from the fields. From somewhere came the clanking of a cowbell. The hospital lay in a long and shadowy pool of silence. But no Bentonite came to inquire whether Wade had survived the murderous attack upon him. Someone had removed Bob Gratwick's body. Frank suspected that it lay in the brush beyond the hospital, covered decently with a blanket, awaiting its recall by the older Gratwick.

Frank sat on the steps of the hospital, his elbows on his knees, one clenched fist pressed savagely against his mouth. He must have sat there for hours, staring blindly before him, conscious only of a great hollow pain in his chest. There had been no doctor to see Wade, no help. Only his brother had sat beside his bed, which was hidden from the rest of the hospital by an improvised screen of sheets and up-ended tables. Each time that Frank had gone into the hospital, Peter had waved him away almost fiercely. "Not yet, not yet," he had whispered. And Frank had exhaustedly returned to the steps and to his contemplation of the deserted road and village.

No one had come to tell him whether Eli had died from his shot. He wanted to know. He wanted to hear that he had done this depraved monster to death. He wanted to look at his hand, and know that it had avenged Wade O'Leary. He sat with his fist against his mouth, and his teeth entered the side of his hand. He sat as rigid as stone and stared before him at the discolored dust where Wade and Bob Gratwick had fallen.

He did not know that from time to time tears ran down his duststained cheeks and made furrows in them. Vaguely, he was sometimes aware that he tasted salt on his parched lips. Finally, in his stony exhaustion, he could not have moved even if he had wished to do so. His body was one vast pain, his mind one flame of hate, one sick surge of grief and rage.

The twilight ran down the hills like water, and now stars began to glimmer in a darkening sky. Frank did not know that Peter had come to him, until the young man sat heavily beside him on the wooden step. Then, with a start, he became aware of him. He grasped Peter's arm, tried to speak. But his dry throat cut off all sound.

Peter shook his head, bowed it upon the backs of his hands. His whole big body expressed his abject misery and sorrow. His blond hair stirred in the evening wind.

Frank's hand fell from Peter's arm, as if it had touched fire. He swallowed drily, over and over, and felt a sinking darkness in him. He finally whispered: "He's—he's—"

Peter's head fell lower, until it was almost on his knees. Lassitude and exhaustion overpowered him. A faint groaning struggled from his throat. But when he finally lifted his head and turned his haggard face toward Frank, his eyes were feverishly bright, unmoistened by tears.

He spoke steadily and hoarsely: "Frank, you've got to get out of here now. Now. Right this minute. If—if Eli dies——if he's dead now, they'll come back and kill you. If—if I had shot Eli, it would have been—all right. I'm Wade's- 'kin.' They'd expect it of me, and let me alone. But you—you aren't 'kin.' If he's dead, they'll murder you. I—I should have thought of it before. Any minute, now, someone'll tell them that it wasn't I who fired that shot."

Stunned, turning cold and completely numb, Frank could only sit without the power to move. Then he whispered: "I hope he's dead."

A mist covered his eyes, and again his grief twisted him in anguish. "Wade," he said aloud, and the word was like a stone. "They killed Wade."

Peter sat upright, and again he was very quiet and self-possessed, proud in his sorrow, composed and dignified. "You've got two hundred dollars, Frank. Take my horse. Ride —ride like hell. Not for Paintsville. They'd expect you to go to the nearest town. Go to Charlottestown, thirty miles to the west. You know how to get there. And don't stop, not for a moment." He stood up, and his face was a white blur in the deepening darkness. "I'll get you some food. You need it. There's no time for coffee or anything else." He paused. His hand fell heavily on Frank's shoulder. He tried to say something, and then was silent. But the pressure of his hand seemed to reach down into Frank's heart, and he put his own hand over Peter's fingers.

PART III

What though the radiance which was once so bright
Be now for ever taken from my sight,
   Though nothing can bring back the hour
Of splendor in the grass, of glory in the flowers;
   We will grieve not, rather find
   Strength in what remains behind;
   In the primal sympathy
   Which having been must ever be;
   In the soothing thoughts that spring
   Out of human suffering;
   In the faith that looks through death,
In years that bring the philosophic mind.

                      —*Wordsworth*

CHAPTER 56

THERE are the years which are faceless, a blur of gray shapes, a long drag of footsteps through lightless tunnels. These are the years which leave no trace in the heart, no mark or scar on the mind, no pool of brightness in the gloom. Is it spring? Yesterday it was autumn. Is it morning? Why, it was midnight only an hour ago. Is it summer? It is impossible; last night it was winter. Have I eaten, slept, drunk, walked, spoken, worked? When? A moment ago I ate my dinner. Yet my stomach is empty. I shaved only a moment ago, yet my chin is bristling. When did I bathe? I do not remember. I do not remember. I never remember. Who spoke to me then as if he knew me? I never saw him before, but he called me by name. This street seems familiar. When did I last walk down it? I saw it this morning—yesterday—two weeks ago, but the sun did not stare at me like this, red and fiery between these houses. It must have been this dawn when I saw it over my other shoulder, yet here it is now, peering down this street. But what has happened to the morning, to the hours between the morning and this minute? Where have they gone? I never experienced them.

I am twenty-nine years old, but, between the year when I was twenty, and now, there must have been time and space, morning, noon and night, all the seasons of the year, all the holidays, the winds, the snows, the rains, the suns. I must have known illness, the sound of the city at night, cold, hunger, work, defeat. I must have known hope. But I know, now, that I never knew hope. It is hope which shines upon the years, measures them, marks them off, records them in time. It is hope which says: Last year, I believed I might have love, or success, or satisfaction. If not this year, then the next. Lying, deceitful, treacherous, inspiring, lovely hope! It is not laughter which distinguishes man from the other animals; it is hope, hope dividing time, projecting the hills which must be climbed, the rivers which must be crossed, creating the morning, creating the soul, setting the eyes beyond the horizon, leaping beyond space, moving the stars, striking upon the heart. Without hope, there is no awareness; there is no time, being, moments, hours, no coming or receding footsteps, no expected face, no shadow falling either to the east or to the west, no promise, no life, no death.

There was a time when each tree changed with the sun, with the dawn, the noon, the evening, when it was a fluid being with a thousand aspects, when it turned white in the wind, folded its arms and bowed its head under the stars, flung itself upwards in the storm, and danced in the bright summer light. But never was it the same, never for even a single minute. Never was there a sunset when this tree cast the same shadow upon the grass or the snow; never were its branches in the same posture as yesterday. So it was with everything. Each day was distinct and vivid in time, cleft from its sisters. The stars never shone with the identical lustre with which they had shone last night, or ten years ago. Even the houses, the streets, the sides of buildings, the gutters, the shops, the sidewalks, were freshly created each morning, glimmering with magic, enchantment, wonder. And the sky, forever, hour by hour, moved with excitement and glory and beauty, whether it was a study in a thousand shades of stormy gray, or streaming with magenta fire in the, dawn, or brooding over the earth at twilight in one long cold arch of limitless green.

But somewhere, sometime, a hand lifted, and the change and the color and the motion paused, became fixed, static, changeless. Yesterday was tomorrow; tomorrow was a year ago, five years ago. The light never moves with a breathless, shining hurry; it darkens or fades, becomes pale or diffused, but it is always the same, and there is no line of demarcation, no intensity. I see shadows, but they have been standing there for eternity, immobile, fixed. I see the sun at noon, but he has never changed his place. If there is a hell, then it is a place where there is no tomorrow, or yesterday, or today, but everything stands still in time, unbreathing, familiar, immutable, a dull painted landscape hanging on the wall of forever.

I am twenty-nine, and I shall soon be thirty. Where are the years of my youth, the golden youth of the poets and the singers and the sentimentalists? Where is the love, the hope, the ambition, the joy, the laughter and the anticipation? I have never known them. I am no longer twenty, as I was yesterday. A decade has passed, but it has passed in silence, in the dark of the moon, and if I have been twenty-three, twenty-five, twenty-seven, I do not remember it.

If I could only feel something, anything, again! If I could only feel despair! If I could only hate! But I feel nothing at all. A man is dead if he no longer is desperate, or hopeful, or even sick to death or full of pain. I look at my hand, and it is unreal to me. It has no substance. I see my face in the mirror, but it is only the shadow of a face that does not exist. Are these my legs, my flesh? They do not belong to me. They never knew me, as I never knew them. My name is Frank Clair, but when I say it, it means nothing to me. I died a long time ago.

CHAPTER 57

THE WINTER twilight darkened over Bison. Long gray shadows plunged themselves deep into the snow, merged with it. The bitter green lake in the western sky had flowed to the east, a depthless sea with a cold and static light. The scattered lamps along River Road began to flicker in the falling darkness.

The big wooden clock on the plaster wall pointed to two minutes of five. Now the great office room of the Dumont Tire and Rubber Company appeared to brighten with the expectation of release. Only half an hour ago, the dank winter air had pervaded the room, dimmed the lights, blurred the tops of the long lines of desks. But now there was expectation in the room; a voice or two spoke easily; someone laughed. The typewriters and the comptometers clattered vivaciously, and papers rustled loudly. It was Friday night, and tomorrow was only a half day. The week-end lay ahead, and the fifty or more young or old, male or female, drab or bright faces, quickened with anticipation. Some of the younger men lighted cigarettes; some of the older men comfortably filled pipes. Some of the younger women opened compacts, dabbed powder on noses, heightened the color of their lips. They were all happy. In these dark and evil days of the Great Depression, they still had jobs.

A blizzard suddenly blew up, with warning flakes of sharp snow, and the big lighted windows rattled. Everyone now stared at the clock, like racers. One minute more, and there would be the wild dash for coats and hats, for purses and gloves and arctics, then the noisy rush down the stairs to the road, where busses awaited them. They could see the busses parked below, lighted and empty. In a few minutes they would be filled to the very doors, and go rumbling and swaying and crunching into the city. Tomorrow was Saturday. Some of the girls were already putting on their tight little felt hats.

Frank closed his typewriter desk, put away his shorthand book, crushed the carbon paper in his hand, threw it into the wastebasket. He returned the unfinished pile of invoices and railroad f.o.b's. to the wire basket on his desk. Now everything was piled up neatly. A shallow wooden box on the right was filled with a high straight stack of completed work. It would be collected in the morning. He put away his pencils and his pen, screwed the top on his ink bottle.

It was five o'clock. The exodus had begun, and the air was full of laughter and calling voices, the stamping of feet. The big doors at the end of the room had been opened, and the office force surged through them. A rush of icy air from the opened doors below gushed into the room. Frank was always the last to leave.

He stood up, went to the rack near him, and put on his hat and coat and arctics. He felt in his vest pocket for his pay envelope. It was there, of course. But on the way home he would feel of it several times. He fished in his trousers pocket for a bus token, slipped it into his palm between his woolen glove and his skin.

The big office building had emptied itself with remarkable speed. Frank was almost alone on the stairs. He could see the backs of the last of the workers, hurrying towards the last bus. He quickened his pace and got into the bus just before the door closed. He shivered, for the air and wind had been like a lash.

He had to stand on the steps of the bus, someone's shoulders pressing into his face. He was always the last, as he had always been the last to leave school. The old instinct for anonymity was still there, heightened during the past few years. "He kept to himself," as Maybelle used to say. He looked at no one, shrinking bitterly and sullenly from any greetings which might come his way. But he was ignored. He was unpopular in the office, for he was reticent, unresponsive, stiff. And shabby.

The girls would not have minded the shabbiness, for everyone knew that "things were tough," and they had decided that Frank must, most probably, have dependents. A mother, maybe, or some kid brothers or sisters. Anyway, he was a man, wasn't he? And why this "high-hat stuff"? Had he been unattractive physically, his reserve would not have irked the young ladies. But, as they said, he had "class." He was "better-lookin' " than almost any other eligible man in the office. He was tall, perhaps too slender, and moved quickly and without any disagreeable awkwardness. How old was he? Looked about thirty, but was probably older, for his dark chestnut hair was touched at the temples with gray. But that did not revolt the girls, who thought the gray "distinguished." No, it was not his shabbiness which had made the girls' first excitement and pleasure in him turn to dislike and ridicule and hostility. It was his coldness, his contemptuous attitude towards everyone, man and woman alike, his avoidance of any social contact with his fellow-workers, his grimness and sullen manners. He attended to his work from morning until night, not speaking, lending his paper, if pressed, sometimes grudgingly extending a cigarette, if asked, but turning away at the slightest and most tentative offer of companionship.

"He thinks he's Mr. Big, the Boy Executive," the girls giggled among themselves. Had he been successful, however, had he risen to a private cubicle along the eastern wall of the office, this, too, could have been forgiven and admired. But he was not successful. He was not "good" at his work. On quite a few occasions, the office manager had reprimanded him for carelessness. It was whispered, on irrefutable information from the pay department, that he had had only one "raise" in five years, and that a meagre one.

Nor were the girls alone in their malicious ridicule and enmity. The men disliked Frank, even hated him. He never joined them at lunchtime for a glance at a racing form, nor was he interested in the Red Sox or the Green, Pink, Yellow, Scarlet or Lavender Sox. When everyone was in a fever of excitement over the autumn football games, and the lunch hour hummed with vehement or protesting opinions over one team or another, Frank sat alone at his desk, sometimes casting an involuntary but noticeably contemptuous glance at the others. Sometimes they caught his eyes, and quite a few shrank in a kind of dismay from the look in them and the glare of disgust which lighted them vividly. He never joined in the angry laughter against President Hoover and his obstinate conviction that "prosperity was just around the corner."

After nine years, no one knew anything more about him than on the first day he had sat at his desk. They did not like his voice, either, though it was low and coldly polite and meticulous as to pronunciation. They heard his faint English accent, and the second-generation Germans and Poles and Italians among the office workers resented it, finding their own slurred and gobbling speech preferable to the correct enunciation of the language. So he became "the Limey," as, in his childhood, he had been "that bloody, bloomin' Englishman."

He gave no sign that he knew of their hatred and hostility. But he was aware of it all. He did not care. He despised these hearty peasants of European stock; he loathed their walk, their voices, the smiles on their coarse features, the sound of their foreign names, their childish prejudices and opinions, their ignorance, their happy, ungrammatical phrases, their cheap slang, their very clothing. He knew that, despite their outward friendliness, there was a deep cleavage among the office workers. The Protestants had inevitably aligned themselves against the Catholics, and deeply suspected them. If a Catholic had a promotion, it was because the "boss" was a Catholic. A new arrival was discreetly cross-questioned until the fact of his religion had been established. If a Catholic, he mysteriously became part of their inner group. If a Protestant, he joined the larger and invisible organization.

Only once had Frank even momentarily joined in a discussion. A group of young men, devouring their lunches, had begun to denounce Communism. They were vague about the principles of the doctrine, but they were vehement in their denunciations. Frank was walking back to his desk from the drinking fountain when he suddenly paused and said, in a mocking cold voice: "Say, what's Communism?"

They had stared at him, astonished at this uninvited interruption from someone they had learned to ignore. They saw his contemptuous smile, and they did not like the way his narrowed eyes danced. But they were willing to enlighten him. One said that Communism was the "nationalization of women." Another said, uncertainly, that it was atheism. Another said, almost with longing, that it meant that the rich guys had all their money taken away from them None of them, it was instantly evident, knew anything about Communism, though they quoted their favorite newspaper copiously. However, they hated it, for one nebulous and erroneous reason or another.

You, thought Frank, are a lot of damn fools. Why don't

you shut your mouths until you know what you are talking about? You ignoramuses. How long did you go to school, any of you? Where did you get your opinions? From the comics? From the movies? From your racing forms? From your churches? Wherever you got them, they are wrong, and just as stupid as you are. Why don't you read a little, sometime? They call this a democracy. It's too bad. None of you ought to be allowed to vote. If they used intelligence tests to determine the right to vote, not one of you would dare enter an election booth. I think democracy stinks. I always did think so, and now I know it.

What he said was: "For God's sake stop talking about something you know nothing about," and he walked away from them, leaving them to stare in dumfounded outrage at his slender retreating back, set in such a posture of contempt. After that, he was "the Bolshie." He was classified, at last. They knew his niche. Five years later, he was "a fascist."

The icy ruts in the road made the bus sway and lurch and tilt. The girls squealed and giggled coyly and staggered with quite unnecessary force against the young men beside them. Some of them, pretending to be too short for the straps overhead, clutched masculine arms. Frank, standing precariously on the step, flung against the door, could hear the shouted conversations beyond him. One of the girls was defending Gary Cooper from a ridiculing male attack. Another was devoted to Greta Garbo. Two masculine voices discussed the chances of the Cardinals next summer. A girl's voice rose on the subject of the new styles. A man shouted his disgust for President Hoover. "I've always been a Republican, just like my dad. But this time I'm a-gonna vote Democratic. Don't care if they put a nigger up. I'm a-gonna vote for him!"

A girl squealed as a male hand gave a playful slap on her buttocks in the press of bodies. Another girl discussed the dance she had attended last night. "O boy, was it hot! There was a dame there, looked like Claudette Colbert, and did she throw her weight around! You oughta seen the fellers go after her. Someone stepped on my new red dress."

A young man announced that he had discovered on Niagara Street a new speak-easy, where "anything goes." He told the name, generously. A card game was arranged between three young men. The air in the bus became warm and fetid, overlaid with the stench of cheap perfume and powder. The lights flickered and flared, showing young, coarse, painted faces with loose reddened lips, and the innocent but gluttonous eyes of animals. Whenever the door opened, Frank had to step down, while girls and men brushed against him. He held himself taut, his nostrils drawn together in detestation. At times, his disgust was like a heady intoxication in his mind. If his eyes were caught by the eyes of another he looked away with open aversion.

The voice of the people! The voice of democracy! This yowling, screaming, ignorant, brainless mob! This slangy, prejudiced, hating conglomeration of beasts, who never read, never thought, never had an idea, were devoid of dignity and humanity, unlettered, proud of their lack of knowledge! The bus steamed with their breath; it was the breath of oxen, of amorphic, castrated souls. These were the murderers of the prophets, the howling animals in a wilderness, male and female bodies that knew lust but never one heroic dream. There they were, hating one another, lusting for one another, bawling and howling to one another, this awful squirming conglomeration called the Masses!

I hate them! thought Frank. Then he paused, held rigid and still. He hated again! Where had his cleansing, purifying, exciting rage hidden all these years? Where had it lurked, like a stunned thing? What had awakened it now? All at once the voices in the bus rushed loudly and with deafening sound into his ears. The lights became vividly bright. He felt the beating of his heart, the sudden pound of exultation in his pulses. Life quickened along his body; he felt the touch of his clothing on his flesh. He seemed to swell, to become strong, contained, invulnerable.

His exultation was like a fire, warming his numbed arms and legs. He bent close to it, eagerly. He hated. He must escape from those he hated. He had endured them, all these faceless years, for he had had no choice. There had been no power in him. He had two thousand dollars in the bank. Never, if he lived fifty years, would he have saved enough to escape from this dreadful raucousness called the People. Even if he starved himself, hoarded every penny, it would not be enough. He must get away! He must escape from the profane touch of their bodies, from the effluvium of their dead minds, from the sound, sight, hearing, being, of them!

But how? He remembered seeing the advertisements of correspondence schools. "Be a certified public accountant, a radio engineer; become an expert in banking, law, public relations—!" He wanted none of this. He knew his aversion for anything pertaining to the business world, mechanics, or finance. But there must be some way of escaping. A man wished to escape, and he found a way. What was his way?

He clung to the handrail. His breath was hot and quick on his cold lips. He was caught up in the urgency and desperate necessity to escape. He repeated the words silently to himself: I must get away. I must find a way! But where, how? Where could he make sufficient money to put a high spiked wall between himself and these others, so that never again would he need to encounter them or look upon them, or be aware that they lived?

My writing. His hand tightened on the rail. I was a writer once. I—I was *good*. They all said so. Once, I knew that I could make money, writing. Then something happened to me. What was it? I don't remember. But it was gone, because my passion was gone, and I no longer hated ugliness, or saw it. I wish my head would stop roaring—I must think this out. Writing. I can go back to it. I can go back to the University and study. I'll concentrate on English and English literature. There must be a way and this is the way. I can do it! Something has come back to me, some great power, some vehemence. I can feel it all through me. I shan't lose it this time! My life depends upon it.

The bus stopped at Forest Avenue, and Frank mechanically left it. The door closed behind him. The blizzard screamed down upon him, a flare of choking whiteness. The wind filled his mouth, his nose, his eyes. He struggled against it. On the sidewalk veils of snow flowed around and away from him. He narrowly avoided being run down by an automobile. He bent double, and found his way to the stinking cheap little restaurant where he ate his meals. Then he paused on the doorstep.

No. 'I'll go to the Statler tonight! I'll treat myself to a fine big dinner. I'll sit in a big lighted room, where the tables are covered with white cloths, and there is music. I will sit among those who have money; I will look at them, and become even stronger and more powerful.

It's only December. I'll go back to the University for the second semester. This time I shall not turn back. This time I'll win my way through!

CHAPTER 58

IN REPOSE, Mr. Endicott Preston's pale slender face resembled that of a tired and cynical camel, for his long nose with its splayed nostrils curved down to a wide and mobile mouth, crooked and bent. His chin retreated gently; he had large and melancholy eyes; the planes of his cheeks sloped backwards to big soft ears. Yet, paradoxically, he was a very handsome man, in his early forties, above average height and weight, his thick gray hair full of graceful and elegant waves. Those melancholy eyes were also large and full and blue, and when he smiled, his resemblance to a camel ceased, and he became all Puck, all humor, all skeptical kindness. His whole intelligent face sparkled, one subtle expression following another until it was sheer fascination to watch him. His voice, sonorous, flexible and full of sensitivity, enchanted the hearer, for nothing he ever said was dull, and his slightest phrase brimmed with color, wit, volatility and brilliance, expressive of the fine mind that glowed behind it like a changing opal.

Like the other professors, his clothing was dun, of medium quality and tailoring, and was evidently bought from a rack in a local department store. He was one of the many wise and distinguished and perceptive instructors on the staff of the University of Bison. Though Frank was later to meet many splendid professors and instructors who taught in greater and more famous universities, it always seemed to him that none surpassed the devoted gentlemen on the campus of Bison's university, none were more kind or understanding, none more eager to discover and help the exceptional student, none more faithful.

This was Frank's third semester, now, in Mr. Preston's English class. Each semester, Mr. Preston would greet him without much surprise, with only a quizzical but pleased quirk of his left eyebrow. Frank was also studying ancient history, French, sociology and logic. He found history somewhat tedious, for dates and battles and events were, to him, dull, though there were moments when he "felt" something living and moving and vital under the dead brown leaves of the past. Dr. Riordon was sometimes a little puzzled and baffled at the sight of Frank coming suddenly alive, and offering an unorthodox opinion on the subject under discussion. Frank never appeared to read the reference books assigned; he returned to class with a look of excitement, and a paper on which he had written his own interpretation of some event, or of some historical personage. His interpretation, Dr. Riordan kindly pointed out, was somewhat unique, and had no accepted authority. Mr. Clair was using his "imagination," and, in history, Dr. Riordan said somewhat drily, imagination was a dangerous thing.

Frank did moderately well in French, though, as he had no high-school background in this language, he had to study and listen with desperate attention to achieve a B-minus each month. Dr. Bontelle, with sorrow, sometimes accused him of inventing a French phrase which, though colorful, would have perplexed a Frenchman.

Frank disputed hotly with Dr. Grayson, who taught sociology. Dr. Grayson was an idealist, and Frank instinctively disliked idealists. Once Dr. Grayson remarked thoughtfully that he was afraid Frank had inadvertently absorbed some fascistic ideas, and that, after all, Mr. Clair, he, Dr. Grayson, was here to instruct and not to enter into furious disputations about ideologies. Dr. Grayson was very anxious about Frank, and spent much time in an attempt to bend his mind to his own. Frank acquired another B-minus each month, and this was given him only by Dr. Grayson's stretching his tender conscience, for Frank never answered any questions, but wrote page after page of philippics, insisting that men who did not understand liberty should not enjoy it, that the weak and the stupid should not be given equal opportunity with the brave and the intelligent, that a man's worth, and not the fact that he had been born, must determine whether he should partake of the privileges of democracy. "Democracy," Frank wrote vehemently, "does not mean that all men, regardless of their mental endowment or worth, shall have a place at the trough, but only that they shall be equal before the bar of legal justice." Dr. Grayson was afraid that Mr. Clair had too narrow and too pragmatic a view, and that he did not quite understand the full meaning of democracy. Frank tired Dr. Grayson very much, for Dr. Grayson's one great passion was his love, boundless and rather naïve, for his fellow-men.

Frank fared a little better with Dr. Herbert Markson, who taught logic. But here, too, Frank failed to heed questions, and to reply to them in an orthodox manner. It annoyed him to discover that validity was not always truth, and he came to the conclusion that logic was a somewhat dreary sister to mathematics. Logic was too patterned, too rigid, to suit Frank. His mind was not the logician's mind, and though he was angered when he was again reminded of his "imagination," and when Dr. Markson hinted that he thought with his emotions rather than with his reason, he took pleasure in refuting logic with passion.

Frank liked and admired them all. But he loved Mr. Endicott Preston. He came back to his class, semester after semester, and each session found him older than the new students. He did not care. In fact, he never saw the newcomers. He came to listen, to work, to feel excitement and joy when Mr. Preston spoke, and literally to tremble when Mr. Preston emphatically praised his writing.

On the appearance of Frank in his class, for the third season, Mr. Preston had called him aside, and had said: "Now, then, this is your third semester here with me, isn't it? I saw your name on the card the other day, and I—I was just a little surprised. You're thirty-two, aren't you? Don't you think you are ready for Dr. Berry now? After all, this is just sophomore English—"

And Frank had replied:, 'No. You give me all I want and need."

Mr. Preston had flushed at this, a little guilty but gratified. He knew all about Frank. He had never had a student like this, and sometimes he accused himself of directing the studies for Frank's benefit. Certainly, each semester was entirely different from the one before, and contained much that would be of distinct advantage to Frank, be peculiarly useful to him. Mr. Preston was very tired. He had some serious heart ailment. He held his classes during the day, and he taught three evenings a week at the Evening Sessions. Sometimes he was so fatigued that he thought death preferable to this aching weariness in his flesh. Yet, at least once a week he had Frank remain for as much as an hour after the class was dismissed, and talked to him, criticized his work, recommended certain textbooks and books on biography, travel and novelized history, inspired him and encouraged him, and gave him the full strong glow of his passion for poetry and great prose, until his own terrible weariness had burned itself away in his selfless desire to help and sustain and stimulate. And Frank would listen, feeling a tumult in himself, an ardor, a joy. They nourished each other, one with comprehension and gratitude, the other with giving, until the hours they spent together became interludes of supreme pleasure and satisfaction.

"I notice," said Mr. Preston once, "that when you express your hatred for hypocrisy and cruelty and stupidity, you write with fire and real literary power. That, then, is a clue for you, the one real clue. But when you merely express hatred, blind, wild hatred, for anything and everything, there is a kind of danger in your writing, a kind of terribleness. You defeat yourself. And you will fail, and you will be sick with your failure, no matter how much money you might make. There is the hatred which is life-giving, the hatred of a Jeremiah, the constructive hatred which is like a goad in the rumps of the apes called malice and bestiality and savagery. That hatred advances civilization and justice, enlightens mankind, helps the animal to rise upon his hind legs and take on the shape and gait of a man. But there is another hatred, which destroys not only the writer but those who read him and hear him, which poisons the well of hope and integrity, and drives men mad. You must look out for that hatred in your writing, and in yourself. It crops up too often, and frightens me. . . . Have you been reading much about Hitler? Listen to him, and you will know what I mean."

At this, Frank's face tightened obstinately and with sullenness. You talk like an old fool I knew once, by the name of Farley, he thought.

He sent three of his stories to some of the more popular and prosperous magazines. They all came back, rejected, but the editors wrote personal letters expressing their belief in his future, and asking for other stories or articles for their consideration. One editor criticized the story submitted to him in almost the same phraseology used by Mr. Preston, and this letter Frank destroyed. He showed the others proudly.

CHAPTER 59

THE Years of the Black Locust had descended upon America, and the national sky was black with them. Under the ominous cloud, the nation crouched in stupefied paralysis. They looked to Washington, as men look to the east during a night of suffering, for Mr. Roosevelt had been inaugurated and a faint and smoldering hope began to burn on the dark horizon. The bank holiday had created a temporary panic, but so firm was the faith of the desperate people that the new Administration would lift the horror from their minds and the paralysis from their arms and the fear from their hearts that even this was regarded as only the first step toward national recovery.

The suicides of Stock Market plungers and once wealthy men were blazoned in turgid headlines on the country's newspapers. But the thousands of suicides of the desperate old and middle-aged who witnessed the foreclosures of their little homes and faced the yawning skull of starvation were noted only in small paragraphs appropriately near the obituaries, or did not appear at all. One heard the rumbling crash of great fortunes from east to west. But one never heard the stifled despair of millions of little men who silently and grimly preferred not to eat rather than to stand at a public trough. They stood in the rubble of a fallen economy and stared about them with dazed eyes, unable to comprehend what had befallen them, able only to move numbly amid the ruins. One by one, the small shops closed; one by one, the factories shut their doors. One by one, and then, the pace quickening, hundreds of banks failed, while the petrified and shabby depositors stood in stupefaction on the cold sidewalks.

Even those who feared Mr. Roosevelt waited to hear what he would say. After all, a danger, like a smoldering fire, began to lick through the streets of the nation; one could smell its smoke. At noonday, the sun was made brazen by it. If Mr. Roosevelt could put out this gathering flame, then even his enemies would be grateful. A radical "crackpot" was better than revolution. If the people's hunger could be stayed, if their bewildered fury could be quieted, there was hope for all the nation. A starving people cannot think. They can only riot and seize and massacre. They can only let loose their latent hatred and resentment for those who live softer, eat heartier, and are more secure. The powerful in the country remembered the guillotine in the streets of Paris, and looked toward Washington, and waited.

Who will sing the saga of a door-to-door salesman during the Great Depression?

Frank Clair sold, or tried to sell, Pure Silk Stockings and Select Pure Silk or Rayon Underthings for Ladies. He carried his heavy valise, order blanks and merchandise books from door to door, in summer heat and winter blizzards. Sometimes he made twenty dollars a week in commissions. Sometimes only ten. The bank account dwindled inexorably. Grimly, from early morning till late at night, he walked the streets, knocking on back doors. Grimly, his arm almost torn from its socket, he walked the several miles back to his wretched room over a meat shop on Grant Street. He had a doughnut and one cup of coffee for breakfast—ten cents. He ate a similar repast at noon. At night, he stopped in at a "hot-dog" stand, and treated himself to a thirty-five cent meal. Then, sometimes, it was too late to return to his room with his satchel. He carried it to the Evening Sessions. The days were steaming or frozen pits of hell. The nights were fragrant islands full of light and sound and hope. But the bank account dwindled to one thousand dollars, to eight hundred, to five, to four.

He found that the poor would buy more readily than the middle-class. Poor women, their worn faces full of fear and compassion, would hesitate at their splintered doors. They would order a pair or two of stockings, for it was not possible to walk the winter streets with bare legs. They would count out their fifty cents reluctantly, but their tired and heavy eyes would be bright with pity as they looked at Frank. They could not afford what they bought. But the universal misery brought out the heroism latent in the people. The parting with a dollar or two might have seemed mean or insignificant. But in all their lives the people performed no more heroic act. Sometimes Frank was invited into a cold and bleak little house or flat, and given coffee or a sandwich from a guarded supply. Sometimes, when he ate at such bare tables, a curious pain came to him, against which he clenched his teeth and tried to steel his heart. He tried not to listen to the sad and desperate tales he heard. He tried to harden himself against them. But they sank like stones into the dark water of his subconscious mind, awaiting the day when he would give them words and being.

He met companions in his despair and hunger and destitution. One day, on lower Main Street, he met old Matthew Sanders. He met him in the fetid little hole of a cheap restaurant where, for thirty-five cents, he ate his evening meal.

Bison's lower Main Street ran obscurely and meanly to the water front through a huddle of dreadful small stores and poolrooms, suspect and filthy little hotels, tiny, squalid restaurants and saloons, and ancient old houses leaning and broken and blind. In one of these houses, almost untenanted, in an attic room, lived Matthew Sanders, who sold photographs in a house-to-house canvass.

Frank was forcing the horrible concoction of stew down his throat when he became aware of the neat little old man sitting near him at the greasy wooden table. Frank was rarely aware of those about him; he shut his eyes and his consciousness against them. But he could not ignore this man, so reserved and quiet was his air, his patched clothing so clean. Despite himself, Frank stared at him with curiosity.

Matthew Sanders, even at the table, appeared very tall and thin in his cheap black suit and frayed old topcoat. He had politely taken off his hat, though no other man in the hot and filthy little hole had removed his. Frank saw a shock of thick white hair, carefully combed. Its uneven edges revealed that he had clipped and cut it himself. He had a long and emaciated face, lined but composed, and his eyes, lifted for an instant to Frank's, were blue and full and curiously gentle and childlike. Frank saw his hands, scoured as to nail and knuckle, tremulous and veined. Above them, his frayed cuffs were white and stiff with starch.

When he became aware that Frank was staring at him he smiled, and his very old face brightened into an expression even more childlike and simple than his eyes. He said, in his croaking voice: "Bad weather today, isn't it?"

"Very," said Frank. The old man nodded and smiled again, as if with pleasure. Then Frank saw how his eyes had fastened on Frank's uneaten bread; for one moment they became tragic. He glanced away and resumed brightly: "But it's healthy, they say. The winter."

Frank hesitated. Then, impatiently, he pushed the bread towards the old man, for he had seen that he had only a cheese sandwich and a small glass of milk. "I don't want this bread," he muttered. "Shame to waste it. Do you want it?"

"Are you sure?" said the other, but his pale mouth twitched and his head trembled with eagerness. "I'm not deprivin' you?"

Frank replied by pushing the bread closer. Then he added, against all his efforts to keep from speaking: "I've got a piece of apple pie coming, but I can't eat it. Do you want it?"

That day marked the beginning of their curious friendship. Frank was bitter and contemptuous toward the old man for his very poverty and futility and hopelessness. But he listened to his story with a queer eagerness which he could not explain to himself. They met every night at six o'clock and talked over the table. Then one night Matthew invited his new friend up to his attic room over the restaurant.

Frank went reluctantly, cursing himself for his weakness. They climbed up a filthy and broken flight of stairs. Then Frank saw the room. It was tiny, windowless, airless. It held an iron Army cot, covered with two filthy brown blankets, grayed and full of holes, a commode with a pitcher and cracked bowl, one broken chair, and a tiny gas heater. One gauntly dim electric bulb swung from the ceiling. The floor was bare; the walls and ceiling and bed literally crawled with cockroaches. In the closet, hanging neatly, were Matthew's few belongings. For this room he paid two dollars a week.

He informed Frank, whom he had ceremoniously seated on the one chair, that he washed his shirts and socks and handkerchiefs in the bowl, which he filled from a stinking bathroom on the first floor, behind the restaurant. Each morning he polished his boots. He spread newspapers between himself and the sheets on the bed. Each night he lit his little gas fire and sat before it. Frank could see him with a vivid clarity, staring into space, rubbing his thin gnarled hands with a dry sound.

Each morning he crept down the garbage-littered stairs, past rooms of obscenity and vice, slipped obscurely past a riotous saloon, glanced aside from the degenerate beings he encountered on the street. He carried a portfolio of photographs from house to house. He was to sell tickets at one dollar apiece for a large and not too-bad photograph. He had to sell ten tickets for the photograph studio to maintain his "salary" of five dollars a week; anything over that would entitle him to a fifty per cent commission. "Silk-linen finished studio photographs," said Matthew to Frank, proudly. Worth two dollars apiece, at least. He also sold passport and automobile license photographs. Sometimes he made ten dollars a week.

Frank, with his writer's sharp and vivid inner eye, could see it all as clearly as if he were present on the rounds old Matthew made. He could see the old man tottering from door to door, tall, shriveled, slightly bent, palely blue and red-rimmed of eye, vaguely courteous and gentlemanly, absent. His toneless flat voice solicited politely, and the pity of the poor went out to him, to this old and weary man. Frank knew that pity, and again the pain assailed him, and again he stiffened against it. He could see Matthew tramping the streets, shivering in the winter wind, crouching exhausted in doorways for a moment's breath, creeping into stores for an instant's warmth until he was evicted. But he made his eight or ten dollars a week. Frank saw that Matthew was sufficiently piteous to excite sympathy even in the wretched, yet refined enough not to rouse that sympathy to the point of exasperation.

Frank's clairvoyant vision quickened. As if he were Matthew himself, he had a queer memory of Matthew's miles of aching and weary plodding through snowy streets, of creeping through back yards, of a gnawing stomach and feet like plagues of living fire, of legs that trembled and a back that broke. He could hear, as if they had been addressed to him, the insults, the rebuffs, sense the closed doors, the old numb despair.

It was all very strange, for old Matthew, in speaking cheerfully to Frank, told him none of this. But Frank felt and knew it in all his bones, in his somber mind, in the depths of his aching heart. He knew that the soles of Matthew's boots had worn through, and that he put cardboard over the gaps in the soles. He knew that Matthew slept on his trousers, that they might be neat and creased. It was cold in this room tonight, despite the hissing little gas fire. Matthew would move in a world of emptiness, without despair, but also without life. Frank knew he prayed. But his prayers were like an old dusty sheet of paper upon which nothing had ever been written, not a single word of hope.

Frank was still young, but he felt Matthew's brittle age, he felt the long and awful years behind him. Frank sat on the broken chair and listened to the old man, absorbed, trapped, enchanted, chained in the other's body, as if his own spirit had entered that ancient flesh and knew all its secrets, all its pain and suffering.

Matthew, who was very simple and unsuspecting, did not know that Frank was one with him, as he sat on that broken chair opposite the old man, who sat on the edge of his cot. He saw only Frank's slightly glazed and attentive eyes, in the glaring electric light. Encouraged by the young man's silence and apparent sympathy, he told him artlessly of his former life.

He and his wife, Eliza, had formerly owned a prosperous little grocery store. Eliza was the businessman. She kept all the records, ordered all the goods, went to the market with him, and bargained sharply. Matthew did not describe Eliza, but Frank could see her with a clairvoyant's vision: lean, tall, stringy, grim-mouthed, straight and firm of glance, her gray hair wound in a bun on the top of her head. Matthew confessed that he was no businessman; he merely stood behind the counter. They did very well, and the customers paid promptly on the first of each month. Eliza saw to that, old Matthew chuckled fondly.

Then had come the depression. The customers either could not pay their bills, or they vanished discreetly from the neighborhood, owing considerable money. Eliza and Matthew struggled along a little while, and then they failed. But something even worse happened. Eliza became ill, very suddenly. It was discovered that she had cancer. She had died in the ward of a local hospital. Matthew had insisted upon paying every bill. He had been left destitute.

Eliza had been "religious," Matthew said tenderly, cracking his knuckles before the gas fire. She had made him pious. She trusted in God. God knew best. Even when Eliza had died, her last words to him, compelling, urgent, stern words, had been to "have faith." Yes, he had always "had faith," he confessed simply. What would he do without God, and his hope that he would soon see Eliza? But Frank, still in Matthew's body, one with his mind, heard Matthew's prayers, methodical, earnest, mechanical, and he knew that the prayers had become repetitions, words without meaning, without peace or hope, and without echo. He prayed as a loving sacrifice to his wife. He prayed for her sake. But there was nothing in him, except his hideous misery, his dumb acceptance, his pain.

"God, my dear Frank, is always the refuge," said Matthew, gazing at Frank with his exhausted pale eyes and smiling. "Always the refuge. Our life here is nothing. Learn the joy of sanctity, my boy. There is always God. What would I do without Him?"

Frank came out of the old man's body and shivered. His pity and compassion filled him with weariness and despair. He said: "Why don't you go on relief, Matt? You'd at least eat, and they'd pay your rent, and you wouldn't have to tramp the streets any more."

Matthew, who had been smiling vaguely to himself, came to with a start of shock and horror. He stared at Frank aghast. "Relief? What would Eliza say? She would never forgive me! We've never eaten a crumb of charity in our lives! Why—why, I'd rather starve to death! I'd never hold up my head again!"

This is where I should feel admiration, thought Frank bitterly. But he saw the empty place in Matthew from which joy and hope and love and significance had departed forever, leaving nothing behind but an attic tenanted by cobwebs, attended only by parching midnight winds, and haunted by voiceless ghosts: the memory of a proud and resolute old woman and the long shadow of a dead God.

I can't stand it, thought Frank, ignominiously shaken and wretched, I'll avoid this poor old fool after this. He went away, after shaking hands with Matthew and hearing a last injunction, "Trust God, and all will be well."

He did not go back to the restaurant for nearly a week. Then, compelled by something he could not explain, he returned and looked for old Matthew. But he was not there. He was not there the next night, nor the next, nor even the following week. Then he asked the fat and dirty cook for the old man.

The cook stared at him blankly for a few minutes. Then he said: "You mean the old feller used to sit at that table with you? Oh, he bumped hisself off one night. 'Bout a week ago." He scowled, "Damned old fool! I warned him; I own this dump. He used to leave that gas-heater on all day sometimes, when he went out. It didn't have no pipe, and it was dangerous, I told him. I said: 'Looky here, Matt, gas costs money. Turn it off when you go out. And turn it off at night. If you don't, you're gonna wake up dead some fine mornin', and it ain't fair to me.'"

Frank felt sick. He said: "And he didn't turn it off—one night, when he went to bed?"

The cook scowled again and nodded. "He was just an old coot. Never could remember nothin'." He scratched his rim of hair under his cook's hat. "Well, maybe he didn't bump hisself off, after all. Just forgot to turn off the heater when he went to bed. Anyway, he was dead one mornin'. Accident, the police said. I let it ride that way."

But Frank, sitting down at the empty table, knew suddenly and clearly that it had not been an accident. He forgot where he was. He was Matthew again, and he knew everything.

Frank went back to his own miserable room, and he sat down and wrote the story of Matthew Sanders. He wrote it all in one night. He sent it to a magazine. It came back to him promptly, with a personal letter from the editor: "Wonderfully and powerfully and compassionately told. But much too depressing, in these days, when everyone needs encouragement and hope for the future. Please send us another story, something bright and gay, full of young love, perhaps—something to take the reader's mind away from the present. Stories of young love are always wanted."

CHAPTER 60

"Young love!" exclaimed Frank bitterly. "Good God! Does the public want nothing but the prurient problems of adolescents?"

Mr. Endicott Preston read the letter from the fiction editor of one of the big national magazines. He pursed his lips in his curiously sad and cynical smile. "This," he said, "is what is technically called 'flight from reality.' " He regarded Frank with long thoughtfulness, wrinkled his eyebrows into little tufts. He saw Frank's thin face and the sunken hollows under the cheekbones which were now flooded with wrathful crimson. He scratched his chin with a corner of the editor's letter, then, looking off into space, he continued softly, meditatively:

"There is something which you must settle in you own mind, Frank, and several opinions of which you must disabuse yourself. Let us first consider literature. What is literature, in the truest meaning of the word? I think it is the faithful reflection of the texture of reality, the fullness and nature of being, written with passion, authenticity and vividness, infused with power and individual truth. By indivdual truth, I mean the honest and vehement conviction of the writer, which doesn't necessarily mean the truth as others see it. But it does mean the truth of the writer, his lack of hypocrisy and time-serving, his fearlessness and strength. Literature, then, is honest and heroic writing. It can be rough-hewn and rugged, even choppy and crude, in the manner of a great statue whose outline and grandeur must be indicated against a wide sky, without overdue attention to fine detail. Or it can be a miniature painted on gold, an ivory figurine. But whether enormous in concept or delicate and minute in execution, it must have integrity, honor, honesty. That is literature."

Frank listened, his impatience and anger struggling with his appreciation of his teacher. Mr. Preston slowly reread the letter. "Yes. Well. There is another kind of writing, which is not so apt to irritate the critics. The critics, I have discovered, are rather annoyed and disconcerted by heroic and ruthless writing, by reality. Sometimes they call it 'turgid,' or 'melodramatic' or 'flamboyant,' or even 'unreal.' And that is a very curious thing, indeed. Reality is often denounced as unreality, and truth as 'tripe.' I read the book reviews, you see. Pardon me, if I seem to wander—I am thinking out loud. Just recently I was induced to read a novel by a dainty woman writer. An eminent critic became very enthusiastic about it. He called it 'finely etched, sensitive, subtle, an artistic triumph, full of grace and an exquisite understanding of humanity.' I ought to have known better, but I spent two dollars and seventy-five cents on that novel. Then I wanted to hang the critic for making me waste the money. I thought I was getting literature; I got drivel. It lacked grandeur and terror and compassion and ugliness, all the things of which reality is composed. Her characters were all very well-bred; her writing was so 'sensitive' that I was never sure what her tale was about. It was all beyond me. She knew no more of humanity than a kindergarten pupil. Lovely illusions about the world are all very well for dreaming children. They are grotesque and hideous in adults; they are revolting."

"Yes. But what has all this to do with me?" demanded Frank, with impatience. He wished Mr. Preston would stop his maunderings and join him in heated rage against the editor.

Mr. Preston continued to stare into space. "Sometimes writers of literature are rewarded with public popularity and become rich. More often they are not, though I was never one to believe that the 'true' artist invariably starves in a garret. Incidentally, a writer is worthy of his hire, and sometimes the public knows it and buys his books. But it is a chance the true author takes. There is a surer way to money." Mr. Preston paused. "You can write what the public wants, or what the editors think the public wants. Sometimes they are the same thing. Writers for popular magazines make quite a lot of money. If money is what you want." He waited.

Frank set his mouth grimly. "It is what I want, as you know."

Mr. Preston sat down in his chair as if very weary. He rubbed his forehead and stifled a yawn. "I may not be a good judge, but I think your style is too strong, too intrinsically and powerfully crude, too passionate, for magazine acceptance. But—you can imitate. Buy or borrow the three most popular magazines. Read them carefully. The people must like them, for they have large circulations. Of course, for you to write such things would be dishonest."

"I want money," said Frank savagely. He looked at Mr. Preston with furiously sparkling eyes. "I've told you! Writing is my only hope of escape from what I hate! I'll write what can be published. I've got to have money! I—I'll die unless I have it."

Mr. Preston did not look at him. He asked, in an absent voice: "Why? What do you want with money?"

Frank stood before his teacher, and stared blindly at the dark, dusty windows which reflected the glaring electric light in the classroom. He spoke, and his voice was low and pent, yet curiously wild: "I've got to get away from poverty, from the smell of it, from everything it means. I—I've got to have some dignity and freedom in my life. I want to be— safe."

"Safe," whispered Mr. Preston, dropping his hands to his knees and gazing at Frank intently.

"I want everything money can give me: a fine house, the company of gentle-folk, books, music, travel, peace of mind, beautiful things—Oh, hell! You know what money can bring a man! Escape—"

"Escape," repeated Mr. Preston reflectively. "I was afraid of that. Escape from yourself: that is what you mean, I think, though you don't know it now."

He stood up, drew out his old silver watch, glanced at it. "I really must go home, Frank. We've been here over an hour since the class was dismissed." His lined face was masklike, but pity and weariness were heavy in his eyes. "I had hoped I was mistaken in you. But I can see now how terribly frightened you are. You are frightened, horribly frightened, aren't you?"

Frank's teeth were clenched in humiliation. "No. Of course not." Ugly, disgusting, repulsive word: fear! "I'm not afraid of anything. I hate fear.'"

When Mr. Preston did not speak, Frank went on in a flood of raging words: "My parents were always afraid! They were loathsome with fear. I detested them for it. They wanted money because they were afraid of life, afraid of everything, afraid of breathing, afraid of every man and woman they saw. I never was. I—I just hate—"

"The same thing," said Mr. Preston gently.

"No! It isn't." Frank was shaking with his mortification.

"My parents wanted money because they were afraid of living. I'm not afraid to live. Oh, God damn it! I can't make you understand."

Mr. Preston shook his head. "Some day, I hope, you will realize that at this time you were very like your parents. Just now you are their son."

The idea was so repellent, so humiliating, to Frank, that he stared at Mr. Preston with something perilously close to hatred. His voice was muffled and stammering when he exclaimed: "If I were so God-damned craven as you seem to think me, I'd be frightened because I have no job. I'd be afraid of—of—tomorrow. I'm not! I don't care that I'm half-starved, and that I live in a stinking hole over a butcher shop. I don't even feel or see these things. I'm shut away from them. I—I'll go out tomorrow and try to sell these bitchy stockings, and I'll sell some. Enough to buy me a few cheap meals, and a little to put away for my rent. Look at my clothes. I'm almost in rags. My parents would have died of terror if they'd ever been in my position. But I'm not afraid. I'm shut away—"

"Yes, said Mr. Preston, "I'm awfully afraid that you are."

Frank opened his pale mouth to speak again, then went abruptly from the room.

The damned, old, sentimental ass! thought Frank, seething. The pedantic scorner of money! He thinks it fine and noble to starve for "art." Art!

He went, the next afternoon, to the old brown public library on Washington Street. Here he had come as a child, dreaming, washed in radiance, carrying his armload of books. Flammarion, Hugo, Haggard, Dickens, Dumas, Thackeray—they had lain in his young arms like a heavy but lovely casket filled with treasure. He had been "shut away" then, too, but he had been shut away in glory, in a resounding and clamorous reality. He had walked through these quiet old rooms, and he had felt exultation and joy. Now he saw only that, though clean and hung with etchings, the walls were shabby; he saw the ancient iron elevator, and despised it. He saw the hordes of men, young and old, who sat about the long tables, and knew that most of them came here for a moment's respite from the weary streets, from the flaying cold, and had not come to read. He saw their hands, slack on the table, or clenched. They stared at the books before them, unseeing, involved in their own terrible thoughts. He turned his head away from them, and climbed up the worn stone steps to the periodicals floor. He had nothing in common with those who were defeated by life. He hated them. The papers termed them "victims of the depression." But he called them victims of their own inadequacy.

He thought he had closed his consciousness against the vision of them. But like gray emanations, like gray wisps of mist, they followed him up the stairs, and he felt their faint slow breath on his back. He hurried a little, planting his feet firmly and loudly on the stone. He thought it was disgust that tightened his throat, made his heart beat so heavily and with such dull pain.

He found the magazines for which he was looking. He sat down and read the gleaming, burnished pages, stared closely at the brilliant colored pictures which illustrated the vapid stories. Young love, triumphant. Young love, full of silly vicissitudes. Young love, in penthouses and night clubs. Young love, defying roaring parents. Young love, at college, in offices, in stately homes. Young love, challenging other young love. A stupid story, here and there, of a "sensitive" child, or of a more-than-human dog, horse, cat, bird. But mostly young love, married, about to be married, discreetly fornicating, indiscreetly "loving"—the saga of lollypops filled the pages, which were interspersed with much more vital and attractive advertisements.

What of the fury which was gathering in Italy and Germany? What of the mountebank Mussolini or the murderer Hitler? An article here and there, hastily short, tucked among the pages of the everlasting, the ubiquitous and saccharine, the omnipotent Young Love.

What of the Depression, of the millions of ruined lives, of the despair of a nation, of the terror, the fury, the paralysis of a whole people? Here and there, accompanied by a small photograph of the President, of Mr. Ickes, Mr. Hopkins or Mr. Wallace, an article by an "authority." But always, and forever—God damn it to hell!—Young Love.

Gritting his teeth against his real nausea, Frank read the tales. And with his rage grew his amazement, his sheer, honest wonder, his awe at this colossal and shameful folly, this shameless seduction of human minds, this pandering to the gross and the stupid and the tawdry. What was love, as depicted in these pages? It was a bauble sold in a ten-cent store, a plated trinket on a moron's arm, a fireside diversion, a cheap tinkle of bells, a pre-adolescent's daydreaming, a pre-puberty excitation! What was the matter with a nation's soul, which, when confronted by the mounting storm of death and horror rising over the horizon, could turn from the lightnings and the shock of distant thunder to a nursery bowl of sweetened porridge?

"Flight from reality," Mr. Preston had called this drug addict's dream of life, this surfeit of "love." Frank pushed the magazines from him. Well, this is what they wanted; this is what they paid for.

He went back to his room, dropping his sample case of stockings on the bare and gritty floor. The walls of the room had originally been papered in a bright orange background, with stripes of brilliant blue. This had now faded to a blurred and bilious tinge, stained, torn and discolored. The one small window, uncurtained, looked out on the narrow and busy traffic of Grant Street, where trolleys clanged vociferously night and day. Frank had a fine view of several cluttered fruit shops and a tailor shop across the street, but he was no longer aware of such views. Just as he hardly saw that his narrow, gritty room was furnished with an iron bedstead, whose filigree work at the head had been painted white but was now a study in peeling gray and black, a square and battered oak table near the window on which stood his creaking old typewriter, a dictionary and a pile of manuscript paper, a straight-back kitchen chair at the table, and a tottering "wardrobe" in a far corner. For this room, steaming in the summer, icy cold in winter, he paid three dollars a week. But he never really saw it.

As he sat at the typewriter he did not remove his winter coat. He blew on his chilled and reddened hands, flexed them, tried them experimentally on the keys. He thrust a clean sheet of paper into the machine. He bit his lip in concentration and frowned at the paper. He would give "them" what they wanted. He would give "them" the corruption they demanded, the poisoned pap which they ate so eagerly in their "flight from reality." Thinking fiercely, he got up, lifted a quilt from his bed, wrapped it about his feet, and sat down again. What should he write? Ah, he had it! Young love, triumphant in the depression. The title? He had it also: "We Were Not Afraid." He wrote the title rapidly, with a sound like a machine gun. Then he paused. Something roiled up in him, black and nauseating, like the contents of a spewing sewer. For the sake of his stomach, he could not write this stuff. Then he clenched his teeth, bent over the typewriter. He must write it, even if he vomited. He waited again. Now he had his characters, a noble and selfless girl thrown out of her job—secretary, store-buyer, which? Secretary, of course.

Her boss had just failed, a handsome youngish man, an architect with silvered temples. Both were penniless but courageous, with a penchant for fine humorous laughter and a way of tossing their heads valiantly, and finding everything great fun.

The typewriter rattled on vehemently while Frank bent over it, his long thin hands rising and falling furiously, his face tight and hard and full of disgust. Why, this was easy! It required no thought at all. The room began to darken, and he stood up and pulled the chain of the naked bulb over his head. Snow began to drift by the window; the panes rattled as if struck by shot. The typewriter rocked, rang its bell; the paper went in and out. The snow became a shivering white curtain at the window, and the room became a narrow, freezing box. The street lamps burst into the quaking darkness, and trolleys rolled and grunted down the street.

At nine o'clock the story was complete. Frank went through it quickly, making corrections with his pen. He slipped it into an envelope, addressed it to one of the major glossy magazines. He stood up then. His knees were trembling with exhaustion, and his head ached poundingly, his eyes smarted. He went out into the March storm, bought stamps, and dropped the manuscript into a letter box. The cost of the stamps had eaten into his rigorously guarded food fund, so he went into a corner "box-car" where, for twenty-five cents, he ate a hamburger and a doughnut, and drank a cup of coffee.

His mind was drained, gray, blotched like a torn piece of blotting-paper. He could not think. He felt dirty, and vaguely thought of a bath. But he was so exhausted that he went to bed, where at least, he could be warm.

But now the thoughts came, heavy, crowding, sickened thoughts. Behind his closed eyelids marched the faceless years of his lost youth, the years of his blankness. He could see them, shadows of shadows, falling into the abyss of time. He saw himself watching them, numb and impotent and voiceless, and he felt their ghostly substance drifting across his face before they vanished.

He thought of his mother, alone now in Manchester, for his grandmother had died two years ago, leaving her rooming house to her daughter-in-law. Frank was not certain how his mother was faring; her infrequent letters were full of complaints. But she must be earning a living, since she had not asked for money. He knew, cynically, that her capital was intact. She was glad she was in England, but England had "changed." It was not the firelit, rosy England of her remembrance. Maybelle complained of this petulantly, as if it were a personal affront.

He thought of his money which the Cunninghams had taken, and which he had never been able to retrieve. He had returned to Bison, leaving Kentucky in a frenzy of flight. He had engaged the services of a cheap and scummy little lawyer, who had written endless letters to the Bowling Green police. But the Cunninghams, as Frank had suspected, had remained in Bowling Green only a week, and then had fled, God only knew where.

The Kentucky interlude, in retrospect, never failed to depress and horrify him. A grotesque light lay over it. What had become of the Sherry Hempsteads, of Isaac Saunders, of Peter O'Leary? Had the mountaineer he had shot, died? What had been his name? Frank could not remember. He could only remember Wade O'Leary with any clarity.

Wade, he thought. Wade, do you hear me? Are you aware of anything, Wade? He saw Wade's lean dark face, but it was stern now, and closed, and unseeing, as if, resolutely, it would not see.

CHAPTER 61

IT WAS April now, a wet, chill April, with an opaline sky at sunset, and foghorns bellowing on the lake front in the foggy mornings. Frank could hear them, great bullfrogs monotonously booming their warnings to the newly arriving boats from other lake cities. He could smell the stale and fetid smell of the dirty quilts which covered him, the dank effluvium of his lumpy mattress and pillow. Then it was, in these mornings, before getting up to go on his rounds through the pouring streets, that he lay bound and rigid in a kind of mental hiatus.

But a day arrived at the end of April, so sweet-smelling, so softly radiant, so mellow and fair, that it touched even Frank's atrophied heart. This was a gilded day, and Bison, shaking off the rain as a dog shakes off water, looked up to greet the morning. Frank got up. Something fragile and quivering, like hope, passed over him. He had the strangest feeling that the hiatus had passed, that events had begun to stir for him. He even hummed a little as he dressed, and was surprised at the alien sound. He treated himself to a good breakfast at the corner "box-car," and with more spirit and verve than in years he began his house-to-house canvass.

The golden promise of the day continued. By noon, Frank had earned, in commissions, over five dollars. A fortune! The day had affected the people of the city, as it had affected him. The depression seemed less ominous today, less terrible and overwhelming. With the dollars in "deposits" jingling in his pockets, he almost forgot the hatefulness of the door-to-door canvasser's lot, the debased humiliation, the inevitable loss of self-esteem, the instant before the opening of an unfriendly door, the first moment of his sales talk, the walking away from the slammed door with that hideous sensation of shame between the shoulder blades, the hot, sick hatred in the pit of his stomach. (How frightful it had been for him to wear that brittle, rehearsed smile, to learn to remove his hat and bow courteously and to speak in a "clear, well-modulated voice" as demonstrated by the sales manager, to smile, smile, smile, at the stupid, the tawdry, the vulgar, the bellicose, the impatient and the superior faces of the housewives, and to smile again at the loud or whining or rough refusal of his stockings, and to smile, endlessly smile, while walking away!) But now he almost forgot. Perhaps it was the new-minted day which had persuaded the housewives to forego their suspicion, and to like, instead of dislike, his sharp pale face and his harsh blue eyes which repudiated the wide tight smile. They had not treated him like a beggar, as usual; some of them had even welcomed him. They had ordered, most of them, not two pair of "Pure Silk Stockings" but three or four, or even half a dozen. He had also sold some rayon "negligées" at six dollars apiece, two dozen rayon "slips" and four dozen pair of men's hose.

This was a better neighborhood than usual, and he met few of his fellow canvassers on the streets this morning. At noon, he found a small clean drugstore on Elmwood Avenue, and ate lunch. Sunlight poured through the street outside; the children were returning to school, and he could hear their happy, released laughter. Sunlight glinted on the bodies and the tops of parked automobiles. Even the streetcars clanged merrily.

He was not far from Delaware Park, and after leaving the drugstore he walked the short distance to it, to look with passionate admiration and pride on the exquisitely beautiful Albright Art Gallery, that almost perfect reproduction of a

Grecian temple. The trees of the park were filled with green and golden haze; grass was brightening under the sun; birds cried happily on brown branches; the drives gleamed and rippled with trickling water. Frank stood and looked at the art gallery, standing in the sunlight in all its white and lovely dignity, looming in delicate strength against a fresh blue sky. All about him rose the chill sweet breath of the awakening earth, the whisper of promise and hope. He felt a sudden exultation, an anticipatory thrill, a strongness of heart. Anything might happen on such a day!

How wonderful it was to feel young again, as he had not felt young for so many years! He forgot that he was nearly thirty-four, that he was a homeless canvasser, that he had almost no money, that he was shabby, emaciated, weary and embittered. He was a boy again, with Paul Hodge standing beside him, sharing his wondering joy in the art gallery. Almost, he could feel Paul's arm pressed against his; he could feel the sweet and innocent emotion at the nearness of his friend. Now he knew sadness, but it was a sweet sadness, a living ache and not a void. He thought of Paul as one thinks of someone who is dead.

After a long time, he turned away with reluctance. But the strength and the hope walked with him, invisible companions of his youth. He returned to the streets. Now he saw other canvassers, furtively and quickly, or slowly, trudging along with their cases, men and women, young and old, shabby and tired and dragging of step. He looked at them and thought: They are afraid. Why, the whole country is afraid, this rich, potent, measureless country! This pride of the world, this hope of the world, this inexhaustible richness and fatness and power, is shocked into impotence by fear! Why? The land is the same, its bowels still swell with vast resources, its wealth is not really diminished, its potentialities lie like thick golden veins in its body, its vigor thunders like a dynamo in its heart, its cogency waits, like a puissant machine, for a hand on the switch. Nothing has really changed, after all. Nothing, except the belief of the people, the faith of the people. What is left, when a people no longer believes in its efficacy and might?

The people of America, the people of all the world, were helplessly and fatalistically projecting another reality now, the reality of darkness and hate and fear. It was as real as the one they had projected before. What they did not know was that they had the power to replace it with another reality, if they so willed. The world was not an inexorable objectivity; it was malleable, capable of infinite mutation, in the hand and the will and the soul of man.

Fear had gone from Frank, though he had never admitted it as fear. He walked quickly through the streets, looking away from his fellow canvassers. He had decided, earlier, not to try to sell more today. But a kind of invincibility was upon him. He knew he could sell now.

He was walking along a low, gray-stone wall, about four feet high, above which immense lawns were banked, like a terrace. Beyond the wall, a hedge of evergreen trees still hid the house. There was an iron gate in the wall, and Frank opened it. He found himself on a long curving drive, and now he saw the house, extremely large and dignified, built of rough gray stone with a small turret on each end of its austere facade. The spring sunlight glimmered upon the small-paned and majestic windows, which gave the house a baronial look, in the English tradition. Frank could see the distant white steps and the grilled door, the red roof and the great stone chimneys which fumed blue smoke against the bright sky.

Then he stopped abruptly. Slowly he put his suitcase down on the drive. It wasn't possible! He had dreamt of this house a long time ago and now here it was, from its gray walls to the glittering conservatory in the rear, from its gardens with long flagged paths to its massive trees and shrubbery. It was all here, its large and quiet aura of wealth lying all about it. But something was wrong; it had been summer in his dream, and there had been a little girl with dark curls and great dark eyes. He had dreamt it when he had been a child, and he had tried to find the house, and it had vanished as all dreams vanish. Yet here it was, just as he remembered it.

He remembered the little girl's name. Jessica. Yes, it had been Jessica! She had run towards him along this very driveway, her hair tied back with a large pink ribbon. He waited. But no one stirred. The windows were blank; the driveway ran with the spring rains.

He felt oddly numb, shakingly expectant. He hadn't dreamt it, after all. He had been here a long time ago. The little girl had told him she was going away to New York with her father. He "played the piano," her father, and her uncle had given her the pink dress she wore. They had sat in a summerhouse in the rear. Frank stepped to one side. Yes, there was the summerhouse, as he remembered it, the rose vines still empty of flowers. They had sat on white furniture, and there had been a white kitten, and the little girl had looked at him gravely, and he had told her that some day he would come back to her. Jessica!

Frank picked up his suitcase. It slipped from his fingers and fell. He picked it up again. It was foolish, but he was trembling. He walked on towards the house. She had been going to New York. There was no possibility that she was here now. The house might no longer be owned by her uncle. After all, it was a long time ago. But his feet hurried him along to the high white door, and he lifted the brass knocker and let it fall loudly so that the sound echoed back from every wall.

He heard the slipping of bolts, and he saw the face of a capped and uniformed maid. She looked at his suitcase and said brutally: "You oughta come to the side door. Besides, we don't want nothin'. We don't buy from people like you."

He looked at her coarse and pimply face, at her piglike eyes, at her slit of a malevolent mouth. He detested her immediately, made his eyes stare at her quellingly.

"Who lives here?" he asked. "I have a message for your mistress."

She had been about to slam the door in his face. Then she paused and eyed him with a cunning grin. "No, you don't! How kin you have a message when you don't know who lives here?"

"Call your mistress," he said, and he put his foot in the doorway. She saw that and was frightened.

"Git outta here, or I'll call the police!" she cried breathlessly. "You goddam thief, you!"

She flung the words at him like stones; livid hatred quivered on her features, slackened and shook her mouth, so that she was no longer afraid of him, but felt for him the instinctive hostility of an inferior.

"I'm not a thief," he said quietly, "and you know it. I have to talk to your mistress." What was the name? Jessica —what? He could not remember.

Neither of them heard the soft gliding of a black limousine up the driveway, nor the quick light step, and both started at the sound of a girl's clear voice: "What is it, Marie?"

Frank turned and saw the young woman, almost at his elbow. Slowly he removed his hat. The maid burst out wrathfully: "It's this beggar, Miss Bailey! I was just gonna call the police. He tried to get in the house!"

The girl looked at Frank with deep, searching quiet, grave and reserved. She was a tall girl, and very slender, with

long and pretty legs and delicate feet. She wore a dress of
pearl-gray wool, and a rich mink coat was slung carelessly
over her shoulders. She had shining hair, coal-black and
polished, and startling against the pure whiteness of her
temples and forehead and throat. There was no color in her
pale face, except for the coral mouth which was at once
firm and soft, thoughtful and gentle. There were pearls in her
ears and a string of pearls about her neck.

Her eyes fixed themselves upon Frank questioningly; they
were exceedingly vivid yet quiet, very dark and radiant, and
now, as they looked at the young man, they lit up a little,
though they did not lose anything of their steadfastness, their
serious intelligence and still humor.

It is Jessica, he thought. It wasn't a dream, after all. It is
Jesscia. The suitcase was heavy iron in his hand; he felt all
his shameful shabbiness, his awkwardness, just as he felt her
assured composure and vitality.

Of course, she did not know him. She had been so young,
all those years ago. She need never know that he was that
enchanted little boy who had sat with her in the summerhouse. He could not tell her, for, if he did, she would look at
him more closely and would despise him for what he had
become. He had only to back away and leave, and there need
not be anything else, nothing at all.

And then he wanted to hear her voice again, her sweet
deep voice. He said: "If—if I could have just a few moments
of your time—" And then he stopped, hating himself.

The girl's eyes did not move over him, but she saw him
clearly and completely, his neat shabbiness, his thin face,
his too-long hair ruffling in the chill breeze. And she felt
something like embarrassed compassion and surprise. She
moved past him towards the door and said courteously:
"Please come in. I have a few minutes to spare." She went
into the house without glancing back, leaving the maid to
stare in furious stupefaction at Frank.

He walked past the maid as if she did not exist, as if she
were a dog whose yappings he had ignored. Miss Bailey stood
in the great panelled hall and removed her gloves. The maid
had slammed the door, and Frank could hear her loud, outraged breath. But Miss Bailey tranquilly removed her coat
and hat, handed them to the woman, and led the way into a
room to the right. Frank followed her, but not without a
glance around the hall, where a fire burned in a black marble
fireplace. He saw the great oaken stairway winding upwards to the second floor; on the landing was a large win-

dow, opening out upon the sky. He heard the warm crackling of the fire, felt the rich thickness of the rug under his feet, saw above the fireplace the dim portrait of a man in a gold frame.

He went into the vast living room where Miss Bailey waited for him, and he saw the exquisite simplicity of the room that denied, rather than affirmed, the existence of unlimited means. Another log fire glowed here, lighting up the pale green walls, whose French windows looked out upon the lawns and the soaring trees. The furniture of the room was pale, and it was skillfully grouped, here and there, on the faded Persian rug with its dim and entrancing colors. Everything was old and exquisitely fashioned, and Frank caught an impression of soft rose, faded blue, fragile ivory, from the French chairs and settees to the faint subdued tints of the draperies that outlined the windows. Every small table bore on it a crystal or silver or bronze lamp, an exotic little box or figurine, or a silver bowl of flowers. On the dimly gleaming grand piano in a distant corner stood a large crystal vase of yellow roses, and on the walls hung excellent portraits and landscapes in narrow golden frames, old and faded. It was an aristocratic room, ordered and furnished by an aristocrat. But, even to Frank's inexperienced eyes, there was something decadent about it, something too tenuous and too refined.

Miss Bailey stood near the fireplace, graceful and composed. She lit a cigarette and nodded toward a crystal box on the low table beside her. Frank put down his hat and case, took a cigarette. His fingers shook a little. For the first time in his life he was really conscious of a woman, conscious of her in his fingertips, his face, his whole body, conscious of her as something sweetly familiar. He could feel the heat in his face, the beat of his heart. Though he did not look directly at the girl, he could sense the shimmer of her silken knees under the pearl-gray woolen dress, the pressure of the wide silver belt about her slender waist, the warmth of her thighs and the movement of her breast. She stirred a little, waiting for him to remove his coat, and he could smell her faint sweet perfume.

It was no use. He ought not to be in this house. He had had his chance to leave, and now it was gone. So that she need suspect nothing, he must go on with this ridiculous farce. He must not show, by the slightest gesture or intonation, that they had ever met before. There was no recognition in her eyes, no perplexity, no wonder. Of course not. How could she remember, anyway? He had only to be calm, give his sales talk, and leave, in ignominy, unremembered, forever anonymous. He had had a dream; it had come to life. He could go away with it, and have it always, unspoiled.

Her face was calm and aloofly pleasant as she sat down. He opened his case on a settee. He tried to begin his sales talk. But before he could speak, she said very gently: "Do you really like this sort of thing?"

There was no condescension in her voice, but a genuine and polite curiosity. Frank's first angry emotion died. He said, with simple sincerity, as he brought out several samples: "No. I hate it. But, just now, I can find nothing else to do."

She smiled. She had a most charming and sudden smile which made her appear very young, though she was apparently in her early thirties. "I'm sorry," she said. "I didn't mean to be—impertinent, of course. But I thought it might be a little out of your line." She paused. "I'm just filled with vulgar curiosity, I'm afraid." She waited, obviously expecting him to tell her his real occupation. Frank regarded her in silence. Should he lie, and tell her he was a jobless certified public accountant, a young executive of some sort, a young businessman who had failed, a clientless lawyer, or even a physician? She was gazing at him with her large shining eyes, which were so kind and so steady.

He said: "I never did anything of any real importance, or I'd not be doing this now. I'm one of the inadequates, I suppose."

She did not speak. She only smiled and smoked, leaning back in her chair, her shimmering ankles crossed. Frank said impatiently: "Do you really want to see this stuff, Miss Bailey, or are you only trying to be kind? I'd rather you wouldn't, you know."

Why did the rich and secure think they had a right to pry into the lives of others less fortunate, and to bestow the patronizing insult of their pity on those who had need of them? Frank held his case in his hands, and only a strong effort of his will kept him from slamming it shut. His eyes almost glared upon the girl, and his thin cheeks were white.

She looked at the cigarette in her slim hand. Now her expression was sad. "Of course I want to see them. I have two friends who are very fine young doctors; they are selling sheets and pillowcases from door to door. A dentist I know has become a handy man, doing odd jobs. One of the sons of a friend of my uncle has a 'swap-shop,' where old junk is exchanged for other old junk. Some people might think it's terrible. I think it is sort of—splendid."

There was real interest in her voice, and she smiled again. She went on: "I think we're very snobbish in America, a very silly kind of snobbery. We don't really have classes, and we have no inherited aristocracy. But we have to have something, it seems. So we call certain kinds of work degrading and other kinds respectable. Work is work. There isn't any distinction." She added, when Frank made no comment: "I should think you'd find your own work very interesting."

"I know." Frank broke in rudely. " 'You must meet so many interesting people'!"

He thought he had offended her, but she suddenly laughed, and after a moment he joined her sheepishly. He sat down opposite her, near the fire. "I don't find frowzy housewives interesting," he said. "I don't find it exciting to have a door slammed in my face. I just want to kill someone, anyone, most of the time. But I like starving even less than I like canvassing. Besides—" He stopped abruptly and flushed. He had been about to tell her of his writing, and caught back the foolish words in time.

He spread the samples on his shabby knees, selected three stockings of various shades, and handed them to her. She examined them carefully, critically. She listened as Frank, in a monotonous voice, quoted prices. She wanted to throw aside the stockings, but she was so acutely sensitive that she knew a careless gesture might hopelessly offend and insult him, so she affected to hesitate and to consider. "I'm not trying to disparage your goods," she said coolly, "but I can buy this quality for fifty cents less in the downtown shops."

Frank was on familiar ground now, and he argued strongly. "Not this quality. Our stockings are pure, unadulterated silk. They will give almost twice the wear of the best-name stockings." To illustrate, he deftly wound a stocking into a rope and gave it a hard pull, a trick taught the salesmen by the sales manager. Miss Bailey pretended to be doubtfully impressed. Frank unrolled the stocking and triumphantly displayed it still unmarred and without a run. Miss Bailey examined the stocking closely and appeared to surrender.

"Well," she said slowly. "Let me see. I'll have a dozen pair of the taupe, half a dozen pair of the Sunbeam, and half a dozen pair of the Autumn Leaf. Size nine."

Frank wrote down her name: Jessica Bailey, and the address. But the pencil jerked in his hand; a wave of scented warmth spread from the girl to him. She sat at least seven feet from him, but he could feel the imminence of her white flesh, the very touch of her breath. He pressed his lips tightly together. His head was bent over his book, and the girl studied him intently, her mouth open a little and her eyes vividly shining. She saw the contour of his narrow head, the hard line of his chin, the set of his wide lean shoulders, and the fine strong shape of his hands. She moved in her chair with a curious restlessness.

Frank gave her the carbon copy of his sales slip, and she read it. Francis Clair. So that was his name. Her life was filled with scores of names. It was very strange that this one should sound so exciting to her, so significant. She folded the slip carefully and put it into her purse.

Frank said: "Do you wish to pay in full now, or give a deposit and pay the rest C.O.D. when the stockings arrive?"

"I'll pay now," she said. She had friends who did this sort of thing, and she knew that the deposit was Frank's commission. She opened her purse and gave him the exact money. She watched him as he stood up and snapped his case shut. All at once, she wanted to detain him, to keep him there for a while longer. She did not stop to analyze the queer impulse, as she usually examined her impulses. It was imperative to her that Frank should not go just yet. But what could she do? Could she ask him to stay for tea? There was no excuse, no pretense, that she could utter and not appear absurd or worse, or which he probably would not misunderstand. But, she thought, drily, would he not really understand? She was a fool. What was the matter with her? She was thirty-two years old, and she had never looked at any young man before except with indifference or with more than the mildest interest. But she did not want Frank to go. Desperately, she tried to find something to say which would keep him there just a little longer. She wanted to know all about him. She wanted to see him again!

She said: "I see you have other things to sell. Why don't you show them to me?"

Frank glanced up quickly. "You wouldn't want them; that's why I didn't show them."

"How do you know? Please let me see them."

He brought out his other sample book, and she held it on her knees. The goods were strong, well-made but coarse. She said: "I like this—negligée. Rose, I think. Size fourteen, And the blue, too. One of each. And the—the—slips. Two white, same size."

Frank stood near her in silence. Then he said grimly: "You don't want them."

She glanced at him swiftly and smiled. "Not for myself, perhaps," she replied candidly. "But one of the maids has a birthday soon, and she'd love these." A dimple twinkled apologetically near her pink mouth. "You might make it size eighteen. Fourteen is my size."

Frank's mouth was tight and unpleasant as he made out another sales slip. She watched him almost humbly. She liked the way he wrote, clearly, sharply, and with no hesitation. He gave her the slip and said: "Fifteen dollars, if you want to pay in full."

She gave him the fifteen dollars, and he put it away in his worn billfold. It did not surprise her that his fingers trembled, though she could not have told why. Something strong and electric ran between her and this queer young man, and she knew he was conscious of it, as she was conscious.

Could she say to him: "Please don't go? Have tea with me now. I want to talk to you. I don't know why, but I must talk to you."

Her mouth felt dry, and something pounded in her throat. How ridiculous I am! she thought confusedly. I'm acting and thinking like an idiot. But it did not matter! He must not go just yet, he simply must not go. He was picking up his hat and his shabby leather gloves; he was turning to her. She said, blurting out the words in a way which would have astonished her uncle:

"Have you always lived in Bison? I have a feeling I ought to know you—"

He regarded her with hard and somber directness. "Yes, I've always lived here, since I was six years old. I came from England with my parents. But I've never met you before."

She was baffled. She drew her fine dark brows together, as if trying to remember. "It's the funniest thing, but I believe I've met you somewhere. Do you know the Crawfords, or the Ansteths, or the Brownes?"

"No," said Frank, "I don't know them. And I doubt if you ever met any of the people I used to know, Miss Bailey. My father was a chemist. He worked for a long time in a shop on Niagara Street near Ferry. You wouldn't be likely to know him."

But her face brightened eagerly. "But, of course! Wasn't that shop owned by a Mr. Farley? We used to live on Porter Avenue, in a big old house, and Mr. Farley had the reputation of selling the biggest and the best sodas in town. My friends and I used to walk over there quite often. It is possible I saw your father—"

But Frank's face had darkened, and was very unpleasant.

Jessica was oddly discomfited by his expression. She stammered slightly as she said: "I remember Mr. Farley very well. He was the sweetest old thing—"

"Yes," said Frank heavily. "He was." Then he was caught by the tense in which they were both speaking. "He—he isn't dead, is he?"

"Why, yes. I remember seeing his name in the paper about twelve or thirteen, or perhaps fourteen, years ago. I was still in pig-tails and middy blouses then. It was sometime after the war."

Frank was silent. Dead. And he had not known. Why, he had intended to see Mr. Farley again! Until now he had not known that he had had this intention. He could not understand the wave of loss and depression that swept over him now. That poor old duffer! He had saved Frank's life. He had understood as no one since had understood. Frank's hands, holding the sales book, felt cold and numb.

"I'm sorry," he said dully. He put on his coat, and he said again, as if he were alone: "I'm terribly sorry. I wanted to see him again."

The girl rose. It was hopeless. There was nothing she could say which would keep him here. But their mutual regret over Mr. Farley was at least something between them. She said earnestly: "I'm sorry I was the one to tell you, Mr. Clair."

She went out into the hall with him and put her hand on the door. Then she said desperately: "Please come back in about two weeks. I might want to buy something more—"

He nodded curtly, without speaking. He went out into the spring sunlight, and she watched him go until a bend in the walk hid him. Even then she stood on the threshold until the breeze chilled her.

She thought: I've seen him before. I've known him before. I know it. But where, where? Why can't I remember? It couldn't have been a dream. I can't let him go.

She clutched the sales slip in her hand.

CHAPTER 62

THE SUNLIGHT seemed less bright and promising now, as Frank walked down the quiet and stately parkway. The suitcase was heavy in his hand.

So, Farley was dead. Frank could not understand his crushing depression. In these past fourteen years he had hardly thought of the old man at all. Something had walled itself away in his mind, shutting out the years of his life from his recollection, shutting out the memory of his father and his mother and the days of his youth. But the thought of Mr. Farley must have lain in that walled, shut place, like a little pool of brightness. Had he really, all the time, unknown even to himself, intended to go to see the old man?

Hardly knowing what he did, he boarded a bus, and then a streetcar. He was vaguely surprised to find himself eventually on Niagara Street, in the vicinity of the little drugstore. What did he intend to do? What compulsion had brought him here? It was nearly five o'clock, and he was hungry. What would it profit him to go into that shop and ask about Mr. Farley and the details of his death? It was ridiculous. But the compulsion had driven him, as it had often driven him when he had been a boy, and in an off moment he had been ruled and directed by it.

The drugstore was as he remembered it, yet somehow it appeared smaller and shabbier. The great red and green jars still stood in the dusty window, but the big flourishing fern Mr. Farley had sentimentally set between them was gone. Shabby, dirty children went in and out, emerging with ice-cream cones or suckers, just as he had sometimes emerged. He went in. Had it always been so dark, so evil-smelling, so dusty, so ill-kept? A big, bluff, middle-aged man in a soiled white coat stood behind a counter of cheap cosmetics. He had a large red face and twinkling blue eyes. He resembled Mr. Farley in some indefinable way, and he said: "Yes, sir?" in the eager, welcoming voice that shopkeepers used during the Depression.

Frank bought a shaving stick, toothpaste, and some razor blades. He went to the soda fountain and ordered a soft drink.

The man waited on him rapidly. Frank drank, then said, idly: "Are you Mr. Farley?"

"Why, yes," said the other, squinting at him. "Don't know as I remember you, though?" He looked at Frank's sample case and his smile disappeared.

"I used to know old Mr. Farley," said Frank. "I suppose you are a relative of his?"

The man's smile returned, and it was quite soft. "I'm his nephew. He left the store to me, and I came here from Detroit with the wife and kids. Fourteen years ago. Yep, he was a good old coot, Uncle Tim."

"I just heard he was dead," said Frank, putting down his glass. "I was sorry to hear it. I knew him very well when I was a kid. My father used to work for him."

Mr. Farley was wiping up the cracked black marble counter with a soiled wet rag, but at Frank's words he suddenly stopped, became rigid. He stared at the young man, narrowing his eyes.

"What's your name?" he asked abruptly.

Frank frowned. "It isn't important, but my name is Clair."

Mr. Farley's face became excited. "Frank Clair? Old Frank Clair's boy? The pharmacist who used to work here?"

"Yes." Frank was curious. "My father died a long time ago, but Mr. Farley and I used to be friends. He took a kind of interest in me."

Mr. Farley leaned his fat elbows on the counter and laughed silently, showing all his yellow teeth. Then he reached out, took Frank's shoulder in his hand, and gave him a push. "Well, I'll be damned! Did you know the lawyer's been lookin' all over town for you? Say, you wasn't in Kentucky one time, was you?"

Something began to tingle in Frank. "Yes, I was."

"Well, I'll be God-damned! Say, the lawyer wrote to the place you was supposed to be at. Nobody down there knew where you was."

"They wouldn't," said Frank, thinking of his flight. "I didn't leave any forwarding address. I've been here for nearly fourteen years, now, but, of course, nobody would know." Why was his throat so constricted? "What did your—your lawyer want?"

"What did he want?" Mr. Farley threw back his head and shouted. "Why, you son of a gun, he only wanted to give you fifteen hundred dollars, that's what! The old man left you the money in his will! Say, look, I'll give you the lawyer's address! No! It's only five o'clock, and maybe you can get him at his office! Wait, I'll get him for you! If this ain't the God-damndest thing—!"

He rumbled off to the telephone booth in the rear. Frank stood up. His knees felt weak. Fifteen hundred dollars! Fifteen hundred dollars! Something blurred his eyes. All these years of semi-starvation, and fifteen hundred dollars had been waiting for him in the bank, waiting cosily, waiting for him to take them! He followed Mr. Farley to the rear of the store. He had to put out his hand against a counter to steady himself. The ball in his throat became huge. My God! he thought.

Mr. Farley, more excited than ever, beaming like a red sun, handed him the telephone receiver. Frank put it to his ear, but the roaring in his head prevented him from hearing clearly. The man at the other end was cackling drily: "—Identification, of course. Formality. Tomorrow morning, at ten o'clock? What did you say? All right, ten o'clock, Mr. Clair. Of course, there are certain small expenses, about a hundred dollars which we spent trying to find you. Ten o'clock."

Frank found himself sitting at the counter again, sweating, shaking. He said, stammering violently: "I—I am afraid—I—didn't get his name. Would—would you write it down for me, Mr. Farley. It's sort of sudden—"

"Yeh. I know," replied Mr. Farley in a rich and sympathetic voice, looking again at the sample case. "Hits you over the head hard, don't it, when you get some unexpected money? Well, I'm damn glad. The good old coot musta thought a lot of you. I've read the will, and he said somethin' that was kind of—well, kind of wonderful. Somethin' like: 'To my dear young friend, who has all my blessings and my prayers.'" Mr. Farley blinked unashamedly. "He didn't have much to leave; he was always handin' out cash to young fellers, God bless him. Left me three thousand dollars and the store, and a little house on Hampshire Street. More than we had a right to expect."

Frank felt weak. "All my blessings and my prayers." He leaned his head on his hand, to hide his eyes. He saw old Mr. Farley's face clearly, sharply, etched on the darkness of his closed eyelids. He saw his smile with incredible vividness and heard his voice over the abyss of the years. "All my blessings and my prayers."

He caught the faint, distant drift of Mr. Farley's nephew's voice: "Died of pneumonia, sudden. Guess it was his heart, too. We come down for the funeral. There was three priests, and even the bishop. You couldn'ta believed it. Like the funeral of one of them plutocrats. You never saw such flowers. The three priests told how he'd helped them when they was kids. The bishop said he was among the angels. Made us cry like babies. Well, that's the kind he was. They don't make them no more."

"Where is he buried?" Frank whispered.

"Out in Mount Calvary Cemetery. He didn't leave no money for a stone, but the Missus and me bought him the damndest best monument in the whole cemetery. A big marble cross six feet high, like this." Mr. Farley demonstrated proudly with his hand. "Flowers all summer, too. We got flowers in our back yard, and we take a load out every Sunday, after Mass. He left money for Masses for his soul, but we pay for 'em, too. Don't want to forget him. That's the kind he was."

Masses for the soul of John Farley. He didn't need Masess. Frank saw the old man's face again, and pressed his hand tight over his eyes.

"Why don't you come out and have supper with us tonight?" asked Mr. Farley, with warm affection. "Seems you're kinda like one of the family."

The street was dark now, in the early spring twilight. Frank still felt weak and hollow, but he was not hungry. He trundled along on the streetcar, and then walked the few blocks to his room. His head was light; his feet did not seem to touch the sidewalk. But his heart was shaking, trembling. He had refused Mr. Farley's invitation to supper. He wanted to be alone to think, to think of old Mr. Farley, and his deliverance. To make his plans. To sit in his dark room, his hands clenched on his knees, and to think, and to plan.

The invincibility he had felt in the morning gathered stronger in him at each step he took towards his room. He was always one in whom reaction was delayed. Now, as he approached the doorway to the stairs that led up to his room, he was shaken by a sudden sense of rapturous power, of exaltation, that made him stop, unable to move. Oh, my God! he thought, something has changed, moved, shifted its position! Something has thundered across the blankness of the years and is here all about me! I'm blinded; I can't see yet. But something has happened. I'm going to be free! My God, my God!

His battered mailbox was just inside the door. Dim electric light filtered down the rotting staircase. There was a letter in his box. With fingers that felt half paralyzed, he pulled out the letter. Probably something from his mother, filled with complaints. He did not care. Nothing mattered now. He was free. Something had shifted, moved with tremendous sound about him.

The letter was long and narrow and thin. A greenish color shone through the glassine window. He tore it open. And then he stared, dumfounded, down at a check for three hundred and fifty dollars, drawn to his order by the editor of the magazine to which he had sent his story: "We Were Not Afraid."

Now he felt violently sick. He dropped his case. He did not feel the impact as it struck his foot. Everything swam before him. There was a slip of paper attached. He could hardly focus his eyes to read it; he did not know that the hoarse and broken sound he heard was his own hysterical laughter.

"We are pleased to send you three hundred and fifty dollars for your story 'We Were Not Afraid.' If you care to send us further stories, and we find them satisfactory and suitable for our publication, we will pay you at the customary rates. Would you, for our information, please send us a short autobiography, so that we may introduce you to our readers? Our subscribers usually like to know something about our authors——"

Frank leaned against the dusty wall of the hallway. He looked at the check. He laughed again, hoarsely, over and over. He could not stop. He had received money for his writing! This was money for his writing! His first money! He sat down on the lower step and laughed and laughed until the tears ran down his cheeks.

CHAPTER 63

ONCE Frank Clair had read a saying by a man, who was very wise, to the effect that if you invent something which the people need you will make a living, but if you invent something which they want you will make a fortune.

He remembered that. It was very simple. The people did not really "need" good books, splendid music or heroic statesmanship, in the true sense of necessity. They could get on in more or less comfort without these things, and certainly with dismaying peace of mind. They did not give their finest and most lucrative awards to the inventors of their necessities, but to the mountebanks who offered them gaudy luxuries, melodramatic politics, or raucous entertainment. Buffoonery was their pleasure and their joy.

Frank investigated the situation thoroughly. He found that there was a small public who awaited, and read, a few excellent books, but that this public was either very frugal or in poor circumstances, and usually borrowed these books from the lending and free libraries or filched them from friends. They rarely bought any, and so the author was usually compelled to earn his living in some other way. Frank remembered that very pertinent remark in the Bible: "Wisdom with an inheritance is good." But few authors were blessed with an inheritance. If one wished to make a good living, and have a few garish luxuries oneself, one must give the public what it wanted.

He found that the reading public preferred two themes: Love (or Sex) and the American Success Story. If one combined both—and it was always clever to do so—the combination was irresistible.

After all, was it not an impertinence to insist that the public should like what it was offered, whether it wanted it or not? Was it not impudent to set up an individual standard, and denounce those who rejected it? If the law of the survival of the fittest was valid at all, what the people rewarded and allowed to survive must be "good." Had not the Greeks said "that which survives is good"? Of course, there was an ambiguous cynicism there, if one wished to study the matter.

Frank now had a very comfortable little apartment in a "private home" on Lafayette Avenue, near Delaware. He had come a considerable distance in the past two years. The apartment was in no wise the garret in which artists are traditionally expected to starve. It was exceedingly comfortable, consisting of a pleasant bedroom-sitting-room, with the bed capable of assuming the bland aspect of a sofa during the day, a private tiled bathroom, and a tiny kitchenette. The family from whom he rented this agreeable little apartment were what Maybelle would have called "shabby genteel." There was an elderly man, with an aristocratic and desiccated face, and his wife, equally aristocratic and desiccated. Their home was filled with antiques, very dark and gloomy, but someone, certainly not themselves, had taken a hand in furnishing the apartment, so that it was cheerful, inviting and quite bright with color. Frank rarely saw them, as he had a private entrance. Relations between himself and the old people were on a grave and ceremonious footing, which he preferred, and when they discovered that he was "a writer" they treated him with dignified respect. He paid them fifty dollars a month for his apartment.

He was averaging three thousand dollars a year now from his short stories for the various magazines. He wrote everything. He did not disdain the Western type of tale, and his experiences in Kentucky helped him there. For the "slick" magazines he wrote endless stories of girls with burnished hair and slim figures, and their male counterparts. For the "little magazines" he wrote "smart" modern poetry, epigrams and tales with a naughty twist or an abrupt, brutal ending. He tried his hand at an article or two proving that a criminal was not really a criminal, but only a victim of his defective glands, that prosperity was really a state of mind, that Hitler and Mussolini were not really menaces but only amusing mountebanks who ought to be ignored by sensible men, that the companionship of a dog was the supreme satisfaction any man could desire, and other articles proving that American women, men, children, bathrooms, movies, restaurants, morals, automobiles, suburban homes, literature libraries, and cities were well-nigh perfect, and an example for all the world.

In short, he gave the people what they wanted, and told them what they wanted to hear. In return, he made a pleasant living, and each check he received was larger than the one he had received before. When a pocket digest magazine reprinted one of his articles which insisted that the rising horror in Europe was none of America's business, that Europe's agony was only a form of "propaganda" to excite the sentimentalists among the American people, he chuckled with gratification.

And now he had the theme for a novel, which he firmly believed would make him both rich and famous. Despite the soothing syrup which was being so sedulously fed to the American people in 1936, there was a poisonous wind of fear abroad, greater than the fear of the Depression. It was rationalized as the fear of war. But Frank intuitively suspected that it was not really the fear of being involved in a major conflict, for he knew that men had never truly despised or rejected war. It was something else. It was tenuous, ghostly, indefinable, but it was there. It was the fear of a people, the fear of a whole world which had lost God, and had not been able to replace Him with any satisfactory substitute. Modern inventions, the ubiquitous machine, had increased man's comfort of body, but had emasculated his imagination, left barren his soul. Mysticism had been discarded, except in the Roman Catholic theology, to which even most Catholics paid lip service only. How was it possible to reconcile supernaturalism with concrete streets, roaring automobiles, screaming airplanes, modern laboratories, movies, electricity? Supernaturalism belonged to the Middle Ages, before astrologers had become astronomers, before alchemists had respectably been converted into chemists, before brooding incantations had taken on the language of psychiatry, and before mystifying phenomena had surrendered to "natural" scientific explanation. In this welter of machines, books, laboratories, observatories and cyclotrons, God was only a dusty litter which had been swept into oblivion.

The suggestion that man had a soul had become much more indecent than had the subject of homosexuality and unnatural eroticism. It was a mark of sophistication to discourse gravely on libidos, sexual suppressions and libidinous dreams, but it was a mark of imbecility to discuss the possibility of the existence of God. In fact, it was actually a *faux pas*, not to be indulged in by the enlightened and the rational. At the charitable least, it evoked a faint, amused smile, or a quick averting of the eyes, as if the speaker had introduced a lewd theme not fit for the ears of the civilized.

Man, left alone among his machines, amid his howling wilderness of science, was terrified. His soul was convulsed with fear. He had found that he was not enough for himself, and that realism was a poor substitute for mystical faith. Perhaps, thought Frank, it is because man is still a primitive barbarian who must be given amulets and incantations against the horror of his instinctive consciousness of infinity and of the unknowableness of the universe which surrounds him. These could only be explained by God, who had been ignominiously banished from the universities and the calculations of scientists.

It was this fear, this godlessness, which now so afflicted the world of men, inspired them to such frenzies of hatred and murder and fury. A strange madness blew among the nations. It blew in America. And as, in these days, everything must be "explained," it was asserted that the fear which so blanched the faces of men was the fear of war.

Americans did not want "war." The country began to be flooded with anti-war propaganda, though, as yet, neither Hitler nor Mussolini had been so bold as to demand or openly threaten it. In an effort to "discover" the causes of war, all the peoples set themselves out to find culprits for past wars and plotters of future wars. They decided that the munitions makers and "international bankers" were really the villains. So, in America, there were feverish "exposures" of munitions magnates and many others.

Now Frank had a theme for a novel which would be eagerly accepted by the American people. He would create a family of "international bankers," men of long, sober American backgrounds, who, from the time of the War of 1812, had cunningly and sedulously plotted wars for their own profit. This was what the American people wanted. Insecure, frightened, mysteriously terrified, they wished a scapegoat for their fear. He, Frank Clair, would give it to them. He would not exhort them to cry "*mea culpa!*" He would put into their mouths the hateful shout: "Lynch him!"

It would not be proper to tell them, in 1936, that if they did not want war they had, even now, only to lift their hands warningly and their voices sternly, to stop both Mussolini and Hitler at once, without the firing of a single gun. The American people were not in a mood to stop anyone, nor to "involve" themselves in "international entanglements." They smelled danger and madness in Europe, and they were afraid. They preferred to find a sacrifice upon which to heap their frightened wrath.

Frank began to write his novel "The Golden Swords." He wrote it at night, and devoted his days to the burnished girls and their handsome males. He invented a whole vicious family, a family of scapegoats, of murderers, of profiteers, of plotters, of sadists and monsters.

Strangely enough, he infused them with life. And now, as he wrote, a kind of hating madness rose in him, too, so that he forgot that he was rationalizing cynically. Out onto the pages he poured the hatreds and pains and sufferings and despairs of his own life, his own disillusionment, his own fear, his own loathing. The story rose, chapter by chapter, into a grotesque but powerful edifice, peopled with Frankenstein monsters, echoing with insane voices, rattling with the sound of counted money.

There was Sex aplenty, and plots to satisfy the most captious.

Never had Frank worked so feverishly, with so much en-

grossment and passion. He was making a comfortable living
with his pen, though he was well aware that he was writing
pure trash. He dedicated the days to the magazines; he
worked at night on his novel. A frenzy was upon him, a kind
of purging of disease. His main character, John Ainsworth,
was his mouthpiece, his alter ego, a ruthless and malignant
creation who expressed Frank Clair's disgust for man, loathing for man, rejection of man. John Ainsworth was the moving spirit of his family, the inexorable beast who manipulated
the fools and destroyed the blameless weaklings. Each chapter found him more invincible, more powerful, advancing
more firmly toward the control of nations. He became, not a
character in a novel, but a living being, endowed with Frank's
own thoughts, his own desires, his own hatreds, his own will
to survive and to conquer. And because he was so alive, so
vivid, the novel took on a kind of horrible magic and verity.

Sometimes, when at dawn Frank had to halt from sheer
exhaustion, he would press his hand down convulsively upon
the pages he had written and would look before him with
wild, bright eyes. Here was his fortune! Here was his hope
of deliverance! It was good. It was powerful. It was strong.
It was full of rage and revulsion. Turgid, perhaps. Melodramatic, most surely. But—it was what the people wanted. And
the people would make him free.

Frank lived for his novel. He wrote the magazine stories
in a kind of abstracted trance. He forgot everything but the
novel. At intervals, he forgot Jessica Bailey. Sometimes he
forgot the day, the week, the month, and when he discovered it was Sunday, or July or November, he was dazed
and disoriented like one emerging from an anesthetic. In a
way, the novel was, for him, a release. In disguised and
larger form, he wrote down his lifelong frustrations and miseries. John Ainsworth overcame them, prevailed over them,
with massive will, by the manipulation of those about him.

Sound and fury, rage and excess, anger and despair, defeated dreams, filled every page of the novel. In rereading
portions of it, Frank was sometimes faintly embarrassed by
the wealth of adjectives and by some of the more thunderous
passages. It was not dull. Critical though he was (with an
eye to publishing), he admitted to himself that the writing
had passion and verve, even if there was a sort of evilness
about it, a kind of corruption, a deliberate twisting of phrase
to gain a dubious point.

The novel had engrossed him. He had lived it. He could
not understand why he felt weak and sick and somehow

polluted when he had written the last long page. When he fastened on the covers, he was conscious of a kind of deflation in which there was no triumph, no satisfaction, no fulfillment. I am tired; it's exhausted me, he thought, pressing his hands hard against his throbbing temples. He wrapped up the manuscript and carefully considered a publisher. No third-rate ones this time! He must have the best. He sent it to Thomas Ingham's Sons.

He had orders for three new stories, one a serial. But he could not write again, not just now. He was inexplicably stunned. He felt as if some virtue, some substance, had gone from him, and that he was a veritable ghost of a man.

But as the days passed, his strange misery lifted, his sense of enormous guilt paled. Then he could not remember either the misery or the guilt, and he awaited each day's mail with rising excitement.

The memory of Jessica Bailey came back to him, full-bodied, alive and warm. He gave himself up to dreams of fame, of meeting Jessica again, on equal terms, on an equal level. He saw himself standing near her, in that faint, dim room, looking down into her large, dark eyes, which smiled so gravely and gently. He knew that she had not married. From time to time, interrupting his stupefied engrossment with his novel, he read of her comings and goings, in the newspapers. He learned that she was the orphaned daughter of the late Mr. and Mrs. James Harvard Bailey, and that she "resided" with her uncle, Wentworth Bailey, who was president of the most important bank in Bison. Once or twice, he saw her face in the newspapers, and he cut out the photographs.

She became, for him, a greater reality than he had remembered. In a way, he worked for her. She was the personification of all that he desired, she and that great quiet house among its secluded trees. He did not know how he knew this, but, with a queer and strong conviction, he believed that she was waiting for him, as he was waiting for her.

He had, so far, seen her only on the day when he had sold her some stockings, when he had learned of Mr. Farley's bequest, when he had received the first money for his writing. A month after that he had had a short note from her, asking him to return with his samples. He had written her stiffly in reply: "I am no longer with that company. I have returned to my profession as a writer."

His first story had been published, and she wrote him, congratulating him, and hinted that she would be delighted to have him call. He held the letter in his hand and engaged in an agonized struggle with himself. Then he went to his closet and looked at his clothes. There were more of them now, but they were cheap. She was accustomed to easy, rough tweeds, exquisitely tailored, on the backs of her friends. These twenty-five-fifty suits would affront her. He thought of buying one expensive suit, but some stern lesson from his parents not to "make a show when you can't afford it, and put on side," restrained him. Some meritorious pride made him shut the closet door firmly, and set his lips as firmly. No. He would wear such suits, and go to see her, when he was in a position to buy not one but several of the coveted garments and not anxiously count the cost.

Twice again, she wrote to tell him that she had seen another of his stories in a magazine. She never explained her interest in him, and he never wondered. It was all inevitable. She would wait, he was certain.

His life was the life of a recluse. He spent hours in the library doing research for his next book, another American Success Story. He ate in good restaurants, and sometimes he bought a steak and cooked a meal for himself in his kitchenette. He walked the hot summer streets of Bison in a dream. It was not the dream of his youth. It was a darker and a stronger dream, and corrupt. From time to time, a sick depression and wretchedness fell upon him, an emptiness. He bought vitamins and iron tonics for his lassitude. He began to suffer from nightmares and vague aches and pains. Sometimes he felt that he was squeezed dry, attenuated. Once or twice a huge pain struck at his heart. He had no friends, no recreations. He was shut in himself, and breathed his own breath.

He was not accustomed to inactivity. More and more he took to wandering the streets restlessly. He tried to begin his new book. But all at once he found himself impotent again, blank, full of nauseous malaise. From his earliest youth he had been familiar with this sensation, but now it took on an ominous and frightening intensity, a physical apathy, a mental emptiness filled only with a sense of calamity and nameless apprehension. Out of the dim memories of his childhood floated the dream, or reality, of the vision he had had on the hearth of his grandmother's home in Leeds. But now the Hand which had launched the opalescent ball into space remained suspended in his mind, incapable of receding, lifting, dropping or disappearing. It hung there in the misty darkness, enormously and cosmically weary, rigid with exhaustion, desiring only nothingness, impelled by some horrible circumstance to remain, to be, never to die. Frank could see that Hand before him when awake or when asleep, and he felt in himself, as an echo, the terrible weariness of God, the desire for death, the desire not to be, the inability to expire and be at peace.

What did anything matter? he thought. What did it matter if he lived or died, succeeded or failed? The sense of insubstantiality, at first faint and passing, became almost constant in him. Objects he saw, people he passed on the street, were painted brittlenesses, and when he looked at them he felt sick and anguished. Nothing was desirable; nothing was desired. He was conscious of nothing now but a kind of awful misery.

He thought of his book, in the hands of Thomas Ingham's Sons, and he turned away from the thought. No, he would not allow this ghastly mood to turn that into stone also. He told himself that when the book was accepted he would feel "differently." In the meantime, it was profoundly necessary not to think of it.

He thought of Jessica, and now there was a ghostly stirring in him. It was early summer. The rich always went away to their summer homes. It was possible that Jessica had gone, too. Though he had carefully avoided the street on which she lived, he took to haunting it, skulking near the heavy trees that lined it, passing quickly by the house and its long drives. Sometimes he saw cars turning in at the driveways, and walked rapidly on, all his body stiffened against a call of recognition. It never came. So she has many visitors, he thought, bright casual people who know nothing of the Depression, of bitter work and defeat and suffering. Once or twice he heard a woman's laugh. It was never Jessica's.

Now his walks past the house became slower, more regular. It seemed violently urgent that he catch glimpses of Jessica. He had the strangest feeling that only such glimpses would redeem him from the illness that had him, which made work and sleep and normal living impossible. He went to the street at night, and sometimes tiptoed into the driveways, where he could see the lights of the house through the trees. He lurked in shrubbery, where cars passed him on the way up to the house. Then one night, by the faint glow of a street lamp, he saw Jessica's face in a car.

She was with a young man. Frank saw her profile, pale, luminous, smiling. He himself was in the shadow of a weeping willow. Perhaps she felt the urgency of his stare, for she suddenly turned her head and looked through the car window. For one instant, Frank saw her eyes, wide and dark, vaguely searching, but eager.

He went away shaken. She knew I was there, even if she didn't see me, he thought. As he walked through the warm night streets, the faint stirring in the emptiness of him quickened, as roots quicken in the black earth in the spring. He was joyful; he was not entirely dead, then. He did not try to work, for fear of killing this new fresh shoot in the wasteland. But every night he returned to the house.

Once he saw her walking from the house down to the street, and he had only just enough time to turn, as if in panic, and walk rapidly in the opposite direction. When he was far enough away to be safe from detection, he glanced over his shoulder. Jessica was standing far down on the street, on the corner, as if waiting for the long stream of automobiles that flowed past the intersection to pass so that she might cross. There came a pause in the traffic. But she made no move to take advantage of it. Lost, forlorn, and completely motionless, she stood on the pavement in her pale blowing dress, as if entranced. He saw her tall and slender figure, the strong but delicate breadth of her shoulders, the long indentation of her waist. The lamplight shone on her dark hair.

Frank stood and watched her. She was standing still, as if waiting. Then, all at once, she turned quickly, as if at a call, and he felt her eyes searching the darkness. He stepped from the pavement to the shadowed curb. She moved a step or two in his direction. She glanced across the street at every corner. She watched every man who approached. Then, slowly, she began to drift back towards the house. Frank, risking death under the wheels of a car, abruptly crossed the street.

She is waiting, he thought exultantly as he went home. She is waiting for me.

Now something sentient and alive, like a growing tree, took root in his mind. The appalling misery and horror of his days and nights lifted, blew away. He could remember the agony of them, but he could no longer feel them. He went, night after night, to Jessica's house, and quite often he saw her strolling, or just standing, near the gates or wall, quiet, sometimes smoking, and apparently undisturbed. She did not go away for the summer, and he had the feeling, perhaps egotistical, that it was because of him.

He wanted to get to work on his new book. But though the sentient presence in his mind daily grew stronger and firmer and more living, he could not write his book.

However, as a writer, he knew that he must wait, that he must allow the growing thing in his mind to take shape, pattern, coherence, before it could be expressed. He had the conviction, too, that that which would finally emerge would not be the book he had planned.

He began to wait for the mails again, with rising and feverish impatience. If the letter he expected fulfilled his dreams, it would be his signal to go to Jessica. But he could not go to her while he still had nothing to offer but himself. That self was nothing, nothing at all, he thought. Not he, but what he had accomplished: only that would be acceptable to Jessica Bailey.

Millions of men, unemployed and hopeless, walked the streets of America. Mr. Roosevelt's desperate panaceas failed to alleviate the universal suffering, for his panaceas could not penetrate to the true sickness of the people. A black cloud of awful rumor hung over Europe. Mr. Roosevelt was reëlected, attempted to "pack" the Supreme Court. A king abdicated his throne for a woman. The newspapers filled their columns with confusions, conjectures, with hideous stories of the concentration camps in Germany, with hints of rising German might.

It all flowed past Frank's feet like faint, unseen water. He lived only for the mails, for the day when he would be delivered from contact with humanity, when, never again, would it have power to hurt or debase him, when he could hate, fully and in freedom, and not fear hunger.

CHAPTER 64

THREE months had gone by, and save for a brief note acknowledging the receipt of the manuscript by Thomas Ingham's Sons, there had been no other word.

Finally, unable to endure the suspense any longer, Frank wrote the publishers a very desperate and somewhat incoherent letter. "I have been writing all my life, and now I am completely discouraged. I have made some money writing trash for the magazines, but it seems almost impossible for me to get started on worth-while work. If this manuscript is rejected by you, I shall destroy it, and never try again—"

Three days went by. Now Frank hardly left his rooms,

cooking his meals himself, and living in a blank vacuum from hour to hour, between the mails. In the morning and afternoon, half an hour before the postman was due to arrive, he would sit by his window and watch, his pale thin face rigid with suspense and passionate anxiety. Faint remnants of his boyhood's intuitiveness returned to him. In some way, he knew that the letter he expected with such immense excitement would not be the usual rejection form. He sat, and the palms of his hands sweated, and unknown to himself, he clenched his knees with his hands, in the old gesture of his father's. A tight knot had taken up permanent residence in the pit of his stomach; a ball of concrete had attached itself to his larynx, so that he could hardly breathe, and food almost choked him when he ate. He waited for the mails as Bluebeard's wife had waited for the coming of her brothers, to save her from death. The street below him was unpeopled, except by shadows. The only reality was the blue-clad postman, going leisurely from door to door. Sometimes, watching that maundering unconcern, Frank cursed the unaware and genial man, and before the latter had rung the bell Frank was halfway down the stairs. But except for a circular, or a small bill, his mailbox remained empty. He would then climb up the stairs to his rooms, weak with the shock of disappointment, aching as if he had grown old, his mouth dry and his eyes dim.

Finally, as he was still young and his nerves still fairly healthy, exhaustion had its way with him one morning, and he slept beyond the hour when the postman was due to arrive. So it was, that when he awakened with a shock, he discovered it to be eleven o'clock. The mails! Still dizzy with sleep and weariness, throwing on his bathrobe, he stumbled down the stairway. Something white gleamed in his mailbox. His fingers, suddenly grown numb, could hardly open the box. There was a square white envelope within. He snatched it out; it fell from his hand. He bent, picked it up. It fell again. He had seen that it was a letter from Thomas Ingham's Sons, and now his legs became gristle beneath him, and he collapsed, rather than sat down, on the bottom stair. His fingers felt enormous and paralyzed as he tore the letter open. He closed his eyes a moment, before looking at the narrow sheet of paper. He braced himself. His eyes swam; the printed words danced and streamed before his vision:

"We must still have a few days in which to consider the book, but I wish to tell you that we have every intention of making you a proposal. It is likely, however, to involve what may seem to you quite radical suggestions. Perhaps you will think them too much. I cannot yet say definitely what they will be, but I think that after consultation we shall be able to work out a satisfactory method. I am just telling you this because your letter made me wish not to keep you any longer in suspense about the question of publication." It was signed "Ever sincerely yours, Cornell T. Hawkins."

His landlord, faded and gray and lean, came out of his own lower apartment, and started when he saw Frank sitting on the stairs. "Good morning," he said, in his frail old voice, and there was disturbed inquiry in his eyes, for he saw that Frank was ghastly white, that he was staring before him as if he had been struck into unconsciousness, and that his whole appearance indicated extreme shock.

"Is there anything wrong, Mr. Clair?" asked Mr. Penseres, tremulously. "A glass of water, perhaps—? Bad news? I hope not—"

Frank stood up; he almost fell against the side of the balustrade. Now his eyes were almost the eyes of an insane man. His voice was loud and shrill as he stammered: "Mr. Penseres! My book! The—the publisher has taken my book! They're going to publish it—!" The ball of concrete suddenly shut off his breath, and he gasped.

"Dear me! Dear me!" exclaimed Mr. Penseres, agitated but perplexed. "Allow me, sir, to offer my congratulations!" He stared at Frank, wondering, uncertain. Frank did not have the appearance of one smitten with great joy. Shock was still gray and twitching on his drawn features.

"My God! My God!" Frank was whispering. Mr. Penseres could see that his forehead was wet, glistening with huge drops. Mr. Penseres was embarrassed. He cleared his throat and said diffidently: "A cup of coffee, perhaps, Mr. Clair? I believe Mrs. Penseres has just attached the percolator—"

The old man came into focus before Frank. Suddenly the young man laughed, weakly, incoherently. "Thanks. Thanks." He paused. Now he smiled, and it was a wild smile. His whole body was shaking violently. "Thanks, never mind. It—it doesn't matter. You see—"

But Mr. Penseres was only staring at him in great perplexity. Frank looked down at the paper crushed in his sweating hand. Then, putting out his other hand to steady himself against the wall, he slowly crept upstairs.

He slumped on the edge of his bed. He sat there a long time. Then he could no longer be still. He began to walk up and down the small bright room, which was flooded with early summer sunshine. He walked with increasing rapidity, whispering over and over: "My God! Thank God! Oh, my God!" He shivered, as if cold, and then he was burning hot. He stumbled against furniture and bruised himself and did not feel it. He wiped his face, only to have to wipe it again, almost immediately. A great trembling filled all his body, so that it was as if his very bones were quaking. He swallowed over and over, in a feeble attempt to eliminate the ball of concrete, which was increasing in size. He wanted to weep, shout, scream, dance, cry out madly. Once, as he walked, he knocked against his table, and caught his typewriter just in time to save it from smashing onto the floor. But his lamp danced crazily. He saw it, and he burst out into loud hoarse laughter.

He read and reread the letter. Cornell T. Hawkins. It was a name written in gold on a silver scroll. It was a name from heaven. It was the secret name of deliverance.

He said aloud, staring before him with protruding eyes: "I am going to be free! I am going to be rich—rich—rich—! I am going to be famous—!"

The world, shut out from him for so long, the world, which could be obtained only by money, suddenly spread before him like a panorama of shining towers, of bright archways, of great paths lit with an everlasting sun. It was to be his! It was all to be his! There was a mighty blazing gate in that panorama that lay before him, and it was open. Music gushed from it, the sound of exultation and triumph. He could not bear it. He flung himself face down on his bed, but the torturing joy lashed him to his feet again, to set him walking, to set him stumbling again on a raceway up and down the room, to set every nerve in his body to thrilling, every hair on his head to arching and tingling. Somewhere his name had been written on the page of those who conquer, succeed, surmount—and live! Somewhere a word has been given which would raise him out of the ruck of misery and darkness and failure and poverty. Somewhere the light had moved again on the golden mountain, and it was pouring down upon him. He, Frank Clair, was seeing his name inscribed with a lighted pen upon the page of life. He saw Jessica Bailey's grave, smiling face.

He pressed the letter convulsively against his chest. He wanted to feel it against his flesh. Had he been a woman, he would have kissed it

He read it again. "—to involve what may seem to you

quite radical suggestions. Perhaps you will think them too
much—"

Too much! Nothing would be too much! Frank paused.
Then a sudden horrible panic seized him. What, if upon
reconsideration, Mr. Hawkins should decide that Mr. Clair
would not care for the "suggestions"? What if the next mail
brought a reluctant letter of rejection?

Cold black horror descended upon Frank. There was but
one thing to do. Disheveled as he was, still in his old gray
bathrobe, he ran down the stairs to his landlord's apartment
and stammeringly requested to use the telephone. He sent a
telegram to Mr. Hawkins: "Any changes you wish to make
are all right. Will arrive in New York tomorrow to discuss
matter with you."

He could hardly see the telephone dial or hold the telephone book on his knees. He called the New York Central
Station, and made reservations on a train for that night.

CHAPTER 65

How was it possible to fill the hours from
noon to midnight? How long did it take to go downtown and
to purchase a really handsome piece of "airplane" luggage,
all gray and amber stripes, fitted with brass, and lined lux-
uriously? How long a time passed while one sat in a cafeteria
and tried to force a tuna-fish sandwich down one's throat,
and drink a cup of coffee which had no taste at all? It devoured no time to buy a new and expensive tie, to watch the
salesman wind it deftly about his fingers to demonstrate the
suave pattern, to watch it shimmer in the broad electric light
overhead, to have it put in a smooth white box, to drop it
into the luggage. A new shirt, a really good one, costing
three dollars, the best of white broadcloth? A moment's
transaction. How about a dressing-gown, a soft Paisley
pattern? Hardly a breath between decision and the passing
of money. A new hat? A sleek gray, with a snap brim,
and an air. Another breath or two. Perhaps buying a new
pair of shoes would consume the time. It was done! Never
had Frank experienced such speed in the shops.

He looked at his father's old gold watch. Why, it was only

three o'clock, and he had spent nearly a hundred dollars! Surely a lifetime must have passed. The knot in his middle, the concrete lump in his throat, were larger than ever. But it was only three o'clock.

He walked down Main Street, carrying his new luggage, wearing his new hat, and he wondered how he could contain himself. He saw the men and women passing him. He wanted to shout out to them: "Look at me! Turn and stare at me! Stop and murmur about me! You pass me now, because you don't know what I am, what I have done, what I am going to be! You think I am only one of you, a shadowless, faceless part of you, as dead of soul and as mean and maggoty of life as yourselves! You think your destiny is mine, grovelling, plotting for little dollars, planning a little fornication or a little adultery, hurrying to your husbands or your wives or your children, hoping that tomorrow you will have a job, or a raise, or a new car, or be able to afford paint for your hideous little houses, or perhaps a new toilet, a new rug, a new fixture for your bedroom. You walk on your sore feet, and you believe my feet are sore like yours, that I breathe the same air with you, that my heart beats as sluggishly as yours. But, look at me! Next week, next month, you will see my face in the newspaper.

Now you shall know, too, you venomous, malignant, contemptible and ugly little world of men, that I detest and despise you, that I have escaped from you forever. I am passing from you, you unspeakable, soulless horror, you animals in the form of men, you brainless caricatures of the angels.

Suddenly he felt that he must tell someone, that he could no longer be mute, prisoning up this mad joy in himself. But who would listen, who would rejoice with him? He ran into a drugstore, fished a five-cent piece from his pocket, bumbled into a telephone booth, and called Jessica Bailey.

While he waited for his call to be answered, he thought he would smother, that his trembling knees would not support him a moment longer. Why had he not done this before? Why had he not called Jessica, Jessica who waited, who would cry out when he told her, who would understand that soon he would come to her? He saw her face, the line of her throat, the black lustre of her hair, the dark light of her eyes. He heard her voice, the little catch in her breath. Why did she not answer? God, why did she not answer, now, when he needed her, when she needed to know?

After a long time a pettish female voice answered the

telephone. Miss Jessica wasn't home, no. She was at her uncle's country house, at the Lake Shore. You want the number? Well, you can have it. But say, listen, she wouldn't be there today, after all. She was goin' to drive down to Rochester today. Someone's wedding.

Someone's wedding, some worthless, stupid, utterly meaningless wedding! It was someone's wedding that pushed his clamoring cry back into his throat, stifled his heart, closed his lips. It was someone's wedding that denied him, mocked him, told him that it was more important than he. Silly orange-blossoms, silly flowers, silly mating of unimportant idiots, empty laughter, defeated him with their raucous and senseless thrusting of themselves between him and Jessica. He crashed the receiver back on its hook.

She ought to have known! Surely, she had known. But she had not waited. She had gone away. To someone's wedding. She had told him that he must wait, that something more important than his affairs was transpiring now. He hated her.

But he must speak, he must tell. Mr. Preston? He had not seen Mr. Preston for nearly three years. He found the number in the telephone book. But the burr was not answered, and again he flung the receiver back on its hook.

There was no one to tell, no friend, no enemy. There was no one. There was no one to grasp his hand and cry congratulations while the eye filled with envy that belied the lying words. There was no one to rejoice with him, to plan eagerly with him, to laugh hysterically with him. No one, no one at all.

He was thirty-six years old, and he had no friend and no enemy, not even an acquaintance.

Where was Paul Hodge? Paul! Frank sat on the narrow ledge in the telephone booth and wiped his forehead. Paul Hodge. Where was Paul? He thumbed through the telephone book. A dozen Hodges, but not an Edward, a Gordon, or a Paul. What had happened to Paul, in all these years, Paul who would understand, who would exclaim with him, who would look at him with pride, and rejoice? There was only Paul, who would know, who would really wait. But Paul had been swallowed in the grave of the years, and there was no trace of him.

Now, in the little security of the telephone booth, Frank was still and quiet. Paul. Why, I've never really forgotten him. He's been with me all the time. Is he married? Does he remember me? We were nearer, closer, than any brothers.

Surely, he hasn't forgotten me. Where are you, Paul? I need you.

Someone rapped impatiently on the glass door, and Frank got up and went out into the hot and noisy drugstore.

CHAPTER 66

HE HAD never ridden in a Pullman before. He arrived at the New York Central Station a full hour before the train was due to leave. Confused by the narrow green corridors of the sleepers, he followed the porter to his berth. But he must, at any cost, pretend to be a seasoned traveller, bored by the necessity for a business trip. Though the night was hot, and the heat in the coaches was hardly lessened by fans, he found he was shivering. He lay rigid in his berth, feeling the stiff smoothness of the sheets on his body, his window-shade up, his eyes staring out onto the railroad yards with their searing lights and glittering tracks. All about him he heard the creaks and rustles, the sighs and snores, of those who slept above and across from him. A bell tinkled softly; the porter murmured to late-comers; baggage was shuffled. Behind his green curtains Frank lay, looking at the lights and the tracks.

Never had he been so wide awake, so tense, with every nerve drawn taut, tingling and throbbing. A dozen times he shifted his pillows, threw back or pulled up the sheet, examined his suit anxiously to see if it was hanging so as not to produce wrinkles. He felt for his wallet under the pillow; he made certain that his hat was in its bag. The train became very quiet now, and the snores sounded louder in the silence.

Sometimes he would rise on his elbow, turn on his light, and look at the time. Almost midnight. He was not prepared, when it came, for the smooth gliding into the night; dazzled, he watched lights flow by him, saw the faces of track workers, saw the silver moonlight on the roofs of shacks. Now he was on his way! Tomorrow he would sign a contract for the publishing of his book. Tomorrow he would be reborn. He would sleep now, so as to be "fresh."

But he could not sleep. He lay there, and the train flowed into darkness. The rails sang gently under him. He heard the purring of the wheels. The fans whirred. But sleep stood far from him, and he could not draw it nearer. He closed his eyes, lay rigid. His head was like a seething pot, and snatches of past scenes boiled up in it. Just when he thought he had made his mind empty, he began to tremble with a violent excitement, and he would clench his hands and open his burning eyes. Tomorrow—no, today, this morning!—he would sit in the publisher's office, and he would sign a contract, and his life would begin. Tomorrow the world would begin to open its shining door, and he would be free. He saw himself talking to Mr. Hawkins. He must not appear a yokel to Mr. Hawkins. He must speak in very measured tones, and now he prayed blasphemously that he would not stammer, that his thick tongue would not helplessly go off into wild and uncontrollable repetitions. He must remember to talk slowly and carefully, to smile coolly, and be calm. He must take time to smother his faint English accent, in order not to arouse the antagonism of Mr. Hawkins, as the antagonism of his associates in Bison had always been aroused by the sound of his broader "a's," his clipped endings, and other shameful Britishisms. In his mind, he practiced subduing the accent. With care, he could pass as an American born. Americans, his father had always said, did not like the English; he must remember.

New York! In a few hours, for the first time in his life, he would see New York. He would see the brilliant towers, the canyon-like streets, the great shops. He would set his feet on the pavements of New York.

It was strange that in the very midst of his beating excitement and tense thrilling he remembered something he had forgotten for almost thirty years. All at once, he was standing in the muddy Common outside the green back door of the yard of the house on Mosston Street. It had been raining, and the sky loomed closely overhead, a rack of gray clouds with dark undersides. He could even feel the cold moistness of the wind in his face, his childish reaction to wind and cloud and muddy earth and the group of little children standing about him. He could not remember their names, but he remembered their faces, pinched, wan, hungry. One or two complained that they had no button-boots for Sunday school, and they looked down at their clogs dolefully. He looked down at his own feet, nicely encased in button-boots, and felt a thin pleasure. "That's because you're poor," he had said.

Poor. He had never uttered the word before. Suddenly, he turned and ran furiously into the house, and found his mother in the kitchen. A cold fright was upon him, and he clutched his mother's skirts in vehement fear. "Mama!" he cried. "We're not poor, are we? We aren't poor like the Dobsons, are we, Mama?"

He had clung to her skirts quite desperately. It was strange that just now, as he lay gently rocking in his berth, he could feel the texture of Maybelle's apron in his hand. He could feel the dampness of dread between his shoulder blades, the ache of his fingernails as they dug frenziedly into his mother's skirts.

Maybelle was cross and preoccupied. She switched herself free from the terrified child. "Of course we're poor!" she said. "And now, go wash your paddies and eat your tea."

How could he ever have forgotten the sheer cold horror that fell on him then, the sensation of vulnerablility, of defenselessness, of real panic? He was hardly six years old, but he was stricken and thrown down, overcome with a very passion of hatred and agonized terror and rebellion. He would not be poor! Never, never, never!

He *had* forgotten, but now, as he lay in his berth, it all came to him and a shadow of his childhood fell over him, and he was sick with depression. He could not stand this. Why had this memory returned to him just now, on the very day of his greatest triumph? He got out of his berth, found water, and swallowed a capsule of nembutal, which his doctor had given him some time ago.

He must have slept, for when he became conscious of himself again the bleak hot dawn of a New York summer morning was blazing into his eyes.

He sat up and looked out. He had missed the Palisades then, and the green Hudson under the sun. He watched the dreary, broken tenements running past his window. He saw the littered corridors of the streets. He saw bedraggled figures creeping below, and had his first sight of New York streetcars and billboards and the high flight of an "elevated." Then a huge apartment house appeared, its hundreds of windows glittering in the sunlight, and another one, and another, until the tenements again streamed by him, unredeemed by a single tree, a single plot of grass. Sometimes filthy windows, blowing with dirty fragments of curtains, pressed almost upon the train, only to give way to a panorama of soot-stained brick walls the space between which was hung with ragged laundry. He could catch glimpses of the hot blue sky.

The porter was fumbling at his curtains, and now he knew

that it was time to get ready. His head pounded, and his stomach was nauseated. But the excitement had returned, until it seemed to him that he would burst the very bonds of his flesh.

The train roared into the tunnel, and in Frank's ears the sound was like the rumble of great triumphant drums.

Out, now, into the station, where he was immediately assailed by a thousand rushing faces, a thousand blurrings of colored dresses and dark clothing, a thousand echoes of hurrying feet and the mutter of a multitude of voices, a very flood of humanity pouring in upon him from every direction as the commuters and the travellers flew by him, birds of passage intent on unaccountable different goals. Overwhelmed by them, choked, smothered, brushed and jostled by them, deafened by the sound and beat and thunder of them, he struggled to the side of the gigantic station and stopped to get his bearings. Incredulous, he watched the cataracts of men and women spewing from scores of different exits, while wan sunlight, through overhead acres of windows, seeped down upon blanched, rouged, intent, scowling, vapid and empty faces, floating and bobbing into infinity. He heard the rumbling shouts of train-callers, the low growl of trains beneath his feet; the stone floor under him trembled. There were ramps here, and ramps there, all seething. Where were they all going? And why? Did it matter? Why this raging and running and hastening? Why all these cross currents, as a river of humanity struck across a river gushing in another direction? They hurried, these ants, out of their labyrinths to their honey-combed nests, the gigantic nests which made canyons of their streets, and which even so early, must be beginning to hum with ant-activity. They hurried, as if they and their ant-lives were important. They hurried, with mass-egotism, into the sun, and never knew that ten thousand of them could be crushed under a toppling nest and the world would not be the poorer for their deaths.

Suddenly Frank felt a clean shame for them, for their debasement, for their outrageous conviction that what they were and where they were going was of any significance at all. If all of them would only halt for a single instant and think: I am nothing, and what I am about to do will not change the current of life in the least, then, and then only, would they, in their humility, acquire a kind of dignity and grandeur, a kind of tragic truth. But they ran and they fled; they panted and they rushed, and in their belief that they were important they were only shameful. A man alone, thought Frank, has a kind of lonely splendor and mystery. But men in the mass lose their souls.

Cold black depression fell on him, and he felt himself dwindling, some virtue drawn out of him and dissipated in the flood that roared by him. It was quite a long time before he came to himself and dully remembered that somewhere he had seen a string of lights leading to the Commodore Hotel. He picked up his suitcase and went on, vaguely wondering why he was so tired, when he had not been tired before, and why there was a kind of ashen dryness in his mouth, a flatness in the soles of his feet.

CHAPTER 67

HE WAS given a pleasant room in the Commodore Hotel, where he could look out upon Forty-second Street, fifteen stories below. The quiet comfort of the room, its blending of green and russet tints, its wide, sun-dazzled window, its glittering white bath, lifted his spirits out of the dark pit into which they had fallen. Never had he been in such a room—and it was his for as long as he wished it, though the cost had momentarily staggered him. He examined the thick white towels in the bathroom, and studied the shower. He felt of the firm soft bed with its heavy green cover. He studied the fine prints on the ivory walls. He stood at the window and saw the seething traffic of men and vehicles below. So, this is what it meant to have money! This is what a man could buy, this dignity and retreat, these luxurious rugs, these massive white towels, this telephone beside the bed, these heavy dark doors! This key in his hand!

His hands shook as he unpacked his few belongings. He glanced at his watch. It was hardly past nine. He went to the telephone and called the offices of Thomas Ingham's Sons. Mr. Hawkins, he was informed, would not be in until ten-thirty. How could he endure it until ten-thirty? He treated himself to a shower, then went downstairs in the crowded elevator full of well-dressed men and women, and found the dining room. He could not get enough of the panelled walls, the Tudor décor, the wonderful rugs, the tablecloths like polished satin. But he could not eat when his breakfast was brought to him, though it was a breakfast of which he had dreamed. His excitement was too profound, too nerve-racking.

It was this which made him think: I am almost thirty-seven years old. It ought to have come to me sooner. What if it is too late?

He could not keep still; it was something in the nature of flight that sent him out into the thronging lobby, where he saw no brute face, no shabby, shapeless clothing, heard no empty brute laugh. These men and women were the creatures of whom he had dreamt in his deepest poverty. They talked softly and suavely; they smiled easily and stood about in casual attitudes. Their clothing was rich and of sharp angles, and even Frank's inexperienced eyes could detect the quality. There was assurance about them, the calm acceptance and awareness of affluence. He moved among them, feeling the inferior quality of his own new suit, the poor leather of his polished black oxfords, the cheapness of his tie. Did they detect all this, as their smiling, wandering eyes touched him? Did they wonder how such as he had been allowed to appear among them? Did those bellboys glance at him with contempt and affront? He was sure of all this, and his face and heart burned with humiliation and anger. Well, a few more days, a few more weeks, and he would walk among them proudly, one of them, entitled to their smiles, permitted to dine with them. Only a little longer, and he could go boldly to Jessica's home, and be admitted, not as a beggarly salesman but as an equal.

He went out into the street, and was stunned afresh at the sight of this incredible city. He saw the colossal towers, the enormous walls, standing above him, their windows sparkling in the sun like countless mirrors. He heard the roar and crash of the traffic; he was jostled by the intent-faced racers on the sidewalks. A wind he had never known blew dust into his eyes. He gasped in the monstrous heat that rose in hot waves from the pavements. Vast shop windows moved beside him, filled with an unbelievable quantity of merchandise. He kept close to them, finding his way to Fifth Avenue. Policemen shrilled their whistles at the corners; busses and cars clattered, honked and bellowed all about him. And on every hand, wherever he looked, the brilliant towers sprang upwards to the burning blue sky and threw sharp black shadows over the streets.

This was New York. He had seen photographs, movies and newsreels of the city. He had imagined he knew it. But imagination was beggared by the reality; imagination was a flat miniature in faded colors. He felt the power of the city, the huge and pounding energy, the fury and the tumult. He stared at the rushing masses of faces, and saw all the men in the world. He was stupefied into unthinking amazement.

He walked down Fifth Avenue in a daze. He saw the great white lions of the Library. Masses flowed in and out of it, converged, were swallowed into other rivers. It did not seem possible to him that there were so many people. He saw how absorbed they were in their passionate aims and thoughts, how unaware of the incredibility of the city they had built and in which they lived and had their being. How tiny and insignificant they were, how vulnerable and meaningless. Yet—they had built this city, a city more impossible and more stunning than the Pyramids, more powerfully impressive than the Parthenon, more wild and colorful and violent than Bagdad, overlaid with more gaudy grandeur than Rome had known. Soft flesh and weak bones, small flaccid feet and little hands—but they had built this city. The terrible and heroic and invincible human spirit had built this city! The dreaming human mind in its frail bony shell had conceived this power and this splendor, this giant and astounding force, this white and shining majesty. It had struck these towers against the sky. It had carved these walls; the fragile hands had raised up these massive canyons of stone and concrete. Oh, dreaming mind of man that could set monuments and palaces in the wilderness and throw arches of magnificence across the desert place!

Frank stood still, and now a furious ecstasy came to him as he thought these thoughts, an ecstasy which shouted from his exultant heart. The darkness which had crept on him that morning retreated at last. It only retreated, and did not vanish. But he could hold it back for an hour, and rejoice, and be exalted and awed by what his species had raised in the voiceless forest. Pride and passion flashed in his eyes. A curious something like love came to him, a love that rose from the walled garden of his childhood and sang all about him with faint but thrilling fervor. Some instinct implored him to hold fast to what he knew, to remember it, and never to forget it, lest he die, for it was a truth he had known and had forgotten.

He found the building in which Thomas Ingham's Sons had their offices. He was surprised at the narrow hall, at the creaking, iron-filigreed elevator. He had expected pomp and circumstance, and this unassuming dignity dismayed him. This was no port of entrance to dreams and triumph. There should have been marble halls and attendants arrayed in livery; there should have been polished doors and thick rugs, and perhaps the smell of incense. But there was nothing save this elevator and an ancient operator with a winged collar and a brooding, disillusioned expression, and the slow drop of teeming, most ordinary, offices as the cage rose upwards.

He was ejected from the elevator onto the fifth floor, and looked about him, dazed with disappointment. He saw a quiet corridor, a desk or two at which girls' fingers scampered over clacking typewriters, and he heard a hushed voice, a footstep on a bare wooden floor. No slumbrous-eyed odalisque floated to greet him, to herald his arrival with a clap of jeweled hands; no scarlet curtains parted to admit him into a vast cathedral room. A young girl with a pert face, glasses and a tousalled head approached him briskly, asked him what he wanted, and took his name. He stood, hat in hand, before a rack of books, and looked at the busy girls, and saw an elderly man or two moving silently in and out of a dim room that vaguely resembled a library.

The girl came back, led him down a narrow corridor past small offices, and into the office of Mr. Hawkins. It was a large, dusty office, with blurred sun glinting on window panes. Frank had a confused impression of a big littered desk, an old swivel chair or two grouped about, and a thin tall man with a felt hat perched on the back of his head. The man rose and smiled, and Frank thought instantly of February, a pale and silent February with a cold blue sky and snow on the ground.

Frank's naïve disappointment sharpened in him, and with it came his old painful muteness, his old morbid self-consciousness, his old fear of the stranger. He looked into Mr. Hawkins' still and frosty eyes, and saw his faint, enigmatic smile, and instantly he was frightened. This man held the power of life and death over him! On his word, he, Frank, would be delivered, or forever imprisoned and lost. If Mr. Hawkins did not like his English voice, if he felt an aversion for him personally, then there was no hope for him!

Mr. Hawkins had extended his lean hand, but Frank was so overwhelmed with his old fears, his old sense of inferiority and nothingness, that he did not at first see the hand. Then he took it, his own chill and damp. Mr. Hawkins was murmuring something in his quiet voice. Frank opened his mouth. Then dumbness seized his vocal cords, and to his terror he knew that even if he did speak his voice would emerge as a stammering blur of incoherent sounds.

Terror-stricken, hating himself, sweating with wild nervousness, he sat down near Mr. Hawkins, his hat on his knees.

And February sat and contemplated him, and knew more than Frank would ever guess he knew. February waited in his reserved aristocracy, one long leg crossed over the other, and the thin patrician face betrayed nothing. But as Frank sat, numb and voiceless in his fear, a faint recognition came to him, a faint sense of familiarity. He knew, confusedly, that this man would not despise him for his haunting English accent, that he would not smile in contempt at his stammer, that he would not turn from him in brute prejudice. This man was of his own blood. This was a man of understanding, who saw and did not detest. He contemplated Frank, and smiled faintly and coldly, and there was no disdain in the pale blue eyes. It almost seemed that he was searching for something, and perhaps hoping for something. This was a gentleman like Wade O'Leary, one of the mature ones, a man who was truly a man, and Frank's tense muscles relaxed, and, in relaxing, ached.

February had no animosity towards this stranger, and this fact alone would have been enough to ease the terrible tightness in the younger man. There had been so few who had looked at Frank with real interest and thoughtful detachment, who saw him as one of their own species. For so long had Frank been the victim of derision, malicious curiosity and stupidity that he could hardly accustom himself to an atmosphere where he was accepted as a man, a man who might be significant and an equal.

Mr. Hawkins said: "I was glad to hear you were coming to New York, Mr. Clair. We can settle things now. I wrote you about certain changes?"

Frank opened his mouth, and to his extreme relief his voice came: "Yes." Emboldened by his success in speaking without a stammer, he went on in a rush of words: "It doesn't matter—Mr. Hawkins. I don't care what changes you make—"

His head was throbbing. The heat and the dazzle of the sun hurt his eyes. He continued eagerly: "I—I just want the book to be published—"

Mr. Hawkins studied him thoughtfully and heard the panic in his voice. "You might not like the suggested changes," he began.

Not like them! Oh, let him take the whole damned book and twist it and change it and make of it what he would! If only the book was published!

"I don't care!" exclaimed Frank, leaning forward. "You—you know what would be best—" And then his voice stopped and he flushed in his agony of muteness.

Mr. Hawkins averted his eyes considerately and waited. Frank struggled with his vibrating but soundless vocal cords. Then he burst out: "You don't know—what—what—this means to me. I don't care what is done with it."

Mr. Hawkins said softly: "It's too long as it is. But it can be cut. Then we can go ahead with setting it up in galleys."

In galleys! Wonderful, magic galleys. The book would be in galleys— Frank's jawbone sprang out under his skin. He swallowed, the lump hard and choking in his throat. His hands clenched on his hat. It was true. They would take the book and publish it.

Mr. Hawkins leaned back in his chair, which creaked. He put his thumbs in the armholes of his vest. His still face expressed nothing. He said: "We have to be careful of libel. You didn't base this book on any actual family of bankers?"

"No. Oh, no. It was all my imagination. A kind of—a kind of—composite. It is all imaginary. Just a story. About the people who cause wars—"

Mr. Hawkins smiled suddenly, slightly, and briefly. Now a faint curiosity stood in his eyes, as they examined Frank. "You think they, all alone, cause wars, that sort of men? You think the people themselves have nothing to do with it at all?"

Was he laughing at him, Frank? But there was no laughter on Mr. Hawkins' face, only an intent interest.

"We mustn't overlook the fact that the Germans have always wanted power and domination over the rest of mankind," said Mr. Hawkins, more in the voice of discussion than of argument or disagreement. "How do you explain Hitler? In terms of the international bankers?"

Frank was silent. He forgot himself, his embarrassment, his stammering, his fear. He regarded Mr. Hawkins, and colored. He knows I don't believe what I have written, or he wonders whether I believe it. I must make him believe it, or perhaps he won't take the book! His voice shook as he protested feebly: "They—the bankers—financed Hitler. They supported him, the bankers of England, France and America."

Mr. Hawkins regarded his desk abstractedly. Then, after a long moment, he said: "Yes. I know. But there's something else, too. If Hitler wants war—and he will want it, it's inevitable—it will be the people who will fight. And it will be because the people, and not the German people only, will want it. There are some who talk of the 'inevitability' of wars. But the 'inevitability' lies in the people's will to war, and, perhaps, in their desire for it. We all talk about man's hatred of war, but the fact remains that wars occur, and will continue to occur, because man doesn't really hate them. The peoples allow the conditions which lead to conflict to arise and to increase; they countenance them and nourish them. Out of this flows the inevitability of wars."

He waited for Frank's comment, but Frank could not speak. Mr. Hawkins went on: "Either the peoples know it, or are too stupid to know it. We could all have made Hitler retreat from the Ruhr if we had wanted to, you know. But we didn't."

Out of his fright, Frank exclaimed: "But the governments of the major powers encouraged Hitler! They didn't want to restrain him! Why? Perhaps it's because they fear Russia. I think that's it. They'll even permit wars because they're afraid of Russia. Why are they afraid of Russia? Is it because they don't want the masses to seize power? I—I think that's it. I even think they are supporting and financing Hitler in the hope that he will attack and destroy Russia."

Mr. Hawkins said nothing. But now he regarded Frank with quickened interest.

"It's the pusillanimity of governments, and their greed and suspicion, which will lead to conflict with Hitler," said Frank, with fear-filled emphasis. Then he paused. "But none of us will fight Germany. We don't hate Germany. We never did." And then his face twisted unconsciously with bitterness, and the faces of the German children he had known in his childhood rose up before him, and he tasted hatred in his mouth. "We don't hate Hitler now, because he's made himself too popular in America, among the cattle, with his anti-Semitism. Cattle must always hate something, and Hitler has given them a defenseless victim."

"It is almost impossible to imagine persecution in these days," murmured Mr. Hawkins abstractedly. "Perhaps we, in America, can't really take it in."

Persecution. I was persecuted in America almost as much as the Jews are now persecuted in Germany! I was persecuted because, among the children of European serfs, I was British, because, among the alien voices of the Near East, of Germany and of Southern Europe, I dared speak in the true language of America! I was an exile in the land of my own people. I was hunted and hounded, tormented and despised, by those for whom my people had fought, by those whom my people had liberated and fed and helped to survive. If the Jewish children run in terror through the streets of Berlin, I ran in terror through the streets which my people had built, past the houses my people had erected to shelter the litter and the scum of Europe. I know persecution!

"We won't go to war with Hitler, because we don't hate him and because Americans don't want to fight Germans." Frank added: "Even if our bankers, all over the world, now finance and arm Hitler secretly."

He had forgotten himself so much by now that in speaking he had hardly stammered at all. The memory of his persecutions and his sufferings, though deliberately smothered a moment ago, still left some trace of itself, so that his face lost its pale fear and his eyes sparkled with suppressed rage. Now Mr. Hawkins studied him with even greater interest, and Frank became aware that the great editor's eyes had taken on a focussed and piercing quality, searching and waiting. For some nameless reason, he was not alarmed but strengthened rather. He became aware, too, of being in the presence of the cool and lofty climate of the mind, tempered and subtle, frostily kind and penetrating. He saw Mr. Hawkins' face, perceived its cryptic and melancholy fatalism, its bleak humor. In spite of his age, Frank was, in many ways, naïvely young, and an impulsive emotion rushed from him to Mr. Hawkins, a blind and artless trust. He wanted to cry out to this strange man: "I want to know you! You look at me, and don't see the grotesque image others see. You see me as I am, and I can trust only those who really know me."

Frank could not know how much Mr. Hawkins saw of this. The editor glanced away with deep thoughtfulness and the sympathetic consideration he had shown when Frank had stammered incoherently. Frank saw this, and he said hurriedly, and with what he later cursed as naïveté: "Have you read the book all through, Mr. Hawkins?"

Mr. Hawkins said abstractedly: "Yes. I think you are a fine storyteller. Your characters live and have vitality. After all, that is the most important thing in a novel. I don't think the subject matter is so important—"

Frank was passionately relieved. It did not matter so much, then, whether or not Mr. Hawkins wondered if Frank believed what he had written. And again, Frank felt the surge of strong emotion. He wanted to hear something else, and now he spoke more diffidently, out of some impulse he could not define: "Thank you. I—I'm glad. But do you think I write well? I mean," he added, coloring again, "do you think I am a—a writer?"

Mr. Hawkins glanced at him swiftly, and said: "Why, yes, of course." He smiled somewhat wryly.

But a gnawing something in Frank was dissatisfied, though he could not tell why. He said: "You see, it's important to me to believe I am a writer." He paused. What did he want? What did he want Mr. Hawkins to say? He did not know, but the urgency to hear it was on him almost desperately.

Mr. Hawkins repeated: "You are a fine storyteller." Why did he look at him, Frank, so curiously, and with the air of one who has been disappointed not only in this young man but in so many others before him?

A "storyteller." The woods were full of storytellers, all the magazines, all the libraries. Just a storyteller. Well, that was enough, wasn't it, if the storytelling brought in enough money? What was more important than money?

"You think I write as well as most—most modern writers?"

Again Mr. Hawkins smiled, as f he knew so much more than Frank knew. "Yes. I should say, yes."

They were both silent. Then, as Frank considered what the other man had said, his old malaise came back to him, dry with futility and undesire. He was frightened. Not now! It must not come back now, when he was about to succeed! What was it, this sickness, this sudden blank emptiness, this disintegration, this fainting weakness and tiredness? He had heard what he had wanted to hear, hadn't he? But had he? And, if not, what was it? Unconsciously, his hands clenched his knees as his father's had done. Mr. Hawkins saw this, and his gray brows drew together as if in anxious pity.

I don't want anything, thought Frank involuntarily. I don't care. It doesn't matter. Then his fright returned. He must care! His life depended upon it.

His wandering eye fell on the pile of manuscript on Mr. Hawkins' desk. It was his own. And beside it he saw a long document with the title of his novel at the head of it, and his name. A contract. The sickness left him, and he was excited again. Mr. Hawkins followed Frank's eye, and his lean hand reached out and picked up the document.

CHAPTER 68

WHAT had he wanted Mr. Hawkins to say to him? It had seemed terribly important. But now he could not remember what it was, or why the not saying of it had left him so bereft, so desolate.

Frank walked endlessly up and down the streets of New York, an unquiet and uneasy figure, oblivious to all that moved around and beside him. He went over and over his conversation with the renowned editor. Mr. Hawkins had said he was an excellent storyteller. He had, with a little prompting, admitted that the tale of John Ainsworth had power, considerable beauty, passion and emotion. What more, then, did any writer want?

The hunger devoured Frank Clair. Something was missing. It was certainly not missing from his pockets, wherin lay the contract and a check for a thousand dollars. Sometimes he would leave the rush of humanity that surged on the bright streets of the city, and find shelter in a doorway, where he would take out contract and check and gloat over them. Or, rather, he tried to gloat. There was an emptiness somewhere, however—a yearning, a hunger, a depression. He told himself it was because he had no one to rejoice with him.

He remembered, then, what his teacher had told him about his writing. "Something is missing." Was it that something which had restrained Mr. Hawkins from telling him, Frank, what he so passionately desired to hear, even though he could not remember it, or dredge it up from the dark depths of his mind? Even though he did not know what it was?

He went back to his room in the hotel and walked restlessly up and down the thick carpets he no longer saw or heeded. He stood at the windows and looked down unseeing upon the great traffic. The magic and the excitement were gone. He said to himself: "It's just the reaction. I'm numbed. It will all come back." He heard his own voice saying this, and it returned to him like an ominous echo.

He went down into the lobby and leafed through the telephone books of every city of considerable size in New York State, searching for the name of Paul Hodge. It was nowhere.

Nor were there any Edward or Gordon Hodges. He went back to his room and wrote a letter to Jessica Bailey.

"I am here in New York, where I have just signed a contract for the publication of my novel *The Golden Sword*. I tried to reach you yesterday to tell you, but you were not at home. But when I return to Bison, I shall go to see you. I am excited just now, as this is the first important thing I have written which is to be published, and though I may be a little too hopeful, I have every reason to believe that the book will be a success. Then, of course, there are the movies to be considered. Mr. Cornell Hawkins, the editor of Thomas Ingham's Sons, has cautioned me about being too optimistic about the sale of the book, but something tells me I don't need to be cautioned, and that I'll make a lot of money from it. That's why I feel I can now go to you, as an equal, that I no longer need feel inferior."

And now, as he wrote, a wave of returning exultation ran over him, and he clenched the pen in his fingers and felt again the heavy lump in his throat. He jumped to his feet and, standing at the windows and clutching the russet draperies at each side, looked down at the traffic. All that below would be his! There was no need any longer to slink through the streets and feel the debasement of insignifance and futility, the hopelessness, the hunger for the things in the shop windows. Why, he could buy a car now, or anything else he wanted! In a very short time he would see his name in the book review sections of famous metropolitan newspapers. He would see the advertisements of his book. The world would know of him, and give him whatever he asked for—wherever he went he would be known!

He stayed several days in New York, on clouds of elation. He bought himself a really good suit and new English shoes. He went to the theatres and the best restaurants. He bought an armful of books. He spent a day in the Metropolitan Museum, and visited the Planetarium. He rode up and down Fifth Avenue on the tops of busses. The smell and the sound and the sight of the city were a delirium of expectation to him.

Not wishing to make a "nuisance" of himself, or to "impose," he did not call upon Mr. Hawkins again, though Mr. Hawkins wondered at his absence. But he passed and repassed the building which housed the offices of Thomas Ingham's Sons as one passes a temple in which dwells a holy joy. Once he saw Mr. Hawkins emerging, and he shrank away into a doorway, praying that he had not been observed.

Mr. Hawkins, of course, would frown at him; it would not "do" to "annoy." It did not occur to Frank that he was behaving exactly as his father had behaved at the sight of poor old Mr. Farley nor did he know that his thoughts were almost identical with his father's thoughts.

He returned to Bison, his mind a fever of plans. Immediately upon his arrival he would call the Bison newspapers. They would be glad to know that a fellow-citizen had so distinguished himself. They would rejoice with him. He would see his name in their pages, and perhaps his photograph. He wanted them to be proud of him.

And he would see Jessica Bailey. He would stand with her in that room, and he would see on her face what he craved to see on every face, though that was something he did not as yet know.

CHAPTER 69

FROM a telephone booth in the station at Bison he called the newspapers. The reporters to whom his call was relayed were properly surprised, pleased and congratulatory. If he stammered, they appeared not to notice it. If he sounded naïve to them, they were politely oblivious, being cynical young men with writing ambitions of their own. They made appointments to visit him at his apartment the next day. The Bison *Evening News* suggested a photographer, and this was agreed to with eagerness on Frank's part.

His quiet and pleasant apartment was filled with morning sunshine. Frank remembered that he had had no breakfast as yet, and he cooked himself a meal. But he could scarcely eat. His excitement returned to him deliriously. If only his father were alive, so that he could choke the old fool with this news! So he was a "failure," was he? He was just "Babbling Bill," was he? His father's wan, pinched face rose up before him, and he shouted his derision and his triumph at the ghost. He was abstractedly surprised at the strength of the passionate hatred that exploded in him at the thought of his father, the contempt, the revulsion. He was too excited, he reflected. But he could not control the spate of his rage against Francis Clair. Why did he have to be dead now? How glorious it would be to see him crawl and grovel before his son today! How servile and placating he would show himself, overwhelmed at the idea of so much money to come, at so much success. Frank could hear him say: "Bank it. Bank it all. You can't tell what rain will fall tomorrow. Bank it. Don't waste a penny of it. Reduce your outgo to nothing; live quietly, spend nothing you don't have to spend. Keep your head down; you might offend somebody. That chap Hawkins: did you behave yourself respectfully? Can't tell what those chaps might do to you if they think you're pushing and forward. How did he look at you? What did he say? What did *you* say? You shouldn't have said that! They might not publish your book— Let me see that check. Best give it to me. To bank for you. Bank it!"

Bank it! "I'll bank nothing!" cried Frank, with hating disgust. "I'll spend every penny of it. I'll live, not die, as you died, you penurious, terrified old ass! I'll take the precious dollars you worshipped and 'tucked away' and buy myself a car, all the clothes I want, a ticket to a thousand miles away. That makes you cringe, doesn't it? You and your bankbooks! What did they give you at the last? A narrow grave in the cemetery, 'tucked away' among 'strangers,' with a mean little stone at your head, and weeds over your body. What did you do with your life except save, except huddle your fears around you like rags? Worst of all, what did you do to me? You sold the years of my youth, and added the dollars to a neat little row in your bankbooks."

Frank hoped his enemies from the old days would see his name in the papers. But they had been such insignificant enemies, and probably they had forgotten everything about him. He regretted that he had no enemies of real consequence. A man, he thought, should make himself some respectable foes, in order to triumph over them and sear them with envy. They were almost more necessary than friends.

When he could control himself, he called Jessica Bailey. After some delay, her voice, quiet and a little subdued, answered him. She congratulated him, and now her voice warmed. Yet he felt something distrait in her, and he was chilled with apprehension. But she invited him to call upon her that afternoon at four.

The sluggard clock finally stood at half-past three. He called a cab and was driven through the warm sunlit streets to the great house he remembered. There was a stricture in his breathing; he sat on the edge of the seat and saw the basking city through a haze of radiance. His thoughts became incoherent, chaotic. Though the day was quite hot, he sometimes shivered. Now a sudden sharp pain, remembered from childhood, struck him a savage blow in the chest, and he pressed his hand instinctively, and with fear, to the spot. Then, slowly and carefully, he slid back on the seat and tried to quiet his breathing. Stop it, he said to himself. Hold on, or you'll die. The pain ebbed away, but he was weakened by it.

When the cab reached its destination, he forced himself to get out slowly, though his instinct was to run. Remembering the pain, he walked up the long winding driveway at a measured pace. It disappointed him, childishly, that his old enemy, the maid Marie, did not open the door for him. An elderly woman led him into the dim and faded living room. Jessica was not there. He spent the moments waiting for her in looking about the room, admiring it, yet smiling at it. It needed a robust dash of crimson about, or a flare of scarlet, the brightness of a vivid blue against that sunny wall. He saw the trees outside; they threw a faint aqueous green light into the room.

He turned and saw Jessica standing near him and was startled. Then he was embarrassed. How long had she stood there, watching him, perhaps smiling amusedly to herself? He felt the flush in his face and could not speak. Then, as they looked at each other in silence, he saw that she had changed.

He had not thought that Jessica would change. In his dreams of her, he had always seen her as he had seen her on that other day, dressed in a gray woolen dress, pearls at her throat, her face calmly composed and lucent, her smooth black hair waved over her white forehead and drawn back into a low knot at the nape of her neck. But she had changed. She wore a plain black dress and no jewelry. She was very pale and quite thin, and seemed much older than he had remembered her. Only her shining black eyes were the same, except that they were more thoughtful now, somewhat sunken in mauve shadows.

She said something, and gave him her hand. He took it dully. He felt the smooth soft fingers in his own. He said something in reply. He heard her invite him to sit down, and she sat down near him. Then they were silent again. Jessica had crossed her shimmering ankles, and he saw her narrow feet in the black slippers.

He had dreamt of bringing her this news. Her smooth and beautiful face would light up; she would cry out something, and hold his hand in both her own, and she would look at him with a dazzling light in her eyes. Then he would confess to her that he loved her, that he had never forgotten her, that he wanted her, and she would smile at him steadfastly, and say— What would she say? He had forgotten. The dream died away, and she sat there opposite him, abstracted and pale, as if she were not aware that he was there at all.

He heard the long slow ticking of the clock in the hall. He heard the warm rustling of the trees outside the open French windows. He felt the old sinking, the old malaise in himself. The dream had lied. Jessica did not care; she was not as he had remembered her. She was bored with him, for he was a stranger.

Jessica gazed at him levelly and inscrutably. Then she was speaking: "I can't tell you how glad I am—about your book." But her voice, if polite, was lifeless. Her eyes surveyed him coolly, indifferently. What a fool he had been! While he had been planning and working, dreaming of her, she had had a life of her own in which he had no part. He was presumptuous; she was probably wondering why he had come to her at all. In a few moments he would have to get up and leave her, while she murmured courteous goodbyes.

No, it could not happen this way! He would not permit it. He would not be cheated now. He would force her, and circumstance, to live up to his dreams. He would make her see him, bring interest to her eyes.

He said: "I hoped you would be glad. You see, I thought of you all the time I was writing it."

She hesitated, and now she smiled briefly. "That is very kind of you." Was that incredulity in her voice, rejection of his impertinence? Was she considering him a low-bred boor, presuming on her time and her attention?

Now he stammered desperately: "You see—I—I remembered that you were kind to me. I—I remembered the letters you wrote me, and the telephone calls—"

She said, and her tone was cold: "You didn't answer them."

She remembered that! Now he felt more confidence, a renewed excitement. "I—didn't want to presume. You see, I was poor—I had no right to impose upon you. You see, you don't know what it is to be poor, to endure humiliation, and—" He smiled miserably.

An opaque shadow fell over Jessica's face, so that her features appeared less distinct and sharp. "You don't know what it is to be poor." She knew, well enough, God knows. Her father, James, brother of her uncle, Wentworth Bailey, had been a musician, one of those unfortunate ones who live and breathe only for music, who have their being in music, but are completely unable to interpret it with soul and passion. No, thought Jessica, he wasn't really unfortunate. He never knew how inadequate he was. He thought, when he sat at his piano, that he was conveying to the ears of his listeners the same lovely wildness and glory that he heard with his inner ear. She saw his fine thin face, moved, transfigured, as he listened to a majesty he was unable to transmit. But he never knew he did not transmit it. In that, at least, God had been kind. He wandered from city to city, securing consistently fewer bookings in consistently smaller towns, his air bemused and exalted, the light of rapture beaming from his tired eyes. She saw him infrequently. He never wrote when away from New York. But somehow, in some way, this frail and delicate man had managed to educate her at second-rate boarding schools, where she had endured the indignity of shabby clothing and very little spending money.

Yes, she had been poor, but she could not tell Frank Clair this. For by some subtle intuition she knew that if she told him she would lose value in his eyes. She stared at him, and her dark pupils dilated. He was a fool!

When her father had died, her uncle had condescended to go to New York for the quiet funeral. He had paid all the expenses and had accompanied her back to her apartment, which he appraised with one swift look. Watching him, Jessica remembered her father's words: "He lives like a stone." A gray, thin, monumental stone, covered with green lichen. He had icy, webbed eyes, and a mouth like a blade. But, curiously, he had appeared to be interested in her, had inquired about her work. Then he had made an astounding suggestion. He wanted her to return with him to Bison, there to act as his private secretary, managing his affairs. In return, he had told her (and she had no way of knowing that she had impressed him most favorably and that she was already established in his mind as his heir) she was to live in his own home, and she would be paid a good salary. Jessica was not "proud" or otherwise stupid. She had a deep respect for money. She had accepted at once. She had never had a moment's reason to regret her decision, particularly not now.

These thoughts ran through her mind in a matter of moments, while Frank sat opposite her, looking at her with such proud misery. She was filled with pity for him. But she was angered also. What could she say to him? It was apparent that he had said something, and was waiting for her to answer.

"I beg your pardon," she murmured. "I'm afraid I was thinking of something else. You see, my uncle was buried yesterday. He died four days ago, quite suddenly."

Frank was taken aback. She saw the line of his jaw spring out under his fair skin; she saw the disappointed tightening of his thin face. He said, with an effort: "I'm sorry. If I had known, I shouldn't have bothered you." He had come on such a high wave of bright exaltation, and now he was defeated, his news as nothing. He added lamely: "It must have been a shock."

"Not really," she said, in her clear voice. "My uncle was a very hard man. I can't help feeling that way about him, even though I have just heard that he has left me all his money and everything else he had. You see, he could have helped my father." She stopped and watched Frank closely.

But Frank had hardly heard her. He was too engrossed in his deflation and disappointment. He said something conventional. All at once, he was exhausted and depleted. This girl was not interested in him. She was a wealthy woman; what he had to offer was nothing. She sat there gazing at him so remotely, forcing herself to be polite and wishing he would go away at once and leave her in peace.

But, he thought in his despair, I can't give you up! She is everything I have ever wanted. She is all I have ever hoped for and striven for and desired.

As clearly as if he had spoken, Jessica followed his thoughts, and now she was sick with her anger. Why do I waste my time with him? Why don't I just get up and tell him to go? He is a snob and a fool; he is as incredulous as a silly child. He is all wrong!

She stood up, and her eyes flashed at him as he slowly rose. "Why didn't you come to see me before?" she demanded, in a hard, stern voice. "Why did you wait until now?"

His expression darkened as he replied: "Because I was nothing. Because it would have been insolent to have come before I had accomplished something. You know what I was when you first saw me. I was selling stockings at your door. If I had come to you before today, you would have had a perfect right to kick me out. I wanted to come here as an equal; I wanted the right to come."

"I gave you that right when I wrote to you and called you!"

"You were only being kind," he said.

She glared at him incredulously. Was he that stupid? Was

it possible for him to be so idiotic? But he was staring at her in confusion, as if he were trying to understand her, and failing.

"You mean," she said, with disgust, "that you thought you didn't 'have a right' because you were poor and earning a living by selling stockings? I told you I had friends who were doing much the same thing, and not losing—caste—or anything else by doing it."

"But your friends were different. They had had money. They had had an education. It was only a temporary matter. But I was nothing from the beginning."

"And you think you are different now?"

"Yes." He said this simply and grimly, and she saw his eyes, like blue stones, and she thought again of her uncle. Then he went on: "My father was a grubby little chemist. My mother was a seamstress. I have done all sorts of work. I've had to acquire an education, of a kind, by myself. I never had anything, until recently, until now."

He will hate me, she thought, if I assure him that he means no more and no less to me today than he did that first time I met him. If I tell him that what he has accomplished is of no importance to me, he will walk out of this room and never see me again, and he will remember me with contempt.

She felt she despised him. She felt that he was insulting her. She said: "You must have a very low opinion of me to think that what you were matters at all."

He smiled unpleasantly. "Because," he repeated, "you don't know what it means to be poor."

She set her mouth in a hard line. She studied him intently. Then she said: "I've read your stories in various magazines."

He colored. He said: "They are trash."

She said, quickly and harshly: "I'm glad you think so. I thought so, too. I was embarrassed. In some way, I knew you could do better than that. I hope this book is an improvement."

They stood facing each other like furious antagonists.

"The people who are going to publish it think so." His voice was bitter.

"What is it about?"

He told her briefly. She listened, her eyes fixed upon his. "That is a silly premise, on which you have built your syllogism of war guilt," she said when he had finished. "And somehow I think you know it. You know very well that wars, and all other such calamities, spring out of the ugliness and evil and guilt of every man, everywhere in the world. You know that it is man's hatred for other men which makes him such a beast. You know that, don't you?"

He had turned very white. He said: "Yes, I know it. But that isn't what the people want to hear. They want to blame anything, anybody, for their own crimes. And a writer makes money by telling them what they want, by furnishing them with a scapegoat." He added viciously: "A victim. Or a romance, preferably full of fornication or adultery. That's what they want, and that is what I am giving them."

"Why, you're a kind of procurer! You—you are shameful!"

He saw her rage, her incredulity, and he could not speak.

"How can you write these things?" she cried. "Why haven't you, why hasn't any writer, the decency to write: 'You, you the reader of this, are guilty of the cruelty and hatred and foulness and lies and godlessness which surround you? You, you alone, are guilty. You are the rewarder of murderers; you are the condoner of concentration camps and wars. You create the criminal politician, the betrayer of peace, the assassin, the thief, the traitor and the dictator. Because you hate. Look at yourself, and know yourself for what you are.' Why don't you write that?"

Frank's mouth became ugly. "Because I want money," he said. Because I want you, he added to himself.

He saw that her smooth face had turned scarlet with her emotions and that her eyes blazed. He was astounded at the passion in her voice, for he had thought her so composed, so cool, so invulnerable, made of different flesh. He had wanted that different flesh, which knew no fear, which was invincible and strong, an alien humanity at once precious and superior and immune. And so he suddenly hated her, was enraged against her for revealing herself to be no more than himself and all the others that he had known. She was a combination of old Tim Farley, Wade O'Leary, Mr. Preston, who believed a man's first service was to his fellows. She was one of those sentimentalists who thought that, for their fat and complacent pleasure, an "artist" should be content to work and starve in a garret, demanding no reward but the satisfaction of giving sustenance and "inspiration." She was one of the maudlin who did not believe that a writer was worthy of his hire.

Now his expression became brutal and savage. His was a nature slow to anger, but vindictive and ruthless when finally aroused. He felt no regret, no alarm, when he realized that he had lost her and all that she was, for he did not believe that he could want one so degradingly like those he had despised for their sentimentality. She was coarse and common. What he had loved in her—her composure, her aloofness, her imagined superiority—did not exist and had existed only in his jejune imagination.

Fearless of her now, he spoke in a hard low voice: "I want money, because it will help me to escape from those I hate, because it will free me from the sight and the smell of them. You don't know the poor; you can't imagine how horrible they are. And I can get money only by giving the people what they want; they give money only to those who serve them. I am not an impudent fool. I'm not so impertinent as to think I know what is 'best' for the public, and I have no right to push things down their throats when they don't want them."

She had become very still, even reflective, as he spoke. She sat down again, very slowly, and looked up at him with quiet and level eyes. She said almost indifferently: "You sound so defiant, as if you really thought wanting money was somehow immoral. That's sentimental."

He was surprised and startled. He had expected anything but this. He could only regard her in silence, frowning.

She laughed a little, abruptly. "Yes, sentimental, and just a trifle precious. Look, now, you know you want money, and you want it terribly, yet some kind of Methodism in your subconscious thinking tries to tell you that wanting money is sort of vicious, and you are childishly defiant. That's all so silly.

"All right, then, you want money. There is nothing dishonorable in that, nothing vile. Every sensible man wants money; I might even say every moral man wants it. I think it is immoral not to want property and affluence of a major or minor degree. Not to want them shows that a man has no self-respect and no desire for his own welfare. Lacking these, he can't possibly have any of the other virtues either. So that makes him immoral, unless he is an ascetic or a saint. A poor man must be contemptible in the sight of the angels, 'poor' in all things."

He was more surprised than ever, then suddenly gratified and relieved. He was wrong, then. She was indeed superior; she had his own contempt for the poverty-stricken and the hopeless. What he did not know was that she read his thoughts very acutely. Now her fine dark brows drew together. I can't reach him, she said to herself. He reads a different meaning entirely into whatever I say.

She went on: "Wanting money, then, for your self-respect and your welfare, is virtuous and moral. But I don't think you want money for self-respect and your own welfare, and that is where you are immoral."

"What do I want it for, then?" he asked angrily.

"I don't know. That is what I'd like to find out. I may be wrong, but I think you think that having money will 'elevate' you to some superior class, or something, and free you from something you hate. In short, I think your reasons for wanting money are disgusting, and that's what makes you dangerous, not only you, yourself, but your writing."

She glanced at the crystal box near her on the table, and he opened it and gave her a cigarette. He took one himself. He lit them both, blew out the match. The maid brought in a silver tray on which stood a seltzer bottle and a bottle of whiskey and two glasses. Jessica glanced at them when the maid had gone. Frank mixed two drinks and gave one to Jessica. He sat down and began to sip his. Jessica seemed to have forgotten him, she was so thoughtful. But his original excitement and sense of power had returned. He no longer stood in awe of her, she had voluntarily come too close to him for that.

"There is no danger in anything I write. There is just money," he said, smiling at her indulgently.

But she frowned as if she thought him childish. "When I read your stories in the magazines, they made me restless. I thought I saw something in them that could be"—she paused—"liberated. I know that is a sentimental word, but I can't think of any other. Something was missing in your writing, but there was a hint of it here and there."

He was angry again. Mr. Mason, Mr. Preston—they both had spoken of the "missing something." This was becoming irritating. Then, for no reason at all, he saw Mr. Hawkins' lean cold face and pale blue eyes.

Jessica continued, almost idly: "What are you afraid of, Frank?"

Afraid! They all came back to that, in a stupid, monotonous refrain.

"I'm not afraid of anything," he replied furiously.

"Yes, you are. And that is why you are so full of hate. And because you hate, you are dangerous. You and Hitler ought to have a great deal in common. It's too bad you can't meet. He is terrified, and so he hates, and because he hates he has to have a victim. He is symptomatic of the German people; he is symptomatic of the whole world. What are we all afraid of? I sometimes think I know. We are afraid of one another, because we know what we ourselves are. We know we are hideous and godless and hopeless, that we are completely evil. We are like condemned prisoners who glare at each other murderously through the bars. Knowing what is in our own minds, we know what is in the minds of others."

She put down her drink and looked at it somberly. "You know, of course, that there will be a war. The attacker will claim to be the attacked. Because he wants to kill. And he wants to kill because he hates, and he hates because he is afraid."

"There won't be a war," said Frank sullenly.

"And if there is, you won't care, will you?"

"No." he added bitterly: "You are wrong. I'm not afraid of anything."

He stood up. The old mysterious depression was on him again, the old flatness and undesire and misery. Jessica watched him. "You must know," she said gently, "that only you matter. If you are to say anything of importance that will help all the rest of us, you've got to begin with yourself."

He laughed contemptuously. "Now you are being sentimental again. Don't you know that no writer is of any importance? Lots of fools think that writers have significance and power, and that they are of value. They aren't. I've had to learn that."

"But you believed it at one time, didn't you?"

He was silent.

Jessica sighed. "It's too bad. Everything's subjective, you know, and I think that if a sane man believes he is of value, he really is."

She stood up and gave him her hand. Her eyes were sad. "Please forgive me if I've offended you in any way. But it seemed awfully important for me to—for me—" She could not go on. Whatever she might say would sound grandiloquent or too intimate.

He held her hand and said: "May I come to see you again, soon?"

"Yes, of course." She appeared very tired.

He had only to relinquish her hand gently and go. But just as his fingers were slackening, some impulse made him grasp her hand more firmly. He felt the pulse in her flesh. He saw her pale and weary face, her beautiful dark eyes and finely molded lips. He forgot his fears, his suspicions, his self-consciousness and inferiority. He exclaimed: "Jessica! Oh, Jessica!"

How terrible, how ridiculous this was, that he and she should stand facing each other like strangers, like two who meet casually and part vaguely, without interest! He did not care if he offended her now, or whatever else happened. He wanted her to know, he wanted her to understand. He went on, in a loud and rapid voice: "Jessica, this is all wrong, everything we've said to each other. You'll probably kick me out, but I've got to tell you. All this time, while I was working, I was thinking of you, and wanting you, and living for the time when I could be here with you. I have an idea that all this—what I've tried to do—doesn't mean much to you, and that you think I've been a fool. Perhaps I have; I don't know. But nothing matters but wanting to be with you, and hoping that you won't turn me away, but that you'll let me come and talk to you sometime—"

Her face changed. In the beginning, she had tried to withdraw her hand, but now it lay in his quietly, even warmly. She smiled; her mouth softened and her eyes brightened. She listened to him eagerly, expectantly. Then she came a little closer to him.

He took her other hand now. She was still smiling up at him.

"You've wasted so much time, coming around to this," she said, with a small, quick laugh. "I've been miserable the last few days. I waited for you to come. And then all we could do was to fly into a political discussion, like a pair of fools! It's amazing, isn't it, that we've seen each other only twice, and yet we seem to know everything about each other—?"

His hands tightened on hers. "You're wrong, Jessica." He sounded breathless. "We met a long time ago. I thought it was a dream, until that day I came to sell you stockings, and I recognized the house."

She exclaimed: "I knew it! But where was it? I, too, began to think it was a dream."

He told her, and she listened intently, trying to remember. But it was no use; she could not even remember the pink dress and the pink ribbon in her hair. What could she tell him, so that he would not be too disappointed? And then she realized that details did not matter. She remembered him, had dimly recognized him, though the circumstances surrounding their first meeting as children might never re-return to her.

She said: "It seems to me that I've always known you. It seems to go back into eternity."

She held up her mouth to him simply, and he kissed her. In a way, his kiss was virginal, for what he had known of women before this had been nothing, a nausea, a revulsion. Here was passion and fulfillment. It was different from anything else he had ever known, and it was incredible.

He said: "I love you." Never in all his life had he ever said those words before, and he felt wonder in himself. He repeated it for the miracle it was: "I love you, Jessica."

"And I love you too, Frank," she said, again lifting her mouth to his.

No one had ever said this to him in all his life, not even his mother. He could not believe it. He said: "Say it over and over, Jessica."

"I love you," she repeated, and now there were tears in her eyes. "Frank, I love you for just what you are, and for nothing else. Just you, Frank. You must remember that."

CHAPTER 70

FRANK CLAIR walked through the streets of Bison, and saw none of them. When he had been a child, he had walked this way, lost yet alive, exalted and unseeing. Once, when he was ten years old, he had read of young beggars who had found strange stones or trinkets on the road, had picked them up, turned them over, and had discovered a magic word that made the world their own. For years thereafter he searched the alleys and the streets and the gutters for the wondrous amulet. And now, as he walked, he remembered and smiled, and thought: I have found it.

He had found it, he knew, because someone loved him. To someone, he was the beloved, the one loved above all others. "I love you for just what you are," she had said. He had no need to "prove" himself; there was no necessity to bring gifts to bribe and attract and compel admiration. It was necessary only to be himself, to be Frank Clair. It did not seem possible; it was a miracle.

It seems a miracle to me, he thought, because, unknown to me until just this minute, I have always believed I was a poor thing, not to be liked for what I am, but always compelled to appease, to do what others wished, to placate, to buy a grudging acceptance. Why was this? Was it because my parents really did inoculate me with their belief that I was worthless, a failure, something to be despised, a kind of monster? If so, why did I believe them? And why has it taken me all these years to realize that I have members and limbs and organs like other men, and that, like other men, I can stand alone to be rejected or accepted? Why have I always been so afraid? I can look at my fear now and know that I have always been afraid, even when I despised fear the most. I repudiated it. It has always been with me. Until now.

He walked on. The sun became a red round ball peering through trees. But he did not see it. The ghost of his father walked with him. It had walked with him before, and when it had done so he had vilified it and defied it and detested it. But now it crept beside him, pathetic, lonely, and very tired. He felt it there, but he did not hate it. He thought: My father walked these very streets, but he saw something I don't see now, though I know I have seen it many times before. He saw Fear.

What must it have been like, to have known that fear, to have lived with it, to have smelt its corruption in every room, in every street, in every trolley car, in every corridor? To have seen it in every face, against windows glancing with sunlight, in every doorway, in the very shadows of the trees, the very corners of every house, in the shape and form of every stranger! To have heard it echo in every voice, in every footstep, in the rustle of foliage, the rattle of every passing vehicle, in every laugh or cry or shout, at dawn, at noon, at night!

What must it have been like, to Francis Clair, this world, this sun and moon and stars? A universe of dread, of apprehension, of terror, full of grotesque threat, of ominous portent, of sinister and personal meaning. What horrible and pathetic egotism must have made Francis believe that the vastness of life was directed towards him with baleful intent, like a single gigantic eye turned only upon him, like a single great hand lifted to smash him, flatten him, crush out his life! No wonder he had hoarded talismans against this enormous menace bent on his destruction: rabbits' feet, pierced coins, four-leaf clovers, a chain woven of dried grass. There was no humor in his hundred magic acts of placating or outwitting a malevolent fate, a universe out to frustrate, defeat or obliterate him. He had infected poor Maybelle with his obscure but looming terrors, so that a normally healthy and courageous young woman had become a gibbering and cruel hag of fear. He had made of his wife a trembling and brutal shadow of himself, concerned with talismans and all the abracadabra of circumventing a ferocious destiny.

How could they have endured living like this? Why had they not died years before of their terrors and their fears? Only the intrinsic toughness of the human body, the iron substance of the human brain, must have kept them alive in that wilderness of menace and fulmination. Frank saw his parents scuttling frantically about their rooms at the unaccustomed sound of a doorbell or a knock. He saw them swiftly and frenziedly pulling down shades, or peeping furtively around the edge of lace curtains, or running away to a back room, there to whisper like fugitives from some secret police, their faces white in the dusk, their eyes strained, their hands clenched together. The caller, a salesman, or a neighbor, would eventually drift away, but it would be quite some time before the shade went up, the curtain was no longer peeped out from behind, the door was unlocked, and voices were allowed once more to rise above a whisper.

My God! thought Frank, his feet pounding faster on the warm July pavements. What was the matter with them? What did they fear? The calamities that come to all men? Why couldn't they understand that pain and suffering and loss and death are the common lot, and that men develop fortitude and faith against them? Why did they believe that they, and they alone, were marked for horror and destruction? They had only to look about them and see the spectres on every doorstep. But within the other houses the men and women laughed and loved, and, in courage, tried to forget the last inevitable moment when they must answer the somber knocking.

Frank thought of his parents again, and now without hatred. The hatred had fallen from him like dried scabs, and though the scars remained, they were beginning to heal. He thought of his parents with pity and compassion and grief. He remembered their cruelty, and he said to himself: They were cruel because they were afraid. They hated and suspected every living thing because they were afraid.

He looked about him and was dimly surprised. He had arrived at The Front. He was standing near a bench on the lip of the long green hill that ran down to the railroad tracks and to the river. He sat down on the bench. The river, mysteriously shadowed under the setting sun, ran in long amethystine waves. Like waves, too, scarlet fire flowed up into the zenith, palpitating. An ephemeral light, spectral and soft, like gray veils, moved over the earth. The trees stood in warm and dusky silence. Now a breeze ran whispering through the paling air, and Frank felt it on his face. He lit a cigarette and smoked. Peace and tranquillity began to stir in him, to come alive. He looked at the running river and the fiery sky, and he saw them as he had seen them in his childhood, deep, portentous, full of meaning and majesty, no longer flat, no longer painted, no longer empty.

Yes, he thought, my parents hated because they were afraid. It is a terrible thing to be afraid. It is a terrible thing to have on your conscience that some man is afraid of you. My father began by fearing his mother. His fear broadened, and darkened all the world for him. It made him vicious and brutal. It finally killed him, but not before he destroyed my mother, and almost destroyed me.

Surely, he thought, if any man has cause to fear you, then count yourself among the accursed of God. If you are a white man, and a Negro lives in terror of you, if you are a Gentile, and a Jew exists under a shadow because of you, if your neighbor watches in dread your coming and going, if a face darkens anxiously at the sight of your face, then you are doomed, and all that you do, all that you believe, all that you think, all your risings and your sleepings, your eatings and your drinkings, your household and your children, are ill-fated and execrable, and you live under the threat of death.

Frank looked at the sky, and a great stillness and dread came to him. Fear lay over the world on this calm and lovely evening. It threw its shadow of hatred over all the cities, over all the seas. Why did man hate his own kind? What evil was born in him, that he wished to destroy his brother? For every man was every other man's brother. It was not some transcendental mystery, some invention of the saints or the angels. It was living and irrefutable fact. The blood of a white man, the blood of a Negro, a Chinese, a Frenchman or an Englishman, was identical, and no scientist with all his tests and tubes could find the slightest difference. The blackest savage in the jungle dark of Africa could exchange blood with the white patrician of the same blood type, and the bloods would harmonize. Man's blood was his link with all other men. Why, then, did his spirit stand in eternal enmity against the spirit of his brother?

Is the secret in myself? thought Frank. Is each man really a microcosm of all the other men in the world? I hated because I was afraid. Why was I afraid? I don't know. I only know that I never really had cause to fear anything. I was not strong enough, not courageous enough, to withstand the shock of reality. Why don't the Churches know that it is not man's animal humility which must be cultivated, but his secret and inner conviction that he is a heroic spirit, invulnerable, immortal, and strong? He knows this when he is a child, for then he is closer to heaven and the fountain of life. The Churches must begin with the child, for once that child fears, he is on the way to destruction, and becomes an instrument of destruction against his fellows.

Not the fear of God, but the love of God. Not the lust for the things of fear: money, position, power, but the lust for the things of the spirit. When the child looks at the sky he dreams, but he does not dream of wealth and security and mastery over others. He dreams of mysteries, and remembers. But when he has been taught fear by those who have forgotten, he stoops like an ape and picks up a stone.

I'm not afraid, now, of anything, thought Frank, because someone loves me. A few hours ago I stumbled around in darkness and was utterly lost. But someone loves me. And my fear went away because I love in return. Life came back to me, full of perspective and color. I can write again as I used to write!

He felt a surge of pure joy and peace and hope. Was it the sky and the river that were trembling in light, or was the radiant trembling in himself alone? He could not tell. Now, down on the tracks below, he heard the long wail of an approaching train. He felt a vibration in the air. The wailing came clearer, louder, more despairing. He listened to it, but he did not put his hands over his ears as he had always done before.

I am free, he thought. I am free, as I was free when I was a child. I feel my strength, my invulnerability, and so I can't be afraid. Nothing can injure me but my own fear, and because that fear is gone I am invincible. I can hate nothing because I am afraid of no man.

Some day I shall find Paul, and I will tell him. I know I shall find him.

The streets were dark and quiet under the warm white moon. Every tree rustled and whispered. Frank heard voices on the verandahs of the houses he passed. He heard the hiss of passing automobiles. He saw lighted shop windows. He heard and saw everything with exultation. His mind burned with his vision of a new book. He had it all now. He would tell of the growth of fear in himself, of terror, and, finally, of hatred. War hung like a black wing over the world. War would come, for man's fear had gone too far. But perhaps, after the madness had passed, there would be hope. If only men could understand. If only they did not invent something to bring greater destruction upon themselves and upon others. If only they could look upon their brothers and know them. It might not be too late even now. It might not be too late even in the midst of the red storm of madness. If only a few listened, it might not be too late. I will do what I can, thought Frank Clair. I may be only one voice, but perhaps, in the wilderness, voices hitherto silent will rise up and join mine.

The summer wind was rising, and the leaves of the trees rose to greet it. Frank reached a corner of a street and saw a great tree before him, standing alone on a long dark lawn. He stood and watched it. And now his heart went out to the great tree, as his heart had once gone out to trees and to all other things. It went out like a wave of love and light, communicating, calling, embracing, encompassing, a long wave of passion and desire and knowing. The tree stood still under the moon, every leaf hanging motionless, every branch heavy with dreams and darkness. Then the wind touched it and broke up its static silence, and all at once the tree moved like a sentient thing waking from sleep, it was all motion, all fluid being, all life. From its branches, from its deepest self, broke forth a soft deep roar, a voice, as if replying, as if responding, to the call that Frank had sent to it, and the leaves turned bright silver in the moonlight, a multitude of small and vivid brightnesses, mirrors of plated glory, shimmering and trembling.

Now the dark and silvered wind struck Frank also, sweeping over and above and about him like a sea in strong motion. He stood and felt it, and looked at the tree, and something of his old passionate exultation replied to the night, something of his old joy and ecstasy and rapturous knowledge.

But he knew, too, as he looked at the tree, and called to it, and the tree answered, that never again could he possess the wonder and the enchantment of the world. The years had struck a black chasm between himself and his youth, and there was no crossing it. The globe of his childhood rolled on into rainbowed space; it was a dream; it was a bewitchment. It was all glory and all delight. It was never to be known by him again in this life, for he was a man, and he knew that enchantment and magic are not part of manhood, and that "the splendor in the grass" is for the eyes of children only.

Never again would he walk a street, and turn over a little stone or a scrap of paper, hoping for the magic word which would give him the world, the fulfillment of dreams, the shining towers of sorcery, the gardens of Circe. Never again would he believe that there were islands of charmed entrancement waiting for the discoverer, full of sweetness and rapture and loveliness. Never again would he climb a hill, expectant of marble walls and golden gates on the other side, and a city where angels walked, clothed in gold, with the sun upon their faces. The world was small; it was hard and concrete with reality. There were no white colonnades full of moonlight to be found in a lost field, and no mountains that rang with music. What there was to be known of the world he knew, and there was no spot "appalled in celestial light."

But for the man of good will, the man who loved and did not hate, the man who knew compassion and grief and understanding, there remained the gentle evening of hope, the sweetness of sympathy, the fruit of peace. Life, for him, would never again be as radiant as the "glory and the freshness of a dream." Ecstasy was no longer to be his companion between sunrise and sunset. But for men of good will there was knowledge, and the faith so to live and so to work that each day would find another stone of anguish lifted from mankind, the faith that the fear and the hatred which beset humanity, and which condemned it to inexorable death, could be transmuted into trust and love—if only a few men desired it and determined upon it.

CHAPTER 71

How INCREDIBLY beautiful it was to wake in the morning with this slow and rapturous content flowing all through one like golden water! To feel filled and fulfilled, waiting, quiet and smiling, to see the sunshine on one's hands as if it had just been newly created, not the sun of yesterday, but a stranger and sweeter light. To look at the walls, familiar yet not familiar, to feel again the emanations of every object, as one felt them in one's youth—that was to be reborn, to have again a child's lovely expectation, tranquillized now, with a more subdued shining, but with a richness not to be know in fragile and uncertain childhood.

This was not peace again, in the new morning, but understanding. It was not ecstasy. It was simply being without fear, fear of tomorrow, fear of every voice, fear of pain, death, defeat, ignominy, frustration. It was, in short, to be free of the fear of one's fellows, their cruelty, malice, brutality and hate. It was to see men crouching in a dark shadow, and to know compassion and sorrow for them, a passionate desire to tell them that he no longer feared them, and that, as he no longer feared them, they had no cause to fear him.

How good it was to know this, and to feel it, and with it the strength and the power granted only to the merciful and the liberated!

It was not possible to forget the balefulness of men, their darkness of mind, their detestableness, their boundless capacity for evil, their envy and avarice, the murder that lurked in them like a watchful beast. But it was possible to feel pity for them, and sadness, and grief—all the preludes to love. Even if they replied with a stone and a Cross, it was nothing at all. Even if they answered with a stake, the fires of hatred they raised might shine with enlightenment upon them, with penitence and awakening.

Each man was immovably scaled in a tree in some dim forest that grew on a wasteland, his real voice choked, his gestures made in wood, his eyes blinded, only a faint rustling heard when he cried out in agony. How was it possible to hate these immured souls, speechless, rooted in the earth they could not escape, striving towards a sky they could not see but could only vaguely feel?

Frank Clair sat on the side of his bed and thought: I was one of them. But now I am free. Some way, somehow, I'll find the words to free these others too. There was a stronger and more vehement stirring in him now, a vast but potent urge. He listened to it, and felt it gathering force and cogency. Into what pattern was it flowing? What would be the words of its articulateness? He did not know. But he felt it growing and expanding, moment by moment, flashing with exultation and purpose, as lightning flashes on mountain peaks, showing, for an instant, the outline of crags and images against an unlit sky. When would the hour come when he would hear the word "Now!" and sit down to write again, to work, to put into words the things he had learned?

He knew he had to wait. The power and the force were

there. They waited as he had to wait. In the meantime, like irresistible roots, they probed deeper into the dark rich soil of his mind, coiling through alluvial deposits, drinking in life, and becoming life themselves.

Old Mr. Penseres called up the stairs to him that the photographer and the reporter from the Bison *Evening News* were waiting for him below. Startled, he saw that it was almost eleven o'clock. He had slept for over ten hours, the deep and dreamless sleep which he had not known for many years.

Later, Mr. Penseres proudly showed him a large item in the morning paper about the acceptance of his novel by Thomas Ingham's Sons. Frank read the item, which he had given to the reporter over the telephone yesterday, and he thought: But that was a dream. It was not that it no longer mattered. It was that since yesterday he had come across eons of space and time, and that the face he had seen in the mirror this morning was not the face he had known before.

It was nearly one o'clock. He would call Jessica and tell her. However poor his words, she would understand and know. But just as he reached for the receiver, the telephone rang, and he answered it impatiently. The man's voice asked for him, and he replied: "Yes. This is Frank Clair."

The voice laughed in a friendly fashion, and now it sounded vaguely familiar.

"Do you remember me, Frank?" asked the voice. "Gordon Hodge?"

Frank's hand gripped the receiver convulsively. "Gordon," he repeated. His own voice came in a wild stammer: "Gordon Hodge! Where are you? I—I've been looking for you—"

"You have?" said Gordon, with mild surprise. Frank could see him, sandy, smiling with indulgent incredulity, good-tempered, yet wary, as he had been when they were children. "Well, I've been here since May. I've been appointed associate professor of English at the University of Bison, and I've been doing some summer work at the University." He paused. "I often wondered what had become of you. I've been teaching in Ohio for the past ten years, myself. And this morning I read about you in the Bison *Courier*, and had to call you immediately and congratulate you. I think it's wonderful, but then, I always knew you would do it, Frank."

Frank stood there, hearing a strong drumming in and about him. His voice seemed paralyzed by the passion that tried to rush across its thin cords. The receiver bit into his hand.

"I'm married now," Gordon went on easily, but with a faint questioning in his tone when he became aware of Frank's silence. "We live near the University, my wife and I, and we have two children. I'd like to have you visit us, so we can talk about a lot of things. You know my father's dead?"

"I—I didn't know," stammered Frank. His knees became weak and he sat down abruptly. He swallowed and said: "I've tried all these years to find you. Gordon, where is Paul?"

Gordon did not answer. The telephone hummed in Frank's ear. He waited, then when he heard nothing else but this, he repeated urgently: "Gordon? Are you still there? Where is Paul?"

Gordon's voice came again, thinner and with a suspicious coldness. "What are you trying to tell me, Frank? That you didn't know that Paul is dead, too?"

All sensation fell away from Frank. He was sitting in nothingness. He heard his voice whispering dryly: "I didn't know. I didn't know."

"Hello?" said Gordon. "Hello, Frank?"

Like a hollow echo, he heard Frank say: "I didn't know. My God, I didn't know!"

Gordon became uncertain and embarrassed. "Why, I can hardly believe it. That was when you were down in Kentucky. You had written once or twice to Paul, while he was in the Navy, and the letters were sent on to me, as next of kin. I wrote you myself, telling you, and the letter was never returned."

That must have been after I ran away, thought Frank, still not feeling anything at all. He said: "When did it happen?"

"It happened a year or so after the war, while he was still in the Navy, transport work. The ship hit a submerged mine, and I believe everyone was killed. I'm awfully sorry, Frank. I thought you knew. It was a long time ago."

No, thought Frank, it was not a long time ago. It was only now. It has happened this very minute. I have just felt the sledge hammer; but that is all I have felt. In a little while I'll realize, because it has just happened now.

Gordon was talking on, in a conciliatory and concerned voice, but Frank heard only a blur of sound which meant nothing. Paul was dead. I'll feel it soon, Frank thought. I'll know it in a few minutes. The blur of sound was again wary and incredulous, faintly rallying, unwilling to believe. That is the way he always talked to me when we were kids, thought Frank. He was always on guard against my "tricks."

Frank hung up the receiver and climbed the stairs to his

rooms. He went to the window and looked down at the hot July pavement. A streetcar passed, and he followed it mutely and helplessly with his eyes. He watched a woman and some children on the pavements. He saw the blue flash of noonday over the buildings opposite. Sunlight glanced from the dusty tops of automobiles, from the steel rails in the street. Now everything began to tremble with the bright outline of a rising agony.

"Paul!" said Frank, aloud. And then, with urgent and terrible questioning: "Paul?"

Only the sunlight answered, and a hot and dusty breath from the pavement below.

"I didn't know," said Frank. "Why didn't I know? Why didn't I feel it? Why didn't you tell me, Paul? I thought of you all the time, and then—and then— There wasn't any answer! I ought to have known then."

He sat down and lit a cigarette abstractedly. It burned in his fingers. He stared before him at the wall, which was patterned in sunshine. He said, still speaking aloud: "I ought to have known when I didn't hear from you. Do you hear me now, Paul? Do you remember all those years, all the walks we had together, all the talks, all the hopes of the future, all the ideas and the dreams and the imaginings? Why, you're my childhood, Paul! You are part of me, more than if we had been brothers. You are an inseparable part, as no one else can ever be a part, not even Jessica. We saw the new world together. Do you remember that spring day in the Canadian woods? Can you still remember those dry, ashen days in November when we walked along the river, and told each other everything we thought and knew, and saw the world through each other's eyes? The books we read, Paul, and the band concerts we used to listen to at The Front, and the sunsets we saw together, and the grave, childish conjectures we had about God and earth and life and being? The weedy Queen Anne's lace that grew along the fence near your home, which to us was a miracle? The games we played, the balls we tossed, the sandwiches we ate in the wet spring grass along the Canadian Creeks, and the way we made designs with our feet in the snow? The candy we bought with our few pennies, and how we tracked down a drugstore that sold penny sodas, and walked the hot summer miles to get them, and how we put crossed pins on the streetcar tracks to make scissors of them? And how we talked of the day when I'd be a 'great writer,' and how we'd buy a house together in which we'd always live, a house in a wood, on the top of a great green hill overlooking cold green water? You believed in me, Paul. Even when you went away that day, that last day, you didn't really go. You always stayed. That day was only a dream, because it never really happened to us."

The sunlight brightened on the walls, on the figured carpet on the floor. There was no sound but that of passing traffic and an occasional child's voice.

"You believed in me, Paul Do you still believe in me?"

There was only silence in the room, but all at once Frank felt a smile. He searched the room with his eyes, clamping down on the anguish which was sharpening in him. "Paul?" he said.

Then the strangest comfort came to him, and the anguish slowly receded, wave after wave. "No, Paul, you aren't dead. I know that now. I know that nothing ever dies. Is that what you're trying to tell me?"

And then, even more strangely, Paul's image in his mind was infused with the images of Miss Jones, old Tim Farley, Wade O'Leary, all those he had known who had felt affection and concern for him, who had hoped for him and believed in him. He saw them all, and they were Paul, and Paul was them. I've been rich all this time, thought Frank. I knew them, and they'll always be with me. They want me to do what I *can* do, what I now *know* I can do. They want me to do it.

He owed it to them, because they had loved him. He saw them all so clearly. They were part of his life, and because they were part, they could never leave him. He had loved them, and so had given part of himself to them forever, and they held it as a hostage.

The power and urgency which he had felt this morning returned to him, and now it had a loud and articulate voice, triumphant and measured. He stood up, shaking with the force that battered in and about him.

He went to his typewriter and tore off the cover. He put a sheet of paper in the roller. He waited. He saw what he must write now, and how it should be written.

After a moment, he wrote the title: "There Was a Time."